OVERKILL

JAMES BARRINGTON

OVERKILL

MACMILLAN

First published 2004 by Macmillan
an imprint of Pan Macmillan Ltd
Pan Macmillan, 20 New Wharf Road, London N1 9RR
Basingstoke and Oxford
Associated companies throughout the world
www.panmacmillan.com

ISBN 1 4050 4176 5 (Hardback)
ISBN 1 4050 4177 3 (Trade Paperback)

Typeset by IntypeLibra, London
Printed and bound in Great Britain by
Mackays of Chatham plc, Chatham, Kent

No one person ever writes a book; it's always a team effort, and I've been lucky enough to find myself working with a first-class team.

I'd particularly like to thank Luigi Bonomi of Sheil Land Associates a real writer's agent – who saw potential where others had not, and Vanessa and Amelia, otherwise known as The Girls In The Basement, for their success in selling the book internationally, even before its British publication.

At Macmillan I couldn't have asked for a better editor than Peter Lavery, and I owe special thanks to him and to the talented and enthusiastic team responsible for the publication of this book.

On a personal note, my thanks go to Bill and Barbara Vine who were, so to speak, there at the birth and who provided helpful and accurate guidance. Thanks also to Rowland, whose last name would be known to many and is omitted here for reasons of professional embarrassment.

Unlikely though it may sound, I'd like to thank my mother-in-law, Betty Lee-Kemp, for providing encouragement and unfailing optimism, despite having to read the flocks of rejection slips as they came home to roost. Particular thanks are due to my sister-in-law Sue Lee-Kemp for what might be termed 'special services' – she knows exactly what I mean – and to my brother-in-law Paul for his enthusiasm and belief.

And in the great British tradition of saving the best until last; to my wife Sally, my first and most vocal critic, and my support for always and for ever.

James Barrington
Principality of Andorra, 2004

Author's Note

This book is a work of fiction, with all the usual disclaimers about people living or dead. However, the central idea is built upon a verifiable factual base, and brief reference has been made to the real American politicians John Kennedy, Jimmy Carter and Ronald Reagan, and to a man named Sam Cohen.

Sam Cohen was employed as a strategic nuclear weapons analyst by the Rand Corporation, a military think tank based in Santa Monica, California. In the late 1950s he effectively created the neutron bomb or Enhanced Radiation Weapon when he proposed removing the outer uranium casing of a hydrogen bomb, creating a nuclear weapon that killed people but left structures largely intact. Details given in the book about the way a neutron bomb works and the theoretical maximum size of the weapon are accurate.

Political and public pressure meant that neutron weapons were neither used nor deployed by America, although a stockpile is still held in the States. Other nations that have stolen, bought or developed the technology for themselves include France, China, Russia, Israel, South Africa and of course Britain.

Red mercury is a real substance, and is exactly as described in this book. It is a mercury compound that has undergone massive irradiation and which, when exploded, creates the levels of pressure and heat needed to trigger a fusion device such as a neutron bomb, eliminating the need for access to a supply of plutonium. Red mercury is comparatively cheap and easy to produce, especially compared to the costs of developing weapons-grade plutonium, and was sold for many years on the black market by Russia to a variety of countries including Iraq.

It is also a fact that, following the collapse of the Soviet Union, the United States began paying billions of dollars for plutonium extracted from Russia's dismantled weapons in an attempt to stop black market trading in the element. It is unfortunately also true that most independent surveys suggest that the Russians have actually been sending the Americans plutonium created as a by-product in their nuclear reactors, and not weapons-grade plutonium. This indicates that either the Russians have not been dismantling their nuclear arsenal, as they claim, or the black market trade in weapons-grade plutonium is flourishing.

We really do live in an uncertain world.

Prologue

Most of the time they didn't fuck about with the executions. A bullet in the back of the head or a blade drawn across the throat and the body left pretty much where it fell. But when Rashid was there it was different. Rashid liked to play.

Bizarrely, Rashid looked more like a caricature of an accountant than anything else – small and slight, hunched, with thick pebble-lensed glasses – but nobody smiled when he was around. He had learnt his trade in the back streets of Baghdad and Basra, and refined his skills working on Russian prisoners seized by the Afghans. The smell of death was on him.

As Sadoun Khamil's enforcer, he would do his master's bidding without question and without compassion. To him it was just work, and he was very good at it. His speciality was the lingering death, what he called *'shwai shwai noum'* or 'sleep slowly', slicing through the victim's spinal cord with a thin and extremely sharp knife. He always knew when he had cut enough, because the body would slump as the nerves were severed. Then they would prop the limp body against a wall or tree and leave it. The man could take days to die, usually of thirst, but occasionally Rashid would enliven the process by making shallow cuts on his arms and legs. The fresh blood and total immobility of the body would attract the birds and the rats and the stray dogs and the insects, and the victim would be literally and slowly eaten alive.

Hassan Abbas hated to watch, but Khamil usually insisted. Knowing what would happen to them if they betrayed or otherwise

1

offended him, Khamil believed, would keep all the members of the cell firmly in line.

Today was different. Khamil had instructed Rashid to make it quick, but painful. The man wasn't part of the cell, wasn't even a full member of al-Qaeda. He was just a courier, a low-level mule, one of the hundreds of thousands of Arabs who shared a hatred of America and an admiration of Osama bin Laden and everything he stood for.

But the courier had committed the unthinkable – he had disclosed the location of Khamil's cell to a friend, a friend who the courier hadn't known was actually a cell member. The friend had immediately informed Khamil, which was why the group was now skulking around a deserted building a couple of miles outside As Salamiyah, instead of their previous and more comfortable quarters in Riyadh itself. Though many Saudis privately – and some even publicly – supported al-Qaeda, the vast majority did not, and Sadoun Khamil had had no option but to move his base as soon as its location had been compromised. For that inconvenience, the courier was about to pay.

The man was lying flat on his back behind the building in the full glare of the early afternoon sun, spread-eagled, wrists and ankles lashed to the corners of a hastily assembled square frame of stout poles. He was naked, and his chest, stomach and thighs bore the bloody stripes of the whipping one of Rashid's 'assistants' had already administered as a taster.

Khamil emerged from the building and strode forward, his white *djellaba* flapping as he walked. He stopped a few feet from the courier and stared down at him. The fresh blood had attracted the flies, and the open wounds bubbled and glistened with their bloated bodies, blackening the man's torso and legs.

The courier appeared to be unconscious, but at a command from Khamil one of the guards strode forward. A sharp crack of the red-stained whip across his chest momentarily scattered the flies which rose in a black circling cloud, buzzing in irritation, before settling back on the body to resume their feast. He forced his eyes open and wailed with the pain, then looked up at Khamil, and fell silent. He had already pleaded his case, and knew that nothing he could say or do would alter his fate.

Khamil stepped back, looked around and nodded to Rashid. The short figure walked forward, stopping in full sight of the man on the ground. In his right hand he held a clasp knife, big and bulky, with a scalpel-sharp six-inch blade. He opened the blade slowly, taking his time, watching the courier's eyes. Then he stepped close to the man, knelt down beside him and began his work.

Eighteen minutes later Rashid stood up, carefully wiped the blood off the blade of his knife, smiled at Khamil and walked away. Khamil glanced once more at the bloody red mess in front of him, nodded in satisfaction, turned and walked back into the shade of the building, Abbas following behind.

In the largest room of the derelict house were a couple of chairs and a battered table. Khamil led the way into the room, sat down and looked up at Abbas, who remained standing respectfully in front of him. After a few moments, Khamil spoke: 'I do not like it. Even now, before we start, before we have any contact with them, I feel uncomfortable about it.' Khamil fell silent, his almost black eyes beneath his red and white checked *keffiyeh* – a potent and visible symbol of his unswerving allegiance to Osama bin Laden – troubled and concerned.

Abbas dropped his eyes, but stood his ground. 'I, too, am unhappy at the implications, at the prospect of working so closely with them, *sayidi*, but we must face facts. We cannot develop this technology for ourselves, at least not within the foreseeable future, and if we buy what we need we will still have the very difficult problem of delivery. My analysis suggests that co-operation is the only option which offers us even a chance of success.'

Hassan Abbas stopped and waited. He had, he knew, staked not only his career but also his life on this single moment. Despite his Western appearance – the light grey suits and glistening black Oxfords he frequently wore, and his fluency in English and French – Sadoun Khamil was still at heart a sand Arab. That meant, amongst other things, that he was accustomed to meting out summary justice to anyone who displeased him.

And what Abbas had suggested was hardly likely to please him. It was, however, nothing less than the truth, and Abbas hoped he knew Khamil well enough to believe that he valued the truth more than anything else. Abbas waited, hardly daring to breathe, staring intently at the floor in front of him. His eyes traced patterns in the dust, concentrating on the insignificant, as he waited to hear what Khamil would say next. Waiting for the words that would either reinforce his position as Khamil's chief of staff or perhaps lead him to the waste ground behind the building to join the courier. Hideous images of Rashid at work span through Abbas' mind while he waited, immobile, for whatever would come.

Khamil stirred slightly in the creaking wooden chair behind the table, then stood up and walked across the room to the small and glassless window. The view was of no interest to him, just dunes and rubble, but Khamil put his hands on his hips and stared out for nearly two minutes. Then he turned round and walked back to the table. He sat down, looked across at Abbas, and uttered a single word: 'How?'

Abbas breathed again, and raised his eyes. 'Money, *sayidi*, money. Always they have needed money, and now more than ever. We have the hard currency they crave, and they have the devices we need. It will be a simple exchange, the one for the other.'

'Hardly simple, Hassan,' Khamil murmured. 'And how long will it take?'

'For everything to be in place, four to five years, *sayidi*.'

Khamil looked up, surprised. 'Why so long?' he demanded. 'Surely the devices are available immediately?'

Abbas nodded. 'The American weapons, yes, *sayidi*, but the devices we require will have to be specially made. But that is not the principal reason for the delay. The problem is the delivery. It is essential that all the weapons are positioned in total secrecy, and that means we must take time, and take care. We will have to lease suitable premises, arrange the proper power supplies and communication systems, all before even one of the devices is positioned. And the devices themselves will have to be delivered piece by piece. If knowledge of the plan leaks out before we are ready, the scheme will fail before we can even begin to implement it.'

Khamil considered this for a few moments. 'I will have to consult my colleague,' he said finally. 'He wanted action sooner than you have suggested is possible.'

Abbas nodded again. He knew, as everyone who worked for Khamil knew, exactly who his 'colleague' was, but nobody ever so much as breathed his name. This was in part respect, or more accurately fear, and in part simple security.

It is no secret that the West's two most important Communications Intelligence monitoring stations – the American National Security Agency at Fort George Meade in Maryland and Britain's Government Communications Headquarters at Cheltenham in Gloucestershire – monitor communications of all sorts, worldwide. The NSA has a weekly output of over two hundred tons of classified data based on communications intercepts alone.

This prodigious 'take' is principally derived from the highly classified Echelon monitoring system, and comprises mobile and satellite telephone calls – probably the easiest of all to detect – radio and signal traffic, internet data-transfer and electronic mail intercepts derived from the Carnivore programme, and even calls between land-line telephones where any part of the transmission involves a satellite or microwave link or passes through a 'friendly' nation. The British Foreign Office, for example, as part of the joint GCHQ/NSA agreement, monitors every international telephone call which originates or terminates in Britain.

With this degree of intercept capability, human monitoring is clearly impossible, so computers do the job instead, listening out for any mention, in any language, of certain names and words. The words are fairly obvious, and are specified by the agency which will be the ultimate recipient of the product, but the names change as the political situation alters. Since the early 1990s, and following the suicide bombings in Jakarta and Lagos, one name in particular has been right at the head of every Western nation's 'most wanted' list with respect to terrorism. For that reason, neither the name Osama bin Laden nor al-Qaeda were ever spoken aloud by any of his followers.

'I have,' Abbas began deferentially, 'another suggestion.'

Ten minutes later Khamil sat back in his chair. The plan Abbas had proposed was outrageous, alarming, stunning in its concept and fraught with logistical and other problems, but it had an undeniable simplicity which he knew would appeal when he proposed it, as he had known immediately that he would, to bin Laden. 'And how long before this could be implemented?'

'Within two years, probably within eighteen months. Some of the assets are already in place. Ready for this, or a similar opportunity.'

Khamil nodded in satisfaction. That was more like it. 'They are fully trained and committed?' he asked.

'Their commitment is not in doubt, *sayidi*, and the training they require is not extensive. In fact,' Abbas added with a slight smile, 'several of them are receiving instruction even as we speak, in America.'

Khamil smiled – the irony was not lost on him. 'What are the chances of failure?'

Abbas smiled again. 'None, *sayidi*. It will succeed.'

Khamil nodded again, then looked sharply at Abbas. 'How do you know? How do you know it will succeed?'

Abbas looked momentarily at a loss for words. 'A figure of speech, *sayidi*. I meant that the plan was almost certain to succeed. The chances of failure are extremely small.'

Khamil shook his head. 'No. I have known you for many years, and you are always exact in what you say. You said you know this plan will succeed. So, I ask again, how?'

Abbas stood silently in front of the desk, his mind racing. He knew Khamil, knew that he wouldn't be satisfied by a vague discussion of semantics. Khamil had an uncanny ability to sniff out truth and false-hood, and infinite patience and persistence in the search. He would, Abbas realized, have to tell him the truth, embarrassing though it would be. 'There is a book, *sayidi*,' Abbas began.

Five minutes later Khamil leaned back in his chair and laughed. 'So, Hassan, now we know where you receive your inspiration: from the ramblings of an infidel who scribbled down his visions five hundred years ago. What nonsense!'

Abbas shook his head slightly. 'You mock me, *sayidi*, but in truth this Nostradamus does seem to suggest that our plan will succeed. And,' he added, 'other prophecies he made have been fulfilled, such as the downfall of the Shah.'

Khamil continued to smile, but shook his head. 'It's all nonsense, Hassan. The future is not pre-ordained, as well you know. If you wish to rely on the obscure words of a Frenchman dead half a millennium, that's your choice. But it does save me the trouble of choosing a code-name for you in our communications. I shall simply call you "The Prophet".'

Chapter One

In the Lubyanka Prison a man lay dying, and he had no idea why. No medical practitioner in the world could have diagnosed his ailment, for he had none, but he was nevertheless dying, and there was nothing any doctor could do to save him. At four fifteen, he had perhaps four hours to live. He knew it. His jailers knew it. And the white-coated technicians preparing the table and equipment in the soundproof interrogation room knew it.

He knew, without the slightest doubt, that he would never see the sun again, never see a blue sky or the waves breaking on the rocky shores of his native Northumberland. His future, short as it was, would be tightly constrained, limited to the four discoloured concrete walls that imprisoned him, and to whatever colours the KGB had elected to paint the basement interrogation room where they were going to kill him.

When they came for him, he was sobbing in despair, but when the guard put a hand on his shoulder to drag him off the stained mattress and on to his feet, he screamed and lashed out blindly, using fists, feet and teeth. The struggle was short and pointless. The captive lapsed into unconsciousness when the blackjack descended on the back of his head, and when he awoke the short journey to the interrogation room was over, and he was strapped naked on the table.

An elderly grey-haired man with twinkling, innocent blue eyes and a short white beard leaned over him, looked down and smiled. 'Good. You are awake. No, don't try and talk yet. You will have plenty of time for that later. First I want to explain things to you.' The Russian's English

8

was fluent, the accent faintly American. He leaned closer. 'I am what you British would call of the old school. I am an old-style interrogator. I do use drugs, the truth drugs, scopolamine and sodium pentothal, but they are unreliable and people can be taught, as no doubt you were taught, to resist their effects. And they can just as easily kill, if they are used in too large doses, or cause such great brain damage that we are left with a gibbering idiot. And we don't want that, do we?'

He chuckled, looking a little like a benevolent Santa Claus, and sat down on a stained plastic chair next to the table. 'So, I only use them if I can take my time, and increase the dosage slowly. But now we need answers quickly, and the best method of persuasion, I believe, is pain. Pain is my profession. I will start with a little pain, to show that I am serious, and then I will ask you some questions. If you answer those, I might not hurt you again, but you will probably lie, or I might think that you are lying, and then I will hurt you more, a lot more, and then I will ask you again. And I will go on like that until I decide that you have nothing more to tell me. If you have helped me, I will kill you quickly, and it won't hurt. But if you have not told me what I wanted to know, then you can take a long, long time to die and you will suffer pain that you will not believe possible.'

He paused and looked down at the Englishman. 'The point, you see, is that I will get the answers I need. I always get the answers. How much pain it costs you is up to you, but I will get the answers. Now, I am going to leave you for a few minutes while you think about what I have said. You must choose, not me.'

He stood up, walked over to the two white-coated figures waiting in the corner and spoke softly to them, then left the room. As soon as he had gone, the technicians moved two trolleys over to the table, and left them in the clear sight of the captive. Each displayed an array of medical equipment – saws, knives and scalpels – as well as more utilitarian tools – pliers, screwdrivers, soldering iron, bolt-cutters and a blowlamp. The Englishman had no doubts about why they had been left there, just as he had no doubt that the interrogator would use any or all of the equipment to obtain whatever information he wanted.

About five minutes later the door opened and the interrogator entered, followed by a white-coated figure carrying a small black bag and a stethoscope, and walked straight to the table. 'Now, to business,' he said. 'I enjoy my work, and I am very good at it, but I would still rather avoid all the unpleasantness of the physical side.' He waved his hand at the two trolleys. 'So, what have you decided? If you help me, I, or my medical friend here, will end it all for you with a simple injection. If not, well, you know what will happen.'

The Englishman was no coward, but neither was he stupid. Faced with a terminal situation, from which there was clearly no possibility of escape, there was only one choice. 'I'll answer any questions you ask,' he said, his voice choked with fear.

'Good, good.' The interrogator sounded gratified. He sat down on the plastic chair, picked up his clipboard, selected a particular page on it and began the questioning. Two minutes later he sat back, then stood up. He did not look pleased. 'That is not what I wanted to hear. I do not think you realize the gravity of this situation. I have explained the options to you, but I must have the information I want.'

The captive shook his head desperately. 'But I don't know the answers,' he shouted. 'I'm trying to answer your questions, but if I don't know the answers, how can I?'

The interrogator looked at him coldly, then smiled again and resumed his seat. 'Well, let's try once again, shall we? But this time, you really must help me.' Again the questions began, but again the answers did not satisfy the interrogator, and after a few minutes he stood up and shook his head sadly. 'I thought you were going to be sensible about this, but I was wrong. I told you that I must have this information, and you will tell me – now or later.'

The Englishman shouted again, naked terror in his eyes. 'I'll tell you anything you want – everything that I know. But these questions – I don't know what you're talking about.'

The interrogator looked down at him and patted his shoulder gently. 'We shall see,' he said softly. 'We shall see.' He stepped across to the wall next to the interrogation table, reached up and clicked on two switches marked, in Cyrillic script, 'video' and 'audio'. Directly above the table, two red lights winked on, showing that the video camera and tape recorder were operating. The interrogator nodded, walked across to the corner of the room, selected a waterproof apron from a peg, and put it on. He motioned to the technicians and the doctor, and they followed his example.

The captive on the table began to scream. The interrogator looked over at him and issued a swift command to one of the technicians, who walked over to the table and roughly applied a sticking-plaster gag. The doctor sat down at the captive's left side, and attached a blood-pressure cuff to the Englishman's arm. He opened his bag and prepared a number of injections, principally stimulants, and taped his stethoscope microphone to the man's chest. With his preparations complete, he nodded to the interrogator.

The technicians waited expectantly by the trolleys, looking at the captive with all the compassion of a couple of butchers contemplating a side of beef. Finally, the interrogator sat down again on the plastic chair and leaned close to the Englishman, who was still trying to scream, even through the gag. 'Quiet, now,' he said. 'You have had your chance to act sensibly. Now you must face the consequences.'

The interrogator spoke briefly in Russian, and leaned forward to watch as the technicians began their work. He enjoyed assessing the resilience of his subjects, and this man, he was certain, would be easy to break. Four minutes later the captive passed out. When the doctor had revived him, the technicians started again. Then they tore off the gag and the questioning began. The answers still didn't please the old man with the innocent blue eyes, so he stepped back from the table and motioned the technicians back to work. When the captive had stopped screaming, the grey-haired man asked him exactly the same questions again.

A little over two hours later they stopped. The captive had mercifully gone into massive shock, and no efforts by the doctor or the technicians had the slightest effect. The interrogator stood and looked down at the wreck of the man on the table for a long moment. Then he selected a thin steel probe from one of the instrument trolleys, and carefully pushed it through the captive's left eyeball and deep into the brain cavity. For good measure, he did the same to the right eye. He pulled out the probe and tossed it back on the instrument trolley, then turned to the chief technician. 'Get rid of it,' he said.

Officially, the *Komitet Gosudarstvennoy Bezopasnosti*, the KGB, has ceased to exist, and certain parts of the organization's old headquarters building at number 2 Lubyanskaya ploshchad – formerly Dzerzhinsky Square – are even open to parties of tourists during the day. The tourists are not allowed into any sensitive areas of the building, and the impression given by their guides is that the huge structure is just a shell, no longer used for any important purposes, a monument to an evil past that has no place in modern, post-*glasnost*, Russia.

But, as with so many things in Russia, past and present, the official position differs markedly from reality. Certainly, the KGB has officially ceased to exist, but a new organization, the *Sluzhba Vneshney Razvyedki Rossi* or SVR, has inherited its mantle – or at least that of the First Chief Directorate – with virtually no visible changes apart from the new name. The SVR occupies the former KGB's sixty-acre office complex at Yazenevo, located close to the orbital ring road in Moscow's southern suburbs, and virtually all the personnel now employed by the SVR are ex-KGB staff, many still in their original offices and doing precisely the same jobs.

In fact, the old building in the heart of Moscow is still used, outside what might be termed visiting hours, for purposes little different from those that characterized the heyday of the KGB. Number 2 Lubyanskaya ploshchad has a grandeur and a presence that is lacking in the featureless new complex, and many of the more senior officers much prefer to operate from it when their duties permit. It is also useful for clandestine meetings or covert actions that would not be practical, or even possible, at Yazenevo.

The grey-haired man left the cellar after removing his waterproof apron and blood-splattered white coat, and ascended in the lift to the third floor. He walked down the light green painted corridor, his shoes rapping on the parquet flooring, then paused and entered a room after a perfunctory knock. He carried the clipboard upon which he had made copious notes in both English and Cyrillic script during the interrogation. The audio tapes would be transcribed later, and the video tape was nestling in his jacket pocket, ready to be hand-delivered to a Ministerial address later that day, but his verbal report of the interrogation was required immediately.

In the room at a massive old oak table, ranged with brand-new office chairs, sat two men. On the left was a tall, thin and sharp-featured man wearing the uniform of a lieutenant general in an artillery regiment. The GRU – *Glavnoye Razvedyvatelnoye Upravleniye*, Chief Intelligence Directorate of the Soviet General Staff, the Russian military intelligence organization – does not have a uniform of its own, and Viktor Grigorevich Bykov continued to wear the uniform of his previous regiment, in which he still nominally served. He was sipping dark Turkish coffee from a fine china cup.

On the opposite side of the table – for the GRU and the KGB have never been willing bedfellows – sat a senior SVR general. Nicolai Fedorovich Modin was the former head of Department V of the KGB – the Executive Action Department responsible for sabotage, kidnapping and assassination. A powerfully built man of medium height, iron-grey hair topping a flat, almost Slavic face, he could have passed in a crowd as just another Russian peasant – as indeed he frequently had done in the early part of his KGB career.

Originally known as the Thirteenth Department of Line F, Department V was reorganized and renamed in 1969, but the KGB slang term for its activities – *mokrie dela* – remained unchanged. The Russian expression means 'wet affairs', because most of Department V's activities involved the spilling of blood. With the creation of the SVR, the General's title had changed, but not his duties.

As the SVR interrogator entered the room, Bykov put down his cup. 'Well?'

The interrogator shrugged his shoulders, walked across the carpeted floor and helped himself to coffee from the American-made percolator. Sipping the bitter liquid, he sat down in a chair at the end of the table. 'I need this,' he said.

The GRU officer drummed his fingers on the table impatiently. 'Well?'

'Nothing.'

'Nothing?'

The grey-haired man shook his head, and put his cup down. He passed the clipboard over. Nicolai Modin took it, scanned rapidly through the notes, then put it down on the table and looked up.

Viktor Bykov reached over, took the board and stared at it. 'Is he . . .?' The interrogator nodded. Bykov tossed the clipboard down angrily, and looked with disgust at three small spots of blood on the interrogator's collar. 'You should have used drugs. We allowed you adequate time for a thorough interrogation. Your methods are crude and out of date.'

Modin intervened. 'How the SVR gets its answers is none of your concern, Bykov. We use whatever methods seem most expedient.'

'I question the expediency of using this animal –' Bykov said to Modin, gesturing at the interrogator, who was sipping his coffee with a pleasant half-smile on his face '– on such a sensitive matter. These days the GRU very rarely has to resort to such crude tactics.'

The interrogator put down his cup and interrupted. 'You miss the point, General. I did not have time for a thorough interrogation – with a resistant subject it could have taken days or weeks to obtain results with drugs, and you needed answers today. The—'

'Nonsense,' Bykov interrupted. 'You could have—'

'No, General, I could not.' The raised voice cut across Bykov's. The smile had left the grey-haired man's face, and his blue eyes were steady, bright and totally devoid of humour or compassion. 'This is my field. I am the expert, and if I tell you something you should listen, and perhaps even learn.'

Modin leaned back in his chair. Despite the seriousness of the situation, and his deep personal dislike of the interrogator, he was almost beginning to enjoy it.

Bykov was furious. 'How dare you address me in such a manner? I am a lieutenant general in the GRU—'

'That is precisely why I can address you like that, or in any other manner that I wish. I am the senior SVR interrogator. Neither you nor any other member of the GRU has any power whatsoever over me, and I suggest you remember that.'

'Enough, both of you,' Modin interjected. He pointed at the interrogator. 'You. Finish what you were going to say.'

'Thank you, General. I would be delighted to do so, and preferably –' he looked sharply at Bykov '– without any further ill-informed interruptions.' He turned to face the SVR officer. 'I agree that my methods are crude, but they are rapid, and they do work. All my interrogations have yielded positive results, just as this one has.'

'Rubbish,' General Modin said, picking up the clipboard and waving it. 'There is nothing here that is of the slightest use to us. There is not a single mention of the project.'

The interrogator smiled. 'Precisely, comrade. Because the subject did not know the answers to any of the questions you instructed me to ask.'

Modin considered this for a moment. 'Are you sure – absolutely certain?'

'Quite certain. If he had known, he would certainly have told me. He would have told me anything. Anything at all.' The interrogator chuckled and picked up his coffee cup again.

Modin stared at him with an expression of acute distaste, then spoke. 'Get out.'

The smile left the interrogator's face for an instant, and his blue eyes stared without expression at Modin. Then he gently placed his cup and saucer on the table, stood up and bowed slightly to the senior officer, and left the room without a word.

When the door had closed behind him, Modin looked across the table. 'He would have known, wouldn't he?' he asked.

'Who?' Bykov was unsure what the SVR officer meant.

'The Britisher. If anyone here in Moscow had known, it would have been him?'

'Definitely. In his position, he had to have known. What other reason could he have had for sending his deputy to Sosnogorsk? What other conclusion could we have drawn?'

Modin shook his head. 'And all for nothing. What a waste.'

There was genuine regret in his voice. Although Nicolai Modin had ordered the termination of many – far too many – men in his long and successful career with the KGB and SVR, he had always been personally satisfied that each of them had deserved to die. His assiduity in checking and double-checking the details of each case before signing the termination order was not just a matter of personal pride; it was also the mark of a professional intelligence officer.

There are few rules in the 'wilderness of mirrors', as the clandestine world has been aptly named, but one obeyed by almost every intelligence service is that opposition agents are never terminated without very good reason. This reluctance does not derive from any sense of compassion or respect for human life, but simply from considerations of operational necessity. The ever-present fear is that even a single execution could lead to an escalating spiral of captures and killings – essentially a private war – something that no service would want. The fear is so prevalent that, if a termination is thought to be essential, it is not unknown for the deceased operative's parent agency to be advised afterwards, with an apology and a justification for the action taken.

Modin had no doubts about the real identity of the man whose body was even then beginning to stiffen in the sub-basement of the building. He knew who he was and the organization for which he had worked, as he had known since the Englishman's arrival in Moscow. If the interrogation had produced the answers that both he and Bykov had expected, Modin would probably have regarded the man's death as justifiable, but the results the interrogator had obtained worried and concerned him.

The GRU officer, sensing the uncertainty of the older man, spoke again. 'Minister Trushenko's orders were most specific, General. We had no option but to obey – to make sure. It was the only way.'

Modin nodded again. 'I know. It's just that sometimes I wonder if we're right – even if he's right.'

'Whatever our personal feelings,' Bykov said, 'whatever our private doubts, we've gone too far now to stop it. We have to carry it through to the end. We have no choice, no choice at all. What we're doing is for the good of Russia, for the good of all Russians.'

Good old Bykov, Nicolai Modin thought to himself. You could always rely on him to quote the party line. He stood up and walked to the window and stared through the bullet-proof glass across Lubyanskaya ploshchad. Early-morning Moscow was quiet, with little traffic and fewer pedestrians. He looked with a sense of sadness towards the centre of the square where, until the madness of *glasnost*, the bronze statue of the founder of the *Cheka*, 'Iron' Feliks Dzerzhinsky, erected by

Khrushchev as a tribute to the KGB, had stared with sightless eyes down what was then known as Marx prospekt towards ploshchad Revoljucii – Revolution Square. They had been better days, but there was, perhaps, just a hope – Modin put it no higher – that they would return, if the project succeeded. Modin squared his shoulders, wheeled round and strode briskly back to the desk, his uncertainty gone. 'He'd better be right. You do realize what this means, don't you?'

Bykov, who was reading through the notes on the clipboard, looked up and nodded. 'Yes,' he said. 'It means that the British don't know, so they can't have told the Americans.'

Chapter 2

'Colonel!' The urgent note in the young officer's voice brought Vitali Yazov across the darkened room at speed.

'Yes, Captain? What is it?' Colonel Yazov asked, leaning over the younger man's shoulder and looking at the displays.

Captain Kryuchkov shook his head. 'It's gone again, sir. A solid but intermittent contact, at high level – not a satellite or debris, as far as I can tell.'

'From which direction, and what range?' Yazov asked.

The captain pointed at his screen. 'There, sir. Almost due north and about five hundred miles out, closing rapidly.' Kryuchkov had inserted five electronic markers into his azimuth display, each corresponding to a single contact detected by the LPAR. Each marker showed the time the object was detected, and its estimated height, speed and heading.

The Large Phased-Array Radar, NATO reporting name Hen House, is designed for ballistic missile detection, satellite tracking and battle management. On the northern Russian border LPARs are positioned at Mukachevo, Baranovichi, Skrunda and Murmansk as well as Pechora. The LPAR is configured to look high, for satellites and Intercontinental Ballistic Missiles, and outwards from Russian territory, and the contact was only being intermittently detected by its lowest lobes.

Colonel Yazov scratched the back of his neck thoughtfully. 'First contact over the Kara Sea,' he murmured, 'and tracking south.' He leaned closer and looked carefully at the calculated speed and estimated height of the unknown return, based upon which lobes of the LPAR had been penetrated. 'At Mach three and above seventy thousand feet.'

He straightened up, gestured at the LPAR display and issued his instructions. 'Record any other contacts with that object. Designate it Hostile One and get me a predicted track across the whole country, immediately. I'm going to talk to Moscow.'

The captain turned round in his seat, surprised. 'Do you know what it is?' he asked.

Yazov nodded. 'Yes. At least, I think I do. But it doesn't make any sense.'

British Embassy, Sofiyskaya naberezhnaya 14, Moscow

'I'm sorry, Mr Willis, but I really don't see what you're doing here. I can assure you that the Embassy staff are more than capable of handling matters at this end.'

The man in the crumpled suit looked across the desk. Diplomats were not his favourite people, and diplomats who thought that their abilities were being called into question were even more touchy than usual. He ran a hand through his unruly fair hair and tried again.

'I assure you, Secretary Horne, nobody is suggesting that your Embassy staff are in any way lacking. I'm here for just three reasons. I have to ensure that the body of Mr Newman is returned as rapidly as possible to Britain. I've also been asked to collect some of Mr Newman's personal effects for his family, but the main reason I'm in Moscow is to carry out an initial investigation into the circumstances of the accident.' He drew a breath and held up his hand to forestall any protest. 'There could be some international repercussions, depending on the degree of culpability of the Russian driver. My company won't be prepared to make any settlement until this unfortunate accident has been thoroughly investigated.'

William Horne, First Secretary to Her Britannic Majesty's Ambassador to Russia and the Commonwealth of Independent States, looked across his polished oak desk, then back to the letter of introduction he had been given some fifteen minutes earlier. Horne was tall and thin, and a well-preserved fifty-five. A career diplomat, with a fastidious approach to life and total dedication to his work, he was expecting an ambassadorial appointment the following year. He was keen to ensure the smooth running of the Embassy, and he didn't like uninvited visitors poking their noses into things that were none of their concern. The man Willis, he was sure, was trouble of some kind – he had a quality of stillness and menace that Horne found quite unnerving – but he couldn't think of a valid reason for having him thrown out. His instinct, however, was perfectly correct.

The man calling himself Willis, whose real name was Paul Richter, knew absolutely nothing about insurance and cared less. He sat patiently, saying nothing, and looking at Horne with disinterest. Richter was conscious of his somewhat crumpled clothing, the result of hasty packing and a long flight in economy class, which Horne's professional elegance threw into sharp contrast. Richter had never been concerned with appearances – his or anyone else's – and Horne's immaculate suit and mirror-polished shoes amused, rather than impressed, him. While serving as an officer in the Royal Navy, Richter had once, and with a certain amount of truth, been described as looking like a badly packed parachute.

Horne removed rimless spectacles from his large and slightly hooked nose and absent-mindedly began polishing the lenses with a spotless white handkerchief. Replacing the glasses, he looked across the desk again and pursed his thin lips. 'It is most irregular. There was none of this fuss when the Second Secretary passed away last year – although, of course, he hadn't been involved in a road accident.'

'He also wasn't insured with my company, sir. We pride ourselves on being as thorough as possible in any case involving accidental death on foreign soil. Unfortunately, there are other companies that take their responsibilities a good deal less seriously.' Richter leaned forward, and assumed what he hoped looked like the expression adopted by an insurance company representative scenting a sale. 'If you are interested, I—'

'No thank you, Mr Willis. All my needs in that regard are already satisfied.' Horne looked at the letter again, then at Richter. 'Very well. What exactly do you want us to do?'

Richter smiled. 'Thank you. I would like sight of Mr Newman's body – not for identification, as that will have to be done formally by his next-of-kin in Britain – but simply to confirm that the injuries as stated on the death certificate issued by the Russian doctor are consistent with those on the body.' Richter leaned forward and lowered his voice slightly. 'It is not unknown, Secretary Horne, for some Russian doctors to issue a death certificate without ever seeing the body to which it relates, simply to "oblige" the authorities.'

'I've never heard of that happening,' Horne snapped.

Nor had Richter, until he'd said it, but he nodded solemnly. 'I would also like to inspect the vehicle in which Mr Newman was travelling at the time of his death, and I would like access to his office and his apartment.'

'Why do you need to visit his office and apartment?' Horne asked.

'Nothing to do with the insurance claim,' Richter said smoothly. 'As I said, my company has been asked by Mr Newman's family to collect some small items of a personal nature which they would like returned in advance of the bulk of his effects. That's all.'

'It is most inconvenient, but I suppose we have little choice in the matter.'

Richter refrained from pointing out exactly how little choice Horne really had and stood up. Horne climbed to his feet, glanced disparagingly at Richter's rumpled clothing and extended a professionally limp hand. Richter shook it and looked enquiringly at him. 'See Erroll. Third door on the right. He will make the necessary arrangements.'

Aspen Three Four

'We're being illuminated – I'm getting intermittent detection of low Hen House lobes, probably from Pechora.'

'Roger,' Major Frank Roberts acknowledged briefly, and again checked his flight and engine instruments. Fifteen miles high and travelling at three times the speed of sound, it was almost entirely silent in the cockpit of the SR–71A Blackbird, the rolling thunder of its two massive engines left far behind. A little over six minutes passed; the Blackbird flew two hundred miles closer to Russian airspace.

'Thirty-centimetre radar,' Paul James, the Reconnaissance Systems Officer, reported.

'OK. Keep it quiet as long as you can.'

Four minutes and one hundred and thirty miles later they couldn't keep it quiet any longer. 'Another thirty-centimetre. And I'm getting two ten-centimetre radars and faint unclassified missile fire control radar. They obviously know we're here. Jamming ten- and thirty-centimetre bands.'

'Yup. The question is, have they got anything around here that can catch us?'

'I hope not. Approaching target area. Stand by starboard turn. Turn starboard now, steady heading two three zero. Cameras and sensors now activated.'

The reconnaissance cameras and radiation detectors started working as the aircraft passed over Vorkuta at 1049, and began to cross the Bolshezemel'skaya Tundra. They would continue to operate until Shenkursk, on the river Vaga south-east of Arkhangel'sk, provided nothing happened to stop them.

Voyska IA-PVO Unit, Arkhangel'sk, Confederation of Independent States

Russia possesses the largest and most comprehensive air defence network in the world. Its Radar Surveillance Intercept Unit organization covers the entire frontier of the huge Confederation of Independent States and comprises literally thousands of air defence radars and surface-to-air missile sites. The colonel at Pechora had been quick to deduce the type of the unknown aircraft, but the IA-PVO Headquarters in Moscow already knew about the intruder when he got through on the direct line. Two of the northern border radars of the RSIU had simultaneously detected the Blackbird at around two hundred and eighty miles north of Amderma. Of course, detecting it and stopping it were two entirely different matters.

Standard operating procedures call for a minimum of two interceptors to be available at every PVO base at immediate notice at all times. In this context, the word 'immediate' means precisely that; the aircraft are fully fuelled, fully armed, and the pilots are pre-briefed and sitting in their cockpits, waiting only for the command to start engines.

The predicted track Colonel Yazov had relayed to Moscow matched that which the PVO had already calculated. Interceptor launch orders had been relayed to the three airfields lying closest to that track – one east of Nar'yan Mar, one south of Salekhard, and the other near Sergino – and operational control of the incident was handed to the Arkhangel'sk District PVO Local Headquarters.

'Understood. We have control,' Lieutenant Colonel Kabalin repeated, put the telephone back in its cradle and looked up sharply. 'Where is it now, Privalov?' he demanded, sliding his wheeled chair to the right so he could see the screen in front of his chief intercept controller.

The Blackbird had just completed its planned turn to the southwest over Vorkuta. 'It's just turned, Colonel. Hostile One's new track is approximately two four zero degrees true, speed is unchanged at Mach three. Unless it turns again, that will take it –' the young Lieutenant quickly scanned the display in front of him '– across the Bolshezemel'skaya Tundra,' he finished, with a puzzled frown.

'Never mind where it's going,' Kabalin snapped. 'Just concentrate on stopping it.'

'Yes, sir.' Lieutenant Privalov pressed buttons to specify the aircraft types of the six airborne fighters, which automatically input their maximum speeds into the track computer. Then he activated the predict vectors, electronically generated lines which showed an aircraft's predicted track based upon its current heading and speed. 'The only aircraft which can get near the American aircraft are the two MiG–29s from Nar'yan Mar, and they can't reach its level.'

'No,' Kabalin agreed, 'but their missiles can. Privalov,' Colonel Kabalin ordered, 'you handle the intercept. Vetrov,' he called to the second duty intercept controller, 'issue immediate launch orders for all interceptors we control. Position them at altitude but do not issue intercept vectors.' Lieutenant Vetrov nodded, pressed a group broadcast button on his console and began speaking into the mouthpiece of his headset. 'Galkin,' Kabalin continued, 'assume control of the four MiG–25s.'

'Do we recall them?' Lieutenant Galkin asked.

'Of course not,' Kabalin replied sharply. 'What happens if the American turns again? Keep them in pursuit. In fact,' he added, 'order them to chase the American at dash speed, and instruct the lead aircraft to radiate its fire-control radar immediately.'

'Why, sir?' Galkin was puzzled.

'Look at your screen,' Kabalin said. 'When he detects the MiG–25 radar, the American might turn away, straight towards the MiG–29s. And Privalov,' Kabalin added, 'the orders from Moscow are quite specific. No warning shots, no requests by us for confirmation. Once the MiG–29s have radar lock, they are to engage.'

British Embassy, Sofiyskaya naberezhnaya 14, Moscow

Simon Erroll, known inevitably to junior Embassy staff as Flynn, looked more like a rugby full-back than a diplomat but proved a good deal more hospitable than William Horne. While he didn't exactly welcome his unexpected visitor with open arms, he did organize coffee and biscuits while he attended to 'certain essential matters, old boy. I'm sure you understand'. Richter assured him that he did, and sat and waited. Richter was good at waiting.

Having dealt with the top three files in his in-tray, Erroll gave Richter his undivided attention for the three minutes it took to sketch out exactly what he wanted. 'No problem. Newman's body is here, actually – we have a small mortuary in the basement – and the Russians delivered him yesterday. We can go now, if you like.'

In the basement Erroll ushered Richard down an antiseptically white corridor to a pair of slatted wooden doors. He opened the right-hand door, switched on the light, and led the way into a tiny chapel no more than twelve feet by ten, with the whole of one side hidden behind two deep purple curtains. The only decoration was a small silver crucifix on one wall.

'Hang on a tick, and I'll get the trolley. Then we can pull him out.' Erroll pressed a button and with a faint hum the two curtains parted to reveal a floor-to-ceiling mortuary refrigerator and a wheeled trolley. The top of the trolley was fitted with two parallel lines of rollers to carry a mortuary tray. He opened the fridge door, rapidly cranked the trolley up to the height of the single occupied tray, pushed it into place and slid the tray smoothly on to it.

'Had a holiday job in a mortuary while I was up at Oxford,' he said cheerfully, as he lowered the trolley to a convenient height and began to undo the safety pins holding the sheet closed over the corpse. 'Fascinating work,' he added, 'if somewhat gruesome.'

He paused before removing the sheet and looked at Richter. 'Only fair to warn you that he's not a pretty sight. He was only wearing a lap seat belt and took the impact with his head, so his face is pretty well pulped. That's the trouble with these cheap bloody Russian cars; they've got no padding on the dashboard at all. It's just bare metal. And then the wreck caught fire, which accounts for the burning of the arms and torso.'

Richter nodded, pulled a notebook out of his pocket, wrote 'Graham Newman' at the top of a clean page, added 'Injuries' underneath, and underlined all three words.

With something of a flourish, Erroll peeled away the sheet.

Aspen Three Four

Captain Paul James detected the Mikoyan–Gurevich MiG–25 Foxbat at 1053. 'Fire-control radar – Fox Fire. Full ECM engaged.'

Sophisticated ECM – Electronic Counter-Measures – have to be employed against the Foxbat. Simple jamming doesn't work because the aircraft's Fox Fire radar relies upon sheer power – a 600-kilowatt output – and jam-proof vacuum tube technology rather than solid-state electronics.

Frank Roberts pushed the throttles fully open. Speed and height were the only things he could vary. The mission planners had made it very clear that, except as a last resort, the aircraft's course had to remain exactly as ordered. 'Where is it?'

'No contact. OK, contact now. Twenty-five thousand feet below and twenty-seven miles behind. Range is opening. No launch detection, no danger. Ease the speed.'

At 1101, with the Blackbird again holding Mach three and eighty thousand feet, precisely on the planned surveillance route, Paul James detected a more immediate threat. 'I'm detecting MiG–29 Fulcrum fire-control radar. Two contacts, both green two zero, range forty and indicating fifty thousand feet, climbing slowly and on an intercept heading.'

'Weapon load?'

'They're probably each carrying AA–9 and AA–10 missiles, plus a thirty-millimetre cannon. The missiles are fire-and-forget.'

'Maximum engage range?'

'Twenty miles for the AA–9s, ten for the others. Maintain height – the Fulcrums can't reach us here – but increase speed now to three decimal three.'

The Blackbird surged forward again as Frank Roberts pushed the throttles wide open. Fifteen seconds later the SR–71A systems detected missile launch.

British Embassy, Sofiyskaya naberezhnaya 14, Moscow

Where it wasn't black, the corpse was white and waxy, the result of post-mortem hypostasis – the blood draining to the lowest parts of the body after death – and he hadn't exaggerated the face. There were no discernible features, just a torn and ripped red mess, teeth and bone showing white. Richter extended a hand and touched the skull, feeling the uneven lumps and ridges where the cranium had shattered.

Erroll looked at him quizzically. 'You've seen bodies before, haven't you?' he asked. 'I was quite expecting you to keel over. Lots of people do, you know, especially the ones you least expect. I suppose you've been in mortuaries before for the identification of clients?'

'Something like that,' Richter agreed, writing 'crushed skull' in his notebook. 'Could you remove the rest of the sheet, please – I'd like to see if there are any other injuries.' Apart from the massive trauma to the head, the body was virtually undamaged by impact. Richter examined the limbs and the trunk, looking for any signs of fracture or dislocation, but with the exception of a broken collarbone and two or perhaps three fractured ribs, he found nothing else to write down in his notebook. The fire had made a mess of the hands, blackening and twisting them into clutching claws, but had caused surprisingly little damage, other than superficial charring, to the rest of the body. He lingered for a few minutes over the corpse, and jotted some more brief notes into his book, but for all practical purposes he had finished the examination long before. The injuries were almost precisely what Richter had expected to find. More importantly, he hadn't found the one thing he was looking for.

Aspen Three Four

'Birds away – four launches detected, almost simultaneous. Probably the AA–9s. Interceptors at sixty-five thousand feet and range twenty.'

'Roger.'

'Jamming and ECM engaged. Missile range fifteen – intercept course confirmed on three. One falling away – probably lost radar lock.' Twenty seconds passed. 'Second missile falling away. Remaining two still have radar lock. Engaging the target generator.'

Radar works by transmitting a pulse towards an aircraft and then receiving the return signal that has bounced off it. The direction from which the return signal arrives gives the bearing of the target, and the time between transmission of the pulse and receipt of the return signal provides the aircraft's range. Range and bearing locate a target precisely, for engagement by a missile or interception by fighter aircraft.

The Sanders Associates' AN/ALQ–100 false target generator is designed to confuse air defence radars by providing a return signal to the radar at exactly the right frequency, but at a much higher strength. This effectively obliterates the real return signal and generates a false target some distance away from the aircraft using it.

Paul James used the Blackbird's Enhanced Radar Warning Receiver to detect the precise radar frequency being used by each of the two approaching AA–9 missiles, fed that data into the AN/ALQ–100, and engaged the system. Then he waited.

'SITREP?' The slight note of tension in Roberts' voice was the only indication of the strain he was under.

'OK. Radar lock lost by both missiles. They've each locked on to the false targets, and they should detonate in under a minute, about ten miles astern. Interceptors now out of effective range. Reduce to Mach three in thirty seconds.'

Voyska IA-PVO Unit, Arkhangel'sk, Confederation of Independent States

'The interception was unsuccessful, Colonel,' Privalov said, leaning back in his chair. 'Interceptor One reported that two missiles lost radar lock, and the other two detonated, but well behind the target,' he elaborated. 'Possibly the Americans used decoys.'

'Where are the other interceptors?' Kabalin asked Vetrov, turning away from Privalov.

'We have six pairs airborne, holding at altitude and awaiting intercept vectors. I have positioned them to try to box the American in.' Vetrov pointed to the screen, indicating the positions of the fighters which had been scrambled. 'Here, sir, at Murmansk, Kirov, Gor'kiy, two pairs north of Moscow, and a pair of MiG–31s at Riga.'

Kabalin mused for a few moments. 'If I were flying that aircraft,' he said, 'I would want to clear this area as quickly as possible.' He projected the Blackbird's track down to the south-west and estimated distances to the edge of the CIS. 'My guess is that they'll try to turn to the west or north-west and break out into Finland. And most of our interceptors are holding to the south of the American's track.' He stroked his chin thoughtfully. 'Well,' he said, and reached for a telephone. 'We'll have to do something about that.'

British Embassy, Sofiyskaya naberezhnaya 14, Moscow

'What's that?' Erroll asked, pointing at the body. Running horizontally across the corpse's chest, a few inches below the shoulders, was a thin and virtually straight line of light bruising.

'I don't know,' Richter replied, looking carefully at the mark on the body. 'Perhaps it was caused by the top of the steering wheel, but the line looks too straight to me.' As Erroll replaced the safety pins, Richter asked how they'd identified the corpse.

'No problem. Newman had been out somewhere and was driving to the Embassy when he ran into the back of a parked lorry loaded with steel girders. He had all his documents on him, and the Embassy pass on what was left of the windscreen. They cut him out, took him to hospital, confirmed he was dead and then called us.'

Richter nodded, and helped him push the tray back into the fridge. In the lift he asked where the death certificate was. 'In my office,' Erroll said. 'Beaky – sorry, the First Secretary – handed the whole lot over to me as soon as he'd done his bit signalling the FCO, drafting the letter of condolence for the Ambassador to send and so on. Between you and me, he's not too keen on the sight of blood. Even likes his steaks well done, if you know what I mean.'

Back in his office Erroll sifted through his pending tray and extracted a buff envelope. 'Here we are. How's your Russian?'

'Sorry. Hardly a word,' Richter replied, lying with a perfectly straight face.

'OK, I'll translate. This section here is "Cause of Death", and it says, er, God, his writing's awful. Ah, yes, "anterior of skull sustained violent impact resulting in numerous fractures, extensive bleeding and extrusion of" – what's that? – "brain matter, with severance of spinal column". I suppose "crushed head" would be a bit brief, wouldn't it?'

'I've never known a medical man use one word where six would do almost the same job,' Richter said. 'Can I take that certificate?'

Erroll frowned. 'Afraid not. It's going in the Diplomatic Bag tomorrow, but you can have a photocopy if that helps.'

Richter actually wanted neither the original nor a copy, but he said that would be fine, and asked if he could see the car immediately, and the apartment and Newman's office straight after lunch.

'Why the hurry?'

'I'm booked on the British Airways flight back to London this afternoon.'

'Oh, I see. Right, here's the report of the accident, with an English translation, and I'll have a copy of the death certificate ready for you this afternoon.'

Aspen Three Four

The cameras had started rolling at 1049, and they completed the run at 1112, just twenty-three minutes covering nearly seven hundred miles of Russian territory. At twelve minutes past eleven the mission was, in a tactical sense, complete, but they still had a long way to go.

Paul James calculated that they would cross the Russian frontier at 1122 just north of St Petersburg – this route would enable the Blackbird to exit into Finnish airspace as quickly as possible after completion of the mission – and then head west into the Gulf of Finland, which meant about another ten minutes of flying over hostile territory after the cameras and detectors were switched off.

'Missile fire control radar! Green three zero. No classification.'

Once again the Blackbird lurched as full power was applied. With the surveillance run complete and tactical freedom restored, Frank Roberts was taking no chances, and as well as increasing speed he turned to port, away from the radar's bearing, and climbed. At ninety-five thousand feet and just under Mach 3.1, the aircraft levelled out.

The missile didn't appear, but Paul James called two further missile fire control radars, both ahead and to starboard, in the next three minutes. Each time, no missile appeared, but the port turns made by the Blackbird to evade took the aircraft progressively further to the south of the planned exit route.

'I don't like this. We're being pushed around.'

'More importantly, we're getting pushed too far south,' Paul James replied. 'It's time we got out of here. Turn starboard heading two nine zero.'

'Roger that,' Roberts replied, as he initiated the turn. 'I get the feeling they've been trying to shepherd us towards something.'

He was right. The 'something' appeared two minutes and fifteen seconds later.

Chapter 3

'It's turning, Colonel,' Lieutenant Vetrov said. 'We have forced the American down to the south, almost as far as Vologda, but now he's turning to the west.'

'Can the Moscow interceptors catch him?' Kabalin demanded.

Vetrov switched in the predict vectors, then shook his head. 'The easterly pair definitely can't,' he replied, 'and the pair to the west are MiG–29s. They can't hope to catch the American spy-plane in a tail-chase.'

'Privalov,' Kabalin ordered, swinging round in his seat, 'take control of the Riga MiG–31s. They're all we have left. For all our sakes, they had better not fail.'

British Embassy, Sofiyskaya naberezhnaya 14, Moscow

In one corner of the parking area behind the Embassy building was a green tarpaulin loosely covering a crumpled wreck. It was just about possible to identify it as a small and somewhat elderly VAZ (*Volzhsky Avtomobilny Zavod*), or Lada as they are known outside Russia. It was about two-thirds as long as it should have been. The bonnet and front wings were crumpled and buckled backwards, the front tyres were slashed and torn on the ruined wheels, and the windscreen was smashed. The driving compartment and front end were blackened by fire. Both doors had apparently been immovably jammed shut in the crash, as the driver's had been cut open, probably by an air-driven ripper gun, to get at the interior.

Like most old cheap Russian cars, it had only lap seat belts, which explained why the occupant had suffered such horrendous damage to his face and head. With the belt done up, the impact would have swung his body violently forward and downwards, pivoting at the hips, and causing his head to strike first the top of the steering wheel and then, if the impact had been violent enough, the top of the dashboard. The rib and clavicle fractures had undoubtedly been sustained by the impact of the torso with the steering wheel on its rigid column.

Richter looked carefully at the floor, and at the pedals. The former was buckled very badly, and the brake, clutch and accelerator pedals were twisted and bent. This was exactly what he had expected from the external damage to the front end of the vehicle, but not at all what would be indicated by the lack of lower limb fractures on the body. The logic was simple enough; if the driver had been intending to kill himself, he would have had his foot hard on the accelerator pedal. If he hadn't been on a suicide trip, he would have been pressing the brake pedal as though his life depended on it. In either case, he would have sustained at least one fracture or dislocation in his right leg.

The fact that there were no fractures meant that the man's feet were clear of the pedals at the moment of impact, which made no sense at all. Or, rather, it made no sense when taken in conjunction with the accident report. It actually made excellent sense to Richter. He straightened up from the wreck, made several notes in his small book, mainly for Erroll's benefit, took down the registration number and put the book away.

'It's not surprising poor old Newman died in that, is it?'

'It was not,' Richter said, choosing his words carefully as they walked together back towards the Embassy building, 'a survivable accident.'

Aspen Three Four

'Radar contact. Green one five at sixty-five. Closing rapidly.'
   'Oh, fuck.'

'No emissions, no classification, high speed. Broad spectrum jamming on; ECM on.'

'Turning away. Keep talking.'

'Stop the turn. Second contact. Red two zero at sixty-two miles. High speed, heading towards. No emissions. Probably two Foxbats, still under ground control. Both are high, above sixty. Contact to starboard designated Bandit One, contact to port Bandit Two.'

The SR–71A had turned to port, but Frank Roberts now straightened out and dived, picking up speed. The aircraft reached Mach 3.2 as it passed seventy-five thousand feet.

'Bandit One green two zero at fifty-six miles, indicating sixty-five thousand; Bandit Two red one zero at fifty miles and sixty-two thousand. Both Bandits now on intercept courses, obviously still under ground control and – wait! Zaslon radar emissions detected from both contacts! Both MiG–31 Foxhound.'

'Shit, that's all we need. Remind me – what are they carrying?'

'Probably four AA–9 Amos and either two AA–7 Apex or four AA–8 Aphids each.'

'What's the optimum engage range?'

'The Apex and Aphids aren't a problem, but the Amos has a range of sixty miles, with snap-up capability. The missiles are semi-active radar homing. Bandit One now green two five at fifty, level at sixty-five; Bandit Two still red one zero at forty-five, climbing slowly.'

The Blackbird was passing sixty thousand feet in a thirty-degree dive. Boxed-in by the Foxhounds, the one thing Roberts could not do was turn away. That would have turned the aircraft back towards the east, and safety lay only to the west, and it would also have slowed the Blackbird significantly, making it an easier target for the missiles carried by the Foxhounds. With no self-defence capability apart from the sophisticated ECM systems, he had to rely on superior performance – superior both to the Foxhounds and to their weapons.

'Bandit One green two seven at forty-five; Bandit Two red one zero at forty. Both now descending to follow us. Not too low, boss, we're getting close to SAM engage limits.'

In fact, the Russian SAM–5 has a maximum ceiling of 125,000 feet – thirty thousand feet higher than the Blackbird's operational ceiling – and can carry a small thermonuclear warhead designed to destroy enemy bombers and missiles within about one hundred miles of the point of detonation. But this lethal missile has only ever been deployed in relatively small numbers around particularly sensitive sites, and the Blackbird's mission planners had calculated a route which avoided all known SAM–5 sites by at least one hundred miles. What Paul James was more worried about were the short-range conventional surface-to-air missiles which were scattered like confetti across the whole of the Asian landmass.

'We're getting out of here right now.'

The Blackbird was indicating Mach 3.3 and passing fifty thousand feet as Frank Roberts initiated the climb. His tactic was simple. The Foxhound is known to have impressive high-altitude capabilities, but due to its reliance upon conventional aerodynamics and relatively unsophisticated engines, it is not particularly agile at high altitudes. In particular, climbing turns tend to bleed off speed very rapidly.

In contrast, the Blackbird is comparatively agile and, having induced the Foxhounds to follow him down – as he had known they would have to if they were to get the SR–71A within their missile engagement limits – Frank Roberts now hoped the Blackbird's superior climbing ability would get him above and beyond the Foxhounds and out of range.

'Bandit One green three zero range thirty-five, five thousand below; Bandit Two red one five at range thirty, three thousand below. Both turning and climbing to follow.'

Voyska IA-PVO Unit, Arkhangel'sk, Confederation of Independent States

There was near-silence in the operations room, just a murmur of voices from the group of officers clustered around the three main consoles, but the tension was almost palpable.

'Interceptor Eight reports that the American is climbing,' Lieutenant Privalov said.

'The Americans are good,' Kabalin said, almost approvingly. 'You can see their strategy. They force our interceptors to follow them in the dive and then they climb so our aircraft lose speed. But we'll have them yet. Don't try to match the American aircraft. Give the MiG–31s vectors for the target's predicted track and authorize immediate release of their missiles as soon as they achieve target acquisition.'

Normal PVO intercept procedure is for the ground controllers to retain control of their interceptors until the pilots report weapons lock.

Privalov nodded and concentrated on his screen display, vectoring the aircraft into the optimum positions for missile engagement. Then he straightened and half-turned from the screen. 'Colonel, Interceptor Nine reports missile lock.'

British Embassy, Sofiyskaya naberezhnaya 14, Moscow

'Well, apart from showing you Newman's office and his apartment, is there anything else we can do for you?'

'A lift to the airport would be appreciated, but if it's any trouble I can take a taxi.'

'No trouble. Beaky said I was to assist you in any way that I could, or words to that effect. I can pick you up from your hotel after lunch, go to Newman's office and apartment and then straight to the airport, if you check out of the hotel first. What time's your flight?'

Richter pulled a ticket out of his jacket pocket and consulted it. 'It's the British Airways flight out of Sheremetievo at around six.'

'OK, bearing in mind that Russian bureaucracy means you'll have to check in at least two hours before departure time, how about having an early lunch at your hotel, and I'll collect you at, say, twelve thirty, and we can go straight to the apartment from there?'

'Suits me. I'm at the Budapesht.'

'Do you need a lift there now?' Erroll asked.

'Thank you, no. It's not that far. I'll see you in an hour and a half or so.'

OVERKILL

Aspen Three Four

'Bandit One is green three zero at thirty, six thousand below; Two is red one five range twenty-five, five thousand below. Both turning north-west.'

'We'll go right between them. At first missile release, we'll head for the one that didn't fire and power-dive towards it.'

'We'll do what?'

'Figure it out. Once one gets a weapons lock on us, heading straight for the other 'hound might bring it within the missiles' radar acquisition range.'

'Yeah, and it might not.'

'You got any better ideas?'

Paul James was silent for a couple of seconds. 'Guess not.'

The SR–71A is called the Blackbird because it appears black – although in fact it's a very, very dark blue – but the colour and type of the fuselage finish was not selected at random; it is an anechoic coating that absorbs radar energy. This, allied to the fact that radar waves are reflected best off a flat surface, and the Blackbird has hardly a flat panel anywhere, means that the aircraft has a very poor radar signature, especially from the front. By heading directly towards the second Foxhound, Frank Roberts hoped to prevent the Russian pilot obtaining missile lock, which would effectively disarm him.

'Both Bandits climbing rapidly. We're still being illuminated by fire-control radars from both. I have full counter-measures engaged.' The closest Foxhound fired almost immediately. 'Bandit Two – missile release. Two birds.'

AA–9 Amos radar-guided missiles are of the fire-and-forget type; the weapon is targeted by the interceptor and released when target lock has been achieved. Once fired, the missile has its own internal radar, but can also be guided by the massive Zaslon phased array radar carried in the nose of the Foxhound.

The Blackbird turned rapidly to starboard and picked up speed in the descent as Frank Roberts aimed the aircraft directly at Bandit One.

'Bandit One on the nose at eight, two thousand below and turning. Keep going like this and he'll be close enough to take us out with a twelve-gauge shotgun.'

'Yeah,' Roberts said, 'but only if he's got one. Where are the birds?'

'Now red four zero at ten, turning to follow. Bandit One dead ahead at three, one thousand below. He's lost radar lock. Two is at red three zero range twenty, same level.'

As James spoke, the first missile detonated, followed almost immediately by the second one, the flashes clearly visible, although the noise of the explosion was inaudible. But at a range of less than a mile, the Blackbird kicked and bucked from the blast wave.

Roberts eased back on the control column and the Blackbird began to climb. From the tiny starboard-side armoured window, Paul James saw the Foxhound designated Bandit One flash past – a barely visible streak of grey against the blue sky, less than half a mile away.

'Good thinking, boss,' James said, admiration mingled with relief in his voice. 'Bandit Two must have used the command detonation on the birds to avoid taking out his wingman. Now I suggest you get us the hell out of here before Bandit One decides to join the party.'

'Roger that.'

The Blackbird was holding a little under Mach 3, and was passing seventy thousand feet in the climb. 'Bandit Two now outside engage range. Bandit One directly astern, range five miles, eight thousand below and in a max rate climb, following us. He now has radar lock. Prediction is he'll try for a tail shot any time now.'

Voyska IA-PVO Unit, Arkhangel'sk, Confederation of Independent States

'Command detonation of both missiles confirmed, sir,' Privalov said. 'Interceptor Eight reports no damage, and the American aircraft is still flying. It may have been damaged by our weapons,' he added hopefully.

Kabalin snorted. 'Don't count on it,' he said. 'Has Eight achieved weapons lock?'

Privalov shook his head. 'Not yet, Colonel, but at any second – yes! Missile lock acquired, but on one weapon only.'

'Excellent,' Kabalin said. 'And at such close range he cannot fail to destroy the target. Instruct him to fire.'

Aspen Three Four

'Missile away – single launch from Bandit One. Possible radar acquisition failure on the second bird. Range six miles, directly astern.'

Frank Roberts had few options. The Blackbird was already travelling at close to its maximum speed. He had a little height above the missile, and he had a little distance, so his only hope was to try to out-run it. He levelled the Blackbird at seventy-nine thousand feet and watched as the needle on the Mach meter slowly began to move.

All air-to-air missiles carry a relatively small fuel load, because of the need for guidance systems, radar equipment and, of course, the warhead, and if a target has sufficient speed it can, in theory, out-run the vast majority of missiles fired at it. As most missiles travel in the Mach 2 to Mach 4 range, very few aircraft actually can out-run them, but the Blackbird could. In fact, that had been one of the philosophies behind the design of the aircraft.

'Missile at six, two thousand below. Bandit One at eight, falling back. Missile has radar lock. I say again, missile has radar lock.'

'I heard you the first time.'

'Range five. Missile speed near Mach four. I estimate impact in about eighty seconds.'

Moscow

The Budapesht Hotel on ulitsa Petrovskie was in fact something over a mile away, on the north side of the Moskva river and almost in the centre of old Moscow, but Richter wanted to walk. Moscow was enjoying the brittle sunshine of early summer, but it still wasn't warm enough to be out without a coat and hat, and he was glad of his leather gloves and fur cap.

He picked up the first tail almost as soon as he walked out of the Embassy grounds. He was on the opposite side of the road about two hundred yards back, heavily – too heavily – muffled against the weather, and as Richter started walking he abruptly lost interest in the newspaper in his hand and began following.

Richter made the second a couple of minutes after he had left the Moskvoreckij Most – the central bridge over the Moskva – and began walking past the eastern wall of the Kremlin. He was about fifty yards in front, walking briskly, and stopping to look around him at irregular intervals like any tourist would, but maintaining his lead comfortably enough. The two of them closed in on Richter as he reached the huge GUM department store opposite the Kremlin and wandered inside, but he wasn't interested in losing them. 'Mr Willis' wouldn't even have known they were there.

Aspen Three Four

The Blackbird's nose tilted downwards as Frank Roberts eased the stick forwards, and the aircraft's speed began to increase more rapidly. Paul James was devoting his entire attention to the radar display.

'Missile still has radar lock. Range now four. Second missile launch confirmed. Range nine, three thousand below.'

The Blackbird reached Mach 3.3 and levelled at seventy thousand feet.

'First missile dead astern, range three decimal five and one thousand below. Bandit One now range fifteen, close to maximum engage range. Full power.'

'This is full power – we're at our limiting velocity.'

'I hope it's enough. Missiles at three and eight, closing more slowly. Bandit One outside engage range at eighteen miles.'

The Blackbird engines howled as the big jet fled westwards. On the ground, thirteen miles below, the supersonic booms from its passage sounded like distant thunder, and people began looking up, puzzled, into the cloudless sky.

'Birds at two and six, both still closing slowly.'

'How long since the first missile launched?'

Paul James was silent for a few moments. 'I don't know exactly, but it must be around five minutes. Why?'

'Just wondering how much more fuel it could have.'

'Enough to catch us, I think.'

Frank Roberts grunted. 'Yeah, I thought you'd say that.'

As if linked by an invisible wire, the big black jet and the white-tipped grey missile powered through the sky. Every sweep of the tail radar showed the missile getting closer.

'Missile speed?'

Paul James didn't need to calculate the answer – he knew it already. 'Mach 3·8, and it's still gaining on us. Range now one decimal five.'

The Blackbird's needle nose dipped downwards as Frank Roberts pushed forward on the control column again and the aircraft's speed increased to Mach 3.4. Then 3.5. 'We're through our limiting velocity,' Roberts muttered. 'I sure hope Lockheed didn't build this baby on a Friday afternoon.'

Moscow

When Richter left GUM ten minutes later, both his shadows were still in attendance, and as he began walking north up ulitsa Petrovka, they dropped back behind him.

The third took a bit more effort to see, but Richter finally identified him as he turned right off ulitsa Petrovka into ulitsa Petrovskie. He was ahead, on the opposite side of the road, wearing loud check trousers three inches too short for him, and carrying a map and a camera – every-man's Yankee tourist.

Richter had been expecting a tail, of course, in view of the circum-stances, but a three-tail was, he thought, something of an overkill. He walked into the lobby of the Budapesht and checked the mail rack – there would be no letters for him, but everyone staying in a hotel checks the mail rack – then turned back to the main entrance and glanced out-side into the street. The two tourists were conferring, while the man with the newspaper was once again absorbed in *Pravda*, leaning against a wall directly across the road. Richter hoped they all had their woolly under-wear on, because it looked like being a chilly afternoon.

Richter walked up the three flights to his floor, stopped at the *dezhurnaya's* table to collect his room key and watched as she logged the time of his arrival, then walked down the corridor to his room. He didn't bother trying to decide if anyone had been in there while he had been at the Embassy, and he had taken no precautions against searchers.

The room was hot and stuffy. With some difficulty Richter pushed open the single window, then tossed his hat, coat and gloves onto the bed. He picked up the accident report and the English translation, took them over to the easy chair by the window, sat down, loosened his tie and started to read. The translator hadn't done too bad a job, only making three minor errors of little importance.

Richter read the report through twice, and was little wiser then. The only conclusion that could be drawn from the stark official phraseology was that the late Mr Newman had been either criminally irresponsible or suicidally inclined, if the facts as stated were correct. He had, it seemed, been travelling at a speed in excess of fifty miles an hour in a narrow back street when he encountered the tailboard, and totally unyielding load, of a parked lorry. Richter smiled humourlessly. Despite the official line, he knew exactly what had happened. He knew the answer, but what he didn't know was the question. He stood up, straightened his tie, tucked the report into his briefcase, locked it and then headed downstairs towards the dining room.

Voyska IA-PVO Unit, Arkhangel'sk, Confederation of Independent States

'Sir, both interceptors dropping back, but the missile is still closing the American aircraft,' Privalov reported. He looked suddenly at the digital display that showed the time each missile had been running.

Kabalin noticed his glance. 'Yes?' he asked. 'What is it?'

'The AA–9, Colonel,' Privalov said. 'If that run-time figure is accurate, it only has fuel for another two or three minutes' flight.'

Kabalin nodded decisively. 'You're right, Lieutenant. How far behind is the missile?'

Privalov spoke into his microphone, then turned back to his superior officer.

'Interceptor Eight estimates under one mile, sir.'

Kabalin thought for a few seconds. 'That's not close enough,' he said. 'Order Interceptor Eight to monitor the missile. If it doesn't catch the American aircraft, instruct the pilot to command-detonate the warhead the instant the AA–9 runs out of fuel.'

That order was the first mistake Colonel Kabalin had made since the Blackbird had been detected, because he had forgotten to allow for just one thing – the Foxhound pilot's reaction time.

Aspen Three Four

Paul James suddenly let out an exclamation. 'Yes! It's out of fuel. Half a mile astern and five hundred below, and falling away.'

In the MiG–31, the pilot was closely watching his radar display and missile telemetry. In the second and a quarter it took him to register the fact that the missile engine had stopped, the Blackbird had travelled just over one mile. In that same second and a quarter, the AA–9 had slowed considerably and had already begun to descend under the force of gravity. It took the Foxhound pilot a further second to lift the guard on the master detonate switch, and another half-second to depress it, by which time the Blackbird was nearly three miles from the AA–9 and over one thousand feet above it.

Frank Roberts was jolted in his seat as the Amos detonated in spectacular fashion, and the Blackbird kicked upwards, then he heaved a sigh of relief. 'Thank God. I thought that fucking missile was going to bury us. Where's the other one?'

'Forget it. Range is four miles, and even if you chopped our speed to three it still wouldn't catch us before it ran out of gas.'

Voyska IA-PVO Unit, Arkhangel'sk, Confederation of Independent States

There was silence in the operations room as the Russian officers watched the radar return of the Blackbird receding rapidly towards the west.

When the telephone rang on Colonel Kabalin's desk, he got slowly to his feet and straightened his uniform jacket before he walked over to pick up the receiver.

Chapter 4

Thursday
Aspen Three Four

Normally Frank Roberts was able to keep a reasonable mental picture of the aircraft's geographical position, but the evasive action and numerous turns, climbs and descents had destroyed it. 'Paul, I've lost the bubble,' he said. 'Where in hell are we?'

Paul James turned his attention away from the radar display and made a swift check of the navigation computer. 'Coastline at Klaipeda in a little under three minutes.'

'Klaipeda? Where the hell's that?'

'North of Kaliningrad – used to be called Königsberg. We've been kicked a long way way south.' Paul James went back to scanning his instruments. After a moment he spoke again. 'Boss, we've got another problem. We're losing fuel.'

'What rate?'

'Slow but steady – looks like around fifty pounds a minute. My guess is that one of those missile detonations ruptured a plate somewhere on the wings, and that's popped a tank. You're getting no handling problems?'

'Not yet, but I'll let you know. What are our choices?'

'I don't think we can make the tanker.'

'Which tanker?'

'Any tanker.'

In reality, the fuel leak had simply compounded the problem. The time spent at full power and the evasions forced on the Blackbird had already driven a major hole through the carefully calculated exit plan. The intention had been to maintain a high-level supersonic cruise westbound down the Gulf of Finland after leaving Russian airspace, across the Gulf of Bothnia, and over Sweden and Norway, before reducing to subsonic speed to link-up with one of two KC–135Q tanker aircraft that were already waiting in holding patterns fifty miles west of Norway's Atlantic coast.

'What are our options?'

Paul James was silent a moment or two, consulting the navigation computer again. 'A rendezvous with either of the tankers isn't advised. If the leak continues at its present rate we could make it to the southern one, but if we hit any problems with the link-up manoeuvring a flame-out is a real possibility.' A flame-out, or engine failure, would mean a double ejection and the loss of the aircraft and, more importantly, the loss of the films and sensor records.

'I'm not happy about a refuel, not with the leak we've got. Let's put it down somewhere.'

'We haven't got many alternatives. We could make it to Oslo easily enough, or Bergen, but we'd have to do a lot of fast talking on the ground.'

'Other options?'

'Back to Britain, and take a Master Diversion Airfield in Scotland.'

'Can we make Mildenhall or Lakenheath?'

'Not advised. They're right on the limit, according to the navigation computer, and we'd have to go subsonic a lot earlier. Plus there's a lot of traffic in East Anglia and Air Traffic Control wouldn't be able to move all of it out of our way.'

'OK,' Roberts said. 'Scotland it is.'

Moscow

The hotel lunch was notable for its quantity, rather than its quality, but it was hot. After he'd finished, Richter returned to his room and spent ten minutes composing a list in his notebook. The first item he wrote down was 'insurance policy' and the last was 'letters'. Then he carried his bags down to the reception desk, paid the bill and sat down to wait in the lobby.

Just after twelve thirty a black Rover with a familiar crest on the door and red number plates, the badge of a foreign diplomatic car, purred to a halt outside. Erroll climbed out of the rear seat and walked into the lobby. 'No parking problems,' he said. 'I've got a driver as well. Here, let me take that one.' Richter surrendered his suitcase and Erroll walked out to the Rover and put it in the boot. They climbed into the back seat, Richter still clutching his briefcase, and the driver indicated and pulled away from the kerb. Erroll noticed his frequent glances into the rear-view mirrors. 'Have we got company, George?' he asked.

'Yes, sir. A black ZIL, three up. They picked us up outside the Embassy as usual.'

Richter peered out of the rear window. About a hundred yards behind a large dark-coloured saloon with at least two people in it was following steadily.

'We get used to it after a while,' Erroll said. 'I don't suppose you get people following you all the time in your line of work, do you?'

Richter looked at him. Erroll was smiling. 'No,' he smiled back. 'Not all the time.'

Erroll sat back in his seat, then fished around in his jacket pocket and pulled out an envelope. Richter opened it, glanced at the copy of the death certificate and put it into his briefcase, where it could keep the accident report company.

Aspen Three Four

The Blackbird stayed at Mach 3 and eighty thousand feet over the southern tip of Sweden and across Denmark as Frank Roberts pointed the aircraft at the east coast of Scotland. Seventy miles out it began to look as if they weren't going to make it.

'Boss, the leak's getting worse. It's now more like one hundred pounds a minute. I estimate that we've got a maximum of twenty minutes up here before it all goes quiet.'

'OK. Let's talk to someone. I'll raise ATC, you tell Mildenhall what's happened.'

While Paul James opened the secure channel to Mildenhall Operations. Frank Roberts set the aircraft's secondary radar transponder to squawk Military Emergency and selected Guard frequency on UHF. 'Pan, Pan, Pan. This is Aspen Three Four with twenty minutes' fuel remaining. Request diversion to the nearest suitable airfield and a priority landing.'

Scottish Air Traffic Control Centre (Military), Atlantic House, Prestwick

The Scottish Military Distress and Diversion Cell is part of the Scottish Air Traffic Control Centre (Military) located at Atlantic House, Prestwick, on the west coast of Scotland. The network of direction-finding heads responded to the call from the Blackbird and the Laserscan equipment pinpointed the aircraft's position on the plotting chart on the wall facing the Cell team. As the assistant guided a laser-produced marker to the indicated location of the aircraft, the duty controller selected the nearest forward radio relay. 'Roger, Aspen Three Four, Scottish Centre. Steer two eight five for Lossiemouth. Request aircraft type and level.'

'Two eight five for Aspen Three Four. We're a military twin-jet, sir.'

'Roger, Three Four. I say again, what is your level?'

There was a pause. 'We're in the upper air, sir.'

The controller's assistant, who had been using the laser marker to update the position of the aircraft with each transmission it made, spoke. 'Jesus Christ, will you look at the speed of that thing. Hey, isn't Aspen a U–2 call sign?'

The controller shook his head. 'That's not a U–2, not going that fast.' He tried again. 'Three Four, I say again, what is your level, and what is your speed?' Turning to the assistant, he told him to contact Lossiemouth for an actual diversion and fuel priority landing, aircraft type not specified but fast USAF twin-jet, and to stand by to take operational control.

Roberts finally replied. 'Sir, Aspen Three Four is supersonic this time, and we're high. There's nobody up here but us.'

The controller gave up. 'Roger, Aspen Three Four. You have forty-three miles to run to Lossiemouth. Decrease speed to subsonic, and descend to maintain Flight Level one zero zero initially. Advise when you're ready to copy the Lossiemouth weather.'

Forty miles east of the airfield, Frank Roberts pulled the throttles back and the big aircraft began to fall, losing height and speed simultaneously.

British Embassy, Sofiyskaya naberezhnaya 14, Moscow

Newman's office was a little bigger than Erroll's, an indication of his slightly more exalted official status. With Erroll watching quizzically from the doorway, Richter began rooting through the contents of the desk.

'Pardon me, but what exactly are you looking for?'

'When Mr Newman's family heard that I was being sent to Moscow,' Richter said, 'they asked my company if I could collect some items of sentimental value and one or two documents that they would like returned to them immediately.' He held up his notebook and displayed a handwritten list. He didn't mention that it was the list he had compiled in his hotel room immediately after lunch. 'What I can't find here,' Richter continued, 'should be at his apartment, which is the reason I want to visit both.'

Richter selected a photograph of a handsome, rather than pretty, woman that stood on the desk, and an address book, and left it at that. He could hardly take Newman's desk diary or look through the filing cabinets with Erroll watching. Someone from Vauxhall Cross was going to have to go through the room with a fine toothcomb, but it wasn't going to be him.

RAF Lossiemouth, Grampian, Scotland

Three Panavia Tornado GR–1 aircraft doing circuits and bumps were told to hold at circuit height until further advised. A fourth Tornado, which had been entering the runway when the line from the Distress and Diversion Cell buzzed, was instructed to turn through one hundred and eighty degrees and clear the runway immediately.

The Lossiemouth Radar Supervisor was talking to the Distress and Diversion Cell Controller and the Director was preparing to take operational control. 'Aspen Three Four is identified. Call Lossiemouth Director on frequency two five nine decimal nine seven five.'

'Two five nine decimal nine seven five for Aspen Three Four. Thank you, Lossie.'

Central Moscow

Newman's apartment was in one of the compounds adjacent to the Embassy. The Rover drove through the gates and stopped outside the building, and the black ZIL – the letters stand for *'Zavod Imieni Likhatchova'* and it's loosely modelled on an old American Lincoln-Mercury saloon – pulled in fifty yards behind on the same side of the road.

Number 22 had the same light grey door as all the other apartments on the second floor, and a small white card, with 'Graham Newman' typed neatly on it, inserted in a cheap chrome frame at eye level. Selecting a Yale-type key from a bunch he produced from his pocket, Erroll opened the door and ushered Richter inside.

The apartment was square and basic. Three rooms in all, the largest being the sitting room and dining area combined, and with a small kitchenette at one end, equipped with a tiny refrigerator and a two-ring electric hob. There were three cupboards over the sink, and the single window offered only a view of the wall of the adjacent building. The dining area boasted a table and four chairs, and the sitting room a two-seater sofa and a pair of easy chairs. Opening off the sitting room was the bedroom, equipped with a double bed, wardrobe and a dressing table with a mirror. The bathroom had two doors, one from the bedroom and the other from the sitting room. Compact, unimaginative and basic.

There was little stamp of personality. There were a few pictures on the walls, quite possibly supplied with the apartment; the carpets were uniform shades, matching the sitting-room furniture, and the few books were a catholic mixture of reference works and a selection of paperbacks, mainly westerns and thrillers.

Richter took the notebook from his pocket and found the right page, then glanced round the sitting room hopefully. There was a small writing desk in one corner, fitted with a drop-down flap, which was up, and locked. On the desk was another picture of a lady of middle years, similar to the one Richter had already removed from Newman's office, so he took that. He looked closely at the lock on the writing desk, but there was no evidence of forced entry. That didn't mean it hadn't already been searched. It isn't necessary to leave convenient telltale scratches on a lock when probing with a pick or skeleton key. In fact, if the metal of the lock is of reasonable quality, it's difficult to mark it at all.

Erroll produced the key, unlocked the desk and dropped the flap. There were six vertical slots inside, three each side of a central section of two drawers. The top drawer produced assorted cuff-links, paper-clips, drawing pins and an elderly bow tie – the elasticized sort, which caused Erroll to sneer slightly – while the second contained about fifty pounds sterling value in roubles. The slots held an insurance policy, which Richter added to his pile, and a group of letters with a Northumberland postmark. He glanced through two or three, and then put them with the photograph.

Fifteen minutes later, having briefly checked every drawer in the flat and the interior of the wardrobe, Richter had finished. He wrote out a detailed list of all the items he had removed, duplicated it, and then he and Erroll signed each copy. Erroll kept one, and the second went into Richter's briefcase. 'That's it. Thank you very much for your co-operation.'

'Not at all, old boy.'

Richter glanced at his watch. 'How long to the airport?'

'It's about twenty miles, so say thirty-five minutes, at this time of day.'

Aspen Three Four

There are slow descents, there are cruise descents and there are fast descents. What Frank Roberts was doing could perhaps have been best described as a plunge descent, with the aircraft losing in excess of twenty thousand feet a minute. The one thing he could not do was to overshoot the field, because they certainly wouldn't have the fuel to get back to it, and he knew the USAF would be really pissed if he dumped the Blackbird down on some Scottish hillside instead of a concrete runway.

At twenty-five thousand feet the sky was clear, but the cloud that the Distress and Diversion Cell Controller had reported over Lossiemouth actually blanketed most of the United Kingdom. It looked like dirty grey soup, and the Blackbird plunged into it twenty-seven miles east of the airfield. The world outside the cockpit immediately went black with zero visibility, but Frank Roberts was already flying solely on instruments.

He was twenty-two miles out when he raised Lossiemouth. 'Lossiemouth Director, this is Pan aircraft Aspen Three Four squawking Emergency. We're IMC in thick cloud, passing Flight Level one two zero in a fast descent on a heading of two eight five, and requesting a straight-in approach to a priority landing.'

RAF Lossiemouth, Grampian, Scotland

In the Approach Room at Lossiemouth the Director, a young flight lieutenant, had been watching the rapid movement of the 7700 Emergency squawk across his screen. The Emergency Services were standing by, fire engines and ambulances waiting on the airfield, engines running, fully manned.

'Aspen Three Four, Lossiemouth Director, all copied. You are identified with nineteen miles to run to the field. Maintain your present heading and continue descent to two thousand feet on QNH two nine decimal eight one inches. Confirm you are now subsonic.'

'Three Four is subsonic and in the drop to two thousand on twenty-nine eighty-one.'

Passing ten thousand feet, the Blackbird crew unsealed their visors and raised the faceplates. As usual, the cockpit smelt of burnt metal.

At fifteen miles range, the squall that had been gathering to the west of the field finally hit, reducing visibility to under a mile.

'Aspen Three Four, Director. We've been hit by a squall and visibility is under one mile with full cover cloud at three hundred feet. This will be a precision approach to runway two three. Turn left heading two five zero.'

The Director broke off as the Radar Supervisor touched his shoulder and spoke to him. Rather than risk losing contact with the aircraft on a frequency change, the Supervisor had decided that the talk-down would be carried out on the Director's frequency.

'Aspen Three Four, you have twelve miles to run to the field. Confirm you are now level at two thousand feet.'

'Confirmed. Level at two.'

'Roger. Squawk standby, carry out Final landing checks and listen out on this frequency for your Final Controller.'

Twelve miles out, the profile of the Blackbird altered as the landing gear was extended, and the aircraft adopted a pronounced nose-high attitude.

'Aspen Three Four, this is Lossiemouth Final Controller. I hold you on precision radar at range ten. Turn left heading two four five.'

'Two four five, Three Four.'

Unlike the clipped and precise instructions given by all other controllers, a precision approach has almost a conversational style about it. This is at least partly due to the fact that the controller talks constantly to the pilot from just before the aircraft starts its final descent until it reaches the runway. 'You're slightly left of the centreline, closing gently on a heading of two four five. Approximately one mile to run to the descent point.'

The talk-down controller paused for a few seconds, then pressed the transmit key forward into the locked position, and began talking. 'Aspen Three Four, seven miles from touchdown, and approaching the descent point. Heading two four five. Slightly left of centreline, closing gently. You need not acknowledge further transmissions unless requested.'

On the twin precision radar displays the Blackbird's return was small and painting faintly, but it was visible. Still below the electronic glide path, the right-hand edge of the return was nearly touching the centreline. The controller watched the return on the elevation screen touch the glide path. The trick was to start the aircraft in descent a little before the centre of the return intersected the glide path. This allowed for delays in the pilot's reactions and the physical time taken by the aircraft to transition from level flight into a descent.

'Six and three-quarter miles from touchdown. Begin your descent now for a three-degree glide path.' The standard three-degree glide path meant that the aircraft descended at the rate of three hundred feet for every track mile flown. 'Six miles from touchdown. Turn left five degrees heading two four zero. You're now on the centreline, but still very slightly above the glide path.'

By five miles out, the Blackbird had settled down on the glide path, and the controller had no need to give descent corrections. As the aircraft got closer to the ground, however, the gusty wind made frequent heading changes necessary. 'Three miles from touchdown, heading two three five, very slightly right of centreline but on the glide path. Confirm final landing checks complete – Aspen Three Four acknowledge.'

'Three Four has checks complete.'

'Roger. Heading two three five, on the glide path. You have been cleared to land on runway two three.'

Passing one mile and three hundred feet above runway elevation, the controller broke transmission. 'Aspen Three Four inside one mile. Centreline and glide path. Confirm visual with the runway.'

In the cockpit of the Blackbird, Frank Roberts was dividing his time equally between monitoring his instruments and looking ahead for the airfield approach lights and runway. He looked ahead again. 'Negative.'

'Roger. I will continue to pass advisory information. Centreline and glide path. Three quarters of a mile.'

Frank Roberts ignored his instruments, concentrating all his attention on the view ahead. Blank, featureless grey murk met his eyes. Then it was as if a carpet had been dragged out from under them, the grey cloud dispersed as if it had never been and the high-intensity approach lights shone clear and bright, directly ahead.

'Centreline and glide path. Half a mile.'

'We have the runway, we have the runway. Thank you, sir.'

'Roger, Three Four. Call Tower on three three seven decimal seven five.'

'Three three seven decimal seven five.'

The Blackbird punched out of the murk at a little under one hundred and fifty feet. The Local Controller, looking out to the east through binoculars, saw an unfamiliar grouping of lights materialize at precisely the same moment that the aircraft called him.

'Lossiemouth Tower, Aspen Three Four.'

The controller lowered the binoculars, made a final visual check of the runway and pressed his transmit key. 'Aspen Three Four, Tower. Confirm landing checks complete.'

'Affirmative. Three Four has checks complete; all green.'

'Roger. Land runway two three. Surface wind green three five at fifteen knots.' The Local Controller raised his binoculars again and focused on the aircraft as it approached the threshold of the active runway. 'What the hell is it? It's a – no it isn't.' The controller lapsed into silence and watched the aircraft's profile become visible as Frank Roberts lifted the nose for touchdown. 'Fuck me,' he said. 'A Blackbird.'

Sluzhba Vneshney Razvyedki Rossi
Headquarters, Yazenevo, Tëplyystan, Moscow

A little over ten miles south-west of the centre of Moscow, not far from the village of Tëplyystan, a black ZIL limousine pulled off the circumferential highway onto a narrow road leading into dense forest. The car passed a large sign that warned the curious not to stop or trespass, and announced that the area was a 'Water Conservation District'.

About two hundred yards down the road the car stopped at what appeared to be a militia post while the driver's, bodyguard's and passengers' passes were examined by armed SVR troops dressed as militiamen. As the electric windows hissed closed, the car surged forward and came to rest in a reserved parking space about a third of a mile beyond. The driver and bodyguard got out immediately and opened the rear doors, but the passengers seemed oddly abstracted, and remained in the car, talking, for a few minutes more.

The two passengers finally emerged, acknowledged the salutes somewhat listlessly, and made their way through the turnstiles in the guardhouse, the only break in the high chain-link fence, topped with barbed wire. Armed sentries from the SVR Guards Division, wearing khaki service dress uniforms, with blue flashes on the lapels and blue stripes on the trousers, inspected the special passes each officer showed. They were buff-coloured plastic cards that showed the bearer's photograph and incorporated coded perforations designating the areas he or she was authorized to enter.

Through the guardhouse, the two officers made their way slowly along the driveway through the lawns and flowerbeds to the SVR building, the former headquarters of the KGB First Chief Directorate. It was designed by Finnish architects and constructed, at least in part, with materials and equipment purchased in Scandinavia. The original seven-storey structure is shaped like a three-pointed star, incorporating a lot of glass and aluminium, with a blue stone trim around many of the windows, but is now dwarfed by a twenty-two-floor extension at the end of the western arm of the building.

The officers passed through the double glass doors and entered the large marble foyer, again showing their passes to armed guards, and walked over to the main group of elevators located in the centre of the building. Once inside, the older of the two men pressed the button for the seventh floor. When the elevator stopped they got out, walked slowly down the carpeted corridor, and entered an office suite.

'Good afternoon, General.' Lieutenant Vadim Vasilevich Nilov, a fresh-faced and eager officer in his late twenties, greeted his superior with his usual mixture of deference and respect, and hurried to relieve him of his uniform cap and greatcoat. He snapped to attention and saluted the other officer, and extended him the same courtesy.

Nilov had, as usual, arrived at the headquarters before seven that morning, had spent two hours reviewing all the overnight signal traffic, marking those of interest, and checking the office schedule for the coming day. He would remain at the headquarters until eight or nine in the evening. General Modin often wondered how much sleep, if any, Nilov needed. He was quite sure he had no social life whatsoever.

Nilov had been aide to General Nicolai Fedorovich Modin since the day the General had arrived at Yazenevo to head Department V of the KGB's First Chief Directorate. The metamorphosis of the KGB into the SVR had caused little change, except that the 'Department V' tag had been dropped and the section renamed.

'There has been priority traffic all morning, General, about the American over-flight. The signals are in the red folder on your desk.'

Modin smiled somewhat tiredly. 'I would have been astounded, Vadim, if there hadn't been priority signals. What do they expect the SVR to do? We have no aircraft or missiles.'

Nilov smiled. 'I could not say, General.'

'No matter. Coffee?'

'Also on your desk, comrade General. I will bring another cup.'

Modin nodded his thanks, led the way into the inner office, picked up the red folder and sat down in a leather armchair by the window. He motioned his companion into the other chair. Nilov returned with a second cup, poured the coffee and set the cups on the low table between the chairs. Then he withdrew, closing the office door quietly behind him. Modin picked up his cup and looked thoughtfully at the other man. 'Well, Grigori. What do we do about it?'

General Grigori Petrovich Sokolov was technically Modin's subordinate, but the two men had known each other for so many years that their working relationship had developed into a firm friendship. Sokolov was short and slim, with a friendly, open face under thick grey hair. He didn't look like a Russian, a fact that had helped his career. An old KGB hand, he had headed the First Chief Directorate's Twelfth Department, a somewhat unusual and very powerful organization staffed by veteran KGB officers who had a remit to identify and pursue their quarry – anyone in any Western military, intelligence, business or government organization who might prove useful to the Soviets – anywhere in the world. As with Modin, the metamorphosis of the KGB into the SVR had changed virtually nothing.

Sokolov put down his cup. 'I don't know, Nicolai, I really don't.' He paused for a few moments. 'What can they discover from the films?'

Modin sighed. 'Not very much, I think. I talked to our technical specialists this morning, as soon as Nilov telephoned, but they do not know how good the American cameras are. However, even if the cameras are excellent, there was little that they could see. What worries me more are the radiation detectors, and also why they flew the spy-plane at all.'

'What do you mean?' Sokolov said, looking up sharply.

'I mean that since *glasnost* the Americans have been very reluctant to carry out any overt intelligence-gathering operations against us. They are very sensitive to world opinion, and do not wish to be seen in an aggressive light. So why would they risk flying their spy-plane across the tundra now, in broad daylight? Of course, they would have been able to detect the last weapon test, but we have been exploding devices for the past year or so.'

'Yes, Nicolai, but they were underground tests. This was the first above-ground test.'

'The first and the last,' Modin said, nodding agreement. 'It is unfortunate that we had to have an above-ground detonation at all, and it wasn't even a test of the weapon, just a confirmation that the triggering mechanism was functioning correctly. But even so, why would the Americans risk the flight?'

Sokolov took another sip of coffee, and then looked across at Modin. 'Do you have a theory, old friend?' he asked, finally.

'It seems to me,' Modin replied, 'that there are only two possibilities. The first is that the Americans are a lot smarter than we thought, and have deduced the nature of the weapon from the recordings of their seismographic devices.'

'I doubt that,' Sokolov said.

'So do I.'

'Of course,' Sokolov added thoughtfully, 'the flight could simply have been a precautionary measure. They would obviously be aware from their seismic records that the weapon does not have the usual characteristics of a strategic fission or fusion weapon, and they might have decided that the only course open to them was to use the spy-plane.'

'Agreed,' Modin said, 'but in the current political climate it seems unlikely.'

'Unlikely, but it is possible, yes?' Modin nodded again, almost reluctantly. 'You said there were two possibilities, Nicolai,' Sokolov went on. 'What is the second?'

Modin lowered his eyes. 'I do not like this, Grigori, but I can see only one other explanation: someone told them about the project. Someone here, or in the GRU.'

'Are you serious?' Sokolov asked. 'Are you really suggesting that there is a *predatel* – a traitor – here?'

'Yes,' said Modin. 'In fact, Minister Trushenko and I have already discussed this, and we both agree that this is the most probable conclusion, based upon the available evidence.'

Sokolov looked across the table and uttered a single word. 'Who?'

'If I knew that, Grigori, I would sleep tonight. This has been the highest-classified project in the country for the last four years. Until a year ago, only Minister Trushenko, General Bykov and I knew all the details – the technicians have obviously known they have been working on nuclear weapons, but not how the weapons were to be used.' He put his coffee cup down and waved his arm in sudden anger. 'This project was so secret that it wasn't even given a name until this year, because if you name something, you acknowledge its existence.'

'And now, Nicolai? How many people know about it now?'

'More than twenty. All with the highest possible security clearances, and most of them known personally to me – and to you. I cannot even begin to suspect any of them.'

Modin picked up his coffee cup, glanced into it and stood up. He looked down enquiringly at Sokolov, who shook his head. Modin walked slowly over to the coffee pot and refilled his cup, then returned to the chair, sitting with a weary sigh. 'The trouble is that every one of them needed to know about the project, now that it is approaching completion. I personally – personally, you understand – approved each one and, naturally, I checked all their records. I even,' he added softly, 'checked your record, old friend.'

Sokolov nodded. 'So you should, Nicolai, so you should. With a matter of this importance no one can be considered to be above suspicion. What now? What will you do?'

Modin sipped his coffee and put the cup on the table, then looked keenly at Sokolov. 'Two things. first, a job for you. It will be distasteful to you, but it must be done. I want you to identify the treacherous bastard who has told the Americans what we are doing.'

'If he exists,' Sokolov said quietly.

'Oh, he exists, Grigori, the traitor exists. Of that I have no doubt. No doubt at all.'

Sokolov looked up, a frown creasing his brow. 'Are you sure I should do this, Nicolai? It is not really my field.'

Modin smiled at him. 'I know that,' he said, 'but I have to have someone I can trust, trust totally, to carry out the investigation. And he has to be someone who already knows about the project. If I call in the security staff, they will have to be told at least the broad outline of *Podstava*, and that will multiply the number of people with knowledge of it to an unacceptable level. No, Grigori. Whoever investigates this has to be someone already indoctrinated, but whose loyalty is above suspicion. You are the best – in fact, you are the only – candidate.'

Sokolov nodded. 'I thank you for your trust, Nicolai. And what is the second thing?'

Modin looked grave. 'This has not been my decision – Minister Trushenko himself has directed my actions. He believes we cannot afford to wait for all the weapons to be placed piecemeal using covert means, so the last weapon is to be delivered intact, despite the risks.'

Sokolov stared at Modin. 'How?' he asked.

'It will be delivered by lorry, as Diplomatic Baggage, but protected by *Spetznaz* troopers.'

'Remind me,' Sokolov said. 'Where is this last weapon to be positioned?'

'London,' Nicolai Modin said. 'It's going to London.'

Sheremetievo Airport, Moscow

It took them just over twenty minutes to get clear of central Moscow and head out to the north-west on the M9 motorway, but that still left plenty of time. At Sheremetievo, Richter retrieved his suitcase from the Rover's boot, shook Erroll's hand and walked away. Erroll looked thoughtfully at his retreating back for a moment, then turned back towards the car. 'Insurance investigator my arse,' he muttered. 'OK, George, let's go.'

The black ZIL pulled up about fifty yards behind the Embassy Rover, and the three men inside watched intently as Richter approached the terminal building. As he passed through the doors, the man in the back seat opened the car door and stepped out. He pulled his overcoat tight around him, then walked across and followed Richter. He had barely entered the terminal before he heard the voice in his earpiece. He cocked his head slightly as if to hear the words better, then smiled slightly and quickened his pace, following Richter deeper into the building.

The British Airways' check-in desk was already open, so Richter produced his ticket and passport and handed over his small suitcase. A professional is always aware of what's happening around him, and Richter was nothing if not professional. As he turned away from the counter, he casually scanned the crowd, looking for anything or anyone out of place, and one pair of hard grey eyes met and held his for just a moment longer than they should have.

Richter ignored the fleeting contact and walked away towards the cafeteria. Eight minutes later, sitting at a corner table and with a coffee and a paperback novel in front of him, he spotted the same man again, standing just beyond the cafeteria. Once can be happenstance and twice may be coincidence, but in Richter's trade coincidences didn't often happen. Usually it meant enemy action.

He finished his coffee, put the novel in his briefcase, stood up and walked into one of the shops. He wandered the aisles and selected a small bottle of the cheapest Scotch he could find. It wasn't a brand he recognized but that didn't matter because he had no intention of drinking it. He put the bottle in his briefcase then left the shop and crossed to the toilets. The restroom was deserted, and Richter acted quickly. He ran to the stall furthest from the door and placed his briefcase on the seat, then closed all the stall doors. He entered the fourth stall, pushed the door closed behind him and climbed onto the seat. Then he waited.

Seconds later, he heard the noise of the restroom door opening, followed by heavy footsteps. The man stopped just inside the room and Richter knew he was looking at the closed stall doors, and was probably down on his knees peering underneath them. After that, the Russian had only one option, and five seconds later he took it.

Richter heard the crash as the first stall door smashed open, then the second and the third. Timing is everything. To kick down a door, the attacker must obviously be standing on only one leg, and a man on one leg is by any definition unbalanced. In the split second before the Russian's right foot connected with the lavatory door, Richter stepped off the seat, pulled the door open and simultaneously launched himself forward, left arm reaching downwards.

The kick that hadn't connected had spun the Russian round on his left leg. Richter's hand hooked neatly under the Russian's right calf and he pulled up and backwards, a basic Aikido move that used the opponent's own momentum against him. The Russian lurched sideways, toppled against the side of the lavatory stall and then fell heavily, legs splayed wide apart. As the man hit the floor, Richter kicked sideways with his left foot, catching the Russian's right arm at the wrist, sending the small black automatic pistol spinning under the wall of the adjacent stall. Then he smashed his fist, hard, into the left side of the Russian's neck, and then it was all over.

Richter pulled the unconscious Russian out of the stall and propped his body against the restroom wall. He reached into the man's inside jacket pocket and extracted a black leather wallet, which he opened. One of the items inside caused him to nod in satisfaction. He replaced the wallet, retrieved his briefcase and extracted the bottle of scotch. Richter cracked open the top, poured the liquor liberally over the front of the Russian's jacket, then placed the bottle by the unconscious man's right hand.

The pistol was a Russian 5.45mm PSM, light and easily concealed. Richter took a handkerchief out of his pocket, picked up the pistol and dropped it into the paper towel waste bin beside the row of sinks. He'd just picked up his briefcase when the restroom door opened and a man walked in. He looked at Richter, then at the figure slumped against the wall.

'Another drunk,' Richter said, in colloquial Russian, walking towards the door.

The man sniffed, then nodded. 'Sometimes you can't walk round Red Square without tripping over them,' he replied.

Richter nodded agreement, opened the restroom door and headed for the departure gate.

Chapter 5

The telephone woke Richter at seven forty. 'Yes?' he muttered.

'Go secure, please.'

'Right,' Richter said, reaching for the telephone base unit and pressing the button. To anyone listening in, it would sound as if both had disconnected.

'Thomas, Duty Officer. How did it go?'

'Fairly well,' Richter said. 'The First Secretary's a bit of a prick, but the Fourth Under-Secretary, a chap named Erroll, is pretty switched on. The car was a mess, and so was the body. The head was crushed beyond recognition, and the hands and arms were badly burnt. The Embassy identified the body by documentation only.' Richter paused and yawned. The voice in the earpiece squawked at him. 'What?'

'I said, was there was any doubt about the identity of the body?'

'No, none at all.'

'Poor old Newman. A pretty futile way to go. He was—'

'Not really,' Richter interrupted. 'You misunderstood me. The identification was conclusive, but only because the body definitely wasn't Newman.'

'What?' Thomas said. 'Are you sure?'

'I wouldn't say it if I wasn't certain.'

There was a short pause, the faint sound of background voices, and then the phone crackled again. 'Simpson wants to see you – now. I'll send a car.'

'Give me an hour,' Richter replied. 'I'm still in bed.'

'Best you get up quickly, then,' Thomas said, his grin apparent even on the scrambled line, 'because the car will be outside your building in about twenty minutes. Come straight up to the Director's office when you get here.'

Richter unscrambled, listened for the dialling tone and replaced the receiver. He glanced at his watch – almost seven fifty – then looked round the bedroom. As usual, it looked as if a bomb had hit it, the bed having apparently been the focal point of the explosion. Richter dragged the sheets and blankets into some sort of order, made a mental note to buy a duvet, and soon, and headed for the bathroom.

ulitsa Novyj Arbat, Moscow

The apartment at the western end of ulitsa Novyj Arbat was small by Western standards, with a floor area of barely one hundred square metres, but for Moscow it was considered vast, particularly for a single occupant. Most Muscovite families thought themselves lucky if they lived in three- or four-roomed flats half that size. Russians are used to cramped living conditions, parents and children routinely sharing bed-rooms, bathrooms and kitchens.

Like most of the other larger properties in this district of Moscow, the apartment was owned by the Russian government and had been allocated to the Ministry of Industrial Production. The Ministry, in turn, had allocated the apartment as the Moscow residence of the Minister himself. Dmitri Stepanovich Trushenko sat comfortably in a leather arm-chair, his long legs stretched out towards the fireplace, where coals and logs were already arranged. His manservant would light the fire early in the evening, before preparing and serving the Minister's dinner. Trushenko was tall and slim, with fair skin and blond hair, and a friendly and somewhat vacant smile that concealed an excellent brain. He looked much younger than his fifty-six years, and his faintly academic air some-times misled opponents into underestimating his cunning and his keen instinct for political and personal survival.

On the low table beside Trushenko were two slim and highly classified files, neither of which had reached him in his official ministerial capacity. One was the report of the interrogation of the Englishman in the Lubyanka, including the audio transcript and the conclusions of the interrogator. This had been accompanied by an entirely unmarked video tape, which Trushenko had already watched twice with a keen personal pleasure.

The second file had originated in the Russian Ministry of Defence and contained a faxed report prepared by the colonel in charge of the Voyska IA-PVO Unit in the Arkhangel'sk Military District, which detailed the over-flight of the Confederation of Independent States by the American spy-plane the day before. The report contained comparatively brief details of the route the Blackbird had taken, but glowing accounts of the prompt and efficient actions taken by PVO officers which, the report stated, had certainly prevented the American aircraft from following its intended surveillance route.

The colonel's report also stated that he believed the spy-plane had been damaged, possibly badly, during its encounters with the Russian interceptors, and suggested that the aircraft had probably not succeeded in reaching safety in the West. Blame for the escape of the spy-plane from Russian airspace was directed squarely at the interceptor pilots for their failure to execute the orders issued by the PVO. The report concluded with a note of the proposed disciplinary action that was to be taken against them.

It was this file which Trushenko had just finished reading, with mounting concern. As soon as he had seen the route details, he knew that the conclusions were rubbish, and that the Americans had photographed exactly what they had wanted to photograph. Privately, he was surprised that any of the interceptors had got close enough to the American aircraft to engage it, far less damage it, and he dismissed out of hand the implied suggestion that the Blackbird had crashed into the North Sea. Obviously, the Americans had found out something about the operation, and had flown their spy-plane to investigate the weapon test site.

Trushenko stood up abruptly and walked to the large lounge windows, which offered an excellent view to the south-west down a long stretch of the river Moskva, and looked out, his hands on his hips. He stood there for several minutes, looking at, but not seeing, the river traffic, then he turned and walked back to his armchair. He reached over and poured a glass of vodka from the bottle of Stolichnaya on the table beside him, and drank it slowly.

When he had finished, Trushenko put the glass down and got up, walked across to a framed Monet print on the wall beside the fireplace and pulled on the left side of the frame. The picture swung away from the wall to reveal the door of a very expensive and secure safe of Swiss manufacture, one of the finest that money could buy. He entered a ten-number combination into the digital keypad and pressed a button. That didn't open the safe, merely released a section of the armoured door to reveal the keyhole.

Trushenko unfastened the top two buttons of his shirt and extracted a slim steel key on a chain that he invariably wore around his neck. He inserted the key in the lock and turned it twice, then grasped the recessed handle on the safe door and opened it. Inside were a dozen or so video tapes plus three bulky files. Trushenko removed the top file and took it back to his chair. The name on the file cover was '*Podstava*', and Trushenko already knew the contents almost by heart.

Hammersmith, London

It was eight forty when Richter got out of the lift on the seventh floor, knocked on the dark green door with the word 'Director' inscribed in faded gold leaf, and walked in. Richard Simpson – the Foreign Operations Director – was waiting for him, looking pointedly at his watch. 'You're late,' he said, somewhat sourly.

'I know,' Richter replied. 'Traffic,' he added. He put his briefcase on the floor and sat down in the armchair in front of the desk.

'I didn't say you could sit,' Simpson snapped.

'That's true.'

So far, the interview was going more or less as usual. Simpson was small, about five eight, with a pink and freshly scrubbed look about him. He'd headed the Foreign Operations Executive for six years, which was four years longer than Richter had been employed there, and throughout that period he'd almost never been known to praise anyone or anything.

Richter still simmered slightly whenever he met Richard Simpson. Four years earlier Richter had been an out-of-work ex-Royal Navy Sea Harrier pilot with a minimal pension and a gratuity that was leaching out of his bank account at an astonishing rate. He'd spent three irritating months scratching about, trying and failing to find any kind of employment that would pay his mortgage without boring him to death. Then he'd attended an interview in London for a courier job that was so intriguing that Richter had just had to take it. It had sounded too good to be true, and it had been.

Sent into France on a courier assignment that nobody, and certainly not Richter, believed made any sense, he had been set up by Simpson as an unwitting target to trap a high-level traitor in the Secret Intelligence Service. Richter had been considered expendable, with no family to make a fuss if he didn't return. Against all the odds, Richter had survived the encounter, which the SIS officer hadn't, and his performance had convinced Simpson that he was too useful to lose. The death of the SIS officer was marked 'unsolved' by the Metropolitan Police and the French authorities, but the file was still open, and Simpson had made it clear that if Richter ever stepped out of line, he would be only too happy to assist the police with their enquiries into the matter.

Simpson stared at Richter from the opposite side of the desk, and Richter stared straight back at him. Behind the row of cacti on his desk – the cacti were about the only things Simpson seemed to have any affection for, and there were more of them in serried ranks on all three window-sills – his face was all Richter could see, his dark, almost black, eyes unwinking. 'Come on, then. I haven't got all day.'

Richter opened the briefcase, took out the notebook he had been using in Moscow and put it on the desk in front of him. The other items could wait until later. 'Right,' he said. 'We got the signal about Newman on Tuesday evening. I flew into Moscow – economy class as usual – on Wednesday morning and checked into the Budapesht Hotel under cover name Willis. I rang the Embassy that afternoon and got an appointment for the following morning with the First Secretary, a man called Horne, William Horne.

'As agreed with Tactics and Equipment, I presented him with the insurance company letter and accreditation, and after a bit of grumbling he passed me on to the Fourth Under-Secretary, Simon Erroll. I inspected the car and the body that morning – the corpse was in the basement fridge – and the office and apartment that afternoon. Then I flew back to Heathrow.

'I took an abstract from Newman's file before I left,' Richter continued. 'He was five feet eleven, weighed about twelve and a half stone, had fair hair and a fair complexion. There is no mention of any distinguishing marks. The body in Moscow was about the correct height and weight, though obviously it was impossible to measure or weigh the cadaver without Erroll smelling a rat. The hair and skin colour looked correct, but the face was completely unrecognizable, and the burning of the hands had destroyed the fingerprints.'

Simpson opened the personnel file in front of him and looked up expectantly. 'So how do you know it wasn't Newman?'

'I'm coming to that. When people talk about distinguishing marks, they think about scars or birthmarks. Newman had no obvious scars or marks, so they probably didn't realize. He had had an in-growing toenail on his right foot removed about ten years ago. The body in the basement mortuary in Moscow had all ten toenails.'

Simpson studied the file for a few moments in silence. 'There's no mention here of a toenail removal.'

'Yes there is,' Richter said, 'in the "Summary of Hospital Treatment". Newman had only had three operations – removal of tonsils and draining of sinuses when he was a kid, and the toenail job. The effect on the toe is quite unmistakable. The nail never grows normally again, because the nail bed is excised, wholly or partially.'

Simpson finally closed the file with a snap. 'Two questions. If the body wasn't Newman, who was it? And where's Newman?'

'Two answers,' replied Richter. 'I don't know – at least, I know what he was, but not who he was – and Newman's dead.'

OVERKILL

Le Moulin au Pouchon, *St Médard, near Manciet, Midi-Pyrénées, France*

The four men had rented the small three-bedroomed house about a mile outside the village some four months earlier, and they had all lived in the property ever since. The reason for this uninterrupted occupation was simple security – although the level of crime in rural France was commendably low, an unoccupied property was still a target and the one thing they couldn't risk was some French low-life breaking in and stealing any of the equipment or, worse, talking about what he had seen inside.

Actually, there wasn't very much to attract a thief to the house. No readily saleable items like TV sets or hi-fi equipment. There was a TV set, but it was at least ten years old, big and bulky, and of little or no value. Hassan Abbas had bought it second-hand from an electrical shop in Aire-sur-l'Adour, the local town where they did most of their shopping. There wasn't even much in the way of furniture. Four single beds, two in each of the largest bedrooms, a table and four chairs in the kitchen. In the living room, two elderly sofas were pushed against opposite walls and on one wall there was a single incongruity – a clear mark showing the direction of Mecca so that prayers could be said correctly. Below the mark there were four highly decorated prayer mats.

There were no curtains at the windows, because the faded wooden shutters were always kept closed, and no signs of anything that might be described as the comforts of home. In fact, the only items of real value lay behind the door of the third and smallest bedroom, at the back of the house. The door to this room was the only one with a lock – a five-lever exterior quality Chubb which had been fitted within a week of the signing of the tenancy agreement at the agency in Aire-sur-l'Adour – and it was always kept locked unless the equipment in the room was actually being used. The room's single exterior window was, like all the other windows, kept firmly closed, as were the external shutters. What was not visible from the outside was the steel grille bolted to the wall inside the room and which completely covered the window opening – another unofficial addition to the property which Abbas had organized.

The other invisible deterrents to a thief were the Glock 17 semi-automatic pistols always carried by each of the four men, and the two AK47 Kalashnikov assault rifles, magazines fully charged, which were kept propped up behind each of the two outside doors. They had also spent some time carefully positioning plastic explosive charges on the inside of the ground-floor doors and windows, to be actuated by trip-wires, and installing a number of high-wattage floodlights under the eaves, powerful enough to illuminate the entire grounds.

There were two reasons why the old mill had been chosen, rather than either of the two other houses that had been on the short list. The first was a unique architectural feature of the property that Abbas had stumbled on almost by accident, and which he devoutly hoped he would never have to use. Just over two miles from the house was the second reason; a small nondescript grey concrete building, it was the automated telephone exchange which served the properties in the shallow valley which opened up to the south of St Médard.

When Abdullah Mahmoud – the name in the genuine Moroccan passport carried by Hassan Abbas when he had stepped off the ferry from Tangier at Algeciras – had decided on the location of the property they needed, he had planned to have an ADSL line installed. An Asynchronous Digital Subscriber Line connection would have provided a permanent Internet connection, but technical requirements meant that the user had to live within about four miles of the local exchange. The other two houses he had been considering were each over ten miles from their respective exchanges, hence the choice of the St Médard property.

In the event, Sadoun Khamil, who had first supported Abbas' decision, had later vetoed the idea of ADSL, simply because it would have been an unusual request in that area and might have attracted attention. So instead Abbas had signed up for Internet access with Wanadoo, one of the French service providers, and relied on a dial-up connection through the V92 internal modem in the 2GHz IBM desktop computer that sat on a rough square table against the wall in the locked rear bedroom of the house.

The PC had been supplied with Microsoft Windows XP, but Abbas had stripped that off because of the potential 'spyware' implications of the Product Activation routine, and had installed Windows ME and Office 2000 instead. The machine had come with Outlook Express and Internet Explorer, which worked well enough despite various security loopholes and which Abbas had left alone, but he had added an anti-virus suite and a firewall for safety. He'd also installed a copy of the PGP – Pretty Good Privacy – file encryption program.

Next to the computer was a small-footprint Hewlett-Packard laser printer, which was used only to print the very rare email messages intended for the group, rather than just Abbas, to see. On the floor next to the table was a large uninterruptible power supply – a UPS – which would provide back-up power to the computer for about half an hour in the event of a mains power failure. Beside the UPS was a black leather Samsonite case containing a powerful laptop computer to be used as a back-up to the IBM machine in case of some kind of major software or hardware crash, and a mobile telephone in case the landline ever failed. And apart from two upright chairs, the room contained nothing else.

Every afternoon Abbas unlocked the door of the back bedroom, switched on the computer, opened Internet Explorer and surfed the Internet for a couple of hours, concentrating on pornographic sites. This he had done ever since they had taken the house, establishing a routine that served to cloak his real activity on the web. He had no interest whatsoever in the lurid images that flashed across the screen, and barely even glanced at them. All he was interested in was one site that he himself had created and that was hosted on a low-cost server in Arizona. He had done nothing to promote the site, so very few people knew it existed, and fewer still bothered to visit it because it was, even by the low standards normally applied to sex sites, remarkably badly constructed and, frankly, boring.

One link on the site generated a 404 error – page not found – but pressing the 'Refresh' button three times within two seconds ran a small piece of code Abbas had embedded in the site. This action didn't produce a new page but simply dialled the classified number of a distant mainframe computer, which Abbas logged on to at least once every week.

As well as surfing the net, Abbas had established himself on several email mailing lists, and every day had to wade through some fifty advertising messages. The majority of these he deleted immediately, but he always read the messages from one advertiser in Germany completely. Some of these messages he deleted after reading, but some he didn't. Although the originating address was German, these emails had actually been sent from a different country, using a series of redirection sites to conceal their true origin.

That morning, Abbas downloaded the overnight messages and found only one from the German email address. He scanned through it carefully, then grunted with satisfaction. About halfway down the page were a few lines of what appeared to be corrupted text. Abbas highlighted the text and copied it into the word processor, then closed his Internet connection and shut down Outlook Express. Then he ran the decryption routine in the 128-bit PGP encryption program on the copied text, using his private key, and read the message twice. Its contents disturbed him, and he knew Khamil had to be told at once.

Abbas spent forty minutes working at the computer, composing and encoding a message for Sadoun Khamil's eyes only, which he embedded in another advertising email, this one with a Spanish originating address. As with the incoming message, Abbas arranged for it to be bounced from server to server before finally being delivered to Saudi Arabia.

Sluzhba Vneshney Razvyedki Rossi
Headquarters, Yazenevo, Tëplyystan, Moscow

It was, Sokolov thought, as he surveyed the pile of folders and files on the desk in front of him, an almost impossible task. He was not even sure that Nicolai Modin was right, that one of the records he was studying was that of a traitor. It was surely possible that the Americans had flown their spy-plane just because they wanted to photograph the weapon test site.

Time was a further problem. Sokolov checked his desk calendar; there were just three weeks to go before the implementation date of

Podstava. Three weeks in which to review the records of twenty-one high-ranking officers of the GRU and SVR, many of whom were personal friends, looking for a single anomaly, a single fact or indication that might suggest that the man's loyalty could be questioned. In fact, including Modin and himself, there were twenty-three officers indoctrinated into the project. There was also Minister Trushenko, but neither he nor Modin had the authority to investigate him.

Sokolov pressed the intercom button and ordered more of the strong black tea that he enjoyed. Then he picked up the draft action plan he had agreed with General Modin and glanced over it. Telephone taps were in place on the home and office telephone lines of all twenty-one officers – that, no doubt, was a complete waste of time, as only an idiot would use his own telephone to pass classified information to a foreign power or agent. Mail intercepts had also been ordered, but again Sokolov had no illusions about the likely results of that. If there was a traitor, Sokolov was sure that the only way he could be detected would be through physical surveillance, by watching where he went and whom he talked to or passed close to in the street or stood next to. The watchers were assigned and ready, and that, apart from scanning the personal files again, was about all that could be done.

The door opened and Sokolov's aide entered, carrying a tray of tea and sweet biscuits, which he placed in front of the general. Sokolov nodded his thanks and picked up the next file. He glanced at the name on the cover – 'Bykov' – then opened it and looked down at the full-face photograph of a sharp-featured man wearing an artillery officer's uniform.

Hammersmith, London

Simpson stood up and walked to the window overlooking the Hammersmith flyover. His small pink hands fussed among the cacti for a minute or so, a sure sign that his mind was on other things, and then he walked back to his desk and sat down. 'Explain,' he snapped.

'First, the body,' Richter replied. 'The head injuries were extremely severe, even for a high-speed, head-on collision. According to the

Russian authorities, the car ran into the back of a parked truck at about fifty miles an hour, but the other injuries to the body don't gel. From the condition of the car, the driver must have sustained lower-limb damage if his right foot was on the brake pedal at the moment of impact. I can conceive of no circumstance in which a driver, knowing that a collision was imminent, would remove his feet from the pedals. His natural instinct would be to brake, and keep on braking—'

'Unless he was suicidal,' Simpson interrupted.

'Yes, but in that case, his foot would almost certainly be on the accelerator. Same difference. No apparent arm injuries, either. And the fire that followed the crash conveniently burnt the body's hands and forearms, obliterating the fingerprints. No, the whole thing stinks. The injuries are certainly consistent with the damage caused to the car, but with the proviso that the driver was unconscious at the time of impact.

'As far as I can see, the only way the body could have received those injuries was by being strapped into the car, feet placed on the floor and hands and arms lying limp or perhaps on the lap. And another thing; when I was examining the corpse, Erroll pointed out a line of light bruising running across the chest, about six inches below the shoulders. At the time, I didn't know what had caused it, but I worked it out on the flight back.'

'What was it?' Simpson asked.

'When they put the man in the car, he was still alive, but unconscious. The seats on the Lada that Newman owned were very upright, and I think they found that he slumped forward instead of sitting normally in the seat. So they tied a length of string or twine around him to hold him upright.'

'Why string? Why not rope?'

'Too strong. What they wanted was a body that looked as if it had died in a road accident. If they'd used rope, that would have left heavy bruising on the body.'

'OK,' Simpson said, 'but you're telling me this man was alive when he was put in the car, but killed by the impact. Dead bodies don't bruise.'

'No, but tissue damage would still occur, and would still be detectable, and might lead to awkward questions being asked, albeit only in private. But they had a better reason for using string. They wanted the victim to die in the crash. If he had been tied upright with rope, he might possibly have survived, and then they'd have had to beat him to death with clubs or whatever to make it look as if he'd been killed in the crash. And it's very difficult to do that without it being perfectly obvious to any reasonably competent pathologist. They must have assumed that we would give the body a post-mortem, just because of who Newman was. By using string to support him, they made sure that at the moment of impact the string would break, and the body's head and upper torso would swing forward and downwards, and make hard – and probably fatal – contact with the steering wheel and dashboard. The bruising was caused by them tying the string a little too tightly, or maybe it was a bit too strong, coupled with the pressure the body exerted on it at the moment of impact, just before it broke '

Simpson considered this for a minute or so, then nodded. 'OK. Go on.'

'It was a set-up. Having snatched Newman, they looked around and found some middle-aged Russian with a similar build and colouring. They knocked him out, dressed him in Newman's clothing, put him in the car and then drove it, maybe by some sort of radio control, into a barrier.

'Then they made sure the face was unrecognizable – part of the lower jaw was missing, and most of the teeth, so even dental records wouldn't have been much help in confirming the identity – and that the body was dead, and burnt the hands and the car. And finally they called the British Embassy to impart the sad news that Graham Newman, Third Secretary and only incidentally Moscow SIS Head of Station, was dead.'

Sluzhba Vneshney Razvyedki Rossi
Headquarters, Yazenevo, Tëplyystan, Moscow

Lieutenant Nilov gave a respectful double knock on General Modin's inner office door, waited until he heard the muffled command to enter, then opened it.

'Yes, Vadim? What is it?' General Modin asked, looking up from his desk.

Nilov walked briskly across the office and stopped in front of the general. 'I have just been informed by the foyer guards that Minister Trushenko has arrived, General.'

Modin leaned back in his chair, an expression of faint surprise on his face. 'The Minister? He's come here?' he said. 'I wonder . . .' His voice trailed away, and he looked up at his subordinate. 'He has, I suppose, come to see me?'

'Yes, General. He's on his way up now,' Nilov replied.

Modin stood up, pulled his uniform jacket straight and began fastening the buttons. 'Well, we must make the Minister welcome, Vadim,' Modin said. 'Coffee and biscuits, please, and show him straight in.'

Six minutes later Nilov knocked again on Modin's door and swept it open without waiting for a response. 'Minister Trushenko, General,' he intoned, and bowed slightly as the politician walked past him and into the office. General Modin stood up respectfully as Trushenko entered. He strode forward and shook the Minister's hand, then gestured to the easy chairs either side of the low table upon which Nilov had already placed refreshments.

'Welcome, Minister,' Modin said, as Trushenko sat down and placed his briefcase on the floor beside him. 'You have not, I think, been to Yazenevo before?'

Trushenko stretched out his long legs before replying. 'No, General, I have not. In truth, I always preferred Dzerzhinsky Square. It was much more convenient there than being out here in the wilds.'

'Yazenevo is hardly Siberia, Minister,' Modin said, smiling. 'We are only a few minutes' drive from the Kremlin.'

'I know, but to me Yazenevo just feels remote.' He nodded as Modin gestured to the coffee pot, and leaned back in the chair. Modin passed the coffee cup over, pushed the plate of biscuits across the table, and waited. He knew Trushenko well, and knew that the Minister would not have arrived – still less arrived unannounced – unless he had a pressing reason for doing so. In all his previous dealings with him, Modin had always been summoned by Trushenko, and they had always met in Moscow, either at the Kremlin or in Trushenko's own spacious office suite in the Ministry.

Trushenko took a sip of coffee, then replaced the cup and saucer on the table and looked across at the SVR officer. 'We have a problem, General,' Trushenko began. 'There has been, I am now quite certain, some kind of a leak. You will recall that we discussed this possibility at our previous meeting, before the Englishman was questioned.' Modin made a gesture of distaste, which Trushenko noticed. 'The English,' Trushenko said, 'have an expression –"you can't make an omelette without breaking eggs." We are not making an omelette, but the same principle applies. The death of the Englishman was inevitable, once he had been taken for questioning. We could hardly send him back to his masters at SIS with knowledge of the questions we had asked.'

Modin put down his coffee cup. 'I do not dispute that, Minister,' he said. 'What I do dispute is the method that was employed to question him. Surely the interrogator could have been instructed to use drugs, rather than the medieval methods that he so obviously enjoyed?'

'No,' Trushenko replied. 'The interrogator was acting under my direct orders, and I allowed him to use whatever methods he felt were the most suitable. He felt that, because time was critical, torture was likely to be the fastest and most efficient technique.'

Modin shook his head. 'I cannot agree, Minister. I don't know what went on in—'

'I do know,' Trushenko interrupted. 'I had the interrogation video-taped.'

'You taped the interrogation?' Modin demanded, staring in disbelief.

'Of course. I like to know what goes on in my name. I have a collection of tapes recorded at several terminal interrogations. I wouldn't recommend them for bedtime viewing, but they are interesting, nevertheless.' Trushenko picked up a biscuit and nibbled it delicately. 'The Englishman was a disappointment,' he continued. 'He offered almost no resistance and obviously had a very low pain threshold. A wimp,' he added, dismissively.

Modin still stared at him. He had been acquainted with the man for nearly four years, and had never suspected this streak of ghoulish, sadistic voyeurism.

'To business,' Trushenko said. 'The Englishman –' he rolled the word on his tongue, as if the mere act of speaking it gave him pleasure '–

77

confirmed what I had suspected. He knew nothing of *Podstava*, which at least means that we will not be forced to implement the plan immediately. Obviously the Americans suspect something – or, to be more accurate, they have been told something – which is why they flew their spy-plane, but they have not shared their knowledge with the British.'

General Modin stopped thinking about the death of the Englishman and concentrated on what the Minister was saying. 'You are certain that they were not simply investigating the weapon test in the tundra?' he asked.

'I don't think so,' Trushenko said, shaking his head decisively. 'In the present political climate they would not have dared over-fly our land-mass just to photograph a weapon test site. To risk the possible political implications, they must have had some overwhelming reason. However, the Americans cannot have detailed information about *Podstava*, other-wise they would not have had to risk the flight at all.'

Modin nodded again. What the Minister was saying exactly matched his own opinion. 'I have already taken steps to try to identify the traitor, assuming that there is one.'

'Oh, there is a traitor, General, of that I am sure. What have you done?'

'I have instructed General Grigori Sokolov to review the files of everyone with a working knowledge of *Podstava*,' Modin replied. 'He has authorized mail intercepts and telephone taps, as well as physical surveillance.'

'Do you expect that to yield anything?' Trushenko asked quizzically.

'Frankly, Minister, no,' Modin said. 'But it will effectively prevent the traitor from sending any further communications to the Americans. That is the best we can hope for.'

'Agreed. Now, if the British had known about *Podstava*, we would have had to begin the immediate implementation of the plan. The leak to the Americans is less critical, as that component has already been completed. Nevertheless, I cannot risk letting *Podstava* run to the ori-ginal timetable, in case the Americans do decide to confide in their European allies.'

'You are advancing the schedule?' Modin asked.

'Yes,' Trushenko replied. 'Complete implementation of Operation *Podstava* will now take place on the eleventh of next month.'

'That's only twelve days from now,' Modin said, glancing across at his desk calendar. 'It leaves very little margin for error or delays.'

'Actually, it leaves no margin at all for error or delays, General. As you know, I was tasked by the Politburo with the planning and execution of Operation *Podstava*, and until now I have been content to simply oversee the various phases. Now, because it is clear that some details of the operation have been leaked to the Americans, and because time is so short, I have decided to take over personal control of all aspects of *Podstava*, including supervision of the assembly of the final weapon and, of course, the actual implementation. Additional security measures will be imposed. No communications of any sort concerning *Podstava* are to be made to any person who has not already been fully indoctrinated. This includes your superiors and subordinates in the SVR, and even Politburo members.'

'Your previous orders forbade any contact with all non-authorized personnel,' Modin pointed out. 'From the beginning of the project you instructed that all communications with the Politburo were to be channelled through you.'

'Correct,' the Minister replied. 'The difference now is that with *Podstava* about to be implemented, any disclosure, of any sort, to anyone, will be regarded as treason. There will be no trial, and the penalty will be death.' Trushenko paused, and smiled bleakly. 'Death may not be immediate. I may take the opportunity to add to my video collection.' Despite the warmth of the office, Modin felt a chill creep over him.

'Finally, General,' Trushenko said, 'I want you to accompany the final weapon to London and oversee its placement.'

'May I ask why?' Modin asked, surprise evident in his voice.

'Yes. You are the most senior SVR officer involved in *Podstava*, and you have my complete trust. The London weapon is in many ways the lynchpin of the European phase of the operation, and I want there to be no mistakes in its delivery or positioning. You have the rank and the ability to ensure that nothing goes wrong.'

'I thank you, Minister, for your confidence.'

'Just ensure that my confidence is not misplaced, General,' Trushenko said, and opened his briefcase.

Hammersmith, London

'Why did we get involved in this?' Richter asked. 'Why didn't SIS get one of their men to investigate it?'

'Simple. Vauxhall Cross didn't want a known "face" poking around over there if this turned out to be anything other than a simple road accident, which – thanks to you – we now know that it wasn't.' Simpson looked down at the file again, then back at Richter. 'Why are you so sure he's dead?'

Richter sighed. Simpson seemed particularly obtuse that morning. That, however, was nothing new. He often appeared slow to grasp what seemed patently obvious to everyone else, but from bitter experience Richter knew that this was just his naturally devious nature manifesting itself. He always wanted to be absolutely certain that an operative making a proposition had considered every aspect of the matter.

'He's got to be, hasn't he?' Richter said. 'They've presented us with a dead body that almost everyone accepts as being the remains of Graham Newman. If they were going to ignore his diplomatic immunity and put him on show, they certainly wouldn't have done that. It would have been a mysterious disappearance, followed a few days later by a cautious leak from TASS, then the usual diplomatic charge and denial that we all know and love. That would have been followed by a trial at which Newman would make a "voluntary" confession to whatever the Russians had in mind. And if it had been a defection, they'd be shouting about it in the world's press, and there wouldn't be a mangled stiff in a Moscow basement.

'No, the only possible reason for giving us a body called Newman is that Newman is dead somewhere, and the only reason for giving us a body that looks like Newman but isn't, is that Graham Newman's remains are not fit for public consumption.' Richter stopped and looked over at Simpson. 'If you want my guess, Newman's in the Lubyanka, and he won't be coming out. They've snatched him for terminal questioning.'

Simpson nodded in a preoccupied fashion a couple of times, then stood up and walked back to the window and fiddled with the cacti on the sill.

'And there's something else,' Richter said.

'What?'

'I picked up tails everywhere I went in Moscow, and I had an exchange of views with one of them at the airport.'

'Who was he?'

'I didn't bother getting his name, but he was carrying an SVR identity card and waving a PSM pistol in my face. The SVR had obviously issued a kill order against me.'

Simpson nodded, returned to his desk, and depressed a button. 'Coffee,' he said.

A few minutes later there was a knock on the door, and Richter got up and opened it. Simpson's secretary was standing outside, a metal tray in her hands. On it were two cups of black coffee, a small jug of milk, a plate with three digestive biscuits, and a bowl of sugar.

'Thank you, Sheila.'

She put the tray down on Simpson's desk and left the office. Simpson reached across, added milk to his coffee and watched Richter take two of the three biscuits. 'It may interest you to know that your appreciation of the situation tallies almost exactly with the Intelligence Director's assessment, given that the body is not Newman.'

'That's why he's the ID, I suppose,' Richter said.

'Don't be frivolous.' Simpson put his coffee cup down and reached for the remaining biscuit. Richter remembered the things he had selected from Graham Newman's possessions in Moscow, opened his briefcase again and piled them up on Simpson's desk.

'What's this rubbish?'

'This rubbish, as you so charmingly put it, is a small selection of the things Newman held near and dear.'

'I realize that,' said Simpson. 'More to the point, why are they on my desk?'

'Because I don't want them,' Richter replied. 'I had to think of a reason for having a quick look round Newman's office and apartment – as instructed by you – and collecting items of sentimental value for his family seemed to be the easiest. I thought you might like to send them off to the SIS or even to Newman's family, if he had one.'

Simpson looked at him. 'There is a next of kin address in the file, as I've no doubt you noted, but Newman wasn't married.'

'I know he wasn't married,' Richter said sharply.

Simpson looked at him quizzically. 'He was the SIS Head of Station. Nobody was stopping him getting married. It's different with us – I never employ field operatives saddled with wives. It's far too hampering.'

'I'm sure it is,' Richter said.

'How I employ my operatives is nothing whatever to do with you.'

'It is as long as I'm one.'

'You're more than a field operative. I recruited you into this organization in order to make use of your unique talents. You, Richter, are one of my secret weapons.' Simpson smiled the way a crocodile does, showing lots of teeth and ill intent. 'I like to think I can aim you at a problem, light the blue touch paper and stand well clear.'

Richter grunted. Simpson showed more teeth, drained the last of his coffee and stood up. 'Leave them with me – the bits you brought back from Moscow. I'll take care of them.'

'Thank you.'

'Well? Anything else?' Simpson said and looked rather pointedly at the door.

'Yes, of course there's something else,' said Richter. 'Having established that the body in Moscow isn't Newman, the big question is why.'

Simpson sat down again. 'You mean why did they snatch Newman?'

'I mean why did they snatch Newman, and why did they snatch anyone?'

Simpson smoothed back his fair hair with a small and scrupulously clean pink hand. 'I asked the Intelligence Director the same question.'

'And what, pray, was the Intelligence Director's assessment of the situation?'

'He was puzzled,' Simpson said. 'There would appear to be no reason why Newman was snatched, rather than any other SIS officer at Moscow Station except, of course, that he was Head of Station. He had had no access to any files of particular interest to the Russians recently, and as far as we are aware he was not involved in any especially sensitive project. Which is to say that he hadn't been tasked by London with anything of that nature. It's pretty quiet at the moment in Moscow, apart from the depredations of the Mafia.'

'Basically, you don't know?'

'I didn't say that,' Simpson snapped. 'We came to the conclusion that it might simply have been a precautionary check. The KGB did occasionally snatch a foreign service operative and pump them dry just to see if they knew anything of interest – although it wasn't common – and it was rare for them not to return the operative afterwards, more or less in one piece. Perhaps the SVR has a more aggressive attitude.'

'So that's it, is it? "Goodbye, Newman. It's been nice knowing you."'

'There'll be a funeral, of course.'

'Delightful. I meant, more specifically, what follow-up action will you be taking?'

'Follow-up action? None. As far as Vauxhall Cross is concerned, officially the body at the Embassy is Newman, and will be buried here as Newman. The Russians couldn't have got anything of major significance out of Newman because he didn't know anything. Therefore, as SIS has not been compromised in any way, we are doing nothing.'

'That will be a great comfort to Newman's shade,' Richter said, and walked out.

Office of the Director of Operations (Clandestine Services), Central Intelligence Agency Headquarters, Langley, Virginia

The outer office door was open, and as Richard Muldoon led the way down the long carpeted corridor he could see straight into the room. Jayne Taylor, the Director's personal assistant – very personal, if some of the rumours circulating in the supergrades' private dining room were to be believed – was talking softly into a telephone while she flicked briskly through a large leather-bound desk diary.

'Yes,' she murmured quietly, as Muldoon paused at the door, 'it looks as if Friday week is about the earliest the Director can see you.

Of course, if you could limit your presentation to fifteen minutes or less we could possibly fit you in before that.'

She looked up as Muldoon knocked, and her eyes widened slightly as she nodded and watched him and the other two men walk in and stand by the window. Muldoon was tall and lanky, and bore an uncanny resemblance to James Jesus Angleton, the agency's notorious former spy-catcher, but today his normally cheerful face was clouded. Jayne Taylor turned away, and resumed her telephone conversation. 'Look, Mike, I have some visitors right now. Could you give it some thought and call me back? Thanks, and you.'

She put the telephone handset down and looked appraisingly at Muldoon, the head of the Directorate of Science and Technology – the CIA division responsible for satellite surveillance and technical intelligence analysis.

Jayne Taylor was undeniably easy on the eye, Muldoon thought, and not for the first time. Dark hair cut fashionably short, wide-spaced brown eyes and perfect lips – an almost elfin face behind which, Muldoon knew, resided an excellent brain. Unlike most of the secretaries and assistants employed by the CIA, who were usually trawled from the high schools of Maryland, West Virginia and Pennsylvania, Jayne Taylor was a B.A. graduate of Vassar College in Poughkeepsie, New York. It was popularly believed that she was only using the CIA as a stepping-stone – just one item on her own hidden agenda.

'Good morning, Richard,' she said with a smile. 'What's this – a mutiny?'

Despite himself, Muldoon grinned. 'Not yet, Jayne,' he said, 'but we have to see Walter, and we have to see him now.'

'That,' she replied, frowning, 'could be difficult. He's involved in a conference call with the National Security Agency right now that should wind up in another ten minutes or so, but he's got appointments booked solidly all morning. How long do you want with him?'

Muldoon shook his head. 'I don't know. At least an hour.'

Jayne Taylor looked at him, and then at the men behind him. She knew them both. Ronald Hughes was Deputy Director of the Intelligence Division, a nondescript figure with a lined face and prematurely grey hair, who looked much older than his fifty-eight years. He had always maintained that the perfect spy was the man nobody noticed, and he seemed proof of his own maxim. Jayne assumed, correctly, that he was with Muldoon because his Director, Cliff Masters, was in Vienna until the following week.

The third man was John Westwood, head of the Foreign Intelligence (Espionage) Staff. Short, red-faced and softly spoken, he looked more like a shopkeeper than an Agency professional. All three men were unusually quiet, not even talking amongst themselves, which Jayne found disturbing. 'You really need this, don't you?' she asked, and Muldoon nodded.

'OK,' she said, and opened the desk diary again. She scanned the page, then nodded. 'He won't like it,' she murmured, 'but William Rush will have to wait.' She picked up the telephone and made two brief calls, then looked up at Muldoon. 'I'll probably catch a lot of flak for that later today – this had better be worth it.'

'It is, Jayne, and thanks. I owe you.'

The three men sat down, waiting in apprehensive silence. None of them was looking forward to the forthcoming meeting. Eight minutes later the light extinguished on the switchboard display and the status light above the mahogany door changed from red to green. Jayne called the Director on the intercom, then looked at Muldoon and nodded. The men got up and entered the inner office.

'Walter,' Muldoon began, as he approached the man at the desk, 'we have a problem, and it's something you need to know about.'

Walter Hicks, Director of Operations (Clandestine Services) of the Central Intelligence Agency, gazed across his desk at the delegation in front of him. He was a big and bulky man, pushing six feet three, and broad across the shoulders. His craggy face, under a thatch of thinning fair hair, carried a tan all year round, due to his passion for sailing, and most weekends he spent at least one day on his forty-five-foot catamaran, occasionally inviting colleagues to join him. It was, he claimed, one of the few places outside the Langley classified briefing rooms where he could say what he wanted.

'I have a feeling,' he said, after a few moments, 'that I'm not going to like this. The CIS went ballistic with signal traffic yesterday. Some major shit's been hitting the fan over there, and the NSA is kinda hoping we can help find out what it is. So I need whatever problem you've got like Custer needed more Indians.'

The office was large and airy, with a conference table positioned in front of the triple-gazed, bullet-proof picture window. Hicks pressed a button on his intercom, asked Jayne to order coffee for four, then walked over to the table and eased his body into the chair at its head, motioning the others to join him. 'OK, Richard,' he said, 'let's hear it.'

Muldoon sat down, glanced over the papers he had taken from his briefcase, and started talking. 'This involves all of us,' he said, gesturing at his companions, 'but it's probably quicker if I act as spokesman. Ronald and John will no doubt correct me if I stray.' Muldoon took a deep breath and began. 'About five months ago the Moscow Station Chief advised Langley that he had developed a high-level source in Moscow.'

'He did what?' Hicks demanded, his brow darkening. 'Nobody told me.'

Muldoon shook his head. 'Nobody told me either. The Station Chief – John Rigby – was adamant that knowledge of the source should be as limited as possible. Apart from him, and until two weeks ago, the only officers who knew about it were the head and deputy head of the Intelligence Division and John here from Espionage. Even the DCI was told only that a new high-level source had been developed, but nothing more.'

'Why?' Hicks asked flatly, reaching for a pack of cigars. 'Bearing in mind,' he added, 'that John is my direct subordinate. How come he knew and I didn't?'

'It was a value judgement,' Muldoon replied. 'Rigby was convinced that the source was very highly placed in the GRU or the SVR. The quality of the data he received was superb, and could only have come from the top, or very near it. Cliff Masters personally approved the list of officers who were to be told about the source. John needed to know because his duties required it.' Muldoon offered a faint smile. 'If you've a beef with that, Walter, you'd better take it up with Cliff, not John.'

'Who's the source?' Hicks grunted.

'We don't know. At least, we don't know exactly who he is, but we know he has to be one of a very small number of SVR or GRU officers.'

'Why?' Hicks asked again. He cut the end off a cigar and dropped it in the ashtray at the end of the long table. 'And how was contact established? Through a cut-out?'

'No. He was a walk-in. Rigby was passed an undeveloped film from a miniature camera while he was browsing round in GUM – that's the State department store in—'

'I think we all know what GUM is, Richard,' Hicks interrupted. He inspected the cut end of the cigar and then stuck it in his mouth. He patted his pockets, then stood up, walked over to his desk and picked up a Zippo lighter. He sat down again, thumbed the lighter and blew a large cloud of blue smoke down the table.

'Go on,' he instructed.

Muldoon flapped ineffectively at the smoke. He was a reformed smoker, and found the smell of tobacco smoke – particularly from cigars – very offensive. He coughed and continued. 'Rigby was off-duty and never even saw the person who gave the film to him. He found it in his jacket pocket when he was leaving the store – it had to have been passed by a brush contact. The point is, the source not only knew who Rigby was, which immediately eliminated most low-level SVR or GRU operatives, but he was able to pass the film completely undetected, which means he's a professional, an agent with field experience.'

Hicks considered this for a few moments. 'And when the film was developed?'

'Christmas,' Muldoon smiled. 'Twenty-four frames, needle-sharp pictures. Twenty-two were of highly classified documents, fourteen originating in the Kremlin itself, two from the GRU and the rest from the SVR. The intelligence we gained has been disseminated within the Agency, but heavily sanitized and on a very restricted distribution list. None has been released outside the Agency except with the Director's personal approval.'

Hicks held up a finger. 'Got it,' he said. 'This is source AE/RAVEN, right?'

'Right,' Muldoon replied. All CIA agents and operations are

identified by a two-letter prefix indicating the country involved – AE for Russia, DI for Czechoslovakia and so on – followed by a randomly generated code-name.

'And the other two pictures on the film?' Hicks asked. 'What did they show?'

'Mainly that our source had a sense of humour, and that he is very near the top. He took one picture of the Meeting Room in the Kremlin, and one of the Walnut Room – that's the room that adjoins it. The documents were impressive enough, but those pictures had Rigby dancing in the street.'

'Yeah,' said Hicks, 'I can see why. There are what, a dozen or so SVR and GRU officers who have access to those two rooms, and they're all right at the top of the tree. OK, all I hear so far is good news. What's the catch?'

'Perhaps I'd better first—' Muldoon broke off as a rap sounded on the door. It opened and Jayne ushered in a middle-aged woman carrying a tray of coffee. Nobody spoke until the two women had gone and the door closed. When everyone had poured their coffee, Muldoon continued. 'Let me first outline the way the relationship developed. Rigby has never seen the contact, and has never made any obvious effort to do so, for fear of alarming him. What he did was to continue visiting shops, cafés and restaurants and generally making himself visible. He would routinely leave his coat or jacket on his chair, or hanging on a hook while he went to the john or to make a phone call or whatever. And, about once a month, an undeveloped film would appear in one of his pockets—'

'Did he attempt to establish any kind of dialogue?' Hicks interrupted.

'Yes. He began putting messages into his pockets, concealed in suitable containers, of course, but the source has never taken one, so it's been a pure one-way traffic flow so far. This continued until about three weeks ago. Then Rigby found another film canister in a pocket – but this time it was the glove pocket of his car. Rigby thought he had left the vehicle locked while he did some shopping, but he can't be sure. Whatever, when he returned to it the driver's door was unlocked, which was why he checked the car.'

Hicks tapped ash from the end of his cigar into the ashtray. 'Why the change in his routine, I wonder?' he murmured. 'OK, what was on that film?'

'Nothing,' Muldoon replied. 'It wasn't a film. When the embassy technician opened the film canister, it contained a small piece of paper bearing a short message.'

'And?'

'You'd better read it,' Muldoon said. 'Ron?'

Ronald Hughes opened the folder in front of him, selected two sheets of paper and passed them over to Hicks. 'That's a photostat of the original, Director,' Hughes said, 'enlarged by a factor of four, and the second sheet is a typed translation of the Russian.'

Hicks took the first sheet of paper and glanced at it, then read the translation of the message. When he'd finished he looked up at Muldoon. Then he read the translation again. 'Jesus Christ,' he said.

Chapter Six

Richter walked into his office on the second floor and pushed the door shut behind him. The room was, like Richter, compact and slightly scruffy. It was small, measuring about twelve feet by ten with an off-white ceiling and a light green emulsion on the walls; the colour was described by Simpson as 'vulture-vomit green', and Richter had to agree he had a point. The single window, triple-glazed and barred, looked south-west, but only provided a view of the wall of an adjacent building and the top branches of an elderly sycamore tree that just about managed to eke out an existence in the side street.

The desk and office chair were next to the window, facing the door, and against the opposite wall was a grey filing cabinet with a non-functioning lock. Richter kept nothing in it but a small kettle, a jar of instant coffee, a container of powdered milk, a spoon and two cups. Next to the filing cabinet, and bolted to a steel plate cemented into the wall, was a large ministry-issue safe fitted with a combination lock. On the desk were 'In' and 'Out' trays, a desk calendar, and two telephones. One had level-nine access which meant that Richter could ring up anyone entirely at the British tax-payers' expense. That was the grey phone. The other one was black, and was a direct line that communicated only with Simpson.

As usual, all the document trays on the desk were empty. Like the Secret Intelligence Service, the Foreign Operations Executive operated a 'clear-desks' policy, which meant that nothing was ever left on a desk in an unattended office. Even if the occupant was only going to the loo, all the files, document trays and even diaries had to be locked in the safe first. It was an irritating, but fundamentally secure, system.

Richter span the safe's combination lock. He reached in and pulled out three documents that had been delivered just before he had left for Moscow. As he did so, the black phone rang.

'Come up, please,' Simpson instructed. He sounded preoccupied.

Office of the Director of Operations (Clandestine Services), Central Intelligence Agency Headquarters, Langley, Virginia

Walter Hicks stood up, walked over to his desk and pressed the button on the intercom. 'Jayne,' he said, 'this is going to take some time. Cancel all my appointments for the rest of the morning, and only put calls through if you can't sort them out yourself.' This meant they wouldn't be disturbed – Jayne was very good at handling callers. 'OK,' he said, as he sat down again at the conference table, 'you people are the experts. I can read what it says, but I need you to tell me what it means.'

Muldoon glanced across the table towards Ronald Hughes. 'This is probably more your field than mine, Ron.'

'The message was apparently written in a hurry, Director,' Hughes said, 'as it's brief and cryptic. But it contains three very specific pieces of information.' He held up his left hand, fingers extended, and counted them off. 'First, RAVEN states that there is a bilateral covert offensive in progress, one part directed against Europe and the other against the States. I emphasize that he says "in progress", not "planned" or "future" or anything like that.'

'My Russian isn't that good,' Hicks interrupted, 'but we must be very clear on this. I presume you've checked the translation with our in-house specialists?'

'Yes. Four separate analyst/translators have studied the wording of this section of the document, and they all agree. There is no doubt about the translation.'

'Go on.'

'Second, he provides a date – the second of this month. Third, a map reference.' Hicks looked at him expectantly. Hughes rubbed a hand over his forehead and looked down at his papers. 'Let me take the three items in order. First, the offensive. As soon as the Espionage Division had this translation to hand, Cliff Masters directed me to run a high-priority check on all military activity within the CIS, looking for any signs of increased readiness. I also checked our current DEFCON status with NORAD at Cheyenne Mountain, and ran a check through all allied intelligence services, concentrating on Europe.'

'That should have covered all the bases,' Hicks said. 'The results were negative, obviously, or I would have known about it.'

'Yes,' Hughes replied. 'We were aware that the RAVEN message specified a covert offensive, but for any type of offensive it would be reasonable to assume that there would be some evidence of heightened military activity. We found nothing. Now, the date and the map reference. The second of the month came and went, and nothing seemed to happen. The position is nowhere. It's just a spot way up in the Bolshezemel'skaya Tundra, pretty much in the foothills of the Urals, and a long way from any sites of strategic interest or importance.'

'Get to the point,' Hicks growled.

'As I said, nothing seemed to happen on the second, but actually something did. Seismic recordings that we obtained showed an explosion of some kind on that date, in more or less the same position as the map reference given by source RAVEN.' Hughes looked over at Muldoon. 'That was when we brought Science and Technology into the loop, because we needed satellite pictures to find out what had happened up on the tundra.'

'We already had some pictures of the location specified by source RAVEN from a Keyhole satellite, taken in the weeks leading up to the second,' Muldoon said. 'The only thing of interest any of these showed was a handful of vehicles close to the map reference. After the event we tinkered with the polar orbit of a Keyhole satellite to optimize coverage. We had some trouble with cloud on the first few passes, but eventually we did get clear shots of the area. All we found was a hole in the ground, and not even a very big hole. Then we ran comparisons with earlier shots of the same area, but that didn't help much either.

'We hadn't got detailed satellite shots of the area – as I said, it's nowhere near anything of any strategic importance – but the wide-angle pictures we had showed nothing but a small hill in the tundra at the grid reference. And that's when two other factors entered the equation.'

'And they were?' Hicks asked.

'The fourth piece of information in the RAVEN message,' Hughes replied, 'and the seismographic analysis of the explosion.'

'I thought you said the RAVEN text contained only three bits of data.'

'No, Director,' Hughes said, shaking his head decisively. 'The message contained three specific pieces of information, which we've already discussed. It also contained three other phrases that were assessed as non-specific, as each was apparently intended to be a question or, possibly, an incomplete piece of data. One translated as "neutron radiation", the second was the proper name "Gibraltar" and the last was the word "demonstration".'

'OK,' Hicks said. 'Give me the rest of it – briefly, please.'

'Analysis of the seismographic records of the explosion suggested that the weapon was slightly unusual,' Muldoon said. 'I won't attempt to go into the technicalities of it because it's not my field, and our in-house experts can provide you with chapter and verse if you need it. However, what bothered our people was the fact that it didn't have the usual characteristics of any known current Russian nuclear weapon, fission or fusion. What it resembled more than anything was a big – a really big – neutron bomb.'

Muldoon fell silent and Hughes spoke again. 'We discussed the satellite pictures with Science and Technology, and ran some probability checks through Intelligence. John tried to do some checking with his sources in the CIS, but didn't get anywhere. The thing that bothered us was the "neutron radiation" statement, which tied up with the seismographic analysis. We tried the usual procedures, using sampling systems in bordering countries and on civil aircraft flying anywhere near the site of the explosion, but got nil results. We didn't understand that, because according to Science and Technology a weapon of the power suggested by the seismograph analysis should certainly have produced significant radiation. As we couldn't detect any, we wondered if the Russians had managed to develop a high-yield but low-radiation warhead – a kind of super neutron bomb, if you like.'

'You will be aware, Walter,' Muldoon interrupted, 'that the neutron bomb – the Enhanced Radiation Warhead – has an extremely small effective radius, usually under two hundred metres. The physical damage it causes is very limited, but the burst of neutrons it releases is immediately lethal within about five hundred metres, and lethal within hours or days to every living thing inside about a mile. More importantly, the radiation dissipates very rapidly and the area can safely be entered quite soon after detonation.'

Hicks stirred impatiently, but Muldoon pressed on. 'The neutron bomb was always intended as a defensive weapon, allowing a numerically inferior force to decimate attacking armour. What concerned us was the possibility that the Russians had managed to turn it into a first-strike weapon of some kind, giving it a high yield without the lingering radiation effects of a conventional nuclear device.'

Muldoon paused, and Hicks looked at him. Hicks took the cigar out of his mouth, looked at the glowing end and then back at Muldoon. 'I get the feeling,' he said, 'that we're coming to the awkward bit.'

Muldoon nodded. 'We decided that the only way to get detailed photographs and proper radiation measurements was to pull a Blackbird out of retirement at Beale and fly it over the tundra.'

Hicks exhaled sharply and blew a large cloud of tobacco smoke down the table. 'That was possibly not a wonderfully bright idea, Richard,' he said. 'I won't ask who suggested it, but I would like to know who approved it.'

'I did,' Muldoon replied.

Hicks nodded and glanced round the table. 'Well, the good news is that at least the rest of you have got top cover. The bad news is that if Richard falls into the shit, he'll have you to land on. What went wrong – I assume something did go wrong?' Hicks stopped suddenly. 'That's it, isn't it? You flew the fucking Blackbird yesterday morning, didn't you? That's why every military radar and radio station in the CIS lit up like a Christmas tree.'

'Yes, we did,' Muldoon said. 'The 'bird carried out the mission, but the crew had a few close calls over Russia – Foxbats, Fulcrums and couple of Foxhounds, I believe – and punched out into Scandinavian airspace with light battle damage. Two, or maybe more, of the fuel cells were punctured, and the crew assessed that they couldn't make it to any of the tankers, refuel safely and get back to Mildenhall.'

'Let's hear the rest of it.'

'The crew didn't have many options, but they managed to put the 'bird down safely at a Royal Air Force base – Lossiemouth – in Scotland. They only just made it. The approach was through very heavy weather and they had to be talked-down all the way. The Blackbird actually ran out of fuel on the runway.'

'Could have been a lot worse,' Hicks grunted. 'They could have landed in mainland Europe, which would have meant a lot of diplomatic hassle, at best, or they could have ended up in the North Sea. Goodbye one very expensive aircraft and crew, not to mention goodbye to the films and detector records. So, what's the problem?'

'The RAF is the problem – or, rather, the RAF and the British Ministry of Defence. They won't let us have the aircraft back until we tell them what it was doing over the CIS.'

Sluzhba Vneshney Razvyedki Rossi
Headquarters, Yazenevo, Tëplyystan, Moscow

Sokolov knocked on the door and waited. After a few seconds, Lieutenant Nilov opened it and ushered him into the inner office. Modin was sitting at his desk, studying an open file, but stood up and smiled as Sokolov entered the room.

'Progress, old friend?' he asked, hopefully.

Sokolov shook his head. 'No, nothing. I can find nothing in the personnel files that should not be there, and none of the surveillance measures has revealed any deviations from normal behaviour – at least, not so far. If there is a traitor, I don't think we're going to find him unless he does something really stupid, like trying to contact an American here in Moscow. All we can do, I think, is watch and wait. And you?'

'I have had Minister Trushenko here,' Modin replied. 'It was not a pleasant interview, for a number of reasons. First, he has ordered that the assembly of the last device be completed no later than Friday next week, and transport is arranged for the next day. He has also brought forward the implementation date of *Podstava* to the eleventh of next month. If there are no delays, that will leave just five days to get the weapon into position.'

Sokolov whistled softly. 'That's tight, Nicolai, very tight. There is little time to overcome any unforeseen problems.'

Modin shook his head. 'You're wrong, Grigori. There is no time to overcome any problems. Everything must go right, first time. The only insurance policy,' he added, 'is me.'

'What do you mean?'

'I will be accompanying the convoy, to oversee the placement of the weapon. It is not a task I relish, but Minister Trushenko was quite specific.'

Hammersmith, London

The courier knocked on Richter's door at ten minutes to four, and placed an armful of files on the desk. Of the twenty-three files, there were seventeen classified Confidential and above which had to be signed for individually in the Classified Documents Register before the courier left. Then Richter took a ruler from his desk drawer and measured the height of the pile of files before ringing Simpson. He answered at once.

'I hope you're not hoping for an answer today on the Newman case,' Richter said, 'because the heap of bumf from SIS sits seventeen and a half inches high on my desk.'

'That's more or less what I expected,' Simpson said. 'Newman would have had some input into virtually every matter that Moscow Station was dealing with. I've got a bad feeling about this, so make the Newman stuff your priority. If you need to shunt your other work around, let me know.'

'OK,' Richter said, and put the phone down. He spread the files out on his desk and started work. Thankfully, a good deal of the information could be discarded after a cursory glance, but that still left a substantial amount of reading matter in the Station files, and he was going to have to cover all that Newman had personally been involved in from his reports. By five thirty in the afternoon he had done little more than sort the stuff out, and decide what he had to read and what he could ignore or just scan through. Then he put the whole lot in the safe, span the combination, signed out of the building and went home. He would start again on Monday morning.

Office of the Director of Operations (Clandestine Services), Central Intelligence Agency Headquarters, Langley, Virginia

Richard Muldoon stopped talking. There was a moment's silence, and then, as if by common consent, everyone looked towards the head of the table.

'So what the hell are they doing?' Hicks asked.

'At the moment, nothing,' Muldoon replied. 'The 'bird is sitting on the ground in a hangar in Scotland. We can't get near it, and we can't talk to the crew except on an open phone line that's almost certainly being monitored.'

Hicks ground out his cigar in an ashtray, then looked up. 'When did the 'bird land?'

'Yesterday morning,' Muldoon replied

'OK, Richard. What have you done since then to get the aircraft back?'

Muldoon coloured slightly. 'Once we knew there was a problem, we tried through the USAFE to persuade the British to co-operate and release the aircraft, but we got nowhere.'

'And what do you expect me to do about it?' Hicks asked.

'You're acting DCI at the moment,' Muldoon said. 'We have assessed that we'll probably need strong diplomatic pressure to get the 'bird released without telling the Brits what they want to know. We'd like you to request the President, through the National Security Council, to try to get the aircraft back.'

Walter Hicks picked up the cigar packet and looked inside. Then he pushed his chair back and walked over to his desk, picked up a fresh pack of cigars and sat down again. 'Kind of "please can we have our ball back, mister"?' he said. Muldoon nodded. Hicks leaned back in his chair.

'OK,' he said. 'Let me summarize the situation as I understand it. We've had a whisper from a source in Moscow—'

'A reliable source, Director,' Hughes interrupted.

Hicks just glanced at him, then continued. 'We've got a whisper from a usually reliable source – I won't put it any higher than that – in Moscow that some kind of covert offensive is being implemented, although we can't detect any signs of it whatsoever. We've got seismograph recordings of a weapon test high in the tundra. And finally, we've possibly got film records of the possible weapon test site stuck in the surveillance cameras of a Blackbird at –' he checked his notes '– at RAF Lossiemouth in Scotland that the Brits won't let us look at until we tell them what the hell the aircraft was doing over-flying north-west Russia, threatening détente and all.' He looked round the table. 'Is that it?'

Three heads nodded.

'It's a crock of shit,' Hicks said flatly. 'It's rumour and unfounded speculation – you've no hard evidence at all. In fact, all the evidence you have says that the RAVEN message is disinformation. You can't start a covert assault without some signs of military activity. I can't take that and try to get NSC or Presidential approval for any further action. Christ, it's going to be difficult enough getting the Blackbird back to Mildenhall without answering a lot of real awkward questions.'

He pulled out another cigar and took his time lighting it. 'Did it ever occur to any of you that RAVEN might be a plant?' he went on. 'That this supposed agent might just be part of a deception operation intended to force us into doing something stupid – which it has? The KGB planners were experts at that kind of thing, and bearing in mind that they all now work for the SVR, do you really think they've lost their touch? Hell, the fucking source probably even works for the SVR!' He looked round the table. 'Well, did you? Any of you?'

Ronald Hughes replied quietly. 'Yes, Director, we did. We did consider it, but the quality of the data we received was so good that we don't believe the SVR would have released it as part of any deception campaign. We've been able to cross-check quite a lot of it, and there are no indications whatever that the source is anything other than what he appears to be – a disaffected officer right at the very top of the SVR or GRU.'

'Good. I'm pleased to see somebody's been thinking. Have we had anything from RAVEN since this note?'

'Nothing,' Hughes said. 'Either the SVR tumbled to him, in which case we've lost the best high-level source we've ever had – in my opinion – or he's having to lie low for the moment. Obviously,' he added, 'we hope he's still in place.'

'OK,' said Hicks. 'In my view, this is probably the SVR twisting our tail, just letting us know that they're still there and still in business. I'll spell it out. First, RAVEN was a walk-in. We don't know who he is or why he's doing it. I hear what you say about the data, Ron, but it is possible that we're being fed disinformation which is being supported by related leaked data that you're using to cross-check it. Kind of like a circular argument.'

'That's not the way I read it,' Hughes said, 'but I'll concede that it is just possible.'

'Second,' Hicks continued, 'the note was handwritten, which is suspicious for two reasons. If RAVEN was caught with the note in his pocket, his handwriting would be identifiable to another SVR or GRU officer at his level. If he is genuine, that would be too dangerous, too much of a risk. And why handwrite it? Why not just photograph the document, the same way he photographed all the other documents? And finally, your checks, Ron, showed no evidence whatsoever of military preparations for any kind of assault.'

There was silence round the table for a minute or so, then Hughes spoke. 'There could be other explanations for the note, Director. It could be that RAVEN has only just been indoctrinated into the operation, that he's only just been told about it. He may have been briefed verbally, and not seen any documents at all. If the project is classified highly enough, no documents describing the entire concept may exist, or there may be just one copy held in a two-key safe which can only be opened by two officers simultaneously; we know the KGB used that technique for added security. So there are several possible reasons why he may have had no option but to scribble brief details down, just to alert us to what's going on. If that is the case, then he will be relying on our ability to pick up the trail and find out what's happening. I wouldn't like to think that we're just going to drop it.'

Walter Hicks gave Hughes a brief grin. 'You misunderstand me, Ron. I'm not going to drop it. I'm just acting as devil's advocate, putting up the obvious counter-arguments.'

Muldoon leaned forward. 'There are a couple of other possible reasons for the lack of military preparations. First, an off-the-wall suggestion,' Muldoon said, looking slightly uncomfortable. 'The Russians could have developed a weapon so powerful that they believe that simply the threat of using it would force the West to accede to any demands they made.'

Hicks laughed. 'Dr Strangelove stuff, Richard? A "Doomsday Weapon"? I don't believe that. Their weapons science is a long way behind ours, unless things have changed a hell of a lot since the USSR collapsed. Besides, we'd need to be convinced that the weapon would work, which would mean a demonstration somewhere – an obvious demonstration, not just a hole in the ground high in the tundra. Even then, what would they do about our retaliatory capability? No, that doesn't hold water. What's the other reason?'

'This is the one that's given me shivers ever since I saw the RAVEN message, Walter. What if they've got weapons in place already, here in the States? Nuclear devices, smuggled in. That could be construed as a covert assault, and it wouldn't involve any kind of military build-up or other preparations.'

Hicks sat silent, digesting Muldoon's suggestion. Then he shook his head. 'That's a sneaky idea, Richard, but to what purpose? Even if they'd positioned a nuclear weapon in every major city in the States, and threatened to detonate them, we could still destroy Russia and the rest of the CIS. It would still be a stalemate, just like in the bad old days of MAD.'

Muldoon shook his head, unconvinced. 'I hope you're right, but my gut feeling about this is that RAVEN is genuine, and that something is going on that we don't know about. We have to take it further.'

'Oh, we're going to take it further, Richard, but I'm not – at least, not yet – going to involve the NSC or the President. What we have to do is recover the 'bird and view the films and detector records. Once we have that data to hand, we can decide what to do next. Right, Science and Technology got us into this – what are your recommendations, Richard?'

Muldoon selected a sheet of paper, glanced over it and then spoke. 'First, I'd like it on formal record that my Division just implemented the request from Intelligence for the surveillance flight by the Blackbird – this was not our plan, Walter, and I will not accept responsibility for it. We—'

'The buck stops anywhere but here, right?' John Westwood said softly, his normally red face growing a deeper shade. 'Your Division produced the satellite film analysis, and you personally recommended taking a close look at the site. The only way to get a closer look was to fly over Russia, which is what Intelligence suggested.'

Muldoon opened his mouth to speak, but Hicks beat him to it. 'This will achieve nothing. If the whole thing does turn to worms, there'll be an internal enquiry, and you can all concentrate on covering your asses then. For the moment, all I'm interested in is retrieving the situation. John, can it. Richard, carry on.'

'Thank you. In my opinion, the most pressing matter is the recovery of the 'bird, because without the film and detector evidence all we have is conjecture. And the longer the aircraft stays in Britain, the more questions are going to be asked – there and here. Don't forget, over flights of Russia were specifically banned by Presidential order in 1960 after the Gary Powers U–2 shoot-down. I know we've largely ignored the directive since then, but the order still stands. And it will also not have escaped anyone's notice that officially the Blackbird was retired from service at the end of 1989. Having one standing on the tarmac at Lossiemouth with obvious battle damage will certainly make people think. The last thing we want is for the British press to get hold of this. They're just as tenacious and prying as the *Washington Post*. I suggest that we instruct the USAFE—'

'I don't think we're in a position to instruct anyone, Richard,' Hicks interrupted.

'OK. I'll rephrase that. We suggest that the USAFE tells the Royal Air Force, and their Ministry of Defence, whatever it takes to get the 'bird back to Mildenhall where we can get things under control.'

'"Whatever it takes" is a pretty broad statement,' John Westwood said. 'What exactly do you mean? You won't let them see the films?'

'If that's what it takes, yes.'

'You can't do that.' Westwood's voice was quiet but firm. He had headed the Foreign Intelligence (Espionage) Staff for two years and no one had ever heard him raise his voice much above a normal conversational level in all that time. 'Remember what RAVEN told us. The covert offensive is two-pronged – one part aimed at us and the other at Europe. Until we get a handle on what's going on, the last thing we need is the Brits getting involved.'

'Why not?' Hicks asked.

'Because until we know more about this offensive, we don't know how we want them to react.'

'They are supposed to be our allies, remember.'

'That's exactly the point,' Westwood replied. 'Whatever this offensive is, and there's precious little to go on at the moment, we should wait until we have the big picture before we tell any of our allies. We don't want the Brits or anyone else blundering into action ahead of time and then have to stage a rescue or support them in some ill-advised action.'

Hicks nodded. 'OK, that's worth considering. However, the reality is that they have our aircraft and the films, and we – or rather the USAFE – will have to satisfy them before we get the access we need.' He turned again to Richard Muldoon. 'Let's look at our options. Can we supply a faked set of pictures – something from the library?'

Muldoon shook his head. 'Not a chance. First, they will almost certainly want the films to be removed and developed under their supervision, so making a switch would be difficult if not impossible. Secondly, don't forget that the Brits have JARIC.'

'Remind me,' Hicks said, looking blank.

'JARIC,' Muldoon went on. 'The Joint Air Reconnaissance Intelligence Centre, their own photographic interpretation unit. Any films we give them will be sent straight there for analysis. Even if we could switch the films, they'd know within an hour of looking at them, and that would only make them intensify their efforts to find out what we were up to. But if we give them the real films, they might write the flight off as a temporary aberration by USAFE, or a proving mission to test Russian reactions, or something like that.'

'OK, but John's objection still stands. When they analyse the films, they'll see—'

'Exactly,' Muldoon interjected. 'They'll see what? They'll see pictures of six hundred miles or so of Russian tundra. They won't know what we were looking for, so they'll concentrate on the obvious – new buildings, activity at known military units and so on. What they won't be looking for is a hole in the ground.'

'They'll do comparison studies with earlier satellite photographs,' said Westwood.

'They'll certainly try to,' Muldoon replied, 'but don't forget that we've denied them access to the footage of that area ever since the last RAVEN contact.' He looked over at Hicks. 'That was just a precaution, Walter, but I think it was wise in the event. They won't be able to see the vehicle concentrations prior to weapon detonation, so even if they spot the hole, all they'll find on the earlier pictures will be tundra and maybe just a few vehicles. And the hill in the tundra was just a hill in the tundra.'

'What reason do we give for the flight?' Hicks asked.

'Nothing at all. If we tell them a story, they'll crack it sooner or later and know that we're up to something. If we tell them nothing, just give them the pictures and let them get on with it, I believe there's a good chance that they'll analyse the films, find nothing of interest, and let the matter drop in a few weeks.'

'Anyone got any better ideas?' Hicks asked. Nobody spoke. 'OK,' he said. 'Do it.'

Turabah, Saudi Arabia

Sadoun Khamil stared intently at the screen of his laptop computer and read the decrypted text from the email message sent by Hassan Abbas three times, then leaned back in his chair to consider it. Like his despised infidel counterpart, Dmitri Trushenko, he had expected one of the Western intelligence organizations to stumble upon the operation sooner or later, as the number of people involved in it grew.

They had, he acknowledged, been lucky so far, but obviously the Americans had suspected or had been told something, hence the flight by the spy-plane. Since the triumph of September 11th, which had worked even better than Hassan Abbas had promised, their security systems had remained on high alert, and they were even more sensitive than before to the possibility of any further attacks. Well, Khamil smiled to himself, it was too late now for them to do anything.

Almost all the preparations were complete, and it only remained for the Russians to conclude their phase of the operation, the delivery of the last two weapons. Then Trushenko would implement the agreed procedure and issue the ultimatum that would permanently humiliate the United States and eliminate the countries of Western Europe as nuclear powers.

Then he and Hassan Abbas would implement their own procedure, agreed to and approved by the al-Qaeda leadership, and about which the Russians knew nothing. And then the world would change, instantly and for ever.

Chapter 7

Muldoon passed the signal from Mildenhall across the table to John Westwood. 'This isn't really your field, John, but you've been involved from the start. You see what it says?'

Westwood read through the text of the signal, then nodded and slid it over to Ron Hughes. 'The RAVEN message is beginning to make a bit more sense. This is presumably based upon an analysis of the Blackbird product – by Mildenhall staff?'

'Yes, with back-up from the recce guys at Beale, who flew across to England a couple of days ago. The 'bird, by the way, was released by the Brits yesterday afternoon, and landed at Mildenhall about nine, local time. The films were developed at Lossiemouth and copies were supplied to the British there. There were no requests to see the radiation detector records, and now we've got the 'bird back we can keep that data to ourselves.'

'Any chance that the Beale people have got it wrong?' Westwood asked.

'Unlikely,' Muldoon said, 'but the films and detector records should be on their way right now from the airport by courier. I've got a couple of our in-house specialist analysts here waiting to look at them. We should have confirmation no later than this evening, but unless they say something different, this is pretty much what we expected, and as RAVEN hinted. The device on the tundra had a calculated yield of about five megatons. That's around two hundred and fifty times more powerful than the twenty-kiloton Hiroshima device, but only about one quarter the yield of the weapons that the old Bear bombers used to carry.

'The yield calculation was based upon the estimated volume of matter in the hill and the degree of destruction shown by the Blackbird photographs. They had to make certain assumptions, including the soil type, the depth at which the device was placed and other factors to do with the method of detonation, and the five megaton figure may have to be modified when they've had time to do a full analysis, but they think it's about right.

'More important,' he went on, 'is the radiation detector result, which was nil. Or, rather, nil significant – there's always some background radiation. The Beale experts calculated the theoretical fallout from a conventional nuclear device of that power, made allowances for the weather patterns over the Asian landmass since the detonation, and for the Blackbird's altitude, but what they expected the detectors to register simply wasn't there. What they expected were traces of radio-isotopes strontium 90, caesium 137 and iodine 131, which are released in all nuclear explosions, but they didn't find any of them in statistically significant quantities. So it rather looks,' he added, 'as if the Russians have managed to develop some kind of high-yield, but very low-radiation, nuclear weapon. What amounts, in fact, to a strategic-power neutron bomb.'

'What I don't understand,' Westwood said slowly, 'is why they'd want to do that.'

Muldoon looked at him. 'Funnily enough, I've been wondering about that too.'

'I'm not with you,' Hughes interrupted.

Westwood leaned forward. 'Think it through,' he said. 'The balance of terror – Mutual Assured Destruction – was based on the premise that if the Soviets attacked us, they would suffer unacceptable losses through our retaliatory strikes, and vice versa. Both sides will lose and nobody will win, so there's no point in launching an attack in the first place.' He pointed at the signal sheet that Hughes was still holding. 'That just doesn't make sense. The yield from that weapon is certainly significantly higher than from our neutron bombs, but they were always intended to be tactical or battlefield weapons, not strategic arms. The fear of nuclear weapons is based on the destructive force of the explosion, but also on the effects of the fallout, the radiation. Take away the radiation, and you take away half the destructive effect of the weapon. And that,' he added, warming to the theme, 'would actually favour the enemy – us.'

'You'd better explain that,' Hughes said.

'Right. Let's suppose that this weapon test was just a demonstration – in fact, the last RAVEN message talked about a demonstration, so this may have been what he meant – and that they had developed high-yield but very low-radiation weapons. Now, if the Russians re-armed with weapons like this, and then attacked the States, we would suffer enormous damage from the detonations. We'd lose whole cities, and the majority of our citizens would be killed, but only – and this is the point – only as a result of the initial detonations and the massive, but short-term, burst of neutron radiation. Nobody would die from the long-term effects of fallout, because there wouldn't be any. Within a few days we could begin to rebuild our cities, without having to wear NBCD suits, and without worrying about contamination.'

'You don't paint a very attractive picture, John,' Muldoon said.

Westwood smiled thinly. 'I know, I know. It's a nightmare scenario, but the Russians must have thought it through. Now,' he continued, 'we don't have any of these fancy new nukes, so if the Russians attacked us we would just have to rely on the good old high-radiation stuff in our subs and ICBMs. And that means that our nuclear response would turn the Confederation of Independent States into an uninhabitable nuclear wasteland. OK, again, nobody really wins and both sides actually lose, but on points we'd be ahead. The CIS might never be able to recover. I mean, just look at them now. Even with all the help the West can give them, they're still trying to sort out the damage caused by the reactor accident at Chernobyl, and that was over twenty years ago.'

Hughes nodded abstractedly. 'I hear what you say, John, but the fact is that the Russians quite obviously have developed a new type of bomb, and I don't believe they did it just for fun. They have to have a specific purpose in mind.'

'That,' said Muldoon, 'is what's been bothering me ever since I read that signal. What the hell are they going to do with it?' Muldoon looked over at John Westwood. Muldoon was a planner and a specialist in technical surveillance techniques, but he knew almost nothing about HUMINT – human intelligence, or espionage. Satellites and reconnaissance platforms provided very precise information about hardware, but no data whatsoever about the intentions of the people who were building that hardware. For that, you needed an agent in place, somebody who could ask the right questions or listen to the right answers.

Westwood shook his head. 'We have no source we can tap about this – apart from RAVEN, of course, and we can't establish a dialogue with him because we don't know who he is. If we're lucky, he might pass further data to Rigby, but we can't rely on that.'

'Definitely not,' Hughes said. 'In view of the last message received from RAVEN, I think the safest course would be to assume that he's been burned. Even if he hasn't, the Russians are bound to have increased security measures after the Blackbird flight, and I doubt he'd be able to pass anything further for a while.'

'Agreed,' Muldoon said. 'So, what do we do? This is your department, John – what's your recommendation?'

Westwood was silent for a minute or so. 'Technical analysis,' he said finally, 'isn't much use to us now. I'd like confirmation from our in-house experts that the conclusions reached by the Beale team are accurate, though I don't have much doubt that they are. What we have to do is find a way to discover what the Russians are planning for their new weapon, and the only way to do that is to tap another intelligence source close to the top in Moscow. As I said, we don't have one, but it's possible that the British, or maybe the French or the Germans, have. My recommendation is that we approach the British first – because of the "special relationship" and all that – and see if they have a line into the GRU or SVR.'

Muldoon smiled. 'I thought you were opposed to telling them anything, John?'

'I am, and I wasn't intending to change my mind, not unless it's unavoidable. I've already cleared it with Walter that I go to London, liaise with our people there, and see if I can get anything. The local Chief of Station should, I hope, have a decent working relationship with their Secret Intelligence Service, and maybe I can find out something through him. This isn't,' he added, 'something we can sort out over a telephone or through signal traffic.'

'How soon would you go? I mean, what's the priority for this?' Muldoon asked.

'I talked with Walter about this yesterday afternoon. Despite the negative feedback we've got, I think whatever is planned is imminent – maybe no more than a month away. If we're to get anywhere, I think we have to move quickly. I've got an open ticket to Heathrow, and I'm planning on leaving no later than Tuesday morning.'

Monday
Hammersmith, London

Richter arrived at Hammersmith just after seven thirty in the morning, and had the first SIS file open in front of him ten minutes later. He was halfway through it when Simpson rang.

'Have you seen this?' Simpson asked, as Richter reached his desk.

Richter looked at the file Simpson passed over to him and read the title – 'Forced-landing of USAF reconnaissance aircraft at RAF Lossiemouth'. 'No,' he replied.

'OK,' Simpson said. 'To save time I'll give you the short version. Last Thursday morning a Blackbird reconnaissance aircraft—'

'A Blackbird?' Richter interjected. 'They've been withdrawn from service for years.'

'I know,' Simpson said, 'and don't interrupt. Last Thursday a Blackbird landed at Lossiemouth with empty fuel tanks, signs of light battle damage and a really close-mouthed crew. Since then the USAFE has been trying everything to get the aircraft back, but the Ministry of Defence, showing an unusual degree of common sense, refused to let them take it away until they were told what the aircraft had been doing. Yesterday, the Blackbird finally flew back to Mildenhall, and a copy of the films it had taken were sent to JARIC.'

'And?' Richter enquired.

'And you can take this file, plot the route the aircraft flew and work out what exactly the Yanks were so keen to photograph, and why they didn't want to tell us anything about it.'

'Is that it?'

'No. Tomorrow you can get your arse over to JARIC and take a look at the films.'

Kutuzovskij prospekt, Moscow

The black ZIL limousine drew into the kerb and stopped. The chauffeur got out, opened the rear door and stood respectfully at attention as a tall slim man emerged from the back seat. For a minute or so the two men stood together, exchanging a few words, then the passenger walked into a shop. The chauffeur closed the rear door, got back behind the wheel, and drove away.

Thirty seconds after the car had disappeared around the corner, the tall man emerged empty-handed from the shop and glanced quickly up and down the street. He nodded as if satisfied, then crossed the road and strode off briskly in the direction opposite to that taken by the car. Three minutes later, and without a backward glance, he entered the foyer of a large, and comparatively elegant, apartment building. The lift had just stopped on the ground floor to disgorge an elderly woman, and the visitor smiled pleasantly at her as he entered the lift. When the doors had closed, he pressed the button for the fifth floor.

Genady Arkenko had been expecting the knock on the door, and opened it almost immediately. Dmitri Trushenko nodded his thanks and stepped into the apartment.

'Dmitri,' Arkenko said, his face splitting into a smile of welcome as the two men embraced, 'it is so good to see you.'

Genady Arkenko was a short, dark-haired Georgian, and was Minister Dmitri Trushenko's best-kept secret. In a country where homosexuality was illegal, and where exposure would mean certain ruin, the two men had been lovers since their schooldays. 'Can you stay?' Arkenko asked hopefully.

Trushenko shook his head regretfully as he sank into a chair. 'I can't,' he replied. 'I have to return to the Ministry this evening.' He looked round the familiar apartment. 'Is everything ready?'

Arkenko nodded. 'Yes. I've installed the radio and it's working well. I haven't transmitted, of course, as you instructed, but I have listened in to a number of transmissions. I have the contact frequencies pre-set on the receiver, all the numbers are programmed into my telephone, and I have memorized all the code-words and responses.'

'And you have everything else you need?' Trushenko asked.

Arkenko nodded again. 'I have plenty of spares for the radio, plus the back-up transceiver. The kitchen cupboards are full of food and I have plenty to drink. Once the operation starts, I will not need to leave the apartment for at least a week.'

'It will be starting, Genady, sooner than we expected,' Trushenko said. 'I have had to bring the date forward – the Americans have somehow found out something about *Podstava* – and I may have to implement the plan at very short notice.' Trushenko noticed the look of concern on Arkenko's face, and reached across and patted him on the knee. 'Don't worry, I'll give you as much warning as I can. In the meantime, you should receive the first message from the ship sometime this evening, and you'll probably have to transmit a number of changes to the vessel's route over the next few days if it is to be in position as planned and on time.'

Arkenko was silent for a moment, then he grasped his friend's hand tightly. 'This will work, won't it, Dmitri?' he asked.

Trushenko nodded. 'We haven't come this far to fail. The Americans can do nothing, and once the last phase is complete we will be able to walk into Europe as if we owned it.'

Hammersmith, London

Amongst the other junk that had accumulated in the bottom non-lockable drawer of Richter's desk was a dog-eared atlas. It was an elderly and somewhat inaccurate document when it came to statistics, populations and political systems, but it served its purpose well enough. After a brief search Richter found it and dusted off the cover. A rapid flick-through revealed the bulging mass of western Russia. Richter opened the pink file Simpson had given him, and noted down the start and stop points of the Blackbird's surveillance run.

He scanned the north coast and soon pinpointed Vorkuta, then he found Shenkursk to the south of Arkhangel'sk. With the start and stop positions identified, Richter took a pencil and ruler and drew a straight line between the two. Then he sat and stared at the map.

After a couple of minutes, Richter realized that either he was missing something or he'd drawn the line across the wrong bit, so he re-checked the data from the file, this time using the latitude and longitude figures given. The first line had been a little out, but not enough to make any significant difference. That didn't make sense, so he rang the Registry and got them to send up the Basic Intelligence Digest (CIS), a remarkably useful document that listed details of every known military or quasi-military installation in the Confederation of Independent States, including those under construction, with maps showing their locations.

When the courier had departed, Richter checked the list attached to the front cover, and noted that the last insertion had been made a matter of ten days previously. Then he opened it up at the map section and carefully compared it with the line he had drawn in the atlas. Then he compared it again.

Ten minutes later, Richter rang for the duty courier and returned the BID (CIS) to the Registry. He sat for a few minutes, looking through the SR–71A file, and staring at the atlas. Then he rang Simpson.

'Yes?'

'Richter. I'm coming up.'

'What for? Have you found something?'

Richter paused. 'I'm not sure,' he said. Then he put the receiver down and headed for the stairs.

That Simpson was busy Richter inferred from the pile of pink files in front of him, obscuring his view of the cactus forest. Richter sat down and waited for him to finish the sentence he was writing.

When the sentence looked like turning into a paragraph he put the atlas and file down on the floor. 'I hope I'm not disturbing you,' he said.

'You're not,' Simpson said, continuing to write. He finished the note, closed the file, initialled the front cover and tossed it into his 'Out' tray. Then he looked at Richter. 'I'm busy,' he said, 'so make it snappy.'

Richter moved three pink files to one side and force-marched the front rank of cacti two paces backwards. Into the space vacated he placed the atlas, open at the appropriate page.

'This line,' he said, 'is the route followed by the Blackbird. According to the USAFE, anyway.'

Simpson looked up sharply. 'Why do you say that? Do you think it isn't?'

'I'm not sure. I can't think why they would try and fob us off with a false route structure – JARIC would bowl that out as soon as they got a decent look at the films. But, assuming for the moment that the route is correct, I don't see why the Americans risked incurring the wrath of Moscow by over-flying that bit of Mother Russia.'

'Explain.'

'There's nothing up there,' Richter said. 'It's just hills and tundra, with a few small towns within camera range, but nothing – assuming that the Basic Intelligence Digest is more or less correct, and it usually is – that is of any military significance whatsoever. And I don't think it's a question of risking the wrath of the Russians. There are details in the route notes of a mid-course acceleration to dash speed, and five gets you ten they didn't do that just to watch the numbers move on the Mach meter. They were being chased by something.'

'Something that didn't catch them.'

'No, but I'm not too surprised at that. The Blackbird was not exactly notorious for hanging about, and the crews weren't fresh out of flying school either. The only things the Russians have got that can get high enough and go fast enough to catch the 'bird are MiG–25s and MiG–31s, and neither of them can match the Blackbird for sustained high speed.'

Simpson sat silent for a few moments. 'So?'

'So I'm curious. As I see it, there are only two possible explanations, assuming that the USAFE Command hasn't fallen off its collective trolley. First, the aircraft was hopelessly off-route, which I don't believe.' Richter paused. 'What do you know about the Blackbird's navigation kit?'

'Nothing,' Simpson replied, 'but I assume it's comprehensive.'

'That's one way of putting it. The Blackbird's principal navigation tool is a computer that permanently tracks fifty-two stars and is accurate enough to guide the SR–71A to any target on earth with an error of under a thousand feet. The aircraft definitely wasn't off-route.'

'So what's the alternative?'

'The only other explanation is that, somewhere along that line, there's an installation that the Americans have detected, but which in their infinite wisdom they haven't seen fit to tell us about.'

Port of Odessa, Chernoye More (Black Sea)

The ten-thousand-ton coaster *Anton Kirov* had been built twenty years ago to run general cargo through the Mediterranean, and time did not seem to have been kind to her. The ship's sides were streaked with rust, the superstructure was pitted and discoloured, and she wore an indefinable air of neglect. In most respects, the appearance of the *Anton Kirov* was an accurate reflection of her condition and usage. The exterior of the ship had been neglected – quite deliberately, because what the ship looked like had no effect upon the vessel's efficiency. But the engines and equipment were a different matter.

The main engines and generators were serviced and overhauled frequently – usually well before the run-time interval specified by their manufacturers – and all the deck machinery, the winches, windlasses and cranes, were in proper working order. The rationale was simple. Efficient engines minimized the length of time the vessel was at sea and made for efficient passages, while the cranes and winches speeded the loading and unloading of cargo, resulting in a shorter turn-round time in port. That made the *Anton Kirov* more efficient, and hence more profitable to operate, than most of her contemporaries.

Unusually, the ship was still secured to a loading berth in Odessa's outer harbour, although the stowage of all her manifested cargo had been completed that morning. All the crew were aboard, but their kit-bags and suitcases were stacked neatly on the jetty, and the master, Captain Valeri Nikolaevich Bondarev of the Russian Merchant Marine, a short, stout man with a face reddened by years at sea, was irritably pacing the bridge, waiting.

It was nearly six in the evening before he sighted the grey coach approaching the outer harbour, and he immediately called the engine room and told the chief engineer to prepare to leave harbour. Then he descended to the deck, walked across to the harbour-side guard-rail and watched as the coach drew to a halt beside the ship.

The front and side doors of the vehicle opened and men began to file out. In front of him, his entire crew, with the exception of his chief engineer and the navigator, started walking down the gangway and on to the jetty. They picked up their bags and formed a line near the coach. This was one voyage they were not going to make.

A tall, thin-faced man with short-cropped black hair had been the first to get out of the coach, and stood watching the new arrivals preparing to board. He was wearing a grey civilian overcoat, but there was no mistaking his military bearing. He noticed Bondarev on deck and strode briskly over to the ship, climbed the gangway and walked over to the captain. 'Captain Bondarev?' he asked, politely.

'Yes,' Bondarev snapped. 'Who are you?'

The man noted the angry edge to Bondarev's voice. 'My name is not important, Captain,' he said soothingly. 'I'm very sorry for having to inconvenience you like this, but I have orders from the highest authority.'

Bondarev nodded. 'Yes, yes, so have I. Just tell me one thing. Have any of your men actually sailed on a working vessel before?'

The tall man nodded. 'Of course, captain. They are all experienced seamen – that's why they were chosen for this mission. You will not have any crew problems on this voyage.'

'I hope not,' Bondarev snapped. 'This will not be a pleasure cruise. I expect to be able to sail within the hour, so I suggest you get your men aboard as quickly as possible.'

Seven minutes later, the engine of the grey coach started and a few seconds afterwards the vehicle began moving slowly away from the *Anton Kirov*'s berth. On board, the new arrivals moved with practised economy and little conversation, rapidly stowing their personal gear and then moving to their assigned positions for leaving harbour.

Thirty-eight minutes after the coach had departed, the *Anton Kirov* slipped away from her berth and headed slowly due east out of Odessa harbour. Once clear of the coast, the ship began picking up speed as she turned south towards Istanbul and the Bosphorus.

Kutuzovskij prospekt, Moscow

Genady Arkenko was sitting at the dining table eating a simple evening meal of black bread and sausage when the alarm sounded on the short-wave radio receiver. He put down the bread, hurried into the small back room, turned off the alarm and put on the headphones.

Two minutes later he removed the headphones, re-set the alarm and walked back into the living room. He walked over to the telephone, consulted a typed list, pressed a speed-dial key combination and waited for the telephone to be answered.

'Phase One is under way,' Arkenko said simply, and then replaced the receiver.

In his apartment a little under a mile away, Dmitri Trushenko put down his telephone handset with a smile of satisfaction. Operation *Podstava* was running to plan. He walked across to the desk in the corner of the room, sat down, opened his laptop computer and switched it on.

Half an hour later he pressed the 'Send' button on his email client software, and despatched one line of encrypted text embedded in a three-page advertising message with an addressee list of almost one hundred. The message would apparently originate in Germany, and because of the six redirection sites it was programmed to visit would take several minutes to reach the only address that actually mattered – Hassan Abbas' mailbox at 'wanadoo.fr'.

Chapter 8

Tuesday
Joint Air Reconnaissance Intelligence Centre, RAF Brampton,
Huntingdon, Cambridgeshire

RAF Brampton is near Huntingdon and usually about an hour and a half from London. It took Richter over two and a half, due to the three sets of traffic-light-controlled roadworks he had to negotiate, and a major accident which had blocked the A1 completely and forced him to take a diversion. At least the time passed pleasantly enough in the Ford Granada Ghia that was all that had been left in the Pool when Richter had appeared at the Transport Officer's door clutching his authorization chit. He had been expecting one of the usual small – and invariably old – Fords and Rovers which made up the bulk of the Pool vehicles, and which were used by the department because, as Simpson explained to anyone who would listen, they were cheap, reliable and invisible.

The Joint Air Reconnaissance Intelligence Centre is a long, low building of one and occasionally two storeys, designed with that singular lack of aesthetic appreciation that characterizes the work of the architects employed by the armed forces. At the main gate Richter was stopped by an armed sentry at the counter-weighted barrier, but a brief enquiry and a perusal of the Royal Navy officer's identity card supplied by the Documents Section produced directions to the Number 2 Officers' Mess Car Park.

Richter parked the Granada in the only vacant slot he could see, put the pass he had been given by the Main Guardroom on the dashboard, locked the car and walked through the picket gate set in the rusty black barbed-wire fence and into the JARIC Guardroom. Inside, a number of elderly and battered chairs were lined up against the left- and right-hand walls, with a small and equally decrepit coffee table covered in old magazines in the middle of the room. In the centre of the wall opposite the outside door was what looked like a steel door without a handle, and to the left of that was a board bearing the word 'Reception'.

Under the sign was an armoured-glass panel fitted with speak slots and a small opening at the base. Behind the glass sat a bulky man wearing sergeant's stripes and the distinctive shoulder flashes of the RAF Regiment. Richter walked over to the panel. The sergeant gave him a neutral stare, and eyed his civilian clothes with a certain amount of dissatisfaction. 'Can I help you? Sir.' The last word was an obvious afterthought.

Richter passed the ID card through the opening. 'Lieutenant Commander Richter. I believe I'm expected.'

'Thank you, sir.' The sergeant looked carefully at the card, and slightly disbelievingly at the photograph. 'What's your Service Number, sir?'

'C021426K,' Richter said.

'Thank you. Please take a seat.' The sergeant passed the card back through the slot and indicated the ancient chairs. Richter picked the cleanest looking and sat down, as the sergeant picked up a telephone. Richter found an antique copy of *Punch* on the coffee table, and was working his way through 'Let's parlez Franglais' when the steel door opened.

The man who entered was a squadron leader, wearing a working-dress pullover. Dark haired and stocky, and with a cheerful and slightly chubby face which suggested a constant diet to keep his waist-line under control, he was about Richter's height.

'Commander Richter? I'm Squadron Leader Kemp. Follow me, please.' The steel door swung open, and Richter followed Kemp across an open compound and into the main JARIC building. On the wall inside the door was a notice in bleak official terminology: 'This is a restricted area. All visitors must be accompanied at all times.' They walked down a long corridor before Kemp stopped and opened a grey-painted door bearing the cryptic message

'SSyO' above the slightly more informative statement 'Squadron Leader J D Kemp'.

Richter preceded him into the office. It was about fifteen feet square with pale blue walls, an assortment of filing cabinets in contrasting shades of brown and grey, and a large grey metal desk behind which was a wood and black vinyl chair, showing signs of age.

'Right,' Kemp said. 'The telephone call I received from a Mr, er . . .' He paused and glanced at a notebook on his desk. 'Here we are. From Mr Simpson yesterday said that you wanted to see the films taken by the American SR–71A that landed at Lossiemouth last week.' Richter nodded. 'May I ask what your interest is in these films?' Kemp asked.

'Certainly,' Richter replied. 'Curiosity.' Kemp looked at him expectantly, so Richter elaborated. 'I'm curious to know why the Americans risked a major diplomatic row, not to mention a very expensive and highly classified aircraft and crew which was, incidentally, supposed to have been withdrawn from active service some years ago, to get detailed photographs of seven hundred miles of Russian tundra, and why they're so damn coy about whatever it is they think is up there.'

Kemp nodded. 'Yes, that puzzled us too. As far as we can tell from the initial analysis, there's no evidence of any new buildings or other structures that might be of any military significance. In fact, it's an extremely boring bit of Mother Russia all round.'

'I'm running a little late,' Richter said, glancing at his watch and then rising to his feet, 'so could I see the films now?'

'Of course. Come with me.'

Heathrow Airport, London

John Westwood walked out into the Arrivals Hall at Heathrow Airport and looked around. After a few moments, a large black man wearing a dark suit detached himself from the wall and walked across to him. 'John Westwood?'

Westwood nodded. 'Yes. And you are?'

'Richard Barron, sir. From the Company. We have a car outside.' Without apparent effort Barron plucked Westwood's heavy suitcase from the trolley and led the way towards the doors. Westwood followed, carrying his briefcase. Outside, two black American Fords carrying 'CD' plates waited at the kerb, engines idling and drivers standing beside them. Barron put the suitcase in the boot of the first car, then opened the rear door for Westwood.

'Hullo, John,' said the man in the back seat. Westwood sat down and looked at him blankly. The thick black hair, deeply lined face, dark blue – almost black – eyes and over-large nose were familiar, but it took Westwood a few seconds to place him. Then he smiled and extended his hand. 'Sorry, Roger,' he said. 'It must be the jet lag, or just a bad memory for faces. It must be – what – seven years?'

Roger Abrahams shook his head. 'Eight,' he replied. 'Bonn. You were Chief of Station, and I was your deputy for the last six months or so before you went back across the pond and moved up in the world.' Abrahams looked towards the front seat of the car. 'OK, Richard,' he said. 'Let's move.'

Barron nodded to the driver, and the car eased away from the kerb and into the mid-morning traffic. Behind, the second car moved out and kept pace about fifty metres back.

'I saw the name of the London COS back at Langley,' Westwood said, 'but I didn't realize it was you. You've done well.'

'Thanks,' Abrahams muttered. 'You gave me a good write-up in Germany, and that helped. Now, what's the problem? What brings the Company Head of Foreign Intelligence all the way to London?'

Westwood took a moment before replying. 'No offence, Roger,' he said. 'I'd rather wait until we're in a secure location. For the moment, let's just say it's a liaison visit.'

Abrahams nodded. 'Understood. I've reserved you a room at the Embassy in Grosvenor Square, but I can book you into one of the local hotels if you'd prefer.'

'No, the Embassy's fine.' Westwood paused for a moment. 'Time's short on this one,' he said, 'so I'd like to get started as soon as possible. We'll need to use a secure briefing room, and I want to talk to you alone first.'

Abrahams nodded. 'No problem. Do you want to sleep or eat first?'

'No, I slept on the plane and I'm not hungry. Just a pot of coffee will do.'

'Right.'

The two cars sped on, mingling with the London-bound traffic on the M4 motorway.

Joint Air Reconnaissance Intelligence Centre, RAF Brampton, Huntingdon, Cambridgeshire

Richter followed Kemp down a short passage which ended in a closed door bearing the legends 'Classified area. No unauthorized personnel permitted beyond this point.' Kemp stopped at a small window in the right-hand wall and addressed it. 'Squadron Leader Kemp. I'd like a visitor's pass for Commander Richter.' He beckoned Richter to the window. 'Sign here, please, and put your name and rank in these columns.'

Richter complied, after which he received a bright red card, plastic covered, bearing a large black letter 'V' and a rather smaller '4' in exchange for his Navy ID card. The door was secured by an electric lock actuated from the other side of the window; it clicked open and Richter followed Kemp through.

In the windowless Viewing Room, Kemp picked up a telephone and dialled a number. 'Squadron Leader Kemp. Commander Richter is with me in the Viewing Room, and we'd like to run the Blackbird films as soon as possible. I'd also like the principal PI officers who've worked on the films to attend. Oh, and rustle up some coffee while you're at it.' He replaced the receiver. 'It'll take about ten minutes or so to set up the projectors with the films, so I'll start off by giving you a general briefing on what you'll be seeing.'

'Thanks,' Richter replied. 'One question before you start: I guessed from your office door label that you're the Section Security Officer – SSyO – but you seem quite familiar with these films and how the RAF got hold of them. Are you a PI as well?'

Kemp walked to a lectern at the end of the room and leaned on it. 'Yes, I am,' he said. 'Virtually everyone here is Photographic

Interpretation trained; Section Security Officer is very much a secondary duty. I spend most of my time peering through a shifty-scope or staring at a computer monitor.'

'What the hell's a shifty-scope?' Richter asked.

'Sorry, RAF slang,' Kemp said, grinning. 'It's a series of stacking magnifying lenses that you place on a photograph or negative on an illuminated table. To increase the magnification you add another lens, and then another and so on. It can be used in both PI and photogrammetrical analysis – that's the use of photographs in survey work. Actually, these days we usually employ computers to analyse images. You'll be pleased to hear that you won't have to use either. We've had everything transferred onto a thirty-five millimetre fine-grain filmstrip which we can run through a high-resolution projector, and that's what you'll be seeing.'

He opened his notebook while Richter looked around. The room was arranged like a grown-up corridor, long and narrow, about forty feet by fifteen. At the far end, beyond the lectern, was a projection screen, with a series of long narrow ceiling-mounted boxes directly in front of it, which presumably held maps or other visual displays.

Kemp took a short stick with a hook on its end and pulled one down, confirming Richter's deduction when a map of north-western Russia unfurled on a kind of roller blind. Richter was sitting in the front row of six rows of seats, with five seats in each. The room's illumination was supplied by fluorescent tube lighting on the ceiling. The wall behind the seats had three small square glass windows through which films could be projected.

'Before I begin,' Kemp asked, 'please state your security clearance.'

'CTS – Cosmic Top Secret.'

Kemp nodded. 'Fine. The majority of this briefing is classified Secret, but there are certain aspects of it that are graded Top Secret, and the caveat UK Eyes Only applies to the whole. Would you please confirm that you understand that?'

'Understood,' Richter replied.

'First, the basic route. As I presume you've already been briefed on this I won't go into too much detail, just remind you of the salient points.' Kemp took a collapsible pointing stick from the lectern, extended it and pointed to the top centre of the map. 'The Blackbird crossed the Russian border about here at Amderma and, from the route details supplied by the USAFE, the filming started here at Vorkuta and the cameras operated until the aircraft reached this point here at Shenkursk, almost due south of Arkhangel'sk.'

Kemp traced the route across the map with the pointer. 'There don't seem to be any particularly good reasons for doing a surveillance run over that region – I can think of lots of bits of Russia I would far rather see in glorious black and white under my shifty-scope – so our first thought was that maybe the Americans were trying to sell us a pup by giving us incorrect route details. However, even a cursory examination of the films ruled that one out. There are numerous points of agreement between the films and the topography of the area, and we're satisfied that the route specified is that actually flown by the Blackbird.

'We also considered the possibility that the aircraft was off-route, but that is so unlikely as to be ridiculous. Apart from the Aurora, the SR–71A is the most advanced surveillance aircraft in the world, and all Blackbird crews are highly experienced. If they photographed this bit of Russia, then this bit of Russia is the bit they wanted to photograph. The final possibility, that of a substitution of films, we also ruled out, as the films were removed from the cameras and developed under JARIC supervision. So, we know that the films show whatever the Americans were looking for. Assuming it's there, of course.

'Total filming time was a little under twenty-three minutes, which gave us a good deal of film to work on. We assumed that the Americans would have started the cameras well before their objective, and stopped them a reasonable distance after the aircraft had passed over it, so we've been concentrating on the central portion of the film, after a preliminary survey of the entire route.

'Four cameras were used by the Americans, of two different types. The two main cameras were the normal high-resolution models as used in most aircraft of this type, similar to those used in the so-called spy satellites. The two in the Blackbird were of a very advanced design, particularly in the optical set-up, and from an examination of them and the films we have assessed that these cameras approach the theoretical maximum possible resolution.'

'Which is?' Richter interrupted.

'It's determined by the laws of physics and the height of the platform. For a satellite at normal orbital elevation, it's just under four inches. The Blackbird flies a lot lower, of course, so the maximum resolution is greater – in this case, a little under two inches. To put that into slightly more comprehensible terminology, if you were sitting on a park bench reading a newspaper and one of these cameras took a photograph of you from fifteen miles up, an analyst would not quite be able to read the headlines in your paper, but he would almost certainly be able to identify what newspaper it was.'

'That,' said Richter, 'is very impressive.'

'You'd be surprised at what the eye in the sky can see, and has been able to see for some time, actually. Those cameras were working independently, taking one frame every half second, one using a very high-speed monochrome film and the other high-speed colour, and covering a narrow strip of territory. The other two cameras were of a much less sophisticated design, and were working together, exposing one frame simultaneously every two seconds. They were obviously intended to supply stereoscopic photographs of the whole area that the Blackbird was flying over.'

As Kemp paused there was a knock at the door, so coincidentally timed that Richter knew whoever it was had waited until Kemp had stopped talking before knocking. The door opened and two men and a girl filed in. Richter looked at her first, because he always looked at women first. She was wearing the uniform of a sub lieutenant WRNS – what used to be third officer in the old days before the Navy began taking women to sea – and Richter was surprised to see her. Not her personally, but a Wren in a highly restricted RAF establishment. She had piercing blue eyes and a mass of blonde hair presently tightly constrained in the regulation bun on the back of her head, but which Richter had no doubt would tumble free as soon as she was off duty. The two RAF officers, in contrast, paled into insignificance. Kemp ushered them all in and made the introductions.

'Lieutenant Commander Richter, let me introduce the team which has been burning the midnight oil over these films since Sunday evening. First of all, Sub Lieutenant Penny Walters, who is here on exchange from the Royal Navy.'

She smiled at Richter. He gave her his nice smile and turned to Kemp. 'I don't know what you exchanged her for, but I think you got the better end of the deal.'

Kemp laughed and she blushed slightly.

'The home team consists of Flight Lieutenant Keith George and Flying Officer Dick Tracey. Dick's real name is William, but he's been known as Dick since the day he arrived at Cranwell, and I think he's finally started to get used to it.'

Richter said he was pleased to meet them all, and got a chorus of 'Good morning, sir' in return. Kemp announced that he had almost finished the general briefing, and invited the three of them to take seats each while he wrapped up the loose ends.

'What you will see,' Kemp continued, 'is an unusual presentation of the photographs we received. As I said, we invariably view stills taken from a picture sequence on an illuminated table through a shifty-scope or on a computer monitor. You're not PI-trained, and we didn't think you would be able to learn anything that way, so we decided to radically change the presentation.

'There was also the problem of the vast amount of material we had available. As you will appreciate, with the cameras taking one frame every half second, the total mass of the film is huge, almost three thousand frames. What we've done is effectively condense it by photographing the frames with a thirty-five millimetre cine camera – video doesn't have the definition we need – and then we can project it as a movie film. The effect you'll see is as if you were actually in the moving aircraft, looking downwards through a very good pair of binoculars at the landscape underneath you.'

Kemp tugged at the base of the map of Russia and it rattled back into its box, then he pressed a button on the lectern and spoke into the microphone. 'Are you ready, projectionist?' There was a muffled grunt from a speaker on the rear wall, and Kemp sat down beside Richter. The lights dimmed – the projectionist obviously had a rheostat control

– and the screen at the end of the room was suddenly brilliantly illuminated by white light. A few flickers, then the title sequence ran. The screen went dark and Richter leaned forward.

Less than a minute later he leaned back again. He didn't know exactly what he had been expecting, but it wasn't the incomprehensible melange of blacks, whites and various shades of grey that were moving jerkily across the screen. It made absolutely no sense to him, and he said as much to Kemp.

'I'm not surprised,' Kemp replied. 'PI is definitely an acquired art.' He went to the lectern and spoke into the microphone. 'Freeze it.' The film flickered for a second or two, then stopped. Kemp pointed at the screen. 'Can you identify anything on that?'

Richter studied it carefully. It looked to him more like a surrealist painting than anything else. A bad surrealist painting, possibly hanging upside down. He shook his head. 'Not a thing.'

'Penny, would you mind?'

'Not at all, sir.' Penny Walters got up and walked forward to the lectern. Taking another pointing stick, this one with a tiny light in the end, she turned to the screen.

Among the blacks, whites and greys on the photograph Richter could pick out three definable features; a meandering line running more or less north-west, assuming that the top of the screen was north which, on reflection, he decided it probably wasn't. There was a small squarish grey blob in the bottom right-hand corner, and a larger, darker oblong patch just above the blob. It was all as clear as gravy as far as he was concerned. Sub Lieutenant Walters, however, seemed unperturbed.

'This was taken early in the run, a few miles to the south-west of Vorkuta. The diagonal line here is the course of a river, and if you look here and here you can clearly see two feeder streams. The river was fairly dry when this film was taken. This is shown by the irregular outline of the banks and the colour changes – the dark in the centre is fairly shallow water while the slightly lighter outline is drying mud. The much lighter area is the riverbank.'

She moved the illuminated pointer down a little. 'This square structure is the remains of a large hut, possibly originally used as a barn or byre. There isn't sufficient left standing to clearly indicate its original purpose, but its size – about fifty feet by thirty – would suggest that it was probably a small barn. The very large dark oblong patch adjacent to the remains is a once-cultivated but now overgrown field. The darker colour is caused by the increased weed and grass growth after the fertilization of the soil that would have taken place during cultivation. There is little else of note on the frame – just fairly typical early summer tundra.'

Richter couldn't think of anything remotely sensible to say, so he didn't. Penny Walters smiled at him. 'That may seem like magic, sir, but I'm very familiar with this film, and I've had the benefit of studying it frame by frame under high magnification.'

Richter turned to Kemp. 'Perhaps you could talk me through the rest of it. It obviously won't make a great deal of sense to me, but I'd like to see it anyway.'

'Certainly. In fact, as Penny is already at the screen, she can supply the running commentary. OK, Penny? Projectionist – run it.'

Ten minutes later lights came on again in the room and Penny returned to her seat. Kemp asked if it had been any help.

'Well, not really,' Richter replied honestly. He thought for a few seconds. 'I suppose you've done comparison studies with previous satellite films of the area?'

'Oh, yes,' said Kemp. 'There haven't been many for the last two months or so, because that area has had a fair degree of cloud cover, but there appear to have been no significant changes since the last set of high-level pictures.'

'OK,' Richter said, 'forget about significant changes. Were there any changes at all?'

'Of course. There are always minor changes, like vehicles parked in different places, houses that sprout sheds or porches, or lose them, but nothing out of the ordinary, as far as I'm aware. Have any of you seen anything that seems unusual?'

The two RAF officers shook their heads, looking slightly bored. Penny Walters didn't shake her head, which Kemp and Richter both noticed.

'Penny?'

She grinned, somewhat shyly. 'Well, there was something, but I'm sure it's of no real significance.'

She paused, and Kemp prompted her. 'Trust the blasted Navy to see something that the RAF missed. Come on, Penny, what was it?'

'Well, it's not anything that's on this film,' she gestured towards the screen at the end of the room. 'It's just I noticed on a couple of the most recent satellite films that there had been a number of vehicles in a location close to the centre of the area the Blackbird filmed.'

'And?'

'And nothing, really. Just a bunch of vehicles.' There was a long and slightly prickly silence. Penny Walters apparently felt the need to defend herself. 'Commander Richter did say he wanted details of any unusual activity.'

'That's true,' Richter said. 'What sort of vehicles – military or civilian?'

'Both,' she replied. 'There was one civilian lorry which appeared in the same place on two successive films, and quite a lot of other trucks, mainly military. Oh, and what looked like construction equipment.'

'What do you mean "looked like"?' Kemp asked sharply. 'Either it was construction equipment or it wasn't.'

Penny coloured slightly. 'It was construction equipment – a digger and a bulldozer – and it arrived on two low loaders. What I meant was that it wasn't used as far as I could see. It stayed loaded on the trans-porters in all the frames I saw.'

'Peculiar,' Richter said. 'Were there any signs of vehicles – these or any others – in the same area in the Blackbird film?'

'No, sir. None at all.'

Kemp nodded. 'I agree. It is peculiar, but it doesn't sound significant. It could, to offer a realistic and simple explanation, mean that the Russians were thinking about starting a housing project there and changed their minds because of problems with the terrain.'

Penny shook her head decisively. 'No, sir, I don't think so,' she said. 'The location was way out in the tundra, nowhere near any proper roads. If they had been going to do any major construction they would have had to spend millions of roubles on roads.'

Kemp nodded. 'OK, let's look at other possibilities. You didn't see the construction equipment used, so its presence there might be irrelevant. Or, perhaps, the civilian lorries had broken down or got stuck in mud and they used the bulldozer to pull them out.'

'But,' Richter interrupted, 'if the site was so remote, what were civilian lorries doing out there? And Penny said there were several vehicles – some of them military. If it had just been a breakdown, they would only have needed a recovery vehicle, or two at the most.'

'That's true,' Kemp replied. 'I'm just exploring possibilities. It might be worth looking into, but I don't think it's worth running the Blackbird film again. Penny has already said there are no vehicles located in that area, so we wouldn't see anything. I think the way forward is for us to run detailed comparisons of all available films of that general area and try to deduce what the vehicles were doing there. In fact, as Penny spotted this, she can do it, because I've got plenty of other work building up.' Kemp rubbed his hands together briskly. 'Well, I think that's it. Unless you have any other questions, Commander?' Kemp seemed eager to get back to his 'In' tray, or perhaps he just wanted Richter off the premises.

'No, I don't think so, but please keep me informed about the comparisons.'

'Of course.'

Richter gave Kemp the section contact telephone number, and they filed silently out of the room.

Richter surrendered his visitor's pass, retrieved the identity card and got back into the Granada. At the Guardroom, he handed in his car pass and drove out of the main gate, turning the big saloon left – to the north and away from London to avoid the roadworks on the A1. He glanced at the dashboard clock and was surprised to find that it was already after one. He hadn't realized that he'd been in the building for so long, and began thinking about lunch.

The two things that saved him were the left turn out of RAF Brampton's main gate, and the bumpy road surface.

When he heard the bang and the jagged lines speared across the windscreen, Richter reacted instinctively and braked hard. When he glanced in the wing mirror, and then the interior mirror, he changed his mind. Richter floored the accelerator pedal, the auto box dropped two gears and the Granada took off like a scalded cat.

What was bothering him was not the fact that the only other car on the road was only about twenty yards behind the Granada – it was the fact that he couldn't see it in the interior mirror because the rear screen had shattered, and slightly off-centre to the left-hand side of the car Richter could see the hole where the bullet had come in.

That definitely bothered him.

Chapter 9

Captain Valeri Bondarev stood on the starboard bridge wing, his sparse grey hair being blown awry by the sea breeze, and looked moodily down at the foredeck. With the ship at cruising stations, a group of the new crew had assembled and, with obvious military precision, was performing energetic callisthenics under the direction of a stocky Ukrainian. He detected movement to his left and turned. The leader of the new crew walked across the bridge wing and leaned on the rail beside him. Bondarev realized he still didn't know the man's name. 'What do I call you?' he growled.

'My name is Zavorin, Petr Zavorin. You may call me Petr.'

'I prefer to use your military rank,' Bondarev said stiffly.

Zavorin looked briefly at the captain, then glanced forward again. 'As you wish,' he said. 'I am a colonel in a tank regiment – that is all you need to know.'

Bondarev smiled slightly, unbelieving. 'And those men,' he said, gesturing forwards, 'I suppose they're all tank drivers and gunners, are they? Learned all about ships from reading books, I suppose. You're all *Spetsnaz*, aren't you?'

Zavorin looked appraisingly at Bondarev. The captain's perception had surprised him – perhaps a more open approach would pay dividends. 'Yes,' Zavorin said, nodding, 'your powers of observation do you credit, Captain. We are part of a *Spetsnaz* company.'

The Russian *Spetsnaz* are the most numerous special forces in the world, comprising some twenty-five thousand troops in all. Most are deployed with the regular Russian armed forces, but a significant number operate permanently or temporarily under deep cover in the West, as athletes, delegates or embassy staff. In the event of hostilities, deep-cover *Spetsnaz* personnel would be ordered to assassinate political and military leaders, disrupt lines of communications by sabotage, seize airfields and undertake other operations to make invasion by Russian regular forces easier. The competence and ability of *Spetsnaz* forces has already been demonstrated. In 1968 they seized Prague Airport immediately before the Soviet invasion of Czechoslovakia, and *Spetsnaz* troops were infiltrated into Kabul in December 1979 to soften up local resistance before Soviet forces entered Afghanistan.

Zavorin glanced round the bridge wing, then looked back at Bondarev. 'I have my orders, Captain, as you have, but perhaps we can work better together if I am frank with you. Not here, though. We will go to your cabin.'

Bondarev nodded, and led the way off the bridge. As soon as Bondarev and Zavorin had left, two of the *Spetsnaz* troops stopped their exercise routine and ran aft. The first trooper picked up a cardboard package about a metre square and twenty centimetres thick, and carried it easily up the external ladders to the bridge. The second man followed with a small toolbox.

With the proficiency born of long practice, the two men climbed on to the bridge roof and began the assembly and installation of a gimballed satellite dish. When the dish was sitting on its mount, one of the troopers began the preliminary alignment process. The final alignment, and initializing communication with the satellite, would have to be delayed until the ship was stationary in harbour.

With the alignment completed, the trooper called to two other men who had climbed up to the bridge. The three of them manhandled four large plywood screens, painted to match the superstructure of the *Anton Kirov*, on to the bridge roof, and then erected them along the edges. The screens completely hid the satellite dish from view, except from directly above.

The second trooper attached a coaxial cable to the LNB on the dish and ran it down the side of the bridge, concealing it in an existing cable conduit. At deck level, he again made every effort to hide the cable, and finally passed the end through a small hole he had drilled earlier. The hole led directly into the forward hold of the *Anton Kirov*.

American Embassy, Grosvenor Square, London

Roger Abrahams swung open the heavy door and John Westwood followed him into the secure briefing room. The long table had seats for ten, but there were only two mugs by the coffee pot at the head of the table. The two men sat down facing each other, and Abrahams poured coffee.

'Thanks,' said Westwood as Abrahams passed the mug over. Westwood unlocked his briefcase, opened the lid and pulled out a large sealed envelope. Taking a clasp knife from his pocket, he sliced through the closed flap at one end and pulled out a slightly smaller envelope. In contrast to the plain brown of the outer envelope, this one was prominently stamped in red ink 'Cosmic Top Secret. NOFORN. By hand of officer only'.

Abrahams raised his eyebrows and nodded towards the envelope. 'NOFORN' was the CIA acronym derived from 'NO FOReign Nationals' which prohibited non-US citizens from seeing a document. 'CTS? NOFORN? What the hell have you got there, John?'

Westwood grinned somewhat wryly as he used the knife on the second envelope. 'We're not really sure,' he replied, pulling out the file. The cover bore the title 'Ravensong'. He positioned the file on the table in front of him, opened it and glanced at the minute sheet on the left-hand side. Then he took a sip of coffee and looked over at Abrahams.

'None of this makes much sense yet, Roger, so you'll have to bear with me while I run through the sequence of events. I'm not even sure if you'll be able to help, but I hope so. We really do need something concrete to work on.'

Abrahams nodded. Westwood glanced down at the file and began his briefing.

Cambridgeshire

The Granada's sudden burst of acceleration had taken the chase car driver by surprise, and the gap between the vehicles had opened from twenty to about a hundred yards. The pursuing car was a Jaguar XJ saloon, the version with the 4.2-litre six-cylinder engine. It was a good car for a chase, and Richter knew there was no way the old Granada could out-run it. Not for the first time, he cursed Simpson's insistence on only using cars at least five years old. That was one of his worries. The other was the rest of the opposition.

If he had been setting up a hit, particularly a mobile hit, Richter would have made sure that he had a back-up vehicle somewhere ahead, just in case the first attempt failed. Richter had no reason to suspect that whoever had organized his attempted demise would be any less conscientious than him, so he knew he had to start going the other way, and quickly.

The dual carriageway was rapidly coming to an end, which provided him with the opportunity he needed. Richter hit the brakes, hard, and watched the speedometer needle unwind as the car's speed dropped. When he had fifty-five showing, he span the wheel hard right, released the brakes, pulled on the handbrake, waited until the car was sliding sideways, then released the handbrake and floored the accelerator. The tyres screamed as the power broke their grip on the road surface and the Ford fishtailed up the opposite carriageway.

As he got it more or less straight, Richter ducked down as low as he could, because the Jaguar was right beside him, going the other way under heavy braking, and he'd seen the man in the back seat, with the dark mouth of a gun pointing straight at him. He heard three shots above the roar of the engine, and the driver's door window fell in a million pieces all over him. One thing was clear – there was no way Simpson was ever going to be able to offer that Granada as a clean one-owner model. Richter straightened up in the seat and checked the door mirror.

He had better than a quarter of a mile on them, and the Jaguar was only just making the turn to follow, so Richter had perhaps half a mile to play with. The XJ6 was still visible in the mirror when Richter took the first left-hand junction, so he knew they'd follow. He started to breathe a little more easily, and started thinking straight.

He had no idea who was behind the attempt to deprive him of his meagre pension, but he was quite determined to find out. He scanned the road ahead, looking for a bend and some kind of cover where he could get the car out of sight. Richter also needed a dearth of witnesses, and luckily there seemed to be almost no other traffic.

Two miles further on, with the Jaguar out of sight behind him, Richter found it. A left-hand curve, followed by a right, with a farm track leading off to the left, past a dilapidated barn. He hit the brakes hard, hoping that the driver of the Jaguar wouldn't notice the skid marks on the road, slammed the box into reverse, and backed the Granada off the road.

He only just made it. Less than three seconds after the Ford had rocked to a halt by the barn, the XJ6 roared past the end of the track. Richter hauled the auto shift into drive and floored the throttle. He forced the car, bucking and kicking, back on to the road. Now he was where he wanted to be – behind them.

Richter was doing fifty as he hit the right-hand curve, and saw the Jaguar a quarter of a mile ahead when he entered the straight, with the speedometer needle hovering around the seventy mark. The Jaguar vanished from sight around a bend, and Richter gave the Granada its head. He couldn't rely on them not seeing the Ford until the last moment, though he hoped they would be concentrating on the road in front, so he had to make up ground when they were out of sight.

The XJ6 was less than two hundred yards in front as Richter came out of the bend, then he lost it almost immediately as the road swung left again. He passed a road sign which brought a slight smile to his lips, announcing bends for two and a half miles, and pushed the Granada as much as he dared.

Then, suddenly, he was right behind them. Richter had practised it often enough, but this was the first time he'd ever had to do it for real. When they saw him, the Granada was less than fifty yards behind them. The Jaguar driver touched his brakes, thought better of it, and put on power again. The shape in the back seat twisted round, gun in hand. Richter watched to see which window he was going for. He moved to the left – he was probably right-handed – so Richter floored the accelerator and swung right.

As the nose of the Granada passed the rear of the Jaguar, Richter swung the car left, still under full power. The XJ6 lurched sideways as the Ford's nearside front wing hit it, and whatever the driver did then, Richter had them.

Anton Kirov

In his sea cabin on the deck below the bridge and next to the radio room, Valeri Bondarev produced two shot glasses and a bottle of Stolichnaya vodka, and gestured Zavorin to a chair. He poured two measures of vodka and passed one to Zavorin; both men drank, knocking the liquid to the back of their throats. Bondarev poured two more glasses and waited.

'Thank you, Captain,' Zavorin said, picking up his glass. 'Now, let me explain what we will be doing. As you guessed, your new crew-members are *Spetsnaz* soldiers. They have cross-trained with the Black Sea Fleet and are all very experienced sailors, which is why they have been selected for this mission.'

'And the mission is?' Bondarev asked.

'All in good time, Captain,' Zavorin replied, taking a sip from his glass. 'Now, your original route was what?'

'One moment.' Bondarev stood up, left his cabin and climbed the stairs to the chart-house at the rear of the bridge, selected a route-planning chart of the Mediterranean and returned with it to his cabin. He moved the bottle of vodka and the glasses to one side and spread the chart across his desk.

'We sailed from Odessa, here,' he said, pointing, 'and we were pro-grammed to route through the Black Sea to Istanbul, then cross the Aegean to Athens, and route west through the Mediterranean to Tangier and then south to Casablanca. We have cargo in the holds for Athens, Tirane and Tunis, and we have scheduled cargo collections at Tunis, Marseille and Tangier for delivery to Rabat and Casablanca. The return voyage is much the same, with cargo to be collected in the western Mediterranean for delivery to Sicily, Greece and Crete.'

Zavorin nodded and studied the chart for a few minutes. 'Well, Captain,' he said at last, 'there will have to be some changes.'

Bondarev grunted. 'I expected that.'

'The first change,' Zavorin went on, 'will be an additional stop to collect cargo – actually special equipment for my men – before we reach Istanbul.'

'Which port?' Bondarev asked.

'I don't know yet,' Zavorin replied. 'This mission was undertaken at short notice, and the equipment will take time to assemble. My guess is Constanta, but it could be Varna or Burgas.' He tapped the names of the three ports, on the Black Sea's west coast, with a pencil.

'No problem,' Bondarev said. 'And after Istanbul and the Bosphorus?'

Zavorin looked thoughtful, and used a pair of dividers to measure distances on the chart. 'I want to keep to the ship's programmed route as much as possible, to avoid attracting attention. Athens should not be a problem, but we will not be able to make Tirane or Marseille if we are to keep on schedule. Yes,' he said. 'Have your navigator prepare a new course from Istanbul to Athens, then Tunis and Tangier, and signal the authorities in Tirane and Marseille that the *Anton Kirov* will not be calling at those ports on this voyage.'

Bondarev was in no doubt that this was an order. 'And after Tangier?' he asked, jotting a note on a pad.

Zavorin smiled. 'I don't think we will make Tangier,' he said. 'The ship will develop engine trouble and will be forced to put in to Gibraltar.'

Bondarev bristled slightly. 'My ship has never had engine trouble.'

Zavorin nodded. 'I know. That is one reason why this vessel was selected. But on this voyage, it will develop engine trouble and we will put in to port to get it rectified.'

'Why Gibraltar?' Bondarev asked.

Zavorin shook his head. 'You do not need to know that, Captain. Let me just say that we will be collecting another item of cargo there – an item of crucial importance to Russia.'

There was a knock on the door. Bondarev slid it open and took the signal from the radioman – one of Zavorin's men – who stood there. He read it and then passed it to Zavorin. 'Good,' Zavorin murmured. 'The equipment will be ready for us at Varna in four hours.'

Bondarev bent over the chart. 'We are now about six hours out of Varna,' he said.

'Excellent, Captain,' Zavorin replied. 'I will go and brief my men.'

American Embassy, Grosvenor Square, London

John Westwood leaned back in his chair, poured himself another cup of coffee and rubbed his tired eyes. The jet lag was starting to catch up with him, he thought, stifling a yawn. Abrahams sat silently, digesting what he had been told. 'You see the problem?' Westwood asked.

Abrahams nodded. 'Yeah. One, your top-level source in Moscow tells you that a covert assault by the CIS on the West is in progress. Two, you can't find any trace of preparations for any kind of assault, anywhere. Three, an attack by the CIS makes no sense in the current political climate. Four, the Russians might have developed a kind of super neutron bomb. Five, if they have, and they deploy it, the weapon will actually favour the Western alliance in any future conflict.' He looked across at his former chief. 'Is that about it?'

'Pretty much,' Westwood nodded.

'That's complete nonsense, so we must be missing something. Somewhere there's a key that will lock that lot, and tie everything together. Right. I understand the background, but what exactly do you want me – or rather CIA London Station – to do about it?'

Westwood looked across the table. 'Nothing much. We've talked the tail off this, and we've got exactly nowhere. What we really need is more data, more information about whatever the hell is going on in the Kremlin or the SVR or GRU or wherever. In short, we need a lead. Do you,' he asked, 'have any contacts with the British Secret Intelligence Service, or MI6 or whatever they're calling themselves these days?'

Abrahams nodded. 'Of course we have. That's one reason why we're here.'

Westwood shook his head. 'Sorry, I'm not explaining myself. I know about the official contacts and information exchange. What I meant was unofficial contacts. Someone who is sufficiently well placed to find out if SIS has any agents-in-place in Russia who could find out what the hell is going on.' As Roger Abrahams looked at him quizzically, Westwood continued. 'Look, at the moment I don't want this on an official level. It could all be some disinformation scheme by the SVR to get us chasing our tails, running round all the Western intelligence agencies, and generally looking like klutzes. That's what I hope. Or it could be real, and RAVEN could be genuine, in which case we have to try to protect him as well as stop this assault. In either case, the last thing we want to do is to start officially involving allied intelligence services. They're still leaky, and if the threat is real and word gets back to the Kremlin that we're on to it, this could turn from a covert assault to an overt one real fast.'

'OK, we might be able to help. I know a guy called Piers Taylor – we meet socially as well as professionally. He's deputy head of Section Nine of SIS.'

'Which is?' Westwood interrupted.

'Responsible for Russian affairs,' Abrahams concluded. 'I'll try and set up a meet.'

Cambridgeshire and London

The Jaguar driver tried to steer to the left, which was the way his car was heading anyway, then realized that was what Richter wanted, so he turned the wheel right. He was too late, much too late. The Jaguar hit the verge, metal screamed against metal, and Richter pulled away, spinning the wheel hard right. The XJ6 bounced off the verge and on to the road, but the tail of the Granada caught its offside front wing and slammed it back to the left.

Richter braked the Granada to a stop fifty yards in front, twisted round in the seat and stared back at the Jaguar. Then he slowly reversed back, ready to take off at the first sign of any hostile movement. The Jaguar wasn't going to move under its own power for a long time. A concrete plinth housing a manhole cover had done most of the damage, and Richter could see that the radiator had gone, steam pouring from the crumpled bonnet.

The driver was unconscious, lolling forward in his seat and still belted in securely, but with blood pouring from a bad head wound. Richter guessed he'd probably hit the door pillar. There was no sign of movement from the back seat, so Richter got quietly out of the Granada, leaving the engine running and the door open, and walked cautiously towards the Jaguar. About halfway there, he picked up a good-sized rock, about six or seven pounds in weight, took a careful grip of it with his right hand. Then he walked to the Jaguar and peered cautiously through what was left of the rear side window.

The passenger was lying on the floor, moaning softly and shaking his head. His pistol – a Colt .45 automatic – lay on the floor beside him, within easy reach of his right hand. Richter knew he'd have to act fast, before the man cleared his head and started shooting. He took a deep breath and pulled open the nearside rear door with his left hand.

As the door opened, the man inside looked up, then grabbed for the Colt, moving much faster than Richter had anticipated. He twisted round, brought up his gun hand and squeezed the trigger. But Richter had been expecting it, and the gunman hadn't been expecting the rock.

Richter parried, the shot tore through the roof of the Jaguar, and with all the force of his right arm Richter brought the rock down on the side of the gunman's head. He dropped, and the gun dropped too. For good measure Richter picked up the rock again and brought it down on the back of the driver's head.

Richter backed out of the car, deafened by the noise of the shot, and shook his head slowly, then took the rock over to the Granada, where he wrapped it in a road map and put it on the floor mat in front of the passenger seat. He reached into the glove box and pulled out a pair of thin leather driving gloves and put them on. Then he took the demisting cloth, walked back to the Jaguar and wiped the door handle where he'd touched it.

Richter picked up the Colt, set the safety catch, and put the pistol in the waistband of his trousers. The man in the back seat had about thirty shells in his jacket pocket, and two spare magazines, both fully charged. From the looks of him, he wouldn't be needing them any more, so Richter took them as well. He checked his pockets, but there was no indication of who he was. No wallet, no credit cards, no nothing. Just around fifty pounds in cash. A pro, but then Richter had guessed that already. The Colt is a weapon for a pro.

The driver was carrying a Mauser HSc in a shoulder holster, which Richter got off him with some difficulty. He had a full spare magazine in a natty pouch on the holster strap, and a dozen or so loose rounds in his jacket pocket, all of which went into Richter's pocket. He, too, was carrying no ID. They were Russian agents, of that Richter was sure, not least because they weren't carrying Stechkins or Makarovs or any other eastern-bloc weapons. The Russians almost never use homegrown weapons in foreign operations. This is because, with the exception of the Kalashnikov assault rifle and its variants, Russian small arms are not sufficiently good to be a weapon of choice for any assassin, so anyone found carrying one is virtually certain to be identified as a CIS agent, even if he's not.

Richter checked the rear of the car. He found three .45 shell cases on the floor, which was probably all there were to find. Richter knew they'd fired at least five shots at him, one which broke the front and rear screens of the Granada, three when he'd reversed direction at the end of the dual carriageway and one when he'd opened the Jaguar's rear door. The Colt was no help – the magazine in the pistol was full, apart from the single shot just fired – another indication that its former owner was a pro. Only amateurs run out of ammunition, and he'd obviously reloaded as they chased the Ford. The fourth and fifth shell cases were somewhere on the road, maybe miles back, and there was no way he was going to start looking for them.

A squawk from the front seat made Richter jump, and he saw a radio transceiver screwed to the dashboard. That suggested he'd been right about the second car, which was probably on its way towards him right then. It was time he was somewhere else. Quite apart from another carload of opposition, Richter didn't want some officious citizen – or, even worse, a brace of woodentops in a Panda car – spotting him there and asking all sorts of questions that he really hadn't got any answers for, so he climbed back into the Ford, put it into gear and took off.

Richter took the first side road he came to and followed it until he found a river. He stopped next to the bridge, checked that he was unobserved and then heaved the rock into the water. Richter knew that forensic experts could pull fingerprints off almost anything, and he wasn't taking any chances. Then he got back in the Granada and drove on. Five minutes and three miles later he pulled the Ford off the road and into a wood. He sat for a few minutes in the car, breathing deeply. From the start of the chase adrenalin had kept him going, kept him concentrating on what he was doing. Now reaction was setting in. His hands were shaking slightly, and a check showed Richter that his pulse rate was significantly higher than normal.

Richter was no stranger to violence. Within days of his first meeting with Simpson, and even before he had been recruited into FOE, he had been sent deep into France with a cover story so thin that it was virtually transparent, and he had been forced to kill just to stay alive. But never before had Richter killed with his bare hands, one-to-one.

The men in the Jaguar were dead, of that he was certain. He had heard, and felt, their skulls shatter under the blows of the rock, and this time there had been no termination order, no official approval. He didn't even know who they were. They had died because they had tried to kill him, nothing more – not much of an epitaph and possibly, Richter realized, not even much of a justification. He knew he was going to have to be careful.

Richter put the guns on the seat beside him, then had a look at the car. It was a mess, at best. The windscreen was laminated, so there was little he could do about the bullet hole, but he knocked out the shattered rear screen, keeping the glass in the car, as he didn't want to advertise that he'd stopped there, for any reason. The driver's door window had shattered as well, and the bits were all over the floor, which was the best place for them.

He looked at the offside of the car and found a bullet hole just below the top of the front wing, and the exit hole near the centre of the bonnet. Richter smeared some mud over the holes – a barely adequate disguise – then threw more at the side of the car. The bullet which had taken out the side window had left the car through the roof, just above the passenger door, and Richter guessed that the third shot had gone above, or perhaps in front of, the windscreen. Under the circumstances, he thought, it had been bloody good shooting.

The left side of the car was very badly bent and twisted, front and rear wings buckled beyond repair. All the lights that side had gone; headlight, sidelights and indicators. The bonnet was jammed shut, so Richter couldn't tell whether the bullet had done any damage in the engine compartment, but as everything seemed to be working he wasn't bothered.

After about twenty minutes Richter was satisfied that he had done all he could to hide the fact that he'd been involved in a running battle. He studied the map for a few minutes, and worked out a route that would get him back to Hammersmith without going anywhere near any major built-up areas until he reached the outskirts of London.

Before he set off, Richter put on the shoulder holster with the Mauser, and put the Colt into the side pocket of his jacket. The magazines and loose rounds went into his pockets. Wearing his gloves again, Richter took the three spent shell cases and dropped them down a rabbit hole near the car. He set fire to the blood-smeared road map and then trod the ashes into the ground. He tossed his gloves out of the window at fifteen-minute intervals as he drove.

An hour and twenty minutes later Richter double-parked the Granada outside his flat, went up and wrapped the pistols, holster and ammunition in a couple of old towels, and put them in a small suitcase. Then he drove to Euston Station and checked the suitcase into the left-luggage office. A man, in Richter's opinion, couldn't have too many guns, especially ones that couldn't be traced to him.

The duty Pool Controller was almost incoherent when Richter delivered the remains of the Granada. He didn't believe it. The duty driver he summoned as a witness didn't believe it either. 'What the bloody hell did you do to it? Look at the state it's in.'

'There was,' said Richter, 'a certain amount of unpleasantness.'

'What am I going to tell the Transport Officer?'

Richter was getting tired and irritable. 'I don't give a toss what you tell him. If he's not happy, tell him to see me.'

Richter went into his office, picked up the direct line to Simpson and waited. After ten seconds he put it down again and looked at his watch. It was after eight, and it was being unduly optimistic to suppose Simpson would still be around at that time in the evening.

Richter shrugged, locked his office door and walked back down the stairs. He called in at the Duty Room and told the Duty Operations Officer what had happened. Or rather, what Richter thought he ought to know about it. The Ops Officer said he would tell Simpson when he got there in the morning.

Chapter 10

Simpson looked very unhappy when Richter appeared in his office at nine the following morning, for two reasons. First, Richter was late and hadn't answered his flat phone, and second, the Transport Officer had been draining all over him since just after eight. 'Sorry,' Richter said.

'Stow it, Richter. Sarcasm I can do without. What happened?'

Richter told him, omitting the fact that he had removed the weapons and ammunition from the car and that he had contributed to the driver's headache and caused the passenger's.

'Who were they?' Simpson asked.

'Pros,' Richter replied. 'Neither had any ID, and it looked like a very tight set-up. The reason I didn't hang around was that I was worried about a second team in another motor.'

'Did you see a second car?'

'Not that I could positively identify, no, but they had a radio in the Jaguar that definitely wasn't there to pick up the racing results on Radio Four. I took off from the crash when I heard a car coming, so that could have been it. I wasn't prepared to take a chance.' That didn't sound too bad. It could have happened.

'Who do you think they were? With reasons.'

'I think the Russian Embassy is short two Cultural Attachés,' Richter said. 'Cultural Attachés who just happened to be trained assassins, who were following me in a stolen car.'

Simpson digested this in silence for a few moments, then spoke again. 'One thing I don't buy – why did they try a mobile hit?'

145

'I don't think they did – it was simply Russian mentality. I drove up to Brampton on the A1 – a hell of a journey, with long queues at three sets of roadworks and a major accident. So I had decided to come back a different route. I was going to cut across country and pick up the A10. But because I'd driven up on the A1, they probably presumed that I would drive back on the A1, queues notwithstanding. After all, queuing is pretty much endemic in Russia.

'I think that somewhere on the A1 between Brampton and London,' Richter continued, 'there was a man with a Mannlicher or a Mauser, waiting for me to drive into the viewfinder of his telescopic sight. No professional assassin would ever try a hit from a moving car against a target also in a moving car – it's virtually impossible to get a clean kill. He would always go for a static hit. So the mobile would have been the last-resort back-up, and they only used it because I turned left instead of right out of Brampton's main gates.'

Simpson nodded. 'What weapons were they carrying?'

'The guy in the back seat had a Colt. The driver I don't know about.'

'Why not something heavier?'

'Probably just prudence. Diplomatic passports or not, the plods take a dim view of foreign hoods wandering about the Home Counties carrying assault rifles or sub-machineguns. Pistols you can hide.'

Simpson nodded, apparently satisfied. He stood up and walked over to his favourite window and looked out. He fondled his cacti for a minute or so, then turned round. 'OK, assuming for the moment that it was a Russian operation, why?'

'I think Newman's death must be tied in with the Blackbird flight,' Richter said. 'Follow the sequence. I go to Moscow, I investigate the death of an Embassy official, and a Russian hood tries to take me out before I even leave Sheremetievo. I come back here and immediately visit JARIC, where any pictures from the Blackbird over-flight would be bound to end up if we had anything to do with it. Then someone else tries to take me out. I gave up believing in coincidence when I stopped believing in Father Christmas. Those events are linked, and the sum added up, from the Russian point of view, to the elimination of Richter.

'I was photographed on arrival at Sheremetievo, as all foreign nationals are, and my guess is that that picture matched a record in the

SVR database, hence the kill attempt at the airport. There'll be a pile of mug shots of me at the Russian Embassy here, and no doubt a directive from the Lubyanka or Yazenevo to watch and report, and obviously a kill order on me if I did certain things or visited certain places. JARIC, presumably, was one of them. The other thing you ought to be aware of,' Richter added, 'is that, if they have been following me, it's quite likely Hammersmith Commercial Packers is now on their watch-list.'

Hammersmith Commercial Packers provided FOE with a thin veneer of cover. The company actually existed, and even employed a small staff to conduct a legitimate business on the ground floor of the building located just north of the Hammersmith Flyover.

'I'll bear it in mind,' Simpson said. 'I can confirm some aspects. The car was stolen three days ago, in London. The Embassy Watch people have confirmed that the two in it were Russians, and from our records they arrived here only the day before yesterday, together with two other new staff for the Russian Embassy, so they could be a professional hit-team. Or, rather, they could have been a professional hit-team. They're both dead.'

'Oh,' Richter said.

'Yes,' said Simpson. 'I suppose they were both alive and well when you left them?'

'I don't know,' Richter replied. 'They were both unconscious, certainly.'

Simpson looked at him doubtfully. 'According to the initial report from the local police, both had suffered fractured skulls, the damage being caused by something like a large hammer or mallet. You wouldn't know anything about that, would you?'

Richter looked straight at him. 'No,' he said. 'Why don't you check the toolkit in the Granada and see if you can find any blood-stained tyre levers or anything?'

'I already have. There was also no sign of the gun you say they fired at you.'

'Really?' Richter said. 'Well, perhaps there was a back-up team in a second car, then, and they shifted the evidence, as it were.'

'Perhaps. And perhaps there's a hammer in a river somewhere with your prints slowly washing off it, and a bag with a gun in it buried in a

147

wood.' Richter looked at him, but said nothing. 'What's the tie-up between Newman and the Blackbird?' Simpson asked. 'Do you know?'

'No,' Richter replied, standing up to leave, 'but I'm going to find out. One thing – I want to draw a weapon.'

'Why?'

'Because if anyone else shoots at me, I want to be able to shoot back.'

Simpson was silent for a few seconds, then he nodded. 'Yes, you can have a pistol.' He shook a warning finger. 'Just try to remember you're not James Bond. Make sure you fire second, if you fire at all, and try to avoid ventilating some innocent member of the public when you do so. I'll ring the Armoury.'

American Embassy, Grosvenor Square, London

Roger Abrahams knocked twice on the bedroom door and walked in, carrying a tray of coffee and a plate of doughnuts. He flicked on the main light and glanced across at the bed, where John Westwood was just opening his eyes. 'Feeling better?' Abrahams asked.

'Not so you'd notice,' Westwood grunted. 'Flying across the pond always screws me up – you'd think I'd be used to it by now.' He looked at the tray Abrahams had placed on the bedside table. 'Some news?'

'Yes,' Abrahams replied, pouring a coffee. 'We have a meet with Piers Taylor in just over an hour, hence the wake-up call.'

Westwood nodded and reached for the cup. 'Good. Where is it – here?'

Abrahams shook his head and smiled. 'No way. Taylor would want a very good reason – probably in writing – to visit the Embassy. We're all going off to feed the ducks in Regents Park, just like characters in a John le Carré novel.'

Westwood grimaced. 'And I suppose we have to indulge in the usual double-speak and then work out afterwards what the hell we were really talking about?'

'Yup. Anyway, eat, drink and get your pants on – the car will be here in thirty minutes.'

OVERKILL

Hammersmith, London

The armourer greeted Richter with a smile and two cardboard boxes. 'Here you are, Mr Richter. One nine-millimetre Browning, with shoulder holster and fifty rounds of ammunitions. as per Mr Simpson's orders.'

'I don't want it,' Richter said, shaking his head.

The armourer looked puzzled. 'But Mr Simpson said that—'

'Yes,' Richter said. 'I do want a gun, but I don't want that bloody thing. The only good thing about a Browning is that it's got a good-sized magazine and doesn't jam as often as other automatics. But at anything over about fifty feet you might as well throw the bloody gun at someone as soon as fire it. I want a pistol that's accurate. I'm not interested in magazine size, and I'm not interested in speed of fire. I want a revolver.'

The armourer looked a little taken aback. 'But Mr Simpson said—'

'I know what Mr Simpson said,' Richter interrupted. 'Ring him up and tell him I want to draw a revolver.'

The armourer picked up the two cardboard boxes and retreated into his office in the corner of the Armoury. Richter was standing on one side of the three-feet-high counter, on the other side of which the department's devices of death and destruction were kept, lovingly cleaned and polished and ready for immediate issue. Richter knew from past experience on the range that FOE held a variety of revolvers, and he knew exactly which one he wanted. The armourer stuck his head out of the office.

'Mr Simpson wants to know which revolver you want.'

'The Smith and Wesson Model 586 in .357 Magnum.'

He repeated this information into the mouthpiece. Richter could hear the strangled squawk from where he was standing. The armourer's head emerged again. 'Mr Simpson wants to speak to you, sir.'

Richter vaulted over the counter and took the telephone from him. 'Yes?'

'Richter? Are you sure you wouldn't like a bazooka, or a small howitzer? What the bloody hell do you want with a gun like that?'

'I want a gun that won't jam. I want a gun that will stop a man if it has to. And I want a gun that I can fire at fifty yards and have a slim chance of hitting what I'm aiming at.'

'What's wrong with the Browning? It is the standard NATO weapon, you know.'

'I do know that,' Richter said. 'I also know that the British Army maintains a centrally heated warehouse in Wiltshire full of bridles and tack for mules, despite the fact that they actually expect to go into the next war driving main battle tanks and three-ton trucks. Just because the Browning is the standard NATO sidearm, it doesn't mean it's actually any use. It's great for making people keep their heads down, or for fights in a confined space, like a telephone box. For anything other than ultra close-range work, it's hopeless. That's why I want the Smith.'

Simpson grunted. 'OK, OK. You can have the 586. Put the armourer back on.'

'Thanks,' Richter said, and handed the phone back.

The shoulder holster was a bulky affair. As Richter fitted the pistol into the holster and shrugged his jacket back on, he realized that he was going to have to make a conscious effort not to walk lop-sided. He put a box of fifty rounds into his jacket pocket and followed the armourer down a flight of steps into the soundproof basement. The armourer unlocked the steel door and ushered Richter into the twenty-five-metre range. He put the range lights on, and the red light outside the door, to show that it was in use, and then gave a thorough briefing on the pistol. Richter listened attentively; he always listened closely to anything that might subsequently save his life.

The gun was big and heavy – the .357 Magnum is a cartridge you can't fire out of a lightweight weapon – but comfortable and well made. The armourer gave Richter a box of twenty shells, and he loaded the weapon. Richter stood facing the target, held the pistol in his right hand, wrapped his left hand around his right wrist, and fired. Even with the ear-defenders on, the report was deafening, and the gun kicked in his hand like a live thing, forcing his arms upwards. Richter aimed and fired again. And again, and again, until he had fired all six rounds.

The armourer had been watching the target through a spotting scope. 'Not bad, Mr Richter,' he said. 'Six hits, with one bull. You seem to be grouping a little low and a little to the right. If you will permit me?' Richter passed him the pistol and watched while he adjusted the rear sight. 'This time take the target on the right and just fire three shots first, then stop. I'll make any further adjustments then.'

Richter loaded three rounds and fired them as instructed, then passed the pistol to the armourer, who ejected the empty cases before adjusting the sights again. 'Elevation seems about right now, but you're still grouping to the right. Try that.' The last three pleased him.

The armourer walked to the end of the range to put up two more targets, then Richter reloaded. He took the left-hand target first, and fired the six quickly, taking the minimum aim necessary – in a fire-fight, the opposition may not be sporting enough to stand silhouetted against a bright light for thirty seconds while you adopt the correct stance and take careful aim – and he was pleased that they were all hits, although the score would have got him nowhere at Bisley. The last two shells he fired at the right-hand target, taking his time.

'Nice, sir. One bull, one nine.'

'Thank you.' Richter put the spent shell cases into the now empty box, reloaded the pistol from the box of fifty and slid it into the holster.

The armourer looked on approvingly. 'Quite right,' he said. 'No point in having the weapon unless it's loaded.' Richter followed him back up to the Armoury, signed the register for the pistol and rounds, and signed the range log to the effect that he had received a full briefing on the pistol and had fired twenty rounds.

Back in his office, Richter examined the pistol again, loaded it and unloaded it a few times, and practised getting it out of the holster quickly. It was clear that Richter was never going to be able to out-draw Billy the Kid, but that didn't worry him unduly – he didn't expect to meet Billy the Kid. What he did expect to meet was a man or men armed with, probably, 9mm automatic pistols, and Richter felt more than a match for them with the Smith.

The problem with a relatively small calibre bullet like the 9mm is that it isn't a man-stopper. The Americans found this out years ago when they issued some of their forces with .32-calibre pistols. Field experience showed that a determined or hyped-up attacker could just keep coming, even after multiple hits with these weapons. But a .357 Magnum – or the Americans' preferred .45 ACP – stopped pretty much anything and anyone. That was the edge Richter wanted.

He made a mug of coffee, put the cup down on his desk, and dialled the Registry. He requested the Blackbird file, the Moscow Station files for the last three months, and the one entitled 'Newman, Graham (deceased)'.

Regents Park, London

The black Mercedes – one of several non-US manufactured vehicles used by the Embassy for unofficial duties – drove out of Grosvenor Square and joined the one-way system in Upper Grosvenor Street, then turned up Park Street, through Portman Street, Gloucester Place and into Park Road. At the western end of Hanover Gardens the car stopped and Roger Abrahams and John Westwood climbed out. 'We'll get a cab back,' Abrahams said, dismissing the driver.

John Westwood glanced at his watch. 'Where are we meeting this guy?'

'By The Holme – it's on the other side of the Boating Lake. We've plenty of time.'

The two Americans walked through Hanover Gardens, past the London Central Mosque, across the Outer Circle and into Regents Park itself. They followed the footpath and the footbridge which crossed the north-west end of the Boating Lake, and then turned right towards Queen Mary's Gardens. The day was seasonably warm and Westwood found that Abraham's brisk pace was causing him to sweat slightly. He removed his jacket and draped it over his arm. As they reached the second footbridge Abrahams touched Westwood's arm. 'There he is,' he said, pointing.

Westwood glanced to his right and saw a tall, slim figure in a light grey suit standing close to the eastern edge of the Boating Lake. As they crossed the footbridge, Abrahams chuckled softly. 'Look. He is feeding the ducks. John le Carré's got a lot to answer for.'

Piers Taylor tossed the last few crumbs of bread into the water in front of him, smiling at the noisy scrambling as the mallards jockeyed for position, then folded the brown paper bag carefully and put it into his jacket pocket. He stepped back from the water's edge and turned towards the approaching Americans.

'Hullo, Piers,' said Roger Abrahams, extending his hand.

'Roger,' Taylor acknowledged, shaking his hand firmly whilst looking at Westwood. 'And this is?' He left the question dangling.

Piers Taylor, Westwood thought, didn't look like much. He had the slightly vacant expression traditionally – and with some truth – supposed to indicate a good public school education, and he was, Westwood mentally concluded, far too young.

'A colleague from home,' Abrahams said smoothly, before Westwood could answer.

John Westwood shook Taylor's hand. 'Call me John,' he said.

'It was nice meeting you, John,' Taylor said, smiled agreeably, turned and walked off.

'Piers,' Abrahams called.

Taylor stopped and turned back. 'Roger,' he said, and waited.

Abrahams sighed and looked at Westwood. 'OK, OK. This is John Westwood. He's the Head of our Foreign Intelligence (Espionage) Staff, and he – we – need some help.'

Westwood looked angrily at Abrahams. 'Was that really necessary?' he asked.

Abrahams nodded, but Piers Taylor answered him, his eyes hard and his face unsmiling. 'Yes, it was,' he said. 'I don't talk to anyone until I find out who they are. I won't ask for ID because you're with Roger, but normally I would want a full recognition procedure. You know who I am?'

Westwood looked again at the slight figure in front of him and nodded. He glanced round to check that nobody else was in earshot, then replied. 'Deputy head of SIS Section Nine, responsible for Russian affairs,' he said.

'Right,' Piers Taylor nodded, his languid manner returning. 'Now we all know who we are, how can we assist our colonial cousins?'

The three men turned as if by common consent and walked towards the Inner Circle. 'It may be nothing,' Westwood began, 'and for the moment I want this to stay on a strictly unofficial level. Can I first ask one question?'

Taylor nodded. 'You can certainly ask,' he said.

'Do you – or does SIS, I should say – have any high-level agents-in-place or other well-placed sources in Russia?' Before Taylor could answer, Westwood continued. 'We basically need either confirmation or denial of the existence of a high-level conspiracy which might – I say again, might – be a threat to the West. If it exists, we believe it has been organized and directed by the very highest echelons of the Russian government.'

Taylor walked on in silence for a few paces, then stopped. 'You do realize what you're asking?' he said.

Westwood nodded. 'Yes. If you have a source at that level we would like you to task him with verifying this information. We do not, of course, require access to your source, or knowledge of the identity of the source, but we would want your assurance that he is in a position to do what we ask.'

Taylor looked up at the sky. 'I had thought this was going to be a good day,' he murmured, almost inaudibly. He began walking again, and the other two followed.

'Let me lay out the problems as I see them,' Taylor said quietly. 'First, I'm not in a position to tell you if we have such a source. Second, if we do have a source at the level you need, trying to get him to verify your suspicions might well result in him being blown to the SVR or the GRU, which is something I'm sure we'd all rather avoid.' Taylor paused and glanced at the Americans, then continued. 'Third, let's look at the logic of this. You believe the Russians might have something nasty heading our way. In the current political climate I personally find that unlikely, but the information you have suggests that to be the case, right?'

John Westwood nodded. 'So,' Taylor continued, 'if our putative source starts asking the wrong sort of questions of the wrong sort of people in Moscow, it will make it obvious to the Russians that we have discovered this plot, whatever it is. What effect will that have?' Neither Abrahams nor Westwood spoke. 'It might,' Taylor said, answering his own question, 'prompt the Russians to implement this conspiracy immediately.'

Westwood suddenly glimpsed the intellect behind the languid mask.

'What do you suggest?' Abrahams asked.

'If I was in your shoes, for which I thank God I'm not,' Taylor answered, 'I would proceed on the assumption that the conspiracy is real and make appropriate contingency plans.'

Westwood was silent for a few moments, then spoke. 'That's good advice, but there are some problems.'

'Like what?'

'Like the fact that we know nothing whatever about the assault. What form it will take, I mean. All we are sure about is that there is no evidence at all that Russian conventional or nuclear forces are involved.'

'What?' Taylor's calm demeanour vanished momentarily. 'It can't be much of a threat then, can it?' He laughed briefly; Abrahams and Westwood didn't. 'Sorry,' Taylor said. 'Obviously you believe it's real, and I noticed you used the word "assault", not "conspiracy", which changes things. Without giving me specifics, what data do you have?'

Westwood shook his head. 'I'm sorry, but I can give you very little,' he said. 'The file classification is "NOFORN". You're not a US citizen, so officially I can tell you nothing about it. But,' he added, 'I can say that the information came from a high-level source in Moscow, and we have not been able to reach that source since we received the data.'

'Hence the need for independent corroboration,' Taylor finished for him, and Westwood nodded. Taylor walked on a few paces, right hand cupping his chin, then stopped. 'Right,' he said, 'I'll do what I can, unofficially, of course. You'll appreciate that I'll have to talk to some people before I can task any source we might have. And,' he added, 'I'm not saying that we have such a source, you understand? I can reach you through Roger, yes?'

'Right,' Westwood replied. 'Oh, there's one other thing that might be some help. One of the pieces of data we received was a single word.'

Taylor looked interested. 'Yes?'

'The word,' Westwood said, 'was "Gibraltar".'

'That's it? Nothing else?'

Westwood shook his head. 'Just the one word. We know what Gibraltar is, obviously, but we've no idea what it means in this context.'

Taylor nodded slowly. 'Very well,' he said, 'I'll be in touch.' He turned away and took a pace, then stopped. 'One final point,' he said. 'If we can't help you, what will you do next?'

Abrahams looked at Westwood. 'If you can't help,' Westwood replied, 'we'll have to try the French.'

Turabah, Saudi Arabia

It all, Sadoun Khamil reflected late that afternoon, seemed to be going reasonably well. The news from Hassan Abbas about the flight by the American spy-plane had been something of a shock, but the apparent absence of any other activity by the Americans – or by anyone else, in fact – suggested that the flight had not revealed anything of interest. And time was passing.

With all the American weapons in position, and with the London bomb almost complete, as far as Khamil could see there was little that anybody could do to stop them. And there was a compelling argument that any further waiting could be counter-productive, allowing a greater chance for some Western intelligence service to penetrate the Russian operation. He had discussed this view with the al-Qaeda leadership, but they had insisted that for the plan to be unequivocally successful, it was essential that all the weapons were positioned as intended, and for the final stages of *Podstava* to be carried through. Only that way could total success be guaranteed.

Khamil concurred with this view, but it still concerned him that something had happened – whether a leak from one of the Russians involved or some indication from a different source – that had prompted the American action. He worried about what they could have found out, but he worried more about what they might try to do if they discovered the full scope of the operation.

The one thing that he and the leaders of al-Qaeda were in complete agreement about was that the implementation of *El Sikkiyn* – the Arab component of the plan – had to be precisely timed and executed. And for that to happen there had to be no American pre-emptive action which might disrupt it, so it was essential that they were informed immediately of any further action by the Americans.

Khamil knew he could rely upon Hassan Abbas to keep him abreast of developments in Russia, through Dmitri Trushenko, and the best source of information about American activity was probably CNN, he reflected with a slight smile. He'd just have to start watching more television.

Hammersmith, London

That afternoon Richter found the first faint evidence of a link. It wasn't much, and he didn't know its significance, but he thought it was worth taking to Simpson. Before ringing him, Richter checked the Basic Intelligence Digest (CIS) and found exactly what he had expected, and a personnel file which only served to confuse him. Then he called Simpson on the direct line and told him he needed five minutes of his valuable time.

'What have you got?' Simpson didn't look up as he spoke, but continued writing notes on the minute sheet of an open Secret file. His desk was covered in pink files, several of them open, and he seemed more preoccupied than usual.

'Not a lot,' Richter replied, 'but I can place Newman's number two in an area virtually in the centre of the Blackbird's flight path, about five days before the aircraft flew.'

Simpson stopped writing, looked up and put down his pen. 'Where, when, and what was he doing?'

Richter sat down in front of the desk and glanced down at the Moscow Station Activities file he had brought up with him. 'The place was Sosnogorsk, and according to SIS he went there as a translator for two days last month.'

'Who was Newman's deputy?'

'Andrew Payne. He's alive and well and currently running Moscow Station pending the appointment of a new head.'

Simpson digested this for a moment or two. 'Right,' he said. 'Tell me about Sosnogorsk, starting with wherever the hell it is.'

'It's a small Russian town in the Komi region, next to a slightly bigger town called Ukhta. It's about four hundred miles almost due east of Arkhangel'sk. It lies to the west of the Severnyy Urals, close to the main railway line from Konosha up to—'

'I'm not going there for a bloody holiday, Richter. Get to the point.'

'You asked. It's nowhere. It gets a nil return in the BID (CIS), and as far as we know it has no intelligence significance whatsoever.'

'Then what was Payne doing there?'

Richter shrugged. 'I don't know,' he said. 'The only installation of interest in that general area is the Large Phased-Array Radar at Pechora, but that's about a hundred and fifty miles to the north-east. He wouldn't have been able to leave Sosnogorsk and get up there without attracting attention.'

Simpson picked up his pen and carefully screwed the top back on. Then he unscrewed it and aimed the nib at Richter. 'Perhaps he did.'

'Did what?' Richter asked.

'Attract attention. Perhaps that's why they snatched Newman.'

'You've never been in the field, have you?' Richter asked. In fact, Simpson wasn't an intelligence professional at all. Prior to his appointment to head the Foreign Operations Executive, he had been a mandarin, a Civil Service high-flyer. Initially, his lack of a 'proper' intelligence background had caused some resentment in both FOE and SIS, but his obvious competence, and completely ruthless approach to his work, had quickly silenced his detractors.

'When I said Payne wouldn't be able to leave Sosnogorsk without attracting attention,' Richter continued, 'what I meant was that he wouldn't have been able to leave Sosnogorsk at all. He would have had one or more minders assigned to him to ensure that he only saw what the Russians wanted him to see – no more and no less. He wouldn't even have been able to leave his hotel room without the *dezhurnaya* reporting it. You can forget about *glasnost* when it comes to foreigners wandering about in Russia, and especially anywhere out in the bundu. The locals are universally suspicious. Take my word for it, Payne didn't leave Sosnogorsk.'

'So what's your suggestion?' Simpson asked, looking irritated.

Richter shook his head again. 'I haven't really got one, but I do think the visit was significant, and I don't think it had anything to do with Pechora. The other thing that bothers me is what he was actually doing, as opposed to what he was supposed to be doing. According to the Moscow Station reports, he went there as a translator to some European businessmen.'

'So?'

'Payne speaks passable Russian. The businessmen were principally British, but there were two Frenchmen and one German in the party.

According to his file, Payne doesn't speak French or German to anything like the level he would have needed to translate for them.'

Simpson played with his pen for a minute or so, then spoke. 'I agree. I don't buy Payne going out as a translator. As Deputy Head of Station he shouldn't even have left Moscow. Get on to SIS and find out what he was really up to.'

Anton Kirov

Once again, Captain Bondarev had had to concede that Zavorin's men certainly knew their trade. The entry to Varna had been as smooth and professional as his own crew could have achieved, and the loading of the cargo had been accomplished in a much shorter time than he had expected. The *Anton Kirov* had two holds; a large one aft, designed for bulk or loose cargo, and a smaller, secure, stowage forward. The special cargo – just one large and heavy box – fitted without difficulty into the forward hold. Bondarev noted that Zavorin had remained on the fore-deck throughout loading and had personally supervised the entire operation. Once the cargo hatches had been secured, Zavorin had telephoned the bridge, ordered Bondarev to put to sea immediately, and had then disappeared for over an hour. Bondarev supposed, correctly, that he had been inspecting the new cargo.

With the *Anton Kirov* heading south again, and Varna becoming only a smudge on the coastline, Zavorin knocked on the captain's door and entered without waiting for an answer. He carried two glasses and a bottle of single malt Scotch whisky. Bondarev looked somewhat quizzically at the bottle.

'I drink vodka,' Zavorin said, with a smile, 'but not from choice. Now this –' he raised the bottle to the light '– is a real drink.' He put down the glasses, poured two large measures and handed one to Bondarev. 'As the British say, "Cheers",' Zavorin said, and took a sip.

Bondarev sipped, nodded appreciatively, then put his glass down and looked over at the *Spetsnaz* colonel. 'So, you have your special equipment. Now where are we going?'

'As planned, Captain,' Zavorin replied, 'we will route through the Bosphorus and probably call at Athens. I am not sure we will have time to make Tunis, but we will see. A lot depends upon our departure date from Greek waters.'

He paused and looked thoughtfully at his glass. 'The deadline is our arrival date at Gibraltar, and I am waiting to have that signalled to me. My guess is we will be instructed to arrive there in about a week.' Bondarev nodded, mentally calculating times and speeds. He picked up his glass again and sipped.

In the forward hold, one of the *Spetsnaz* officers, who held a degree in electronic engineering from a West German university, checked that the coaxial cable from the satellite dish on the bridge roof was securely attached to the high-frequency DBS-band receiver. The dish had been aligned and a test message received from the satellite within fifteen minutes of the *Anton Kirov*'s arrival alongside the loading jetty.

The officer made a final check of all the connections, then snapped shut his precision toolkit and nodded to two troopers standing beside him. They picked up and replaced the side panel of the large crate and then dropped the lid back into position. The device was functioning normally, and could be safely left unattended until it reached its final destination.

London

The Foreign Operations Executive officially didn't exist, and was officially nothing to do with SIS, although in reality its sole function was to carry out deniable operations on its behalf. The Secret Intelligence Service, popularly and incorrectly known as MI6 – also didn't officially exist, which meant that Richter worked for a non-existent organization which worked for another non-existent organization. It was no wonder the manager looked at him quizzically every time he walked into the bank.

MI6 was effectively created in July 1909 on the recommendation of a sub-committee of Haldane's Committee of Imperial Defence. The intention had been to set up a single Secret Service Bureau, but this proved unworkable, and by 1910 the present division into MI5 and SIS was already well established. MI5, more properly known as the Security Service, was charged with counter-espionage within the United Kingdom, while SIS was responsible for running espionage operations abroad.

Since 1910, both organizations have evidenced a marked lack of co-operation with each other, which has on occasion degenerated into open hostility. It was this hostility which was responsible – at least in part – for the creation of FOE, as a separate and secret executive arm of SIS. Giving FOE the dirty jobs enabled SIS to deny its involvement if an operation turned sour, and didn't give MI5 anything to get its teeth into.

In 1994, SIS moved from Century House, an anonymous twenty-three-storey block near the Lambeth North underground station and known to almost everyone as 'Spook House', into a new building on the Thames at Vauxhall Cross, the avant-garde design of which has prompted some unkind nicknames – 'The Aztec Palace' is perhaps the least offensive. Like FOE, entry is strictly controlled at Vauxhall Cross, and a similar clear desks policy is applied. SIS also operates a 'no talking in the lift' rule, just in case the man in the corner with the bucket and wash-leather is a Russian Cultural Attaché on assignment, and not Bob the window cleaner.

And like Bob the window cleaner, Richter couldn't just walk into Vauxhall Cross. The Russian Embassy maintains a watch group whose sole function is to photograph everyone who enters or leaves the building. They have another group watching the US Embassy in Grosvenor Square, another across the road from Thames House, a substantial stone-built 1930s block north of Lambeth Bridge and the headquarters since the mid 1990s of MI5, others in South Audley Street, Grosvenor Street and Gower Street, where MI5 maintains offices. Further groups watch some of the covert addresses used by SIS elsewhere in London, and a large team monitors the SIS training establishment at Fort Monkton, near Gosport in Hampshire.

To return the favour, as it were, SIS has permanent watch teams in place outside the Russian Embassy at 13 Kensington Palace Gardens, the consular and trade section at 33 Highgate West Hill, and others covering the rest of the foreign Embassies in London.

The principal beneficiary of all this activity is of course Kodak, but it means that FOE operatives are forbidden to enter Vauxhall Cross, all other MI5 and SIS buildings, and the American Embassy, to prevent their picture from appearing at SVR headquarters in Moscow. That in turn meant that any meetings between FOE operatives and SIS, MI5 or CIA officers had to take place elsewhere.

And that was why at three ten in the afternoon Richter was sitting in the lounge of the Sherlock Holmes Hotel in Baker Street, looking over a coffee pot, milk jug, sugar bowl, two cups and a small plate of assorted biscuits at the slightly vacant expression on Piers Taylor's face. Richter had known Taylor for about eighteen months, and he knew that his expression was wholly deceiving. Taylor possessed one of the sharpest brains in SIS which was why, at only thirty-eight, he was the Deputy Head of Section Nine, responsible for Russian affairs.

Taylor absent-mindedly plucked a thread from the sleeve of his jacket, glanced round the lounge, which was empty apart from a group of American tourists loudly discussing their theatre-going of the previous evening, and leaned forward. 'It was just routine,' he said, softly.

'Come on, Piers,' Richter replied, just as quietly. 'Deputy Head of Station Moscow doesn't just wander off halfway across Russia with a bunch of European businessmen on a whim. He had a reason for going there.'

Taylor shook his head. 'No, we know why he went there – Newman told him to – but he wasn't tasked with anything very exciting. I had Payne flown back to London on Monday to introduce him to his new head and to give him a current briefing. He told me then about the trip to Sosnogorsk.'

'What did he tell you? I mean, Newman must have given him some indication of what he expected him to do there.'

Taylor nodded. 'Yes, he did. Newman told him that if anyone approached him and introduced himself as Karelin, Nicolai Karelin, Payne was to give him a one-word message and note the reply, which should also be a single word.'

Richter waited. Extracting information from Piers was sometimes a long and tiring process. 'Is there any reason I shouldn't know what Payne's message was?'

'No, no reason. It was *Schtchit*.' Taylor looked at him. 'Do you know what it means?'

'Of course I know what it means,' Richter said. 'It's Russian for "shield", and it also means the type of double-exposure film sometimes used by GRU operatives.' He took a sip of coffee and pondered for a moment. Taylor looked at him in silence.

'Newman didn't tell Payne what other action he should take if this Karelin turned up – or even if he didn't turn up?'

'No. Just the message he was to pass, and to note the reply. Nothing else.'

'And did Karelin contact Payne?'

'Yes.'

Blood out of a stone. 'And?' Richter said.

'And what?'

'And what was the message this Nicolai Karelin passed?'

'Not one word, as Newman had briefed him to expect, but two – *Stukach* and *Chernozhopy*.'

Richter thought for a moment. 'Fine,' he said. 'Do they mean anything to you, because they certainly don't to me?'

'Your Russian getting a little rusty, is it?' Taylor asked, smiling.

'Piers,' Richter said, 'I can read it and translate it, and speak it well enough to get by, but I'm not fluent, and probably never will be.'

'*Stukach* is Russian slang for "secret informant" or "stool pigeon", and *Chernozhopy* translates as "black-arses". That's a derogatory term applied to coloured people of all nationalities. About the only interesting thing about it is that the term is most often used by officers of the GRU.'

Richter opened his mouth, but Taylor held up a hand. 'Before you ask, yes, we have checked them. We ran both words through the computers here. *Stukach* wasn't listed and the only code-word *Chernozhopy* we found was the title of an aborted operation run by the Red Army as the Germans approached the gates of Moscow in the Second World War. We're quite satisfied that the word was chosen precisely because it was effectively meaningless, but sufficiently unusual not to be mistaken for anything else.'

Piers sat back, as if satisfied. Richter wasn't. 'And when Payne got back to Moscow?'

'Nothing. By the time Payne returned to the Embassy, Newman was already dead.'

'What conclusion did you and your analysts draw from all this?'

Piers shrugged his shoulders. 'Most of it was obvious. Payne was tasked with checking all Newman's files and documents when he got back to Moscow, for obvious reasons. He found nothing significant, by the way. According to notes in Newman's work diary and from the station files, Nicolai Karelin is the name of an established British source in the Sosnogorsk area. He's a computer operator who used to work at the Pechora LPAR site and passed us some useful low-grade intelligence in the past. According to Newman's notes, he's now working on another project in the area, but we don't yet know what.'

'And the code-words?' Richter asked.

'That was simple enough as well, because it was in Newman's work diary. *Schtchit* was Payne's recognition signal to Karelin, and the response *Stukach* meant that Karelin had succeeded in identifying another potential source at Pechora, something Newman had asked him to do. Payne was just being used as a messenger boy.' Taylor leaned back.

'And *Chernozhopy*?' Richter asked.

'That,' Taylor admitted, 'is what we don't know. Payne couldn't find a reference to the word anywhere in Newman's files or records. Our best guess is that the word was intended to be used as a recognition signal for the new agent Karelin was trying to recruit.'

'OK, I'll buy that,' Richter said, after a moment. 'One other question. According to Payne's file, his French and German are nowhere near fluent, so how did he manage to translate for the group of businessmen he was with?'

'No problems,' Taylor replied. 'Apparently the Frenchmen and the German understood English well enough to cope.' Richter reached for the coffee pot and poured two more cups. 'By the way,' Taylor asked, his voice even quieter, 'why are you tooled up?'

Richter's jacket had swung open to reveal the substantial butt of the Smith and Wesson, and he hastily concealed it. 'I'm having trouble with the bailiffs,' he said.

Taylor grinned at him. 'These would be Russian bailiffs, perhaps?'

'Perhaps,' Richter agreed. Taylor frowned slightly, and Richter leaned forward. 'Yes?' he said, encouragingly.

'I'm not sure that it's relevant,' Taylor said, 'but some of our Cousins were scrabbling around looking for favours this morning.'

'The Company?' Richter was surprised. 'I thought it was usually the other way round. What were they after?'

'Mainly,' Taylor said, 'access to a high-level source in Moscow.'

Richter's eyes widened. 'They don't want much, do they? They don't want the keys to the Kremlin as well?' Richter glanced round the lounge. 'Have you such a source?' he asked.

Piers Taylor shook his head. 'You know I can't tell you,' he murmured. 'Need to know, and all that. However,' he went on, 'I think you can assume that if we had such a source we would not willingly risk compromising him without very good reason.'

Richter nodded. 'And the Company couldn't come up with a good reason?'

'Not good enough,' Taylor replied. 'Just a lot of unsubstantiated stuff about a covert assault on the West.'

Richter sat straighter. 'Covert assault? That's sounds serious enough to me. What data did they supply?'

'That's the problem. They supplied almost nothing. They claim to have cultivated a high-level source of their own in Moscow, and that source started the hare running. The whole thing is subject to a NOFORN caveat, and they can't, or won't, be specific about any of it.'

'Why don't they get their source to confirm the data?'

Taylor shook his head. 'They can't,' he replied. 'They've had no contact with him since he sent this assault message.'

'Hence the reason for them sniffing round SIS,' Richter said.

'Exactly.'

'Have you told them you can't help?'

'Not yet,' Taylor replied, 'but we're going to.'

Hammersmith, London

Richter delivered a negative report to Simpson.

'So where does that leave us?' Simpson asked.

'No further forward,' Richter replied. He was almost thinking aloud. 'If Payne's presence at Sosnogorsk was simply to service an existing source, it can have nothing to do with the Blackbird over-flight a week later.'

'We know that,' Simpson interjected suddenly, 'but the Russians didn't.'

Richter looked at him with sudden respect. 'That's right,' he said slowly. 'They didn't. Maybe it was just a horrible coincidence. If they have got something devious going on in that area that the Americans know about and haven't told us, and if they had identified Payne as the Moscow Station Deputy Head, his visit to Sosnogorsk could easily be interpreted as an investigation by SIS. In that case, snatching Newman, as Payne's superior, for questioning does make some kind of sense.'

They sat silently for a moment, both considering the matter from this new angle. 'Recommendations?' Simpson was suddenly icily efficient.

'Two,' Richter said. 'First, I think I should talk to JARIC again and see if the vehicle concentrations they noted were anywhere near Sosnogorsk. Second, I wonder if we're missing the obvious. The Americans are the ones who started this hare running when they flew the Blackbird. I think you should talk to the CIA London Chief of Station and try to find out what the hell it is that they think they've found up there.'

Simpson nodded. 'Good idea. I'll catch him at the next meeting of the Joint Intelligence Committee.'

'Has anything come in since about the Blackbird surveillance films – from the Americans, I mean?'

Simpson shook his head. 'Nothing. We had a brief note – sent direct from Langley to SIS, in fact – stating that the results had been negative. That was a couple of days after we released the films to them.'

'Did you believe that?'

'Of course not. Would you?'

'No,' Richter said. 'There's no way that the Americans would have made an over-flight of Russian territory in the Blackbird, risking a major international incident, unless they were certain that there was something there to find. And they certainly wouldn't then simply drop the whole thing like a hot brick and do nothing about it. Something is going on, and I get the distinct feeling that we're about to be handed the shitty end of a heavy stick. There's something else you should know,' he added, 'which may make you decide to talk to the CIA London Chief of Station sooner rather than later.'

'What?'

'According to Piers Taylor, the Cousins have information that some sort of covert assault is in progress, directed against the West by Moscow.'

'Details?' Simpson snapped.

'That's the problem. There aren't any. The Cousins are really cagey about it, Piers said, not least because Langley has slapped a NOFORN caveat on the whole thing. But they are serious,' Richter continued. 'They actually asked Piers if SIS had a high-level source in Moscow who could confirm the data they have.'

'Jesus Christ.'

'You move in more exalted circles than me,' Richter said. 'Have you heard any whispers? Anything at all?'

'Nothing,' Simpson replied. 'Has Taylor any corroboration of this assault?'

Richter shook his head. 'No, but he's definitely taking it seriously. He thinks SIS will be tasking us with investigating it any time now.'

'Right,' Simpson said. 'Try your contacts in the CIA. See if you can get any hint of what's going on from them. Then try JARIC again – there must be something on those bloody films. I'll try to get some sense out of the CIA Chief of Station or his deputy.'

Theatreland, London

Harvey Sharpe did not fit the popular image of a CIA officer. Short, balding, around fifty pounds overweight, and perspiring freely in the

London heat, he gazed pinkly at Richter through thick-lensed glasses from the far side of his second dry Martini. He mopped ineffectively at his brow with a large green handkerchief, and Richter ordered him another drink from a passing waitress.

'I wish you limeys would discover air conditioning,' Sharpe complained. 'This room is hot even without the crowd.' It was seven twenty, and they were sitting at a tiny corner table in a packed wine bar just off Drury Lane, where the buzz of conversation made anything they said to each other completely inaudible to anyone else.

'We've got a lot to learn from you, I'm sure,' Richter said, and Sharpe gazed at him suspiciously.

'Why the meeting, Paul? I've got a wife and kids I'd like to get back and see.'

Richter looked at him for a moment. He had three possible contacts in the London CIA – two in the Intelligence Division, and Harvey in Research. In fact, 'Research' was something of a misnomer, as the Division was in charge of technical intelligence, which included atomic weapons technology and, crucially, satellite and surveillance aircraft photographic interpretation. Harvey was a photographic and technical analyst – if anyone knew about the Blackbird films, he would. 'Harvey,' Richter said, 'we have a problem. We don't seem to be getting the co-operation from your Company that we used to. In fact, we seem to be getting nothing at all.' Sharpe gazed back at him, and took another sip of his Martini. 'You heard about the Blackbird?' Sharpe nodded, somewhat reluctantly. 'Do you know what the films showed?' The American nodded again, more slowly. 'Care to share it with me?'

Sharpe drained his glass and, as the waitress appeared with the Martini Richter had ordered, he seized it gratefully. 'I can't,' he said finally.

'Why not?' Richter asked. 'We've exchanged before, Harvey. I've passed you a lot of good, solid data. We really need to know about this, and I'm calling in the favours.' Sharpe shook his head again. 'Harvey,' Richter said, his voice hard and cold, 'don't freeze up on me. We lost our Moscow Head of Station over this.'

Sharpe looked up, startled. 'You mean—'

'I mean terminated, Harvey,' Richter replied. 'With, as you used to say, extreme prejudice. Probably in the Lubyanka, and that's a real hard way to go.'

Sharpe took another swallow of his drink, and Richter thought that his face had paled slightly. Around them the pre-theatre crowd ebbed and flowed, a meaningless constant background babble. 'I heard he died in a road accident,' the American said, almost defiantly, 'before the Blackbird flew.'

'That's the official story, Harvey, but we're quite certain he died under interrogation, and we're satisfied that there's a link. I can't give you specifics, but we had an SIS officer close to the centre of the 'bird's flight-path a week or so earlier, and we guess that the Russians connected that with whatever the hell they're doing out in the tundra. And your people must know something's going on up there, otherwise you'd never have flown the Blackbird.' The American sat silently, sipping his drink and looking anywhere except at Richter. 'Harvey.'

'I can't tell you.'

'Harvey, please.'

Sharpe took another drink, mopped his brow again and leant forward. When he spoke, his voice was so quiet Richter had to strain to hear what he was saying. 'OK, listen to me. We got copies of the films here last week, but they weren't like the usual stuff out of Keyhole – the KH–12 satellite. These were restricted circulation, Paul. Analysts and Head of Sections only, and a NOFORN caveat. You know what that means?' Richter nodded. 'Usually they're just the usual US/UK EYES ONLY,' Sharpe said. 'And we had a specific directive from Langley – no sight, no discussion with any non-US personnel. It's my job if I tell you, Paul.'

Richter had an idea. 'Did you ever play charades?'

'What?'

'Charades. You know, the parlour game. I'd like to try a variation. I'll ask the questions, you tell me "yes" or "no". That's all, Harvey. "Yes" or "no". OK?' Sharpe stared across at Richter. 'You wouldn't be telling me, Harvey. I'd be telling you. That's not a discussion, is it?'

Sharpe shook his head slowly. 'No, I guess not.'

'OK. Let's try it.'

Richter paused and marshalled his thoughts. 'First,' he said, 'you know we've got copies of the films?'

'Yes.'

'We've noticed some vehicular concentrations in one area. Is that important?' The American nodded. 'Are the Russians building something there?'

Sharpe smiled for the first time. 'No, they're not.'

The way he said it made it obvious to Richter that he was way off beam. 'Were they destroying something?'

Sharpe nodded slightly. 'Yes.'

'Something new?'

'No, very old.' He leant forward again. 'And I do mean very old.'

'What – pre-war?'

His reply staggered Richter.

'No,' Sharpe said. 'Pre-Christian.'

'What?'

Sharpe shook his head. Richter thought for a few moments, then continued. 'Was what they destroyed important?'

'Completely worthless.'

Richter sat back. He hadn't expected answers like that. 'Do the films show this thing before they destroyed it?'

'Which films?'

'The ones from the Blackbird.'

'No.'

'What about the Keyhole satellite pictures? We have some taken about a month ago. Do they show it?'

'Yes.'

Richter was getting very confused. 'I'm getting lost, Harvey. The Russians have destroyed something that was over two thousand years old, but of no value whatsoever, miles out in the tundra, and for that the Company pulled a Blackbird out of retirement at Beale and flew it over the CIS?'

Sharpe nodded. 'Think laterally, Paul. There are two components to this equation, and you've only asked about one of them. Look at the films you've got, but don't look for something that's there – look for something that isn't there. I can't say any more.'

Sharpe stood up, and a final thought struck Richter. 'We didn't receive any data from the radiation detectors on the Blackbird, Harvey. Is that important?' Sharpe nodded. 'Do they show a high level of radiation?' Sharpe shook his head. 'Do they show any radiation?'

'No.' The American leaned forward and almost whispered. 'Normal background radiation only. Nothing else. Remember that – nothing else.' He eased his way out of the corner. 'That's it. I'm going home. Good luck, and remember, you didn't get it from me.'

Richter sat there, lost in thought, as the American pushed his way through the crowd towards the door.

Chapter 11

Thursday
Hammersmith, London

The following morning Richter saw Simpson again. Simpson didn't understood what Harvey had been driving at, which wasn't surprising because Richter didn't understand it either, and he was the one trying to explain it.

'Who is this guy?'

Richter shook his head. 'I protect my sources. He's an analyst with CIA London, and that's all I'll tell you.'

'But he knows what he's talking about?'

'Yes. Definitely.'

'And the films are significant – they do show something?'

'Yes – or rather, they don't show something, and that's what my source told me we should look for.'

'Don't confuse me any more. I'll contact JARIC and tell them we're coming up.'

'We?' Richter asked, surprised.

Simpson smiled slightly. 'I do get out of this office sometimes, Richter. Yes, we'll visit the Crabs and see these films. Ring the Pool and tell them we'll be taking the Jaguar.'

American Embassy, Grosvenor Square, London

'Anything yet from that Taylor character?' John Westwood asked, as the two men entered the secure briefing room.

'Nope,' Roger Abrahams replied. 'Don't forget it'll take him a while to talk his bosses into letting us access any source they've got.'

'If at all.'

Abrahams nodded. 'Yes,' he said. 'If at all.'

'What have you got now?' Westwood asked.

'Langley came through with some new data on the secure link. You saw the preliminary report on the Blackbird films and detectors?'

'Yes,' Westwood nodded. 'Just before I left.'

'Well,' said Abrahams, 'the Langley in-house experts have gone through the films and the seismic records again. I think you said the preliminary assessment was that it was a weapon in the five-megaton range?'

'About that, yes.'

'OK,' Abrahams said. 'They've had to re-think it a bit. Further analysis of the seismic records suggest that the detonation was actually about six or seven megatons. What is troubling everyone is that any radiation that was produced had to have been real short-term stuff, because the detector records on the Blackbird showed no significant radiation. That means that either it's a radiation-free nuclear weapon, which as far as we know is impossible, or the radiation it produces dissipates astonishingly quickly. So whatever this device is, it's brand new. At least, a weapon with that yield and that speed of radiation dissipation is brand new. The short version is that this looks like some kind of a super neutron bomb. What bothers them,' he finished, 'is that nobody at Langley has any idea why the Russians built it, or what the hell they're going to use it for.'

Abrahams paused. 'Langley also came up with a new instruction, John. I don't think you're going to like it, but the Company has lifted the NOFORN caveat and authorized full disclosure of all data to the British, initially only at Joint Intelligence Committee level.'

Joint Air Reconnaissance Intelligence Centre, RAF Brampton, Huntingdon, Cambridgeshire

Simpson drove fast but competently, and saw the radar speed trap on the A1 before Richter. They went through the beam at precisely fifty-nine miles per hour, and Richter touched his forelock to the two constables as the Jaguar passed their pursuit car.

'Bloody woodentops,' Simpson muttered. He had a very low opinion of the British police force. On the other hand, he was scrupulously fair – he had a very low opinion of almost everyone. Richter had the Smith under his left arm, and watched the duplicate passenger mirror like a hawk for any sign of HIS – Hostile Intelligence Service – activity, but saw nothing.

Simpson turned into the main gate at Brampton at precisely eleven fifteen, and the two men went through the usual security procedures. Kemp was waiting for them in the JARIC foyer, and extended a somewhat frosty greeting. Richter guessed that Simpson's call to him had been couched in fairly peremptory terms. As Simpson preceded him through the doorway, Kemp asked Richter in a low whisper what Simpson's rank equivalent was. Richter told him Air Vice Marshal, which in fact elevated Simpson a couple of steps, but would at least ensure that FOE got any necessary cooperation.

In the viewing room, Kemp introduced Penny Walters, who was waiting by the screen. Simpson smiled briefly and insincerely at her, then turned to Kemp. 'Right, get on with it.' Kemp took up a position behind the lectern and began his preamble. Richter could see Simpson start to turn slightly pink, a sure sign of irritation, so he interrupted.

'Squadron Leader, I think you can take it that Mr Simpson knows the details of the flight, and I can confirm his security clearance as Cosmic Top Secret. What we would like to see is what, if anything, you have found on the films.'

Kemp looked slightly confused, and beckoned to Penny. 'I haven't been involved in further analysis of this material,' he said, 'but I believe that Sub Lieutenant Walters here has had some success.'

Penny stepped forward and smiled nervously at Simpson. 'The most obvious thing I've spotted isn't something that's there – it's something that isn't. That sounds awfully confused, sir, but I'll try and explain.'

Simpson sat forward. 'That,' he said, 'is what we hoped you would say. We have had indications from another source –' he glanced over at Richter '–that the significance of these films is what they don't show, rather than what they do show.'

Penny looked puzzled, but nodded and ploughed on. 'On the satellite pictures of just over two months ago, there was a small hill, just about here.' She pulled down the map of north-west Russia that Richter remembered Kemp using on his previous visit, and pointed. Kemp looked interested.

'So?' he said.

'Well, on the Blackbird film, the hill isn't there any more. I thought at first it had been levelled for some sort of agricultural development, but it's a bit too far out in the wilderness for that. And there are no major roads anywhere near it, so I don't think that it can be for any sort of construction.' She stopped, and shrugged her shoulders. 'That's all, I'm afraid.'

'Where's it near?' Richter asked. 'I mean, what's the closest settlement?'

Penny looked at the map, measuring distances with her eyes. 'There's really not a lot up there,' she said. 'The site's right in the western foothills of the Severnyy Urals. I suppose the closest would be Anyudin, and that's about forty or fifty miles down to the south-west. But it's pretty small.'

'What about the closest cities?' Simpson asked.

'Pechora to the north-west, I suppose, or maybe Ukhta due west. They're both roughly the same distance from the site.'

There was silence for a few moments while Richter and Simpson digested the information, then Kemp spoke. 'I wonder. Could it be the first step towards the construction of a military establishment? But there should be reasonable road access – it would be prohibitively expensive to fly construction equipment to a site so remote – and that means—'

Simpson interrupted him. 'Wrong. We know it's not a proposed site. Our informant has stated categorically that the significant point is the removal of the hill.'

Kemp looked at Simpson for a moment or two, then turned to Penny. 'OK, Penny. Get the projection room to set up for binocular projection of the last satellite picture with the Blackbird film frame of the same area.'

She returned after five minutes or so, by which time the coffee Kemp had presumably ordered had arrived. Kemp acted as mother. Richter was handed a slightly chipped white mug bearing an indecipherable legend. Simpson got a cup and saucer, plus two biscuits.

'All ready.'

'Good,' said Kemp. 'Projectionist – ready?' The lights dimmed. Simpson and Richter looked at the images, and Penny supplied the commentary.

'The frame on the left is the satellite picture; source, USAF; picture taken four weeks ago; vehicle, the KH–12 Reconnaissance Satellite, more familiarly known as Keyhole. The Keyhole satellite automatically converts images into digital form, then transmits the data to one of a number of communications satellites in geo-stationary orbit above it.'

'And where does it go from there?' Simpson asked.

'Depending upon the location of the Keyhole, the communications bird beams the signal either directly, or indirectly via another communications satellite, to the Mission Ground Site at Fort Belvoir, near Washington, D.C. From Fort Belvoir, the images are passed to the National Photographic Interpretation Centre – that's N-PIC, the Americans' equivalent of JARIC – located in building 213 in the Washington Navy Yard. Keyhole technology means that the US planners and battle staff can get their pictures in as near real-time as makes no difference, usually no more than a few minutes after the picture was taken.

'We,' Penny added, 'usually have to wait a good deal longer than that to receive images from across the pond. At best it's hours, but usually it's days or even weeks. The height of the satellite at this location is approximately one hundred and thirty-five miles, but as you can see the picture quality is good. This is due to the excellent cameras, and the KH–12 provides an exceptionally stable platform for long-range surveillance photography. The frame on the right is from the Blackbird film, and it covers only the central section of the satellite picture.' She picked up a microphone from a wall bracket and spoke into it. 'Increase magnification on the left-hand frame by a factor of ten.' The picture wobbled slightly, and then seemed to accelerate towards the viewers. 'Stop. That's fine.'

She spoke to Simpson. 'We can't greatly increase the magnification of the satellite picture through the projection system, or we'll start to lose definition, but I think the two frames will now illustrate what I wanted to show you.' She picked up the microphone again. 'Superimpose the grid overlay.' The two frames, looking only slightly alike to Richter, suddenly sprouted vertical and horizontal lines; letters vertical, numbers horizontal. 'Reduce grid size on the left-hand frame by thirty per cent. Stop. Hold it there.' She walked over to the screen and took up her illuminated pointer.

'Despite their different sizes, the two gridded areas represent the same geographical area, as near as makes no difference. They look different primarily because they have a different orientation; the left-hand frame is aligned to true north, so north is conventionally at the top of the screen. The Blackbird frame, however, is effectively rotated about one hundred and ten degrees anti-clockwise, so the top of the frame is almost due east.'

She jabbed the pointer at the screen. 'First, the points of coincidence. In grid Alpha Four, this small black patch is an outcropping of slightly darker rock.' She pointed at a small blob on the left-hand frame, and then indicated a similar feature on the Blackbird still. Richter took her word for it, because the picture was still a confused blur as far as he was concerned. He wondered how long it took to train a PI Officer.

'Here we have a small spur formation, in Hotel Seven, and a similar formation up here in Papa Eighteen. Now, the hill is quite clearly visible here on the left-hand frame.' The pointer traced a dark area more or less in the centre of the frame. Richter looked over to the other picture, and he could see that there was no dark area in the corresponding grid squares – there was, in fact, a lighter patch in about the same position. Penny continued. 'On the Blackbird frame, the hill has vanished, and there appears to be a slight depression in the same position.'

Kemp interrupted. 'For Mr Simpson's benefit, could you indicate the size of the hill.'

'Certainly. To an error factor of plus or minus fifteen per cent, it is – or rather was – around two hundred feet high, five hundred feet in diameter, more or less circular, and in cross-section similar in shape to an inverted bowl.'

Kemp got up, walked to the screen and studied the two frames intently.

Simpson turned to Penny. 'Richter tells me that you detected an unusual number of vehicles in one location in these films. Is that location anywhere near this hill?'

'Yes, sir. They were about a mile away, down to the south-east.'

'Anything unusual about any of the vehicles or the loads they were carrying?'

'Nothing really, sir. As I told Commander Richter last time he was here, there were a couple of low loaders carrying a bulldozer and a digger, but all the other vehicles had rigid cargo areas. In one of the shots the civilian lorry had its rear doors open, and it looked as if it might have been carrying a small satellite dish as part of its load, but that's all.'

'Satellite dish? Are you sure?'

'Frankly, sir, no. That shot was taken on a sunny day and even though the rear doors were open, the interior of the vehicle was in deep shadow. What I saw was a light-coloured disk about one metre in diameter. It looked like a satellite dish, but it could have been a small picnic table or even a big drum for all I know.'

Kemp interrupted. 'I can't see any evidence of tracks that would have been left by heavy wheeled vehicles in either frame, and if the hill had been flattened immediately after the satellite snap, there should still be clear traces in this frame of the presence of the machinery they used.' He looked again at the screen. 'What I can see, though, are some tyre marks close to the hill in the KH–12 frame. They look as if they've been made by a medium truck – say about a three-tonner.'

Kemp tapped the left-hand picture and addressed the room. 'It takes a lot of very heavy-duty gear to shift something that size, you know. A hill like that isn't like a sand castle on the beach that you can just kick over. Even using demolition charges – and they would have had to – it would have taken at least a month to shift the earth and debris. Doing a rough mental calculation, we're talking about over one and a half million cubic metres of earth. Which is another point – where did they put it?'

'Perhaps they dug a hole and buried it,' Richter said. Penny giggled, and Simpson flashed him a look that could have fried an egg.

Simpson got up, walked over to the screen and looked at both pictures. 'We aren't, I suppose,' he asked, after a moment or two, 'looking at a nuclear weapon test site?'

There was a brief silence before Kemp replied. 'Not if it was any kind of a conventional nuclear weapon, no. Underground tests always leave a depression, like these pictures show, but they also leave a telltale circular perimeter of disturbed earth some distance from the epicentre. There is no sign of such a perimeter in these pictures.'

'What about an above-ground test?'

Kemp shook his head. 'The Russians almost always conduct underground tests. The few above-ground tests they have done have always followed the same pattern – they build a tower around a hundred feet high and detonate the weapon at the top of it. There was no evidence of a tower in any of the Keyhole pictures.'

He looked over at Penny, who shook her head decisively. 'Definitely not,' she said. 'The towers are quite unmistakable.'

'Plus,' Kemp went on, 'above-ground tests show distinctive aftertraces, and we haven't seen anything like that in the Blackbird films.'

'What about a surface detonation?' Richter asked.

'Sorry? What do you mean?' Kemp looked puzzled.

'Suppose the Russians didn't bother erecting a tower, but just stuck a weapon on the ground or maybe just below the surface, lit the blue touch-paper and walked away?'

'Why would they do that?'

'I've no idea,' Richter replied. 'I'm just offering a suggestion. Suppose that's what they did. What evidence would you expect to see on the ground afterwards?'

'I don't know,' Kemp said slowly. 'If the hill was at the centre of the detonation it would presumably be vaporized, but I would still expect to see other traces, like disturbed earth further out.' He shook his head. 'I may be wrong, but I don't think a nuclear device did this. It would be worth checking the seismic records, though, just to make sure.' Kemp paused, and then made another suggestion. 'I suppose we are looking at this from the right angle?'

'What do you mean?' Simpson asked, looking puzzled.

'Well, we have two photographs here, one showing a fairly substantial hill, and the second one, taken two months later, showing no hill and no indication as to how it was removed. We are assuming – or at least I've been assuming – that the hill has been levelled for some sort of installation which will be built in the future. But suppose we've got it backwards, and that what we are seeing is not the site of a future installation, but the site of a past one.

'Suppose the hill wasn't a hill. Suppose it was simply a camouflaged structure housing some sort of installation that the Russians have had up there for years. That could have been removed without the use of the heavy equipment needed for earth moving, couldn't it? And it would also provide the answer to the question I asked earlier, about where they put the earth.'

Simpson looked interested, glanced again at the pictures, then over at Richter, who shook his head. 'My informant stressed the fact that the artefact removed was completely worthless and old – very old. He said it was pre-Christian, and I don't think he was joking. I don't believe he just meant something like a pre-war bunker. I think he did mean something hundreds or thousands of years old – I think the hill was just a hill.

'And,' Richter continued, 'if it was artificial, what sort of installation could it have been? Bear in mind that if it was manned the people there would need food, changes of personnel, replacement equipment and spare parts. Even if it was purely some sort of monitoring station it would still need periodic checking and, presumably, repairs at odd intervals. There would have to be some evidence of transport to and from the area, even if it was only an occasional helicopter, and if there has been, I presume you haven't seen it.' He paused. 'I suppose you would have seen it?'

'I would say yes,' Kemp replied. 'We get a regular sighting of KH–12 and other surveillance satellite films, courtesy of the NSA and CIA, and even if there's too much cloud cover for normal films to show much, the infra-red detectors would easily pick up anything the size of a man in the area. A helicopter would stand out like – if you'll pardon the expression, Penny – a dog's balls.'

Richter had a thought. 'Are there any UK surveillance satellites covering that area?'

Kemp laughed. 'There wasn't any need to add the last three words. Apart from communications satellites and the geo-stationary type used by Rupert Murdoch to beam Sky television at us, the only stuff we've got going round this planet is scientific, and I mean really scientific, not

Russian scientific. We measure cosmic radiation, take pictures of stars and listen for the extra-terrestrial babblings of bug-eyed monsters, from what I can gather. What we don't do is take pictures of Mother Russia, or anywhere else.'

'I see. So we are totally dependent on the Americans for pictures of this area?'

'In a word, yes.'

Richter beat Simpson to the obvious question by about half a second. 'Have there been any significant gaps in the supply of films? I mean, any break of more than, say, a week?'

Kemp thought for a moment, then stood up. 'Lights, please. I can't recall any breaks, but I'll just go and make sure. Excuse me.'

He left and Richter put his coffee mug down. Penny walked over and sat down beside him. Simpson looked at him disapprovingly. 'What are you driving at, sir?'

'I'm not sure I know at the moment,' Richter replied. 'We're definitely missing something, and I don't know what it is. What is obvious is that the Americans had to have had some indication of something going on in north-west Russia to make them fly the Blackbird. And, as we're in the dark about what it is, it seems logical that they may have spotted something via satellite that they don't want to tell us about. If that's the case, they might therefore have simply omitted to let us see the relevant films. They might have pleaded some kind of mechanical malfunction for the critical period when whatever happened was going on.'

'Yes, that makes sense. But what is it that they don't want us to see, and why?'

Richter shook his head. 'At this moment, I've absolutely no idea.'

Sluzhba Vneshney Razvyedki Rossi
Headquarters, Yazenevo, Tëplyystan, Moscow

'When will you leave, Nicolai?' Sokolov asked.

'I will join the convoy at Minsk, on Sunday morning,' Modin replied. 'My old bones ache if I have to spend more than an hour in the back of a car. Minister Trushenko has instructed me to accompany the convoy, but he did not say from where. So, I will join it at Minsk – I can fly there on Saturday and get a good night's sleep before the journey.'

Sokolov nodded agreement, then opened the first of the folders he had brought with him. Modin looked expectantly at his old friend and comrade, but Sokolov shook his head. 'No, I haven't found the traitor, Nicolai, and I am still not really sure that there is one. We have no hard evidence, none at all. The wiretaps, intercepts and surveillance have revealed nothing, so even if one of the people indoctrinated into this project has betrayed it, he has not been in contact since the start of this investigation.'

'So what is in the folders?' Modin asked.

Sokolov held them up in front of him. 'As well as trying to find out who could have been in contact with the Americans, I also looked at the problem from the other side. I have been able to identify some officers who could not have been in contact, because of their postings to areas where no Westerner is allowed, for example. I had to assume that no traitor would be stupid enough to send evidence of his crime to the American Embassy by mail.'

Modin smiled thinly. 'Particularly not Russian mail,' he said.

'Exactly. And the same applies to telephone calls. Most long-distance calls still have to be connected by an operator, and the called numbers are always recorded. It would be too much of a risk.'

'And the result was?' Modin prompted.

'I could eliminate eight officers only,' Sokolov replied. 'Including the two of us and Minister Trushenko, that still leaves sixteen people.'

Modin sat in silence for a few moments. 'Grigori,' he said finally, 'forget about the physical evidence. You have reviewed the personal files of all the officers?'

Sokolov nodded. 'Yes, of course.'

'And you know most of them personally?' Sokolov nodded again. 'I have relied upon your intuition before,' Modin continued. 'Do you not have a feeling – however slight or irrational – about any of the officers? Let's assume that you had to pick just one of them.'

Sokolov smiled. 'You mean, if somebody told me that so-and-so was the traitor, which name would surprise me least?'

'More or less, yes.'

'I admit that I have never liked the man,' Sokolov admitted, 'and I am trying not to let that cloud my judgement, but if I had to pick just one, I would choose Viktor Bykov.'

Modin nodded and smiled bleakly. 'We always thought the same way, Grigori,' he said. 'I have already had Bykov seconded to my staff here, and he will be accompanying me to London with the weapon. If he is the traitor, he will have no chance to communicate with the Americans until the plan is implemented. I will see to that.' Sokolov nodded, his relief evident. 'However,' Modin continued, 'Bykov may be absolutely innocent, so continue your researches, old friend.'

'Of course. Now, what is the next step?'

'Apart from the placing of this weapon, all that remains is to indoctrinate the *rezidents* in the target cities into the plan and instruct them on the procedures they are to follow. That is being done as we speak.'

Joint Air Reconnaissance Intelligence Centre, RAF Brampton, Huntingdon, Cambridgeshire

'You're right,' Kemp said. 'There was one short period of about eight days, just after the last set of KII–12 pictures that this frame came from. There was a "command failure" which took a week to rectify, during which time no pictures were received from the satellite.'

Penny smiled at Richter. 'I didn't realize you were psychic,' she said.

'I'm not,' he replied, 'I'm just a real good guesser, and I'm prepared to lay money that whatever alerted the Americans took place during that period when they are claiming that the satellite was out of action. Probably they detected more evidence of vehicular movement in the area, and that sparked their interest. Then when the hill vanished from the KH–12 pictures, they flew the Blackbird to get a closer look at the site.'

'There's another point as well,' Kemp added. 'Although we've been getting KH–12 pictures since the command failure, we've received none showing this location, or anything within about a hundred miles of it.'

'I'm not entirely surprised,' Richter said.

'So now what?' Kemp fired the question at Richter, but Simpson fielded it.

'From JARIC's point of view, I think that's it. I don't think there's anything more to be gained from analysis of these films. We've identified the fact that the hill has vanished. What we now have to do is find out how the Russians managed it, and why the Americans don't want to tell us about it. And that's our job.'

Babushka Restaurant, Central Moscow

John Rigby had been an agency professional for a long time, and had easily spotted the tail as he left the American Embassy on Novinskij bulvar, but he had made no attempt to shake it. A golden rule for any covert operative is never to shake a tail, because doing that identifies the person being followed as a professional, which immediately blows his cover as a covert agent. A professional who believes he is being followed will simply proceed about his lawful business or, if he was actually en route for some kind of nefarious activity, abandon his plans and do something completely innocent and legal. John Rigby was just going out for lunch, so he ignored the man in the dark blue VAZ as he looked for a parking space.

The Babushka Restaurant just off Nikitskaja ulitsa was small and intimate, and a popular lunchtime venue for foreign diplomats and newsmen. Rigby was a regular there, and nodded to several acquaintances as he hung his overcoat on the end peg just inside the restaurant doorway. Rather than join any of the people he knew, Rigby selected a small table for two in the far corner. He sat with his back to the wall, facing the restaurant entrance, ordered his meal and then buried himself in a two-day-old copy of the *Wall Street Journal*.

Despite his apparent absorption in his paper, Rigby was paying close attention to the comings and goings at the restaurant, and particularly to the area near the coat rack. Ever since the last message from RAVEN he had been making himself even more visible than before, eating three meals a day in various Moscow restaurants, taking walks in Gorky Park, shopping in GUM or just wandering the Moscow streets. His duodenal ulcer had been complaining ever since this routine had started, and he was beginning to lose sleep as well.

As he ate the rather plain meal and drank the glass of milk that was all he could tolerate without reaching for his bottle of pills, Rigby wondered if Langley was right. Initially he had been instructed to make absolutely no attempt to identify RAVEN, for fear of alarming him, but since finding the message in his car, Langley had been frantic to get any indication of the identity of the disaffected Russian. Rigby had spent hours memorizing the faces of the most senior officers in the GRU and the SVR plus, where photographs existed, those of their principal assistants, friends and associates. That hadn't helped identify RAVEN, although Rigby had detected certain liaisons of which CIA Moscow had not previously been aware.

At every meal, and every time he went out anywhere, Rigby had tried, as surreptitiously as possible, to be aware of anyone who approached him, his overcoat – which he invariably took off in every bar and restaurant he visited – or his car. To date, his vigilance had yielded absolutely nothing, because RAVEN had simply failed to make contact.

Rigby drank the last of his milk, and then went into the toilet at the back of the restaurant. When he returned to his table, he called for the bill, paid it, and collected his coat. He glanced carefully around the restaurant before he left, but paid no particular attention to the grey-haired man sitting alone at the far corner of the bar, head buried in his newspaper, which was perhaps unfortunate. The man's face would have been almost as familiar to Rigby as his own, and if he had identified him, the CIA's search for source RAVEN would have been over.

It wasn't until he was outside in the street and walking away from the restaurant that his probing fingers detected the small cylindrical object in his overcoat pocket. Rigby returned immediately to the restaurant, and looked closely at everyone there, even checking the restroom. As he turned to leave for the second time, he noticed that the bar stool in the far corner was unoccupied, the newspaper and an empty glass sitting innocently on the bar top.

Kutuzovskij prospekt, Moscow

'Hullo?' Genady Arkenko said as he picked up the telephone.

The voice at the other end didn't bother with introductions, just passed the message. 'Phase Two has been truncated. Implement Option Two Alpha immediately.'

Genady Arkenko repeated the message and put down the telephone. Then he removed a single page from a large notepad and placed it on a piece of hardboard, which he had already confirmed would not register the impression of anything written on it, sat down and composed a short message in block capitals. He walked over to the radio, took a one-time pad from a locked drawer, sat down again at the table and encoded the message.

The radio set Dmitri Trushenko had provided included a squirt or burst transmitter – a device which allowed messages to be compressed to a fraction of their proper length, transmitted, and then recorded and expanded by the receiving equipment. Arkenko initialized the system, and input the encrypted message into the transmitter's tape recorder using a Morse key. Then he re-recorded the message on to the second, high-speed tape deck. When he pressed the transmit key, the red 'transmit' light illuminated for less than a quarter of a second, barely time enough for any detection equipment to register the transmission, and nowhere near long enough for any kind of fix or triangulation to be obtained.

In the corner of the room, tucked behind a bookcase, was a small paper shredder. Arkenko took the page from the one-time pad, and the sheet of notepaper he had used to compose the message, and fed them both through the machine. Then he opened the shredder's receptacle, removed the thin strips of paper, took them over to the fireplace and burned them. Finally, he used the master erase function on both the tape recorders in the radio installation to obliterate the two copies of the message he had sent.

Six minutes after he had received the telephone call, no trace of the message he had relayed could be found anywhere in the room. Genady Arkenko was a very careful man.

OVERKILL

Cambridgeshire and London

In the XJ6 on the way back to London, Simpson sat silent most of the time, which Richter ascribed to perhaps one glass of wine too many at lunch – certainly he had tossed Richter the keys as they had made their way back to the car park. However, as the Jaguar approached the northern suburbs Simpson seemed to rouse himself. 'Conclusions?' he asked.

'At the moment I haven't got any,' Richter replied, 'but I think I'm beginning to see what's going on. More importantly, I can understand why my CIA source was telling me that the problem had two components, and that I was looking at the wrong one.'

'Go on,' Simpson nodded.

'Since we got involved with this, we've been looking for things on films. We looked at the hill on the KH–12 films, and at the hole where the hill used to be on the Blackbird footage. In fact, I think the hill's irrelevant. What's important is how the Russians destroyed it – that's the second component of the problem, and that's what my source was trying to tell me.'

Simpson mulled over this for a few minutes. 'What are your intentions now?' he asked.

'Research. Shifting that much earth had to cause a bang, so the first thing I'm going to do is check the seismic records. Then I'm going to have to think about it.'

Simpson nodded. 'Don't think for too long. I'm getting a bad feeling about all this, and I think it's time we started taking some action.'

Anton Kirov

The *Anton Kirov* had made good time. The transit through the Bosphorus had been completed by early afternoon and by 1500 local time the ship was crossing the Marmara Denizi, the short stretch of water between Istanbul and the Dardanelles. Captain Bondarev was sitting down to a late lunch in his cabin when Zavorin knocked briefly and entered. 'Valeri,' he said, 'there has been a slight change of plan.'

187

'Yes?' Bondarev put down his fork and looked up.

Colonel Zavorin smiled. 'Nothing too drastic. We have been ordered not to call at Athens. Moscow wants us to make best speed across the Aegean and the Mediterranean, and our first port of call will probably now be Tunis.'

Bondarev grunted. 'Did our lords and masters say why?'

'No, but I presume that our arrival time in Gibraltar has been brought forward.'

Bondarev grunted again. He wasn't fond of Athens, but he was finding it increasingly irksome being a ship's captain who was not allowed to take any decisions. 'Very well,' he said. 'I will make the signals.'

Le Moulin au Pouchon, *St Médard, near Manciet, Midi-Pyrénées, France*

Unusually, there were three emails containing encrypted messages for Hassan Abbas to decode that afternoon. All from a German address, they had actually originated in Moscow, sent from Dmitri Trushenko's spacious office at the Ministry. As a minister, Trushenko was entitled to a single unmonitored telephone line with international access. All the other office lines went through one or more switchboards where, Trushenko was quite certain, either or both the SVR and the GRU – and maybe even the CIA and SIS – had placed taps.

The secure line was checked for bugs daily, and he was certain it was safe. Early in his term at the Ministry Trushenko had telephoned a trusted colleague and, with his agreement and – for the safety of both men – with witnesses present at both ends of the line, the two men had engaged in a pre-scripted conversation so blatantly traitorous that no monitoring organization could have failed to take immediate action. Nothing had happened. Nobody had kicked in his door in the early hours of the morning, or frog-marched him out of the Ministry to the cells at the Lubyanka. He had repeated the exercise a couple of times a year ever since then, with precisely the same absence of results.

The line was intended to allow ministers to converse frankly with colleagues without fear of being overheard and subsequently forced to listen to taped statements that they should never have made. Trushenko used the line sparingly for telephone calls, partly because he was supremely conscious of the security implications of the operation in which he was involved, but mainly because he was essentially a loner and not much given to chatting with colleagues.

However, virtually every day he connected his laptop to the telephone socket next to his desk, because that enabled him to send and receive email messages with as much security as was possible in Moscow. And with *Podstava* now approaching its final stages, close liaison with the ragheads, as Trushenko dismissively termed them, was essential.

The first two emails Abbas decoded were simple enough. One confirmed that the last device – the London weapon – was as good as finished and would be ready to leave the factory in Russia the following evening. The second advised him that the route of the small freighter carrying the demonstration device had been changed so that the ship would arrive in Gibraltar earlier than had originally been planned. Abbas read them, opened a spreadsheet on his computer and input the dates and times. Then he spent some time composing and encrypting an email for Sadoun Khamil which relayed the same information to him.

It would have been easy enough for Dmitri Trushenko to have sent copies of his emails simultaneously to Khamil, but from the start the leaders of al-Qaeda had insisted that the liaison with the Russians would be handled solely by Hassan Abbas, to avoid any possibility of compromising any other members of the organization.

The third email was the most interesting, and Abbas read it several times before composing his message to Khamil. Trushenko had couched his information in guarded terms, but his analysis of the implications of the over-flight by the American spy-plane was thorough. When he'd received the first brief message which simply stated that an over-flight had taken place, it had been immediately obvious to Abbas, as it had been to Trushenko, that some kind of a leak must have occurred. Trushenko's considered opinion now was that this leak was an irritant, nothing more, because the operation was so nearly complete, with only two weapons still left to be positioned, and after some thought Abbas was inclined to agree.

In fact, from the point of view of al-Qaeda, everything they required was already in place, so whether the London weapon was successfully delivered or not made little or no difference to them.

Hammersmith, London

When Richter got back to the office, he jotted down some dates on a piece of paper. Then he called the Registry and requested the Seismic Activity file and the Moscow Station activity files.

When they arrived, Richter went back through each for two months, and read all the subsequent reports. Then he checked the dates he had noted against one of the seismic reports, and then he knew why the Blackbird had flown, and why it had been so important for the Americans to take pictures of a hill that wasn't there any more. The only things Richter didn't know were how the Russians had done it, and what their next move was likely to be. The answer to the first question he might be able to find out by research, but the second Richter could only guess at. And his guess frightened him.

Richter made a long telephone call to a contact at the Ministry of Defence, then he called Simpson on the direct line and told him he was coming up.

Office of the Director of Operations (Clandestine Services), Central Intelligence Agency Headquarters, Langley, Virginia

Clifford Masters, Director of the CIA's Intelligence Division, knocked and walked into the office. 'We've heard from RAVEN again,' he began without preamble.

Hicks looked interested. 'About time. The same transmission method?'

'Yes,' Masters replied. 'And again it wasn't a film, just a short note in a film canister. It was passed to John Rigby in a Moscow restaurant at lunchtime today, in broad daylight.'

'Did he see who delivered it?' Hicks asked.

'No,' Masters shook his head. 'As usual, Rigby hung up his overcoat when he arrived, and tried to identify anyone who went anywhere near it. He saw no known opposition personnel in the restaurant, and only left the table to go to the john – he says he was away for less than five minutes – but when he left the restaurant he found the film canister in his overcoat pocket. He went straight back inside, but saw nobody he recognized.'

'Well,' Hicks said. 'At least we know that RAVEN is still alive and operational, which has to be good news. What was the message?'

Masters opened the file he was carrying and extracted a sheet of paper. 'We've had the Russian translated, and double-checked. Like all of RAVEN's messages it's very brief and cryptic. It contains a single word and two short sentences. The single word is *Pripiska*.'

Hicks looked blank, and Masters nodded. 'Yes, this puzzled our analysts as well. It's actually a slang term dating back to the bad old days of the collective farms and Ten-Year Plans. It means the falsification of records and other documentation to do with agricultural and industrial production. In those days, cooking the books was about the only way the farms and factories could meet the targets and quotas specified by Moscow.'

'And the sentences?'

Masters looked at Hicks before replying. 'They translate as "Last component enters west on 9th. Implementation date 11th." And that,' he added, 'is exactly seven days away.'

Hammersmith, London

'I think I've worked it out,' Richter said.

Simpson nodded encouragingly and looked at his watch. 'Make it snappy. There's an extraordinary meeting of the Joint Intelligence Committee in under an hour, which means I've got to leave here in exactly twenty minutes.'

'OK,' Richter said. 'I'll give you the short version.' Simpson motioned him to a seat. Since the beginning of the investigation, their relationship had improved considerably. Richter still couldn't say that he actually liked the man because he didn't, but at least they weren't sniping at each other quite as much as before. 'Why,' Richter asked, as he sat down, 'is there an extraordinary meeting of the JIC? And why so late in the day?' Richter had checked his watch, and it was already nearly five.

'I don't know,' Simpson said, 'but I'll let you know if it has any bearing on this.'

'Thanks. Right, I think I've worked out when they moved the hill. The last KH–12 film that JARIC received prior to the Blackbird's flight was taken a month ago, and they didn't receive any further films at all from the KH–12 for eight days, and they've still had no further pictures of the area round the hill. I believe that the films shot by the Keyhole satellite showed something so unusual that the Americans decided a "command failure" was necessary. Again I don't know, but logic suggests that this was the placement of a device in or on the hill.'

'Device?' said Simpson. 'You obviously mean some sort of a bomb.'

'I do mean some sort of a bomb,' Richter agreed, 'but I don't know what sort, except that it's something totally new. I'll explain later why it has to be new. The Blackbird flew last week, so whatever happened out there on the tundra had to have taken place between four weeks ago and last week, and most likely closer to four weeks ago.'

'Why?' asked Simpson, then shook his head. 'I'm not thinking straight,' he said. 'It had to be three to four weeks because of the lead-time needed to mount the Blackbird flight.'

'Exactly. Just sorting out the logistics of getting a plane out of mothballs at Beale and across the pond probably took at least a week.' Richter held up the Seismic Activity file. 'I went back two months in this, just to make sure, but there was nothing significant reported from anywhere in the Eurasian landmass throughout that period, but on the second of last month there was—'

'Don't tell me,' Simpson interrupted. 'Let me guess. A major explosion was detected in the Bolshezemel'skaya Tundra.' Richter nodded. 'So?'

'That was the easy bit. The seismic record shows that the Russians detonated a medium-size nuclear weapon way out in the tundra. What doesn't make too much sense is the rest of the data. The Seismic Activity pack usually only contains traces from the seismograph recorders plus a summary about the likely source from one of the scientists, but this incident generated a number of highly technical little notes from the boffins at Aldermaston.'

Simpson looked at his watch. 'And what do these notes say – briefly?'

'I'm not a scientist,' Richter went on, 'but the gist of the matter seems to be that the nuclear explosion was unlike anything the Russians have detonated before. The seismic signature doesn't match anything they are known to have developed for their nuclear arsenal. It also doesn't correspond to any weapon type developed by the Americans, so the obvious implication is that the weapon is entirely new.'

Richter paused and Simpson looked at him appraisingly. 'So what?' he asked.

'That's precisely the point,' Richter replied. 'So the Russians have developed a new bomb, but so what?'

Simpson looked at his watch again. 'I've got to go,' he said, and stood up. 'So what have we got?'

'I still don't really know,' Richter said. 'What I've read in the files and what Kemp at JARIC said about the lack of normal post-weapon test traces on the tundra suggests that the Russians have developed a completely new form of nuclear bomb. What I don't understand is why that should make the Americans so cagey about telling us.'

'Well,' said Simpson. 'I might be able to tell you that tomorrow, because this extraordinary JIC meeting has been called on behalf of the London CIA Chief of Station.'

Chapter Twelve

Friday
Hammersmith, London

Richter received a brief call at home just before eight in the morning from Sheila, Simpson's PA. 'Committee Room Two at nine, please.'

When Richter reached the third floor, it was clear that he hadn't been the only operative to receive a summons. The Committee Room seated twenty-four, and there were only five seats spare once he'd sat down. Simpson was at the head of the table, the Intelligence Director on his right. Simpson looked round the table, checking that everyone was present and correct, nodded to himself and then began. 'We have a problem,' he said, without preamble. 'To date the only people who have been aware of this matter have been Richter and myself, although the ID has been consulted about certain aspects of it. Some of you will have heard about the death of Graham Newman, the SIS Head of Station Moscow.'

There were murmurs of sympathy from around the table. 'What you will not know is that Graham Newman did not die in a car crash. That was, and will remain, the official version. Richter's researches indicate that Newman was almost certainly snatched by the SVR, and we have concluded that he died under interrogation in Moscow.' The murmurs turned to angry whispering. 'That is unusual enough, especially in the current climate of better east–west relations, but there is more. Last week a Lockheed SR–71A Blackbird spy-plane was pulled out of retirement to make a covert flight over north-western Russia. The aircraft was slightly damaged during the flight and was very short of fuel when it cleared Russian airspace. It was unable to rendezvous with any of its support tankers or to reach its airfield of departure – Mildenhall – and it was forced to land at RAF Lossiemouth.'

The room was entirely silent, everyone hanging on Simpson's words. 'The photographic intelligence experts at JARIC analysed copies of the Blackbird films that were supplied – under a certain amount of duress – by the Americans. They also ran comparisons between KH–12 satellite pictures they had on file and the SR–71A films, but their initial report was inconclusive. No new installations were detected, and there seemed no adequate reason why the Americans had wanted pictures of the terrain over which the aircraft flew.' Incomprehension was showing on a number of faces. 'Richter visited JARIC to examine the films, and on leaving was attacked by an assassination team, later and posthumously identified as Russian.' Simpson looked straight at him, as did everybody else round the table.

'I was lucky,' Richter said. 'They ran out of road.'

'Quite,' Simpson said dryly, and continued. 'Richter is well known for his wide and somewhat eccentric contact list, and he was able to persuade a CIA analyst to give us some pointers about the Blackbird films, despite their NOFORN caveat. His source stated that it wasn't what was showing on the films that was important, but what wasn't. Further study by JARIC staff showed that a hill deep in the Bolshezemel'skaya Tundra had vanished.

'We considered the possibility that the hill hadn't been a hill at all – that it had been some sort of camouflaged installation – but we have concluded that this was not the case. Richter's informant was quite specific in stating that the object removed was both completely worthless and very old, and none of the satellite photographs on file at JARIC showed any sign of activity at the location. So, we have to conclude that the hill was just a hill.'

Simpson poured himself a glass of water. 'Yesterday Richter checked the seismic recordings. These showed that on the second of last month seismic activity of an unusual sort was detected in the vicinity of the hill. I don't pretend to understand the technicalities of it, but the boffins here got quite excited. The hill was apparently destroyed by a nuclear weapon, but one without a known signature. In other words, a new type of bomb.'

He changed tack. Simpson had always given good briefings – short, concise and precisely to the point. Nobody ever fell asleep when he was talking. 'Last night I attended an extraordinary meeting of the Joint Intelligence Committee, which was extraordinary in more than one sense of the word. First, it was called by the CIA Chief of Station – Roger Abrahams – who was accompanied by a man called John Westwood. He's the Head of the CIA Foreign Intelligence Staff – a Langley big wheel. Secondly, it was a meeting without minutes. All secretarial staff were excluded, and restrictions were placed on all attendees.

'Roger Abrahams and John Westwood took the chair, as it were, and told us a very interesting story. It's a story at the moment without an ending, which is why you're all here now. The CIA needs our help, for reasons which will become clear later.

'First, a history lesson, which I'll keep as brief as possible. Following the accession to power of Gorbachev and Yeltsin, the entire fabric of Russian society changed. The nation opened up to the West and to Western ideas, but this actually created more problems than it solved with, for example, member states of the former USSR breaking away to try to do their own thing. Names like Chechnya, Kazakhstan and Uzbekistan entered the languages of the world, usually associated with violent protests against Moscow and Russia.

'Obviously nobody anticipated the Westernization of Russia would proceed without difficulties, but there were actually far more obstacles than anyone expected. Instead of the optimism that might have been expected, a significant proportion of the peoples of the Confederation of Independent States began protesting against the new regime. Their argument, reduced to its simplest form, was that although things had been bad under Communist rule, at least everybody knew where they were and what was going on. Under Gorbachev and Yeltsin, the situation was entirely new, and they felt cut adrift, their normal points of reference removed. This mood led to the attempted *coup* against the new leaders.

'That,' Simpson said, 'is the history. The CIA has maintained intense surveillance of Russia throughout this period, and has come up with some interesting data. First, overt defence spending in the former USSR has slowed considerably. The CIA and all other Western intelligence services have noted a reduction in the build rate of combat aircraft, submarines and ships, and a lot of building has stopped entirely. This should have freed significant amounts of capital into the general economy, but neither the CIA nor anyone else has been able to detect any evidence of this. The queues outside the shops in Moscow are just as long – in fact, most of them are a lot longer – and the food shortages are just as apparent. What the CIA has been trying to find out is where the "spare" money has been going.'

Simpson glanced round the table again. 'The CIA has come up with a controversial hypothesis. If it is assumed that actual defence spending is the same as previously, then the secret development of a new weapon is a real probability. Further, if this hypothetical new weapon is sufficiently unusual that it makes existing weapons obsolete or nearly so, then it is possible that *glasnost* is just a front to lull the West into a false sense of security, and that Russia is actually planning some kind of first-strike against us.'

American Embassy, Grosvenor Square, London

'We've heard from SIS,' Roger Abrahams said, closing the briefing room door behind him.

'And?' John Westwood looked up from the file open in front of him.

'And nothing. Officially, the Secret Intelligence Service regrets that it is unable to assist, but requests that we keep Piers Taylor fully informed.'

Westwood considered this. '"Unable to assist" – does that mean that they can't, or that they just won't?'

Abrahams shrugged. 'Whatever. It could be either, but my guess is that they can't. Either way, we're going nowhere here. Do you want me to keep Taylor in the loop?'

Westwood nodded his head. 'Yes. The directive from Langley was clear enough about that,' he said. He slapped the file closed and looked at his watch. 'I'd better talk to Langley, and now I'll have to go see the French. Signal the Paris Chief of Station that I'm coming, and then get me on a flight to Paris tomorrow morning.'

Hammersmith, London

There were sharp intakes of breath around the table and two people started to ask questions. Simpson stopped them. 'Questions later. I should say that I don't personally subscribe to this first-strike theory, and I would normally assume that it's just the usual CIA paranoia. However, the killing of Newman, the attempted assassination of Richter, and the vaporization of a hill in the tundra have to be considered. We can ignore none of these. Something is definitely going on, and we are going to find out what. The Americans have come to the same conclusion as us about the bomb used to vaporize the hill, according to John Westwood. They believe it's a new weapon, but not one offering an unusually high yield. That appears to be the limit of their knowledge. They don't know how it works or what its significance is.

'The final point is the most important, and is the real reason why Westwood is here in Britain. The CIA has acquired a high-level source in Russia, and this source claims that some form of covert assault against the West has actually been launched by Russia.' In the silence which followed, Simpson held up his hand, and began ticking points off on his fingers. 'To save time, I'll run through the obvious questions, and what we believe the answers are.

'First, the "first-strike" option. I don't believe – and I don't think the CIA really believes – that this actually is an option, despite this covert assault business. Whatever the type of bomb, it still has to be delivered, and all Western defence systems are designed to detect not only weapon launches, but all the build-up beforehand. We simply could not fail to be aware of the increased ballistic missile submarine activity, higher alert states at bomber airfields, missile bases and so on that would have to be a precursor to a first-strike. So, if the Russians are planning something sneaky, it has to involve an unconventional delivery system.

'Second, the bomb itself. A bomb is a bomb. It goes bang and causes damage; everything else is a question of degree. The seismograph records – both the ones we have seen and those acquired by the CIA – indicate that although this weapon has some unusual characteristics, its yield is about the same as a small to medium-sized conventional nuclear bomb, around five to seven megatons, so it's difficult to see what advantage could be gained by its use, rather than a weapon which already exists.'

Richter put his hand in the air. Simpson looked at him, then nodded. 'The other thing my CIA source emphasized was that the radiation detectors on the Blackbird gave nil results,' Richter said. 'Whatever the weapon was that the Russians used, it didn't emit the fall-out that a conventional nuclear bomb would have generated.'

After a short silence, Simpson nodded and spoke again. 'Oddly enough, neither Roger Abrahams nor John Westwood mentioned that, and they really should have known about it, shouldn't they?'

'If my source knows,' Richter replied, 'they know, no question. I know John Westwood,' he added, 'and he's sharp and very competent. If he didn't tell you, it's because he didn't want you to know.'

The Intelligence Director stirred uncomfortably and offered a contribution. 'That data, if substantiated, could radically influence any subsequent actions taken by the Russians.' He always talked as if he was delivering a lecture to a class of university students. 'MAD – Mutual Assured Destruction – was predicated on the twin premises that any aggressive action would be matched by retaliation in kind, and that no nation could survive the nuclear winter that would follow any significant exchange of nuclear weapons. The nuclear winter, of course, would be caused primarily by the radiation products of the weapons themselves. If you remove the radiation, to some extent you remove the nuclear winter.'

Simpson nodded agreement. 'True enough, but that somewhat misses the point. If the Russians have developed a radiation-free weapon with a yield equivalent to a normal fission or fusion weapon – a kind of strategic neutron bomb, in fact – and if they equipped their armoury with it, that could actually encourage the West to launch a pre-emptive attack. If we take that scenario to its logical conclusion, the West would be able to lob bombs willy-nilly on to the Russian landmass, rendering it uninhabitable for possibly centuries to come, whilst the Russians would only be able to retaliate by launching what would amount to very large conventional weapons. In other words, if Richter's informant is correct, the development and deployment of such a weapon would actually disadvantage the Russians.' Simpson paused and drummed his fingers on the table. 'We're missing something here, and I don't mind admitting that I don't know what it is.'

His thought processes were interrupted by a respectful double tap on the door, which opened to reveal Simpson's PA. Simpson nodded, and she retreated briefly before shepherding in two of FOE's elderly female retainers pushing Ministry-issue tea trolleys. When all the people sitting round the table had selected either lukewarm tea or lukewarm coffee, and paid excessively for it, the retainers shuffled out again and the door closed firmly.

Simpson took a sip, then put down his cup with a grimace and continued. 'So, what have we got? In summary, we've got a weapon which the Russians seem desperate to stop us finding out about, and which, if they deploy it, would apparently benefit the Western alliance. I don't need to tell you that that is complete nonsense. Any thoughts?'

He glanced round the table encouragingly. The Intelligence Director opened his mouth to speak, but apparently thought better of it and closed it with a snap.

'What I don't like about this,' Simpson went on, 'is that I personally think that the Americans do know what's going on, or at least they know more than they're telling us. I think they're trying to drive us in a particular direction for reasons of their own. What those reasons are I don't know, but I am sure we're being misdirected. The ball, as it were, is in the air, and that's what we're watching, but what we should be looking at are the players. However, I think this is probably a side issue, and one that we will be able to resolve later. The important thing is that we are now involved, and we have things to do. Any comments on the central issue?'

Nobody spoke. Simpson didn't seem put out by the lack of useful response, and continued briskly. 'Right – actions. There are a lot of peculiarities about this situation, and I intend to launch some immediate actions to find out what's really going on.' He opened the briefcase on the table in front of him, and began tasking operatives, passing each a slim pink folder containing assignment details. Clearly he had spent most of the night in the building preparing for this meeting. His strategy was comprehensive but simple, intended to ascertain Russian intentions and if possible the true nature of the weapon.

One liaison officer was appointed to work directly with MI5 to look at Russian activity in Britain, and several to perform the same function with SIS, studying Russian operations abroad. Others were to work with the Naval Intelligence Department and the intelligence arms of the other armed forces, two with the Foreign and Colonial Office and a further two with CIA London. Another was to go to Aldermaston and to a specialist at the Science Museum to discuss the seismographic evidence, which just left Richter.

'Richter,' Simpson said, sliding a folder down the table towards him. 'It looks like a nice day for a drive. You have an appointment in Cambridge at two thirty this afternoon.' Simpson looked round the table. 'Until this matter is resolved, Thomas, Williams and Lowry will act as Duty Officers, working a three-watch system and will collate the data gathered. Assessment of the information will be handled by myself and the Intelligence Director. We will have a brief meeting every evening at seven, and another in the morning at nine to discuss overnight developments. All available operatives are to attend both.'

Simpson wound up the briefing. 'One last point. The attempt on Richter's life at Brampton is an indication of the seriousness of this situation. With immediate effect, operatives are to be armed at all times. Those of you who are not currently carrying weapons are to report to my outer office immediately after this briefing for the issue of carry permits and other documentation. You are then to visit the Armoury to collect pistols and ammunition and to fire the weapons. This is to be completed before you leave this building for any reason.' He looked directly at Richter, then continued. 'Unless any of you object, you will be issued with Browning nine millimetre semi-automatic pistols.' Simpson looked at the clock over the door. 'Right, briefing completed at ten zero three. Let's get on with it.'

American Embassy, Grosvenor Square, London

'What do you think, John? Is it can't or won't?' Walter Hicks asked, his voice echoing on the scrambled transatlantic line.

'I don't know for sure,' Westwood replied, 'and nor does Roger, but if you asked me for my guess, I'd say it's probably a bit of both. We've no indication that SIS has got a highly placed source in Moscow. There's been nothing in any of the British intelligence summaries I've seen in the last six months to suggest they've got anyone other than the usual low-level informers on the fringes of the government and military. Plus, we've really got nothing to go on, no hard evidence to show SIS, so even if they had a source, they probably wouldn't agree to risk him, despite our disclosures to the JIC. And,' he added, 'I wouldn't blame them.'

'No, I guess not,' Hicks agreed.

'OK, John, we have some good news and some bad,' Cliff Masters said from Langley. 'The good news is that Rigby was contacted again by RAVEN yesterday.'

'Yesterday?' John Westwood asked. 'Why the delay in letting me know?'

'The usual reasons,' Walter Hicks said. 'First we had to get the message from Moscow to Langley, then get it translated – which caused some problems – and checked. Then we had to decide what to do about it. This one, John, was very specific.'

'Yes?'

'RAVEN states that the last component will enter the West on the ninth of this month – that's next Tuesday. He also says that implementation will take place two days later, on Thursday the eleventh.'

'What does he mean by "component"?' Roger Abrahams asked.

'We don't know,' Masters replied, 'but the consensus here is that he must mean a weapon of some sort.'

'Jesus Christ,' Westwood muttered. 'Did the message say anything else?'

'That was the entire text, apart from a single Russian word – *Pripiska*.'

'And what the hell does that mean?' Abrahams asked.

'That was the word that caused the delay in translation,' Hicks said. 'According to the Linguistics Section, it's old-Russian slang and it means generating false statements about agricultural and industrial production. "Cooking the books" is about as close to an accurate translation as we can get.'

'I don't see what possible connection that can have with this assault,' Westwood said.

'Nor do we,' Hicks said. 'Our analysts' best assessment is that *Pripiska* is simply the Russian code-name for the operation, but that's really just a guess. OK,' Hicks continued, his voice brisk, 'we now have a date, something to aim for, but it doesn't really change anything. I still want you to go to Paris, John, and see if you can get anything out of the French. Roger – talk to your SIS man again, and pass the substance of this new message to the Joint Intelligence Committee. I don't suppose it'll do any good, but you never know.'

'What are you going to do?' Westwood asked.

'We have very few options, John,' Hicks replied. 'The Director of Central Intelligence is still away, so I'm presently the acting Director. I have a meeting with the President in a little less than two hours, and as far as I can see I don't have too many options. I'm going to suggest he treats the threat as real and kicks the military into action.'

East Anglia

Richter drove up to Cambridge on the Old North Road, the A10, rather than the faster A1(M) or M11 motorways, and was approaching Ware when he spotted the grey Vauxhall. Four cars behind the elderly Escort supplied by the Motor Pool – the Transport Officer obviously still hadn't forgotten about the Granada – Richter saw the Cavalier. A common, even unremarkable, car, but what bothered Richter was that he had seen the same vehicle three times before on the journey, always well behind him but, essentially, always behind him.

He patted his left armpit to reassure himself that the Smith and Wesson was snug in its holster, and decided what to do. There was always the chance that the driver was entirely innocent, and that it was simple chance that he was following the same route, but Richter didn't believe in chance.

First, confirm the tail. He checked the road ahead and selected a garage a quarter of a mile in front. He indicated left, pulled on to the forecourt, stopped beside the pumps, climbed out and watched the road closely. The Cavalier drove past, its two occupants seeming to take no notice of him whatsoever. Richter shrugged. Maybe he was getting paranoid. But, he reflected, just because you're paranoid it doesn't mean they're not out to get you.

Richter pumped ten pounds' worth of fuel into the Escort's tank, paid at the kiosk, started up and pulled out, heading north. He checked every driveway and turn-off he passed for the next five miles and saw absolutely no sign of a Vauxhall Cavalier, grey or any other colour. He shrugged again, and dismissed the incident from his mind.

He was near Buntingford when he decided to stop for lunch. He pulled into the car park of the next pub he came to, locked the Escort and walked into the lounge bar. He ordered a club sandwich and a coffee, and sat down at a corner table from which he had a good view of the pub door and the road outside. About a dozen cars parked outside while he was eating, none of them Cavaliers, and the pub's bars filled steadily.

Richter finished his lunch, stood up, brushed the crumbs from his jacket, nodded a farewell to the barman and walked outside. As he turned towards the parking spot where he'd left the Escort, Richter glimpsed a grey Vauxhall Cavalier about fifty yards down the road, well out of sight of the pub's windows. He'd taken only a couple of steps further when something hard was pushed into the middle of his back and a hoarse and unmistakably Essex voice murmured in his ear. 'A word with you, my son.'

Richter froze, his mind figuring the angles before he started to move. Then he saw a second man approaching from his right. Big, bulky and with the kind of face even a devoted mother would have a job cradling to her bosom. He was wearing a brown coat over his shoulders like a cape, but not because the day was cold. He had the coat on to help conceal the whippet – a sawn-off double-barrel twelve-bore shotgun with a pistol grip – he was carrying in his right hand. The chances were, Richter realized, that the object pressing against his spine was the other half of the pair, and that changed the odds, seriously.

Richter's ace in the hole was the Smith, but before he could even think about using it, he had to get these two comedians where he wanted them – in front of him.

'Over 'ere,' the man in the brown coat said, inclining his head towards the waste ground at the rear of the pub. His accent confirmed Richter's suspicion that he was dealing with a couple of contractors hired from the underworld by a cut-out, not SVR agents or professionals. That, he hoped, would help a little.

The man behind him shoved Richter forwards, and he walked in the direction indicated, his arms held wide apart. At the edge of the wood which extended up the hill at the back of the pub, they told Richter to stop. He did so, and turned to face the two men. Both were holding whippets, and both were smiling, but they were the kind of smiles that didn't reach their eyes.

'We 'ear you've bin a bad boy,' the man with the brown coat said, menace apparent in every syllable. Good God, Richter thought, they've been learning their dialogue from the television. 'A very bad boy, and my colleague 'ere is goin' to teach you a lesson.'

The other man placed his whippet carefully on the ground, then reached into his coat pocket and pulled out two lengths of iron pipe each about a foot long. Never taking his eyes off Richter, he slowly and carefully screwed the two lengths together, then hefted the weapon in his hand.

Richter knew exactly what they intended to do. This was going to be a mugging that went wrong. No knife wounds, no bullets, just a few well-placed blows from the pipe and he'd be dead inside two minutes, his wallet gone and the police with even less clues than usual. What he had to do was get the man in close, close enough to disable him and so close that the other man wouldn't be able to fire his weapon. But he also had to increase the distance between himself and the whippet. The advantage of the weapon was also its disadvantage – at anything over about ten feet it's a genuine scatter-gun, ideal for blowing away an opponent but useless if you're trying for accurate shooting.

The man with the pipe took off his jacket and dropped it on the ground, then walked slowly over to where Richter stood. As he closed, Richter let a look of panic and fear spread across his face, and he took a couple of steps backwards, subtly increasing the distance between himself and the whippet.

The thug smiled again, raised the pipe and swung it in a vicious arc, the iron singing through the air. It wasn't intended to hit Richter, just frighten him even more. Richter looked over the man's shoulder to where the second thug stood, still smiling, the whippet dangling from his right hand. He estimated the distance at about twenty feet; far enough, he thought.

Richter stopped moving. The thug swung the pipe again, but this time Richter didn't flinch. A look of puzzlement crossed the man's face as he raised the pipe for a killing blow. Richter stood there, gazing levelly at him, arms by his sides, hands open and ready, his left foot slightly advanced. An *aficionado* of martial arts would have recognized his posture as the *hidari-hanmi* position, one of the Aikido preparation *kamae*, or stances, but Essex Man probably thought Aikido was something on the menu of a Chinese take-away.

Aikido is probably the most unusual of the oriental martial arts, in that it is essentially defensive in concept and its primary weapon is the attacker's own strength, which an Aikido expert will use against him. Attacking an Aikido master is a bit like trying to punch smoke – frustrating and ultimately pointless. Richter wasn't a master, but he had the basic skills.

The man grunted, stepped forward and swung the pipe down and sideways, a hard, savage blow that would have broken Richter's neck if it had connected. But it didn't connect, and the reason it didn't was that at the moment Essex Man moved, so did Richter. What surprised his attacker was that he moved forward, not back.

Richter stepped inside the blow, turned to his left and placed his back against the thug's chest. He stretched up his right hand, fingers splayed until the web of his hand contacted his attacker's swiftly moving right arm. Richter slid his hand down until he reached the wrist, where he clamped his fingers tight. He pulled the man's arm down, bending sharply from the waist as he did so. The man's own momentum pitched him forward, and Richter's steady pull on his right wrist did the rest. He tumbled over Richter's body and slammed into the ground on his back, pipe tumbling away and the breath instantly knocked from his body.

Richter kept moving. Still gripping the man's wrist he braced his right foot against the man's armpit and pulled, instantly dislocating his shoulder. Richter looked up. The second man had watched his actions with a kind of dumb disbelief, but the sight of his colleague lying incapacitated on the ground prodded him into action. He raised the whippet towards Richter and began to squeeze the trigger, but his target was already diving to one side.

The shotgun boomed, pellets hissing through the leaves, and Richter felt some tugging at his jacket as he hit the ground, but none, as far as he could tell, had injured him. But he knew the weapon had a second barrel, and that he had to deal with the situation quickly.

He rolled once, then came up into a crouch. In a single fluid motion Richter hauled the Smith and Wesson out of the shoulder holster and sighted down the barrel. The heavy recoil from the whippet had forced the thug's arm upwards and back, and as Richter stopped moving he swung the weapon down again. But before he could squeeze the trigger Richter had completed his move. The pistol boomed once, the recoil kicking Richter's arm up, and the .357 magnum round took the thug squarely in the chest, knocking him backwards. He was dead before he hit the ground.

The noise of the shots echoed and faded and Richter knew that within seconds the occupants of the pub would be pouring out into the car park to find out what was going on. But he only needed seconds. He stepped across to the first attacker, who was trying to sit up, moaning over the pain of his dislocated shoulder. Richter kicked his good arm from under him and the man slumped back on the ground. For a brief moment time seemed frozen, then Richter pointed the pistol straight at the man's stomach and pulled back the hammer, the sudden click unnaturally loud.

'Who sent you?' Richter asked, his voice quiet and level as he spoke for the first time since the encounter had begun.

For a moment it looked as if the man would refuse to answer, then he shook his head. 'The people you owe money to,' he said sullenly. It was pretty much as Richter had guessed. The old story – a man running up gambling debts which he can't or won't repay, and a couple of bruisers sent to straighten him out. The only thing that surprised him was that the Russians had stooped so low.

'I hope they paid you in advance,' Richter said, holstering the Smith and Wesson, 'because if it's by results you're not going to make much of a living doing this. Sorry about your boyfriend,' he added as he walked away towards his car.

Oval Office, White House, 1600 Pennsylvania Avenue, Washington, D.C.

'Walter, isn't it?' the grey-haired man asked, rising to his feet and advancing from behind the massive mahogany desk as Hicks entered the room.

'Yes, Mr President.'

'You know the Secretary of Defense?'

Hicks turned and nodded towards the man sitting in one of the Oval Office's comfortable armchairs. 'Yes, I do. Good day, Mr Secretary,' he said.

'Right, Walter, let's hear what you have to say.'

Hicks sat down and opened his briefcase. 'This will sound un-believable, Mr President, but we have information which suggests that an assault is about to be launched upon the United States by Russia.'

The Secretary of Defense rose abruptly to his feet. 'What in hell! Is this some kind of a sick joke?' he demanded.

Hicks shook his head wearily. 'No, Mr Secretary, it isn't any kind of a joke,' he replied. 'I wouldn't be here now if it was.'

The President was still standing, looking appraisingly at Hicks. 'Go on, Walter,' he said quietly. 'What kind of assault, and what is your evidence?'

Hicks pulled out a file bearing the title 'Ravensong' and began to speak.

Cambridge

Richter spent a busy ten minutes on his mobile explaining to Simpson what had happened on the A10, and Simpson agreed to let the

Metropolitan Police lean on the Cambridgeshire Constabulary. The story they worked out between them was that the incident was a shoot-out between gang members, which wouldn't be that difficult for even a policeman to believe. When he got to Cambridge – late – Richter parked near the railway station, then took a cab to the Department of Theoretical Physics.

Expert assistance from the academic world is surprisingly often required by a variety of government departments, including what is usually called the Illegal Section. As a result, following a covert security check known as Negative Vetting, certain leading authorities in numerous and diverse fields are approached and asked to act as consultants to the government as required, in return for a predictably small annual retainer.

Since the Second World War, and increasingly through the sixties and early seventies, with the embarrassment caused by Burgess, Maclean, Philby, Blunt and others of their ilk, the security forces of the Western world have greatly increased their emphasis on checking and screening people who will have access to sensitive material.

This was something that the British had never been very good at. The system's failings could largely be laid at the door of the old school tie, and to the peculiar belief that, even if it was perfectly obvious to anyone with half an eye that a particular individual was an habitual drunk, a raging queen with a boyfriend called Boris or Ivan and, in some cases, a card-carrying member of the Communist Party, the fact that he had been to Winchester and Cambridge somehow outweighed all this evidence. Indeed, for some years about the only consistent qualifications for membership of the security establishment appeared to be unusual sexual proclivities and a general sympathy with Stalin's long-term aims.

Eventually and despite, rather than because of, the system, vetting was improved and a new breed of security man evolved – the Screener, as he is colloquially known. Screeners are usually ex-service officers of a fairly senior rank who have shown some aptitude for what one might call ferreting, and they spend their working lives checking, cross-checking and then checking again, all relevant details of the personnel whose files appear on their desks.

There are two types of security checking procedure which may be undertaken, and the one used depends almost entirely on the intended employment of the individual in question. The more usual procedure is Negative Vetting, which is a covert operation. Virtually all the Screener does is to confirm that stated details are correct, by checking birth and marriage certificates, details of the individual's immediate family, school records and so on, and weeding out any obvious insanities like an uncle who's the Secretary of the local Communist Party. Negative Vetting is the normal procedure for people entering the armed forces in an officer rank, and is generally considered to provide clearance up to Secret.

Positive Vetting is required for anyone needing access to Top Secret, Atomic Secret, Cosmic Top Secret or any of the other thirty or so grades and classifications above Secret, and starts more or less where Negative Vetting finishes. The co-operation of the subject is essential, and the process ensures that the entire life history of the individual is scrutinized, starting from conception and ending the day before the screening started. Family and friends are interviewed in depth. Past employers are contacted and receive a visit, and even the sex life of the subject is placed under the microscope. The process is thorough, lengthy and moderately distasteful, but it does work, which is the intention.

However, despite the fact that some of the civilian consultants used by the government work on projects which are technically of a much higher security classification than Secret, usually only Negative Vetting is applied. The rationale behind this is that as these consultants would only have a limited view of one aspect of a project, rather than an overview of the whole thing, they do not need to be investigated thoroughly. The truth is that it was felt that the uproar and predictable howls about civil rights which would accompany the Positive Vetting of scientists would be more trouble than the resulting clearance would be worth, and so it is only applied in situations where there really is no other option.

Richter turned in through the open double doors, walked across to a glass-fronted booth labelled 'Porter', but found it deserted. On the wall beside the staircase was a list of the building's inhabitants, and Richter scanned rapidly down it until he found 'Professor Hillsworth' listed as having a laboratory on the third floor. The building consisted of a central stairwell, with a long corridor of rooms on each side of the stairs. On the third floor Richter flipped a mental coin and chose the left-hand corridor. It would have been quicker if he'd gone right, but he finally found the door he was looking for by dint of looking at about twenty others that didn't have 'Professor Hillsworth' written on them. Richter knocked, heard a muffled call from inside, and entered.

Richter didn't know quite what he had been anticipating, but both the room and the man were unexpected. The room because it looked nothing like any laboratory Richter had ever been in. No test tubes, no retorts, no Bunsen burners, not even a slide rule or a calculator. After a moment, Richter realized that he shouldn't have been surprised; theoretical physics, and particularly theoretical nuclear physics, could only find a very limited use for such mundane equipment. Nuclear reactions in the laboratory are not phenomena to be encouraged.

The room was oblong, one wall consisting almost entirely of large windows, giving the place a light and airy look. Underneath the windows was a built-in table, covered in books, pieces of paper and writing implements of various sorts, and a small photocopier. At one end of the table was a sink and, adjacent to it, a kettle, mugs, instant coffee and a bag of sugar. A milk carton and a box of teabags completed the set.

The chairs at the long table appeared starkly uncomfortable in contrast to the armchairs which comprised the furniture for the rest of the room. At the far end was a partly screened area, in which Richter could see three computer keyboards and monitors, plus a new high-tech wipe board and rather more traditional blackboard. On the walls were three framed photographs, two of elderly and no doubt distinguished scientific gentlemen, and the third showing the typical mushroom cloud of an atomic weapon detonation.

The professor had been sitting in one of the armchairs, a drink in his hand and looking at a copy of *Penthouse*. He stood up as Richter walked in.

'Professor Hillsworth?'

'The same. You must be Mr Richter, from the Ministry of Defence.' Hillsworth was a short, tubby man, with jet black hair parted on the right-hand side and prominent laughter lines on his face. He looked more like a stand-up comic from a working man's club than a professor of anything, let alone theoretical nuclear physics. He was casually dressed in a tweed jacket and grey slacks, light blue shirt with dark blue stripes and a dark blue tie bearing a motif which appeared to be a small, but accurately drawn, pig with wings. He waved Richter to a chair. 'First things first. How do you like your tea?'

'Coffee, if possible. White, no sugar,' Richter told him, and Hillsworth busied himself with the kettle, cups and a packet of short-cake biscuits for a couple of minutes.

'Now,' he said, when Richter had tasted the drink and declared it to be to his liking, 'what can I tell you?'

'What were you told on the telephone, Professor?'

'Only that a Mr Richter from the Ministry of Defence would be along this afternoon, and that it would be appreciated if I could make myself available. That I have done.'

'Fine,' Richter said, and launched into the rather pompous spiel which Simpson had provided in the pink folder inside his briefcase. 'If I may, I'll just sketch out the background for you first. The Ministry of Defence, as you are no doubt aware, keeps a watching brief on numerous topics not directly connected with defence. We've recently received information which suggests certain developments have been taking place in the field of nuclear research which could have a pronounced effect on our defensive capability. I'll return to that topic a little later, if I may. First of all, I would be grateful if you could establish the ground rules, as it were, by giving me a brief run-down on the way an atomic weapon works.'

'Certainly, Mr Richter. Before I start, could you please show me your identification, just in case I trespass into classified areas.'

One point for the professor. Richter pulled out his wallet and selected a card which he passed over to Hillsworth. He looked at it carefully, confirmed Richter's likeness to the photograph, and then handed it back. 'Where did your scientific education stop?'

'At school,' Richter replied. 'GCE – Ordinary Level Physics. I passed,' he added.

'Well, I suppose that's something,' Hillsworth said, doubtfully. He settled back into his chair, drew out a long curved pipe from his pocket, and began filling it from a leather pouch. 'Let me,' he said, 'begin at the beginning.'

Kutuzovskij prospekt, Moscow

Genady Arkenko replaced the telephone receiver carefully, and walked over to the table. He was becoming very concerned. Despite all of Dmitri's assurances, *Podstava* kept on changing. The last message he'd received meant that the planned arrival date of the *Anton Kirov* in Gibraltar had been advanced yet again. Even more worrying was the fact that he hadn't seen Dmitri – hadn't even spoken to him on the telephone, apart from repeating the messages – since Monday. Arkenko hoped, desperately, that Dmitri was all right.

The apartment, once so comfortable and secure – a meeting place where the two men could lie together in a familiar embrace – was feeling more and more to Arkenko like a prison. A comfortable prison, but a prison nevertheless.

With a sigh, he reached for his notepad and began to prepare the radio message.

Cambridge

The professor was well established into his lecture. 'Matter, of course, can neither be created nor destroyed. What can happen is that matter can be converted into other sorts of matter, or into energy, as matter and energy can be considered to be different forms of the same thing. This conversion is what happens when you burn coal on a fire, for example. The energy released when the coal is burnt is the energy stored in the various sorts of chemical bonds holding together the molecules which constitute coal. That's a simplification, of course, but it's accurate enough for the purposes of this discussion.

'As well as the release of energy, the products of the combustion process are radically different from the original components of the coal or whatever the fuel is. Carbon compounds will burn to produce carbon monoxide and dioxide, nitrogen compounds to give various nitrous and nitrogen gases, and so on. But the point is that if you have carbon in the original material, you will have exactly the same amount of carbon in the combustion products. OK?'

Richter nodded, and wondered how long it would be before he started dozing off. 'Now, in a nuclear reaction, that statement is no longer true. The elements which are present on the left side of the equation are not the same as those on the right. Matter is actually changed from one element to another, just as the old alchemists were trying to do in their search for the Philosopher's Stone centuries ago. Our sun is a vast nuclear furnace, meshing atoms of hydrogen together to create helium. The same thing happens in the detonation of a nuclear weapon. One element is turned into another, with the release of enormous amounts of energy. And it's the energy release which marks the practical difference between conventional explosives and nuclear weapons. A suitcase of dynamite could flatten a building. A suitcase of uranium would flatten a city.

'This fundamental difference between the two types of explosion is because in a conventional explosive, the energy released is that which binds molecules together, whereas in a nuclear blast it's the forces which hold the very atoms themselves together which are ruptured. The stronger the bond which is broken, the greater the energy released, and the atomic bonds are very, very strong.' Hillsworth got up and walked over to the wipe board. 'The actual value of the energy released is given by the mass-energy equation, with which I've no doubt you're familiar.' He wrote '$E = mc^2$' on the wipe board with a red magic marker, and looked at Richter, who nodded and tried to look intelligent.

'"E" is the energy released; "m" is the mass of the material used, and "c" is the numerical value of the speed of light, which is then squared. There's no need to bother about the units involved; suffice it to say that the value of "c" squared is very high, which is why "E" is so vast.'

Hillsworth resumed his seat. 'Now, to build a nuclear weapon, you must first of all find some suitable material. It must be fissionable, which means it must be able to be readily converted into other elements, with the consequent release of energy, which in practice means that it must be one of the very heavy radioactive materials, like uranium or plutonium.

Radioactive materials, as the name suggests, emit sub-atomic particles and certain types of radiation and some, like the isotope uranium 235, have what is called a critical mass. To put that in simple terms, if you simply assemble more than a certain amount of uranium 235 in one place, it will go critical and a nuclear explosion will result. That, in a nutshell, is the theory of the atomic bomb. Simply find yourself enough uranium, smash it all together at the desired time and place, and wait for the bang.

'The mechanics, of course, are much more complicated, which is probably just as well. The normal detonation methods utilize shaped charges, amongst other things, which enable a bomb to be produced using substantially less fissionable material than in the early days. The bombs I've mentioned so far are fission bombs, where a heavy element is broken down into two or more lighter elements. The hydrogen bomb, on the other hand, combines hydrogen atoms to produce heavier elements, in exactly the same way as the sun functions. Do you want me to go into that as well?'

'Thank you, Professor. I would appreciate it.' Richter had learnt nothing new, and nor did he expect to at that stage of the discussion, but one of the first rules of friendly interrogation – that is, interrogation of a non-hostile subject – is to ask so many questions that it is difficult for the person being questioned to discern what you are really trying to find out. As far as Richter was concerned, the more Hillsworth said the better, and he seemed to be settling nicely into his lecture routine.

'Right,' Hillsworth said. 'A hydrogen bomb uses a fission trigger wrapped in hydrogenized material to initiate a fusion reaction.' He paused as the sound of muffled ringing became audible.

Richter muttered an apology and retrieved his cellular phone from his jacket pocket. 'Richter,' he said.

'This is the Delivery Section,' the voice at Hammersmith said. 'We've just received a category-four delivery for our main customer.'

On an open line – even for a call routed to a GSM digital cell phone, which was effectively scrambled by the transmitting cell – the proprieties had to be observed. 'Main customer' was America, and a 'category-four delivery' was code for DEFCON – DEFence CONdition – FOUR.

There are five stages in the DEFCON process. The normal peacetime state is DEFCON FIVE; DEFCON ONE means that the American armed forces are in a state of maximum preparedness for combat, or are actually at war. DEFCON FOUR kicks the American military machine into a significantly higher state of readiness, and is the inevitable precursor to any outbreak of hostilities.

'Oh, shit,' Richter replied. 'When?'

'About twenty minutes ago.'

'What action?'

'Back here as soon as you've finished where you are.'

Richter snapped the phone closed as Hillsworth got up and made another drink, then he cut to the chase. 'We have heard, Professor, that the Americans are starting to experiment with a new device which will produce about the same yield as a conventional nuclear weapon, about five megatons, but emit little or no radiation. I can't reveal the source of this information, and we have at present no idea of the way in which such a weapon could function.'

Richter couldn't tell him the source of the information principally because no such information had been received. Hillsworth sipped his tea slowly, looking keenly at Richter over the rim of his mug, then smiled. 'I thought the Americans were on our side?'

'They are, Professor,' Richter replied, 'and that's why we're interested. You always know what an enemy will try to do. It's much more difficult to tell what your friends are intending, which is why we always look very carefully at any rumours we hear.'

Hillsworth nodded. 'Very wise, no doubt.' He looked thoughtful. 'It's an interesting idea, but unfortunately impossible.'

'Impossible?' Richter queried.

'Yes. The physics won't let it work. Whenever a nuclear explosion takes place, radiation products are emitted, and there's nothing anyone can do to stop that happening. The radiation is as much a part of the equation as the uranium or plutonium.'

Hillsworth paused and scratched the back of his neck. 'As we've briefly discussed,' he continued, 'there are three principal types of nuclear weapon: the fission bomb, the fusion bomb and the neutron bomb, which is also a fusion device. All emit radiation of various sorts, including gamma rays, x-rays, alpha particles and neutrons. In fact, the neutron bomb is specifically designed to emit huge quantities of high-speed neutrons which are lethal to all living things, but it's only a tactical weapon, with no strategic potential.'

'Why is that?' Richter asked.

'Because in a conventional nuclear weapon the neutrons released when the weapon detonates are absorbed to increase the energy of the explosion, to increase its yield. In a neutron bomb, the neutrons are allowed to escape, which severely limits the maximum possible size of the weapon.'

'How high a yield could a neutron bomb have?'

'The theoretical limit is about nine megatons, but most neutron devices were designed to be fired from large-calibre artillery pieces or mounted on small battlefield-use missiles, so it's usually down in the few kilotons range. As I said, it's strictly tactical in its application.'

'And what about the radiation?'

'It's known as an Enhanced Radiation Weapon or ERW, and was always intended to be used to defend the West against a numerically superior attacking force. The neutrons would kill the attacking troops, but the low yield of the bomb means that it would cause little structural damage, which could be important if you were fighting on your home territory. And the radiation dissipates quickly, which could also be an advantage.'

Richter was, he thought, perhaps not actually able to see the light at the end of the tunnel, but he was at least beginning to make out the tunnel walls fairly clearly.

Anton Kirov

'Not another change of plan?' Valeri Bondarev asked, somewhat peevishly.

Colonel Zavorin nodded. 'I don't like it any more than you do, Valeri,' he said. 'I am running to a schedule, but it is dictated by Moscow.'

'So,' Bondarev said. 'Now we do not go to Tunis either.'

'No. We have been told to head straight for Gibraltar, and to signal Moscow with our estimate as soon as possible. My signalman has already cancelled our berth at Tunis.'

'Thank you very much,' Bondarev replied, with patent insincerity.

Cambridge

'So what's happened to the neutron bomb?' Richter asked.

'Well,' Hillsworth said, 'it's always been very controversial, because it's a people-killer. It was specifically designed to decimate enemy troops, and its intended deployment by the Americans in Europe caused an uproar. The Russians apparently thought it was unfair that their vastly superior invasion forces could be defeated by a handful of troops armed with nothing more exotic than howitzers and a few rockets.

'The fact that the weapon only had defensive potential and so would only be used to kill the Russian hordes if those same Russian hordes first swept into Europe riding main battle tanks was deemed to be irrelevant. The Americans didn't deploy the weapon, although they did stockpile them in America to be used in the event of hostilities over here.'

'And the Russians? Did they build any?'

Hillsworth nodded. 'Of course they did. In the nineteen eighties they announced that they had built and tested neutron weapons. What the state of play is now I have no idea, but I strongly suspect that some-where in Russia some new kind of neutron bomb has been tested in the fairly recent past.'

'Why is that, Professor?' Richter asked, sitting forward slightly in the chair.

'Because you're here, sitting in my chair drinking my coffee and eat-ing my biscuits and telling me a pack of lies about American designs for a super-bomb.'

'Oh, yes?' Richter said.

The professor smiled. 'I'm not an idiot, Mr Richter. I know about Anglo-American co-operation in defence projects – apart from anything else I'm a member of one of the Steering Committees – and if our cousins across the sea were developing a new weapon I promise you I would know about it. I don't, so therefore they're not, but the Russians probably are. QED.'

'Ah,' Richter said, and drank the rest of his coffee. He reflected that you don't get to become a professor at the age of thirty-two, which Hillsworth had achieved, without being a pretty sharp cookie, but Richter somehow hadn't expected quite this degree of sharpness. 'Without wishing to confirm or deny—' Richter started in his best Civil Service voice, but Hillsworth interrupted.

'Let me finish it for you,' Hillsworth said. 'I've heard it often enough. In brief, you are not prepared to confirm the source of your information, nor the quality of that information, nor even, if pushed, the existence of that information. Right?' Richter nodded. 'In short, you've heard a story, or seen some kind of report, and you want an independent opinion as to its veracity?'

'Yes.'

Hillsworth shook his head. 'I don't know why you didn't say that at the beginning instead of going all round the houses and sitting through a rather boring lecture on basic nuclear weapon theory. I suppose you enjoy all the cloak and dagger aspects of it.'

Richter nodded again, somewhat sheepishly. 'We like to keep in practice, Professor,' he said. 'OK, having cleared the air, is it possible that the Russians have managed to develop a strategic neutron bomb?'

'Anything's possible, I suppose,' Hillsworth said. 'But there's one very obvious problem if they have developed such a weapon and decide to re-arm with it.'

'Yes,' Richter prompted. 'What's that?'

'Well, if they have, the Russians would obviously place themselves at a very severe disadvantage in any future nuclear exchange. But,' Hillsworth added, 'there are three other aspects about this that might be relevant to your enquiry. First, does the name Sam Cohen mean anything to you? Second, what do you know about America buying Russian weapons-grade plutonium? And have you ever heard of red mercury?'

Hammersmith, London

Richter reached Hammersmith just after six thirty, parked the Escort in the Transport Pool's underground garage, checked in with the Duty Officer, then went straight up to Simpson's office. Simpson was sitting at his desk, studying a file, which he snapped shut when Richter walked in.

'Well?' he demanded.

Richter sat down heavily in the chair in front of the desk. 'It's like this,' he said, and started to explain what the professor had told him.

Glavnoye Razvedyvatelnoye Upravleniye *Headquarters*, the 'Aquarium', Khodinka Airfield, Moscow

Since the effective end of the Cold War, the number of Russian surveillance satellites which has been launched has dropped considerably, but there are still several vehicles, all operated by the Directorate of Cosmic Intelligence of the GRU, established in polar orbits which do little but watch the American landmass. Like the early American Big Bird satellites and the current KH–11 and KH–12 Keyhole vehicles, the Russian platforms are equipped with sophisticated optical devices and an assortment of other detectors working in the non-visible electromagnetic spectrum, and are primarily designed to detect any military activity which might be considered a threat to Russia.

The kind of activity which falls into this category includes precisely the actions taken by the American military machine when the DEFCON state is increased, and five hours after America went to DEFCON FOUR the first satellite pictures arrived at the Aquarium.

Thirty minutes after that, the GRU duty commanding officer was en route to the Kremlin with a sheaf of pictures and a hastily prepared intelligence appraisal.

Stepney, London

Richter left Hammersmith an hour and a quarter later, after the evening meeting, told the duty driver that he was taking the Escort, and drove back to his apartment. Richter's London home was in an undistinguished building, lurking in the warren of streets that lay north of Commercial Road, which had originally been a grand town house for some unknown Victorian merchant. Richter had taken a lease on one of the two top-floor apartments shortly after he had started working for FOE. It was small, anonymous, fairly central, but above all reasonably cheap, at least by London standards, all of which seemed to Richter to be pretty good reasons for staying there.

In the flat, he pulled off his jacket and hung it over the back of a chair, kicked off his shoes and stretched out on the couch. He needed time to think, time to try to tie some of the loose ends together. Just after eleven thirty the telephone rang and Richter stumbled off the couch and went into the hall to answer it. The FOE duty driver wanted to collect the Escort, unless Richter still needed it.

'No,' Richter said. 'Help yourself. It's parked right outside my building.'

As he was on his feet, and getting hungry, Richter walked into the kitchenette, opened the freezer door and surveyed the contents with a marked lack of enthusiasm. He selected a frozen lasagne, read the instructions, put it in the microwave and returned to the living room.

The 'ping' of the microwave timer came several minutes later, and was followed almost immediately by a muffled but loud and echoing thump that Richter couldn't identify. What he knew was that the noise hadn't come from inside the apartment.

He peered out of the windows, but could see nothing unusual, so he walked down the hall to the windows which overlooked the main road. The first thing he saw was two men running across the road, towards his building, and a few seconds later he heard the distant wail of a siren, getting closer. Then he looked down at the street directly below him. It was only then, when he saw the blackened, twisted pile of metal that had once been the Motor Pool's Escort that he knew just how far wrong things had gone.

221

Chapter Thirteen

Saturday
Stepney, London

Richter took another brief glance downwards at the ruins of the car, turned away and walked back into his apartment. He closed and bolted the door on the inside, then walked through into his bedroom. His face was set and icy calm, and he moved with swift and deliberate purpose.

He peeled off his grey trousers and tossed them on the bed. Then he opened the wardrobe door and pulled out a pair of blue jeans, a black leather motorcycle jacket, a pair of black trainers, a dark blue polo-neck sweater and a small grey haversack. He put on the jeans, fastening the waist with a broad leather belt, pulled on the sweater and laced up the trainers. Then he reached up to the top of the wardrobe and pulled down a dark red motorcycle helmet and a pair of leather gloves, which he placed on the bed.

Walking back into the living room, he put his mobile phone in the haversack. Then he walked across to a desk set against the wall opposite the main windows and pulled open a drawer. From it he took a pair of rubber surgical gloves, a glasscutter, a roll of black adhesive tape, a small flashlight and two spare batteries, and put them all into the haversack.

He pulled the shoulder holster on over the sweater, then checked that the Smith and Wesson was fully loaded and put the pistol into the holster. He put six spare rounds into one of the pockets of his jeans, and the rest of the bullets into the haversack in their cardboard box.

He ate the cooling lasagne and drank about half of a pint carton of milk. Then he walked back into the bedroom, put on the leather jacket and picked up the helmet and gloves. He shrugged the haversack on to his back, snapped off all the lights except the low-wattage bulb in his hallway, and walked to the main door of his apartment. For just over a minute he peered through the spy-hole out into the hallway on his floor, then pulled out the Smith and cautiously unbolted and pulled open the apartment door.

Looking down from the head of the stairs, Richter saw and heard nothing. The locks on the building doors were good enough to keep casual thieves out, but he doubted that the people who had wired the explosive to the Escort's ignition system came into that category.

Satisfied, he pressed the call button for the lift and waited. When it arrived, he slid inside and pressed the button for the garage floor and watched as the numbers unwound. The garage lights were activated by motion detectors, and were out when the lift doors slid open and Richter emerged. Nevertheless, he checked carefully around the perimeter before walking across to the far side of the parking area, where a bulky shape lurked under a green tarpaulin.

When he'd first arrived in London, Richter had come in a car. Within a month he'd realized that four-wheeled vehicles were much less use than he'd anticipated, and he'd returned to his first love – motorcycles. At the place he still called home – a ramshackle cottage on the east side of the Lizard Peninsular in Cornwall – he kept an immaculate Vincent Black Shadow and a Velocette Venom Thruxton in a securely locked pre-fabricated garage.

Wonderful though these bikes were, they were useless in London, being too valuable, too attractive and simply too unreliable to be practical forms of transport. In London, Richter rode Japanese. Cheap, old, fast Japanese.

He pulled the tarpaulin off the Honda 500–4 and tossed it on to the garage floor, swung his leg over the saddle, stuck the key in the ignition, turned it and pressed the starter button. As always, the engine burst instantly into life, then settled down to a steady, even tickover. Used to a long series of British-built motorcycles, it had taken Richter a long time to come to terms with the total reliability that characterized most Oriental machines, but now he just accepted it as normal.

He settled the haversack more comfortably on his back, pulled in the clutch, snicked the gear lever into first and moved quickly away towards the door. Richter stopped by a pillar, reached out a gloved hand to press a button, waited as the electric motors swung the double doors open, then switched on the Honda's lights and accelerated up the ramp and away into the silent streets, heading for Aldgate and London Bridge.

Turabah, Saudi Arabia

The email from Hassan Abbas, which contained the complete transcript of Dmitri Trushenko's analysis of the implications of the American over-flight of the weapon test site, plus Abbas' own comments, pretty much confirmed what Sadoun Khamil had already deduced. As soon as he'd been told about the flight of the spy-plane, Khamil had copied Abbas' email, added his own take on the incident, encrypted it and had sent it to his contact with the al-Qaeda leadership, Tariq Rahmani, a dour, secretive man even by Arabic standards, who remained almost permanently in the background. Although Khamil had explicit instructions to contact only this one man, he had actually met Rahmani only twice in his life.

He knew little about him, not even which country he lived in, as he used a web-based email service and a mobile phone registered in Saudi Arabia. What Khamil did know was that Rahmani was very close to the top of the al-Qaeda leadership, and that his decisions had the force of law within the organization. And that made Khamil tread very carefully around him.

Now, with Abbas' very detailed and explanatory email on the screen in front of him, Khamil thought carefully before composing his own message. Like Abbas, he didn't see what practical difference the American over-flight of Russia made to their own, secret, operation, the part of the plan that al-Qaeda had named *El Sikkiyn*.

Finally, he shrugged. He wouldn't, he decided, say anything at all. He'd just forward the message from Abbas in its entirety and leave it at that.

Battersea, London

Richter pulled into the kerb in Fenchurch Street and checked carefully that no other vehicles stopped anywhere near him. He'd watched the mirrors of the Honda constantly since he'd ridden it out of the garage, and had seen no obvious signs of pursuit, possibly because the watchers – and there would definitely have been watchers – would probably have been looking for a man in a suit, not a black-clad figure on a motorcycle.

Satisfied, Richter pulled out his cell phone and rang the Duty Officer. Using the vague and woolly double-talk necessary when speaking about a highly sensitive matter on an open line, Richter finally managed to acquaint him with the essential details, and also told him that he would be telling Simpson about it.

'It is after one o'clock, you know,' the Duty Officer reminded him.

'I know.'

'He won't like being woken up.'

'That's my problem, not yours. Just tell the Pool and you'd better have a chat with the Met as well.'

Simpson, predictably enough, was a bachelor and lived in a service flat in Battersea, and the Duty Officer had been quite right. Richter had tried to call him immediately after he rang off from Hammersmith, but just got the ansaphone. When he arrived at the building, it took the better part of five minutes to get Simpson to respond to the entry phone before Richter even got into the building. Simpson's face, as he edged his apartment door cautiously open, was puffy and full of sleep, and his greeting was notably lacking in warmth. 'What do you want? Do you know what time it is? And what the hell are you dressed like that for?'

'Yes,' Richter said, 'I do own a watch. I want to come in. I'm in a hurry, and I've got some bad news for you.'

Simpson stared at him suspiciously. 'What kind of bad news?'

'The kind I don't want to talk about out here in the hallway.' Richter pushed the door open impatiently and walked in.

Simpson slammed it shut behind him. 'What's going on?' he demanded.

Richter told him the night's events in clipped tones. Simpson thought for a second and walked over to the telephone. He dialled, switched in the scrambler, held a very brief and subdued conversation, replaced the receiver and walked back. 'The driver was Brian Jackson,' he said. 'They had to do a run down to Manor Park, and decided to collect the Escort on the way back. He'd only been married three months.'

Richter nodded. Simpson got up again and walked over to the drinks' cabinet. He pulled out a bottle of malt whisky and splashed a generous three fingers into a tumbler. He held the bottle up towards Richter.

'I know you don't normally, but—'

'I don't ever,' Richter said. 'I'll make myself a coffee.' The kitchen area was small but well equipped. Richter spooned instant coffee into a mug and switched on the electric kettle. While he waited for it to boil, he went back into the lounge. Simpson was sitting in his armchair, looking old and tired. He took a long swallow of his Scotch and looked up.

'This has got to stop,' Simpson said. His eyes were like black coals in his pink face. Richter nodded. For the moment they were in complete agreement, but Richter doubted if they would be when he told him what he was going to do. The kettle emitted a high-pitched scream, and Richter returned to the kitchen and poured water into the mug. He added milk from the fridge and sat down in a chair.

'What's going on?' Simpson asked, for the second time that night.

'I think I've worked most of it out, now,' Richter said.

Oval Office, White House, 1600 Pennsylvania Avenue, Washington, D.C.

His Excellency Mr Stanislav Nikolai Karasin, Ambassador Extraordinary and Plenipotentiary of the Embassy of the Confederation of Independent States, sat somewhat stiffly in the leather armchair and looked over at the President of the United States of America.

'Mr President,' he began formally, 'I thank you for agreeing to see me this evening at such short notice, for the matter is grave.'

The grey-haired man opposite him smiled slightly. 'It is always a pleasure to see you, Mr Ambassador. How can I help?'

The Russian diplomat paused briefly. When he spoke, he sounded almost embarrassed. 'Mr President, we have, as you know, bilateral agreements which require each of our countries to inform the other in advance of any planned major military exercises or operations. Despite this, our technical surveillance systems indicate that you have ordered your armed forces to a higher alert state than normal – what you refer to, I believe, as Defence Condition Four – and there appears to be significant activity at many of your military establishments. Have your staff, perhaps, forgotten to inform us of some exercise you have planned?' Karasin stopped and waited.

The President looked at him levelly. 'We have no exercise planned, Mr Ambassador,' he replied. 'It is true that we have moved our forces to a higher alert state, but this is just a precautionary measure.'

'A precaution against what, Mr President?' Karasin asked sharply.

The President waited a few moments before replying. 'I was hoping,' he said finally, 'that you might be able to tell me.'

Battersea, London

When Richter had finished, Simpson got up and poured himself another Scotch. 'Are you sure? It sounds bloody unlikely to me.'

'I'm as sure as I can be,' Richter said. 'In any case, as far as I can see, it's the only explanation that covers all the facts we have. If you've any better theories, let's hear them. All I'm saying is that the explanation I've just advanced seems to me to be the simplest and most likely, and until a simpler and more likely one comes along, I'm going to work on the assumption that it's correct.'

Simpson paced up and down in front of the coal-effect electric fire. 'OK,' he said. 'Assuming that your hypothesis is right, why are the Russians trying to hit you, and what are they going to do next?'

Richter took a mouthful of coffee. 'I don't know for certain, but I can guess. Follow the sequence of events. They snatch and torture to death the Head of Moscow Station. I turn up to investigate, ostensibly as an insurance company representative. Either somebody in Moscow recognized me or they guessed I wasn't an insurance rep, hence the attack at

Sheremetievo. Then my picture is relayed to London, to the Russian Embassy, with watch orders. Perhaps I was tailed from Heathrow when I landed. Perhaps they've even tapped my telephone – I wouldn't put it past them to have someone at Tinkerbell.'

Tinkerbell is an anonymous grey building in Ebury Bridge Road, opposite Chelsea Barracks, which is responsible for tapping telephones in Britain. It was the subject of controversy in January 1980 when it was alleged on excellent authority (in fact by the people employed there to carry out the work) that illegal tapping of telephone lines was common. Tinkerbell's equipment can monitor and record well over a million lines at any one time. The building is officially used by the Post Office for equipment development, which is true, but tells only half the story.

'What I am sure,' Richter continued, 'is that they found out where I lived and worked. The next thing I did was turn up at JARIC, which is a place that very few insurance company investigators have ever heard of, far less been to. The Russians know – obviously – about the Blackbird flight, and having seen that I've been involved both with Newman's death and the photographic intelligence centre, they must have assumed I was getting too close.'

Richter swallowed the last of his coffee and put the cup down. 'Now I'm guessing. The kill directive must have been included in the Moscow Centre orders, because they tried to hit me as soon as I came out of JARIC, and presumably intended me not to have the opportunity to pass on anything I'd learned to you or whoever they think I work for. That attempt failed, and the two low-lifes they sent after me when I went to Cambridge didn't do any better. I guess they've been waiting for another opportunity, but it's not all that easy to carry out a hit in London, with the traffic and the crowds. And they don't know which route I'd be taking to and from Hammersmith, or how I'd be travelling – I've been constantly altering my timing, method and route as a precaution, and there are three separate exits from my apartment block to confuse them as well.'

Simpson interrupted. 'But they must know – or at least assume – that by now you have passed on what you know to me or to SIS, so why are they still trying to eliminate you?'

'The oldest reason in the world,' Richter said. 'Revenge. Two Cultural Attachés, or whatever they were calling themselves, came back in boxes from East Anglia, and I can't believe that the Russians don't think it was my fault.'

'OK,' Simpson said, after a moment. 'That does make sense, but it still doesn't answer the question. Why was there a kill directive? What is so desperately important to them that they're prepared to break all the rules and risk the consequences?'

'I don't know for certain,' Richter replied, 'but I believe that they've got something really big building and they can't, under any circumstances, allow any word of it to reach government level.'

'I don't buy all this covert assault crap that the CIA is banging on about,' Simpson said. 'So what could be that big?'

'I don't know, but I think I can find out.'

'How?'

'I'm going to go and have a talk with Orlov,' Richter said.

Simpson just stared at him. 'You're joking, of course.'

'I was never more serious in my life. I'm fed up with sitting around and letting them take pot shots at me, and I've got Brian Jackson's blood on my hands. Someone's going to pay for that, and Orlov looks to me like the prime candidate.'

Simpson stood up. 'For God's sake, man, think of the consequences! You snatch – I presume that's what you mean – Orlov, and as soon as the Russians realize he's gone they'll start yelling the place down. And think what'll happen when he goes back to them. Think of the repercussions then.'

Richter sat back in the chair and looked up at him. 'You misunderstand me, Simpson. Orlov isn't going to go back to anyone. Once I've got him, that's it.'

Oval Office, White House, 1600 Pennsylvania Avenue, Washington, D.C.

Karasin sat silent for a moment, his face pale in the light from the desk lamp. 'How do you expect me to be able to tell you that, Mr President?' he asked.

'Because, Mr Ambassador, we have received definite information –
and I regret that I cannot disclose the source – which suggests that an
imminent assault is planned by your country upon mine.'

Karasin turned white. 'What?' he almost shouted, and stood up,
protocol forgotten. 'What? What do you mean – assault?'

'I cannot be any more specific, Mr Ambassador,' the President
said smoothly, motioning Karasin back to his seat, 'but we do have the
information.'

The Russian sat down, slowly, his eyes never leaving the American's
face. 'Mr President,' he said, 'I have no knowledge, no knowledge at all,
of any such operation. The suggestion is –' he searched for a word '– is
simply monstrous. Relations with your country have, I believe, never
been better. Why would we risk any conflict now?'

'Why indeed, Mr Ambassador?' the President said. 'Nevertheless,
that is the information we have.'

Karasin looked stunned. He shook his head and got to his feet. 'I
must take advice,' he said. 'Urgent advice. In the meantime, Mr
President, I must urge you, in the strongest possible terms, to do nothing which would exacerbate this situation.'

The President looked at him. 'We will do nothing that we do not
need to do,' he replied, 'but this situation is, we believe, entirely of your
country's own making.'

Karasin shook his head. 'I know nothing of this,' he repeated.
'Nothing. Thank you, Mr President. I will contact you as soon as possible.' The Russian shook hands briefly, and walked briskly out of the
room.

'Well?' the President asked.

Walter Hicks, who had been sitting silently at the back of the room
facing the long windows throughout the meeting, rose and walked
slowly towards the President's desk. 'You know him much better than I
do, sir,' he said. 'What's your impression?'

The President sat down again, this time behind the desk. 'I've
known Karasin for three years,' he said. 'Normally, he's the model of
diplomacy, never a word out of place. I've never seen him like this
before. If I didn't know better,' he finished, the words coming slowly, 'I'd
say he doesn't know anything about it.'

OVERKILL

Orpington, Kent

Vladimir Illych Orlov was the possessor of a diplomatic passport and was officially Third Secretary at the London Embassy of the Confederation of Independent States, with special responsibilities for Cultural Exchange and Industrial Development. Third Secretaries, generally, are pretty low on the pecking order at most embassies, but Orlov lived in a large house with a bodyguard and chauffeur, and was regularly to be seen at important Embassy functions, where he was treated with marked deference by everyone from the Ambassador downwards. The reason was simple enough – Orlov was a full colonel in the SVR, and was head of the large staff of SVR officers employed in the Embassy. He also ran at least three separate and distinct spy rings – mostly comprising low-grade sources in industry and the fringes of the military – that SIS knew about, and probably others as well.

He was quite literally the most powerful Russian in Britain, and FOE had a dossier an inch and a half thick on him at Hammersmith. Richter knew that talking with him wasn't going to be easy. There was a clip of photographs of the house in the file. It was detached, surrounded by thick hedges and a brick wall on the side of the property adjoining the road, with double gates, electrically operated with remote control switching both from Orlov's official car and from the house itself. All the downstairs windows were barred, and the doors front and rear were lined with steel. It was not, Richter knew, a tempting place to crack.

He pulled the Honda into the side of the road a hundred yards or so from the house and switched off the engine. He pulled the bike on to its stand, removed the ignition key, secured his helmet to the lock below the seat, switched off his mobile phone and started walking. It was a fairly bright night, the moon only occasionally vanishing behind clouds, which was more or less what he wanted. Richter didn't anticipate that anyone in the house would be awake, and the moonlight would certainly help him avoid falling into any ditches or other obstacles Orlov might have strategically or accidentally positioned in the grounds.

He felt the brickwork on the top of the wall, but could find no trace of glass, barbed wire or, more importantly, any indication of an alarm system. He checked the road carefully in both directions, then pulled himself up and dropped down on to the lawn on the other side. He removed the haversack, opened it and transferred the glasscutter, torch and adhesive tape to pockets on his leather jacket. Then he pulled down the jacket's zip so that he could reach the Smith and Wesson easily, pulled on the rubber gloves and moved off.

Richter kept to the edge, near the hedge, all the way, keeping his eyes on the house and looking and listening for any sound of movement. There was a light burning downstairs in the hall, which he could see through the narrow vertical windows either side of the front door, and another upstairs, but no lights were visible in any of the bedrooms. Richter made three complete circuits of the house before he was satisfied.

It was a substantial red-brick property, as an estate agent would have described it, and the bars on the ground-floor windows would certainly have given Richter peace of mind if he'd been thinking of buying it. With his present intentions in mind they were, at best, a nuisance. The first floor looked a good deal more promising, with no bars as far as he could see, and a balcony area at the rear of the house, above a bay window.

Richter thought briefly about the best entry point, and decided that the balcony was it, as long as he could get up on to the top of the bay. There were no convenient creepers or ivy – Richter would have been surprised if there had been – so he looked around behind the garage and the shed at the rear of the house for a ladder or anything similar. He didn't find a ladder, but he did find a warped twelve-foot scaffold plank, presumably discarded after some work on the property. Richter examined it carefully, but apart from the twist in it there were no other obvious signs of weakness, so he carried it out from behind the garage to the house. He rested one end on the top of the bay and jammed the other into the soil of a flowerbed adjacent to the wall.

Then he started his ascent. The plank had looked steady enough when he had put it in place, but with Richter's weight on it, it wobbled enough for him to be very glad of the wall on his left-hand side. He hoped he would be able to leave by the front door.

On top of the bay, he looked cautiously through the window with the aid of the torch. There was a large double bed against one wall with blankets neatly folded at one end. Richter could see a wardrobe, three chairs and a dressing table, but nothing that suggested that the room was anything other than what it seemed – an unoccupied spare bedroom. The window was double-glazed and the catches closed, but that was what he had expected.

Richter took the roll of sticky tape and pulled a length of about a foot off it. This he stuck on to the window pane next to the catch, after doubling the centre four inches of the tape, so that he ended up with eight inches of tape stuck to the glass with a 'handle' about two inches long in the centre of it. Then he took the glasscutter and described a circle around the tape, big enough to get his hand and arm through. He ran the cutter round twice in the groove, then replaced it in his pocket. Holding the tape firmly in his left hand, Richter gave the glass a sharp rap with his right fist. There was a splintering sound, and the circle slid inwards. Carefully he brought the circle of glass outside, and placed it flat on the top of the bay.

Richter repeated the operation on the inner pane and placed the second circle of glass on top of the first. Then he slid his right arm inside, and felt all the way round the opening section. If there were any wires, he didn't feel them, so he slowly released the catch and gently pulled the window open.

No alarm bells rang or lights flashed. Richter climbed through the window and into the room. He pulled the window closed behind him and secured the catch – the last thing he wanted was for it to bang shut in a gust of wind and scatter glass all over the floor. Richter worked his way carefully round the room, and found absolutely nothing of interest.

He walked to the door and listened for a minute or so. The house was silent. Richter turned the handle and pulled the door towards him. He peered through the widening crack out onto the landing area. All was silent. Just the light burning and closed doors.

Richter knew that Orlov had a staff of only three – his chauffeur and bodyguard, who accompanied him almost everywhere, and a cook/housekeeper who lived out and was helped in the running of the house by two daily women who handled the cleaning and so forth. He knew that because one of the dailies was on the SIS pay-roll. Richter didn't anticipate any trouble from the cook, who should be at her home and in bed, but the two heavies might prove more difficult. His intention was simply to snatch Orlov, and with him under his gun, convince the other two men to surrender their weapons. If they didn't, Richter believed that the Smith could persuade them in a permanent fashion.

He guessed that Orlov would sleep in the large bedroom at the front of the house – FOE and SIS held detailed plans of all the properties leased by Russian citizens – so Richter walked along the landing corridor until he came to the door. He took the Smith out of the shoulder holster and turned the door handle slowly. As the door opened, he could see no light in the room, but he could hear the sound of gentle snoring. Even if it wasn't Orlov, it would do no harm to incapacitate the occupant. Richter eased the door shut behind him and started walking across the floor towards the sound on the other side of the room.

He was about halfway there when the main lights came on and something hard prodded him in the back. A voice from behind Richter spoke softly. 'Good evening, Mr Willis. We've been expecting you.'

Chapter Fourteen

Saturday
Orpington, Kent

The basic training given to men who become members of elite combat forces, like the Royal Marines Commandos and Special Air Service, lays a very considerable stress on proficiency in a hand to hand combat situation, because taking someone out with the use of a knife, fists or feet is, generally speaking, silent and anonymous. Every bullet fired from a gun identifies the gun, but the best a forensic scientist can do with a stab wound is to say that the knife had, say, a single-edged blade at least four inches long, which covers a positive multitude of weapons. As well as being taught to attack and kill in silence, such men are also taught to counter-attack in the same sort of situation.

Early in Richter's term of employment with the Foreign Operations Executive he had spent a painful five weeks with the SAS in Hereford, learning what the instructors had called the dirty tricks of the trade. One thing he remembered very clearly was that in a close combat situation, anyone who sticks a gun in your back is as good as dead. It's all to do with speed of reaction and speed of movement. The technique is simple. With a pistol pressed into your back, even if the holder has his finger on the trigger, there is no way he can pull it faster than you can move providing that he doesn't know you're going to move. By the time his brain has registered the fact that you are moving, and has instructed his finger to squeeze the trigger, your move should have been completed, and by then he's either dead or unconscious.

If you're right handed, twist your body to the left, bringing the blade of your left arm back and down across his gun arm. That

235

will knock the weapon off aim and even if it does fire the bullet won't hit you. Continue the twisting movement of the body, and bring your right hand down hard – the harder the better – on the side of his neck. Dead simple. Dead being the operative word, if you do it right.

Two things had surprised Richter when the lights went on. The first was the fact that whoever it was behind him had used the name 'Willis', until he remembered that that had been his cover name in Moscow, and would be the name under his photograph in the Moscow Centre files. The second thing that surprised Richter was that the man behind him should have pressed his pistol into his back. But Richter hadn't even started to move when the voice spoke again and the pressure vanished. 'Don't, Mr Willis. Just drop the gun and then put your hands on your head, fingers interlocked.'

His training had been as thorough as Richter's, by the sound of it. Richter had absolutely no option anyway, because by then he'd seen the other two occupants of the room. Orlov was sitting in an easy chair in pyjamas and dressing gown, with a smile on his face, and a second man was standing behind him, wearing a somewhat crumpled shirt and slacks, and pointing an automatic pistol at Richter's stomach. He looked as if he knew how to use it.

No man should ever surrender his weapon to an armed adversary unless there is absolutely no alternative. Richter calculated that he could, possibly, shoot the man standing in front of him, but if he did that he would certainly be immediately killed by the bodyguard standing behind him. Even a short extension of life is always preferable to instant certain death, so he tossed the Smith on to the thick pile carpet, and put his hands on his head.

The room was obviously a man's bedroom. The walls were light blue, with hunting prints in silver frames, and the carpet a darker blue. There were two large built-in double wardrobes, no dressing table, a desk and chair in one corner, and a double bed with twin bedside cabinets against one wall. There were four other chairs – one easy chair in which Vladimir Orlov was comfortably seated, and three more or less upright chairs, one facing Orlov, the other two either side of it. It looked like a prisoner's chair in front of a jury and Richter knew that was almost precisely what they had in mind. Orlov nodded and Richter received a hefty push in the back which propelled him to the chair.

'Sit down, Mr Willis,' said Orlov, speaking for the first time. His voice was low-pitched and bore only traces of his native Georgian accent.

Richter sat. With the bodyguard behind Orlov still pointing his gun directly at Richter, the second one pulled off the surgical gloves, then went through the pockets of his jeans. He found and spare rounds for the Smith, but allowed Richter to keep his comb and handkerchief, as the Russian presumably thought that neither could be turned into any kind of weapon. Unfortunately, Richter agreed with him.

Orlov nodded again, and the bodyguards sat, one on each side of Richter, who saw them both for the first time. They were very similar. Tall, dark, and well built, and both looked very professional. Richter couldn't see how he was going to get out of the house alive. There was a moment of silence while the three Russians looked at him, then Richter spoke. 'Good evening, Vladimir. I'm from the Gas Board, and I've come to read your meter.'

Oval Office, White House, 1600 Pennsylvania Avenue, Washington, D.C.

'If you're right, Mr President,' Walter Hicks said, 'then that's the worst possible news.'

'Explain,' the grey-haired man said, looking up sharply.

'If Ambassador Karasin genuinely knows nothing about this assault – whatever the hell it is – then we can only assume we're dealing with some kind of freelance operation.'

The President frowned. 'You mean it's some sort of terrorist attack?'

Hicks shook his head. 'No, sir. All the information we have received from our informant, and the data we have obtained from technical surveillance, point to official involvement of some sort. A private organization simply would not have the resources or the ability to detonate a nuclear weapon in the tundra.'

'So what do you mean?'

'What I mean is that this assault might be the brainchild of the SVR or the GRU or even of some Russian minister. What I don't think, assuming that Ambassador Karasin is being truthful, is that it is official Russian government policy. There's also,' Hicks added, 'some circumstantial evidence which might support his denial. Ambassador Karasin is one of the most senior and important Russian diplomats, and I simply do not believe that Moscow would knowingly leave him here in Washington if any sort of conflict were imminent. They would have recalled him on some pretext weeks ago.'

The President nodded. 'Yes, that makes sense. Right, in the absence of the Director, what are your recommendations, Walter?' The Director of Central Intelligence, an old friend of the President, was out of town. In fact, he was in Florida recuperating from a mild heart attack, and had not been consulted about the situation, on the President's explicit orders.

Hicks shrugged his ample shoulders. 'We're not getting very far, sir. Our own operatives haven't been able to obtain any further data from our source in Russia, and the British haven't so far been of any help.' He paused, deducing that the President was seeking some approval, however tacit, for the actions he had already taken. 'I would not presume to advise you about the political stance you have adopted, Mr President – that is not a function of my office – but I do think we should maintain a higher military alert state. In the absence of any definite information, escalating our operational readiness to DEFCON FOUR was, I believe, the wisest – and possibly the only viable – course of action. I think we should maintain at least that status until the implementation date quoted by our Moscow source.'

'Or until the threat is actually implemented?' the President asked, with a wintry smile.

'Or, as you say, sir, until the threat is actually implemented,' Hicks agreed.

OVERKILL

Orpington, Kent

'Please don't try to be funny, Mr Willis,' Orlov said.

'Who told you I was coming here?' Richter asked.

Orlov smiled, his thin lips parting to reveal excellent teeth. He pulled his dressing gown more tightly round his spare body and raised his hands in a gesture of mock surprise. 'Told me, Mr Willis? What is your real name, by the way?' Richter told him – as far as he could see it wouldn't make any difference whether the Russian knew or not. 'No one told us you'd be coming, Mr Richter,' Orlov said, then paused. 'We've never met before,' he added, 'but I know quite a lot about you.'

'I'll bet you do,' Richter said.

Orlov chuckled. 'Oh, yes. It was a matter of simple deduction. When our bomb caught the wrong man this evening, we anticipated that you might be tempted to stop being on the defensive and do something rather more positive. It was, if our information about you is correct, entirely in character. You are a very dangerous man, Richter. The men we sent after you last week were two of the best we had. We brought them in especially to terminate you, and for what you did to them you're going to die very slowly. Very slowly and very painfully.'

'I didn't think you went in for that kind of thing, Vladimir,' Richter said. 'Not if our information about you is correct, that is.'

Orlov smiled again. 'I don't personally,' he said, and gestured to the man on his left. 'One of the men you killed was Yuri's brother. When I've finished talking to you, I'm going to give you to Yuri. Yuri will enjoy it, but I doubt if you will.'

Richter looked at Yuri. The Russian smiled, but it wasn't the smile of a man who is enjoying life. It was the smile of a man anticipating future pleasures, and Richter didn't like the look of it one bit. 'So how did you know I was coming tonight? I could have come tomorrow, or the day after.'

Orlov shook his head. 'No, Richter. It had to be tonight. You were annoyed about the bomb – so were we, by the way – and in any case, your superior would probably have forbidden you to try, if you'd spoken to him first.'

That was the only glimmer of light so far. They didn't know Richter had spoken to Simpson, and therefore they didn't know that Simpson knew as much as he did. Richter knew that if he never got out of the house alive, Simpson would know why, and Simpson was a very, very vindictive man. It was a cold comfort for Richter to take to his grave.

'This house is an expensive property, Richter,' Orlov continued, 'and it has a very sophisticated burglar alarm system. Oh, I've no doubt you fumbled around looking for wires and so on, but these days we're a good deal more subtle than that. There's a photoelectric cell warning system, working in the infra-red spectrum, which is triggered as soon as anything bigger than a cat comes over the wall or the gate. That system is linked to three night-vision cameras covering the grounds and the approach to the house. As soon as my men realized we had an intruder, they dressed and then we just sat here and waited for you to arrive. If we'd known for certain that you were coming, we would have left the ladder out for you. I don't think that plank is at all safe, you know.'

Richter grunted. 'I didn't think it was either. Why didn't you open the front door and invite me in?'

Orlov shook an admonishing finger. 'No, no, that's not in the game at all. We just waited for you to climb in through a window. All the first-floor rooms have a system of sequenced photoelectric cells. If you go to open the window from inside the room, you break one ray, which switches off the second ray covering the window area. But if you come in from the outside, you break the second ray first, and the alarm goes off. We have a main alarm panel downstairs in the lounge, and three repeaters up here in the main bedrooms.'

Richter didn't need telling who occupied those three bedrooms. Orlov pointed to the wall above the desk, and there Richter saw a small square grey box, on which one tiny red light was winking. 'Very clever, Vladimir,' Richter said. 'What else did you get for Christmas?'

For the first time a cloud of annoyance crossed the Russian's face. 'I would suggest that you refrain from remarks of that sort, Richter. Yuri will shortly be making life very unpleasant for you, but just how unpleasant depends to a large extent upon how you behave in this room. Rule one is you don't annoy me.' He paused. 'What I want to know, Richter, is just how much you and your organization know.'

'About what?' Richter asked.

The smile left Orlov's face. 'Please don't be coy. You know perfectly well what I'm talking about.' He signalled to Yuri, who got up and walked over to Richter. 'I'll ask you once again. How much do you know?'

'I don't know what you're—'

Richter saw it coming, but there was nothing he could do about it. Yuri's fist smashed into the left side of his face. Richter saw stars for a moment, then tasted blood on his lips. His face felt numb – the pain would come later. Yuri changed his position slightly, and applied the same treatment to the right side.

The first rule of interrogation, from the point of view of the subject, is never say anything. That may sound trite, but it is a perfectly valid piece of advice. Once you tell an interrogator anything at all, he can build on it and if he's any good he can confuse you to the extent that you can't remember what you told him, how much he knew already, and how much he's guessing. And if you reach that stage you have no hope at all of recovering the situation.

Orlov knew the rules just as well as Richter did, and as far as Richter could see the best thing he could do, bearing in mind that they were going to kill him anyway, was to try to mislead them as much as he could. Unfortunately for Richter, it was going to be a painful process, because before he could spill the fake beans, to confuse a metaphor, he was going to have to be 'persuaded' by Yuri. If Richter had been in Orlov's position, he would have been very suspicious indeed of a rapid surrender.

'Once again, Richter. Tell me what you know.'

Richter shook his head. Yuri was smiling again and Richter realized he was just beginning to enjoy himself. Two more blows rocked Richter's head from side to side, and the stars started getting brighter. Despite what may be seen in films, there is a limit to the number of severe blows to the head that can be tolerated before unconsciousness supervenes. Yuri was very big and very strong, and Richter could feel himself getting near the point where the blackness would envelop him.

He was dimly aware of hands lashing his arms to the side of the chair, and then the work began in earnest. After the fifth or sixth blow Richter stopped counting and concentrated on keeping awake. When Yuri finally stopped, after a sharp command from Orlov, Richter hung his head and played dead. The way he was feeling, it wasn't any effort at all. Someone grabbed Richter's hair and pulled his head back. 'He's out. You want me to wake him?'

'Leave him for a few minutes. I doubt,' Orlov added, chuckling, 'if a few slaps across the face are going to bring him round. There are some smelling salts in my bathroom cabinet, on the bottom shelf. Get them. Oh, and bring some towels and put them on the carpet. He's bleeding quite a lot.' Richter's face was still too numb for him to feel anything as delicate as a stream of blood running down it, but he could still taste the blood in his mouth. He wondered briefly and inconsequentially what sort of a state his clothes were in.

When the towels had been positioned to Orlov's liking, Yuri thrust the bottle of smelling salts under Richter's nose. He snorted, then opened his eyes. Or rather, his eye. His left eye seemed to be struck tightly shut, probably by drying blood. Orlov was still smiling. 'And again, Richter. What do you know?'

Richter tried to speak, but all he managed was a croak.

'Water. Get him a glass of water.'

Richter took a couple of sips, and coughed.

'We're waiting.'

Richter tried again. 'Did you hear about the Irish tap dancer? Fell in the sink and—'

Yuri started again, harder this time if anything, and Richter could feel himself slipping away. Orlov stopped him.

'Well, Richter?'

Richter shook his head. Yuri started again, alternating between Richter's face and stomach. And the pattern was repeated, time and again. Richter passed out at least twice, possibly three times, and was revived each time with the salts. His whole head throbbed, as if some great pump was inflating and deflating it, and his stomach ached as if he'd been kicked by a donkey. Richter could feel his will to resist slowly ebbing away.

All he wanted, all he wanted in the world, was for them to stop. Silently Richter cursed Yuri, and he cursed Orlov and most of all he cursed Simpson for getting him into this thing in the first place. The one thing Richter couldn't do was blame himself because he had to keep angry if he was going to have any sort of control left, and he had to have that control because when he finally told them, he had to tell them what he wanted to, not what he knew. So Richter cursed, and he cursed again and again.

Yuri's fists must have been aching by that time, because Richter was dimly aware that the blows had changed. Instead of the solid thump of flesh and bone, it was a stinging, slicing pain. He opened his eye cautiously and saw that Yuri had a bucket of water and a hand towel. He had moved his chair round so that he was more comfortable, with the bucket in front of him. Two blows, one left, one right, wet the towel, wring it out, two blows, one left, one right, wet the towel. Yuri looked as if he could go on all night. Richter knew, quite certainly, that he couldn't. He had to stop it, and he had to stop it soon.

And suddenly it did stop. The reeking, penetrating odour of the salts forced Richter's head up, and he looked at Orlov. 'That, Richter, was just for starters. Yuri is now going to start breaking your bones, starting with the fingers. Unless, of course, you feel like talking a little?'

Summoning what strength he had, Richter nodded. He couldn't allow Yuri to do anything to his hands. He couldn't see any way out of the house, but if Yuri smashed his hands, that would be it. He would definitely die, without being able to do a thing about it. With his hands, there was always a chance.

'You mean you will talk, Richter?' Orlov asked and Richter nodded again.

'Good, good. I thought you'd see things my way, eventually. Wipe his face, Yuri, and then give him another drink of water.'

If Richter had been looking for a ministering angel, Yuri would have been right down at the bottom of his list of likely candidates.

Wipe Richter's face he did. He used the wet towel, but to Richter it felt like he had taken a rough file to it. A file wielded with most of his very considerable strength. The only benefit seemed to be that by the time he'd finished Richter could open his left eye again. The glass of water helped, but only a little. Richter knew that what he had to do was to take as long as he could to tell the tale. That way he could recover some of his strength before Yuri took him away to play.

Orlov spoke. 'Well, Richter? We're waiting.'

Richter coughed and shook his head. 'Where – where do you want me to start?'

'At the beginning, Richter, at the beginning. Where else?'

Situation Room, White House, 1600 Pennsylvania Avenue, Washington, D.C.

As soon as Walter Hicks left the Oval Office, the President moved over to the desk and depressed a key on the intercom. 'I'm on the way down,' he said, and walked out of the office. Two minutes later he entered the Situation Room, a small, wood-lined underground chamber, some twenty-five feet long by twenty feet wide, located in the basement of the West Wing of the White House, directly under the Oval Office. It is not, by any stretch of the imagination, a hardened or bombproof facility, and is only designed to be used in the early stages of a crisis.

'How's it going, John?' the President asked, walking across the room.

John Mitchell, the tall grey-haired Vice-President, looked up from his copy of the *Washington Post*. The Vice-President is invariably placed in charge of crisis management and he had been running the Situation Room since Walter Hicks' first meeting with the President. 'Absolutely nothing new, Mr President. Despite what the CIA believes, there are no indications of any unusual military activity anywhere in the CIS. We're just sitting here twiddling our thumbs.' He gestured at the White House staff and senior military officers sitting at desks in the room.

'I've just seen Karasin,' the President said.

'And?' Mitchell looked interested.

The President shrugged. 'And nothing. He asked to see me because Russian satellites had detected our escalation to DEFCON FOUR and wanted to know what it was all about. He claims to know nothing about any threat to the US, and I think he's probably telling the truth.'

Mitchell grunted. 'I've said it before, Mr President, and I'll say it again. I think the CIA is paranoid about this so-called covert assault. I don't believe there is a threat to America, and I think we're just wasting our time. More importantly, we've now alarmed the Kremlin for no good reason, which will do nothing for our international relations. My recommendation, Mr President, is that we stop this nonsense, stand down to normal readiness, and tell the Russians it was all just a false alarm.'

The President nodded. His Vice-President was no fan of the CIA, or any of the other intelligence organizations. 'I hear what you say, John, but I disagree. As long as there is even the slightest possibility of any threat to the security of the United States, I'm going to take whatever steps I think are justified. Right now, that's DEFCON FOUR, and a meeting of the National Security Council here at the White House in thirty minutes.'

Orpington, Kent

Richter told Orlov about Newman, and the suspicions SIS had entertained about his death. He went slowly through his time in Moscow, telling him about the few inconsistencies he had found on the body – the injuries that weren't there but should have been.

Orlov interrupted. 'That's not enough, Richter. I grant you that one of his legs would have been likely to break, but there is no certainty in the matter.'

'Quite right, Vladimir,' Richter said. 'Perhaps I should have pointed out that by then I was just looking for indications as to how the man had been killed. I knew as soon as I looked at the corpse that it wasn't Newman.'

'How?' Orlov's voice was a soft, silky purr.

'Attention to detail, Vladimir. That's where a lot of high-powered schemes fall down; attention to detail. Your SVR colleagues picked some poor sucker who was unfortunate enough to be about Newman's height, weight and colouring, and I've no doubt they checked to see if Newman had any distinguishing marks. Because none were obvious – no scars, tattoos and so on – they assumed that he hadn't got any. If they had bothered to look, they would have found that he had had an in-growing toenail removed years ago. The corpse your people thoughtfully provided for the Embassy had all ten toenails.'

'I see,' Orlov said. 'I take your point. The whole scheme, of course, was not of my doing but I was kept informed of the operation. I will see to it that the appropriate steps are taken in Moscow to reprimand the operatives responsible for this.'

Richter nodded. 'I'm sure you'll enjoy that, Vladimir.'

The Russian made an impatient gesture. 'Continue.'

Richter asked for more water, more as a delaying tactic than because he actually wanted any, then finished off Moscow and told him what SIS knew about the over-flight of north-west Russia by the Blackbird. Richter sang the praises of the SR–71A fairly loudly, partly because he wanted to annoy Orlov just a little, to try to make him slightly less critical of the lies he was soon going to start telling, and partly because dragging the story out bought him just a little more time, and time was something he needed a lot of.

'Yes, yes,' said Orlov, impatiently. 'The American spy-plane can fly high and fast, we know that. It was fortunate for the Americans that we were not prepared for such an intrusion. It would have been a different matter if they had met any of our MiG–31 interceptors.'

'No doubt, Vladimir, no doubt,' Richter said. Orlov looked at him sharply, but Richter wasn't smiling. He couldn't smile. He didn't think, the way his face felt, that he would ever smile again.

He covered the diversion of the Blackbird to Lossiemouth, and dealt with the insistence of the Ministry of Defence on seeing the films shot by the aircraft cameras. Up to that point, he hadn't really told Orlov anything of importance, or anything he hadn't already known or hadn't guessed. The difficult bit was just about to start.

'So,' Orlov said, 'what did your so-called experts think of the films?'

'They were puzzled,' Richter replied, which was true. 'And they still are.' Which wasn't quite true. 'The only significant feature on the films shot by the Blackbird was the removal of a small hill which had been on previous satellite films of the area.'

Richter saw Orlov stiffen almost imperceptibly. 'So?'

Richter tried to inject a little puzzlement into his voice. 'The Americans believe the hill was the test site for a new type of nuclear weapon, but that's not our take. Our experts' reading of the seismograph records suggests that the weapon test was just a blind, using a conventional medium-yield weapon to conceal what you've really been up to.'

'Which is what?'

'We still aren't sure, but we believe that the hill wasn't a hill at all. We think that it was a camouflaged site, covering some sort of covert installation, which you have since decided to remove. Then you detonated a surplus nuclear device to cover up the fact that the hill – or rather the installation – had vanished.'

Richter could see Orlov start to relax, so he spun him the rest of the yarn that he had been working on ever since the lights had come on in the bedroom. He told him that SIS suspected that the installation had been a test site for a portable phased array radar unit, designed for early warning of either orbital or sub-orbital missiles or intruders. He expounded on the potential of such a device to avoid detection by reconnaissance vehicles, its value to Russia and the possible illegality of such a radar under the terms of the SALT agreements.

Orlov started nodding before he got halfway through the tale, and Richter hoped it was to convince him that he was right rather than an expression of his appreciation for Richter's ingenuity.

'We obviously don't know any more than that at the moment, but we'll find out, I promise you,' Richter concluded.

'I don't think you will, Richter,' said Orlov, speaking the absolute truth. 'You, personally, certainly won't.' He paused for a moment. 'Why are you so certain that the hill was a camouflaged site?'

'We aren't, but we applied simple logic,' Richter said. 'You've very rarely carried out above-ground nuclear weapon tests, and only then after a lot of preparation and work. We saw no signs of such preparations near the site. No, what happened in the tundra had all the hallmarks of a hasty cover-up, using a bomb blast to remove the evidence of what you were doing up there previously. It's the only scenario that makes sense.'

Orlov nodded slowly. 'Very good, Richter, very good. Your logic is impeccable, but the premises upon which you based your argument are wholly invalid. But, you are almost right, and you may take that comfort with you to your grave. What I will say is that it wasn't a phased array radar, but something much more interesting.' A careful man, Orlov, giving nothing away even though he knew that within minutes Richter was going to be in no state to ever tell anyone anything. The Russian glanced behind Richter. 'Yuri, he's all yours,' he said.

Richter looked round and Yuri smiled at him. Richter didn't need any prompting to know why he was smiling. He turned back to Orlov. 'I've told you what you wanted. If you're going to kill me can't you just shoot me?'

Orlov shook his head. 'I'm sorry, Richter,' he said in a tone which made it quite clear that he wasn't, 'but I promised you to Yuri, and he's been looking forward to tonight ever since the day you visited JARIC. And anyway,' he added, 'we don't want gunshots echoing out over the Home Counties, do we? Lowers the tone of the area.'

Richter tried again, leaning forward in the chair as far as his roped arms would allow. 'Orlov, please. Hasn't he hurt me enough?'

Orlov's smile turned to a sneer of contempt. 'Our conversation, and your life, is at an end. Yuri, take him away. Try not to make too much of a mess downstairs.'

As a sentence of death it left a good deal to be desired, Richter thought.

Moscow

Dmitri Trushenko glanced around the apartment for what he knew would probably be the last time. He had packed enough clothes and toiletries for a couple of weeks into a lightweight suitcase which was standing by the apartment door, and he had just made a final check of the contents of his briefcase. As well as the portable computer with its built-in modem, he had his mobile telephone with a spare battery and charger, plus the Ultra Secret classified *Podstava* file. He knew that simple possession of the file would be enough to justify his immediate arrest, and he was relying upon his credentials as a government minister to avoid problems.

He had left a brief note for his manservant on the dining table, confirming that he would be away, staying with friends in St Petersburg, for the next week or so, and adding that he would telephone when he knew the date of his return. The note was virtually a duplicate of the one on his secretary's desk at the Ministry, except that his secretary had also been given his contact address in St Petersburg. It was all perfectly normal – a part of the routine that Trushenko had carefully established over the previous seven months.

There was a brief knock at the door. Trushenko opened the door and handed his suitcase to his chauffeur, then picked up his briefcase, locked the apartment door and followed him into the elevator.

The drive to the station took only a few minutes in the light early-morning traffic, and Trushenko arrived in good time for the express to St Petersburg. The chauffeur took the suitcase out of the boot of the limousine and accompanied Trushenko into the station. Trushenko handed over the ticket – purchased for him by his secretary – to the railway official, who removed the top copy and handed the rest back. He took the suitcase from his chauffeur, walked on to the platform, and climbed on to the train without a backward glance.

Orpington, Kent

Yuri and the anonymous thug released Richter's arms, and he slumped forward out of the chair on to the floor. His one hope was to convince everyone, and especially Yuri, that he was in no state to resist anything. That might, just might, make them a little careless.

They picked him up and Yuri twisted Richter's left arm up and behind his back. The second man made to help him, but Yuri shrugged him away with an impatient gesture. 'He's mine,' he growled, in heavily accented Russian. 'I do not need your help.'

Richter believed him. So did Orlov. 'Do as he says. Just open the door for them.'

Yuri dragged Richter out of the room and to the top of the stairs. Richter wondered briefly how he was supposed to get down them. He found out. Yuri simply gave him a hefty shove. Richter stumbled off balance, grabbed for the banister and missed, then tumbled. He had enough presence of mind to tuck his head well in as he fell, and he tried as far as possible to roll rather than bounce, but by the time he reached the half landing his body felt as if it had gone over the Niagara Falls in a barrel.

Richter moved cautiously, but nothing seemed to be broken. Yet. He had got to his knees by the time Yuri reached him. The Russian kicked out, his foot catching Richter in the stomach, and he crashed and rolled his way to the bottom of the stairs. From the throbbing agony in his lower abdomen, Richter decided that if Yuri ever tired of being a bodyguard, there was definitely an opening for him on the football field. Richter was quicker this time, and he was on his feet before Yuri reached him, but still bentalmost double clutching his stomach.

Yuri grabbed Richter's arm and jerked him upright, and Richter moaned softly. It wasn't hard to do. It would have been hard not to. Yuri punched him in the stomach a couple of times for good measure, and gave him another shove. Richter reeled across the hallway and fetched up against a panelled door. Yuri grabbed him, twisted him round and smashed him face-first into the panels, then turned the handle and pushed him into the room.

Richter stumbled over something and fell to the floor, knocking the back of his head against a table leg as he did so. What made it worse was that the table leg didn't move. As the lights came on he looked at it and saw why. It was a billiard table, covered in a dust-cloth that reached down almost to the floor. The one thing Richter needed then was a weapon, any weapon, and he suddenly realized that he might have found one.

Richter looked over at Yuri. He had turned round to close the door and was taking off his shoulder holster, the better to enjoy his work. Richter reached his right hand up, under the cloth, to where the corner pocket was, praying that the balls would be in the pockets and not in a box in some cupboard, because if they were in a box he was dead.

His probing fingers found the mesh of the pocket, and then the smooth round hardness of a ball on the rack just below the pocket. Just the one, but one was all he needed. He closed his fingers around it and dropped his arm just as Yuri turned back towards him.

Yuri had the door key in his hand. He smiled at Richter and slid it into his trouser pocket, then walked over towards the table. He stopped about three feet away and looked down. 'I'm going to enjoy this, English. My brother was a good man, a good Communist. You are going to wish you had never been born. Get up.'

Richter was leaning against the leg of the billiard table, his right arm twisted round behind him, the ball held tight in his fist. He shook his head. 'Can't,' he gasped. 'Can't move.'

Yuri snorted with disgust and stepped closer. Richter hoped the Russian wanted him on his feet first, so that he could have the pleasure of knocking him down again. Most thugs preferred that, in Richter's experience. Yuri reached down and seized the lapels of Richter's leather jacket in both hands. 'I told you up, English bastard.'

Yuri was strong, and Richter knew that he was only going to get the one chance. If that failed Yuri would break both his arms and then beat him to a pulp. Yuri began to pull. Richter could feel his weight coming off the floor. He looked at the Russian's face, judging distance, keeping his right arm and shoulder low. As Richter planted his feet flat on the floor, he moved.

His right arm was still below the level of his knees, and he brought it up, up with every ounce of strength that he possessed, straightening his legs as he did so. Richter's right fist, holding the heavy ball tightly, swept up between Yuri's arms and caught him under the chin, hard. The Russian's head snapped back, and he crashed to the floor.

Moscow

Fifteen minutes before the St Petersburg express was due to leave, Trushenko climbed down from the carriage and hurried back along the platform. At the barrier he explained that he had to make an urgent telephone call and was directed towards the far wall of the station.

Twenty-three minutes after that, Trushenko was in another railway station, sitting in a carriage on a train that was going to an entirely different destination.

Orpington, Kent

Richter didn't wait. As Yuri tumbled backwards Richter kicked his right foot up into his groin as hard as he could, then went for the head. He wasn't thinking, by that stage. He was an animal, an animal fighting for its life, and he was going to make no mistakes.

When Richter stopped, Yuri's head was a red, battered mess, and he didn't need a stethoscope or a doctor to tell him that the Russian was dead. He had probably been dead after the first blow with the ball that Richter still had clutched in his right hand. A blow like that has a definite tendency to break necks, if it's delivered hard enough, and Richter couldn't have delivered it much harder.

Richter staggered, panting, to the nearest chair, and slumped into it. He needed a rest, just for a few minutes. Richter looked at the bloodstained ball in his hand. It was a snooker ball, a red, which

seemed somehow appropriate, bearing in mind the political persuasion of the man on the floor. Richter smiled, or thought he did – his
face ached so much that it was difficult to tell what the facial muscles
were doing – and put the ball into an ashtray.

Then he started thinking again, and picked it up, pulled a handkerchief out of Yuri's pocket and wiped the ball thoroughly before
putting it back into the pocket of the billiard table. Richter pulled the
door key out of Yuri's trouser pocket, still using his handkerchief to
avoid leaving prints, and put it in the lock. He took the Russian's pistol, an Austrian Glock 17 semi-automatic, out of his shoulder rig and
without bothering about prints – he would wipe it later – checked it
over and made sure that the magazine was full. He found two spare
magazines in a pouch attached to the other side of the shoulder holster
strapping, so Richter took them as well, though he didn't think he was
going to need them. There was a silencer in Yuri's jacket pocket.
Richter took it and screwed it on to the pistol barrel. With the gun
in his hand he felt better, and sat there in the chair for another twenty
minutes or so, gathering his strength.

When Richter's breathing had slowed to normal, and he felt a bit
more of a going concern, he got up and listened at the door. There was
no sound outside, so he turned the key slowly in the lock and eased
the door open, taking care to use the handkerchief again. The hall was
quiet and empty, with the single light still burning. Richter removed
the key and locked the door from the hall side, then wiped the key
thoroughly and dropped it into a tank of tropical fish that stood beside
one wall. Richter knew that immersion in water would certainly not
help define any partial prints that he might have left on it.

He walked to the foot of the stairs and listened carefully – there
was no sound from above. He hadn't expected any, but Richter had
only lived as long as he had by never assuming anything and never
trusting anyone. He could, he realized, have just walked through the
front door and got away on the Honda, but he had come for a talk with
Orlov, and he intended to have a talk with Orlov.

He started up the stairs, keeping to the side nearest the wall,
where any creaks from the treads would be minimized. At the half
landing he paused to gather breath and listened again. Still nothing.

He continued to the top, and walked slowly over to the door of Orlov's room.

Pressing his ear close, Richter could hear the soft sound of voices, so he assumed that Orlov and his bodyguard were in conference. Richter slid the pistol into his pocket, wiped the sweat from his palms on a clean handkerchief, took the Glock out again, took a deep breath and opened the door.

Orlov was sitting at his desk, the bodyguard standing to his right and a little behind him. They seemed to be studying something on a piece of paper on the desk, and neither turned round, no doubt because they were only expecting Yuri.

Only a fool gives an enemy an even break, so Richter raised the Glock, took careful aim, and shot the bodyguard in the back. The Russian pitched forward and sideways, smashing into the corner of the desk before sliding sideways to the floor. Richter aimed again and shot him carefully in the stomach, twice, then once in the head.

Then he turned his attention to Orlov who sat, frozen, an expression of stark terror on his face, like some tableau in a waxworks. 'Hullo again, Vladimir,' Richter said, his words slurring through his battered lips. 'I'm not really from the Gas Board. I'm an ornithologist and I'm collecting new specimens. You're my little Russian canary, and you're going to sing, sing, sing.'

Chapter Fifteen

Saturday
Ickenham, Middlesex

'Just what the hell happened to you?'

Richter tried a grin that turned into little more than a twitch of his facial muscles, and looked across the room into the worried face of David Bentley, Lieutenant Commander Royal Navy, and the current Naval Liaison Officer at Royal Air Force Uxbridge. He and Richter had gone through the Royal Naval College at Dartmouth together, and had kept in touch – albeit somewhat sporadically – ever since. They were less than friends, but more than acquaintances, and Richter knew that he could rely on Bentley to help, and not to ask too many questions.

He had had practically no options anyway. Simpson's apartment was possibly being watched by then, and Richter knew that his own apartment building had been under surveillance for some time. And after what he'd done to Orlov, the Russian dogs would be out in force. Bentley's RAF married quarter had been the only place he could think of running to when he'd staggered away from the house in Orpington.

'I can't tell you, David,' Richter said, his words slurred and indistinct. 'It's dangerous enough for me – I can't expose you to the same risks I get paid to take.'

Bentley looked at Richter's battered tragedy of a face. 'Whatever they're paying you, Paul, it's not enough.'

Richter lifted the mug of coffee cautiously to his lips and took an exploratory sip. The scalding liquid played hell with the cuts and abrasions he could feel inside his mouth, but it was welcome for all that.

'OK,' Bentley said. 'I'll go and put your motorcycle in the garage, then we'll see what we can do to make you a bit more comfortable.'

Richter nodded his thanks, and eased back in the chair, wincing as eddies of pain shot through his torso. The journey through London and out to Ickenham had been a slow and painful nightmare. The beating he'd received had left him weak and dizzy and aching in every joint, and twice he'd had to stop the Honda and wait for his head to clear.

He'd stopped for a few minutes in Clapham and rung Bentley from a public telephone box, just in case the Russians had somehow managed to tap into the GSM mobile system and could trace the numbers he called. He'd hung on for better than twenty rings before Bentley had picked up the receiver, and he'd told him almost nothing, just asked him to watch out for his arrival and to let him into the house without delay. Bentley, typically, hadn't commented, just said that he would, and had rung off.

The side door of the house closed. Richter heard the sound of a key turning in a lock, and then Bentley was back in the living room. 'Can you stand?' he asked, and Richter nodded.

With Bentley's help, Richter slowly removed the haversack, then eased his arms out of the leather jacket. Bentley looked quizzically at the Smith and Wesson in Richter's shoulder holster. The Mauser HSc, which Richter had liberated from Yuri's deceased colleague before leaving Orlov's house, was stashed in the haversack. Richter had reduced the Glock 17 that he had used on Orlov and the bodyguard to its component parts and dumped them in several widely spaced rubbish bins between Orpington and Ickenham.

'Is that loaded?' Bentley asked, gesturing at the Smith. Richter nodded, pulled the pistol out of the holster and shook the shells into his palm. Bentley took them from him, and put the pistol, holster and bullets on the sideboard.

Getting the sweater off Richter's battered body proved much more difficult than the jacket, and eventually Bentley went into the kitchen and returned with a large pair of scissors, which he used to slit up the back of the sweater. The shirt was, by comparison, easy.

'You're a mess,' Bentley said shortly, looking at Yuri's handiwork. Most of Richter's chest and stomach was a montage of blue and vivid purple bruises. 'I'm surprised you managed to ride that bloody motorbike of yours all the way here.'

'I nearly didn't,' Richter said, and sat down again.

Bentley vanished into the kitchen for a few minutes and came back with another mug of coffee, a plastic bowl of warm water, and a selection of soft cotton cloths. He looked down at Richter and shook his head. 'I'm no medical man,' he said, 'but I really think you need to see a doctor. You could have broken ribs, a cracked sternum or anything under that lot.'

'No,' Richter said. 'I just need a place to rest and hide for a while, that's all.'

'OK. Now,' Bentley went on, 'this is probably going to hurt, but I'd be obliged if you didn't scream, because Kate's still asleep upstairs, and you really don't want to wake her. If she doesn't get her full eight hours she's not a lot of fun to be around.'

'I'll bite on a bullet,' Richter said, trying another smile, and leaned slowly backwards as Bentley began to gently bathe his cuts.

It didn't hurt as much as Richter had feared, but the water in the plastic bowl quickly turned a deep red, and he could see the concern on Bentley's face as fresh blood flowed from the wounds. 'I won't say it again, but you know what I think,' he said, getting up and carrying the bowl into the kitchen. He came back moments later with a first-aid kit, spread antiseptic cream on the wounds on Richter's face and covered them with soft pads which he secured with a bandage wound round his head. 'I can't do much about your chest and stomach,' he said. 'I guess you'll just have to sleep lying on your back for a while.'

'Thanks, David.'

'Don't mention it. And I really do mean don't mention it, and especially not to the people who did this to you. Now, can you make it up the stairs?'

'If there's a bed up there with my name on it,' Richter said, 'I can make it.'

*

Richter awoke with the sunlight streaming through the windows, from which the curtains had been drawn. For the briefest of moments he lay still, trying to work out where he was. He didn't recognize the room, and the pyjamas he was wearing were an unfamiliar pattern. Then everything fell into place. He turned to look at his watch on the bedside table and winced as a spasm of pain shot through his neck. He tried again, more cautiously. Almost eleven. He lay back slowly, luxuriating in the warmth.

The ache from his stomach had eased somewhat, but his whole body was stiff and sore, and his face hurt like hell. He was wondering whether to try to get up by himself, because the one place he was definitely going to have to get to, and soon, was the toilet, when the bedroom door swung open and David Bentley walked in, bearing a laden tray. 'Breakfast,' he said, and put the tray on top of a chest of drawers.

Richter tried a smile that almost worked. 'Thanks, David. Actually, what I need more than breakfast is the bathroom.' With Bentley's help, Richter levered himself into a sitting position, and then to his feet. Three minutes later, and much relieved, he sat down again on the bed and leaned back against the headboard.

'Coffee?' Richter asked, took the cup from Bentley and put it on the bedside table.

'I wasn't sure what you wanted, so I've just brought toast and marmalade. If you want anything else, it's no problem.'

'No, that's fine,' Richter said. 'I've never got much of an appetite in the morning.'

Richter ate the toast and drank his coffee. Bentley poured a second cup and handed it to him. 'What are you going to do?' he asked.

'First of all,' Richter said, 'and if you don't mind, I'm going to take this cup of coffee and go and have a long soak in the bath. After that, I'll let you know what my plans are. Always assuming,' he added, 'that I've worked any out by then.'

Richter looked at himself in the full-length mirror before he climbed into the bath. He was not, by any stretch of the imagination, a pretty sight. The bruises, although not aching quite as much, looked a damn sight worse than they had the previous night, and there were very few areas of his body which were free of some purple blotches. He pulled off the bandage and looked at his face. It was a mess, puffy and red with livid wheals on both cheeks – caused by the wet towel wielded by the late and unlamented Yuri – overlying the deeper bruises resulting from the early stages of his interrogation. The good thing was he still seemed to have all his teeth, and he could feel no evidence of deeper damage. What he wasn't going to be able to do for a while was shave.

Richter lay in the bath, feeling the heat of the water beginning to ease his aches, drank the coffee and then started thinking. He needed to talk to Simpson, face to face, and quickly. The problem was how. He knew Simpson was going to be at Hammersmith for most of the day, because he had told him so the previous night. Richter wanted to keep out of sight as far as possible, which meant he couldn't risk going to Hammersmith, because there would certainly be a hostile watch there, and even if he got inside without being hit, there would definitely be a man with a rifle waiting for him when he came out.

So he had to set up a meet, on neutral ground. Richter still wasn't happy with the telephone situation, either. It was at least possible that his flat line had been tapped, and if it had, then he had no guarantee that the Hammersmith building exchange hadn't got a few bugs as well. So, Richter knew he had to contact Simpson some other way.

Richter walked slowly and carefully down the stairs, wearing a vivid blue dressing gown he'd found hanging in the wardrobe in the bedroom. Bentley was sitting in an armchair, reading a copy of the *Daily Telegraph*, and looked up as Richter walked into the living room. 'Kate?' Richter asked, interrogatively.

'Weekend shopping,' Bentley replied briefly. 'Normally I go with her, but as you're here . . .'

'Is she OK?' Richter asked.

Bentley nodded. 'Yes, she's fine. She knows the sort of work you do, so she's not too enthusiastic about having you in the house, but that's all.'

'If there was anywhere else I could go, David, I'd be out of here in a minute. The last thing I want to do is cause you or Kate any problems.'

'It's no problem, Paul. Just relax. Oh, and don't, for heaven's sake, let her see that pistol. You know what she's like about guns of any sort.'

'Of course not. It's tucked away in my haversack upstairs.'

'Good. Now, would you like another coffee?'

'I never say no,' Richter said. 'Have you got some writing paper and an envelope? I need to send somebody a message.'

Bentley gestured towards a roll-top desk in the corner of the room. 'Help yourself,' he said, and walked out into the kitchen.

Richter wrote out a note with some care. He handwrote it, so that it could be verified against the samples of his handwriting held at Hammersmith, and prefixed it with the code-word 'TESTAMENT', which he knew would capture Simpson's undivided attention. 'TESTAMENT' was a code-word only used when the sender of the message had information which was believed with reasonable certainty to be likely to involve major powers in conflict or, to remove the top-dressing of Ministry of Defence verbiage, information likely to lead to war. The word had not, to Richter's knowledge, been used at FOE since the formation of the department, but in the circumstances it was certainly justified.

Richter read the note several times, ensuring that the contents were clear and unambiguous, then sealed it in an envelope and addressed it to 'Hammersmith Commercial Packers'. At the top of the envelope he added in block capitals 'For the personal attention of Mr Simpson', and underlined 'personal' twice. He asked Bentley to ring one of the numerous motorcycle despatch firms working in west London and to request a rider as soon as possible.

The front door bell rang forty minutes later, and two minutes after that Richter watched through the living-room windows as the black-clad rider climbed back onto his Suzuki and roared away towards the Uxbridge Road.

OVERKILL

Situation Room, White House, 1600 Pennsylvania Avenue, Washington, D.C.

'Gentlemen,' the President began, 'the folders in front of you contain the latest information we have about this alleged Russian assault. The code-name "Kentucky Rose" has been allocated to this, and the data is subject to a "Top Secret, US EYES ONLY" classification.'

He looked slowly round the table at the three other statutory members of the National Security Council – the Vice-President, the Secretary of State and the Secretary of Defense – and at the Chairman of the Joint Chiefs of Staff, one of the two statutory advisers to the National Security Council. The other statutory adviser, the Director of Central Intelligence, was absent.

'You should also know,' the President continued, 'that Ambassador Karasin has denied all knowledge of this threat. It could be argued, of course, that he would have been instructed by Moscow to make such a denial, which is certainly possible. However, I've known Karasin for three years, and I don't think he's following the party line. I think he really doesn't know. If we take that as fact,' he went on, 'then the situation is even more dangerous than the Cuban crisis. At least then Kennedy knew who he was dealing with. This time, I don't think we do. Accordingly, despite the fact that we still have no independent evidence to support the data the CIA claims to have uncovered, I propose to invoke SIOP with immediate effect.'

The Single Integrated Operational Plan is the central and most secret part of the West's nuclear deterrent. Despite the fact that SIOP has existed, in one form or another, since 1960, it is so secret that even the acronym 'SIOP' is classified and the plan has its own dedicated security classification – 'Extremely Sensitive Information' or ESI. SIOP has evolved from a simple 'launch everything and blast the Commies to pieces' strategy to a finely tuned and infinitely variable plan which would, in certain circumstances, permit nuclear exchanges between the superpowers to continue for weeks or even months.

The plan identifies in excess of forty thousand potential military and civilian targets within the Confederation of Independent

261

States, and contains a vast number of options and sub-options for both major and minor strikes. The American nuclear arsenal contains over ten thousand deliverable strategic nuclear weapons ranging in size from around fifty kilotons, or just over twice the size of the bombs dropped on Hiroshima and Nagasaki, up to weapons yielding over nine megatons. The accuracy of the missiles varies from less than six hundred feet to nearly one mile. SIOP factors-in the yield, accuracy and number of available missiles, and combines that with the type and number of suitable targets, and allows the nuclear commanders to select a multiplicity of possible responses to an attack.

'We are now,' the President continued, 'at DEFCON FOUR. I propose to leave decisions on timing of increased readiness to the Secretary of Defense, but I require us to be at DEFCON ONE – maximum force readiness – no later than sixteen hundred hours Eastern Standard Time on the tenth.'

Paris

The British Airways Boeing 757 landed at Paris' Charles de Gaulle airport fifteen minutes early, but the black Lincoln with CD plates was already there when John Westwood walked out of the terminal building. He didn't know the junior diplomat who had been tasked with meeting him, and he only made small talk on the drive south through Paris to the US Embassy at 2 avenue Gabriel, just off the avenue des Champs-Élysées. Westwood hadn't been to Paris before, although he'd visited France on three separate occasions, once professionally and twice as a tourist, and he looked with interest through the tinted windows at the bustle of the city.

To an American, accustomed to the heavy traffic, but generally tolerant and competent drivers stateside, French driving habits were frightening – almost lethally aggressive. Cars swerved from lane to lane without warning, drivers gesticulated and hooted at each other, and the few pedestrians he saw crossing the roads were quite clearly taking their lives in their hands. 'Is it always like this?' Westwood asked the diplomat.

The young man smiled and shook his head. 'No, sir. This is mid-afternoon at a weekend – it's quiet and peaceful. If you want to see it busy, stay here till next Friday and go stand at the Arc de Triomphe at about five thirty.'

'Jesus,' Westwood muttered.

At the Embassy, he was ushered through the security doors at the rear of the building and taken to a guest suite. He was unpacking his suitcase when there was a gentle knock on the door. 'Come in,' he said, turning around from hanging up his jacket.

A short, grey-haired man wearing rimless spectacles opened the door and walked into the room. 'Miles Turner,' he said, by way of introduction. 'I'm Chief of Station,' he added.

'John Westwood. Pleased to meet you, Miles,' Westwood replied, striding across the room and shaking his hand.

'I know why you're here, John,' Turner said. 'I had a classified signal from Roger Abrahams in London yesterday afternoon, and there's a conference call with Langley scheduled in an hour or so. What I'm not sure about is whether you've had a wasted journey. The French are as prickly as hell about anything to do with es-pionage. If they had an agent who was valet to the head of the SVR, I doubt if they'd even tell you what colour pants he wears.' Westwood grunted. 'Anyway, we'll do what we can,' Turner contin-ued. 'I've arranged a meeting with the DGSE for Monday afternoon.'

'Remind me,' said Westwood.

'The DGSE is the *Direction Générale de Sécurité Extérieure*,' Turner said. 'It used to be called the *Service de Documentation Extérieure et de Contre-Espionage*, or SDECE, until Mitterand's election in 1981. As well as being partisan and reluctant to talk to anyone who isn't French, it's also made some spectacular blunders, like sinking the *Rainbow Warrior* in New Zealand waters a few years back. The DGSE has been quiet of late, which may mean it's up to something. Or,' he added after a pause, 'it may not.'

Ickenham, Middlesex

'I'm really sorry to be a nuisance, Kate,' Richter said, as Bentley's wife walked into the kitchen carrying two bulging shopping bags.

She put the bags down on the worktop and began pulling groceries out of them. 'You're not a nuisance, Paul,' she said, dark eyes flashing under her fringe of black hair. 'You're a friend and we're glad to be able to help. It's just that you're dangerous – well, not you personally, but it's the work you do and the people you associate with. That's what worries me.'

'I know,' Richter said, 'and I'll be out of here just as soon as I can. Probably tomorrow, or Monday at the very latest.'

'You don't have to leave until you're ready, Paul,' Kate said, but Richter could detect the relief in her voice as she realized that he would soon be out of their house.

After lunch, while Kate busied herself in the kitchen, Richter outlined what he was going to have to do the following morning, and what he was going to have to ask David Bentley to do to help him.

'It seems bloody complicated,' Bentley said when Richter had finished.

'It is bloody complicated,' Richter said, 'but I have to be sure that the man I'm going to meet has shaken any tails – lost anyone following him, I mean – before he meets me. I can tell you, with absolute certainty, that if I get seen by the wrong people, I'm dead.'

'You do lead an exciting life, Paul,' Bentley said, but there was absolutely no trace of envy in his voice. 'On the whole, though, I think I'd rather just shuffle files at Uxbridge all day then come back home and mow the grass.'

'To each his own,' Richter said, 'though right now I'd trade places with you if I could.' He paused. 'I know what Kate thinks, but could you help me tomorrow for an hour or two? Your part will, I guarantee, be risk-free. All you'd have to do would be to deliver me to the service area on the M4, and then pick me up after the meeting.'

Bentley grinned at him. 'I don't see a problem. I think tomorrow it would be prudent if we took you along to the local hospital for a check-up. That way she'll never know.'

'Thanks, David. I really appreciate it.'

'One question. Why are you meeting in a motorway service area?'

'Because on a motorway you can be very sure if anyone is following you. If my man pulls in, and any of the cars he has had following him pull in as well, he'll simply put some petrol in his car and then drive off. He'll only meet me if there's no indication of any pursuit. You can't, you see,' Richter finished, 'front tail or double back on a motorway, not without making it quite obvious, and not without risking a motorway patrol breathing down your neck.'

Bentley looked doubtful. 'Yes, I can see that, but what happens if he is followed, and just drives away?'

'Then I'm back to square one,' Richter said.

Minsk, Belorussiya (White Russia)

Nicolai Modin unlocked the door of his stateroom with relief. It had been a busy day and a long evening. He had spent the morning in a final, but inconclusive, session with Grigori Sokolov. Sokolov had been apologetic, but he had still found no positive evidence to indicate the identity of the SVR traitor. Privately, he confided to Modin, he still thought Viktor Bykov was as likely as anyone, but he had discovered absolutely nothing incriminating about him.

The afternoon flight from Moscow had been delayed nearly an hour, as far as Modin could see for no good reason, and the drive from the airport to the local SVR headquarters had seemed interminable. Bykov seemed to have taken charge of the journey, and had appeared delighted to have been seconded to Modin's staff.

Out of courtesy, Modin had dined with the SVR senior officers, and had only retired at midnight, pleading the next day's long drive as the excuse. Viktor Bykov, he noted to himself somewhat sourly, was still in the dining room.

American Embassy, 2 avenue Gabriel, Paris

'I don't believe it,' John Westwood said into the telephone handset. 'Surely not even the GRU could mount an operation without some sort of approval from the Kremlin?'

'You may well be right,' Hicks replied. 'All I'm telling you is what the President thinks. It's possible that Karasin is a far better actor than we're giving him credit for, and that this is a carefully concocted operation approved of, and directed by, the Kremlin.'

'Nothing new from RAVEN, I suppose?' Roger Abrahams asked from London.

Hicks grunted. 'Nope,' he said. 'Rigby is still making himself as visible as possible, but he's had no further contact.'

'So where do we go from here?' Westwood asked.

'We carry on,' Hicks said. 'We assume the threat is real and do everything we can to combat it. You keep chasing the French while Roger tries to get something out of the British intelligence services. We're increasing satellite surveillance of the Asian landmass, but as we don't know what the hell we're looking for, that's probably a complete waste of time.

'I discussed this with the President, and his orders were quite specific. The security of the American people is paramount, so we're going to move from DEFCON FOUR all the way up to DEFCON ONE no later than the tenth. The President will launch the bombers and support tankers that evening. They'll fly to their Positive Control Points and hold there, awaiting a Presidential decision to either proceed and deliver their weapons or return to base.

'The Navy will get the boomers into position no later than the morning of the ninth, and all serviceable strategic nuclear missiles will begin countdown on the tenth. The missiles will be held at five minutes' notice to launch until the Russians implement their threat, or until the President is satisfied either that the threat doesn't exist or that the crisis is over.

'The President will probably remain at the White House throughout, or may decide to retreat with his family to Camp David. He wants to create as little speculation in the media as possible, and he thinks that if he remains in Washington that should help to reassure the American people. Whatever he decides, he has already ordered his principal military advisers to get airborne in the Nightwatch aircraft during the afternoon of the tenth.'

Walter Hicks paused for a moment. 'Gentlemen,' he said, 'the United States military machine is assuming a full war footing, and at the slightest sign of any provocation from Russia the President intends to attack at once.'

Chapter Sixteen

Sunday
Minsk, Belorussiya (White Russia)

The civilian stewards at the SVR headquarters had set out a separate table adjacent to the windows for the visiting senior officers. When Nicolai Modin walked somewhat stiffly down the stairs just after six, he found Viktor Bykov already seated, drinking thick black coffee and reading a local paper. The two men nodded to each other, and as soon as Modin was seated, a steward hurried over to take his order. Modin looked at the plates of black bread, cheese, salami and pastries that were already arranged on the table, and just asked for coffee.

'So, General,' Bykov said, 'today we begin the final phase.'

Modin nodded and reached for a pastry. 'It will be a long and tiring journey, Viktor,' the older man said. 'Nilov – my aide at Yazenevo – prepared a schedule for me. He prepares,' Modin added thoughtfully, 'schedules for almost everything.'

Bykov nodded and smiled. 'So I've heard,' he murmured.

Modin looked at Bykov and smiled gently. 'I would be somewhat lost without that young man,' he said. 'Anyway, he has calculated that we have about eighteen hundred kilometres of driving before we reach the French border, so we have little time in hand if we are to get to London on schedule. Nilov's estimate for the French border is mid-morning on Tuesday, and London on Wednesday morning.'

'What time have you ordered the convoy to leave?' Bykov asked.

'Six thirty,' Modin replied. 'We have two drivers for each vehicle, so we can realistically expect to be able to travel for twelve hours a day, if necessary. Nilov estimated an average speed on the road of fifty kilometres an hour, which shouldn't be too difficult to achieve. A lot,' he added, 'depends upon the border crossings, but our diplomatic status should ensure we receive some priority.'

Bykov nodded. Both men ate in silence for a few minutes. Then Modin put down his coffee cup, wiped his mouth on his napkin and glanced at his watch. 'Six twenty,' he said. 'We should move.'

Bykov nodded agreement and stood up. A steward walked over to the two men and handed Bykov a large brown paper bag. Modin looked at him. 'Snacks and soft drinks,' Bykov explained. 'As you said, General, it will be a long drive.'

The two men walked out of the building by the back stairs and into the rear courtyard. An articulated lorry was parked adjacent to the far wall, its engine idling. Two light blue Mercedes saloons were parked nose to tail almost in the centre of the courtyard, and a black Mercedes limousine was waiting at the bottom of the steps.

As Bykov and Modin appeared, the driver of the limousine stepped out of the car, opened the rear door and saluted briskly. Modin acknowledged the salute, but did not immediately get into the car. Instead he walked over to a small group of men – all *Spetsnaz* troopers but wearing civilian clothes – standing next to the Mercedes saloon cars. 'All well, Captain?' Modin asked, as he stopped beside a tall, well-built man.

The men came smartly to attention, and the man Modin had addressed saluted, then nodded. 'Yes, General. We are ready.'

'Very good,' Modin replied. He strode across to the articulated lorry, exchanged a few words with the drivers, and then walked back to the limousine. 'Right, Viktor,' he said, taking his seat, 'let's go.'

Thirty seconds later one of the blue Mercedes saloons pulled smoothly out of the courtyard, followed by the articulated lorry and then the second saloon. Bykov nodded to their driver, and the limousine joined the group at the rear. The four vehicles cleared the outskirts of Minsk at seven fifteen and headed south-west for Brest on the Polish border, some two hundred miles distant. Nilov's schedule suggested that they should reach it at about eleven thirty. As the convoy picked up speed, Modin wondered just how accurate his estimates were going to prove.

Anton Kirov

Colonel Petr Zavorin broke the seal on another bottle of Scotch whisky and poured healthy measures into two short glasses. 'Your health, Captain,' he said, and took a sip.

Valeri Bondarev obediently raised his glass and drank. He didn't particularly enjoy the fiery amber liquor – of which Zavorin appeared to have an inexhaustible supply – and would have much preferred a decent vodka. However, Zavorin was in charge, and Bondarev saw no real harm in humouring him.

'We have done well, Valeri,' Zavorin said, putting his glass down on the side table. They were, as usual, sitting together in the captain's day cabin. The message from Moscow had arrived half an hour earlier, and the anonymous sender had declared himself pleased when Zavorin – roused from sleep – had responded with the current position of the *Anton Kirov*.

'No more changes of plan, Colonel?' Bondarev asked.

Zavorin shook his head. 'No, no more changes. We make for Gibraltar, to arrive no later than Tuesday morning. We have ample time, I think?'

Bondarev nodded agreement. 'Yes, we have plenty of time. And what then?'

'We wait,' Zavorin replied. 'We wait at Gibraltar until we are instructed to proceed.' He took another sip of his whisky. 'I should not really tell you this, Captain, but we have been working well together, and I think, perhaps, that you have earned the right to know.'

He paused, and Bondarev leaned forward expectantly. 'First, one of the equipment boxes that we loaded at Varna is to be delivered to a small company in Gibraltar which is run by one of our operatives. But the real reason for visiting Gibraltar is that we are to collect a piece of American cryptographic equipment – a cipher machine – which our agents have managed to obtain. This will be delivered, probably by a small boat, whilst we are alongside. As soon as this machine has been loaded we will be able to leave Gibraltar.'

Zavorin smiled pleasantly and Bondarev nodded. It was more or less what he had expected. His ship had effectively been hijacked for use in some spy game that Moscow was playing, and there was nothing he could do about it. At least the end was in sight. Once the cipher machine had been loaded, the *Anton Kirov* could turn east again, and head back towards the Black Sea. Perhaps, Bondarev thought, he would suggest to Zavorin that the ship should pick up some legitimate cargo on the way. A matter of camouflage, almost. He wondered, for the first time, if the voyage might become something other than a total waste of his time. Bondarev stood up and smiled. 'I thank you for your confidence, Colonel. Now, if you will excuse me, I have to return to the bridge.'

'Of course.' When the captain had closed the door behind him, Zavorin drank the last of his Scotch. He was rather pleased with his story of the cipher machine; the idea had come to him whilst re-reading one of the very first James Bond novels. Zavorin smiled to himself, then picked up the bottle and left the cabin.

Middlesex

After an early breakfast of coffee and toast, Richter made himself as presentable as possible by covering the more offensive-looking abrasions on his face with plasters which were more or less skin-coloured. His jeans were a mess and his shirt and sweater had been shoved straight into the dustbin as soon as Bentley had managed to pull them off him. Bentley rummaged around in his bedroom wardrobe and emerged carrying a white shirt and a clean pair of jeans. The jeans were a little big around the waist, but the belt ensured they'd stay up. Richter dressed in his bedroom, assisted by Bentley, and as soon as he'd pulled the jeans on he opened the haversack and extracted the shoulder holster and the Smith and Wesson.

'Is that going to be necessary?' Bentley asked, as Richter pulled the holster into place.

'Christ, I hope not,' Richter replied, loading the pistol with six shells, 'but I'm not about to start taking any chances.'

Bentley gave him a hand with the leather jacket, which completely covered the shoulder rig, then unearthed an elderly trilby-type hat and offered it to Richter.

'Not exactly a picture of sartorial elegance,' Richter said, looking at his reflection in a mirror, 'but it does cover some of the damage.'

Bentley grinned at him.

'What?' Richter asked.

'Nothing,' Bentley said. 'Just shades of Philip Marlowe.'

'Before we go,' Richter said, looking straight at Bentley, 'I'd feel happier if you were armed, just in case.'

'Just in case what?' Bentley demanded. 'You told me my part of this little escapade would be completely risk-free.'

'It should be,' Richter said, 'but I'd feel happier if I knew you were carrying, that's all.'

Bentley looked at him for a long moment. 'OK,' he said, finally. 'Hand it over.'

Richter delved into his haversack and pulled out the little Mauser HSc and its shoulder holster. While Bentley pulled on the holster, Richter quickly showed him how to operate the Mauser. The Navy man was used to the Browning 9mm pistol, an altogether bigger weapon, but very similar in operation. He was still somewhat apprehensive about carrying the pistol, and Simpson would throw a fit if he knew. Neither Richter nor Bentley wanted to think about Kate's reaction if she found out.

Richter had fixed the rendezvous at the service area for ten twenty – only a fool or an amateur ever has a meet on the hour or half hour – and they drove a tortuous route out as far as Reading in Bentley's red Saab Turbo before turning south to join the M4 at junction eleven. By that time Richter was absolutely certain that there was no one on their tail. It just remained to check that there was nobody on Simpson's.

Richter had told Simpson to leave London in the Jaguar on the M4, losing any tails if possible, and drive out as far as junction ten, where he was to turn round and head back towards the capital, timing his arrival at junction ten at nine twenty as near as possible. Richter reckoned it was a comfortable forty-five minute drive from junction ten to the Heston service area, beyond Heathrow, which meant that Simpson should arrive there at about five past ten.

With Bentley at the wheel of the Saab – Richter wanted to devote his entire attention to watching, as if his life depended on it, which it did – they turned left onto the eastbound carriageway of the M4 at eight fifteen, and settled down to a relaxing fifty miles per hour cruise. Few cars travel at fifty on a motorway, and those that do tend to be very conspicuous.

Everything Richter spotted as possible opposition passed them, and by the time they approached junction nine he was certain that this final check was also negative. They pulled off the motorway at junction seven, and Richter told Bentley to park on the southbound flyover, above the westbound carriageway, and pretend to look at a map for a few minutes while he watched the westbound traffic.

Richter checked his watch. Eight fifty. Just about right. At five minutes to the hour he saw the dark green XJ6, a shadowy figure at the wheel. For the moment, Richter wasn't interested in him, but he was in the cars behind him. A grey Rover was overtaking, so he discounted that, but listed seven possibles – two Ford Orions, an old Metro, a light blue Transit van (a favourite vehicle for watchers, because you can park it almost anywhere without too many questions being asked), a Renault Laguna and two BMWs – a three-series and a five-series.

Richter turned to Bentley. 'Wagons roll, David. And could you wind it up a bit once we get on to the motorway?'

'No problem. I hate driving at fifty.'

'I've noticed that.'

They closed the gap rapidly, and by the time they reached junction nine Richter had eliminated the BMW 325, because it had overtaken the Jaguar, and the first Orion, because it had expired in a cloud of steam on the hard shoulder. At the junction, the Transit and the five-series BMW turned off, as Bentley and Richter did, and headed north towards the A4, so that just left the second Orion, the Metro and the Renault in trail behind the Jaguar.

Richter told Bentley to pull the same map-reading effort again, and they stopped on the northbound flyover so that he could watch the eastbound traffic, waiting for the Jaguar to show again. It did, at twenty to ten, and Richter waited until he was sure that the three cars he had seen westbound were no longer in company before telling Bentley to start the engine.

They pulled onto the motorway and held position about a mile behind the Jaguar. Richter was still constantly checking cars, both in front of them and behind, but by the time they approached junction four, the Heathrow turn-off, he had only spotted two possibles, a Volkswagen Passat and a Renault Safrane, both of which had appeared on the motorway at junction six and had then held position in front of the Saab and behind the XJ6.

Richter's mobile phone rang as they passed junction four. 'Yes?'

'Simpson. Are you in a red Saab?'

'Yes.'

'Right.'

The phone went dead, and Bentley looked enquiringly at Richter. 'That was the man I'll be meeting,' he said. 'He's spotted us, but I don't think he's seen any other possible tails.'

The Jaguar's left-hand indicator came on as it approached the Heston service area, and Richter watched the two cars he had been watching drive on towards London. 'Right, David,' he said. 'I think we're clear. Pull in and park where we can see the Jaguar, but where you have a clear run to the exit, just in case the opposition have been cleverer than I thought.'

They pulled up on the end of a rank of cars and Richter saw Simpson walk away from the Jaguar and head towards the cafeteria area, feeling in his pocket, presumably for some change. That was a good sign, as it indicated that he hadn't spotted any chase cars either, apart from the red Saab he knew Richter had been using.

Richter and Bentley sat in the Saab, watching for any sign of cars that he had previously seen, but by the time Simpson emerged, Richter had still no indication of any possible watchers. At eighteen minutes past, he reached for the door handle, then turned to Bentley. 'If there's any sign of trouble, any sign at all, don't hang around, just take off and get back home. And if when I get out of the Jaguar I walk towards the cafeteria, go, because that will mean I've spotted someone. OK?'

'OK, Paul. Just be careful.'

'I will,' Richter promised. 'I've got a pension I'm determined to collect, if only to piss off my boss.'

Bentley smiled and nodded, and Richter opened the door and stepped out.

Biala Podlaska, Eastern Poland

Modin was pleased. The convoy had encountered no significant hold-ups on the road to Brest, and the crossing into Poland had taken less than fifteen minutes. The Poles knew better than to delay vehicles bearing diplomatic plates, especially Russian diplomatic plates.

Warsaw was about one hundred and twenty miles ahead, and they were actually ahead of Nilov's schedule. Modin instructed the *Spetsnaz* escort to radio approval for a meal break and driver change. The lead Mercedes driver pulled off the road where it looped north around the town of Biala Podlaska, and parked his car at the far side of the parking area of a small café. The articulated lorry followed, then the second Mercedes saloon and the limousine.

'Thirty minutes,' the *Spetsnaz* escort said into the microphone. 'Remember the standing orders. One person to remain in each vehicle at all times. No talking in the café.'

Modin nodded his approval, and he and Bykov got out of the limousine and walked towards the double doors of the café.

Middlesex

Richter opened the nearside rear door of the Jaguar and climbed in. There was an audible clunk as Simpson used central locking to secure all the doors. He turned to face Richter. 'I'd like some answers, Richter. I've had the Met on my back all morning, wanting to know if I knew anything about the late Mr Orlov and two of his associates who were found dead by their cook this morning. The Met Super said he'd never seen such carnage. He said Orlov had twelve bullet wounds, just as if someone had shot bits off him.' Richter nodded. 'What happened to your face?' Simpson asked.

'I walked into a door. Why did the Met contact you?'

'Because Orlov was an alien, and a Russian alien at that. They said the Foreign and Commonwealth Office thought that SIS might know something, and the idiot SIS Duty Officer gave the plods my phone number. I'll be sorting him out later.'

'And what did you tell them?'

'I told them I'd look into it,' Simpson said. 'And unless you've got some pretty fancy answers, I'm going to point the finger straight at you. I told you last night not to touch Orlov.'

'I thought you said you couldn't afford to do without me?' Richter asked.

'I'll give it a go, Richter,' Simpson snarled. 'Now tell me a tale, and it had better be a good one to justify all this bloody cloak and dagger crap and TESTAMENT.'

'It may be cloak and dagger crap to you, Simpson, but it means my life, so if it's all right with you, we'll just keep on with it, OK?'

Richter leaned forward in the seat and told him what Orlov had told him or, rather, what he had started to tell him after Richter had shot off both his kneecaps, and what had then been forced out of him with further 9mm encouragement. When Richter finished, he leaned back and waited. Simpson looked ashen. 'You're sure? You're absolutely sure?'

Richter nodded. 'I am sure that Orlov believed what he was telling me. I do not believe that anyone in his position would have been able to invent such complicated lies which would tie in so well with what we already know.'

Simpson sighed. 'Dear God. Dear God help us all. What are we going to do?'

Richter shrugged. 'That's not up to me. We have to tell the French, obviously, because they're already involved. We should tell the CIA officially – I know they've been aware that the Russians have been up to something for some time, but if we tell them what we know it might get us a bit of co-operation. As for retrieving the situation, I suppose we could make strong diplomatic noises at Moscow, not that it would do much good if the Kremlin knows as little about this as we did. The only thing Orlov couldn't tell me, because he didn't know, was when the final phase is going to happen, but I think we have very little time left.'

'How long?'

'Four days, at a guess, perhaps five. No longer.'

'That hardly leaves enough time to go through diplomatic channels, does it?'

'No,' Richter said, 'but what other course of action is open to us?'

'Only one,' said Simpson, 'just as you suggested. First, now that we know what we're up against I'll get everything sorted at FOE. Second, I'll brief Vauxhall Cross so that they can tell the CIA here in London, and everyone else who needs to know. Third, we stop the last device, and that means we send you to France.'

'Me? Why me?' Richter asked. 'You haven't forgotten I'm at the top of the SVR's kill list, have you?'

'No, Richter, I haven't forgotten, but it has to be you. You know more about this than anybody else in the department, because you've been involved right from the start, but the real reason is that you're the best man I've got for this kind of work. I'll get you a diplomatic passport, for what it's worth, and give you a couple of bodyguards, but you've got to go.'

Richter grunted. 'I don't like it,' he said.

'I'm not asking you to like it,' Simpson snapped. 'I'm just telling you what you're going to do. Can you see any alternative?'

'No,' Richter conceded, 'I can't. Don't bother about the bodyguards; they'd only draw attention to me. If I've got a diplomatic passport I can carry a weapon anyway, and there's no need to risk anyone else.'

'If that's the way you want it,' Simpson said.

Richter got out of the Jaguar and waited until Simpson had driven away. Then he walked over to the Saab, climbed back in and told Bentley they could go.

'Is everything all right?' he asked.

'I don't know yet,' Richter replied. 'I've got to go away for a few days.'

'Where to?'

'Home, James,' Richter said.

'No. I meant, where are you going?'

'I can't tell you that, either, but it's between here and Spain.'

'I see,' Bentley said, then paused. 'No, I don't,' he added. 'Why France?'

'I have to look in the back of a lorry.'

'That's it?'

'That's all I can tell you,' Richter said. 'You shouldn't really even know that much – for your own sake.'

Razdolnoye, Krym (Crimea)

Dmitri Trushenko closed his email client software, initiated the shut-down routine for his laptop computer and leaned back in his chair. The message he had just sent, concealed within a typical piece of junk email and bounced round a succession of servers in three different countries, just told the ragheads that he was in position.

They had no idea where he was, and they didn't need to. The final phase of *Podstava* simply required him to be in a secure location, outside Moscow, with access to the Internet. Once the *Anton Kirov* had arrived at Gibraltar, and the last weapon had been successfully delivered to London, Trushenko would be able to initiate the demonstration he had planned from the start and then issue the ultimatum that he was quite convinced would instantly neuter America.

And then, as predictably as night follows day, Europe would fall. Her armies would be destroyed or simply disarmed, her governments faced with no alternative but to accept whatever demands Moscow should choose to make. As the man who had engineered *Podstava*, Trushenko would be fêted and acclaimed and, in due course, the mantle of leadership of the Confederation of Independent States might well fall upon his shoulders. If he wanted it, of course, and he wasn't entirely sure that he did. Because there was an alternative, an alternative that he had been considering more and more seriously for the past few weeks.

If the idiots in the Kremlin failed to seize the opportunity he had presented them or, even worse, decided to denounce what they could legitimately consider his treason, Romania, Bulgaria and Turkey were all within easy reach. He could simply run, and nobody would ever find him. And the more he thought about it, the more attractive this option seemed to be.

Trushenko smiled as he walked towards the kitchen to prepare a light supper. Money would not be a problem. *Podstava* had been a long-term project, and at the very first meeting with the oily Hassan Abbas, Trushenko had grasped both the scope of the operation and its potential for his personal enrichment. The funds the ragheads had so liberally provided had been used as they had intended, to construct and deliver the weapons to the locations Abbas had specified, but from the start

Trushenko had creamed off a healthy commission, and his three Swiss and two Austrian bank accounts – he had never believed in concentrating any kind of asset in a single location – held between them more than enough funds to allow him to live out the rest of his life in considerable comfort.

He had planned the final phase of *Podstava* with considerable care, and well in advance. The *dacha* he had rented for ten days – ample time – was large and spacious, situated on the western tip of the Crimea and with inspiring views across the Karkinitskiy Zaliv, the arm of the Black Sea which lies to the south-east of Odessa. It was an ideal place to wait during the last few days while the final weapon was positioned.

He had anticipated that sooner or later – in fact, it had been later – the Americans or somebody would discover that something was going on, simply because of the increased activity that was an inescapable part of the last phase of the operation. In the latter stages, too, more people had had to be told about it, which increased the potential for leaks, either deliberate or accidental. With hindsight, he wondered if he should have insisted on the above-ground weapon test in the tundra, but he had believed, and still did, that the final test was essential, if only to confirm that the satellite firing system was working properly.

Trushenko walked back into the living room with a tray on which was a dish of *solianka* that he had prepared – meat soup with added tomatoes, cucumber, olives, onions, capers, lemons and sour cream – and two slices of black bread. Though he rarely cooked for himself, Trushenko was competent and creative in the kitchen, and in the short period since his arrival in the Crimea he had been indulging himself.

He put the tray on a side table, poured a glass of vodka and sat comfortably in an armchair, gazing out of the large windows and over the *dacha*'s grounds which sloped down to a small jetty, and across at the distant lights of Port-Khorly and Perekop. He wondered how much the Americans knew, or had been able to deduce, and what they would do about it. At some stage, he presumed, they would talk to the Kremlin, and that would be when the fun would really start, when they found out that the Kremlin knew even less about it than they did. He smiled to himself again in the gathering dusk.

The trail he had laid so carefully in Moscow led straight to St Petersburg, and he knew that there was no surviving trace of his journey to the Crimea. From his *dacha* he could control all of the final stages of *Podstava*, without risk, and after the Gibraltar demonstration he doubted if there would be any problems with the Americans or anyone else. His only regret was personal – he missed dear Genady and their weekly couplings – but it was essential to have one trusted friend in Moscow to handle the communications with the ship, and Trushenko trusted no one as he trusted Genady Arkenko.

'Genady,' Trushenko sighed, raising his glass, 'I do miss you, old friend.'

Then he cheered up somewhat, and promised himself that he would watch a video from his Lubyanka collection, the pick of which he had brought with him. Perhaps the German – though that was rather long – or maybe the Georgian. Yes, Trushenko mused, the Georgian, and he felt his body stirring with anticipation.

Wroclaw (Breslau), Poland

The first major delay the convoy encountered was about five miles west of Wroclaw, heading for the Czechoslovakian border in the early evening. Modin heard the bang quite clearly even though the limousine was over a hundred metres behind the lorry, and as soon as he saw the articulated vehicle lurch he knew that a tyre had blown.

The limousine cruised to a stop behind the lorry, and Bykov and Modin got out. It was a typical heavy goods vehicle problem; the tyre had shed its tread in chunks, and then the carcase had ruptured. Not a problem, just a delay that they didn't need. The lorry was carrying two spare wheels and the heavy-duty jacks and wrenches needed to change a wheel, but Modin stopped Bykov when he instructed the *Spetsnaz* troopers to effect the change. 'No,' he said. 'Ring a tyre service company.'

'Why, General?' Bykov asked.

'Because it's safer,' Modin replied. 'We have a long way to go once we cross the German border, and I do not want to attract any attention once we enter the West. If we have a problem like this there, we can attend to it ourselves, and not call on anyone for help. Here in Poland, things are different.' Bykov nodded, acknowledging the rationale of the decision.

The service vehicle arrived forty minutes later, but two of the nuts had jammed and fitting the new tyre to the wheel took nearly two hours in all. The convoy was not ready to move on until almost ten thirty. Before any orders were given, Modin gestured to Bykov and the two officers consulted a map. Nilov's schedule, and the planned route, called for the convoy to cross into Czechoslovakia at Jakuszyce, and then route via Prague and Pilsen to Waidhaus on the German border.

'We do have one alternative,' Bykov suggested, pointing. 'We could turn back towards Wroclaw and then head north-west on the E22 autoroute past Legnica.'

'And then?' Modin prompted.

Bykov pointed again at the map. 'Through Boleslawiec to Zgorzelec.'

'And into Germany at Görlitz,' Modin finished. 'Yes, that has some advantages, because we could then use the E63 and E6 autobahns down to Nürnberg, and that would certainly be quicker than going through Czechoslovakia.'

Modin looked at his watch, then back at the map, considering. 'No,' he said finally, 'I think we should continue as planned. This route was selected precisely so that the convoy would enter Germany as far west as possible.'

'Agreed,' Bykov said. 'That is the safest option.'

'It's too late to carry on tonight. We'll drive back to Wroclaw,' Modin finished, yawning, 'and stop somewhere there. We will still be able to cross the Czech border tomorrow morning.'

Middlesex

Bentley and Richter went out in the Saab just after eight that evening to buy a take-away Chinese meal, and to allow Richter to use a public call box to contact Hammersmith. The Duty Officer, after Richter had identified himself, said simply, 'Nine forty at the Dover Court Hotel,' and rang off.

Chapter Seventeen

Monday
Ickenham, Middlesex, and Dover

Richter was awake at six, and walked stiff-legged but fully dressed into Bentley's kitchen just after six thirty. He still ached abominably, but he was mobile, and knew he wouldn't have too much of a problem riding the Honda.

He was on the road by seven. He picked up the A40 within three minutes of leaving the house, and turned east for central London. Just over an hour later, he pulled the Honda into a garage on the A2 in Bexley and filled the tank. The early-morning traffic was building up, but most of it was heading into the city, and Richter was going the other way. At Strood he joined the M2, but continued to keep his speed low, as he had time in hand.

At nine thirty he rode the Honda into the car park of the Dover Court Hotel, and stopped the bike in a corner of the car park. He switched off the engine, removed his helmet and locked it to the seat. At nine forty exactly he walked into the lounge, found a table and ordered a pot of coffee. Richter spotted the two FOE contacts the moment they walked in through the door, and waved a friendly hand.

If you are organizing a meet in a public place – and the lounge of the Dover Court Hotel at that time in the morning was fairly full – it looks far more suspicious if you try to be sneaky about it. A meeting between two businessmen who know each other, on the other hand, attracts almost no attention whatsoever. Not that Richter looked much like a businessman. The jeans and leather jacket had already attracted one or two stares which stopped just the safe side of being hostile, and the fresh plasters on his face didn't help either.

The two men came over to Richter's table and sat down. Richter glanced round the lounge, and spoke in a low voice to the senior FOE officer – Tony Deacon, who ran the Far East desk. Mark Clayton, the second FOE man, sat back in his seat, checking for watchers or listeners. 'Do you need to give me a verbal briefing on the operational stuff?' Richter asked.

Deacon shook his head, his eyes still fixed on Richter's battered countenance. 'No,' he replied. 'It's all in the briefcase, plus details of your contact and fallback arrangements. Your car's in the corner of the car park. It's a Granada Scorpio which replaced the last one you used, and you-know-who said he wanted it back in one piece this time.'

He passed Richter a key fob with a label attached. 'Here are the keys. Your diplomatic passport, ferry tickets, insurance details and Green Card are also in the briefcase, plus a couple of credit cards and enough cash to keep you going. There's a letter of introduction – sealed – which should stay that way until you deliver it, and a copy of the letter for your eyes only. Read it and destroy it before your meeting. Also sealed is a copy of the operation file, fully updated, and there are seals and envelopes for you to re-seal it once you've read it. There's a suitcase of clothes in the boot, hopefully in your size.'

'Thanks.'

'What happened to your face?' Deacon asked.

'I was mugged,' Richter said, and Clayton laughed. 'Anything else?'

'No,' Deacon said. 'You have an open return ferry ticket, and as long as you get to the rendezvous on time you can go when you like. You might like the choice of accommodation we've booked for you. It proves that the Cashier's got a sense of humour after all.' He looked around the room, as if anxious to be away.

'Anything else?'

'No, that's it. Have a good trip.'

'Just one thing,' Richter said. 'I arrived here on a motorcycle. Can either of you ride it back to Hammersmith for me?'

'I've got a licence,' Clayton said. 'Where is it?'

'Far corner of the car park,' Richter said, passing over the keys and eyeing Clayton's city suit. 'The helmet's locked to the seat, and there's a pair of weatherproof coveralls in the pannier. I know it's old, but I'm attached to that bike, so please try not to bend it.'

'Right.'

They stood up, shook hands with Richter because that's what businessmen do, and left. The briefcase Deacon had been carrying stayed under the table. It was a neat black leather attaché case, complete with a handcuff and keys allowing it to be chained to the wrist. Richter wondered if he would be able to hang on to it after the job was over.

Jelenia Góra, Poland

Despite an early start, the convoy encountered increasingly heavy traffic after leaving Wroclaw. As they approached the major junction at Jelenia Góra, where the roads from Wroclaw, Prague, Görlitz and Boleslawiec meet, they saw the reason. Two lorries had met more or less head-on, and the rescue services were still trying to cut one of the drivers free. Although they had dragged the other vehicle to the side of the road, the junction was partially blocked, and the police were filtering traffic through one lane at a time.

Modin briefly considered taking the road to Görlitz and directly into Germany, bypassing Czechoslovakia altogether – a variation on the route suggested by Viktor Bykov the previous evening – but again rejected the idea. With the cargo they were carrying, the planned route still seemed the safest. So, they waited in the queue with all the other vehicles, and took their turn across the junction.

Dover

Richter looked round the car park, spotted a dark grey Scorpio in the far corner, and walked over to it. He checked the registration number, unlocked it, opened the door and climbed in. Inside, he opened up the briefcase and examined the contents. The ferry tickets were in the name of Beatty, and Simpson had thoughtfully provided a diplomatic passport in the same name, bearing a reasonable photograph of Richter's face before Yuri had started work on it. There was, as Deacon had said, a letter addressed to Sir James Auden, British Embassy, Paris, stamped 'Strictly Personal, Private and Confidential' and sealed with wax. The copy for Richter's information was in a separate envelope, also sealed.

Richter signed the two credit cards and put them in his wallet, together with the cash which amounted to about £500 in euros. He also found a permit issued by the Metropolitan Police, and endorsed by a senior Gendarmerie officer, in the name of Beatty authorizing the carriage of the Smith and Wesson, and a personal search exemption certificate which, together with the diplomatic passport, should avoid any problems with Customs on either side of the Channel. The FOE file was enclosed in two sealed envelopes, one large and one slightly smaller, as is mandatory for classified files which are taken out of a secure building. Richter wouldn't open that until he reached his destination.

He stepped out of the Ford, glanced round the car park to check that he wasn't being observed, opened the boot and dropped the haversack inside. From the suitcase of clothes he extracted a dark blue blazer which he swapped for his leather jacket. He had to wear a jacket simply because of the shoulder holster, and the blazer was more in keeping with the Granada than the motorcycle jacket would have been.

Richter started the car and drove down into Dover. He found his way to the Western Docks, where he presented his ticket and was directed into a line of other vehicles waiting to board the Calais ferry. Twenty-five minutes later he was aboard the P&O vessel and sitting in a corner seat in the Club Class lounge.

Richter ordered coffee, but ignored the newspapers and opened the briefcase. He made sure he couldn't be overlooked, then read the copy letter of introduction to the Ambassador at the British Embassy in Paris. He read it twice, then put it into his jacket pocket. Immediately before disembarkation he would visit the loo, tear the letter into very small pieces and flush it away. That was not the recommended disposal method for a document of that classification, but entirely adequate in the circumstances.

He also looked at the faxed confirmation of his accommodation arrangements, and could immediately see what Tony Deacon had meant. The Cashier had booked Richter four nights in a cabin at Davy Crockett Ranch, one of the accommodation areas at the Disneyland Paris resort. However, a note attached to the fax from Simpson showed that the decision had received his approval, and there were actually good reasons for it.

First, Disneyland Paris was directly linked to the centre of the city, where only an idiot or a Frenchman would drive a car, by the very efficient rail system – the RER – which meant that Richter could reach the British Embassy in well under an hour. Second, by the very nature of the place, the car parks at Disneyland were always occupied by a varied selection of vehicles from all countries in Europe, so the Granada would be less likely to stand out there than it would in Paris itself. Third, Richter's battered face would be less conspicuous in the relative privacy of a log cabin in a wood than in some left-bank hotel. Finally, Richter thought, bearing in mind the general absence of any sense of humour in the Russian psyche, Disneyland was not a place where they would be likely to look for him.

Overall, it was probably a good choice.

10 Downing Street, London

'How certain are you about this?' the grey-haired man asked. It was the first thing he had said since Simpson had stopped speaking three minutes earlier.

Sir Michael Geraghty, the current 'C' – Secret Intelligence Service chief – looked across at Simpson, who was sitting on his left, in front of the desk in the Prime Minister's private office. 'It's assessed as Grade One intelligence, Prime Minister,' Simpson replied. He didn't need to explain further. All British Prime Ministers are required to be familiar with the terminology and procedures of the intelligence services, and the Cabinet's most secret intelligence group, the Overseas and Defence Committee, is chaired by the Prime Minister.

The grey-haired man nodded. He removed his spectacles and rubbed his eyes, then replaced the glasses and looked over at Simpson. 'You're quite certain?' he asked again. 'There's no possibility of any kind of error? It's not some form of deception operation or anything of that kind?'

Simpson shook his head and opened his mouth to speak, but Geraghty cleared his throat and replied first. 'We're quite satisfied that what Simpson's organization has uncovered is a real and potent threat to the security of the Western alliance and, more importantly, to Great Britain, Prime Minister,' he said. 'Simpson has outlined the measures he has put in train to resolve the immediate problem, that of the weapon intended for London, but that does not—'

'I appreciate that, Sir Michael,' the Prime Minister interrupted. 'I just wanted to be absolutely sure.' He picked up a fountain pen from the silver holder in front of him and removed the cap. He wrote a short note on a sheet of paper and then replaced the pen. 'I was aware,' he said, 'from the last JIC meeting that the CIA was very disturbed about something going on in Russia. Now that Mr Simpson's group has identified the substance of the threat, we at least know what we are up against. What is not clear to me at the moment is what we can do about it. Obviously this matter will have to be discussed at Cabinet level,' he added, 'and we will need to carefully consider our military options. Apart from the operation in France, what other measures would you think appropriate?'

Sir Michael Geraghty shook his head. 'There is little more that the intelligence services can do, Prime Minister. We have no direct access – official or unofficial – to the SVR or GRU, and even if we had I don't know what steps we could take to resolve the situation. In my view, the only possible actions available to us now are political and military. Political, to put pressure on the Kremlin to stop this operation before it can be implemented, and military to provide a viable counter to the threat in the event that political persuasion fails.'

The Prime Minister nodded. 'The Independent Nuclear Deterrent?'

'Yes, Prime Minister,' Simpson said. 'We park two of our missile-carrying nuclear submarines off the Russian coast and tell the Kremlin that if they implement this nasty little plan we'll reduce the CIS to radioactive rubble.'

'Er, quite,' Geraghty said, looking a little startled. 'Somewhat colourfully put, but Simpson has, I think, expressed it rather well.'

American Embassy, 2 avenue Gabriel, Paris

Westwood was just finishing an early lunch in the Embassy commissary when Miles Turner hurried in. 'We've just received this Immediate signal from Langley, John, marked for your attention,' Turner said, handing over the flimsy.

Westwood took the paper and read the single line of text: 'CONFERENCE CALL SCHEDULED FOR 0700 EST.'

'What time is the meeting with DGSE, Miles?' Westwood asked, looking at his watch and juggling time zones in his head.

'Three, local time. Zero seven hundred Eastern Standard Time is one o'clock here – that's in fifteen minutes – so unless the conference is very long it shouldn't be a problem.'

'Right,' Westwood said, swallowing the last of his ice cream, 'let's get down to the Communications Room.'

Jakuszyce (Polish/Czechoslovakian border)

Modin had hoped that the traffic would diminish once they had cleared the accident site, but they still made very slow progress. The journey from Jelenia Góra to Jakuszyce took over two hours, and there was a queue at least a mile in length at the border itself. When the convoy finally came to a halt, Bykov and Modin climbed out of the limousine and walked up to the lead Mercedes. The *Spetsnaz* officer in charge got out of the car and awaited orders.

'Go forward to the border,' Modin instructed. 'Show the border guards your diplomatic passport and advise – no, tell – them that this is a diplomatic convoy which must not be delayed. Tell them,' he added, 'that if we are still not cleared through the border within thirty minutes, I will personally file a report individually naming every single border guard and accusing them of gross dereliction of duty and wilfully obstructing a diplomatic mission.'

The *Spetsnaz* officer nodded and hurried off. Modin wondered if the threat would be taken seriously. Russia no longer had the sway over her satellites that she had once enjoyed.

Fifteen minutes later, with all eastbound traffic halted and the road cleared, the convoy was waved through the Polish border and, almost without a pause, across the Czechoslovakian frontier as well.

American Embassy, 2 avenue Gabriel, Paris

There was a problem with the secure satellite link between Langley and CIA London, and it was almost zero seven fifteen Eastern Standard Time, thirteen fifteen Central European Time, before the conference call circuit was completed.

'Basically, John,' Walter Hicks began, 'this is an update briefing on RAVEN and his last message. We think we may know a bit more about him now. OK, Cliff, this is your ball.'

'Right,' Masters replied. 'First, we looked again at RAVEN. We still don't know who he is, but now we think we know what he is. We believe he's a Russian with a conscience and a bad case of guilt.'

'Come again?' Abrahams asked.

'We ran the entire sequence of events, and sanitized copies of the messages, past three of our tame shrinks. The most significant single factor, they agreed, was the last message. The initial stuff we received was high-grade intelligence, no question, and obviously RAVEN had had plenty of time to prepare it and to make the deliveries to Rigby. The message placed in Rigby's car,' he continued, 'was different. That showed definite signs of haste. A man in a hurry, or a man who thought he might be observed. A frightened man, perhaps, or one who had just learned what was going on. The last message, though, was more like the earlier stuff. It was a note again, not a film, but obviously RAVEN had been able to prepare it at his leisure.'

'So?' Westwood asked.

'So if that is an accurate assessment, why is the message so cryptic? He could have said "bomb" or "nerve gas" instead of "component", and told us exactly what the threat really is. He could have been specific about the "implementation". Are we talking about an actual invasion, or a first-strike or some other kind of threat?'

'I follow you,' Westwood said. 'You mean that RAVEN could have told us precisely what the operation comprises, but something – his loyalty to Mother Russia or whatever – held him back.'

'Exactly,' Masters said. 'What we have here, the shrinks believe, is a Russian who doesn't like what is happening, but who is still not prepared to go the whole hog and completely betray his homeland. He's salving his conscience by providing us with data, but not enough for him to feel like a traitor. He probably thinks that if we work out what's going on and stop it, he will have helped us in the name of humanity, or something like that. On the other hand, if we don't solve the problem and the implementation or whatever goes ahead, then he can step back and say, "Well, I tried, but they just weren't smart enough."'

'OK,' said Westwood. 'I guess we'd better make sure that we are smart enough. That helps a little with RAVEN. What about the message – or rather what it says?'

'It's still puzzling,' Masters said, 'and it looks as if we are dealing with a most unconventional assault – if that really is the right word. The fact that a "component" is being delivered to the West does not suggest a first-strike, or anything involving a normal weapon delivery system – missile, aircraft, submarine or whatever. It seems more likely to us that we're talking about a slow and conventional form of transport.'

'What, a ship or train or something?' Abrahams asked.

'Exactly. It looks like whatever this weapon is, it's being mailed to us.'

Abrahams laughed, briefly, then stopped.

'I'm still listening,' Westwood said. 'What you say makes sense. Presumably the delay between the component entering the West, as RAVEN puts it, and the plan to be implemented, is to allow time for the weapon to be placed in position and primed or whatever.'

'Yes,' Hicks interrupted, 'and for an ultimatum to be delivered.'

After a brief silence, Westwood spoke again. 'I agree with your conclusions. What I'm not sure about is where we go from here. We have no idea – I presume – about exactly what this "component" is, what it looks like, where it's coming from or where it's going to, so where do we start looking? And how the hell do we find it by tomorrow?'

'There's another problem,' Hicks growled. 'RAVEN's message refers to the "last component", which implies that there are others already in place. Finding and stopping delivery of the final component may not stop the implementation of whatever the hell this operation is.'

'Exactly,' Cliff Masters said. 'If what we're looking at is a number of bombs that are already strategically placed in American cities, whether the last one actually gets delivered to Washington or wherever is irrelevant. There could already be a high enough tonnage of weapons in place to ensure that the President would have no option but to accede to whatever demands are made.'

'You believe that?' Westwood asked. 'You believe the President would just roll over and play dead?'

'He might have no option,' Hicks replied. 'Put yourself in his position. If the Russians announce that they've positioned one strategic-yield nuclear weapon in the centre of every major city in the States, and that they're going to detonate them unless he agrees to whatever they want, what else can he do?'

'It would be a first-strike without any warning,' Masters added. 'There could be no warning, because the weapons are already here. The first we would know about it would be the detonation of the first bomb.'

'I'm having a job coping with this,' Westwood said. 'If you're right, then this completely negates all of our defences.'

'Well, not exactly,' Hicks replied. 'I've had two meetings with the President already, and he's quite prepared to go to the edge on this. We've already discussed the military preparations he's approved. The threat of us implementing those measures might be enough to defuse this situation.'

'It might,' Westwood said, 'but I wouldn't put any money on it. Any progress with that Russian word – *Pripisha* or whatever it was?'

'*Pripiska*,' Hicks said. 'No. We're still looking into it, but so far nobody here has had any bright ideas.'

'So what the hell are we going to do?' John Westwood asked, leaning back in the padded chair in the Paris Embassy Communications Room. The room was air-conditioned and cool, but he was sweating.

'OK,' Walter Hicks said. 'What we need is data – any data. At the moment, we have no idea what we're up against. What I don't believe is that nobody's noticed anything. Christ, we've got spy satellites peering into everyone's backyard, we've got the NSA reading just about every diplomatic signal that passes through the States, and the British GCHQ listening-in every time somebody takes a crap. Somebody, somewhere, must know something.

'John, you have to lean on the French. Forget about diplomacy, protocol, Gallic sensitivity and all the rest. Kick ass if you have to, but get some answers. Roger, the same applies to you in London. Get back on to that Taylor guy and get SIS moving. You've both got top weight on this – I've already talked to SIS and the DGSE, and the President will be calling the British Prime Minister and the French President today.' There was silence for a moment or two. 'Questions?' Hicks asked.

'No,' Westwood replied, echoed a second later by Abrahams.

'OK,' Hicks growled. 'Get to it.'

Office of Commander-In-Chief Fleet (CINCFLEET), Northwood, Middlesex

Flag Officer Submarines (FOSM) is the head of the Submarine Branch of the Royal Navy and exercises operational control of some twenty-five nuclear- and conventionally powered submarines, and is responsible for training and maintenance aspects of the Trident missile-carrying nuclear submarines. Operational control of the Trident boats, however, is vested in Commander-in-Chief Fleet (CINCFLEET), which is why the Top Secret, Military Flash signal from the Chief of the Defence Staff (CDS) was sent to CINCFLEET as the Action Addressee, and was copied to FOSM for information.

Communication with submarines is difficult, because water acts as a barrier. The greater the depth of water above the boat, the more difficult it is to communicate with it. Standard procedure is for all patrolling nuclear submarines to trail a short aerial which is designed to receive Extremely-Low Frequency (ELF) signals at the vessel's normal operating depth. The disadvantage of ELF is that it is very slow, and only a limited number of characters can be sent in a given time period – normally about one letter character every fifteen to thirty seconds. This is not enough to pass a complete operational message, but what

ELF can do is transmit a warning message to one or more submarines in coded form.

These warning messages are usually repeated sequences of just a few characters. The decoded text will tell the captain that his operating authority has a message to pass to him, what time the message will be sent, and how the message will be transmitted. At the appropriate time, the submarine will reduce its depth in preparation. Depending upon the transmission method selected, either the submarine will trail a long aerial which will float immediately below the surface of the sea, or the boat will extend an aerial above the surface from the top of the sail. The former method is the more secure, but reception is slow, while the latter allows high-speed transmissions to be received, albeit at the risk of the aerial being detected by radar from a hostile vessel or aircraft, or even visually in calm seas. Under no circumstances will the captain acknowledge any message – submarine communications are strictly one-way, to avoid compromising the vessel's position.

Forty-five minutes after CINCFLEET received the signal from the CDS, a Group Warning Signal was transmitted via the ELF radio relay station just outside Rugby in Warwickshire. Thirty and thirty-five minutes after that, two Military Flash Operational Tasking Signals were sent via a communications satellite to HMS *Vanguard* and HMS *Victorious*, the two Trident boats on patrol. Fifteen minutes after receiving the signals, the two boats, in their widely separated patrol areas, were back at their normal operating depth and moving at increased speed on new headings.

Marne-la-Vallée

Disneyland Paris is difficult to miss. Quite apart from the Mickey Mouse symbols and road signs advising travellers of their proximity to the Magic Kingdom, the unlikely towers of Sleeping Beauty's Castle can be seen from a considerable distance on the autoroute. Davy Crockett Ranch lies to the south of the A4, the opposite side to Disneyland itself. The approach is down a private road, under an arch proclaiming the identity of the place, and into a car park outside the reception area.

Inside, they spoke good English, which was just as well because Richter had left his French behind at school. He was given keys to his cabin, a number code to open the barrier which protected the camp from unauthorized visitors, or at least from those arriving in cars, a map of the place, and a three-day Disneyland passport. Richter doubted that he would be making much use of the last item, but he thanked them anyway, climbed back into the Granada, and drove on into the heavily wooded site.

The cabin, when Richter found it, was surprisingly comfortable and well equipped. He visited the general store, called the Trading Post, and bought coffee, tea, milk and biscuits, then returned to the cabin. He locked the door, drew the curtains and unpacked his suitcase, then reviewed his plans while the kettle boiled. The schedule drawn up by the FOE planners was simple but comprehensive. They had organized a meeting with the Ambassador in Paris at nine fifteen the following morning, and immediately afterwards a discussion with the SIS Head of Station. By the time that had been completed, the Embassy should have sorted out an appointment for Richter with the French authorities, which was crucial. If he encountered difficulties with that, he had real problems.

Richter opened the sealed envelopes containing the operation file, and read it. It was a new file that had been compiled from the separate FOE packs containing details of the Blackbird flight, Newman's death and the other related matters. Simpson had obviously had a hand in the compilation of the last few entries, as it contained a detailed statement of the information Richter had obtained from Orlov, and notes on the plan of action they had decided upon. Richter noticed that the new file had been given the code-name 'Overkill'.

Direction Générale de Sécurité Extérieure *Headquarters, boulevard Mortier, Paris*

The boulevard Mortier runs almost parallel with the north-eastern *Péréphérique* – the Paris inner ring road – between the Porte de Bagnolet and the Porte des Lilas. The headquarters of the DGSE is located in a disused barracks near the junction of the boulevard with the rue des Tourelles, close to a large municipal swimming pool. This juxtaposition has not escaped the notice of the other French security forces, and the DGSE has acquired the slightly pejorative nickname '*piscine*' as a result.

The journey from the Embassy at avenue Gabriel took nearly an hour because of the increasingly heavy Paris afternoon traffic, and it was nine minutes past three when John Westwood and Miles Turner climbed out of the Embassy Lincoln and looked at the unprepossessing building before them. 'Are you sure this is it?' Westwood asked, a puzzled frown on his face.

'Yup,' Turner replied. 'The DGSE likes to keep a low profile.'

'Much lower than this,' Westwood said, 'and they'll be completely submerged.'

Anton Kirov

Captain Valeri Bondarev knocked on the second mate's cabin door and waited. The second mate, of course, was somewhere in Odessa, Bondarev knew, probably having a much better time than if he had still been on the *Anton Kirov*. The door slid open smoothly and Colonel Petr Zavorin looked out enquiringly.

'You asked to be informed, Colonel, when we were one hundred and twenty miles out of Gibraltar,' Bondarev said. 'We've just reached that point.'

'Good.' Zavorin nodded in satisfaction. 'Reduce speed to eight knots, Captain,' he said. 'We don't want to arrive too early.' Bondarev nodded obediently and turned away.

'Captain,' Zavorin called after him, 'I know you haven't much enjoyed this voyage, but you should remember that we are all acting on specific instructions from Moscow, and your role is vital to the success of this mission. Take heart also, Captain,' Zavorin added, 'that we will soon be returning home, and you can then resume your normal life.'

Bondarev nodded. Now that, he thought, was much more important to him than any of Moscow's spy games.

Direction Générale de Sécurité Extérieure *Headquarters, boulevard Mortier, Paris*

Westwood shifted uncomfortably in the upright chair and wondered again whether they were just wasting their time. The colonel who had been appointed to meet with them had not arrived until almost three thirty, and had pointedly failed to apologize for keeping them waiting. This, Westwood thought, was almost certainly because he and Miles Turner had been slightly late themselves. Turner had addressed the colonel – his nametag said 'Grenelle', but he had not formally introduced himself – in workable, though not fluent, French. Grenelle had affected incomprehension, and there had been a further delay whilst a bilingual DGSE officer was located. When Westwood had finally been able to state the purpose of their visit, Grenelle had insisted upon delivery and translation one sentence at a time. It had been a long, slow process.

'So, Monsieur Westwood,' the translator said, 'you want to know if we have any high-level agents who can verify the information your Central Intelligence Agency has received?'

'Yes,' Westwood replied. 'Or any indication from any source of any unusual activity in Russia, or any abnormal movements of men or equipment from Russia into any Western country. Or anything else that seems in any way odd,' he finished, rather lamely.

Grenelle spoke briefly to the translator, reinforcing Westwood's belief that the former at least understood English. 'The colonel wishes to inform you that he is unable to divulge any information about French operatives.'

Westwood shook his head in exasperation, but kept his voice low and reasonable. 'I thought I'd made it clear that I'm not asking for information about operatives. I don't care if the DGSE has bugged the Russian President's crapper and has every Kremlin valet on its payroll. All I'm interested in is whether the DGSE has received any relevant information.'

The translator paused slightly before reverting to French, but Grenelle interrupted him almost immediately. 'The colonel wants to know why you need to know.'

'Because,' Westwood said, with as much patience as he could muster, 'we believe that the Russians may be planning an attack of some sort on the West, and that it will probably involve France as well as every other country in Western Europe.'

The translator relayed this to the colonel, who paused thoughtfully before speaking. The translator looked slightly happier when he addressed the two Americans. 'Colonel Grenelle says that the DGSE has no information about any such Russian plan, and that we have no operatives who would be able to assist. However, he has heard that there have been some slightly unusual movements of equipment from the former Soviet Union into and through France during the last year.'

Westwood glanced across at Miles Turner. 'What movements?' he asked.

The translator smiled across the table. 'That, Monsieur Westwood, we cannot say. The function of the DGSE is limited to operations outside the borders of the hexagon.'

'The hexagon?' Westwood muttered. 'What the hell's the hexagon?'

'France,' Turner replied. 'It's a colloquial name for France.'

'OK,' Westwood said. 'So who do we talk to now?'

Grenelle smiled a small, tight smile and spoke in English for the first time. '*The Direction de la Surveillance du Territoire*, Monsieur Westwood. The DST – that's who you talk to now.'

Office of the Director of Operations (Clandestine Services), Central Intelligence Agency Headquarters, Langley, Virginia

'What progress?' Walter Hicks asked, rubbing his hand across his tired eyes. He had been at Langley all day, and he had an evening meeting scheduled with the President in a little under two hours.

'Not a great deal, Director,' Ronald Hughes replied.

'That isn't what I wanted to hear, Ron,' Hicks growled. 'I have to see the man this evening and I have to tell him something, like whether we punch the bombers into the air in two days' time and point them at Moscow. "Not a great deal" is not the kind of thing I need to hear right now.'

Hughes shifted slightly in his seat. He, too, hadn't left the building in some twenty hours. 'Specifically,' Hughes said, 'Roger Abrahams in London has got nowhere with SIS, but he thinks this is simply because they don't know anything, not that they won't tell. The only significant piece of data he did manage to obtain is that one section of SIS is actively investigating an incident which may be related.'

'What incident?' Hicks asked, looking interested.

Hughes shrugged. 'I'm not convinced there's any connection, but the SIS Head of Station in Moscow was reported to have died in a road accident last week. SIS sent someone to investigate it and the word is that the body the Russians handed over definitely wasn't the SIS man. The suggestion is that he was snatched by the SVR and pumped dry.'

Hicks looked at him over the desk. 'That's unusual, to say the least. Are they certain?'

Hughes nodded. 'The identification of the body was positive – positive, that is, that it wasn't their man. Some kind of distinguishing mark wasn't present, I think.'

'OK,' Hicks muttered, 'we have to accept that SIS will know their own man, so if they say the stiff wasn't him, it wasn't. What I don't see is any connection with RAVEN.'

'Nor do I,' Hughes agreed, 'but I've told Abrahams to keep us in the loop just in case there does turn out to be a link.'

'What about France?' Hicks asked.

'You know what the French are like,' Hughes said. 'John had a meeting with the DGSE – that's the foreign espionage section of the French security forces – this afternoon. It didn't go well. They were a few minutes late arriving, and John said the French colonel apparently took umbrage. The only thing the French admitted was that there had been some non-typical movements from the CIS into and through France.' Hicks opened his mouth but Hughes forestalled his question. 'The DGSE wouldn't tell him. Any operational matter within France, they said, was the concern of the DST and nothing to do with them.'

Hicks grunted. 'All assistance short of actual help, by the sound of it.'

Hughes nodded. 'Anyway, he's on it, but I'm still not sure if he's just wasting his time. Non-typical movements might just mean that the Russian Embassy in Paris is having new crappers fitted.'

Pilsen, Czechoslovakia

The convoy stopped for the night at a small hotel just outside Pilsen. As usual, one *Spetsnaz* trooper stayed in each vehicle, sleeping as best they could.

'Not a good day,' Modin remarked, as he and Bykov sat together in a deserted corner of the lounge after dinner.

Bykov shook his head. 'We seem to have spent all day on the road and got nowhere,' he replied.

'It could be worse,' Modin said. 'We are now only about sixty kilometres from the German border at Waidhaus so, unless we have a repeat of today's performance, we should be inside Germany by mid-morning tomorrow.'

'I hope so,' Bykov replied. 'The weapon must arrive in London on schedule.'

Chapter Eighteen

Tuesday
American Embassy, 2 avenue Gabriel, Paris

John Westwood woke just before seven, dressed and walked down to the Embassy commissary for breakfast. Over coffee, ham, eggs and hash browns, he and Miles Turner reviewed the situation. 'We have to talk to the DST today,' Westwood said. 'Why that DGSE colonel played so hard to get I don't know. I just hope the DST people have more sense.'

'I'll ring at nine – that's the earliest there's likely to be anyone there apart from the night duty staff – and set up a meeting this morning,' Turner said. 'There haven't been any overnight developments at this end, but it's buzzing like a hornets' nest in the States. Walter Hicks has arranged another conference call for three this afternoon, our time, to up-date us on what's happening Stateside, and to receive progress reports from us.'

Westwood grunted. 'Well, I'd be happy to be able to report some progress, but on past form it isn't likely.'

Marne-la-Vallée and Paris

Richter's alarm went off at seven, and he was driving into the Disneyland resort before eight. He had managed to shave for the first time since his visit to Orlov, and looked fairly presentable. Disneyland was quiet – the doors weren't open to the public that early – and Richter parked close to the main entrance, then walked in and down to the RER station.

He reached the centre of Paris at eight forty, and climbed up into Châtelet-Les Halles and into the sunshine. The station is only a few metres from the eastern end of the rue St Honoré, and Richter walked north-west along it until he reached the crossing of the rue Royale, which runs from place de la Concorde to Sainte Marie Madeleine. On the far side of the rue Royale the rue St Honoré becomes the rue du Faubourg St Honoré, and the British Embassy is at number 35, on the south side of the road.

Entry was painless, due to the persuasion afforded by both the diplomatic passport and Richter's appointment – as 'Mr Beatty' – with the Ambassador. They showed him into a comfortably furnished waiting room and he sat there clutching his briefcase until ten past nine, when a junior staff member appeared and said that the Ambassador would see him. Richter followed her down a corridor and into a large, high-ceilinged room with tall, elegant windows looking south, towards the Seine. A small man with silver hair, immaculately dressed in a charcoal grey suit, was seated behind a large, and obviously antique, rosewood desk. He rose and extended a hand as Richter was ushered in, but he didn't smile. He didn't, Richter thought, look particularly pleased to see him. 'Mr Beatty?' His hand was cool and somewhat limp.

Richter nodded and sat down in the chair the Ambassador indicated in front of his desk. 'I have been advised – perhaps instructed is a better word – to afford you all the assistance you require,' Sir James Auden began, speaking clearly and somewhat pedantically. 'What the Foreign and Commonwealth Office has declined to do, for reasons which may become clear later, is to tell me why. Perhaps you can enlighten me.' Before Richter could speak, the Ambassador added apologetically. 'I am sure that your credentials have already been checked by my staff downstairs, but I would like to see your identification, if you wouldn't mind.'

'Not at all,' Richter said, and handed over the Beatty diplomatic passport.

The Ambassador opened the passport and inspected the contents, glancing over at Richter to ensure that his face bore at least some resemblance to the photograph in it. Then he closed the passport and passed it over the desk to Richter. 'That seems to be in order, Mr Beatty,' he said, 'though I must say that you certainly don't look like a diplomat.'

Richter took that as a compliment. 'In fact, I would have been somewhat surprised if you did,' Auden continued. 'I am aware that you have an appointment to see Mr Herron this morning, and I am sure that it is no coincidence that he is the senior Secret Intelligence Service officer here – what you would probably term the Head of Station.' Sir James Auden was obviously no fool. 'I presume, therefore, that this matter involves some form of covert action.'

'Probably more overt, in fact,' Richter replied.

Auden's eyebrows rose a millimetre. 'Indeed. Perhaps you would care to explain.'

'Better than that, Ambassador, I have here a letter which I think will clarify things.' Richter handed over the sealed envelope.

Auden looked at it with interest, particularly at the seal, then he selected a silver letter-opener, slit the top open and extracted the three sheets of paper it contained. He looked first at the signature block and scrawled signature at the end, then at the crest on the first page. He glanced over at Richter, and began to read. At the end of the first sheet he looked up. 'I can assume that this is not some sort of a joke?'

'No, Ambassador. It's not any kind of a joke – I wish it was.'

Sir James Auden shook his head and carried on reading. Finally he put the pages down and stared across the desk. He looked suddenly older, and his hand was shaking slightly. 'This is monstrous. It's unbelievable.'

'You have to believe it, Ambassador. It's the truth, and I need your help if it isn't going to become a reality.'

Auden looked at the letter, then back at Richter and shook his head. 'You are sure?'

'Quite sure.'

The Ambassador spoke quietly. 'The letter does not deal with the specifics of the matter, only the overall concept. I do not, I think, wish to know the specifics, which you will no doubt be discussing with Herron. What exactly do you want me to do?'

Richter told him, and five minutes later walked out of the Ambassador's office for his appointment with Tony Herron, Paris Head of Station. The Holy of Holies – that section of the Embassy used by Secret Service officers – was small in Paris, and the staff was similarly tiny. This was due to the fact that the French are, at least nominally, on the same side as the British. Richter had never met Tony Herron, but he knew his name from SIS reports.

Herron was six feet tall, sandy haired and, like Richter, appeared slightly rumpled. He welcomed Richter into his inner sanctum, and they settled down to business. 'I've had several Flash and Immediate Top Secret signals from SIS London,' Herron began. 'From these I gather that something is afoot with our eastern neighbours, despite *glasnost* and all the rest.'

'Spot on. Do you want the background now, or wait until we talk to the French?'

'It can wait. One question, though. What grade is the information you have?'

'Grade One – no question.'

Information obtained by all Secret Services is graded according to source and type. Under the United Kingdom grading system, Grade One data is absolutely, one hundred per cent correct without any possibility of error; Grade Two is probably correct; Grade Three is possibly correct; Grade Four is unlikely to be correct, and Grade Five is known to be incorrect. Most of the information Richter had obtained had been unwillingly provided by Orlov, and he had no doubt at all of its veracity.

'I was afraid you'd say that. It's the—' Herron broke off as the telephone rang and he answered it. He identified himself, then listened without speaking for a couple of minutes. 'Thank you, Your Excellency,' he said, replaced the receiver and looked at Richter. 'You certainly got the Ambassador's attention. That was His Nibs – we have an appointment in fifteen minutes with DST operational staff at the rue des Saussaies.'

The *Direction de la Surveillance du Territoire* is France's counter-intelligence agency, which functions like a combination of the British Special Branch and MI5. It is controlled by the Ministry of the Interior and freely employs the resources of the *Renseignements Généraux*, the General Intelligence section of the French police service. It was the DST which in late March 1987 rolled up the Soviet-bloc espionage network that had been passing data on the HM–60 cryogenic rocket motor designed to launch the European Space Agency's Hermes space vehicle.

Richter looked at his watch. 'How long to get there?'

'No time at all – it's just around the corner, off the place Beauvau,' Herron replied. He pressed a button on the telephone, told the duty officer where he was going, then grabbed his jacket and headed for the door.

French Ministry of the Interior, rue des Saussaies, Paris

Herron and Richter were escorted to a small conference room on the second floor where three people waited, seated at a long table. The man at the end announced, in perfect English, that he was the senior officer, Colonel Pierre Lacomte, introduced the other two Frenchmen as DST officers, and requested that the Englishmen sit down. Tony Herron briefly outlined the reason for their visit, introduced Richter as a colleague from SIS London, then handed over to him.

'We have a problem,' Richter began, 'and so do you.' He opened his briefcase, pulled out the operation file and opened it on the table in front of him. 'We have code-named this operation "Overkill", which is actually quite appropriate. What I'm about to tell you will probably sound most unlikely, perhaps even impossible, but I can assure you that it isn't.' Richter glanced at the other men in the room – none showed any signs of dozing off. 'Before I explain the present situation, I have to give you some background information – a bit of history, if you like.' Richter looked at the two DST men. 'Some of this is moderately technical, so please stop me if there are any words you do not understand, and perhaps Colonel Lacomte could then translate for you.'

Lacomte nodded agreement. 'Back in 1958,' Richter said, 'a man named Sam Cohen, who was employed as a strategic nuclear weapons analyst by the Rand Corporation in California, started looking into the secondary effects caused by the detonation of large thermonuclear weapons. One thing that struck him was the very high level of neutron emissions that was essentially a by-product of the detonation of a fusion weapon. Normally a hydrogen bomb has an outer casing of uranium which is irradiated by those neutrons and which contributes to the explosive yield of the weapon. Cohen theorized that if a bomb was designed without the uranium casing, the released neutrons would travel considerable distances and could penetrate pretty much anything. As neutron radiation has a high lethality, such a weapon would be an excellent people-killer, but due to the lower explosive yield of the weapon, it would cause much less structural damage on detonation.

'And there was another benefit. Nuclear fallout is mainly caused by the products of fission reactions, and this weapon was by definition a fusion device triggered, like all fusion weapons, by a very small fission explosion. So, a bomb of this type would release only about one per cent of the radiation of a fission bomb of comparable size, causing minimal fallout, and the neutron radiation disperses very quickly, which would mean that the area could be entered comparatively soon after detonation. This was the birth of the Enhanced Radiation Weapon or neutron bomb.'

'The ERW, Mr Beatty? This is hardly news, is it?' Whatever Colonel Lacomte had been expecting, it clearly hadn't been a lesson on the physics of nuclear weapons.

'No, Colonel, it isn't news, but it is essential background. Anyway, the neutron bomb became a political football. The Kennedy administration decided not to build any such weapons because it might affect their relations with the Soviet Union, but when the Russians broke the existing moratorium on nuclear weapons tests they changed their mind. The first American ERW was tested in 1962 and large-scale manufacture began in the 1970s, when President Carter proposed installing neutron warheads on Lance missiles and howitzer artillery shells to be deployed in Europe. That decision caused such political turmoil that Carter eventually backed down, indefinitely deferring any such deployment. Reagan was more of a hawk, and re-authorized the production of ERWs, but with the caveat that they would be stored in America and only deployed to Europe if hostilities broke out. The Russians, who were largely behind the "ban the neutron bomb" campaign, had secretly developed their own ERWs. France had tested its own version of the weapon by 1980 and began series production in 1982.'

'Your information is out-of-date, Mr Beatty. We ceased production of these weapons in 1986, and that is not a secret.'

'Agreed, Colonel. But France didn't destroy her existing stocks, did she? Nor did the Americans, who still hold in excess of seven hundred neutron warheads, all of tactical, not strategic, size. The latest information we have suggests that China, Israel and South Africa, at the very least, all have stockpiles of neutron weapons of various sizes and yields.'

The DST men seemed to be keeping up with Richter, but Tony Herron looked moderately confused. Richter smiled at him. 'That's the history, and most of the background. There are just a couple of other things you need to know. First, since *glasnost*, America has been paying billions of dollars to the Russians in exchange for plutonium from dismantled nuclear weapons. They had the best of motives – if the USA could buy all their plutonium, then the Russians wouldn't need to sell it on the black market with the risk of it ending up in the hands of terrorists. Unfortunately, all the expert independent evidence shows that the Russians have actually been handing over material produced in their nuclear power plants, and not weapons-grade plutonium. That suggests very strongly that the Russians, contrary to their public statements, have not been dismantling any of their nuclear weapons.

'Second, it's well known that to construct a fission bomb you need uranium-235, but to build a fusion weapon or a neutron bomb you have to have access to plutonium. That's a well-known fact, and it's completely wrong.' Richter paused and looked at Colonel Lacomte. 'Have you ever heard of red mercury?' he asked.

National Military Command Center, The Pentagon, Washington, D.C.

By five fifteen a.m., local time, the last of the Joint Chiefs of Staff and their aides had assembled in the National Military Command Center – a suite of offices on the third floor of the Pentagon. The noisiest section of the NMCC is the office which handles the raw data, because of the rows of clattering telex machines that bring in reports and information from sources worldwide. It has a bank of clocks set for a variety of world time zones and a permanent display of maps showing the dispersal of strategic assets and troops of all major national armed forces. Quiet by comparison, the Emergency Conference Room is next door.

The ECR is a split-level room. On the lower level, the duty officers, known as the Battle Staff, sit on both sides of the 'leg' of a vast T-shaped table, collating data. Four Emergency Action officers sit at purpose-built consoles along the top of the 'T', each with communication links to American forces around the world. The Joint Chiefs of Staff, the President's military advice team, sit on a raised platform slightly above and to the left of the table used by the Battle Staff. On the opposite side of the room, and in front of the Joint Chiefs, are six huge colour screens on which can be displayed maps of any area of the world, as well as plans, charts, surveillance and other photographs, details of troop concentrations and any other type of graphic which would help to clarify a developing situation.

The NMCC, like the White House Situation Room and the hardened facilities at Cheyenne Mountain, the Underground Complex at Offutt, and Raven Rock, forms part of a single vast command structure, linked by telephones, faxes and telex machines, satellites, radios and computers. Although the briefing was being delivered in the Pentagon, staff at the other linked locations would be able to hear every word that was said.

An army general was the Senior Duty Battle Staff Officer, and would normally have conducted the briefing of the Joint Chiefs. The situation, however, was not normal.

'Gentlemen,' the general began without preamble, 'we have an unfolding situation possibly involving disaffected elements within the former Soviet Union. A definite threat, not involving overt troop or conventional military manoeuvres, has been made against both the United States and Western Europe. This briefing will be in two parts. First, Mr Walter Hicks, the Central Intelligence Agency's Clandestine Services Director of Operations, and currently the acting DCI, will brief you on the history and substance of the threat. When he has concluded and answered any questions you may have, I will advise you of the White House's response to the situation, and what the President intends to do next.'

The general looked up, glanced to his left and nodded. Walter Hicks stubbed out his cigar in the ashtray by his left arm, got to his feet and walked over to the lectern.

American Embassy, Grosvenor Square, London

The internal telephone on Roger Abrahams' desk rang at nine fifty. He put down the file he had been studying and picked up the handset. 'Abrahams.'

'This is the switchboard, sir, and I have a call holding for you. The caller won't identify himself, but says it's urgent and a personal matter,' the Embassy operator announced.

'What nationality?' Abrahams asked.

'British, sir, definitely.'

'OK,' Abrahams said. 'Make sure the tape's running and put him through.'

There was a click and a brief silence. 'Hullo,' Abrahams said.

'Good morning, Roger,' the familiar voice said, and Abrahams could detect the urgency behind the casual drawl. 'I presume you're taping this, so I won't bother repeating myself.' The voice paused, then spoke three words. 'Anatidae. Ten ten.'

The line went dead, but Abrahams had completely understood what the caller meant. He looked at his watch, then pressed the speed-dial code for the motor pool's number. 'This is Abrahams. I need a car, now.'

Le Moulin au Pouchon, St Médard, near Manciet, Midi-Pyrénées, France

'Excellent,' Hassan Abbas murmured, reading the decrypted email message from Dmitri Trushenko for the third time.

In fact, there had been two messages from the Russian. The first had simply confirmed that he had reached his secure location but did not, of course, reveal where that location was. When Abbas had read that, he'd heaved a sigh of relief. Obviously the comparatively long silence from the Russian had been caused by nothing more sinister than Trushenko's journey from his apartment in Moscow to wherever he had chosen to hide whilst the final stages of *Podstava* were played out. Abbas suspected privately that Trushenko might even have left the Confederation of Independent States, maybe gone to Greece or Turkey.

But it didn't matter where he was, as long as the Russian authorities couldn't find him.

The second message contained the specifics of the positioning of the last two weapons. The Russian coaster was exactly on schedule for its planned arrival in Gibraltar, and the convoy carrying the London device should, according to the latest mobile telephone message from the escort, arrive in Germany that morning. Unless something totally unforeseen occurred, both weapons would be positioned precisely on time.

Abbas rubbed his hands together, opened up his word processor and began preparing the text of the message he would sent to Sadoun Khamil in Saudi Arabia.

French Ministry of the Interior, rue des Saussaies, Paris

The colonel sat straighter in his chair. 'What, exactly, is red mercury?'

'Red mercury was the substance that frightened Sam Cohen most. It's a mercury compound which has been subjected to massive irradiation in a nuclear reactor, and which when exploded creates tremendous heat and pressure. Exactly the same kind of heat and pressure that's needed to trigger a fusion weapon. So you no longer need access to weapons-grade plutonium, or any plutonium at all, in fact. And red mercury is cheap, especially by comparison with the cost of plutonium.'

'And?' Lacomte asked.

'And the Russians have been making it and selling it on the black market for years, although all sales stopped about four years ago. One of their biggest customers was Iraq, which is enough to make most people lose some sleep straight away.'

Lacomte looked puzzled. 'I hear what you're saying, Mr Beatty, but I still don't understand what any of this has to do with us. Why are you here? What, exactly, is the nature of any threat to us in Western Europe?'

Richter nodded. 'I'll explain that in a moment. That's the end of the history lesson. Last week a USAF SR–71A Blackbird reconnaissance aircraft was pulled out of retirement at Beale Air Force Base in the States and made a totally illegal over-flight of a section of territory in north-west Russia. We believe that the Blackbird encountered opposition fighters during its flight and had to take evasive action. Precisely what happened we don't know, but certainly it suffered battle damage and there was virtually no fuel left in its tanks when the aircraft landed at an Air Force base in Scotland. The Americans were very reluctant to explain the aircraft's mission, but we finally discovered that the Blackbird had been sent to photograph a hill that wasn't there any more.'

Tony Herron still looked puzzled, and the DST men looked totally confused. 'Hill? What hill, Mr Beatty?' one asked.

'Just a hill,' Richter said, 'deep in the Tundra. Let me explain. The Americans were puzzled, because the hill had been destroyed by a nuclear detonation of an unusual sort. The Blackbird flew to photograph the hole where the hill had been, but its principal mission was to take radiation measurements of the area. After that they had to sit down and think it out.' Richter poured water into a glass and resumed the story. 'We got involved after a man called Newman disappeared from the British Embassy in Moscow. He had apparently been killed in a road accident, but when we examined the body it was immediately apparent that it wasn't Newman's. That was significant enough, but when added to the fact that Newman was the SIS Head of Station in Moscow, it became obvious that something was going on. We surmised that he had been snatched by the SVR for terminal questioning.

'We checked our files, and found that Newman's deputy had acted as a translator, and had accompanied a party of Western businessmen on a tour in north-western Russia, a tour which took them to within a mere hundred miles or so of the site of the hill. Then a CIA source advised us that the radiation analysis didn't make sense. The Blackbird flew a fairly short time after the explosion, but the aircraft detectors registered no significant radiation.

'Finally, there was the short and turbulent history of the neutron bomb, the evidence that the Russians demonstrably weren't decommissioning their arsenal of nuclear weapons, and the fact that black-market sales of red mercury by Russia stopped about four years ago. We put all that lot together, and we came up with a theory.'

OVERKILL

The Gold Room, the Pentagon, Washington, D.C.

The Joint Chiefs had left the Emergency Conference Room as soon as Walter Hicks and General Rogers had completed the briefing. Despite its name, the ECR was not designed for conferences, only for briefings, and the Joint Chiefs had immediately moved into the so-called 'Gold Room' conference suite, also on the third floor of the Pentagon.

The Secretary of Defense had not been present at the Kentucky Rose briefing, because he had been closeted in the White House Situation Room with the President, but by mid-morning he, too, was in the Gold Room. After a lengthy telephone conversation between the Secretary of Defense and the President, the Joint Chiefs of Staff elected to upgrade the alert status of the US forces immediately to DEFCON THREE.

Because of the time zone differences between Moscow and the east coast of America – eight hours – and because source RAVEN had specified the eleventh of the month as the actual date of implementation, the Joint Chiefs also instituted a formal countdown. It began at 0600 Eastern Standard Time on the ninth, and assumed that implementation of the assault would take place at midnight Moscow time – sixteen hundred EST – on the eleventh. That was designated H-Hour, and it was exactly thirty-four hours away. The clock was running.

Regents Park, London

The black Mercedes surged away from the traffic lights, drove rapidly down Park Road and stopped with a squeal of tyres at the western end of Hanover Gardens.

'Wait, please,' Abrahams said to the driver, and strode off briskly through Hanover Gardens towards Regents Park. He was a few metres from the second footbridge when he saw the slim figure beside The Holme. Piers Taylor wasn't feeding the ducks. He was pacing up and down beside the Boating Lake and when Westwood stepped off the footbridge he strode forward to meet him.

'Good morning, Piers,' Roger Abrahams said.

311

'It isn't, actually,' Taylor replied. 'Thank you for coming. You had no trouble with my simple little code?'

Abrahams shook his head. 'No,' he said. '"Anatidae" – family name of the class of swimming birds normally known as ducks. Besides, I recognized your voice.'

Taylor grinned, briefly.

'So,' Abrahams asked, 'what's up?'

Piers Taylor looked round, checking that nobody else was within earshot. 'That matter we talked about with your American colleague,' he began. 'Now we think we know what it's all about.'

French Ministry of the Interior, rue des Saussaies, Paris

Richter had the undivided attention of everyone in the room. 'About four years ago, something happened in Russia. What, we don't know, but whatever it was caused the stoppage of all external sales of red mercury. The obvious conclusion is that the entire production of the substance was diverted into a new project, a project that we're seeing the results of now. What we think is that the Russians for some reason had a sudden need to manufacture a large number of strategic-yield neutron bombs, but didn't want to use weapons-grade plutonium, either because they would have had to pull it out of existing nuclear weapons or because the refining process would have taken too long, or attracted too much attention. They needed the plutonium for something else, which I'll get to in a moment.

'The vaporization of the hill showed clearly enough that the neutron weapon would work, but we are moderately certain that that was just the last in a series of tests, but the first which the Russians had conducted above ground. The yield of the weapon was calculated to be at least five megatons, which makes it far and away the biggest neutron bomb ever detonated, and classifies it firmly as a strategic weapon. But that still left two questions unanswered. First, if the Russians had perfected a strategic-yield neutron bomb, how did that help them? It would have a higher yield than any ERWs in our inventory, but we couldn't see how the weapon would benefit them if they went to war with the West.

'If the Russians re-equipped their missiles with the new war-head and simply fired off their ICBMs and other assorted arsenal in the usual Doomsday fashion, the Americans would retaliate before their missiles were halfway across the Atlantic and the Russians would suffer unacceptable losses. Granted, the loss of life on the American continent might be somewhat greater than our colonial cousins would have been expecting, but that wouldn't help a hundred million incinerated Russian citizens. So, there had to be something else.

'Secondly, the lack of radiation emitted by the new device would favour the West, not the Russians. The balance of terror – Mutual Assured Destruction and all the rest of it – has always been predicated on the basis that neither side could win a nuclear war. Any significant nuclear exchange would turn both nations into radioactive wastelands, so neither could win in the conventional sense of the word. If the Russians used the new weapon, it would just cause massive damage and loss of life in America, but not render the country uninhabitable. That simply didn't make sense. Using the new weapon would actually benefit the West.'

'So there was something else?' Tony Herron asked.

'Oh, yes,' Richter said. 'There was definitely something else.'

8th Arrondissement, Paris

John Westwood's mobile telephone, supplied by the Embassy in London, rang as he and Miles Turner turned right into avenue de Marigny from avenue Gabriel. Their appointment at the French Ministry of the Interior was at eleven thirty, and they had decided to walk. 'Westwood,' he said, moving to the side of the pavement away from the traffic noise.

'John, it's Roger in London.'

'Yes, Roger?' Westwood knew the matter had to be urgent, other-wise Abrahams would have used one of the secure communications links at the Embassy itself. He also knew Abrahams would have to be circumspect in what he said. Although calls made using digital mobile telephones are effectively scrambled, sophisticated equipment can still decode conversations.

'I tried you at the office, but I must have just missed you,' Abrahams said. 'I have some business news for you. Our English friends think they've found the solution to our problem, and they suggest you contact their chief sales executive, Mr Beatty. He's in Paris at the moment, and you can reach him through the Paris office of the English company.'

Westwood nodded. 'That's excellent news. Thank you, Roger, I'll do that. See you.' Westwood terminated the call and slipped the telephone back into his jacket pocket.

Turner looked at him. 'News?' he asked.

'Yes,' Westwood said, glancing round cautiously. 'Roger says the Brits have found out what the Russians are up to, and they've got a man here in Paris now, working out of the British Embassy. Guy name of Beatty. Do you know him?'

Turner shook his head. 'Nope, but it could be a work-name.' He looked at his watch. 'We'll go see the DST now, but I'll call the Embassy and have them talk to the local SIS men.'

French Ministry of the Interior, rue des Saussaies, Paris

'We even looked into the possibility of a co-ordinated satellite-launched attack which would do major damage in America before a retaliatory strike could be ordered. As I'm sure everyone in this room is aware, the Americans monitor all Russian satellite launches, and then disseminate the information to the British government and other interested parties. But analysis showed no unusual activity. All we found was a single new communications satellite – or what the Russians said was a communications satellite – in geostationary orbit over the eastern Atlantic. That could certainly not be construed as a threat to anyone or any country.'

'So what is it? What are they going to do with the new weapon?' Lacomte asked.

'I'll come to that in a moment. We believed until a few days ago that some kind of action was imminent.'

'Just a minute,' Tony Herron interrupted. 'You said that you believed some kind of action was imminent. Do you mean that it now isn't imminent, or have you definite information concerning an attack?'

Richter nodded. 'Definite information, yes, but not of an attack – at least, not the way you mean it. We decided to return the favour over our man in Moscow, and pulled the SVR London *rezident*.'

'Orlov? You pulled Vladimir Orlov?' Tony Herron sounded appalled.

'Yes,' Richter said.

'What have you done with him? You can't hold him for ever.'

Obviously word had yet to reach Paris. 'Comrade Orlov,' Richter said, 'did not survive his interrogation. The important thing is that Orlov revealed everything he knew about the plan.'

'And?'

Richter shrugged his shoulders. 'Really, it's all a matter of perspective. For years everyone has assumed that any future conflict would be between the superpowers, Russia and America. ICBMs and other weapons were targeted from one nation to the other. The rest of NATO, and of course the French, followed suit with their own forces. But why should that be the case? What good would it do Russia to attack America? It would be far more sensible for the Russians to simply neutralize America, to eliminate the States from any conflict—'

Tony Herron interrupted. 'We never assumed Russia would attack America. We always thought Soviet ground forces would advance on Western Europe.'

'Yes,' Richter said, 'but when allied forces were forced to retreat because of the sheer numerical superiority of the Russian forces, what would happen then? The defence strategy of every European nation is wholly based on the assumption that if the attacked country can just hold on for a few hours or days, the US cavalry will charge in to the rescue. No cavalry – no rescue. If there's not going to be a rescue, what's the point in fighting?'

'So what are you saying? That America has been neutralized, and that the Russians are going to take Europe?' Colonel Lacomte expressed it very well.

'That's it exactly,' Richter said. 'Russia wants neither a war with America nor a war in Europe. What it wants is Europe without a fight, and the whole purpose of this scheme is to achieve that.'

The room was silent again as his audience digested this. Finally, Tony Herron spoke. 'But what about *glasnost* and the liberalization of the USSR? What about that?'

'We believe that this plan is not, and never was, part of official Russian strategy. Piecing it together from what Orlov revealed, it looks as if the scheme was a strictly private venture, concocted by the SVR and the GRU, possibly under the auspices of Group *Nord*.'

'Group *Nord*?' Lacomte asked.

'Group *Nord*,' Richter replied, 'was formed in the mid-1970s by Yuri Andropov when he was Chairman of the KGB. The Group's members were the chiefs of all the KGB's operational divisions and it met once a month. The declared object of Group *Nord* was to shatter the western alliance, isolate the United States of America, and so weaken or otherwise disable America that the country would no longer have the will to resist the Soviet Union. "Overkill" has all the hallmarks of a Group *Nord* operation.'

'Just a moment.' Colonel Lacomte was looking puzzled. 'We seem to have missed the main point. You said that America had been neutralized. How?'

'This information I have not had confirmed,' Richter said, 'mainly because the Americans either don't know or won't talk about it. However, according to the late Comrade Orlov, the Russians have spent the last four years carefully installing a selection of high-radiation conventional nuclear weapons in every major city in the United States.' Tony Herron gave a gasp of astonishment. Richter carried on. 'A thoroughly nasty idea. The Americans were spending billions on buying non-weapons-grade plutonium from the Russians, which was effectively a waste product they pulled out of their nuclear reactors, while the Russians were sending the plutonium the Americans thought they were getting to America, but inside live nuclear weapons. And you remember the communications satellite I mentioned – the one in geostationary orbit over the Atlantic?' Lacomte nodded. 'That's the firing link. All the weapons have radio-controlled triggers, which the Russians can pull any time they want.'

'How the hell did they get them into the States?'

'A combination of smuggling and misuse of the Diplomatic Bag – it doesn't have to be a briefcase carried by a Queen's Messenger, you know. It can be anything from an envelope to an articulated lorry.'

Tony Herron spoke slowly. 'I can see why they're neither confirming nor denying it. But you said those were standard nuclear bombs. What about these high-yield neutron bombs? I thought that was what this was all about?'

'It is,' Richter replied. 'The American weapons are only half of the story. The problem with taking Europe is that Britain and France have retained their own nuclear deterrent. That means that, even if America has been taken out of the equation, Russia could still suffer massive losses if her troops were to invade Western Europe. So the problem the SVR and GRU faced was to eliminate the British and French nuclear deterrents, but still not turn Europe into a nuclear wasteland. And for that, the strategic neutron bombs are tailor-made because of the high yield and very short-duration radiation. They could detonate a device under the Eiffel Tower and walk down what was left of the Bois de Boulogne five days later. You'd have to step over a lot of corpses, but you wouldn't need to wear an NBCD suit or a mask.'

Colonel Lacomte shook his head. 'This is unbelievable,' he said.

'It is,' Richter agreed, 'but it's nevertheless true.'

'Assuming for the moment that it is,' Lacomte continued, 'what can we do about it? And how far have the Russians got with the scheme?'

'What we can do,' Richter replied, picking up the 'Overkill' file, 'is stop them delivering the last neutron bomb – which is destined for London – because that will stalemate the situation and keep the British independent nuclear deterrent as a counter-threat. And the reason it's your problem as well as our problem is that, according to Orlov, the Paris, Toulouse, Nice and Bordeaux devices are already in place.'

Chapter Nineteen

Tuesday
French Ministry of the Interior, rue des Saussaies, Paris

The knock at the door sounded unnaturally loud in the silence that followed. Lacomte gestured to one of the DST men who walked over and opened it. He held a brief conversation with someone outside, then walked back and murmured to Lacomte. The colonel looked up at Richter and Herron, then spoke briefly to the DST officer, who immediately left the room. Lacomte smiled briefly. 'We have some visitors,' he said, 'who may be able to corroborate some of what you are saying.'

'Who?' Herron asked, looking at Richter.

'Two gentlemen from the American Central Intelligence Agency,' Lacomte replied, as the door opened to admit John Westwood and Miles Turner.

Westwood stopped just inside the door as his eyes swept the room and then settled on Richter. 'Paul?' he said, his voice uncertain.

'John Westwood,' Richter said. 'Long time no see. How the hell did you get here?'

Rozvadov, Czechoslovakia

The convoy came to a halt just west of the town of Rozvadov, about a mile short of the German border and at the end of the queue of vehicles waiting to cross. Most, Modin noted, were lorries, which probably meant delays while their loads or manifests were inspected and approved by the German Customs officers.

'We cannot, I suppose,' Bykov asked, 'attempt to get across any quicker, because of our diplomatic status?'

Modin shook his head. 'No,' he said flatly, 'not across the German border. Don't forget, Viktor, the lorry is supposed to be carrying furniture and fittings for our London Embassy. It would be difficult to argue that these goods constitute any kind of a priority load. We wait, and we take our turn.'

French Ministry of the Interior, rue des Saussaies, Paris

'Any questions on any of that?' Richter asked.

'No, not at the moment. Thank you for recapping,' Westwood said. He and Turner had paled noticeably when Richter described the placement of the nuclear weapons in American cities. Richter's second explanation had been much briefer than his first, and the Americans had already known at least some of the background data, which helped.

'Would they have the ability to construct these devices – I mean the bombs back home and these new neutron devices – and get that satellite into orbit?' Miles Turner asked.

'Yes, without question,' Richter said. 'The GRU has an almost unlimited budget, and the SVR – like the KGB before it – is still the nation's biggest single employer. We know they'd have the resources to do it. The Kremlin relies on the SVR, just as it used to rely on the KGB, to tell it what's going on in the country. If the SVR doesn't tell the Kremlin, the Kremlin probably won't find out, because it's got very few other sources of information. As long as this plot has been conceived at a high enough level it wouldn't be too difficult to keep it quiet.

'We believe that somebody – probably somebody in Group *Nord* – looked at Western Europe four or five years ago and saw the answers to all the problems of their nation. The fields of France could feed the world, if the political will existed to organize it. The German industrial machine could dominate the global economy, if it was given sufficient muscle. The resources were there; all that was necessary was to devise a plan to take them. We believe that the originator of this operation planned to annex most of Western Europe, incorporate it into an expanded Soviet bloc, and then continue with the age-old dream of Communist expansion throughout the world. They probably thought that by seizing Europe's assets they could at last make the Communist system work, and demonstrate to the world that Lenin, Marx and all the rest of them had been right all along. We know better, of course. Given Communist management, or rather mismanagement, Germany would be a subsistence economy within five years, France in two.

'The problem they had was to make Europe give up without a fight. A Germany or France devastated by war was not what they wanted, which is why they seized on the two-pronged assault. First neutralize the USA by the potent threat of the total destruction of almost every major city in America, using weapons that were already in place, and which could not, therefore, be detected in flight, intercepted or countered. Then, with America out of the fight, threaten Europe with similar devastation, but without the fallout and radiation problems.'

'Mr Beatty,' Lacomte held up a hand, 'I don't know about my colleagues, but I am getting both confused and worried. I am confused because almost everything you have told us is new to me, and I freely admit that I do not understand all of it, and I do not know if I believe any of it. But I am getting worried because, if what you say is true, then this meeting should be pitched at a much higher level than a mere colonel.' He looked at Richter keenly, then glanced at his watch. 'As it is nearly half past one, I suggest we break now for lunch and resume this afternoon at three. I will ensure that the Minister of the Interior or the most senior available member of his staff joins us then. Would that be satisfactory?'

'Perfectly,' Richter replied. 'Could I make two requests for you to discuss with the Minister prior to our meeting this afternoon?' Lacomte nodded, and poised his pencil over a sheet of paper. 'First,' Richter said, 'I would like the route of the road convoy carrying the weapon destined for London to be watched and its position advised to us at frequent intervals. I presume that would not be difficult?'

'Not at all,' Lacomte replied. 'That can be done on my orders, without bothering the Minister. Can you supply details of the route and identify the vehicles?'

'The route, yes, but not the vehicles, although I can make an informed guess. I can do that this afternoon.' Richter paused. 'The second point might prove more contentious,' he said.

Lacomte nodded encouragingly. 'Go on, Mr Beatty.'

'We have to stop this convoy, and detain all the personnel associated with it. I am requesting permission to utilize a unit from the British Special Air Service to help do this.' Richter heard Tony Herron's quick intake of breath, and Lacomte bristled visibly.

'I do not think the Minister would accept that, not without very compelling reasons. Why would you wish to use the SAS?'

The one thing Richter couldn't tell Lacomte was that the SAS were the best in the world – French pride would never admit that any non-Frenchman was the best at anything.

'Three reasons,' Richter said. 'First, I will have to direct at least some phases of the operation against the convoy, as I'm the only one who knows exactly what we will be looking for. I believe that the load may be booby-trapped, or worse. I don't speak French, and I may have to give orders that will be acted on immediately and without question – the SAS would respond instinctively, and far faster, than anyone whose first language is not English.

'Secondly, the SAS specializes in this kind of operation, and would be able to give valuable assistance to the men you would detail to carry out the assault. I only want a standard four-man patrol unit, comprising one officer and three troopers. I would anticipate using a group of ten to fifteen men to actually halt the convoy, so the SAS men would only be acting in an advisory or supporting role to the French assault team.'

'Third, if this convoy is not stopped, the weapon will reach London and could conceivably destroy most of the population of the city. That makes it a problem for Britain, and I believe that British forces should have an active role in preventing that happening.'

Lacomte considered this for a moment, then nodded slowly. 'Yes, Mr Beatty, what you say does make sense. I will recommend that the Minister accedes to your request.'

8th Arrondissement, Paris

Richter left the Ministry with Tony Herron and John Westwood. Miles Turner had left immediately for the American Embassy to call Langley and take instructions. The three men walked along the road until they found a reasonable-looking restaurant that had a table free, then sat down and ordered lunch.

'I hope you know what we're doing,' Herron said, as the waiter moved out of earshot.

'So do I,' Richter replied, taking a bite out of a slice of baguette.

'You two know each other, I gather,' Herron added, looking from Richter to Westwood and back again.

'We got involved in a chase across France a few years ago,' Richter said. 'What are you doing here, John?'

'I was sent over here to try to find out what the hell's going on.'

'And did you?' Richter asked.

'No, we didn't,' Westwood said. 'CIA London was told about it by SIS this morning.'

'What are you going to do?'

'Back home, I've no idea – that's someone else's problem,' Westwood said. 'As far as I'm concerned, I was told to find out what was going on, which I suppose I've done, so now I'm just going to hang on for the ride. Unless Langley tells me any different, that is.'

Richter nodded. The restaurant was busy, and they were able to talk quietly together without being overheard above the hum of conversation. 'OK,' Richter said. 'Now that the pleasantries are out of the way, let's get back to the job in hand. We're running short of time. We have to stop that lorry tomorrow, which means we have to get the SAS team over here tonight at the latest.'

'Suppose the Minister doesn't approve their use?' Herron asked.

'Then they'll have a very short holiday in France. We just have to assume that he will give approval. Can you get a car and one of your Friends from the Embassy to meet us here before we go back into the Ministry, to get things moving as soon as possible?'

In the peculiar parlance of the clandestine world, a 'Friend' is a British Secret Intelligence Service Officer, usually one based in an Embassy.

'Yes,' Herron said. 'I'll call now.' He pulled out his mobile telephone, dialled a number and held a brief conversation. 'No problem,' he said. 'They'll be here at two fifteen.'

Waidhaus, Germany

When the convoy reached the head of the queue, the Czechoslovak Customs officers waved the vehicles through with merely a glance at the passports. The Germans were more thorough.

'Why,' the senior Customs officer asked Modin, in English, their only common language, in one of the border post interview rooms, 'are there three vehicles escorting a lorry-load of furniture across Europe?'

Modin shook his head. 'This is not an escort,' he said. 'The lorry is making a routine delivery of furniture and fittings to our London Embassy. There have been similar deliveries recently,' he added, 'to Russian embassies elsewhere in Western Europe.' He didn't add that some of these deliveries had included one item which had not appeared on the load manifest.

'Why does the London Embassy require furniture to be sent out from Russia? Are there no furniture shops in Britain?'

Modin nodded. 'Of course there are,' he replied. 'But you must appreciate the fragile nature of the Russian economy since *glasnost*. Our government has ordered that all embassy furniture and fittings are to be purchased in Russia, not from companies in the West.'

The German grunted. 'I notice that the ruling by Moscow does not extend to the vehicles you are driving.'

'That is different. We are unfortunately compelled to purchase cars manufactured in the West for our European embassies. There are always delays, you understand, with obtaining spare parts for Russian-made vehicles. Our Embassies cannot take the risk of having official cars unavailable for prolonged periods. The same applies to our international lorries – we cannot afford to have broken-down vehicles waiting for days or weeks by the roadside.'

'And the sixteen people?' the German officer persisted.

'Simply a coincidence,' Modin said smoothly. 'There is a major staff change in progress at our London Embassy.'

'Why didn't they fly into London?'

'For reasons of economy,' Modin replied. 'The vehicles were being transported by road, and it seemed foolish to purchase airline tickets when there were empty seats in the cars.'

The German looked steadily at Modin for a minute, then stood up. 'Very well,' he said, and handed back the Russian's diplomatic passport. He had little choice in the matter, and he and Modin both knew it. 'Proceed,' he said.

8th Arrondissement, Paris

When the car arrived, the three men climbed into the back seat and Herron instructed the chauffeur just to drive around for a few minutes. As they pulled out into the traffic flow, Herron briefed the SIS officer sitting beside the driver, and then turned to Richter. 'Right, what do you want done?'

'At this stage,' Richter said, 'I'd just like to get the SAS moving. Can you send a signal from the Embassy to FOE London, attention Director, information SIS and Stirling Lines, requesting the immediate activation of a four-man SAS team. If he's available, I'd like Captain Colin Dekker to lead it. Detailed tasking and briefing will be carried out in Paris, but the team should prepare weapons and equipment suitable for operations against an armed road convoy. Transport to Paris should be by road, in a civilian vehicle, and preferably a "Q" van.'

The SAS 'Q' vans are disguised vehicles, usually Leyland Sherpas or Ford Transits, fitted with uprated suspension systems, highly tuned – and usually very large – engines, long-range tanks and all the rest. They also have hidden compartments for weapons and equipment, and will pass more than a cursory inspection by police or Customs officers. The disguises are many and varied, everything from a church minibus to a builder's van.

'Two questions,' the SIS officer said. 'What classification and precedence for the signal, and what rendezvous point do you want in Paris?'

Richter thought for a moment. 'The signal should be classified Secret, and the precedence Military Flash. Oh, and could you insert "Operation Overkill" in the subject field. The rendezvous, I think, should be tonight at my accommodation. Yes,' he said, and smiled. 'They'll like this. The rendezvous will be at Davy Crockett Ranch at the Disneyland Paris resort. Include a statement in the signal that I will book accommodation for them there. A party of four, in the name of, oh, "Robbins".' Richter gave him the cabin number, on the 'Cherokee Trail'. 'Say that the SAS contact point is that cabin, immediately after arrival at the Ranch. Do not,' Richter added, 'give my name. Just state that I am their Briefing Officer.'

Westwood smiled at Richter. 'You're staying at Disneyland? Now I've heard everything.'

He chuckled, and Richter grinned at him. 'If you were leading a Russian hit team, would you think of looking for me there?'

Westwood's smile slowly faded. 'No,' he said, shaking his head. 'I guess I wouldn't.'

Anton Kirov

'Gibraltar, Gibraltar, this is the motor vessel *Anton Kirov*. Over.' The *Spetsnaz* radio operator adjusted one of the dials on the radio and listened.

'MV *Anton Kirov*, this is Gibraltar. Go ahead. Over.'

The voice from the overhead speaker was tinny and slightly distorted, but perfectly understandable.

Petr Zavorin nodded, and the operator replied. 'Gibraltar, this is the *Anton Kirov*. We are out of the port of Odessa bound for Tangier with a mixed cargo. We have experienced a small fire in the engine room and we request permission to put in to Gibraltar to effect repairs. Over.'

There was a brief silence before the Gibraltar operator replied. 'Do you require assistance, *Anton Kirov*? Over.'

'Negative, Gibraltar. We will have to replace one fuel pump and some fuel lines, but we do not require any form of assistance. Over.'

'Wait.'

There was a pause of perhaps two minutes. '*Anton Kirov*, this is Gibraltar. Permission granted. What is your estimate for Gibraltar? Over.'

Zavorin looked at Bondarev.

'About three hours, unless you want to increase speed.'

Zavorin shook his head. 'No, we will maintain this speed. Tell them three hours.'

'Gibraltar, this is the *Anton Kirov*. We estimate about three hours. Over.'

'Roger. Proceed to a position one mile west of Gibraltar, hold there and await a harbour tug. You will be berthed at the North Mole. Over.'

'Thank you, Gibraltar. Out.' The radio operator removed his headphones and nodded to Zavorin.

'Excellent,' Zavorin said. 'We have just entered the final phase of the operation.'

French Ministry of the Interior, rue des Saussaies, Paris

The car dropped them at the rue des Saussaies, and they walked back to the Ministry, arriving at three. They were again escorted to the conference room, where Lacomte waited expectantly. Miles Turner and the two DST officers were already there, and a minute or so after Richter, Herron and Westwood walked in, four other men entered. Lacomte greeted them somewhat formally, and made the introductions in French and English, then turned to Richter.

'The Minister is away from Paris this afternoon, but we are expecting him back early this evening. Monsieur Giraud –' he gestured to the elderly man who had just taken a seat at the head of the table '– is the senior adviser to the Minister, your equivalent of a Permanent Under-Secretary of State, and I have explained the situation to him and to his aides. He has discussed the matter with the Minister on a secure telephone line. The Minister has empowered Monsieur Giraud to take decisions on his behalf, as time is short.' Lacomte paused. 'The Minister has not decided whether to permit the use of your Special Air Service personnel on French soil, but will leave that decision to Monsieur Giraud. Monsieur Giraud will decide after he has heard your detailed proposals.'

'I see,' Richter said, and Tony Herron looked at him. Richter wondered how much of an uphill struggle the afternoon was going to be.

'Monsieur Giraud,' Lacomte continued, 'understands English, but because of the technical nature of this matter he has asked that I translate what you say into French, to avoid any possible misunderstandings.'

And also, Richter thought, to emphasize that they were in France and should therefore, by any Gallic definition, be speaking French.

'Before we begin,' said Lacomte, 'I have one or two questions I would like to ask.' Richter nodded. 'We understand that much of the information about this matter has reached you by indirect channels, shall we say, and some of it could be construed as circumstantial. What is the source and grade of your information about the devices on French soil?'

Richter bet that question had come straight from Monsieur Giraud. 'That information came directly to us from the SVR London *rezident*, Vladimir Orlov,' Richter said. 'The information is assessed in our system as Grade One – that is, one hundred per cent reliable without any possibility of error.'

Lacomte looked at Monsieur Giraud, who nodded. 'Are you aware that the Russians do not have any diplomatic representation in some of the cities you mentioned? In Nice, for example? Where would they position a weapon?'

'With respect,' Richter said, 'this is just detail. Orlov didn't know and so couldn't tell us exactly where any of the devices were positioned, only that they were in place. I imagine that the Russians have set up a front company which has leased a warehouse or an office somewhere, and the weapon will be located in that.'

Lacomte loaded that into French and rapid-fired it at Giraud. Giraud nodded, and replied quietly. Lacomte asked another question. 'Have you any independent evidence that what Orlov told you is the truth?'

Richter shook his head. 'No,' he said, 'we have no independent evidence that directly corroborates what Orlov told us, but I cannot imagine him telling lies in the circumstances of his interrogation.' Giraud grimaced slightly. 'What I can say is that most of what Orlov told us has been indirectly corroborated by the other data we have been able to collect. I've already mentioned the Blackbird over-flight, the snatching of our Moscow Head of Station and so on.'

'Can I add something here?' John Westwood asked.

'Of course,' Lacomte waved a hand.

'The one thing nobody in this room knows, except for Miles Turner here,' Westwood said, 'is that the Company – the CIA – received advance warning of the Russian plan, some time before the Blackbird over-flight.'

There was a short and somewhat hostile silence.

'Did you now?' Richter said, quietly. 'But you didn't think of telling us, did you?'

Westwood shook his head. 'Not my decision,' he said. 'It was Company policy.'

'What was the source of this information?' Lacomte asked.

'I can't tell you,' Westwood said, and held up a hand towards Richter, who had opened his mouth to speak, 'simply because we don't know. Our Moscow Station Chief was contacted by a walk-in who slipped a film into his jacket pocket. We've had further drops from this source, but we still don't know who he is. What we do know, because of what was on the first film, is that this source is very near the top of either the GRU or the SVR.'

'OK,' Richter said. 'We haven't time to go into that now. What was the warning this source passed to you?'

Westwood shook his head. 'That was the problem,' he replied. 'That's why we've been running round like headless chickens looking for help. The warning was non-specific. It simply said that a covert assault on the West was in progress, but gave no useful details. What it does do, though,' he added, looking at Lacomte, 'is corroborate what Mr Beatty has been saying.'

Lacomte looked at Giraud, and then both of them looked at Richter. 'The one piece of hard evidence that is available,' Richter said, 'is the one that I do not have at present.'

'The lorry?' Lacomte prompted.

'Exactly,' Richter said, 'the lorry. When that is stopped, if the back only contains the collected works of Lenin, or whatever the Russians have put on the manifest, then I will apologize humbly and take my delusions home to bed. But I'm quite certain we'll find a nasty little nuclear weapon in a steel box, with a delivery address of Harrington House, 13 Kensington Palace Gardens, London, W8.'

'Which is?' asked Lacomte.

'The official residence of the Russian Ambassador Extraordinary and Plenipotentiary to the Court of St James.'

There was a short silence, broken by Giraud, speaking English for the first time. 'So,' he said, 'you have to stop the lorry?'

'Yes,' Richter replied, 'we have to stop the lorry.'

Anton Kirov

Zavorin pushed open the steel door leading to the engine room and walked in ahead of Bondarev. He slid quickly down the steel ladder to the deck below, and strode across to the starboard side. Three of his men were assembled close to the starboard fuel pump, around which had been packed a selection of oil-soaked rags and paper.

'Is this really necessary?' Bondarev asked, his voice almost plaintive.

'Yes, Captain, it is,' Zavorin replied. 'We do not know whether or not the staff at Gibraltar will insist on helping us. If the engine room shows no sign of damage, we would not be able to allow them on board, which would look suspicious.'

Zavorin looked at the troopers. 'Ten minutes, no more,' he said, 'then douse the flames. Make sure you leave fire-extinguisher foam around the pump, and snap the input pipe.' He nodded to the second trooper, who was holding a gas lighter. The man snapped the lighter open, kindled the flame and ignited the paper. 'Now,' Zavorin said, looking with satisfaction at the growing flames, then turning back and glancing up at Bondarev, 'we have some real damage we can show them.'

Ansbach, Germany

The convoy had picked up the autobahn just beyond Hartmannshof and taken the route to the south-east of Nürnberg. Just south of Ansbach, Modin called a halt in a rest area for refreshments and a driver change. Again, he and Bykov consulted the map.

'I think we will make one small change, Viktor,' Modin said. 'We were to route through Stuttgart, which is the most direct route, but I think that will take longer than staying on the autobahn.'

'Yes, I agree,' Bykov said, tracing the route on the map with his finger.

'So,' Modin continued, 'we will continue heading west, through Heilbronn and up to Walldorf, and then south past Karlsruhe and Baden-Baden to Strasbourg. Brief the drivers.'

French Ministry of the Interior, rue des Saussaies, Paris

Giraud turned to one of his aides and spoke rapidly in French, then after listening to the reply he turned back to Richter.

'This, Mr Beatty, is the situation as I understand it. You have what you believe to be compelling evidence that a section or sections of the Russian security forces are attempting to blackmail America and then force Europe to submit to what amounts to a non-military invasion from the east?' There was nothing wrong with Giraud's English, or with his grasp of the situation.

'Correct,' Richter said.

'But neither you nor the American CIA can offer any independent support for this interesting theory, other than what amounts to some circumstantial evidence which is possibly indicative of something going on?' Richter nodded. 'And the only hard evidence that can possibly be provided is in the back of a lorry which is about to make its way through France?'

'Yes,' Richter said.

'A lorry which will, unless I'm very much mistaken, be travelling under the legal protection of diplomatic status and, probably, with the physical protection of armed couriers, who will also be carrying diplomatic passports? Is that a fair summary?'

'Yes,' Richter said, 'but—'

Giraud ploughed on relentlessly. 'You are doubtless also aware that any interference with such a vehicle is tantamount to a severance of diplomatic relations with the originating country? And that there would be most severe – I say again, most severe – international repercussions if your theory turned out to be a fiction?'

'Yes.' There wasn't anything else Richter could say.

Giraud fixed him with a penetrating look, then turned to Lacomte and spoke briefly in French. Richter glanced over at Tony Herron and shrugged his shoulders. Giraud turned his attention back to Richter. 'I suppose your Special Air Service personnel are already en route?'

'Er, yes,' Richter said. 'Actually, they are, or should be.'

'We expected that,' Lacomte said, nodding. 'With the time-scale you have outlined they would have to be about to leave, or have already left, Hereford.'

'I had to make some assumptions,' Richter said. 'I had to assume that you would give permission. They can be stopped, of course, probably before they reach Calais.'

'I wouldn't do that, Mr Beatty,' said Giraud. 'I think that you probably will need their help to stop that lorry.' He favoured the group with a wintry smile, gestured to his aides and stood up. When the four men had left the room, Lacomte relaxed visibly.

'What made him agree?' Westwood asked.

'The possible diplomatic repercussions, I think,' said Lacomte. 'If he had refused permission for the lorry to be stopped, and it later turned out that you had been right, his career would be at an end.'

'Everyone else's career would probably also be at an end,' Tony Herron interjected.

'Quite,' said Lacomte. 'But by allowing your SAS to participate, if it all goes wrong he can claim that it was some sort of a British cowboy action that he knew nothing about. In fact,' he continued, 'he has instructed me to ensure that the SAS personnel take charge of the assault on the convoy, and that French involvement is to be kept to a minimum.'

'To make it more deniable, of course?'

Lacomte smiled. 'Of course.'

'Machiavellian old devil,' Richter said.

'Yes. That is his reputation.' Lacomte rubbed his hands briskly and gave instructions to one of his colleagues, who left the room. 'To business,' he said. 'Let's start with the convoy.'

'Right,' Richter agreed, and opened up the file again. 'First, the route. Orlov wasn't completely certain about it, but the point of departure was almost certainly going to be Minsk. It will have travelled through Poland, probably Czechoslovakia, and then into Germany and should enter – or have entered – France at Strasbourg.'

Lacomte glanced at his watch. 'I don't think it has entered France yet,' he said. 'I gave instructions this morning for a total watch operation to be put in place on all French overland borders apart from that with Spain, for obvious reasons, and for any vehicles demanding diplomatic immunity to be delayed as much as possible without making it obvious.'

'Thank you,' Richter said, nodding approval.

'We have heard nothing, so I think we can be sure that the convoy is still in Germany. What time-scale did Comrade Orlov give you?'

Richter referred back to the file. 'He said that the London weapon was scheduled for positioning the day after tomorrow.'

'Right, and with point of entry Strasbourg. I think the roadworks at Strasbourg are going to cause the convoy some delays in getting on to the autoroute. I think we can guarantee that it won't reach Reims until tomorrow mid-afternoon at the earliest.'

'And are there roadworks at Strasbourg?' Westwood asked.

'There will be in less than an hour,' Lacomte replied, and gave instructions in French to the remaining DST officer. As he left, the other DST man returned, arms laden with maps of northern France, which he spread out on the conference table.

'And after Strasbourg?' Lacomte asked. 'What route then?'

'Orlov believed the convoy would stay on the autoroutes as much as possible, so it will probably route from Strasbourg either to Metz or possibly Châlons-sur-Marne and then on to Reims. After that there's not much scope for diversions. It will almost certainly pick up the A26 autoroute to St Quentin, and then route past Cambrai to Calais for the Channel crossing to Dover. The crossing will certainly be from Calais, and they're probably aiming for a night sailing, tomorrow.'

Lacomte had been tracing the possible routes on the map while Richter had been speaking. When he stopped Lacomte smoothed out the central section and looked at it with interest. 'So where do we stop them?' he asked.

'To be perfectly honest,' Richter said, 'I haven't got that far yet. I was thinking about faking a diversion off the autoroute, and hitting the truck on some quiet road somewhere. I thought maybe the assault team could pose as French truck thieves.'

Lacomte looked at him. 'I won't pretend that we don't have gangs who specialize in stealing entire lorries, but it would, I think, be a very optimistic or very stupid gang which took on a diplomatic-plated lorry and two or three cars full of armed couriers. No, I think we apply a bit of cunning here.' He thought for a few moments. 'I like the idea of the diversion,' he said, 'but let's do it backwards.'

'Backwards?' Richter asked.

'Instead of diverting the convoy off the autoroute, we divert everything else off it, except the convoy.'

'That's sneaky,' said Tony.

'It's brilliant,' Richter said. 'That gives us plenty of room to work and a complete absence of eyewitnesses. Can you fix it?'

'Of course,' said Lacomte. 'We've done it before.' He took a pencil and paper and drew a rapid sketch. 'First,' he said, 'we choose a section of autoroute without service areas, and we flush all vehicles out of the parking areas on both carriageways. Then, we wait for the convoy to pass here,' he said, drawing a parking area to the south of the section he had marked, 'where we will position one of our vehicles with a radioman. As soon as he signals confirmation of the convoy's position, we prepare for action.' He pointed at the drawing of an intersection. 'As soon as the convoy passes this junction, we block the inbound access and erect barriers across the carriageway to divert all the following traffic on to the national roads. The convoy will be slow, and they should soon be the last vehicles on the northbound section. If any other vehicles do lag behind it, we will have them stopped and detained by gendarmes.'

Lacomte was warming to his theme.

'As soon as we close the northbound carriageway we will also close the southbound section, two junctions to the north, to ensure there are no witnesses to the operation. Then, when all the traffic is clear, your SAS men and our assault forces will stop the truck.'

If you said it quickly, it sounded easy. It could even work, but Richter wasn't certain it would be quite as simple as Lacomte seemed to believe. 'Fine,' Richter said. 'I have no problems with any of that. But stopping a lorry isn't that easy. If the driver simply decides to keep going – and he will probably have orders to do exactly that – what then?'

'We arrange an accident,' Tony Herron said.

'What do you mean?'

'We have to allay their suspicions. The Russians will probably notice the absence of traffic heading south, and the fact that nothing is overtaking them going north, and they will be expecting trouble of some sort. So we arrange an accident – a big one, one that blocks the northbound carriageway altogether – and put rescue vehicles on the southbound side. Lots of flashing lights and confusion, people running about.'

'Yes,' said Lacomte. 'That should work.'

'The convoy will have to stop, and with all the vehicles stationary it should be fairly easy to immobilize the escort. Perhaps a gendarme could approach the cars and ask if anyone is a doctor, or demand their first-aid kits or something. Something to distract their attention.'

'That's good,' Richter said, and turned to Lacomte.

'Can you organize that?' he asked.

'Yes,' he replied. 'We'll take two articulated lorries and jack-knife them across the carriageway, as if they collided when one was overtaking the other. It happens often enough in France,' he added.

'We can leave the details of the actual assault until I have spoken to the SAS officer,' Richter said. 'But we should identify the location of the operation now so you can prepare.'

Lacomte nodded and turned his attention back to the maps. The other DST man returned to the room and advised them that a main water pipe had burst just outside Strasbourg and that access to the autoroute for all heavy goods vehicles was very slow. Private cars, he added with a smile, were able to get through without too many problems.

Half an hour later they had identified the site. The operation would take place between Chambry, junction number 13, just to the north of Laon, and the Courbes junction, number 12, on the A26 autoroute between Laon and St Quentin. There was even a convenient military camp just south of the autoroute between Vivaise and Couvron-et-Aumencourt, which could possibly be explained away as the origin of any small-arms fire which might be heard.

'Who will you use for the assault?' Richter asked.

'*Gigènes*,' Lacomte said, 'GIGN – *Groupe d'Intervention de la Gendarmerie Nationale*. They have a base in the south-east of Paris, at Maisons-Alfort.'

The GIGN was formed on the 3 November 1973, principally in response to the siege of the Saudi Arabian Embassy in Paris that year. The force has always laid great store on personal marksmanship, and this was vividly demonstrated at Djibouti in February 1976, when GIGN snipers simultaneously shot at and killed five Somali Coast Liberation Front terrorists who had seized a school coach containing thirty children aged between six and twelve. The marksmen had to wait over ten hours for a clear shot at all the terrorists at the same time. The only casualty was a little girl who was butchered by a sixth terrorist who boarded the bus after the shooting; he did not survive the subsequent storming of the vehicle by GIGN personnel.

'We thought,' Lacomte continued, with a smile, 'that your SAS men might like to experience working with true professionals.'

It was after six when Richter and Herron emerged from the Ministry and climbed into the waiting car. Westwood waved a hand and walked away towards the avenue Gabriel. Back at the British Embassy, Herron looked through a sheaf of signals, including one from Stirling Lines – the signal address of the SAS Headquarters at Hereford – which he passed over to Richter. It confirmed that the unit requested would arrive no later than 2359 GMT that evening. No date, no place, no names. Typical SAS brevity.

Marne-la-Vallée

At ten minutes to midnight there was a gentle double tap on the cabin door. Richter pushed everything into the briefcase and locked it, eased the Smith out of the shoulder rig and gently pulled the curtain away from a window. Outside was a white Transit van with 'Uxbridge Vehicle Hire' printed on the side and a handwritten sign in one of the windows advising any interested onlooker that the occupants belonged to the Rotary Club (Pinner, West London, Division). With the Smith held out of sight behind him, he unlocked and opened the door. Richter almost didn't recognize him in his suit and tie, but Colin Dekker knew Richter instantly, despite the state of his face.

'Paul Richter,' he said. 'I might have guessed.'

'Come in, Colin,' Richter replied.

Dekker stepped up into the cabin, and watched Richter put the Smith back in its holster. 'This looks serious,' he said. 'You don't normally carry a piece.'

'I don't and it is,' Richter agreed. 'Where are your men?'

'Out there,' he gestured with a thumb. 'Making sure we aren't disturbed or overheard. So what's this all about? Nothing to do with British lamb and French farmers, I hope.'

'Not exactly,' Richter said. 'We're going to attack an armed road convoy and seize a nuclear weapon that the Russians are trying to deliver to London.'

'Fuck a duck,' Colin Dekker said, and sat down.

Chapter Twenty

Wednesday
Marne-la-Valée

Colin Redmond Dekker, Captain, Royal Artillery, and nearing the end of a three-year detachment as Commander, Troop 3, D Squadron, 22 Special Air Service Regiment, sat in an easy chair and watched a film of the Main Street Electrical Parade, with commentary in German, on the Disneyland Paris resort closed-circuit television system.

Richter put the kettle on and sat down opposite him. 'You'd like a drink, I take it? What about your troop?'

'Yes, thanks, and they would too,' Colin Dekker said. 'I'll leave one man outside just in case, but I think we should be safe enough here.' He opened the door, stepped outside and whistled softly. A figure approached silently, murmured to Dekker and then stepped inside. A second followed him. A third man approached, talked briefly to Dekker, then melted into the darkness. Colin Dekker walked back inside and stood beside the two newcomers. His stocky, compact figure looked smaller than Richter remembered, but it might just have been the contrast with the size of the other two men. 'Introductions, I suppose. This is Trooper Smith, and that is Trooper Jones. As you can probably guess, the man outside is Trooper Brown.'

Richter nodded. Standard SAS procedure.

'Troopers,' Dekker began, 'this gentleman is a member of Her Majesty's Secret Service, but that's a secret, so don't tell anyone.' The two men smiled politely but disinterestedly. 'Before you both dismiss him as just another desk jockey with delusions of adequacy,' Colin Dekker continued, 'you should also know that he has been through the full course at Hereford, starting with the Battle Fitness Test and finishing with the Fan Dance.'

The Fan Dance is named after Pen-y-Fan, the highest peak in the Brecon Beacons. It's a twenty-four-kilometre run over the Beacons. You start at the bottom of Pen-y-Fan, run up to the top of the mountain, down and around another mountain called the Crib and along a Roman road to the checkpoint at Torpanto. Then you turn round and do the whole thing again in reverse. The memory of it still gave Richter occasional nightmares.

'He also spent some days on the range and a week in the Killing House, and his scores were easily good enough to get him into the Regiment.'

The Killing House at Hereford is the Close Quarter Battle training range. Its interior can be modified to simulate almost any environment from a suburban semi to the passenger cabin of an airliner, and it offers the most realistic combat environment possible, short of an actual firefight. The troopers were looking at Richter with a little more interest.

'Whilst I am reluctant to break into this paean of praise,' Richter interrupted, 'we do have things to discuss. Oh, and for the duration of this operation, my name is Beatty, OK?'

The kettle boiled. Richter made coffee and handed round the mugs. Dekker flopped down again in his chair, took a sip and then put his mug on the table beside him. The two troopers sat side by side on the sofa, silent and watchful. 'It's been a very long day,' Colin Dekker said, 'and we nearly didn't make it. We got the Flash activation signal from your Secret Squirrel outfit at just after fourteen forty, UK time. We sent the van on its way within twenty minutes, which was bloody good going, and then we sat down and worked out what we were going to need.' He took another drink. 'Drawing the gear and checking it took over two hours, then we had to sort out passports, money, Channel Tunnel tickets and all the other stuff, so we weren't ready to get into the chopper until well after five.'

'Where did you fly to?' Richter asked.

'Manston,' Dekker said. 'The van was waiting for us, so it was a quick blast down to Folkestone, hop into the Chunnel train and then explore the delights of the French autoroute system, which isn't that bad, actually.' He smiled at Richter. 'I hope you're impressed.'

'By what?' Richter asked.

'By the fact that neither I nor Trooper Smith nor even Trooper Jones have asked what the hell we're doing sitting in a log cabin in a wood at a holiday resort in France watching Disney cartoons at nearly one o'clock in the morning, while Trooper Brown wanders about outside guarding a van which contains enough ordnance to start a small war.'

'Only a small war?' Richter asked.

'It's only,' Dekker replied, 'a small van.'

'It's camouflage,' Richter said. 'Hopefully no one will think of looking for us here.'

'Well, I wouldn't look for you here,' Dekker said, after a pause, 'so you might be right. Who exactly do you think might want to find us?'

'At the moment, only the SVR and the GRU, but if it all goes wrong tomorrow you can probably add the entire security apparatus of la belle France.'

Trooper Smith blinked once, but that was the only reaction Richter could detect. Colin Dekker swallowed the last of his drink and put down his mug. 'I think,' he said, 'that you'd better tell us everything we need to know.'

Forty minutes later Richter folded up the map and put it back in his briefcase. Dekker looked at him thoughtfully, then turned to his men. 'Trooper Smith can give us his recommendations before he goes out to relieve Trooper Brown. Your thoughts, John.'

The man called Smith looked at them both, then spoke softly and economically. 'It doesn't look difficult,' he said. 'The only problem is not knowing the actual opposition strength, but we can handle it.' Looking at him, Richter thought he probably could.

Dekker nodded to him, and he left the cabin as silently as he had entered. Trooper Brown came in a minute or so later, walked straight to the kitchen and switched on the kettle.

'Make yourself at home,' Colin Dekker said. 'Oh, I see you have.'

Brown walked into the lounge carrying a mug of tea and sat down next to Trooper Jones. He was more Dekker's build, compact and wiry, but looked just as competent and capable as his companions. Colin

Dekker outlined the task ahead, and Brown just nodded. 'No problem,' he said.

Richter coughed politely. 'I have no wish to dampen this mood of unbridled optimism,' he said, 'but you should remember that we are likely to be facing two or three armoured saloons occupied by *Spetsnaz* troopers, probably carrying automatic weapons, plus an armed crew in the cab of the lorry and maybe other armed guards inside the cargo bay. There are exactly four of you, and you'll also have to avoid shooting a number of GIGN personnel who'll try and get in on the act.'

Brown looked at him coldly. 'I said, no problem.'

'Fine,' Richter said. 'Colin?'

'Trooper Brown, as you've probably noticed, is not one to be bothered by the odds, but he does have the experience to back up what he says.'

'I don't doubt that for a moment, but I don't think it's going to be a picnic.' Richter took a fresh sheet of paper. 'We have a meeting at nine thirty tomorrow morning with DST and GIGN personnel in Paris, where we'll sort out the details of the actual assault, but I would like to get some feedback from you first. Are you happy with the basic plan – stopping the lorry and the escort using the fake accident?'

'Yes,' Dekker said. 'That's good, and it should minimize the risks.'

'So the next question,' Richter said, 'is how to immobilize the truck and the escort.'

'Right. The truck first, as that's the most important. What size vehicle is it?'

'We'll know tomorrow morning, but my guess is an articulated lorry.'

'Good,' said Dekker, 'that makes it easier.' He thought for a moment. 'The two most important things, I take it, are that the load the lorry is carrying isn't damaged, and that the vehicle is completely immobilized as quickly as possible?'

'Yes,' Richter replied. 'I doubt if any external cause could detonate the weapon, but there would be obvious radiation hazards if the container was breached.'

Trooper Jones spoke for the first time. 'We can slice the main driveshaft.'

'How?' Richter asked.

'Easy. A small piece of plastic, wrapped around it and detonated. The shaft's hollow, and that would snap it like a twig. Without the drive-shaft, that truck's going nowhere.'

'That's good,' Colin Dekker said. 'That's very good. And you'd deliver the explosive as soon as the truck has stopped at the accident?' Jones nodded.

'OK,' Dekker continued. 'That takes care of the truck. Escort?'

'Again,' Richter said, 'we won't know until tomorrow what the strength is. The DST has mounted surveillance of all overland border crossings, and will then operate a long-tail on the convoy as it travels through France. I'm expecting a minimum of two escort vehicles, possibly three, so probably at least ten armed opposition personnel.'

'How do you want them?' Colin Dekker asked. 'The escort? Alive or dead?'

'I don't personally care,' Richter said, 'but I think preferably alive. It doesn't make such a mess on the road and that might irritate the French a bit less, and one or two of them might have something useful to tell me.'

'OK,' said Dekker. 'Subject to GIGN or DST veto, we'll aim for a co-ordinated assault, using stun grenades and CS gas, the go signal being the detonation of Trooper Jones' lump of plastic on the truck's drive shaft. Then the application of the minimum force necessary to achieve the objective. Textbook stuff.' Dekker looked at his watch. 'Two thirty,' he said. 'Bed, now. I'll meet you here again at – what – seven?'

'Seven will be fine,' Richter said, and the three men filed quietly out into the night.

Oval Office, White House, 1600 Pennsylvania Avenue, Washington, D.C.

'Have you briefed the Joint Chiefs yet?'

'No, Mr President.' Walter Hicks shook his head. 'I wanted to tell you first.'

The older man gestured. 'Go ahead.'

'I wish we could claim the credit for this, Mr President,' Hicks began, 'but the fact is that we can't. The British put this together themselves from the data we released to them about the Blackbird flight, the implications behind the murder of an SIS man in Moscow, and some other bits and pieces. They then persuaded a senior SVR officer to fill in the gaps.'

'Really? How did they persuade him?' the President asked.

'You really don't want to know that, sir,' Hicks replied.

The President looked up and shook his head. 'No,' he said, 'perhaps I don't. Carry on.'

'Our source in Moscow – RAVEN – was quite right. There was and is a covert assault in progress against us. The problem is that there's almost exactly nothing we can do to eliminate the threat. What the Russians have done is sneak a whole bunch of conventional nuclear weapons into major cities here in the States and tie them all to a trigger in a communications satellite.'

'They've done what?' the President shouted. Hicks didn't reply. 'Jesus Christ.' The President stood up abruptly, his face flushing red with anger. He leant across the desk and pressed a switch on the intercom. 'Get that bastard Karasin here as quickly as you can,' he ordered. The intercom squawked. 'Yes, I do mean fucking Ambassador fucking Karasin. I want him here now.' He almost shouted the last word, and snapped the switch back angrily. Fists clenched, he stood silent for a moment, then sat down. The anger had vanished, and he was again the calm, calculating man Hicks had come to know. 'Which cities?' he asked.

'That's the problem,' Hicks said. 'We don't know which cities, and even if we did that wouldn't help us to find the bombs. You're only talking about something the size of a small car, even with its back-up power supplies. You could hide it almost anywhere. Almost any crate in any warehouse could contain a weapon.'

'How did they get them here?' the President asked.

'As far as the Brits know, it was a mixture of discreet smuggling and improper use of the Diplomatic Bag.'

The President nodded, not really hearing Hicks' answer. 'So,' he muttered, almost to himself. 'What do we do?' He raised his voice slightly. 'And what do they want?'

Hicks gave a shrug. 'That, Mr President, is the point. The Russians don't actually want us to do anything.'

The grey-haired man looked up sharply. 'They haven't gone to all this trouble, smuggling nuclear weapons into America and launching a satellite, for nothing,' he said. 'There must be a purpose behind it.'

Hicks nodded. 'Oh, there's a purpose, Mr President, but the Russians really do want us to do nothing. They want us to stand aside and watch as they march into Western Europe.'

Marne-la-Vallée

Colin Dekker knocked on Richter's door at seven exactly, came in and sat down. They ate a scratch breakfast of toast and marmalade, washed down with English tea – Dekker had brought the bags with him.

'One question,' Dekker said, as they stood up to leave. 'Are we authorized to carry side-arms before the operation?'

'Probably not,' Richter replied, 'but I'm wearing the Smith, and in view of the situation I suggest that you should all carry personal weapons.'

'Good enough,' Dekker said, and vanished outside to brief his troops, two of whom he would be leaving at the camp to 'mind the store'. When he reappeared, Trooper Smith in tow, the three men climbed into the Granada and retraced Richter's route of the previous day, driving over the autoroute to Disneyland, parking the car and catching the RER to Paris.

French Ministry of the Interior, rue des Saussaies, Paris

They arrived outside the British Embassy at eight fifty. Tony Herron and John Westwood appeared five minutes later, and the group walked into the French Ministry of the Interior exactly on time. Lacomte was already in the conference room, studying a map, and beside him stood a tall, well-built man with close-cropped hair, who Lacomte introduced as Lieutenant Erulin of the GIGN. Dekker and Trooper Smith eyed him with interest. 'Fortunately,' Lacomte said, 'Lieutenant Erulin speaks English, so we will have no language problems.'

The way he said it made Richter wonder if he was anticipating any other kind of problems. Richter introduced Dekker as Captain Colin of 22 Special Air Service Regiment, and Trooper Smith as Trooper Smith, and they got down to business.

Lacomte began by providing a summary of overnight events, which amounted to very little. Monsieur Giraud and the Minister had summoned him late the previous evening and requested an update, and he would be seeing Giraud again immediately before lunch. The French President had been informed, and had also been in consultation with the American President and the British Prime Minister. 'The Minister reinforced what Monsieur Giraud said, Mr Beatty,' Lacomte said. 'He wants minimal French involvement in this matter.'

Out of the corner of his eye Richter could see Erulin stiffen. 'Colonel, with respect,' the GIGN officer began, 'this operation is already using significant French resources. We will be closing both carriageways of a busy autoroute for a distance of some forty kilometres and a period of, probably, four or five hours. We will be using two articulated lorries and numerous emergency vehicles, not to mention the gendarmes and others who will have to be at the scene to provide local colour. It seems pointless to me to pretend that it is an unauthorized British operation. GIGN personnel are perfectly capable of handling this entire matter.' He waved a hand dismissively towards Dekker and Smith.

Lacomte regarded him levelly for a moment. 'I think you may well be right, Lieutenant,' he said. 'I suggest that you call the Minister and Monsieur Giraud immediately and tell them that they are wrong.' Erulin stared at him for a moment, then dropped his gaze. 'No?' Lacomte continued. 'Right, then we do it their way.'

Erulin lapsed into a sullen silence. Richter wondered how his attitude would affect the co-operation they were going to need with GIGN personnel, and he knew Dekker would be thinking exactly the same.

'As the subject of manpower has been raised,' Lacomte continued, with a glance at the GIGN lieutenant, 'this might be an opportune time to look at the forces available to us.' He looked over at Dekker. 'I understand you have three men with you?'

'Yes, sir,' Dekker replied. 'A standard four-man patrol.'

Lacomte nodded. 'Lieutenant Erulin is in command of a GIGN strike team, which is all the French involvement that Monsieur Giraud wishes. For those of you not familiar with GIGN operating procedures –' he clearly meant all of the non-French in the room '– that's two five-man intervention forces, plus a dog and handler. I don't think we're going to need the dog today, as I'm sure we can all find a lorry on a deserted autoroute.' Dekker rewarded him with a polite smile. 'So that gives us a total of fourteen personnel, plus Captain Colin, Lieutenant Erulin and, of course, Mr Beatty and myself. I assume,' he said, looking at Richter, 'that you, Mr Herron and Mr Westwood are not intending to participate in the actual assault?'

'Certainly not,' Richter said, looking at Colin Dekker. 'No point in having a dog and barking yourself.' Erulin sneered at him.

'I'm out of this,' Westwood said. 'My boss wants me to keep a watching brief, but he didn't say anything about me being shot at.'

'Very well,' Lacomte continued, 'I don't want to discuss the actual tactics of the assault at this stage, as until we know the composition of the opposition it would only be speculation, but what we can do is assess distances and average speeds.' He looked down at his map. 'Strasbourg to Metz is about one hundred and fifty kilometres, Metz to Reims around two hundred, and Reims to Laon about fifty. If we add, say, another ten kilometres from the Laon intersection to the site of the operation, that gives a total of just over four hundred kilometres.' He glanced round the table. 'How fast can a lorry travel?'

'Too bloody fast, in most cases,' Dekker said.

'We're not talking about an average trucker with a deadline to meet,' Richter said. 'This is a large, heavy and very dangerous load, and it's not just the truck, it's also the cars. They'll all have to make stops for food, fuel, toilets, sleep and all the rest, so I'd have thought we should estimate a fairly low average speed. They'll also probably stick to the speed limits, because the last thing they'll want to do is attract attention.'

'If they do it'll be about the only lorry in France that does obey the speed limits,' Tony Herron murmured.

'Let's have some numbers, then,' Lacomte asked. 'Mr Beatty?'

'My guess would be no more than eighty kilometres an hour, overall.'

Lacomte did a quick calculation on the paper in front of him. 'That gives a total journey time from Strasbourg of about five hours.' He thought for a moment. 'Let's give ourselves a reasonable time frame. What's the fastest possible speed we could expect the convoy to achieve? One hundred kilometres an hour?'

'Make it one ten,' Dekker said.

'Right. One hundred and ten – that gives a time of about three and a half hours. So we can work on the basis that the convoy will arrive here,' he tapped the ringed section on his map with the pencil, 'between three and a half and five hours after departure from Strasbourg.'

'So all we need now,' said Colin Dekker, 'is the time the lorry is going to clear Strasbourg and start heading this way.'

Right on cue there was a knock at the door and a DST man entered with a sheet of paper, which he handed to Lacomte. They all waited expectantly while the colonel scanned it. 'Excellent,' he said. 'The Gendarmerie in Strasbourg has reported that the Russian convoy arrived early this morning, but the delays caused by the roadworks have held all the vehicles at Strasbourg. They do not expect the convoy will be able to continue its journey until mid-morning at the earliest. More importantly for us, we now know what we're up against.'

Autoroute E42, Strasbourg, France

Unlike the crossing at Waidhaus, getting over the German/French border had been a mere formality. All four vehicles had been ordered to stop, probably because of their Moscow plates and because they were quite obviously travelling together, but all the French Customs officers and gendarmes had done was inspect their passports. They hadn't even bothered asking what the lorry was carrying or why twelve Russian diplomats were driving together across Europe.

The border crossing had been easy, but getting through Strasbourg had been a nightmare. As far as Modin had been able to discover, a water main had burst just to the west of the border by the Rhine. They had reached the end of the traffic queue whilst still on the autoroute and approaching Kehl, and by that time they had little choice. They couldn't turn round on the autoroute, and the only two junctions they could have taken off it wouldn't have helped. The one to the south ran down to Lahr and Offenburg, and the northerly turning would have taken them through Rheinau and on to Rastatt, but neither offered any crossings of the Rhine or of the border. They had had no option but to carry on through Strasbourg.

The city was in a state of chaos. The gendarmes had been doing their best, but Strasbourg was virtually gridlocked and all traffic was subject to diversions. Local traffic was being allowed through the centre, but all vehicles in transit had been forced to head south out of eastern Strasbourg on minor roads, through Plobsheim and Erstein, before being allowed to join the N83. From the junction to the west of Erstein, traffic had been flowing freely in both directions. Modin had hoped there would be no further problems around Strasbourg, but once they had joined the autoroute A35 past Illkirch-Graffenstaden, traffic had again come to a virtual standstill because of vehicles leaving the autoroute to get into the centre of the city.

'At last,' Bykov said, as the limousine accelerated away. The Mercedes was the last vehicle in the convoy, then heading north up the autoroute A4, taking the loop past Brumath and Hochfelden rather than the more direct, but much busier, road to Saverne.

'Chaos,' Modin agreed. 'Total chaos. We have probably lost two or three hours. Order the convoy to increase speed. Aim for one hundred and ten kilometres an hour. We must make that ferry tonight.'

Le Moulin au Pouchon, *St Médard, near Manciet, Midi-Pyrénées, France*

Hassan Abbas read the decrypted text from the email he had just received from Dmitri Trushenko and grunted in satisfaction. The *Anton Kirov*, Trushenko reported, had arrived safely at Gibraltar without apparently arousing any suspicion, and the weapon would be removed from the vessel within two days. The crate containing the device would be burnt and carefully broken and then removed from the dockyard along with the damaged fuel pump, associated fuel lines and other fire-damaged equipment from the *Anton Kirov*'s engine room, probably in a skip. It would then be delivered to a small warehouse in Gibraltar already hired by a local SVR agent. Meanwhile, the convoy carrying the London weapon was about to cross the German-French border, and delivery of the device to London should occur on schedule.

Abbas thought carefully before relaying the new information to Sadoun Khamil, and his message, when he had composed it, was much longer than usual. As well as the purely factual data provided by Trushenko, Abbas also included a proposal that he had discussed previously with Khamil but without reaching a decision. There was, Abbas reasoned, no reason to wait any longer. The Gibraltar device could now be detonated at any time and, though the positioning of the London weapon was crucial to the Russian operation, it made very little difference to the hidden agenda formulated by al-Qaeda. Therefore, Abbas concluded, there was no reason why they shouldn't initiate the detonation sequences immediately.

He pressed 'Send' and checked to make sure the message was successfully transmitted. Then he shut down the computer, shut and locked the bedroom door and walked down the stairs to prepare a meal. It would, he knew, be at least two hours before Khamil would reply.

French Ministry of the Interior, rue des Saussaies, Paris

Dekker took out a pen and prepared to write.

'French Customs stopped the lorry and the escorting cars, purely for a routine documents check,' Lacomte said. 'There are two young men in the cab of the lorry, which is, as we guessed, an articulated unit. There are three escorting cars, all Mercedes and all, in the opinion of the Strasbourg Gendarmes, armoured.'

'Personnel?' Colin Dekker asked.

'The two saloons each contain a driver and three passengers, all young men, all with diplomatic passports.'

'Those will be the *Spetsnaz* escort,' Richter said. 'What about the third car?'

'The third,' replied Lacomte, 'is a long-wheel-base Mercedes limousine, containing a driver and escort in front of the partition and two passengers behind it. The Gendarmes report that one is a gentlemen of about sixty, and the other a man of about forty-five to fifty years old. As with the others, all four are carrying Russian diplomatic passports.'

'Do we have an ID on that car – a registration number?' Richter asked.

Lacomte looked back at the sheet of paper. 'Yes,' he replied, 'but you can easily identify it – the two saloons are light blue in colour, but the limousine is black.'

'What are you thinking?' Colin Dekker asked.

'Those two passengers obviously aren't *Spetsnaz*,' Richter said. 'My guess is that they're ranking SVR or GRU officers, along for the ride and to see the device positioned correctly. Those two, I really would like to talk to.'

'I'm sure we can arrange that,' said Dekker.

With the strength of the opposition known, Lacomte turned to the assault plan. Immobilization of the truck would be carried out as suggested by Trooper Jones, using plastic explosive. The Mercedes saloons were a different problem. There was no point in immobilizing them and it would, in fact, suit their purposes very well if they drove off at the first sign of trouble, but nobody seriously expected that to happen.

'The thing about an armoured car,' said Colin Dekker, reflectively, 'is that in most cases it's designed only to protect the occupants against their attackers. What isn't generally realized is that it also protects the attackers from the occupants.' He glanced round at a number of puzzled faces. 'What I mean is, if the *Spetsnaz* troopers want to shoot at us, they'll have to wind down a window, and if they do that the vehicle is no longer secure. I understand that your speciality,' he said, turning to Erulin, 'is accurate shot placement.'

'Yes,' Erulin nodded. 'All our personnel have to score a minimum of ninety-three per cent on a two-hundred-metre range.'

'And at, say, twenty to thirty metres?'

Erulin smiled somewhat grudgingly. 'I would personally discharge any GIGN NCO who failed to achieve a perfect result.'

'OK,' said Colin Dekker. 'So what I suggest is this. We bow to the wishes of the French Minister of the Interior, and my team hits the convoy. There are only four of us, and four vehicles to be attended to. Under normal circumstances, those would not be unreasonable odds, but these are not normal circumstances. I'm worried about crossfire, and about opposition personnel getting out of their vehicles on our blind side. We also don't know what order the vehicles will be in. My guess would be Mercedes saloon, truck, limousine, second saloon, but that might not be the case if they sense trouble. They'll certainly be linked by radio, and they might send both saloons ahead and let the limo drop back. It's still all rather vague.

'What I propose, therefore, is that Trooper Jones plants his plastic on the truck drive-shaft, lights the blue touch-paper and then retires a safe distance. It's just conceivable that he might be able to do that unseen, especially if both saloons have gone on ahead, but I wouldn't count on it. He will then cover the truck cab with his weapon. That's Phase One, if you like. Phase Two starts when the plastic cuts the drive-shaft. Troopers Smith and Brown will lob CS gas grenades at the two Mercedes saloons, aiming to lodge them under the engine compartments of the cars.'

'How will that help, against an armoured vehicle?' asked Lacomte.

'Simple. The bodywork is armoured, but the air-conditioning system takes in air from outside the vehicle. It's a hot day, and the cars will almost certainly have the systems running. Even if the driver switches it off immediately, the interior should get a good dose of gas, and that should hopefully be that.' Colin Dekker looked round. 'However, let's assume that it doesn't. The grenade rolls too far, or the occupants have anti-gas respirators in the car and manage to get them on, or something else goes wrong. We will be carrying Hocklers – Heckler & Koch MP5 sub-machineguns – which are highly efficient weapons against personnel outside their vehicles, but of no use against an armour-plated Mercedes. Mr Beatty –' he gestured at Richter '– would prefer the opposition to walk, rather than be carried, away from the scene, and so would I, so I don't want to use armour-piercing rounds or anything heavier than the Hockler.'

'So what do you propose?' asked Lacomte.

'One CS gas grenade for each car, shoot out both tyres on the side facing us, plus a demand for immediate surrender. If they don't surrender, that's where Lieutenant Erulin's GIGN are going to carry the day. If any window opens on any of the vehicles, except the limo, I want a stream of bullets going in before anything nasty can come out. The Hockler isn't accurate enough for that, but your team –' he turned to Erulin '– shouldn't have any trouble.'

'None at all,' the Frenchman confirmed.

'And the truck?' Richter asked.

'That should be the easiest of the lot,' Colin Dekker said. 'As soon as the charge detonates, Jones will fire two rounds from his Arwen up into the cab.'

'Arwen? What's an Arwen?' Herron asked.

'It's a nasty-looking piece of work,' Richter said. 'Like a short-barrelled twelve-bore shotgun, but with a five-shot magazine like a revolver. It's basically designed for anti-riot work, but it can handle an interesting cocktail of ammunition, lethal and non-lethal. My guess is that the first round will be armour piercing and the second a CS gas grenade. Colin?'

'Exactly.'

The brief silence was broken by Lacomte. 'Has anybody any better ideas? No?' He turned to Dekker. 'What about personnel disposition – where do you want the *Gigènes* to be?'

Dekker shook his head. 'At the moment,' he said, 'I don't know. I'm sure Lieutenant Erulin would agree with me that force dispositions are better sorted out on the spot.' Erulin nodded agreement.

'I must be getting old,' Richter said. 'I've been so tied up working out how to stop the convoy, I've forgotten the other essential. We also have to stop the convoy personnel contacting Moscow as soon as they meet trouble.'

Lacomte looked puzzled. 'Do you think they'll have a radio link to Moscow from one of the vehicles?' he asked.

'No,' Richter said. 'There are good reasons why they won't be using long-range radio, although as Captain Colin said earlier they'll probably be using short-range walkie-talkies for contact between the vehicles. But what they will have is a lot simpler and more effective.

They'll have a mobile telephone – or more likely several mobile telephones.'

'Of course,' Lacomte nodded. 'Digital mobile phones will work almost anywhere along the autoroute, and they could actually talk to Moscow in clear with one, because of the digital transmission system – it works almost like a scrambler.'

Dekker nodded. 'Quite right,' he said, 'but easy to fix.' Lacomte raised his eyebrows in enquiry. 'It's simple,' Dekker said. 'You just knock out the local cells serving that section of the autoroute. No operative cells, no calls. With the authority you've got,' he added to Lacomte, 'that should be no problem at all.'

The Frenchman nodded slowly, then smiled. 'No, no problem at all,' he said. 'Leave it to me.' As Lacomte reached for the telephone, it rang. He picked up the receiver and held a brief conversation. Then he replaced it on its rest and looked up. 'The clock,' he said, 'is running. The convoy left Strasbourg at eleven fifty this morning.'

Chapter Twenty-One

Wednesday
Autoroute A26, vicinity of Couvron-et-Aumencourt, France

Richter, Dekker and Trooper Smith were sitting in a British Embassy car and heading east out of Paris fifteen minutes later, with Westwood and Tony Herron following in a second car. Dekker was muttering quietly into his personal radio, briefing the troopers at Davy Crockett Ranch that the group was en route and organizing weapons and equipment for the operation. He also told them to buy sandwiches and drinks, something Richter hadn't thought of. 'Why not?' Dekker said. 'This could turn out to be another very long day.'

At the Ranch they disembarked from the cars, which Herron sent back to Paris. Dekker and Trooper Smith went into their cabin to get changed; Jones and Brown were ready and waiting, dressed in camouflage clothing, not the jet-black combat suits normally worn by the SAS on operations. Herron, Westwood and Richter waited and watched as Brown made a final check of the equipment. Dekker and Smith emerged from the cabin and trotted over to the Ford. 'Right,' Dekker said, climbing aboard. 'Reims, go.'

Jones slid the Transit into first and drove out of the Cherokee Trail and down the road out of the Ranch. He turned right on to autoroute A4, and held the Transit at a steady one hundred kilometres an hour, heading east. The run to Reims, about ninety kilometres, took just under an hour, and when they turned north onto the A26 Richter knew they had time in hand. As the Transit approached the Vallée de l'Aisne junction, Richter noticed three yellow autoroute maintenance vans clustered together on the hard shoulder, with a group of men sorting out cones and *'Route Barrée'* signs. Lacomte's diversion plan was under way.

353

The rendezvous was at thirteen forty at the parking area just east of Laon, in the Forêt de Samoussy, and they pulled in five minutes early. Jones found a quiet spot at the rear of the area and parked. At thirteen forty a dark blue Renault Trafic van with *'Gendarmerie Nationale'* signs pulled in next to them. Erulin was the front-seat passenger, and he got out and walked round to the Transit's rear door. 'Ready, Captain?' he asked Dekker, who nodded. 'Right,' Erulin continued. 'We'll go on to the ambush site. I'll lead, you follow. When I pull over, you stop just in front of me, so that it will look as if I've stopped you for a motoring offence.'

They followed the Trafic along the autoroute for about another ten kilometres, past junction thirteen. When the Trafic's indicator began to flash the Ford overtook it, pulling off on to the hard shoulder just beyond the Renault. Colin Dekker hopped out and went back to the Trafic to consult with Erulin. Richter looked up and down the autoroute. It wasn't an ideal place for an ambush, as it was almost dead straight, but he hoped the 'accident' would give them the edge they needed.

There was some cover to the north of the autoroute, where men could be concealed, and the central reservation had established shrubs, which would act as a shield between the two carriageways. Dekker returned to the Transit and looked inside. 'Right,' he said, 'this is it. The two artics will be positioned about two hundred yards ahead of where we are now.'

'Where are they now?' Richter asked.

'Patience,' Colin Dekker said. 'According to Erulin, they're on their way to the parking area we used for our rendezvous. They'll wait there until we know the convoy is a bit closer.'

Dekker called the troopers out of the Transit and stood with them by the side of the autoroute, shielded from the view of passing traffic by the van. By his gestures Richter knew he was trying to decide on force disposition and arcs of fire for his men, and probably also for the Gigènes snipers. Richter looked back at the Trafic van, where a group of a dozen men in camouflage clothing were standing. He could see two were carrying 7.62mm FR–F1 sniper rifles fitted with flash suppressors and laser sights – the standard GIGN weapon.

'Nervous, Paul?' John Westwood asked.

'Of course I'm nervous,' Richter said. 'I don't ambush armed Russian convoys carrying nuclear weapons every day. There's a hell of a lot riding on this.'

'Granted. What do you think of the site?'

'It's not perfect. I would have preferred a sharp bend immediately before it, but you don't get sharp bends on French autoroutes.' Richter looked at the passing traffic and then at the terrain to the north. 'Once the traffic stops, it should be quiet enough. No houses in view, no awkward farmers ploughing fields. It should do. In fact,' he added, 'it will have to do.'

Oval Office, White House, 1600 Pennsylvania Avenue, Washington, D.C.

News of the crisis had, of necessity, spread. Key congressmen had been summoned to either the Pentagon or the White House and been briefed on the situation. The Secretary of Defense was still flitting between the White House and the Gold Room at the Pentagon. They had adequate communications between the two establishments, but the President preferred face-to-face discussions. You can't, he often said, tell what a man is thinking if you can't see his face.

'I think,' the President said, at the end of a meeting at the White House, 'that it's time to start taking preventative measures.'

The Secretary of Defense nodded. 'Agreed, Mr President. I'll implement JEEP as soon as I get back to the Pentagon.'

Autoroute A26, vicinity of Couvron-et-Aumencourt, France

Five minutes later Lacomte arrived in an unmarked light blue Trafic van, parked in front of the Transit, got out and walked back to Erulin's Trafic. He returned with the GIGN lieutenant, motioned to Dekker, and then to Richter and the other two men. The back of Lacomte's Renault was a mobile command post, with radio and other communications equipment. Two operators sat in swivel chairs wearing headphones and listening intently. As they clustered together at the back, one of them raised a hand and then addressed Lacomte. 'Valmy,' he said.

'*Qu'est-ce que c'est que ça?*' Lacomte responded, picking up a map.

'*Ils sont à Valmy. Près de Sainte Menehould.*'

'*Bien,*' Lacomte said, then switched to English. 'The convoy's on autoroute A4 and we're getting a position report every time it passes a junction or service area. It took the northern route, through Metz, as we thought it probably would, and it's now between Sainte Menehould and Châlons-sur-Marne, heading west. We have what I believe you would call a revolving long-tail, Mr Beatty. Six vehicles, swapping places regularly, sometimes ahead of the convoy, sometimes behind. The drivers pull in for fuel or just into a rest area to get behind the target, then overtake again later. As a matter of interest,' he went on, 'the convoy has been averaging almost exactly eighty-five kilometres per hour.'

'Fine,' Richter said. 'What's its disposition – where are the escorting cars?'

Lacomte addressed the question to one of the radio operators, who replied at once in rapid French. Lacomte translated. 'The Mercedes saloons have been swapping positions fairly regularly, but generally they have one in front of the lorry and one behind, about a hundred metres distant. The limousine has always been the last vehicle in the group, sometimes as much as a mile behind.' The radio operator spoke again and Lacomte paused to listen. 'They've just changed places again. It looks as if their standard procedure is for both cars to accelerate in front of the lorry if they see any sign of problems ahead.'

'How far ahead do they go?' Richter asked.

Lacomte waited for a response from the radioman before replying. 'It looks like about one kilometre. Why?'

'Just an idea. What do you think they'll do when they see our little accident?'

Lacomte shrugged. 'If they do what they've done up to now, the two saloons will accelerate ahead to investigate it.'

'Exactly,' Richter replied. 'We're not really interested in the cars – it's the lorry and the limousine that we want, so let's isolate them.'

'How?' Colin Dekker asked.

'First,' Richter asked Lacomte, 'have you got radio links with the lorry drivers?'

'Of course.'

'Good. Let's revise our original plan. We don't use the articulated lorries to block the autoroute in front of the convoy. We use one to block the autoroute in front of the lorry, but behind the two saloons, and the other to shut the back door, to block the road behind the limousine. I don't want that car doing a U-turn and vanishing somewhere in northern France.'

They considered this for a few moments. 'That's better,' said Dekker. 'Separating the cars from the truck makes good sense, and might avoid some problems. But we still need to rig an accident or something else to entice the saloons ahead.'

'Time is running out,' Lacomte interrupted, looking at his watch. 'If we are to implement this change we will have to do it quickly. I will have to re-brief the lorry drivers and the road crew by radio, and the convoy is probably now only around a hundred and ten kilometres away. That's just over an hour.'

'How's this?' Richter said. 'Our lorries are waiting at the parking area in the Forêt de Samoussy, near Laon?'

'If they aren't there now they will be within about five minutes,' Lacomte replied.

The radio operator interrupted again. '*Saint Etienne-au-Temple,*' he said.

Lacomte nodded, glanced at the autoroute map on the inside rear door of the Trafic and checked his watch. 'They've speeded up a bit. That puts the convoy due north of Châlons-sur-Marne, with about one hundred kilometres to run. Carry on,' he said, looking at Richter.

'Your plan was to get the lorries moving ahead of the convoy, block the road and wait for it to arrive, yes?' Lacomte nodded. 'Change the orders,' Richter said. 'Tell the first driver to move out as soon as the Russian lorry has passed the parking area, and the second to pull out after the limousine. When they get to the ambush site, the Mercedes saloons will probably accelerate ahead. Once the driver of the first lorry sees them do that, he should pass the Russian artic, get about a hundred yards ahead of it but still behind the two cars, and then brake hard, slewing the lorry across both lanes of the carriageway and the hard shoulder. That shouldn't be a problem, should it?'

Lacomte smiled slightly and shook his head. 'No. That particular driver spends most of his spare time racing trucks on international circuits – that's why we selected him for this job. It will not be a problem. And the second lorry will block the road in the same way, but behind the limousine?'

'Exactly.'

'What happens if the escort cars don't accelerate in front of the lorry?' Dekker asked.

'Then we're back where we started,' Richter said. 'No worse off than before.'

Erulin spoke up. 'I would like the two lorry drivers out of their cabs as soon as possible after they have stopped,' he said. 'They should be briefed to climb over the central reservation, cross the southbound carriageway and lie flat in the scrubland off the autoroute. I don't want them in the firing line.'

Lacomte nodded. 'Agreed. They're wearing orange jackets, as you requested, so you can identify them.'

'*La Veuve*,' the radio operator said.

Lacomte noted the position on his map. 'They're now north-west of Châlons,' he said.

'So what do we use for our accident?' asked Dekker.

'How about your Transit?' Richter suggested. 'As long as the Queen wouldn't mind.'

'Hopefully,' Dekker said, 'she won't find out.'

Richter turned to Lacomte. 'How's this? The lorries proceed as we've just discussed. Your vehicle can be positioned on the hard shoulder to the east of the ambush site, well out of the way, with the bonnet open as if you've had a breakdown. We position the SAS van at the ambush site, slewed sideways across the right-hand lane, so that it looks as if it's been involved in an accident. Lieutenant Erulin's Trafic can be parked on the hard shoulder just behind it, blue lights flashing. The hazard warning lights on both vehicles should be switched on, warning triangles displayed, and a line of cones placed so that traffic is forced into the outside lane.' Richter paused. 'Just a normal, daily, minor accident on the autoroute.'

'That should work,' said Lacomte. 'Any criticisms or suggestions?'

'Only one,' Tony Herron said. 'We won't need the rescue vehicles or any of the other personnel we were going to use for the big accident, so I suggest you withdraw them. The less friendly bodies there are out there the better, in my opinion.'

Lacomte nodded, turned to the radio operators and began issuing detailed instructions as everyone else climbed out of the van. Dekker nodded to Erulin and they walked off together, still discussing their force dispositions. After a couple of minutes the SAS officer came back. 'Right,' he said. 'I think we have agreement. Erulin will position seven of his men on this side of the autoroute, at about one-hundred-metre intervals, and the other three on the south side of the central reservation, closer to where we'll park the Transit.'

Tony Herron interrupted. 'Isn't one hundred metres rather wide spacing?' he asked.

'I couldn't agree more,' Dekker said, 'and if you can show me exactly where each of the vehicles is going to stop, we'll tighten up the spacing. We've got to hedge our bets. By covering nearly one kilometre with that separation we're hoping that we'll have at least one sniper within about fifty metres of each vehicle. The plan is that, once the vehicles have stopped, the *Gigènes* personnel will close up into optimum positions.'

'They'll probably be seen when they move,' Richter said.

'A risk we have to take. What Erulin is hoping is that the convoy drivers will be looking ahead, at the two vans, and not into the scrubland beside the autoroute.'

Lacomte left the back of his van and walked over to them. 'They're approaching Reims,' he said. 'They passed the Aire de Reims-Champagne six minutes ago.'

Washington, D.C.

The Top Secret Joint Emergency Evacuation Plan, or JEEP, is an evacuation plan for selected personnel who live and work in Washington. As soon as the Secretary of Defense reached the Gold Room, he ordered JEEP Preps to begin.

Fifty-five minutes later the last of the designated Army and Air Force helicopters was in position at the Pentagon heliport and on the paved terrace between the Pentagon building and the Potomac River. JEEP cardholders are specially selected military officers and civilians who are capable of running the United States during and after a nuclear war. They are required to be on permanent stand-by and in peacetime hold regular exercises to ensure that they can always get themselves to their designated collection points. There are two categories of JEEP cardholders – One and Two – reflecting the relative importance of the individuals concerned.

The first group of forty-four elite men and women, the government officials, scientists and technicians who held JEEP-1 cards, was airborne thirty minutes later. Some went to the Alternate Emergency Command Center in Raven Rock, also known as SITE R; others to the civilian government emergency bunker, known as the Special Facility, in Mount Weather in northern Virginia.

Four hours later, all but four JEEP cardholders had been flown to their assigned locations. Fifty-nine were at the Special Facility at Mount Weather, and one hundred and ninety-four had arrived at SITE R in Raven Rock. The remaining four cardholders were from the Federal Emergency Management Agency, the government civil defence agency, and were still en route to the civil defence National Warning Center at Olney in Maryland.

Autoroute A26, vicinity of Couvron-et-Aumencourt, France

'What about Trooper Jones?' Richter asked. 'Where is he going to be crouching with his wad of plastic and his Arwen?'

Colin Dekker shrugged. 'Flip a coin,' he said. 'That bloody lorry could stop anywhere in about a five-hundred-metre length of autoroute. He'll just have to do a bit of sprinting.'

Richter shook his head. 'Not necessarily. I can tell you where it's going to stop.'

'How?' Dekker asked.

'Easy,' Richter said. 'Borrow one of Erulin's snipers and tell him to take out one of the truck's tyres as it approaches, preferably one of the twin tyres on the tug – we don't want it to crash. If the driver's any good it should be stationary in under eighty metres.'

The rear door of the light blue van opened and one of the radio operators gestured to Lacomte. He walked over, listened a moment, and then returned. 'Reims,' he said. 'Now we just have to wait for them to make the turn off the A4 and onto autoroute A26. After that, there's really nowhere for them to go but here.'

Dekker and Erulin summoned their men and ran through the briefing one final time, then ordered them to suit-up. They donned bullet-proof Kevlar waistcoats under their combat jackets and checked their weapons and ammunition packs. Finally, they retuned their personal radios to a frequency specified by Lacomte, which would allow direct communication between all personnel and the radio van. That done, they sat down on the grass beside the hard shoulder, waiting for the go signal.

Richter and Westwood walked over to Lacomte's van, and reached it just as he opened the rear door. 'They've passed La Neuvilette,' the Frenchman said. 'They've made the turn, and I estimate arrival here in about thirty-five minutes.'

'Right,' Richter said, and walked over to tell Colin Dekker.

'How soon do we move?'

'Lieutenant Erulin can deploy his men as soon as he likes,' Richter replied, 'and so can you, but don't position the Transit until the convoy's about ten minutes away.'

'Understood,' Dekker said, and began issuing orders.

A long ten minutes passed before Lacomte's radioman announced that the convoy had passed the Vallée de l'Aisne junction. That would be the last check until the vehicles passed under the D977, just to the east of Laon, and just minutes after that they would be on them.

'Close the autoroute,' Lacomte ordered, and Richter relayed the news to Dekker and Erulin, who were still waiting beside the Transit. Lacomte had emerged from the rear of his vehicle, and was walking over towards Richter when the radioman shouted. He doubled back quickly and listened intently to the message.

'What is it?' Richter asked.

'They've pulled off the autoroute,' Lacomte said.

Oval Office, White House, 1600 Pennsylvania Avenue, Washington, D.C.

Ambassador Karasin had known the American President for three years, and believed he knew him well. He was also, from necessity, able to interpret body language and to use his intuition. And what his intuition told him, as he sat in one of the Oval Office's comfortable leather chairs, was that, despite the President's placid exterior, he was consumed with fury.

'Mr Ambassador,' the President said smoothly, 'are you absolutely certain that Moscow knows nothing of this matter?'

The Russian shook his head. 'Nothing, Mr President. Nothing at all.' Walter Hicks, sitting in a chair towards the back of the room, nodded to himself. He thought Karasin was probably telling the truth. 'I spoke with the President himself,' Karasin continued, 'and he gave me his personal assurance, his personal assurance,' Karasin repeated, emphasizing the words, 'that he had authorized no action of the sort you suggested.'

The American looked at him for a moment before speaking. 'Well, Mr Ambassador, that's certainly good to know,' he replied. Karasin relaxed slightly in his seat. 'Unfortunately,' the President continued, just as smoothly, 'that does present us with something of a problem.' Karasin looked at him, but said nothing. 'When we last discussed this,' the American said, 'I told you that we had information that an assault was being planned by Russia upon America.'

'Yes, Mr President,' Karasin said, nodding. 'I remember our conversation. I hope you also remember that I said at the time I had no knowledge of this alleged assault. I repeat that now, with the further assurance from our President.'

The American spoke softly. 'Quite so, Mr Ambassador. The problem is that we now have it on unimpeachable authority that this assault has not just been planned.' He paused. 'We now know – not believe or think, but know – that this assault has already been implemented.'

Karasin clenched his fists, his face growing white. 'I assure you, Mr President—'

'Assurances, Stanislav,' the American said, using Karasin's first name quite deliberately, 'are no longer sufficient. I have no choice but to advise you that, unless we receive an unequivocal guarantee from your President that the assault has been halted, no later than fifteen hundred hours Eastern Standard Time – that's twenty three hundred hours Moscow time – today, then one hour later we will launch our strategic bomber force without any further notice or reference to you.' Karasin shook his head. 'You should also be aware, Mr Ambassador, that the United States will go to DEFCON ONE in –' he looked at his watch '– a little over eight hours from now. You are aware, I hope, of what that implies.'

'Yes, Mr President. We know what that means. I repeat, our President has assured me he knows nothing of this assault. How, then, will he be able to convince you that it has been stopped? And how can he stop it?'

The American stood up. 'Those, Mr Ambassador, are his problems, not mine. I have told you what we will do. Our position is non-negotiable. Good day to you.'

Autoroute A26, vicinity of Couvron-et-Aumencourt, France

'What?' Richter demanded. 'Where? You mean they've turned off it?'

'No,' Lacomte said. 'They've pulled into the service area just north of junction fourteen.'

Richter relaxed. 'Probably just a fuel or food stop,' he said.

'I hope so,' Lacomte replied, 'but what concerns me is the traffic. I've just ordered the autoroute closed north of that junction.'

Richter thought for a moment. 'We have to preserve the illusion of normality at all costs,' he said. 'I think you'll have to open it up again until they get going.'

Lacomte nodded and jumped back into the van. Richter told Dekker his men could relax for a few more minutes, and climbed into Lacomte's van to wait for news. The messages they were getting from the driver who had followed the convoy into the service area didn't seem to indicate anything suspicious. The lorry had been refuelled, as had the cars, and the occupants were visiting the toilets and the shop, always leaving one person in each vehicle. After fifteen minutes, they started their engines again, and eased out into the traffic stream.

Lacomte waited until the pursuit car driver radioed that the convoy was established westbound, and then ordered the autoroute closed once again. 'Now we wait,' he said.

Twelve minutes later the radio speaker crackled and, behind the French, Richter could hear the sound of a big diesel engine. 'The truck's just passed the Forêt de Samoussy rest area,' Lacomte said. 'Our first truck is pulling out to follow.' A minute later the second truck moved out to follow the limousine, then running about half a mile behind the second Mercedes saloon.

Richter opened the van door and called out to Colin Dekker: 'Go.' The SAS officer gave a thumbs-up sign and climbed into the Transit, started the engine and drove off slowly along the hard shoulder, hazard lights flashing. Erulin got into his Renault Trafic and followed.

'Time we organized your breakdown,' Richter said to Lacomte. They went round to the cab of the van and opened the bonnet. Then Richter turned on the hazard lights, took a warning triangle from the rear compartment and placed it about fifty metres behind the van.

The traffic flow had reduced markedly as the closures Lacomte had put in place at junctions 12, 13 and 14 took effect, and only an occasional vehicle passed in either direction. Richter looked up the autoroute. About three-quarters of a mile ahead, he could see one of the GIGN men placing cones in a narrow triangle to protect the Transit. To Richter, it looked convincingly ordinary, but his opinion wasn't the one that mattered. He climbed back into the van, closed the rear doors, put on a headset and thumbed the button. 'Colin?'

'Here. SAS check-in.' Three voices acknowledged in sequence.

'Lieutenant Erulin?'

'Here.'

The radio operator spoke to Lacomte, and he tapped Richter on the shoulder. 'Chambry,' he said.

'All positions,' Richter said into the microphone. 'This is Control. The target vehicles have passed Chambry. We estimate they'll be with us in four minutes. Stand by.' Erulin repeated what Richter said, in French, to the GIGN troopers. The rear doors of the Renault had small windows, and Richter stood up and looked back down the autoroute. The road was empty, no traffic moving in either direction. Lacomte told one of the radio operators to get out and fiddle with the engine of the van – an added touch to lend veracity to the scene.

Then Richter saw them. The lead Mercedes was just passing under the flyover that carried the D967 between Laon and Crécy-sur-Serre, and as he watched the second saloon moved into view from behind the bulk of the articulated lorry. Richter pressed the transmit switch again. 'All positions, Control. Two minutes.'

Richter turned his attention back to the autoroute. The road was almost perfectly straight, and he couldn't see either of the French trucks, but he could see both blue saloons. 'Both Mercedes are ahead of the truck and accelerating.' Richter looked back through the window. Behind the Russian truck he could just see the cab of another articulated lorry coming into view, obviously accelerating to overtake. It looked to Richter as if he had left it too late.

'Something's wrong,' Bykov said.

Modin had been dozing quietly. 'What?' he asked.

'Something's wrong,' Bykov repeated. 'There's too little traffic. I have a feeling—'

He broke off, lowered the limousine's partition and spoke urgently to the escort in the front seat. 'Send the two Mercedes ahead. Tell the crews to look out for anything unusual.'

'They've already started moving,' the escort reported.

Bykov turned to the driver. 'Ease back. Stay well behind the lorry.' Bykov twisted round in his seat. Nothing behind but a single articulated lorry, about five hundred metres back. In front, another French-registered artic was just passing the Russian lorry. On the opposite carriageway, nothing moved.

'It's probably just another accident,' Modin said, stifling a yawn. 'We've seen two today already.'

'No. This is different,' Bykov snapped. He reached for the car phone clipped below the partition. He looked at the status display, then showed it to Modin. The tiny grey-black letters proclaimed 'No service'.

'All French autoroutes have excellent cellular coverage,' Bykov said. 'Somebody has disabled the local cells.'

Modin rubbed his chin thoughtfully, sat up straighter in his seat and peered ahead up the autoroute. 'You might be right, Viktor,' he said softly. 'I think we may have a problem.'

'One minute.' The Mercedes were coming, one in each lane, the two lorries about half a mile behind them. 'Thirty seconds.' Both Mercedes, running almost side-by-side, swept past the Renault and on towards the Transit. 'Twenty seconds.'

The French lorry had eased in front of the Russian vehicle and was moving back into the nearside lane. The Renault shook, twice, as the two heavy goods vehicles roared past. Richter turned his attention to the autoroute in front, and looked through the front screen of the Trafic. 'Ten seconds,' he said. He was guessing, but that should be near enough. As Richter released the transmit button, the leading articulated lorry's brake lights went on, and then everything seemed to happen in slow motion. The lorry lurched to the left, and Richter could see the smoke of burning rubber from its tyres. The trailer skidded and slipped, almost hopping, and turned broadside on to the carriageway. Speed dropping all the time, the cab just brushed the steel barriers on the central reservation.

The brake lights flared on the Russian truck. The driver had reacted late, but he had reacted. The leading lorry halted, completely blocking the carriageway and obscuring the view of everything beyond it. The cab door opened, and a diminutive figure wearing an orange jacket jumped out, vaulted the central barrier and disappeared from sight to the south of the autoroute. It had been one of the most impressive pieces of driving Richter had ever seen.

The Russian truck was slowing gradually, then lurched to the right. Richter saw the puff of dust and rubber as a tyre exploded under the impact of the 7.62mm round, and the cab start to weave. But its speed was already low enough for there to be no real danger.

Richter glanced quickly out of the rear windows. The other lorry was parking, the driver taking his time, broadside on to the carriage-way about half a mile back, and between it and the Renault van Richter saw the black limousine for the first time.

Anton Kirov

The *Spetsnaz* trooper halted outside the door of the Second Mate's cabin and knocked twice. After a few seconds Colonel Zavorin slid the door open. 'Yes?'

'He's gone, sir. Captain Bondarev has gone ashore.'

'Good. Tell the technician I'll meet him outside the hold.'

'Yes, sir.' As the trooper hurried away, Zavorin closed the cabin door and followed. It was time for the final check on the weapon before it was unloaded, and Zavorin was keen to ensure that Bondarev knew nothing about it. Zavorin had been embellishing the cipher machine story in their recent conversations, and was certain that Bondarev believed it.

But if Bondarev found out that the *Anton Kirov's* cargo included a nuclear weapon that was going to be unloaded the next day and left, primed and ready, when the ship departed from Gibraltar, Zavorin was not sure what he would do. Sometimes, ignorance was best for all concerned.

Autoroute A26, vicinity of Couvron-et-Aumencourt, France

'There has been an accident,' a calm voice reported from the front dash-board speaker in the limousine. 'Two small trucks are involved, but the road ahead is not blocked.'

'Look behind you,' the escort shouted into the microphone.

'We've burst a tyre,' the lorry driver yelled, 'and some idiot Frenchman has just slewed his truck right across the road in front of us.'

A babble of voices burst out of the speaker. 'Quiet,' Bykov shouted, grabbing the microphone. He looked behind, and saw the second lorry just completing its manoeuvre.

Modin smiled faintly. 'I think, Viktor,' he said quietly, 'that someone has found out.'

'Convoy,' Bykov called, ignoring the older man. 'This is Bykov. Assume an attack is imminent. Await my command to respond.'

Richter looked ahead. The Russian truck had stopped, and as he watched a figure rolled out from underneath the trailer and sprinted off over the hard shoulder and into the scrubland. Behind. The limousine was coasting to a stop, around fifty metres behind the Trafic. Ahead. For a long moment nothing moved. The Russian truck sat idling, exhaust fumes just visible above the twin silencer boxes behind the cab. No noise, no movement. Then the plastic explosive detonated with a crack that Richter heard even through the headphones.

'Go!' he shouted into the mike. 'Go! Go! Go!'

The figure in camouflage gear stood up beside a bush just off the hard shoulder and pointed a stubby, bulky weapon at the cab of the artic. The figure recoiled as the gun spat flame and the right-hand-side door window disintegrated. A second round followed, and suddenly the cab was billowing with the distinctive white fumes of CS gas.

A long way ahead Richter heard the sudden crackle of small-arms fire.

Colin Dekker ducked down behind the steel barrier at the side of the autoroute as the rear window of the leading blue Mercedes saloon slid down six inches. All SAS personnel are required to be expert in weapon identification, and he knew instantly that he was looking down the barrel of a Kalashnikov assault rifle. He raised his Hockler, selected semi-automatic, flicked off the safety catch, sighted quickly and fired two rounds at the vehicle.

His first bullet slammed into the rear door of the Mercedes, scattering flecks of paint and leaving a dent which confirmed that the vehicle was armoured. The second round went higher and hit the partially-lowered window, but by then the Kalashnikov had added its deeper voice to the exchange, and Dekker tumbled flat on the ground as bullets ploughed through the steel barrier within inches of where he lay. Where the hell were Erulin's men?

Even as the thought crossed his mind, Dekker heard two sharp cracks, then a third, as two of the *Gigènes* fired through the partially open window of the Mercedes, the bullets bouncing around the inside of the armoured vehicle. Dekker heard a sudden scream, a cry of pain, and then silence as the Kalashnikov's muzzle dropped out of sight.

Richter tore off the headset and looked behind. Fifty metres away the limousine was starting to make a U-turn, to head back to the east. Richter kicked opon the rear doors and pulled out the Smith, but at that range it was useless. One of Erulin's GIGN snipers was crouching behind the Renault and Richter shouted to him. 'Stop him,' he yelled. 'Shoot his bloody tyres!' The GIGN trooper looked round blankly. Richter cursed. What the hell was French for 'tyre'?

Lacomte jumped out of the van. '*Les pneus!*' he shouted. '*Tirez sur les pneus!*' The sniper nodded, took aim and fired. The echoes of the shot had hardly died away before he fired again, and when Richter looked the limousine was lurching drunkenly towards the hard shoulder, both left-hand tyres in shreds. Erulin was right about the shooting skills of his men. Richter shouted to Lacomte as he took off at a run down the autoroute. 'Check with Colin.'

Richter didn't think the occupants of the limousine would want to abandon their car and head off on foot into rural France, but he wasn't going to take a chance on it. He stopped about ten metres short of the car and directly behind it. Richter could clearly see the faces of the two men in the back seat looking at him, and at the Smith and Wesson he was pointing at them. He heard running footsteps and glanced to his left. Two of the GIGN snipers were approaching. Richter waved one to his left and the other to the right; they stopped in line with him, crouched and sighted their rifles at the Mercedes, covering both sets of doors.

'It's over,' Richter shouted in Russian at the car, reinforcing his words with gestures. 'Open the doors and step out. Left rear seat passenger first.'

'That's it,' Modin said.

'What? We just give up?'

'Viktor,' Modin snapped. 'Use your eyes, and then use your head. We're outnumbered and out-gunned. If we fight, we die.' He nodded to Bykov. 'Get out,' he said. 'And Viktor,' he added, 'try not to do anything stupid.'

Modin leaned forward to the driver. 'Switch off the engine,' he said.

Richter saw the movement and turned towards the sniper on his right, but the trooper was way ahead. His rifle cracked twice and both right-hand tyres blew. The Mercedes was going nowhere. 'The next ones go into the fuel tank,' Richter shouted. 'Get out now.'

The left-hand rear door opened, and the passenger slowly emerged, his arms held high above his head. 'Walk towards me,' Richter commanded. When he reached about five metres away Richter shouted again. 'Stop. Lie down, face down, hands and feet apart.' The Russian hesitated. Richter raised the Smith and Wesson and Viktor Bykov looked straight down the barrel. 'Your choice,' Richter said. 'You'll lie down, alive or dead.' Bykov lay down.

Richter followed the same routine, straight out of an American police basic training manual, with the second passenger, and finally the driver and escort. While Richter ensured the co-operation of the prisoners with the intimidating presence of the Smith and Wesson, one of the GIGN snipers lashed their hands together, behind their backs. No rope, no wire, just cheap plastic cable ties. Virtually unbreakable, and no keys to lose.

Richter tucked the Smith back in the shoulder rig, left the four Russians lying in the road and trotted back to the Renault van. Lacomte met him halfway there. 'The limousine OK?' he asked.

'Yes,' Richter said. 'Any problems with the lorry?'

'No. The cab crew got a good dose of CS gas, and came down without any trouble. Both of them have lacerations of the head and neck caused by flying glass, but nothing serious. Our problem is the two Mercedes.'

'What happened?'

'They stopped when the lorry started the blocking manoeuvre, but Erulin thought they might try and make a run for it, so his men shot out the tyres.' The GIGN snipers seemed to be getting quite good at that.

'And?'

'The occupants of one of them opened fire, so the *Gigenes* fired a few rounds through the windows which stopped them. We don't know whether they're dead or alive inside the car, but at least they're not still shooting. The second car is just sitting there. The men inside have weapons available – we can see them through the windows – but they aren't using them, and neither do they seem to want to come out peacefully.'

Richter thought for a moment. 'Leave it to me,' he said. 'Tell Colin and Erulin not to take any action yet.' He turned back towards the limousine.

'Where are you going?' Lacomte asked.

'To consult a higher authority,' Richter said. He walked past the GIGN guards and knelt down beside the older of the two men lying on the tarmac. 'Are you the senior officer?' Richter asked him, in Russian. Nicolai Modin nodded. 'Right,' Richter said. 'Let me help you up.' Richter got Modin to his feet and walked him back towards the limousine.

'We have a problem,' Richter said, and pointed up the autoroute. 'Both your escort vehicles are sitting immobilized about half a mile up the road, full of *Spetsnaz* soldiers armed to the teeth and surrounded by our men, also armed to the teeth. There's already been an exchange of gunfire and I guess some of your men will need medical attention quickly.

'Now,' Richter continued, 'we can do this the hard way, or we can do this the easy way. The hard way is they stay in the cars, and we pop an armour-piercing round through each window and follow it with a grenade. That makes a mess on the road and means I've got a lot of boring forms to fill in.'

'And the easy way?' Modin spoke for the first time, and in English.

'The easy way is you get on the radio –' Richter pointed through the window of the limousine '– and tell them to leave their weapons in the cars and get out, one at a time.'

'And then?' the Russian asked.

'And then we have a little talk,' Richter said. 'If your men surrender I can guarantee they won't be harmed.'

'Do I have much of a choice?'

'Frankly, no.'

'Can you release me?' Modin asked.

'I'd rather not,' Richter said. 'Not just yet. I'll operate the radio for you. My Russian,' he added, 'isn't fluent, but I promise you I'll know if you say anything you shouldn't.'

Chapter Twenty-Two

Wednesday
Autoroute A26, vicinity of Couvron-et-Aumencourt

By five they had the situation sorted out. Two *Spetsnaz* troopers had been found dead when Dekker's men opened the rear doors of the Mercedes; the other two occupants had serious wounds and were on their way to hospital. The two lorries that had been used for blocking the carriageway had gone, as had the tractor unit from the Russian artic. A new tractor, summoned by Lacomte, had been hitched to the Russian trailer and driven into the next rest area, a few kilometres further up the autoroute. The Mercedes cars had been winched on to breakdown trucks and were parked in the same rest area, awaiting new tyres. Both carriageways of the autoroute were closed to all traffic between the Chambry and Courbes junctions, and were going to stay that way until everyone was ready to leave. The Minister of the Interior was expected imminently, by helicopter, to inspect the cargo in the Russian lorry.

The surviving Russians, with two exceptions, were sitting with their wrists bound with cable ties and locked in the back of Erulin's Renault van. The first exception was the senior officer who had ordered the *Spetsnaz* personnel to surrender without a fight. He was sitting comfortably enough at a stone picnic table, thoughtfully provided by the French autoroute operating company, and eating one of the sandwiches left over from Colin Dekker's lunch. Trooper Smith was standing ten feet away, watching him carefully, his Hockler at the ready.

Richter was sitting in the back of the Transit van, looking at the second exception – the younger of the two Russian passengers they had pulled from the back seat of the limousine. 'My name is Beatty,' Richter said, 'and I represent the British government.' A somewhat sweeping,

373

and almost entirely inaccurate, statement, but there was nobody around who could dispute it. 'Can I please have your name?' Richter asked politely.

The Russian stared at him. 'You have seized my passport,' he said. 'If you can read, you will see that it is a diplomatic passport, and that by holding me you are in breach of international regulations. I have nothing further to add.' He turned to look out of the window.

Richter picked up the passport and glanced at it. 'According to this document,' he began, 'your name is Petr Lavrov and it states that you are a diplomat. I do not believe either of those pieces of information. I do not believe that your name is Petr Lavrov, because I heard your superior address you as "Bykov". And I do not believe that you are a diplomat because real diplomats do not attempt to smuggle nuclear weapons into another country.

'Perhaps, Comrade Bykov,' Richter said, after a few moments, 'it would help if I explained the facts of life to you. The operation to halt your little convoy and prevent you positioning a nuclear weapon in London was a joint effort. We used a detachment from our Special Air Service, a squad from the *French Groupe d'Intervention de la Gendarmerie Nationale* and the whole thing was co-ordinated by the French DST, that's the *Direction de la Surveillance du Territoire.*'

'I do know what the acronym stands for, Mr Beatty,' Bykov said.

Richter nodded. 'I thought you probably would,' he said.

'So why are you telling me this?' Bykov asked, looking puzzled.

'I'm telling you so you realize that the operation has involved people of two different nations who don't share a common language. Because we don't speak the same language, we have had some problems with communications. None of the organizations involved in this matter have filed their reports yet,' Richter continued, 'but when they do they will probably all incorporate a recommendation that any future joint operations include interpreters. That way, unfortunate accidents and misunderstandings might be prevented.'

'I really don't understand what you're talking about. What unfortunate accidents and misunderstandings?'

'Well, that rather depends on you,' Richter said, after a short pause. 'If, for example, you give me some answers – preferably truthful answers – to a few simple questions, then in a couple of hours you and your colleague can get back in your comfortable limousine and continue your journey, or return to Mother Russia, or go wherever else your whim or your conscience dictates. We'll even,' he added, 'pay for four new tyres for you.'

'And if I refuse?' the Russian demanded.

'Well, that's the problem,' Richter said. 'I really do need to get some answers from either you or your colleague. If you refuse to talk to me then I have to hope that he will be sensible. What I might have to do is arrange for you to be, say, shot while trying to escape, to encourage him to see reason. That's the kind of unfortunate accident I'm worried about.'

Bykov's glare was still defiant, but his face seemed a shade paler. 'You wouldn't dare. That would be murder, simple cold-blooded murder.'

'It certainly would,' Richter agreed, 'but I'm sure you've done worse in your career.' Bykov opened his mouth to speak, but apparently thought better of it. 'France,' Richter said, 'is a civilized country, where all citizens are subject to the rule of law. Please believe me when I tell you that in this parking area the rule of law has been temporarily suspended. Here, we can do exactly what we like.' He pointed out of the window at Trooper Smith. 'You see that man there? He's a member of 22 Special Air Service Regiment. He has spent all of his adult life in the British armed forces, and he is now a member of arguably the most professional and proficient elite Special Force in the world – not excluding your *Spetsnaz*.

'I have a story which might interest you. In December 1974 a four-man IRA gang took a couple hostage in Balcombe Street, Marylebone – that's a district in London. The gang was well armed – in fact, they had sub-machineguns – and showed no inclination at all to come out. The Metropolitan Police believed they faced a long siege, which might conceivably end with the killing of one or both of the hostages and general mayhem and havoc. However, before any major actions were taken by either side, an enterprising police officer leaked a fictitious story to the BBC and one of the national daily newspapers. The story stated that operational control of the incident was about to be transferred to the SAS. Do you know what happened when that news was broadcast?'

'No, of course I don't,' Bykov snapped.

'The gang surrendered. Immediately and without conditions. And do you know why?' The Russian shook his head. 'Because they knew perfectly well that if the SAS took over the siege, their chances of getting out alive were nil. Zero. More recently, in April 1980, a group of six terrorists seized the Iranian Embassy in London. When they started killing hostages, the SAS stormed the building, with the press of half the world watching. When it was over, five of the six terrorists were dead, and the sixth only survived because he pretended to be a hostage and was only properly identified outside the building after the SAS had cleared it.

'What I'm trying to tell you,' Richter went on, 'is that the SAS don't take prisoners. The Regiment is our force of last resort. They are sent in when all other remedies have failed, when the only sensible course of action left is to blow away the bad guys. All their training, all their tactics, are geared to that objective. You are undeniably a bad guy. Compared with what you had planned to do, the Iranian Embassy terrorists were just a bunch of naughty schoolboys.' Richter paused. 'Now, bearing all that in mind,' he said, and pointed again at Trooper Smith, 'what do you think he would do if I dragged you out of this van and told him to shoot you?'

'I don't know.'

'Wrong,' Richter said. 'You do know. He would shoot you immediately, and without question. The only consolation you would have is that it would be a quick death – the SAS only shoot to kill, never to wound.'

'You'd never get away with it,' Bykov spluttered.

'Wrong again,' Richter said. 'My report would say that Trooper Smith acted instantly to protect a senior officer – that's me – from an assault by a Russian terrorist – that's you. Trooper Smith and I would both know that the truth was somewhat different, but if you think either of us would lose any sleep over it you're wrong. The reports filed by our French colleagues standing over there –' Richter pointed at a group of *Gigènes* near Erulin's Renault '– would say exactly the same, because they wouldn't have understood anything I said to Trooper Smith or he said to me. That's the problem with not having a common language.'

Richter leaned forward, his eyes cold and hard. 'Here and now,' he said softly, 'we are the law. Anything I do to you can be justified, because anything I could do is totally insignificant compared to what you tried to do. Please believe that, because I'm going to ask you the same question now that I asked ten minutes ago, and if I get the same answer you're leaving here in a pine box. And that's a fact.' Richter stared at him, and Bykov's eyes shifted from his gaze. 'Right, Comrade Bykov, we start again. Can I please have your full name?'

The Russian looked at Richter and said nothing. Richter picked up the passport and opened both rear doors of the Transit. He had got one foot on the ground when he heard the Russian's voice. 'Bykov,' he said, with a sigh. 'Viktor Grigorevich Bykov.'

Fifteen minutes later Richter helped Bykov out of the Transit – his wrists were still tied – and led him to the stone picnic table, where he could remain under the watchful gaze of Trooper Smith. The older Russian stood up as they approached. Richter nodded to him. 'Just a few questions, please.'

As they walked away Bykov spoke – a single sentence that caused Richter to turn and look at him again. 'It's not over yet, Mr Beatty,' he said.

The Kremlin, Krasnaya ploshchad, Moscow

The Moscow traffic police began stopping vehicles long before the approaching cars could be seen or the sirens even heard. The motorcade – two of the huge ZIL limousines still favoured by some Russian officials, and accompanied by four police outriders astride BMW motorcycles – swept across Teatral'nyj proezd and swung right into Manezpaja ploshchad. They crossed ploshchad Revoljucii, passed the massive fourteen-storey-high red granite and white marble Moskva Hotel, and on into Krasnaya ploshchad – Red Square. The long, wide, red wall of the Kremlin extends down the right-hand side of the Square in a straight line, the ground sloping away. Opposite the Kremlin wall, the huge Gothic building which is the GUM department store fills the whole of the other side of the Square.

The motorcade drove on into the Kremlin complex through Saviour's Gate, the principal official entrance, in the left corner of the Kremlin wall. The Kremlin is a city within a city, occupying a seventy-acre site high above the Moskva River in the centre of Moscow. Basically a three-sided fortified citadel with a north-facing point, dominated by the Sobakin Tower, it is completely surrounded by a wall some fifty feet high reinforced by eighteen towers and pierced by four gates. There are three buildings in the northern section of the Kremlin. To the east is the smallest, the Kremlin Theatre. Half concealed behind the Theatre is the building of the Council of Ministers, ostensibly the home of the Russian government.

The third building is also the biggest; an extended rectangle pointing north and lying along the western façade of the Kremlin, behind the spiked outer wall and overlooking the Alexandrovsky Gardens. In the southern end of this building is the Armoury Chamber or Arsenal, a museum renowned for its collection of antique and pre-Revolutionary weapons, highly jewelled icons, delicate clocks and jewellery. Immediately behind the Arsenal all the interior walls are solid, and there is no internal access to the upper floors of the building. To reach those floors, visitors must pass through the tall wrought-iron barrier that guards the space between the Arsenal and the Ministers' Building.

The upper Arsenal forms a hollow rectangle, four storeys high. Inside the building is a narrow courtyard aligned north–south that divides the area into two narrow sections. On the third floor, about halfway up the eastern block, overlooking the courtyard and hidden from prying eyes, is the Meeting Room. About fifteen metres long and eight metres wide, it's decorated in the heavy, ponderous style which characterizes most Russian government buildings. In this room, every Thursday morning, the Politburo – the exclusive group of men at the pinnacle of the Central Committee of the Russian Communist Party and still the real power in Russia – meets and sits at the long green baize-topped table to discuss the government of the three hundred million citizens of the Confederation of Independent States. Adjoining the Meeting Room is the more intimate Walnut Room, with a smaller table and more comfortable seats, which is used for meetings when the full Politburo is not present.

The motorcade stopped beside the western end of the Council of Ministers building. The motorcycle outriders parked their machines in a protective circle around the cars and waited. At a signal from one of the outriders, both limousine drivers leapt out and opened the rear doors of their cars. Three men emerged from the first ZIL, and two from the second; all five walked briskly through the gateway and were quickly lost to sight.

Fifteen minutes later, a black Mercedes limousine stopped outside the building. One man got out and walked through the gateway.

Autoroute A26, vicinity of Couvron-et-Aumencourt

The older Russian followed Richter to the Transit without comment and sat down where he indicated. Oddly enough, he seemed relatively cheerful, bearing in mind what he'd been through that afternoon. 'Let's begin with some identification,' Richter said. 'My name is Beatty, and I am an agent of the British government.'

The Russian's lips twisted in a gentle smile. 'You seem to be a man of many names, Mr Beatty,' he said. 'Despite your somewhat battered appearance, I seem to recognize you from a slightly blurred photograph. But the name you gave then was Willis.'

Richter smiled back at him. 'You have a good memory,' he said, 'and perhaps the cameras at Sheremetievo need adjusting. I used that name on my last visit to Moscow. May I ask who I am addressing?'

'You have seen my passport, Mr Beatty.'

'I know, but my question stands,' Richter said. 'Who are you? I don't,' he added, 'really want to trawl through all our file photographs of GRU, KGB and SVR agents and officers. Apart from anything else, that would delay your release considerably.'

The Russian looked at him appraisingly. 'Very well, Mr Beatty. My name is Modin, Nicolai Fedorovich Modin, and I am a senior SVR general.'

'What are you prepared to tell me about the operation?'

Modin hesitated. 'I should not really tell you anything,' he said, 'but the fact that we are sitting here means that you obviously know almost everything already. I also have no doubt that Bykov provided a good deal of information.'

'I do know most of it,' Richter replied, 'but getting anything out of Viktor Bykov was very hard work, and there remain some details that I would like you to clarify. You will also notice that we are alone in this vehicle, and I assure you that nothing you say will necessarily be passed on to any third party.'

'So you say, Mr Beatty. So you say.' Modin didn't sound even slightly convinced.

'Was it,' Richter asked, 'a Group *Nord* operation?'

Modin shook his head. 'No. In fact, Group *Nord* has been disbanded for several years. Operation *Podstava* – you would probably translate the word as "provocateur" – was directed from the start in great secrecy by Minister Dmitri Trushenko, acting on the direct orders of the Politburo. The plan was executed by a joint task force of SVR and GRU personnel.'

'Isn't that rather unusual?' Richter asked. 'A joint SVR–GRU operation?'

'No, Mr Beatty,' Modin said, 'it's not unusual – it's unheard of. But, if I may mix my metaphors, desperate situations make for strange bed-fellows. We needed facilities that only the GRU could give us, and if the plan was to work, we had to work with them. It was not a particularly edifying experience.'

Richter changed tack. 'Why are you in France? Wasn't that something of a risk for a man in your position, even carrying a diplomatic passport?'

Modin nodded. 'It was a risk, yes, but I had been instructed by Minister Trushenko to witness the placement of the weapon myself. Viktor Bykov came with me ostensibly because he has been posted as the London GRU *rezident*, a post I cannot now imagine him occupying. In fact, he has been the principal GRU liaison officer on this project since its inception.'

'You said "ostensibly",' Richter asked. 'Why did you use that word?'

Modin smiled, then actually laughed. 'Excuse me,' he said, 'I will explain. First, may I ask you a question?'

Richter nodded. 'I can't promise to answer, but you can certainly ask,' he said.

'Thank you,' Modin said. 'Have you discussed this matter with the Americans?'

'Yes,' Richter replied. 'In fact, we have a senior CIA officer here as an observer.'

'Perhaps it might be better, Mr Beatty, if he was present before I say anything else.'

'Why?' Richter asked.

'Because it will save time, and time is something you don't have a great deal of.'

Richter thought for a few moments. 'OK,' he said, opened the rear door of the Transit and called John Westwood over, taking care to use only his Christian name. 'General Modin, this is John, from the CIA. John, this is General Nicolai Modin of the SVR,' Richter said.

'Did you,' Modin asked Westwood, 'tell the British that you had developed a source – I believe you would call it a "walk-in" – in Moscow? A high-level source?'

Westwood looked somewhat sheepishly at Richter, then nodded. 'We did,' he replied, 'although only very recently. We were trying,' he went on, 'to clarify the situation without involving our allies. That was possibly a mistake.' Richter nodded in agreement.

'We knew about the "walk-in",' Modin said. 'I briefed a colleague to try to identify the traitor. He spent a great deal of time and effort in trying to find anyone who could have passed information to the Americans, but he was not successful. However,' Modin added, 'he and I both agreed that the most likely candidate was Viktor Bykov, which is the real reason why Bykov was with me and why he was travelling to take up a post in London.'

Richter looked puzzled. 'I understand that, General,' he said, 'but you seem to find it amusing that Bykov has been suspected of being a traitor. What's funny about that?'

Modin's grin grew wider. 'It is funny, Mr Beatty,' he said, 'because Bykov is not the traitor that my colleague believes him to be.'

'How do you know?' Richter asked.

'Because, Mr Beatty,' Modin replied, 'I was the "walk-in", not Viktor Bykov.'

The Walnut Room, the Kremlin, Krasnaya ploshchad, Moscow

The door opened and a short, slim, elderly man with thick grey hair walked in. He looked round the room and nodded respectfully to the five figures seated at the table. At the head sat the Russian President. Flanking him were Yevgeni Ryzhkov, Vice-President of the Supreme Soviet, and Anatoli Sergeyevich Lomonosov, Chairman of the Council of Ministers. At the far side of the table sat Yuri Baratov, Chairman of the SVR, and his deputy, Konstantin Abramov. The President gestured the newcomer to a seat at the end of the table.

'General Sokolov,' the President rumbled in his gravelly voice, 'we have a problem.'

Grigori Sokolov sat down and looked enquiringly up the table, but said nothing. He was far too experienced to speak until he knew exactly what was going on, and the peremptory summons he had received had given him no clue.

'Where is General Modin?' Baratov asked, his voice quietly penetrating.

Whatever Sokolov had been expecting, that wasn't it. 'General Modin?' he murmured. 'You know where he is, Comrade Baratov. He is on his way to London.' Sokolov watched Baratov's face carefully as he replied, and as soon as the words were out of his mouth, Sokolov realized that Baratov did not know, and had not known, where Modin was. None of the men at the table knew, and Sokolov suddenly understood that something was very, very wrong.

'Why,' the President asked, 'is he going to London?'

Sokolov stood up and bowed his head. 'Comrade President,' he replied, stammering slightly, 'I will assist you in any way that I can, but I do not think I am the person to whom you should be speaking.'

'Then who should we be addressing?' Ryzhkov asked.

'Minister Dmitri Trushenko,' Sokolov replied. 'General Modin and I have been carrying out the Minister's specific instructions. General Modin believed – and I believed – that the Minister was properly following Politburo directives.'

'And what instructions did Minister Trushenko give?' the President asked.

Sokolov straightened and looked directly at him. 'Minister Trushenko has been co-ordinating Operation *Podstava*,' Sokolov said quietly. 'Operation *Podstava* was designed to neutralize America and let our forces walk into Western Europe without a fight. General Modin,' he finished, 'is overseeing the final phase of the operation.'

Autoroute A26, vicinity of Couvron-et-Aumencourt

Westwood shook his head. 'So you're source RAVEN? We had a list of possibles,' he said, 'and you were on it purely because of the access we knew you had. We never seriously thought it could be you.'

Modin shook his head. 'I am not a traitor,' he said. 'At least, I don't think I am. The information I passed to your man in Moscow earlier was genuine – it was not what you call disinformation – and I revealed it for one reason only. I had to establish a track record with the CIA, so as to be sure that when I told you about this operation you would take my warning seriously. I had to be sure that you would take action to stop it. *Podstava*,' he went on, 'would not have worked. I began to doubt the wisdom of our actions earlier this year, and I even made representations to Minister Trushenko.' He shook his head. 'But it was like trying to stop a train – once it's in motion, it's impossible. In the beginning, it all seemed so simple, so obvious. Frighten America off the stage. Take Europe without a fight, and at last we would have a platform from which we could truly dominate the world. Make Communism work, really work. Fulfil the dreams of Lenin and the rest.'

He smiled. 'I don't know when it was, but I realized that it wouldn't work – couldn't work, in fact. We could take Europe – that would be easy enough – but it was the aftermath. Russia already has ample natural resources, but the fact is that we can't even feed our own people. Without the grain we buy from America every year, our people would starve. Adding the territories of Western Europe would increase our resources, but we would have to absorb their populations as well, and that would simply mean yet more mouths to feed. We would actually make the situation worse, not better. I opposed *glasnost*, you know. I didn't believe that opening our borders to the West would help Russia. Now, I think that Gorbachev and Yeltsin were right. Russia cannot remain a fortress, isolated and remote from the rest of the world, from progress, any longer. If we try to, we will just slip further and further behind. The time has come for Russia to – if you will pardon the expression – come out of the closet.'

'So you decided to tell us about it?' Richter asked.

Modin nodded. 'Yes. It seemed the only way to avoid a conflict that neither side could win. In this matter,' Modin added, his voice dropping, 'you and the Americans must work closely together – very closely. Do you understand?'

Richter shook his head. 'I'm not entirely sure I do, General,' he replied.

'Never mind. Just remember what I said. You must work with the Americans.'

'When were you going to tell us about the weapons in the States?' Westwood asked.

'This week,' Modin said. 'Minister Trushenko is to deliver the ultimatum, and he is only waiting for confirmation from me of the placement of this weapon in London.'

'The weapons in America are controlled by your new communications satellite?' Richter asked. 'The one in geostationary orbit over the eastern Atlantic?'

'Yes,' Modin replied. 'The weapon test in the Tundra, which the Americans flew their spy-plane to investigate, was not actually a test of the bomb – it was a test of the firing mechanism. We had already run exhaustive underground tests of the new weapon. You know,' he added, 'that we have developed a strategic-yield neutron bomb?'

'Yes,' Richter said. 'Comrade Bykov was somewhat evasive on this point, so I will ask you. Why can't the Americans simply destroy the satellite? Send up a Shuttle with a laser or something and burn it up?'

'Because our scientists have been much more cunning than that, Mr Beatty. The Americans will have a vested interest in keeping that satellite alive and well. The satellite does not contain a triggering device,' Modin continued. 'It contains a hold-fire device – it's a fail-unsafe system. The satellite receives a signal from an uplink station in Russia, and radiates that signal to the United States. Each weapon is linked to a satellite dish and receiver. As long as the signal is received, the firing circuits are disarmed. If the signal fails, an automated sequence arms the firing circuits and the weapon will explode.'

Richter thought for a moment. 'You mean if the satellite is destroyed, or even badly damaged, the weapons you have placed in America will detonate?'

'Exactly, Mr Beatty.'

Westwood stared at him. 'Holy shit,' he said, shaking his head. 'Did the genius who conceived this plan stop to think about what would happen if the satellite suffers a power failure, or gets struck by a meteorite or some space debris?'

Modin shrugged. 'There are safety features,' he replied.

Richter sat silent for a minute or two. 'Would you really press the button?' he said, finally. 'Would you really reduce America to a smoking ruin?'

A shadow seemed to cross Modin's face. 'That would not have been my decision, Mr Beatty. I have explained, I hope, why I took the actions that I did to try to stop it. This operation,' he continued, 'is an abomination. When that lorry slid sideways across the road in front of us I actually felt relieved, because I knew then that someone had finally worked it out, and that meant it could be stopped.'

'Oh, we'll stop it,' Richter said. 'That's a promise.'

'You mentioned safety features on the satellite,' Westwood said, his voice still angry. 'Are you prepared to explain what they are?'

'Yes. I am not a technician, so I can only describe in broad terms how they work. First, there are two satellites, not one, co-located in the same orbital position. This will reduce the chance of system failure, due to external or internal causes. Both radiate the same signal from the uplink station, and we have calculated that the chances of both becoming unserviceable at the same time are virtually nil. The satellite signal has to be interrupted for some time – over forty-eight hours – before the firing circuits on the weapons are armed. That delay is intended to allow time for emergency action to be taken should both satellites fail simultaneously.

'Finally,' he said, 'we have over-ride systems that can be enabled to temporarily or permanently disarm the weapons. These systems can be actuated either by signals from the satellites or manually, on the ground. That is all I can tell you.'

Richter thought about this for a few moments, then changed the subject again. 'Comrade Modin, we have to decide what to do with you, with Bykov and your *Spetsnaz* colleagues. You are all – even the drivers – carrying diplomatic passports, so holding you captive is going to get more embarrassing for everyone with every hour that passes. Besides, we don't want to hold you. We have the weapon, and that was what this whole operation was designed to achieve. My own inclination is to simply let you all climb back into your cars and leave, but in this matter my wishes are subordinate to those of the DST, and the DST, in turn, will have to be guided by the Minister of the Interior and, ultimately, by the French government. What I will do, though, is make representations to my DST colleagues and recommend that we just let you all slip away quietly.'

'Thank you,' Modin replied.

Richter looked at his watch, then turned to Westwood. 'We're expecting the French Minister of the Interior any time now,' he said. 'John, could you check and see what time he's due to arrive?' When Westwood had closed the van door behind him, Richter turned back to Modin. 'General, there is one other small matter that I would like to clear up now.' Richter told him what he wanted to know, and then he told the Russian why he wanted to find out. After a moment's hesitation Modin gave Richter the answer he needed.

'I think I know what you intend to do,' Modin added, 'and I have no objection.'

'Would you assist me?' Richter asked. 'A letter would be a help.'

Modin looked thoughtful. 'Yes, Mr Beatty,' he said. 'I will write you a letter.'

The assault team had collected and examined all the bags from the Russian vehicles earlier, and Modin's briefcase was standing with the others just beside the Transit. Richter jumped out and collected it, and passed it to the general. Modin opened it and selected a sheet of paper headed with his office details. He took a fountain pen from his pocket and wrote rapidly. When he had finished, he read through what he had written, then passed the sheet over to Richter. 'I think that will suffice,' he said.

Richter read it. 'Yes,' he replied, 'that should do very well.'

Richter passed it back to him. Modin signed the page, then placed the letter in an envelope, which he sealed. He referred to a small black book, then wrote an address on the front of the envelope, added 'By Hand' underneath it, and handed it over. 'I don't like unfinished business, Mr Beatty. Good luck.'

Richter put the envelope in his pocket, and as he rose to leave he heard the sound of an approaching helicopter. 'That will probably be the Minister now, General,' Richter said. 'Please stay here while I talk to my colleagues.'

The Walnut Room, the Kremlin, Krasnaya ploshchad, Moscow

When Sokolov completed his detailed explanation of Operation *Podstava*, there was an appalled silence in the room. The Russian President passed a weary hand over his brow and looked down the table at the SVR general. 'You may be interested to learn, General, that America will be increasing its military alert state from DEFCON THREE to DEFCON TWO any time now, and to DEFCON ONE in –' he glanced up at the wall clock '– just under four hours. I have also been told that the entire American strategic bomber force will be airborne and on station, fully armed and with support tankers and fighter escorts, no later than twenty-three hundred Moscow time today.' He paused. 'The bombers, of course, are only a part of the American response to this operation that Minister Trushenko decided to instigate. I don't even want to think about the silo-based ballistic missiles or those in their nuclear submarines which are no doubt already in position.'

Sokolov had turned pale, and was sitting down again. 'Well, General,' Baratov said, 'you obviously know far more about Operation *Podstava* than anyone else in this room. What do you suggest we do about this situation?'

Sokolov shook his head. How had the Americans found out? He roused himself. 'Operation *Podstava*, Comrade Baratov,' he replied, 'was specifically designed to eliminate America from any future conflict. I can only assume that the warning to them has not yet been delivered, because the plan called for Minister Trushenko to contact the Americans only after placement of the last weapon in London. Once the ultimatum has been delivered, I am confident that the Americans will stand down their forces.'

There was another prolonged silence, then Baratov spoke again. 'You may be confident, General, but I am not. Nor are any of us. I do not believe that America will stand its forces down. I think – we all think – that the American President will do exactly what he has threatened, and will not just tamely surrender as Minister Trushenko apparently expects.'

'So, General,' Anatoli Lomonosov spoke for the first time, 'we have to stop this ill-conceived operation, and stop it right now.'

Sokolov shook his head helplessly. 'I don't think,' he said slowly, 'that we can.'

Oval Office, White House, 1600 Pennsylvania Avenue, Washington, D.C.

'I still think it's a mistake,' the Vice-President said, standing obstinately in front of the desk.

The President passed a hand wearily over his face. 'I don't care what you think, John. I'm not prepared to take any chances. The two National Command Authorities are myself and the Secretary of Defense. By sending you up in one of the Nightwatch planes I'm creating a reserve Commander-in-Chief and an additional NCA. I hope it's just a precaution,' he added.

John Mitchell looked levelly at him. 'And where will you be? And where are you sending the Secretary of Defense, for that matter?'

'I'm staying here,' the President said, and held up a hand to forestall the protest he could see forming in Mitchell's mind. 'I'm staying here in case Karasin or the Kremlin come up trumps.' He paused and glanced at his watch. 'The Secretary of Defense will be leaving from the Pentagon for SITE R in about three hours. That will give you adequate time to get established aboard the Nightwatch aircraft.'

John Mitchell shook his head. 'Very well, Mr President. If that's the way you want it.' He extended his hand across the desk, and the President shook it. 'I still think you're wrong,' Mitchell said.

'I hope I am, John. More than anything I've ever wished for, I really hope I'm wrong.'

Twenty minutes later, the white-topped Marine Corps helicopter from the Quantico base – about thirty miles from the White House – settled gently on to the grass of the White House lawn. The pilot signalled to the group of men standing some fifty metres away, and they walked briskly towards the aircraft.

When the cabin crew reported that all the passengers were properly strapped in, the pilot pulled up on the collective and the big Sikorsky climbed into the afternoon sky. Once airborne and well clear of the buildings, the pilot swung the helicopter south for the flight to Andrews Air Force base, twenty miles and eleven minutes away, where the Nightwatch Boeing 747 waited. Unofficially known as the 'Doomsday Plane' or 'Kneecap', an acronym derived from the aircraft's official designation of National Emergency Airborne Command Post, the Nightwatch 747 provides an awesome array of communications facilities.

From the aircraft, which can stay airborne for as long as seventy-two hours with in-flight refuelling, the National Command Authority can directly control virtually all of America's armed might. The Nightwatch plane carries a battle staff capable of duplicating all the Presidential codes for nuclear weapon release, and copies of all the procedures and operational plans to conduct a nuclear exchange.

The President or Vice-President is also able to communicate with the Strategic Air Command's airborne command post, originally called Looking Glass, but today code-named Cover All. One Cover All aircraft is airborne at all times, commanded by a SAC general, and has the ability to launch the entire Minuteman missile force. In times of crisis, at least another two Cover All aircraft are scrambled.

The Vice-President looked back briefly towards the White House, wondering if he would see it or the President again, then turned his mind to the task in hand.

Autoroute A26, vicinity of Couvron-et-Aumencourt

Twenty minutes later the helicopter lifted off again, the Minister having peered approvingly at the Russian prisoners and with displeasure into the back of the lorry. Richter had told Lacomte that he thought they should just release the Russians and pretend nothing had happened. After a moment he agreed, and so did the Minister once Lacomte had explained the reasons to him.

Monsieur Giraud, who had remained a respectful one pace behind the Minister throughout his visit, had one additional suggestion. 'We will take photographs,' he said, 'of the weapon in the back of the lorry, and pictures of all the Russians who accompanied it. Still pictures and videos, so that there can be no possible doubt about the crime.'

While Lacomte organized a DST photographic unit, Richter returned to the Transit. 'Good news,' he said to Modin. 'The Minister has approved your release.' He explained about the photographs that would be taken, and Modin smiled.

As Richter stood up to leave, Modin spoke again. 'Mr Beatty,' he said, 'there are three other things we should discuss.'

Richter sat down. 'Yes?' he replied

The Russian seemed lost in thought for a second, then he looked over at the Englishman. 'There will be a delay while we wait for the photographers, and we are still waiting for the new tyres for our vehicles, but I would imagine we will be allowed to leave here in about three or four hours. Would that be a reasonable estimate?'

'Yes, probably,' Richter said. He couldn't see where the Russian was heading.

'So, we can probably expect to reach Calais no later than, say, about two o'clock tomorrow morning?' Richter nodded. 'The Calais to Dover ferries run all night, so we will probably reach London by about five or six tomorrow morning. In view of what I am about to tell you, you may wish to delay our release from here, although you obviously cannot hold us indefinitely. Our London Embassy is expecting us no later than tomorrow midday, which is the estimate I passed to them when we finally got out of Strasbourg.' A thought struck him, and he smiled slightly. 'I should have guessed then. The roadworks were a delaying tactic – a device to hold us up while you organized this?' He waved a hand at the people outside.

'Not my idea,' Richter replied, 'but the DST thought it was worth doing.'

'It was, and it was well done.' Modin's smile vanished, and he leant forward. 'You must realize,' he said, 'that I am a patriot, not a traitor. I have provided you with information about this matter only because I believe the plan to be ill-conceived and, as I have already said, I actually want it to fail.' Modin stopped, apparently trying to come to a decision. He opened his briefcase again, tore a scrap of paper from a notebook and scribbled on it. Then he handed the scrap to Richter; on it was a single Russian word – *Krutaya*.

'What's this?' Richter asked.

'That,' Modin said, 'is all I can do for you, Mr Beatty, without placing my own life in even more danger than it is already. You will need to work out for yourself why that word is important. But,' he leaned forward again, 'you will need to act quickly, and you will need to work with the Americans. Remember, you must work with the Americans.'

Richter looked at him, and tucked the scrap of paper into his wallet. 'This word is to do with Operation *Podstava*, I assume?' he said.

'Yes,' Modin replied. 'It is central to it, but that is all I will say. I have not, and I will not, tell you anything that I believe would harm Russian interests.'

'General,' Richter said quietly, 'I haven't asked you about anything else.'

'I know, and I thank you. When we reach London, we will proceed immediately to the Embassy, and I will have to compose a priority message to Minister Trushenko advising him of the seizure of the London weapon and the discovery of the plot. I will have no choice in this matter – that is my duty, and I will have to obey.' Richter nodded, and Modin looked over at him. 'You disabled the cellular telephone cells in this area?' he asked.

'Yes,' Richter replied.

'I would suggest,' Modin said, 'that you remove the cards from all the telephones we are carrying, and so disable them. If you don't, there is nothing to stop me making a call direct to Moscow as soon as we land in Britain to alert Minister Trushenko. A cellular telephone would be secure enough to permit that. If you do that,' Modin continued, 'then I can delay sending the message until we reach the London Embassy because I will have to use secure communications. However, Bykov will certainly suggest driving south and sending it from our Paris Embassy.'

'I can probably arrange for the DST to escort your vehicles to Calais and insist on your departure from French soil,' Richter said.

'That would be a sensible move,' Modin replied. 'That is the first point. The second matter is more difficult to assess. I cannot predict what effect my message to Minister Trushenko will have,' he continued. 'I explained before that I tried to stop this scheme and I failed. Whether your discovery of the plan at the eleventh hour will be sufficient to stop it I do not know. My guess is that it won't, and that Minister Trushenko will simply implement it slightly sooner than he originally intended.'

Richter was starting to feel cold, despite the sunshine. 'Even with the British nuclear deterrent in place, and no weapon positioned in London, he would still go ahead?'

'Probably,' Modin replied. 'You must realize that Dmitri Trushenko has dedicated the last four years of his life to Operation *Podstava*, and he will not willingly see the plan fail. He is a driven man, Mr Beatty, and driven men are dangerous. I think he will go ahead because it is his plan, and his plan might still work. It might still work,' he added, 'because Europe is Europe and Britain is Britain. Whatever your European Parliament might say, and despite the Channel Tunnel, Britain is still an island and it is possible – or Minister Trushenko might believe it is possible – that Britain would not intervene if Russian forces invaded Europe.'

Richter digested this for a moment. 'You said there were three things, General. What is the third?'

Modin looked at him. 'Really, it's another aspect of the same thing,' he said. 'You haven't asked all the right questions, Mr Beatty, and there is one answer that you really do need. You know about the American devices, and you know about the neutron weapons in Europe, but you haven't asked about how the plan was to be initiated, about how

Minister Trushenko was going to convince the nations of Western Europe to agree to our demands.'

'Go on,' Richter said.

'In final stage of *Podstava* statements will be issued to all Western European governments. These will specify what we want, but Minister Trushenko didn't seriously expect that just telling the governments would be enough. So he's planned a demonstration first.' Modin waved his hand in irritation. 'I tried to stop that too, or at least get it moved somewhere else, and I failed in that as well. I wanted him to detonate it in a desert or somewhere where there would be little or no loss of life, but he over-ruled me. Trushenko wanted a location that was sufficiently far from major centres of population to avoid a catastrophic death toll, which might provoke an immediate nuclear response from either the French or the British in retaliation. But he also wanted a significant loss of life, to prove his serious intent, and he also wanted a really spectacular demonstration of the power of the strategic neutron bomb.'

Richter's mouth was going dry. 'Where is it?' he asked. 'Where is the demonstration?'

'Gibraltar,' Modin replied. 'A Russian freighter – the *Anton Kirov* – has already arrived there with "engine trouble". The crew is almost entirely *Spetsnaz*, and the ship's hold contains a neutron bomb with a calculated yield of seven megatons, sufficient to reduce a large proportion of the "Rock" to rubble and certainly sufficient to kill every living thing in Gibraltar as well as most of the populations of La Linea and Algeciras. The *Spetsnaz* have orders to defend the ship and its cargo with their lives. The weapon is scheduled to be unloaded at Gibraltar tomorrow and positioned in a local warehouse, but it can be detonated while still aboard the ship.'

Modin passed a hand over his brow. 'I cannot be certain, Mr Beatty, but I think that within hours or perhaps even minutes of my message reaching Moscow, Minister Trushenko will detonate that weapon by signal from the satellite.' He looked at his watch. 'It's now seven in the evening. My guess is that you have no more than twelve hours to stop Gibraltar from being blown off the face of the Earth.'

Chapter Twenty-Three

Wednesday
The Walnut Room, the Kremlin, Krasnaya ploshchad, Moscow

The Russian President looked across at Yuri Baratov, Chairman of the SVR. 'Find Minister Trushenko,' he growled. 'Immediately.' Baratov said nothing but stood up, nodded respectfully towards the head of the table and left the room. The President looked, in a somewhat hostile manner, down the table at General Sokolov, and Sokolov could feel himself start to tremble.

'General Sokolov,' the President said, 'in the absence of any evidence to the contrary, I am prepared to accept that neither you nor General Modin were aware that this Operation *Podstava* was not official government policy. However,' he added, 'if any such evidence is subsequently found, well – I need hardly dwell upon the consequences.' He bestowed a wintry smile upon the old man. 'Now,' the President went on, 'we have to formulate a course of action to recover the situation. Yevgeni, what are your recommendations?'

Yevgeni Ryzhkov, Vice-President of the Supreme Soviet, glanced round the table. 'We have, Comrade President, only two options, as far as I can see. The first option is to make a clean breast of it. Contact the White House on the hot-line and explain that the whole thing was an unauthorized venture, which we will stop as soon as we are able to do so.'

The President looked unconvinced. 'From what Ambassador Karasin has told me,' he said, 'I'm not sure that the Americans will accept that. And even if they accept that what we're saying is true, that does not mean that they will stand down their forces.'

'And what is the other option?' Anatoli Lomonosov asked.

'As the Americans would say,' Ryzhkov replied with a shrug, 'we go with the flow. We implement *Podstava*.'

Autoroute A26, vicinity of Couvron-et-Aumencourt, France

Richter jumped out of Transit van as soon as Modin stopped speaking, and took Colin Dekker and Colonel Lacomte off to a secluded section of the rest area. He told them what Modin had said, and what they had to do. Dekker contacted Hereford on a secure circuit using Lacomte's comprehensive communications equipment and explained the situation. Immediately, operational control passed from him to the major in charge of the duty troop. Dekker was told to await further orders, but to begin formulating plans for an assault on the Russian ship.

This seemed to Richter a somewhat pointless exercise, as they knew nothing about the number of the freighter's crew, or the vessel's size, type, or even location at Gibraltar, and Modin wasn't much help when Richter went back to the van to ask him. He thought the crew numbered about twenty-five, but all he knew for certain was that they were all – apart from the captain and perhaps one or two other ship's officers – *Spetsnaz* personnel. However, Colin Dekker dutifully sat down with Trooper Brown at a picnic table and started work.

Ten minutes later, Trooper Jones told them that Hereford had activated the three remaining four-man SAS patrol units from the duty troop, and that they would be flown by helicopter from Hereford to Northolt, the RAF airfield located a few miles north of Heathrow airport in north-west London. They would then fly to France by a C–130 Hercules transport aircraft from the Special Forces Flight of 47 Squadron, Royal Air Force, departing Northolt no later than nineteen hundred hours local time – seven in the evening. Permission was sought by the RAF, and immediately granted by Lacomte, for the Hercules to land at Reims, the closest airport to their position on the autoroute.

Lacomte raised the French Minister of the Interior at home and, using a scrambled circuit, explained the new development and what he proposed to do. When he had received the Minister's approval, he instructed his Headquarters to make the necessary arrangements for the Hercules' arrival at Reims, which would include briefing the French area radar units on the unscheduled flight. He also told his staff to organize a *carte blanche* clearance for the C–130 to depart from Reims that evening and route directly to Gibraltar. 'No delays, no re-routes, no exceptions,' he said. 'If you get any objections from anyone – and I do mean anyone – refer them immediately to the Minister of the Interior himself.'

'What about the Spanish authorities?' Richter asked.

'The Minister will make sure they won't give you any problems. At least, not if they still want anyone to be alive in Algeciras tomorrow night.'

Richter spent half an hour in the back of Lacomte's Renault talking to FOE on a secure circuit. First he briefed the duty officer on the day's events, then waited while he arranged a conference call which brought in Simpson and the Intelligence Director. Then they discussed the bomb at Gibraltar, and what they were going to need.

'I don't know what time the Herky-bird will get there,' Richter said, 'so we need Gibraltar airfield kept open until further notice. We'll need accommodation of some sort there – HMS *Rooke*, the Naval base, would do nicely. We'll need transport from the airfield to *Rooke* for twenty people, including the Hercules crew. At *Rooke*, we'll need a conference room or similar as soon as we get there to conduct the final briefings and then, depending on where the freighter is moored, dories or inflatables or something to get us out to the ship. If it's not at anchor they won't be necessary, but we do need to know as soon as possible, so can you drag the Gibraltar harbour master out of whatever bar he's in and ask him.'

'Is that it?' Simpson asked.

'No,' Richter said. 'We're sitting here by a French autoroute with a Russian nuclear weapon in the back of a lorry, and there are two things I want sorted out. That weapon, according to General Modin, is identical in most respects to the one in the hold of the freighter at Gibraltar. I want someone to come out here and show me how to disarm the bloody thing, so I know what colour wire to cut tomorrow morning.'

'We're way ahead of you,' said Simpson. 'We've had a team from Aldermaston on standby since you went to France. They're on their way out to you now.'

'Good. What's their ETA?'

'About seven thirty tonight, French time. They're coming by road, because of the X-ray gear and other equipment they're bringing.'

Richter thought for a moment. 'Then you're going to have to organize another aircraft to get me down to Gibraltar,' he said. 'The SAS will be leaving Northolt at seven, which means arrival at Reims about half an hour later, which is actually eight thirty French time, and my guess is they'll just pick up the SAS guys here and head south. I doubt if the Aldermaston boffins can crack the system, and explain it to me in words of one syllable, in much less than two or three hours.'

'Wait,' said Simpson, and Richter could hear murmurs as he consulted with someone.

'Right,' he said, coming back on to the line. 'We'll have an RAF Tornado fly into Reims and wait there until you're ready to go. You can fly down in the navigator's seat.'

'What about Diplomatic Clearance?' the Intelligence Director said. 'Technically, we'll need—'

'Don't worry about it,' Simpson snapped, irritation evident in his tone. 'Richter can get the DST to sort that out from the French end – right?'

'Shouldn't be a problem,' Richter said. 'Lacomte has the ear of the Minister on this, for obvious reasons. If I'm flying in a Tornado,' he added, 'you'll have to provide the RAF with my measurements for the flying suit – it has to be reasonably tight-fitting.'

'Right. You said two things,' Simpson said. 'What's the second?'

Richter told him, which produced a loud protest from the Intelligence Director. 'You can't do that,' he said.

'Why not?' Richter replied. 'We'd only be pointing the same gun in a different direction, so to speak.'

'I like it,' Simpson interrupted. 'Yes, it's sneaky and devious, and that's usually the best way to work. Leave it to me. Now, is that it – as far as the weapon is concerned?'

'Probably not,' Richter replied, 'but it's about all I can think of at the moment. But there are a couple of other things we need to sort out.'

The Gold Room, the Pentagon, Washington, D.C.

'And that is your unanimous recommendation?' the Secretary of Defense asked. The Chairman of the Joint Chiefs of Staff shook his head. 'Not unanimous, Mr Secretary, but that is our majority view.'

The Secretary of Defense nodded slowly. 'Very well,' he said finally. 'We go to DEFCON ONE now.'

Defence Readiness Condition One is the ultimate state of emergency. It ensures maximum force readiness and implies that the country is either at war or about to go to war.

Four minutes later the Secretary of Defense was talking on a secure telephone to the President. 'The Joint Chiefs have recommended escalation now,' he said, 'so, subject to your veto, we're going to DEFCON ONE immediately. Do you agree, sir?'

'Yes. Implement it immediately.'

'I'm leaving with the Joint Chiefs for SITE R as soon as the choppers get here, and the NMCC will revert to skeleton manning with immediate effect.'

'I had hoped it wouldn't come to this,' the President replied. He sounded more depressed than the Secretary of Defense had ever known.

'Still no word from Karasin?'

'Nothing,' the President replied. 'I contacted the Kremlin on the hot-line telex link about an hour ago, but they told me that the Russian President is still in conference. I don't know,' he added, 'exactly what that means.' The Secretary of Defense didn't reply. 'I was intending to stay here throughout the crisis,' the President went on, 'but I've changed my mind. I've ordered a helicopter to take me to Camp David. My family's gone there already, and I can conduct operations from there as well as from here.'

Camp David has an underground emergency operations centre designed to operate as a nuclear war command post. The centre is linked to SITE R by armoured underground communications cables.

'Very good, Mr President,' the Secretary of Defense said. 'We've already activated the Mystic Star and Nationwide secure communications systems. The Joint Chiefs are linked with the Cover All and Nightwatch aircraft, Cheyenne Mountain, SITE R, USStratCom at Offutt and the other centres, and I'll get Camp David added. I'll make sure that you can contact me, the Vice-President and your nuclear commanders as soon as you get there.' There was a short silence on the line. 'Mr President?'

'Sorry. Just thinking. My staff will tell Karasin where I'm going, and the Kremlin too. Is there anything else we can do?'

'Nothing, Mr President,' the Secretary said. 'All we can do now is wait and pray.'

Le Moulin au Pouchon, *St Médard, near Manciet, Midi-Pyrénées, France*

Sadoun Khamil actually took over six hours to draft a reply to Abbas' email, and as he read the decrypted text Abbas guessed that the delay had been because Khamil had been in prolonged consultation with senior al-Qaeda personnel.

Khamil's response was unequivocal – they would wait for the last phase of the operation to be implemented, for the London weapon to be put in place, for the Gibraltar bomb to be detonated and for Trushenko's ultimatum to be delivered. Only then was Abbas authorized to take charge of the integrated weapons system the Russians had so obligingly constructed for them, and change the world.

Camp David, Maryland

The President settled himself wearily into an armchair in the underground bunker and glanced around. His wife and children were still above ground, watching an afternoon movie in the comfort of the Camp David house. There would be, the President knew, ample time to bring them down into the bunker when – and if – necessary. Sitting about ten feet away from him was a Marine Corps major, clutching a black attaché case which was chained to his left wrist. Known colloquially as The Football, the case contained everything the President needed to wage global thermonuclear war – the current SIOP options, the President's Decision Book and, most importantly, the Top Secret Gold Codes.

The Gold Codes are a jumble of random letters and numbers issued on a daily basis by the National Security Agency. One copy of the Codes is delivered to the White House, or wherever the President happens to be, for inclusion in The Football, and simultaneously duplicate sets are delivered to all American nuclear command posts, including the Cover All and Nightwatch aircraft. Possession of the Gold Codes, and access to one of the secure communication networks, is all the American President – or anyone else, in fact – needs to authorize the release of nuclear weapons.

The Marine Corps major, one of three officers assigned to The Football detail, had a simple job. He was to stay with the President at all times, day and night, until the President was either incapacitated or dead, when he would immediately transfer his allegiance to the next appointed Head of State.

'Cheer up, Marine,' the President said, a somewhat forced smile on his face. 'It may never happen.'

'No, sir,' the major replied, doubtfully.

An Army colonel approached the President. 'The Secretary of Defense, sir,' he said, 'on the Mystic Star console.'

The President walked across the floor and picked up the headset. The Secretary of Defense's voice was scratchy and echoed in the earphones – a function of the scrambling system used – and the President had to concentrate to hear what he was saying.

'We're established at SITE R, Mr President. Any news?'

'Nothing yet,' the President said. 'Karasin and the Kremlin know where I am.' He paused. 'I just get the feeling they're going to go all the way on this one.'

There was a brief silence on the line. 'Mr President, in my judgement you've been right about most things since you took office, but this time I really hope you're wrong.'

Autoroute A26, vicinity of Couvron-et-Aumencourt, France

'What time will you begin the assault?' Simpson asked.

'That depends upon what we find when we get there,' Richter said, 'and will in any case be decided by the SAS officer in charge. My guess, for what it's worth, is the early hours of the morning.'

'Anything else?' Simpson asked.

'Yes,' Richter said, and fished a scrap of paper out of his wallet. 'General Modin was very insistent that I noted down a Russian word. The word is *Krutaya*.' Richter spelt it out.

'What does it mean?'

'If I knew that,' Richter said, 'I wouldn't be asking you. I've no idea if it's the name of a person, a place or even a description of something. Modin won't explain it further.'

'Can't you lean on him?' Simpson asked.

Richter thought for a moment. 'No,' he said, finally. 'I don't think I can. He's been far more co-operative over this matter than we had any reason to expect, and this is too public a place to start applying much pressure. Also, I think it might be useful in the future to have established fairly friendly relations with a senior SVR general.'

'Agreed,' Simpson said. 'So, what do you want us to do about *Krutaya*?'

'Find out anything you can,' Richter replied. 'Run it through our computers, and do the same with the SIS and MI5 databases. Try GCHQ and the CIA, FBI, DIA and NSA systems. It must mean something to someone, somewhere.'

'What priority is that?' the ID asked.

'Very high. Modin insisted that it is central to this operation, and that makes it very urgent. Don't forget,' he added, 'disarming the Gibraltar weapon doesn't solve our problem – it just buys us a little more time. We've still got to stop *Podstava*.'

Camp David, Maryland

'Mr President. It's time, sir.'

'Right.' The President glanced at his watch, then got up from the chair where he'd been sitting reading a series of intelligence briefs forwarded from the CIA at Langley. He beckoned to the Marine Corps major and walked across to one of the secure consoles. The Secretary of Defense was already on the net when the President put on the headphones. 'Do we need to discuss SIOP options?'

'I really don't think so, Mr President. What we're doing isn't responding to any kind of a first-strike, which is what SIOP is intended to counter. The Russian weapons are already here, primed and in place, and there isn't anything we can do about them. I think our only possible response, if the Russians don't back down, is total retaliation. We've got to be prepared to fire everything we've got at them, and make sure they know it.'

'They know it,' the President said. 'I've explained it to Karasin twice already. So, what's the immediate next step?'

'We need to brief USStratCom Command Center to increase the alert state of the ICBMs. Pretty much everything else has been done, as far as I know.'

'What are they at now?'

'Alert Twenty. They should be moved up to Alert Five in stages over the next two hours. I recommend going to Alert Fifteen now.'

'Agreed. I'll send the codes.'

On a command from the President, the major opened the black attaché case and extracted the Gold Codes. The President selected the code he needed and instructed that it be transmitted to USStratCom Command Center as an Emergency Action Message from the National Command Authority.

Autoroute A26, vicinity of Couvron-et-Aumencourt, France

The Aldermaston group – five scientists and three bomb-disposal specialists in a Leyland Sherpa minibus, plus two Transit vans con-

taining their equipment – arrived at seven twenty, after having been
halted by the gendarmes guarding the closed section of the autoroute for
ten minutes while they sought approval from Lacomte to let them
through. They drove the wrong way down the autoroute, on the northbound carriageway from the Courbes junction to the rest area, and
pulled up next to the Russian articulated lorry.

They clambered out of the minibus and stood looking with interest
at the Russian vehicle. As Richter walked over to them, a stooping grey-
haired man – presumably the senior scientist – detached himself from the
group and ambled over to meet him.

'Are you in charge here?' he asked.

'I suppose I am more or less keeping up the British end,' Richter said.

The scientist extended a hand. 'Dewar,' he said, 'like the Scotch.
Professor Dewar, Aldermaston. We know what's in the lorry, but we
don't know what you want us to do with it. Give me a clue.'

'Three things,' Richter said. 'First, I want the device made safe, but
not disabled. I want any firing circuits rendered temporarily inoperative.
Second, I want you to explain to me how to do exactly the same thing on
another weapon of the same type.'

'Where is it?' Dewar interrupted.

'It's at Gibraltar,' Richter said. 'I won't bore you with the details, but
that weapon is likely to be detonated within about ten hours unless we
do something about it, so I need answers bloody fast. Third, my instructions are to have this weapon transported to Britain as soon as possible.
We have a tractor unit and escort coming out this evening, but I'd like
your team to accompany the lorry as well.'

'Right, then,' Dewar said. 'We'd best get on with it.'

The SAS team had broken the seals and opened the back of the truck
as soon as they had parked it in the rest area to check that it did contain
a nuclear weapon, and not, for example, a consignment of caviar and
vodka for a Russian Embassy staff party. The trailer had been fully
loaded to enable it to pass a cursory inspection if it was ever stopped
and examined by an authority which would not accept its diplomatic status. After they'd emptied out all the cardboard boxes and bits
of furniture from the back, the only thing left was a large steel box,
padlocked. One of the GIGN men had cracked the padlock with a pair

of bolt-cutters, checked carefully for any wires or switches that might indicate a booby-trap, and then they'd peered inside the box. Then they'd shut the trailer. Now they opened the rear doors wide and most of the Aldermaston team climbed in. Richter left them to it and went off to talk to Lacomte.

'I'd like a helicopter,' he said.

'Where and when?' Lacomte asked.

'As soon as the boffins have finished, to fly me to Reims to catch the Tornado. My guess is it will take them at least a couple of hours, but I'd like it on standby here sooner than that.' Lacomte nodded and rattled off instructions in French to the radio operator beside him.

Colin Dekker walked over and stuck out his hand. 'We're off,' he said. 'It's seven forty, so we're leaving for Reims now. I wouldn't,' he added, 'want to miss the Hercules and all the fun down south.' Lacomte and Richter shook his hand.

'Have a good trip,' Richter said. 'I hope I'll reach Gib about the same time you do, but I'll definitely be there well before the assault.'

As the Transit drove out of the rest area and headed south for Reims, Lacomte radioed the gendarmes at the Chambry junction and ordered them to escort it to Reims airport. Lacomte and Richter walked over to the lorry to check on progress. The professor was directing operations from behind, in the best military tradition.

'How's it going?' Lacomte asked.

Dewar turned round and looked at him. 'Difficult to say,' he said. 'We've identified three anti-handling devices so far, and I suspect there'll be at least one more. When we've disabled those we'll be able to get at the weapon.'

'Time is very short, Professor. Can you give me any idea how long this will take?'

'No,' he snapped. 'We're working as fast as we can, and we won't be helped by you two standing there asking stupid questions.'

Lacomte started to speak, but Richter took his arm and moved him away. 'Better we leave them to it,' he said.

One of the radio operators walked over to Lacomte and passed him a message. 'Things are moving,' Lacomte said. 'The Hercules left Northolt a few minutes ago, and its estimate for Reims is eight fifteen.

Your helicopter is on its way from the *Gigènes'* base at Maisons-Alfort, and should land here in about twenty minutes. Finally, your Tornado is flight-planned out of RAF Honington and that will reach Reims no later than eight thirty our time.'

'Good, and thank you,' Richter said.

'I'm out of here, Paul,' John Westwood said, walking over to Richter. 'I'm going back to Paris now, then on to London. From there, I don't know. It all depends on what happens down in Gibraltar, I guess, so good luck.'

'Thanks,' Richter said, shaking his hand. 'I think I'm going to need it.'

10 Downing Street, London

'The London weapon has been stopped in France, Prime Minister,' Sir Michael Geraghty began, as he walked into the private office at number 10 Downing Street. 'There were no casualties on our side, and the operation was entirely successful.'

'Excellent news,' the Prime Minister said, rubbing his hands and looking cheerful.

'It isn't all good news, unfortunately,' Geraghty went on. He had been briefed by Simpson about Gibraltar only minutes earlier. 'The architects of this scheme have arranged a demonstration of the weapon's power in Gibraltar, and we are racing to disarm the device before it can be detonated.'

The Prime Minister sat down, and motioned Geraghty to a chair. 'Explain, please.'

'There is a Russian ship there, Prime Minister, called the *Anton Kirov*,' Geraghty began, and reached into his briefcase for his notebook.

Autoroute A26, vicinity of Couvron-et-Aumencourt, France

It was nearly nine thirty before the Aldermaston team finally completed the disarming of the weapon, and Dewar beckoned Richter over. 'All done,' he said. 'Sorry it took so long, but we obviously didn't want any accidents.'

'Quite,' Richter replied. 'Will it take me as long with the Gibraltar weapon?'

Dewar shook his head firmly. 'It shouldn't do. Our main problem was not knowing how all the anti-tamper devices were rigged. You should be able to disable the other weapon in about ten minutes. Now, come with me and I'll show you.'

They climbed into the back of the lorry and looked at the Russian bomb. It was much smaller than Richter had expected, and didn't look like a bomb at all. The outer steel box was about ten feet long, four feet high and five wide. At one end of it were three large lead-acid batteries, wired in parallel, while the weapon itself was a virtually invisible three-foot-diameter cylinder underneath a tangle of wires and cables in the centre of the box.

'Right,' said Dewar. 'The first thing is the bank of batteries. Do not under any circumstances disconnect those, as they power the anti-tamper devices. If you interrupt the power supply, all four circuits are made simultaneously, and the explosive charge will detonate. It won't,' he added, 'trigger the bomb, but you won't be around to appreciate it.'

He pointed at the mass of cables. 'You have to cut the following seven wires, in this sequence,' he said, and gave Richter a sheet of paper on which he had written the colour coding of the wires, and the order in which they were to be severed.

'And that disarms the bomb?' Richter asked.

'Of course not,' Dewar said, shaking his head. 'That just means you can shift all this crap –' he gestured at the wires '– and see the weapon. Now watch.' He bent down and undid four butterfly nuts, then lifted out a large aluminium plate in the centre of which was a sealed box and around the box most of the wiring. 'The box,' he said, 'contains about four kilos of plastic explosive, but once the wires are cut there's no further danger from it.' He put the plate down carefully on the floor beside the box, and they both looked inside again.

'This weapon,' he began, 'wasn't armed. That is to say, the firing circuits and all the other components are present, but the connections hadn't been made. I presume that this would have been done once the weapon had been finally positioned.' He pointed at a black plastic box with eight cables emerging from it. 'This box is the link to the power supply. The weapon can be powered either by a mains supply – one hundred and ten or two hundred and forty volts alternating current, or by a twelve-volt direct current from a battery pack like the one in this container. In fact,' he continued, 'we believe it would normally be powered by the mains with the battery pack as a standby, as the circuitry incorporates a battery charger.

'Now listen carefully. When you look at the weapon in Gibraltar, you will probably see a cable entering the box, just here.' He pointed. 'That will be the power supply. Again, as with the anti-handling devices, don't interfere with it. This weapon doesn't incorporate any kind of timing device, so we assume that it can only be detonated by an external signal of some sort.'

'That is what we have been told,' Richter assured him.

'The trigger,' Dewar said, 'is here – this black cylinder with the four leads attached to it. On the Gibraltar weapon, there will also be one or more other wires which will be attached to whatever radio or communications device they are using to actuate it.'

Richter looked where he was pointing. The cylinder was about six inches in diameter and a foot long, and stuck at right angles out of the centre of the cylindrical bomb casing. 'Do not attempt to disconnect or interfere with any of these leads. The only safe way to disarm the weapon is to physically remove the trigger.'

He looked at Richter. 'Are you good with your hands?'

'I hope so,' Richter said.

'So do I, because if you cock this bit up there'll be a sodding great bang and most of Gibraltar will disappear. You,' he added, 'will be the first to know about it.' Dewar wasn't smiling. 'The trigger is held in place by six Allen bolts – or rather Russian variants of them. These look like normal Allen bolts, with recessed hexagonal sockets in the heads, but differ in one important way. They have a left-hand thread, instead of the usual right-hand. That means that to undo the bolts you turn them clockwise.'

'Why have they done that?' Richter asked. 'Just to be bloody awkward?'

Dewar glanced briefly towards the rear of the trailer. 'If this was a French device, I'd agree with you,' he said. 'French engineering makes a point of complicating everything for no readily apparent reason. In this case, though, I think it's just to ensure that the correct bolts are used. The pressures generated within a nuclear weapon at the moment of detonation boggle the mind, and it is essential that the trigger assembly remains in place for the period intended by the designer. These bolts have been specially made and have enormous tensile strength.'

He selected a ratchet handle from a socket set and attached a six-inch extension to it. Then he fitted an Allen bolt key to the end and snapped it into the head of one of the bolts. 'You'll find that they'll take some shifting,' he said. 'We calculated the torque setting used at about three hundred foot-pounds. We removed all these earlier, so there's no problem.' Working quickly, he undid and removed five of the six bolts, then steadied the cylinder with one hand while he removed the last one. Then he put both hands around the cylinder and eased it slowly out of the bomb casing.

'It's quite heavy,' he said, 'but the important thing is to avoid it touching the sides of the casing as you remove it. If you do that, you could earth the cylinder and that might activate the trigger. I'm not saying it would, but it could, and I wouldn't want to try it.'

'Nor would I, thanks. And then?'

'You're almost there. With the trigger out of the sphere, put it on the floor and cut the four leads attached to it.'

Richter was puzzled. 'Won't that fire the trigger?'

'Yes, of course. Oh – I see what you mean. This isn't an explosive trigger; it's mechanical.' He held it up so that Richter could see it, and pointed at the sides. 'These four bolts are recessed at present,' he said. 'When the trigger fires they will extend simultaneously and make contact with four electrically active panels on the inside of the hole in the bomb casing. That will complete the electrical circuit which triggers the explosive charge that actually fires the weapon. It's an unusual system,' he mused, 'and there are some odd features in the design of the weapon itself.'

'You might,' Richter said, 'get a chance to look at it more closely later on. Anything else I should know?'

'Only to keep your fingers out of the way of the four bolts when you cut the wires attached to the trigger,' he said, 'but otherwise, that's it.'

'What about radiation from the weapon?' Richter asked. 'Once the trigger's been removed, I mean.'

'We've measured it, and it's not significant,' Dewar replied. 'The fissionable material is obviously shielded within the bomb casing itself.'

'OK, I'm happy with the disarming instructions, but please give me your mobile phone number now, and leave the mobile switched on for the next twenty-four hours. That's just in case I meet any other problems down in Gibraltar.'

'Of course,' Dewar said. He wrote a number on a slip of paper and gave it to Richter.

'Oh, one last thing,' Richter said, 'can I borrow the socket set and your pliers?'

Reims airport, France

The Alouette dropped out of the darkening sky and settled on to a concrete hardstanding to the north of the main runway at Reims airport. The ground marshaller dropped his light wands into the 'park' position – in a cross below his waist – and the pilot commenced the shutdown sequence. As the clattering of the rotors died away, Richter unstrapped and climbed out. A figure standing beside the marshaller walked over to him. 'Mr Beatty?'

'Yes.'

'Squadron Leader Reilly, 9 Squadron. I believe I'm your driver.' They walked over to a small building adjacent to a hangar and entered. Inside, another RAF officer was waiting. 'Flight Lieutenant Peter Marnane, my navigator.'

'Beatty,' Richter said.

Reilly pointed to a set of flying clothing draped over a chair. 'We were given your measurements, so hopefully that lot should fit,' he said. 'While you're dressing, a few questions.'

Richter took off his jacket, and there was a noticeable pause as the RAF officers saw the Smith and Wesson in the shoulder rig. Richter took it off and undid his tie. 'Fire away.'

'Have you flown in a fast jet before?' Reilly asked.

'Yes,' Richter said. 'I'm ex-Navy and a qualified Sea Harrier pilot, and I've also flown Jet Provosts, Hawks, Jaguars and a MiG–29 Fulcrum.'

'Jesus Christ,' said Marnane.

Richter grinned at him. 'I was joking about the Fulcrum,' he said. Richter pulled on the long underwear and long-sleeve pullover, then climbed into the g-suit, designed to keep the supply of blood to the brain as constant as possible during high-energy manoeuvres, while Reilly went through a pre-flight safety briefing. The life-saving jacket was an unusual design with sleeves to accommodate the arm restraints Tornado crews wear to protect them if they have to eject at high speeds. Finally he put on the helmet and gloves.

'Before we go out to the Tornado,' Reilly said, 'I have to remind you that it is a two-crewman aircraft, and isn't designed to accommodate a pilot plus a passenger. I know you're a qualified pilot, but not on the Tornado, and there will be some operations that you will have to carry out for me. Obviously I will talk you through them, but Peter has prepared a kind of idiot's guide to the switches and controls for you.'

'OK.'

'Finally, I am aware that you carry substantial authority, otherwise I'd be tucked up cosily at home in Lincolnshire instead of standing in an unventilated hut in the middle of France. But I must emphasize that I am the aircraft captain, and all decisions relating to the safety of the aircraft are mine. You must obey any and all orders I give without question, unless of course you don't understand them.'

'Agreed,' Richter said.

Reilly smiled. 'And if I say "eject", and you say "pardon"—'

'I know,' Richter finished it for him, 'I'll be talking to myself.'

The Panavia Tornado GR–1 was parked on the adjacent hardstanding. Marnane clambered up the steps positioned against the port side of the aircraft and leant into the rear cockpit. 'He's switching on the Inertial Navigation System and warming up the radar,' Reilly said, then walked round the aircraft carrying out external pre-flight checks.

Marnane helped Richter get into the rear seat, which was easier than he had expected. Strapping into the Martin-Baker Mark 10 ejection seat was slightly non-standard. First, the personal survival pack, which actually forms the seat cushion, was attached to a lanyard on the life-saving jacket, and then Marnane fastened the negative-g, lap and shoulder straps. Then he attached the leg restraints which hold the legs firmly against the seat in the event of an ejection and fastened the arm restraints to the life-saving jacket. Finally, Richter put on the helmet, plugged the communications lead into the intercom system and attached the oxygen mask.

Reilly was already sitting in the front cockpit, and as soon as Marnane tapped him on the shoulder and gave him a thumbs-up sign, he called on the intercom. 'Ready, Mr Beatty?'

'Ready,' Richter said.

'Your mobile is switched off and your weapon and other equipment are stowed?'

'Yes,' Richter replied. 'They're in the storage compartment.'

'OK. Closing the canopy.' Richter heard the whine as the electric motor drove the canopy down into the closed position, and Reilly talked briefly – and in French, Richter noted – to the ground crew, who were linked to the aircraft's intercom, and started the starboard engine, then the port. 'You'll feel some bumps and shudders now,' Reilly said on the intercom. 'I'm running the BITE program.'

'What's that?' Richter asked.

'It's a computer-driven pre-flight check which exercises all the flight control surfaces in sequence, plus the intake control system,' he replied. 'Once it's finished, the aircraft lets us know if it wants to fly or not.'

'Really?' Richter said. 'Let's hope it's in a good mood.'

Reilly chuckled. 'OK,' he said, a couple of minutes or so later. 'Systems check complete, we're ready to roll. Remove your pins, please.'

As briefed by Peter Marnane, Richter extracted one safety pin from the ejection seat, arming it, and another from the MDC – miniature-detonating cord. This is a single filament cord which runs longitudinally down the centre of the canopy. In the event of an ejection, the cord detonates and blows a hole in the canopy to permit the ejection seat to pass through it.

'Normally the navigator would input start position data into the navigation computer,' Reilly said, 'but Peter has already done that, and it really doesn't matter much anyway, as Gibraltar's a bit too big to miss.'

As the Tornado moved along the taxiway, Richter looked at the two screens in front of him. The one on the right was showing a track display, while the left exhibited a plan view of the intended route of the aircraft. At the end of the runway Reilly stopped the aircraft while he waited for take-off clearance, then turned the aircraft on to the runway and lined up. He ran the engines up to maximum cold power, holding the Tornado on the toe brakes, then engaged full after-burner and simultaneously released the brakes.

Just over ten seconds later, as the airspeed indicator reached one hundred and forty-five knots, Reilly rotated the aircraft ten degrees nose-up and they climbed away. Within another few seconds the Tornado's speed had built sufficiently to allow him to disengage the after-burners, and the noise level dropped considerably. At three thousand feet he levelled out, turned the aircraft south, and instructed Richter to select three one seven decimal six megahertz on the UHF radio box beside his right thigh.

'I'll be off intercom for a couple of minutes,' Reilly said. 'I have to talk to Mazout Radar to advise them we're now en route for Gibraltar and to get clearance to climb.' A couple of minutes later the intercom crackled. 'Back with you,' he said. 'We're going up.' The aircraft's nose pitched higher and they continued the climb to twenty-three thousand feet and increased speed to five hundred knots, heading south in the deepening night.

North American Aerospace Defense Command, Cheyenne Mountain, Colorado

Construction of the Cheyenne Mountain base began in 1958, following the launch of Sputnik by the Russians, but the base did not become operational until 1966. Workmen used a million pounds weight of explosives and removed nearly seven hundred thousand tons of granite to create the four-and-a-half-acre site. The entrance is located about seven thousand feet above sea level, and leads into a tunnel fourteen hundred feet long. The tunnel cuts a curved path through the granite, and is designed to let the pressure wave from a nuclear detonation traverse its length. More or less in the centre of the tunnel, and parallel to the direction of any blast, are two immense steel doors, each over three feet thick and weighing twenty-five tons, fifty feet apart and set into concrete pillars. Behind these doors lies the NORAD complex; fifteen steel buildings, inter-connected by steel walkways, and each resting on huge steel springs designed to resist the effects of shock waves. The complex is effectively self-contained. Electric power is provided by six diesel generators with fuel supplies for about thirty days. Drinking water, food and sleeping accommodation are all available on site.

On a normal day, Cheyenne Mountain is occupied by about eight hundred staff. When Brigadier-General Wayne Harmon had assumed the watch at two that afternoon, the staff tally list showed that twelve hundred and forty-three people were in the complex, either on duty or waiting to relieve duty staff. Harmon heard the murmured conversations of Air Force officers of the North American Aerospace Defense Command, and the clipped, precise messages they were relaying over their radio and satellite links. NORAD had already passed alert and update messages to its worldwide network of early warning radar sites. These included Fylingdales in Yorkshire, England, Diyarbakir in Turkey, Shemya and Clear in Alaska, Thule in Greenland and the thirty-three sites of the Distance Early Warning system – the DEW line – the ageing warning stations that stretch across the entire width of the northern Canadian border.

General Harmon took a last look around the active suites, then turned and walked into his private office. He sat down in his leather swivel chair and loosened his tie. Despite the air conditioning it was hot, and it had already been a very long day.

Gibraltar

At eleven thirty-three local time the Tornado banked to port as Reilly turned left base leg. There was no view ahead, because the pilot's seat completely obscured it, but out of the left-hand side of the cockpit Richter could see the lights of Gibraltar, with La Linea just to the north, the two complexes separated by the dark mass of the airfield, its landing and approach lights barely distinguishable at their present range. The Tornado was at four thousand feet over the Bahia de Algeciras, about two minutes from touchdown.

Five minutes later the whine of the engines stopped as Reilly applied the parking brake in the dispersal area they had been allocated. A C–130 Hercules was parked about a hundred yards away, so Richter assumed that the SAS had arrived. Richter replaced the seat and MDC pins, on Reilly's instructions, then unstrapped, opened up the storage locker and grabbed the pistol and toolkit, and clambered out. The ground marshaller gestured towards a Sherpa van with 'Air Traffic Control' written on the side, and they walked over to it and climbed aboard.

Chapter Twenty-Four

'Before we start I think we should just establish the ground rules, as it were,' Richter said, looking across the Wardroom dining table at Dekker and the senior SAS officer, Major Ross. 'My instructions in this matter are quite specific. We are to seize that vessel, and we are to disarm the weapon it carries. All other considerations are subordinate to that. If we encounter any resistance we are to overcome it using whatever force we consider necessary. That's the official terminology. In real terms, it means that we shoot the bastards, starting with any sentries they've got posted and finishing with the ship's cat. Do I make myself clear?'

'Like crystal,' Ross nodded.

'Right, Major,' Richter said, 'where's the *Anton Kirov*?'

The ship was alongside the North Mole, which made the approach easy. If it had been at anchor in the bay or alongside the Detached Mole – an elongated hyphen almost linking the encircling concrete arms of the North and South Moles – they'd have needed boats.

Ross considered two different attack strategies. 'As I see it we have only two choices,' he said. 'Either we try a diversion – a fire or something on or near the Mole – which might allow us to get aboard undetected or we go for a straight frontal assault. Let me clarify that – a quiet straight front assault. Colin – your recommendations?'

'I agree about the two options, but I don't favour a diversion,' Dekker said. 'It would either involve additional personnel who might get in the firing line, and who we haven't got anyway, or we would have to use some of our troopers which would deplete the number available for the assault. And diversions tend to attract attention. I wouldn't want to wake up the entire crew of the *Anton Kirov* to watch a bonfire on the Mole, say, on the doubtful grounds that while they're watching that they aren't going to be watching out for us.'

Ross nodded, then turned to Richter. 'Mr Beatty?'

'I agree with Colin. Don't forget that, according to Modin, the crew have been instructed to defend the vessel against any possible assault. The crew are experienced *Spetsnaz* personnel who probably outnumber us by slightly more than two to one – if we start a major diversion, my guess is that at least some of them will realize that it is a diversion and actually expect an attack. And that's the last thing we want.' He paused. 'However,' he added, 'perhaps a minor diversion would assist.' Ross nodded, so Richter told him what he had in mind.

Autoroute A26, vicinity of Couvron-et-Aumencourt

'At last,' Modin muttered, as the Russian convoy, now equipped with new tyres and with Gendarmerie vehicles in front and behind, was finally waved out of the parking area, en route to Calais. The articulated lorry was still in the parking area, waiting for the arrival of the tug and escort that had been sent from Britain.

'Where will they take it?' Bykov asked, glancing back at the lorry as the limousine pulled away. He had been very subdued since the convoy had been stopped, worried, Modin supposed, about his future career. Modin wasn't worried. He knew his own career was over.

'Britain, I expect,' Modin said. 'No doubt they will want to examine the weapon.'

'I wish,' Bykov said, 'that we had been able to contact Moscow. The Minister will want to be informed.'

'I'm sure he will,' Modin replied. Minister Trushenko would not, he hoped, be informed about the seizure of the London weapon for some hours yet. Once he found out what had happened, Modin was not at all sure what Trushenko might do.

Gibraltar Harbour

The black combat suit supplied to Richter by 22 Special Air Service Regiment wasn't exactly Savile Row. The bulletproof vest was bulky and heavy, but the Smith in its shoulder rig nestled comfortably under Richter's left armpit. As well as a Hockler MP5SD – the version of the 9mm MP5 fitted with a silencer – on loan from 22 SAS, Richter carried a grey nav-bag he had borrowed from Peter Marnane. Inside that he had stowed Professor Dewar's wire-cutting pliers and the contents of his socket set, carefully wrapped in four linen napkins borrowed from the HMS *Rooke* dining room. In their steel box, Ross had said, they rattled, and he was very keen on not having anything around him that rattled.

Ross had also made it very clear that he was as far as possible to stay out of harm's way, which Richter thought was an excellent idea. Richter had briefed Colin Dekker on the disarming sequence for the bomb and given him copies of Professor Dewar's notes, in case he did get taken out, but Dekker hadn't looked enthusiastic about doing the job himself.

They were ready to go at one twenty. Richter rang Air Traffic Control and extracted a slightly sleepy promise to send the van to the Wardroom immediately. It arrived ten minutes later, and by one fifty they were all assembled at the harbour. There was virtually no moon, and there was a good deal of cover on the North Mole – piles of crates, cables, wires and even a few cars and vans – and they got to within about seventy metres of the *Anton Kirov* without any possibility that they had been spotted from the ship. Ross, Dekker and Richter crouched behind a large crate that smelt strongly of fish, even through the filtering effect of their anti-gas respirators, and studied the target through night-vision glasses.

The Russian freighter was moored bow-on to them, a rather rusty ship that looked deceptively peaceful through the glasses. Richter could see no sign of life on board, but Colin Dekker had better eyes. 'Two sentries,' he said quietly, his voice sounding hollow through Richter's earphones. 'One on the bridge – I saw his cigarette – and one aft, by the gangway.'

'Options?' asked Ross.

'The bridge is sealed, and the glass is armoured – against the weather, not bullets, but the effect is much the same – so we can't take him out from here. I think the decoy option offers us our best chance.'

'Agreed,' said Ross. He turned and waved a hand.

A minute or so later a couple of SAS troopers staggered past them, arms round each other's shoulders, and exhibiting all the characteristics of a pair of happy drunks, even to the loud and tuneless singing. Their combat outfits were discreetly hidden beneath dark blue Royal Naval raincoats that Richter had liberated from the cloakroom at HMS *Rooke*. They watched in silence as the two men approached the ship. Richter saw a flash from behind the bridge windows and tapped Dekker on the arm. 'Got it,' Dekker murmured, and focused the night-vision glasses again. 'We aren't the only ones using these,' he said. 'The bridge sentry is watching our two amateur thespians very carefully.'

The two men had reached the stern of the *Anton Kirov* and appeared to be having an argument, the sound of their voices carrying clearly in the still night. Richter saw the second sentry for the first time as he moved into the glow of the deck lights. The men clutched each other, weaved about, and then began making their unsteady way up the gangway. The sentry immediately moved forward to stop them. Dekker was ignoring the drama and still watching the bridge through the glasses. 'The bridge sentry's gone,' he whispered. 'With any luck he's on his way down to help the guy on the gangway.'

The three men met more or less in the middle of the gangway, and Richter could clearly hear the Russian's voice as he remonstrated with the intruders. 'This wrong ship,' he said, in heavily accented English. 'You must get off.'

'It's a bloody foreigner,' one of the troopers said, in a thick Glaswegian accent. 'Where's Jock? He should be on duty tonight.'

'What have you done with Jock, you German bastard?' shouted the other, and lunged clumsily at the Russian. Richter saw a second figure approach the gangway from the deck, and as he reached the side of the ship the decoy operation was completed. Richter heard two almost simultaneous subdued coughs from the silenced Browning Hi-Power 9mm pistols carried by the troopers, and both the sentries fell.

OVERKILL

Camp David, Maryland

'Anything?' the President asked, walking back into the underground bunker, the Marine major on Football detail a respectful five paces behind him. The President had been spending a few minutes up in the house with his wife as the children were put to bed.

The senior officer present, an Air Force general, stood up as the President approached, and shook his head. 'Nothing, sir. We're just sitting around here waiting. We're at DEFCON ONE, we've got just about everything airborne and heading east that's got wings and an engine and can carry anything bigger than a grenade, and the Russians are doing zip.'

'No response at all?'

'Nothing, Mr President. Our technical resources – principally the Keyhole satellites – show absolutely no unusual activity anywhere in the CIS. The Russians must know that we're holding at maximum readiness, but they're not responding in any way at all.'

The President looked at the tote boards and video screens ranged along the longest wall of the bunker, and shook his head. The general was right. Every board showed long lists of American strategic military assets – the teeth of the Triad – in the air, out at sea or sitting, primed and ready, in underground silos. All were waiting for his single word of command, translated through the Gold Codes, to deliver a blow from which Russia might never recover.

'I never thought I'd see this,' he muttered, almost inaudibly. 'At least, I hoped I never would.' The enemy activity totes were, as the general had said, completely empty. Nothing that could in any way be construed as hostile was moving anywhere within the Confederation of Independent States. The President shook his head again, walked across to a leather armchair and sat down. The general watched him for a few seconds, then turned back to his console.

Gibraltar Harbour

'Go,' Ross said into his helmet microphone, and the SAS troopers behind Richter began to move forward, Ross in the lead, Dekker a few yards behind him. Even with no apparent opposition, they still moved in combat fashion, one group stationary, weapons at the ready, while another group moved. One trooper slid down beside Richter and covered the ship with his 7.62mm Accuracy International PM sniper rifle fitted with a Davin Optical Starlight scope.

The first group had boarded the ship and was regrouping on deck when it all started to go wrong. Richter heard a muffled noise from somewhere near the bow, and then the distinctive metallic crack of a Kalashnikov AK47 assault rifle firing single shots. Two SAS men fell immediately, and the others dropped, rolling into what cover they could find while they searched for the gunman. The trooper beside Richter found him immediately. His rifle fired once and the Kalashnikov fell silent, but by then the advantage of surprise had gone, and lights were coming on all over the accommodation section at the stern of the freighter.

On deck, Ross was deploying his men ready for the firefight to come. The accommodation section was accessed by a door on the centreline of the ship, and Richter knew there was at least one other door on the starboard side because he could see it. He guessed that the starboard door was mirrored by one on the port side, which meant the SAS had three entrances to cover. The plan they had hoped to implement was for a stealthy entrance to the accommodation section and, as far as possible, silent elimination of the opposition, cabin by cabin. But that was before the man with the Kalashnikov alarm clock woke everyone up.

Ross had briefed two contingency plans. The first had assumed that the assault team would be detected after boarding the ship, and the second that they would be spotted on approach to the vessel. As Richter watched, the troopers swarmed silently around the accommodation section, smoothly implementing the former. Brief commands and acknowledgements sounded in his earphones.

From behind his crate Richter had a good view of the centreline door. Two troopers stood by it, and even at a distance Richter could see the characteristic stubby shape of the Arwen carried by one of them. The second man was working on the door, on the hinge side, moulding plastic explosive and implanting detonators. As Richter watched, the troopers moved away from the doors, into shelter, and seconds later three explosions ripped through the night. Ross's contingency plan had called for simultaneous assaults on all possible entrances, and it sounded as if that had worked.

Through the smoke and debris Richter saw that the centreline door had gone, replaced by a gaping black oblong. The troopers ran back to their previous position, and one lobbed something through the doorway. The flat crack of the stun grenade sounded louder than the plastic explosive, magnified by the steel bulkheads of the accommodation section. The whitish fumes of CS gas poured out of the doorway, and when Richter could finally see clearly again, both the troopers had gone.

The SAS man beside him was quartering the ship with his Starlight scope, looking for signs that any *Spetsnaz* personnel had already got out of the accommodation area. Richter spotted another crate about twenty-five yards from the gangway, grabbed his bag and machinegun and sprinted for it.

The deck area appeared quiet, two troopers covering a third as he worked on the two SAS men who had fallen when the AK47 had opened up – all SAS personnel receive comprehensive medical training – but the accommodation section of the *Anton Kirov* was echoing with shots. Richter looked up at the bridge area, then further astern, and knew it was time for him to move.

'This is Beatty,' he said into the microphone. 'I'm coming aboard.' As Richter stood up he saw a brief flash from the bridge wing, and dropped flat behind the crate. Half a second later a bullet whistled through the thin wood beside him and ricocheted off the concrete of the Mole and away into the night. One of the SAS troops fired his sniper rifle. Richter cautiously eased his head out from behind the crate and looked up. Another flash, and two more shots from the Mole. Richter saw a dark figure tumble backwards and slump against the bridge wing door.

'Thanks,' he muttered, left the nav-bag where it was, moved the Hockler into the firing position, stood up and ran. He reached the gangway and ducked down beside it. No shots. He stood again, sprinted up the gangway and crouched down against the steel side of the accommodation section. One of the troopers on deck raised an arm in acknowledgement.

'Beatty. I'm going up to the bridge.' A steel ladder ran down the side of the section, and Richter ran over to it. He looked up, but could see no signs of opposition. One SAS trooper moved to the side of the ship to provide covering fire if needed, and Richter started to climb. The ladder was in three sections, joined by intermediate platforms of perforated steel, and he made the first without problems. Richter waited briefly on the platform, checking above and below, before he started up the stairs again.

Halfway up, a shape moved above him, and Richter span round, landed on his back on the stairway and jammed his feet out sideways to stop sliding down. He saw the movement again, and opened up with the Hockler on automatic at the same instant as one of the snipers on the Mole fired his sniper rifle. The figure above Richter slumped down, his Kalashnikov tumbling from his grasp and falling past Richter to the deck below.

He got to his feet again and continued up. The *Spetsnaz* soldier was lying facedown on the second platform, the back of his seaman's jersey soaked with blood. It looked as if he had taken five or six bullets through the chest. Richter felt briefly for a pulse in his neck, found none, and started up the third flight.

The last set of stairs ended on the bridge wing, where another figure was slumped. As Richter stepped on to the wing he thought he saw the figure move. He dropped, just as he had been taught at Hereford, and fired a double-tap – two rounds – with the Heckler & Koch. Richter got to his feet, walked over to him, checked for a pulse and moved on. The bridge door was unlocked. Richter opened it and slid inside. There were no lights on, but he had a good idea where he was going. At the centre rear of the bridge was a sliding door, closed.

Richter checked that the Hockler was selected to single shot and that he had about half a magazine left, and slowly slid the door open, admitting the light from the passageway. Richter saw him before he saw Richter, but it didn't matter because the Russian fired first. The Kalashnikov round ripped through the wooden door and took Richter full in the chest. It felt like a kick from a bull, and he tumbled backwards into the darkness of the bridge, the sub-machinegun spinning from his hands.

The Walnut Room, the Kremlin, Krasnaya ploshchad, Moscow

There was a brief knock at the door and then Yuri Baratov walked in. 'We haven't found Trushenko,' Baratov said as the Russian President looked at him enquiringly, 'but we think we know where he is. When we went to his apartment, his manservant said he was in St Petersburg, and when we finally found his secretary at the Ministry he confirmed it. He's spending a few days with friends in St Petersburg. We got the address from the Ministry, and I've alerted the local SVR headquarters. They're on their way to pick him up now.'

Anatoli Lomonosov snorted. 'They can only arrest him if they can find him,' he said sardonically. 'It is, I suppose, just a coincidence that the Finnish border is only a hundred miles from St Petersburg. Your SVR men may find that the bird has already flown.'

'Why should he?' the President asked. 'He doesn't know yet that *Podstava* has been discovered. Or does he?'

'What have you decided to do, Comrade President?' Baratov asked.

'Nothing,' the President replied. 'We are going to do nothing at all for the moment. I have used the hot-line telex to tell the American President that I have no knowledge of this alleged assault, which is very nearly true. We are not going to take any military measures to respond to the American sabre-rattling.'

'Is that not dangerous?' Baratov asked. 'If we don't respond, we are defenceless.'

'Defenceless against what?' Yevgeni Ryzhkov asked. 'The one thing we do know about the Americans is that they would never dare initiate a first-strike. Let them fly their bombers in small circles over the Atlantic and Pacific, let them sneak their nuclear submarines around. There are two very good reasons not to respond. If we initiate any military actions, the Americans might use that as an excuse to launch a pre-emptive strike against us.'

'And the second reason, Comrade President?'

'According to General Sokolov, ultimate control of *Podstava* lies in the hands of one man – Minister Dmitri Trushenko. If we can't find him, he will presumably activate it when his own timetable so dictates. So, if we can't find a way of stopping it, we are going to have to let *Podstava* run its course.'

Anton Kirov

Richter lay crushed up against the front of the bridge, his left shoulder against the base of the binnacle, trying to get his arms working. He had no idea where the Hockler had fallen, but he still had the Smith and Wesson and he was expecting the *Spetsnaz* trooper to push through the bridge door any second to inspect his handiwork. Richter's right arm seemed heavy, almost too heavy to move, and it took all his strength to seize the butt of the revolver and pull it out. He dragged the pistol on to his chest, panting from the effort.

The bridge door flew open, and Richter struggled to lift the Smith into a firing position. But he was too late – aeons too late. Back-lit by the passageway lighting, the Russian looked down at him over the barrel of his Kalashnikov. '*Das vidaniya* – goodbye,' the Russian said, walked over to Richter and tucked the assault rifle more tightly into his shoulder.

Richter tried to lift the Smith, but the pistol was just too heavy. He tensed, then heard the crash of a shot, but from his right. The Russian suddenly had no head, just shoulders and a spray of blood. He toppled to Richter's left and fell sprawling on the bridge floor. A small, black-suited figure ran from the bridge wing and knelt beside Richter. 'You OK?'

'Don't know. Chest.' It was all Richter could do to speak. His chest didn't hurt – it was just numb, and he couldn't seem to draw breath. The SAS trooper felt cautiously under the vest, which Richter hoped had worked as advertised, then pulled out his hand and waved it in front of Richter's face. 'No blood,' he said.

'Good. What gun?' Richter gestured feebly at the body lying beside him.

'Arwen,' the SAS trooper replied. 'Buckshot, more or less. You should see what it does with a chest shot.'

'No thanks.' Richter's breath was coming more easily, and he still had work to do. 'Help me up,' he said.

The SAS trooper checked round the bridge and down the passageway before lowering the Arwen to the floor. With his help and the support of the binnacle, Richter got back on his feet. He felt as if he'd been through a combine harvester. The trooper picked up his Arwen, moved across the bridge and then returned with Richter's Hockler. 'You OK now?'

'Yes,' Richter said. 'I owe you. Just give me a minute to get my breath.'

'All part of the service. You're Beatty, right?' Richter nodded. 'Did you get to the Radio Room?'

Richter shook his head. 'I didn't get that far.'

'Right. Follow me.'

Richter followed him off the bridge and down the passageway. There were three doors off the passageway, all open. They checked each room, but found them all empty. None of them was the Radio Room. A steel staircase led to the deck below. The trooper crouched flat on the floor, peering down the staircase and looking for any opposition. Satisfied, he stood up and made his way slowly down. On the next deck down there were only two doors on opposite sides of the passageway, one of which bore lightning-flash symbols indicative of high voltages and the Cyrillic legend 'Радио Офис' – Radio Office.

Richter pointed at it. The two men moved to the door and took up positions on either side of it. Richter stretched out his arm, turned the door handle gently, and then pulled. The door didn't budge, but suddenly the clamour of an automatic weapon erupted and a pattern of holes appeared, ripped through the wooden door at chest height.

They flattened themselves against the steel bulkhead. Richter caught sight of a movement opposite, and saw the other door start to open. He was still slow and hurting, but he brought up the Heckler & Koch and selected auto. As the muzzle of the Kalashnikov turned towards them, Richter opened up. The machine pistol took just under a second to fire the eight 9mm rounds he had left in the magazine. A tight pattern appeared in the wooden door, and the AK47 dropped. As Richter dropped the magazine out of the Hockler and inserted another one from his belt pouch, the SAS trooper took out his Browning, ran over and kicked open the door. He slid inside, and Richter heard a single shot.

'No problem,' he said, as he emerged and took up his position again on the other side of the Radio Office door. 'Nice shooting.'

The trooper opened the magazine on the Arwen and inserted two shells from his belt pouch. 'Stand back,' he said. He stepped back into the passageway, took aim at the bottom steel hinge on the door and fired. Richter had time to see that the hinge remained more or less intact, but the wood on the door beside it had simply disintegrated, before he fired again, at the top hinge. The door toppled slowly outwards into the passageway, and as it fell the trooper lobbed a stun grenade into the Radio Room.

Three seconds later they were inside. The sole occupant was lying in a corner, AK47 beside him. He was alive, but the stun grenade had ensured that he would take no part in the proceedings for a while. The trooper pulled out his Browning, but Richter stopped him. 'I have to ask him if he used the radio,' he said.

Richter picked up the Kalashnikov, put one round through each radio set, extracted the magazine and cleared the breech. The communications equipment installed was comprehensive, but in no way unusual. All the radio sets had appeared to be switched on, but again that was probably normal practice. Richter's hope was that the man lying in the corner was simply a crewmember who had taken refuge in the Radio Office, and not the ship's radio operator. What bothered him was the unmade cot in one corner of the room.

The Russian showed signs of coming round, and Richter knelt beside him. 'Listen to me,' he said, in Russian. 'Can you hear me?' The Russian shook his head, trying to clear the fog. 'Did you signal Moscow?'

'What?'

'Did you signal Moscow?' Richter repeated.

The *Spetsnaz* trooper looked up at Richter then, his pale blue eyes defiant. 'Yes,' he said. 'As soon as you attacked. I sleep here, and those are my orders.'

Richter stood up. 'I've got to get to the hold,' he said. 'Deal with him.'

As Richter picked up his Heckler & Koch and walked out of the Radio Office and down the stairs, he heard another shot from the trooper's Browning. 'Ross, this is Beatty,' Richter said into the microphone.

'Ross. Where are you?'

'Coming down from the Radio Room. They signalled Moscow, so if they're going to detonate the weapon we can expect it at any time.' He paused, still catching his breath. 'Have you reached the hold yet?'

'No. We've eliminated most of the opposition apart from a group on the first deck of the accommodation section. I've got men above and below them, but we can't get them out.'

'Don't worry about them,' Richter said. 'If we can't get into the forward hold we're all going to die.' He had reached deck level. 'I'm on the main deck now, starboard side. Can you meet me there?'

'On my way.'

Richter saw a trooper standing beside the guard rail, and a figure in civilian clothes seated beside him. 'Who's that?' he asked.

'Ship's officer. He wasn't on board — we caught him as he came running down the Mole when the fire-fight started.'

'Good,' Richter said. 'Bring him along.' The trooper yanked the man roughly to his feet and pushed him forward. 'My name is Beatty,' Richter said in Russian, 'and I would like your help.' The Russian spat at Richter's feet. The trooper kicked him behind his left knee, then dragged him to his feet again. 'Please listen to me,' Richter said. 'The hold of this ship contains a very powerful nuclear weapon which I believe will be detonated within minutes by radio signal from Moscow. You and the *Spetsnaz* troopers were probably never intended to get off the ship or unload the weapon. You were unknowing suicide bombers. Can you help us disarm it?' The Russian continued to stare. 'Right,' Richter said. 'Bring him.'

Ross stepped out of the accommodation section. 'Who's that?' he asked.

'A ship's officer – or maybe a *Spetsnaz* officer,' Richter replied. 'He was grabbed by your men on the Mole. I'm hoping I can talk him into unlocking the forward hold for us.'

'You're sure it won't be in the aft hold?'

'No,' Richter said. 'That's for bulk cargo – it's got no security at all. The weapon will definitely be in the forward hold, and the hold will certainly be locked.'

They descended three decks before they found it. A steel door labelled, in Cyrillic characters, 'Forward hold. No unauthorized personnel'. It had concealed hinges, two large padlocks, one top and one bottom, and in the centre a combination lock. 'Shit,' Richter said. The padlocks wouldn't be much of a problem, as long as they could find some bolt-cutters, but the combination lock was a different matter. Richter turned to Ross. 'Get someone to find some bolt-cutters and a welding kit – try the engine room. And I need my nav-bag. It's on the Mole behind the crate opposite the gangway.'

While Ross gave the orders, Richter turned his attention back to the Russian, who was watching with a slight smile on his face. Richter opened a door behind him – it opened on to a small storeroom. 'In here,' he told the trooper. The SAS trooper roughly shoved the Russian into the room. Richter followed, switching on the light and closing the door behind him.

'What's your name?' Richter asked.

'Zavorin,' the Russian said.

'Well, Comrade Zavorin. We will get through that door into the hold,' Richter said. 'The only thing I don't know is how long it will take. What I do know is that if we can't get in before your masters in Moscow decide to press the button, we will die. All of us on board this ship will die. So will most of the population of Gibraltar, and of La Linea and Algeciras in Spain. People you've never met, people who know nothing about this, people sleeping peacefully in their beds. Innocent bystanders.'

'There are no innocent bystanders,' Zavorin said. At least he was talking.

'I have only one question. Do you know the combination of that lock?' Zavorin said nothing, just stared. 'I'll ask you again,' Richter said, 'but if you don't know or won't tell me you're just going to get in the way.'

He moved the firing selector on the Hockler to single shot, slipped the safety catch off, and levelled it at him. 'Five seconds, Comrade Zavorin. Do you know the combination?'

Zavorin said nothing for ten seconds. He was probably relying on the fact that English gentlemen don't shoot unarmed men. Richter had never claimed to be a gentleman, and was more Scots than English, so he lowered the Hockler and fired one round through Zavorin's right thigh. It probably shattered the femur, because the Russian fell instantly, screaming.

Kutuzovskij prospekt, Moscow

The alarm bell rang softly and persistently in the top-floor apartment, but it was several minutes before Genady Arkenko heard it. He had drunk perhaps a little too much vodka the previous evening, and had been deeply asleep. When the sound finally penetrated, he rolled over in bed, glanced at the bedside clock and got groggily to his feet. Cursing, he walked across the living area and into the small back room of the flat. Arkenko sat down in front of the short-wave radio set, turned off the alarm, put on the headphones and played back the message which had been stored on the automatic tape recorder.

Three minutes later he was back in the main room, notepad in hand, pressing the speed-dial code of Dmitri Trushenko's mobile telephone. His hands were shaking, and it wasn't because of the vodka.

Anton Kirov

'There's a reasonably good hospital in Gibraltar,' Richter said, raising his voice above the noise Zavorin was making. 'You can be out in a few weeks. You'll be limping, but you will be able to walk.' He paused. 'If I put the next round through your knee, you'll probably never walk again. Let's try one more time. Do you know the combination of that lock?'

Zavorin stopped screaming and spat at Richter.

'I'll take that as a "no", shall I?' Richter said. He raised the Hockler again, and pointed it at the Russian's left knee. 'This really is your last chance,' he said.

'Wait, wait,' Zavorin shouted.

'Yes?'

'I don't know the combination,' Zavorin lied. 'It was sealed when we left Varna.'

'Was that where they loaded the device?'

The Russian nodded. 'The crate was supposed to be off-loaded here, tomorrow.'

'This is your last chance. You really don't know the combination?' Zavorin shook his head. 'Then I'm sorry,' Richter said, shot him twice in the chest, opened the door and stepped back into the passageway.

'Any luck?' Ross asked.

'No,' Richter replied. 'He said he didn't know, though I'm not certain I believed him.'

The noise of firing from above stopped abruptly, and Ross used his radio to find out what had happened. 'That's it,' he said. 'The last of the Russian crew have been secured.'

'That's secured as in shot, right?' Richter asked.

Ross nodded. 'What we call nine-millimetre handcuffs,' he said.

Three minutes later an SAS man severed the hasp of the second pad-lock, while another dragged an oxy-acetylene kit down the passage. 'Cut around the lock,' Richter said. 'If we can punch it out, we can probably lever the bolt out.'

Razdolnoye, Krym (Crimea)

The sound of a telephone ringing was skilfully woven into Dmitri Trushenko's dream, and only gradually impinged on his conscious mind. Then he woke rapidly. Only Genady Arkenko knew the number of his mobile telephone, and he had strict orders to ring him only in an emergency. Trushenko reached out, picked up the mobile and pressed a button. 'Yes?'

'It's Genady, Dmitri. I've had a message from the *Anton Kirov*. They claim –' Arkenko swallowed '– they claim that the ship is under attack.'

'What?'

'Under attack, Dmitri. They said the ship was under attack. But,' Arkenko added, 'I thought that the *Anton Kirov* was at Gibraltar, so that can't be right.'

Trushenko didn't reply for a moment, then responded abruptly. 'Thank you, Genady,' he said. 'I'll take care of it. Don't you worry about it. Good night, my old friend.' His voice was calm and controlled, but his mind was racing. If the *Anton Kirov* was under attack, that meant that someone, somewhere, must have found out almost everything about *Podstava*.

Trushenko ended the call, got out of the bed and stood up, his clenched fists the only outward sign of his inner rage and turmoil. Four years of planning, of scheming, of concealment, and at the eleventh hour somebody – some Western Intelligence service, he supposed – had discovered what was going on. There had to be a leak, Trushenko knew that without a doubt. Knowledge of the *Anton Kirov*'s special cargo was confined to four people only, apart from Trushenko himself, Hassan Abbas and the *Spetsnaz* personnel actually aboard the ship: Genady Arkenko, and the three principal military officers involved in *Podstava*.

The leak wasn't Genady, of that Trushenko was quite certain, so it had to be one of the three soldiers – SVR Generals Nicolai Modin and Grigori Sokolov, and GRU Lieutenant General Viktor Bykov. When this is all over, Trushenko promised himself, I'll see all three of those bastards on the table at the Lubyanka. Then Trushenko smiled to himself, because despite this unwanted interference in his plans, it still wasn't too late. The American weapons were already in place and the strategic neutron bombs were positioned all over Europe, except for the London weapon, but that didn't matter. Implementation, Trushenko decided, would just take place a little sooner than he had originally planned, that was all.

Anton Kirov

It was a warm night, and it got a lot hotter in the narrow passageway with the oxy-acetylene torch running. Like all watertight doors, the hold access was solid steel, about half a centimetre thick, and the torch made slow progress. It took nearly fourteen minutes to cut a rough circle round the lock. Wearing heavy gloves, because the cut edges of the metal were still red hot, the trooper tried pushing the lock through the hole, but it wouldn't budge.

'Try a kick,' Richter suggested. The trooper kicked hard, hitting the combination dial with his heel. This time, the lock moved. A second kick, and the lock went straight through the hole, the bolt pulling out of the bulkhead recess. They opened the door and stepped inside. Richter looked round the hold, a seemingly cavernous structure, three decks high. There wasn't by any means a full load of cargo, but there was enough to make the immediate location of the weapon impossible. He found a switch and flooded the hold with light.

Ross had followed Richter inside. 'What are we looking for?' he asked.

'A steel chest,' Richter said. 'It's about ten feet long by four feet high and five feet wide. But it'll probably be inside some sort of a crate, so look for something with slightly larger dimensions than that.'

Four minutes later one of the troopers called out. 'Here.' They moved over to the corner, picking their route through the other hold cargo.

'That's probably it,' Richter said. Predictably enough, the wooden chest was locked, but the bolt-cutters swiftly disposed of the padlock, and the trooper swung back the lid, dropped the side panel and they all peered inside. The steel chest looked exactly like the one that had housed the London weapon. The trooper used the bolt-cutters to sever the hasp of the padlock, and Richter lifted the lid of the chest cautiously. Another trooper brought Richter's nav-bag over, while he read through Professor Dewar's instructions one more time.

'I suppose there's no point in taking shelter anywhere?' Ross asked.

'Not,' Richter said, 'unless you're a sodding fast swimmer and can make it around to the other side of the Punta de Europa in about ten minutes. Even then I wouldn't want to guarantee you wouldn't fry. This baby –' he pointed into the chest '– was designed to turn the Rock into the sort of stuff you put in egg-timers.'

'Ah,' Ross said.

Richter referred again to Dewar's notes and picked up the wire-cutters. He took his gloves off, checked the wire colour coding, identified and located each of the seven wires that controlled the anti-handling device, and took a deep breath. 'Here we go,' he said.

Razdolnoye, Krym (Crimea)

Trushenko walked briskly out of the bedroom and into the lounge where the dying embers of the fire still glowed. He snapped on the light, sat down at the table and opened up his laptop computer. He plugged in the data cable, and attached the other end to his mobile telephone, then switched on the computer and waited patiently while the start-up programs loaded.

Anton Kirov

Richter's hands were sweating. He wiped them on a napkin, and picked up the wire-cutters again. 'Would you read out the sequence of wires for me?' he asked. 'And hold the paper so I can see the list as well.'

'Right,' said Ross. 'First – yellow with a green stripe.' The cutters were sharp, and the wire parted easily. 'Second – plain blue.' The last wire was red, and when Richter cut it, Ross heaved a sigh of relief. 'Thank Christ for that,' he said. 'Let's get out of here.'

'Sorry,' Richter said. 'That didn't disarm the weapon. That just made sure I wouldn't get blown to pieces trying.'

'What?'

'That was only the anti-handling device,' Richter said, undoing the butterfly nuts. He lifted off the aluminium plate and put it to one side, where hopefully nobody would tread on it. Ross and the two troopers peered into the box. 'This,' Richter said, pointing, 'is the bomb.'

Razdolnoye, Krym (Crimea)

'That's it,' Dmitri Trushenko muttered, watching the screen. Through his mobile telephone, the laptop had logged into the mainframe computer

433

nearly fifteen hundred miles away. His identity and password had been accepted, and it only remained to select the weapon and initiate the firing sequence.

Anton Kirov

Richter traced the wires attached to the trigger, and carefully snipped off all the ties securing them, taking extreme care not to damage the wires themselves. Freeing the wire ties would mean he could place the trigger on the floor outside the bomb chest. Assuming he got it out, of course. He took out the socket set and assembled the ratchet handle with the Allen key in the end, and carefully inserted it in the head of the first of the six bolts holding the trigger assembly in place. He steadied the ratchet with one hand and started to pull with the other.

'Stop!' Ross shouted. 'You're turning it the wrong way.'

Richter stopped and looked at him over the open chest. 'They're left-hand threads.'

'Oh. Sorry.'

Dewar hadn't been exaggerating about the torque needed to undo them. Richter could feel his chest tightening with the effort, and stopped. 'Here,' he said to one of the troopers. 'You're a bloody sight stronger than I am. You do it.'

'Me?'

'Don't worry. I'll tell you exactly what you have to do.'

The trooper took the ratchet, pulled apparently quite gently, and the first bolt began to turn.

'Good,' Richter said. 'I'll unscrew it the rest of the way. Now undo the bolt diagonally opposite to that one.' With the full force of the trooper's impressive shoulders behind the ratchet, the first four bolts shifted easily. 'Now,' Richter said, 'we come to the tricky bit.'

'Yes?'

'There are now only two bolts holding the trigger in place. We have to remove those, but we must hold the trigger steady. If it moves sideways, it could detonate the weapon.'

'Understood.'

The trooper inserted the Allen key in the fifth bolt head. Richter wrapped his hands around the trigger and nodded. The trooper pulled, and the bolt gave. 'Don't unscrew it yet,' Richter said. 'First loosen the last one.'

The trooper repeated the process, then unscrewed each bolt a half-turn at a time, until they were only finger-tight. 'Right,' Richter said, and took a firm grip on the trigger. 'Take both of them out, all the way.' The trooper bent forward and began to unscrew the last bolts.

Razdolnoye, Krym (Crimea)

Trushenko's face was set with concentration as he identified the device he wished to trigger and entered the first authorization code. As a fail-safe, two authorization codes had to be entered before any weapon could be activated, and the mainframe computer requested the second immediately after acceptance of the first.

Trushenko looked at the screen and paused for a few seconds. He thought about Gibraltar – a place he had never visited – and of the unsuspecting thousands of people there, sleeping, working, making love or whatever. People he had never known, and now would never know. Then he thought about *Podstava*, and the triumph that would inevitably follow its implementation.

'You can't,' he muttered, 'make an omelette without breaking eggs.' Trushenko referred back to his book and carefully entered the second authorization code. Then he logged off and switched off his laptop computer. The system had been exhaustively tested, and Trushenko knew that detonation of the weapon would take place in less than ninety seconds.

Anton Kirov

The trooper pulled the last bolt clear, and Richter rotated the trigger assembly very slightly, just to ensure that it hadn't got stuck in position. 'Nobody say anything, nobody move.' As Richter began, millimetre by millimetre, to ease the trigger out of the bomb casing, Ross pointed silently at the back of the assembly. An orange light had just illuminated. Richter glanced at the Cyrillic script below it. 'Oh, shit,' he said. 'That's the start of the detonation sequence. Someone's activated the weapon.'

The trigger unit seemed longer and heavier than the one in the London weapon, but Richter knew it wasn't. He moved faster, and the unit was almost halfway out when the red light illuminated.

'What's that?' Ross asked, his voice hoarse with fear.

'Preparation for firing,' Richter said. The green light came on the instant Richter pulled the trigger clear of the casing, and with a metallic clang the four recessed bolts slammed into the fully extended position. The force was so great that he dropped the trigger, but it fell harmlessly beside the bomb casing.

'If anyone,' Richter said, slumping down beside the bomb, 'wants to change their trousers now, that's fine by me.'

Gibraltar Harbour

On the Mole, chaos reigned. The noise of the small arms' fire and stun grenades had echoed round the harbour, and the Ministry of Defence police, two fire engines and an ambulance were in attendance. So, too, were the crews of most of the other vessels moored along the North Mole. Three of Ross's troopers were standing in line abreast, a silent threat, their sub-machineguns pointed in the general direction of the crowd. An MoD police inspector was standing in front of one of the troopers, making a lot of noise and demanding to see identity cards, weapon permits and authorizations, but nobody was actually listening to him.

Ross and Richter walked down the gangway. Colin Dekker was waiting for them at the bottom, sitting on a bollard.

'SITREP?' Ross asked.

'We lost Carter,' Dekker said, standing up. 'He took a head shot from the Russian on the bow when we boarded. Flemming was hit at the same time, but his vest saved him – he's walking wounded. We've got five other injured troopers, all minor.'

Colin Dekker looked at Richter. 'Is it done?'

'Yes,' Richter said. 'It's done.'

Chapter Twenty-Five

Thursday
Gibraltar Harbour

Richter sat on a pile of wooden boxes on the North Mole and called London on his mobile telephone. Simpson was asleep on a camp bed in his office, but was in on the conference call within two minutes. Richter felt bone-weary, and it showed in his voice. 'The Gibraltar weapon is disarmed,' he reported.

'Any casualties on our side?' Simpson asked.

'Yes. One dead and half a dozen minor injuries. The opposition,' he added, 'came off rather worse than that.'

'I'm sorry about this,' Simpson said, after a pause, 'but we need you back here as soon as possible. We have another problem.'

'What problem?' Richter asked.

'Not over an open line,' Simpson said. 'Your friendly RAF pilot is waiting for you at the airfield – we got him out of bed half an hour ago. Get back here as quickly as possible. There'll be a car waiting for you at Northolt, and you can come into the building at the back, through the secure garage.'

'Colin,' Richter said, putting the phone in his pocket, 'I have to go.'

'OK,' Dekker said. 'Come and do the Fan Dance next time there's a Selection.'

Richter smiled at him and shook his hand. 'Not, if I can help it,' he said.

Reilly was waiting at the airfield when Richter got there ten minutes later, and he had the Tornado airborne fifteen minutes after that. They landed at Northolt fifty-three minutes later. Richter climbed into the waiting Rover, still wearing the g-suit, leaned back in the seat, and closed his eyes.

Camp David, Maryland

The President was dozing in the leather armchair in the corner of the bunker when the message came through. 'Mr President,' the Army colonel shook him gently by the shoulder.

'What is it?' The grey-haired man was instantly awake.

'A secure telex message from CIA London, sir.' The Colonel handed over the flimsy. 'Yesterday the British intercepted a nuclear weapon in transit through France which was intended for positioning in London, and about an hour ago they also located and disarmed another weapon in Gibraltar Harbour, aboard a Russian freighter.'

'Did they now?' the President said, scanning the paper quickly.

'Perhaps more importantly, sir, an attempt was made to detonate the Gibraltar weapon by remote control, presumably by the Kremlin. The trigger was actuated as the British were removing it from the weapon.' The colonel shook his head at the President's unspoken question. 'No, sir. No casualties – it was an electro-mechanical trigger.'

The President stood. 'Inform the Vice-President and the Joint Chiefs,' he said, 'and everyone else on the Command Net. Then locate Ambassador Karasin and tell him I want to speak with him.' The President paused and smiled grimly. 'And then,' he concluded, 'I'll have a little chat with the Kremlin and see what they have to say about all this.'

Hammersmith, London

Simpson's office was large enough to include a small conference table, and when Richter got there Simpson was sitting at the head of it, the Intelligence Director to his right and a long-haired, bespectacled man wearing jeans and a CALTECH T-shirt, and who looked faintly familiar to Richter, on his left. The only vacant chair was at the end of the table, facing Simpson. Richter had changed out of the g-suit in his office, where he kept some spare clothes. 'Do you know James Baker?' Simpson asked, by way of introduction.

'I think I've seen you around the place,' Richter said, stood up and shook his hand.

'Probably. They usually keep me locked up in the basement.'

'Of course,' Richter said. 'You're one of our computer experts.'

Baker grinned at him. 'They normally call me the computer nerd.'

'Well done,' Simpson said, 'in France and Gibraltar. Both were handled very competently.'

'You can thank the SAS for that,' Richter said. 'I was really only along for the ride.'

'If you say so. Right, that was the past; now we have to look to the future. I've asked Baker along because I hope he'll be able to help, but first things first. We will be re-routing the London weapon as you suggested. It should be in place within four or five days.' The Intelligence Director looked disapproving. 'Second, the word Modin insisted you remember – *Krutaya*. We've run it through our database, or rather Baker has, and we came up with nothing, or almost nothing. We tried SIS, MI5 and GCHQ – all negative. A tame source in CIA London tried it through the CIA, DIA and NSA systems with the same result. It's not a code-word that we know about, and it isn't the real name, or the work-name, of any known Russian operative.'

Richter interrupted him. 'You said we had almost nothing on it. What did you find?'

'The only *Krutaya* listed was in the gazetteer,' said Simpson. 'It's a small settlement in the Komi district of Russia, at the southern end of the Timanskiy Kryazh. It's virtually at the end of a road that leads to another settlement called Voy Vozh but goes nowhere after that.' He was looking absurdly pleased with himself.

'Yes?' Richter said, encouragingly.

Simpson was determined to spin it out. 'We checked the BID (CIS) and found nothing, and we checked with JARIC at Brampton. No major developments, nothing of apparent military interest. Apart from what appear to be new telephone cables and some renovation work on a couple of buildings, nothing of any interest appears to have happened in the past year or two – or perhaps for the last two hundred years – at Krutaya.'

'Simpson, stop grinning like a Cheshire cat,' Richter said. 'Stop telling me what you haven't found, and tell me what you have found.'

'Where do you think Krutaya is near?'

'I seem to have forgotten to bring my pocket atlas of the world with me,' Richter said. 'I've no idea.'

'Ukhta,' said Simpson triumphantly.

Richter sat in silence for a moment. The name rang a distant bell, but he couldn't place it. 'Sorry,' he said. 'That means nothing to me. Give me a clue.'

He seemed to have spoilt Simpson's moment. 'Your memory's going, Richter. What about Sosnogorsk?'

Light dawned. 'Where Newman's deputy went as a translator?' Richter said.

'Exactly. Krutaya is about fifty miles to the south-east of Sosnogorsk.'

'Is that it?' Richter asked.

'More or less, yes.'

Richter stared at him. 'I'd hoped for something a bit more interesting than that,' he said. 'As far as I can see, we've been given the name of a town in Russia. A town which appears to have no military significance whatsoever. The only possible link, which could be entirely coincidental, is that last month an SIS operative visited a town about fifty miles away.'

Simpson was still smiling. 'Baker has a theory,' he said. Baker was grinning too. Richter was beginning to feel like the only one in the room who hadn't understood the punch line of the joke.

'OK,' Richter said. 'Let's have it.'

'First,' Baker said, 'let me take you back to the French autoroute, when you talked to General Modin. A question. When he gave you the word *Krutaya*, did you think he was serious? I mean, did he toss the word out to see if you'd catch it, or did he really emphasize it?'

'He was serious about it, no doubt,' Richter replied.

'Did you think he was trying to help you, or was it a ploy to mislead you, to force you to waste time looking in the wrong place?'

Richter thought for a few moments. 'I think he was trying to help, not hinder.'

'Right,' Baker responded. 'Now let's take the situation a stage further. If we accept that Modin was genuine, then the word or the place *Krutaya* must be important. Because of his position in the SVR, Modin probably has a reasonably good idea of the data held on allied intelligence service computers, and he would have been able to assume that the only *Krutaya* we would find would be the village at the foot of the Severnyy Urals.' Richter nodded. 'So, a reasonable working hypothesis would be that *Krutaya* the place, rather than, say, *Krutaya* the code-name, is important, despite what the BID and JARIC say.'

'I don't see where you're heading, but I'll accept that for the moment.'

'JARIC reported only building renovation work, and new telephone cables being laid. The telephone cables were laid underground, in a trench. The Russians usually run them using telegraph poles.'

Richter was beginning to get confused. 'Maybe it's an attractive area. Maybe they decided not to cover the landscape with telegraph poles. Maybe they've run out of bloody trees to make the poles – I don't know.'

'Maybe,' said Baker, 'but there could be another reason. They could be important telephone cables. Cables that they didn't want to string from telegraph poles in case some drunken peasant drove his tractor into one and brought the lot down.'

Richter thought this through for a minute or so. 'The road goes nowhere,' he said slowly, 'apart from running to the other settlement. If we assume that these cables are important for some reason, they must link something in Krutaya with somewhere else. They can't just be vital telephone links that simply pass through the village.'

'Precisely,' said Baker. 'And so?' he prompted.

'So if we accept that Modin was on the level, then there is something in Krutaya that we need to find out about.' Richter looked at Simpson. 'I'm not going tramping round the bloody Urals disguised as a Russian potato farmer, if that's what you've got in mind,' he said.

'There won't be any need for that,' Simpson said, and nodded to Baker.

'So what is it?' Baker asked. 'What could the Russians put in a nowhere village that's important enough to link to the outside world with armoured telephone cables? OK,' he said, as Richter opened his mouth to challenge his assumption, 'I don't know that they're armoured, but I think that they probably are.'

Richter shook his head. 'Look,' he said, 'just assume I'm a congenital idiot and tell me what you're leading up to. I've been up all night and I want to get to bed some time today.'

Baker looked disappointed. 'A computer,' he said. 'A big computer.'

Simpson interrupted. 'Put it all together, Richter. Modin's insistence on you investigating the clue he gave you; the Russian plan; the underground cables; the fact that Krutaya is way out in the sticks, well away from any strategic target, and the visit to Sosnogorsk by Newman's deputy. Add that lot up, and what do you get?'

'A headache,' Richter said.

'You get,' said Baker slowly, 'the very real possibility that one of the buildings in Krutaya houses the computer that controls the satellite that controls the weapons that the Russians have planted.'

The Walnut Room, the Kremlin, Krasnaya ploshchad, Moscow

The Russian President put down the telephone and grimaced. 'The Americans,' he said, 'have the expression "plausible denial". I think we are getting very close to the point where nobody is going to believe that we knew nothing about *Podstava*. That,' he added, 'was Karasin. The American President has told him that the British intercepted a nuclear weapon in France, obviously the one General Modin was escorting, which was destined for London. More significantly, British Special Forces boarded the *Anton Kirov* in Gibraltar Harbour last night and disarmed the weapon it was carrying.' He looked round the room. 'That would be bad enough,' he said, 'but the British also reported that an attempt was made to detonate it.'

'By whom?' Yuri Baratov asked.

'That is not known,' the President replied, 'but the weapon was linked to a satellite communication system on board the ship.'

'Trushenko,' Ryzhkov said.

The President nodded. 'Exactly,' he said. 'General Sokolov told us that the Gibraltar weapon was to be detonated as a demonstration only after the London weapon had been positioned and twenty-four hours after the *Podstava* ultimatum had been delivered.' He paused. 'So that means that somebody must have told Trushenko that things were going wrong. We have to find this person.' He turned to Baratov. 'Nothing from St Petersburg?'

The SVR chief shook his head. 'No,' he replied. 'The address Trushenko claimed he was staying at does not exist. We have widened our search, but so far without success.'

'I wonder,' Konstantin Abramov said, tentatively. 'Someone must know where he is, and that someone must have been contacted either by the London convoy escort, or by the crew of the *Anton Kirov* when the vessel was attacked. Nobody else knew.'

'That is obvious,' Baratov said. 'So?'

Abramov leaned forward. 'Finding this man could be almost impossible, because if he is simply sitting in a building with a short-wave radio, he could be anywhere in the country. But he must have a means of communicating with Trushenko, and that could be the link we are looking for. Trushenko has a mobile telephone. I know, because all requests for ownership of such equipment have to be approved by the SVR – even requests from ministers. And all—'

'Yes, of course!' Baratov almost shouted. 'I should have thought of that myself. All calls to and from mobile phones are logged automatically. We can find out exactly who Trushenko has been talking to, and we can place him anywhere in the world to within about ten miles, because of the cells.'

'What cells?' Ryzhkov asked.

'The mobile telephone system operates using cells. All the time a mobile phone is on, it's in communication with the local cell and, through the cell, with the central computer system. And the numbers of all calls to and from every mobile phone are recorded.'

'I do not fully understand what you are saying,' the President said, 'but do you mean that you can find Trushenko?'

Baratov nodded. 'We can quickly find out more or less where Trushenko is. We can also identify everyone he has called or who has called him, and we can pull them in for questioning. And,' he added, 'once we know Trushenko's approximate location, we can instruct the local cell to disable his mobile telephone. That will force him to use a landline phone, and once he does that, we can take him.'

The internal telephone rang and the President answered it. 'I will come down,' he said, and replaced the receiver. Baratov looked enquiringly at him. 'The Americans want to talk to me on the hot-line,' the President said. 'This time, I think I will have to tell them about *Podstava*. And,' he added, with a wolfish grin, 'I can explain that the traitor Trushenko will shortly be apprehended.'

Hammersmith, London

Richter sat up straighter. 'Proof?' he asked.

'None yet,' said Baker, 'but I might have something soon.'

'Clue me in on this,' Richter said. 'How exactly can a computer stuck in a building in a hick town like Krutaya control these weapons?'

Baker switched to lecture mode. 'First, as it looks like this was what you might call an unofficial plan and not one officially sanctioned by the Kremlin, the computer has to be somewhere like Krutaya. If it was in the Lubyanka or down at Yazenevo, somebody who wasn't privy to the plan would be certain to notice it and start asking awkward questions. Second, with the data transfer facilities available today, the controlling computer could actually have been placed anywhere – not even necessarily in Russia.'

He paused and checked to see if Richter was listening. He was. 'Now, there are two major components of this system, plus the weapons themselves. The most important component is the Krutaya computer itself. That contains a big and complicated program that controls every aspect of the system, from the functioning of the weapons to the positioning of the satellite in geostationary orbit over the middle of the Atlantic.

'The second crucial component is the satellite, because that actually controls the operation of the weapons, acting on instructions from the computer. The satellite and the computer are inextricably linked. The computer will be constantly monitoring the weapons via some kind of feedback system, and also watching the station-keeping parameters of the satellite to ensure that it stays in its designated position.'

Richter had a question. 'How do they communicate with each other? Where's the link?'

Baker shrugged. 'The how is easy, the where I'm not certain about. They communicate through a facility called an uplink station. That's basically a big satellite dish pointed permanently at the Atlantic satellite. It sends signals to the satellite, and receives messages back from the bird. I don't know where it is, but my guess is Pechora.'

'And if they decided to fire the weapons?'

'Each bomb will have a unique identifier, just like the Sky card in your satellite TV receiver at home. If they want to fire the Los Angeles weapon, the operator selects the code for the Los Angeles bomb, chooses "Detonate" or whatever, and a couple of minutes later a substantial part of Los Angeles turns into a cloud of dust. If they want to fire them all at once, they just select all the weapon codes simultaneously and go through the same routine.'

There was a long silence. 'The operator?' Richter asked. 'Where is he? At Krutaya?'

'He can be anywhere,' Baker said. 'That's the point of the armoured telephone cables. They carry the signals to and from the uplink station, but they also allow authorized access to the computer from anywhere else in Russia, or in fact from anywhere in the world. The guys actually sitting in the building at Krutaya looking at the computer screens will probably be mainly low-grade maintenance staff. Their job is simply to monitor the physical health of the computer, if you like. They'll be the ones doing tape back-ups of the program and data files, running diagnostic utilities, checking that the air-conditioning is working and that the lavatories aren't leaking over the power supply, that kind of thing.

'The real operators,' he continued, 'are in Moscow, probably at Yazenevo. They log on to the Krutaya computer via the telephone lines, and give instructions to the program from there. They never need go to Krutaya – in fact, there's no need for them even to know where the computer actually is. All they need is a telephone number, a username and a password. That's the beauty of the system. That's its flexibility. It's also,' he added, 'our way in.'

'Oh yes?' Richter said.

'Modin told you that the satellite could disarm the weapons, temporarily or permanently. All we have to do is hack our way into the Krutaya computer, convince it that we're an authorized user, and then instruct it to permanently disable all the weapons.'

They all looked at him. 'And how easy is that going to be?' Simpson asked.

'If the Russian programmers were any good,' Baker replied, 'it'll be sodding difficult. Finding the computer's telephone number is the easy bit – one of my computers is doing that now, which is why I've got the time to sit here and explain it all to you. The problem is the username and password.'

'And how do you get them?' Richter asked.

'Well, the system itself may help us. A lot of very powerful computer networks actually provide help screens so that a new user can work out how to use the system. I think it's unlikely, at best, that the Krutaya computer will have a facility like that. Assuming that it hasn't, we're back to trial and error – we just try every username and password that we can think of. That's standard practice for computer hackers. There are a few tricks of the trade that we can try, but unlike most hackers we do have one big advantage – we know a lot of the names associated with this project. Modin, Bykov, Trushenko and so on. One of the almost infallible rules of computer science is that if you tell anyone to think of a password, they invariably use a name or a date or a place known to them. All we have to do is find which name, date or place they selected. And that,' he added, looking across at Richter, 'is where you come in.'

10 Downing Street, London

'I understand what you are saying, Mr Prime Minister,' Mikhail Viktorovich Sharov, the Russian Ambassador Extraordinary and Plenipotentiary to the Court of St James, said, somewhat petulantly, 'but the whole tale sounds to me like a work of fiction. Certainly I have no knowledge of any of the matters you have talked about.'

Sharov had been summoned, peremptorily, from his official residence at Harrington House in Kensington Palace Gardens, and was not in the best of tempers. His mood was matched by that of the Prime Minister, who had concluded an interview with Sir Michael Geraghty, the Secret Intelligence Service chief, some fifty minutes earlier.

'This is not fiction, Mr Ambassador,' the Prime Minister said, his voice hard and cold, 'this is fact. The proof was found in the back of a Russian lorry we had stopped in France. We can show you the device itself, if you wish, together with photographs of the alleged Russian diplomats who were accompanying it.'

'Photographs can be faked,' Sharov said, with a faint smile.

'Of course they can,' the Prime Minister snapped, 'but the nuclear device cannot.'

Sharov shook his head. 'A deception operation, Mr Prime Minister,' he said. 'It is a crude ploy by the American CIA to discredit us.'

The Englishman leaned forward. 'It would have to have been a very clever deception operation by the Americans, Mr Ambassador, to have also planted an identical nuclear weapon in the locked hold of a Russian cargo ship.'

Sharov looked shocked. 'What Russian cargo ship?'

'The *Anton Kirov*, Mr Ambassador, which we seized in Gibraltar Harbour a few hours ago. This weapon was to be detonated at Gibraltar as a demonstration of the power of these new nuclear devices your scientists have developed, and to encourage the rest of Europe to fall into line.' The Prime Minister lowered his voice. 'You may also be interested to learn that we disarmed this weapon a matter of seconds before an attempt was made to detonate it.' He paused, and looked straight into Sharov's eyes. 'If the weapon had been successfully detonated,' he said, 'we believe that virtually the entire population of Gibraltar, and most of the Spanish living in La Linea and Algeciras, would have been annihilated.

'What you should also know,' the Prime Minister went on, his voice like steel, 'is that these deaths – these needless deaths of completely innocent people – would not have been the last. Most of the population of Moscow, St Petersburg and Gor'kiy would have shared their fate within minutes.'

'I am not certain I follow you, Mr Prime Minister,' Sharov said.

'It's quite simple, Mr Ambassador,' the Prime Minister said, a slight, and completely mirthless, smile on his face. 'I have issued most specific orders to my nuclear commanders. The moment any nuclear weapon is detonated anywhere in Europe, the entire ballistic missile inventory of the two British nuclear submarines – *Vanguard* and *Victorious* – will be launched without delay and without warning.'

'You cannot do that, Mr Prime Minister,' Sharov said, rising to his feet, red-faced and almost shouting.

'I can, and I have. I suggest that you convey this information to your masters in Moscow immediately. You can also tell them that all the Trident missiles in both submarines have been re-targeted. No military installations have been included, only Moscow, St Petersburg and Gor'kiy. We are aiming for the total destruction of these three cities and the maximum possible loss of life.' There was a short, appalled silence before the Prime Minister continued. 'Your masters should also be informed that both these submarines have been ordered to patrol areas very close to the coast of the Confederation of Independent States. The missile flight time, I have been told, will only be a few minutes, perhaps five minutes at the most.

'You have my most solemn assurance,' the Englishman added, 'that the three principal cities in Russia will cease to exist no later than ten minutes after any of the devices your agents have planted in Europe is detonated. Russia,' he concluded, 'is not the only country that can play at nuclear blackmail.'

Hammersmith, London

Richter had never been into the Computer Suite before, and Baker gave him a swift guided tour. 'You noticed the door as you came in?' he asked.

'Not particularly,' Richter replied.

'It's sheathed with copper,' Baker said, 'with bonding strips on the hinge side to ensure a good contact. The entire room – walls, floor and ceiling – are also lined with copper. Basically, you're inside a huge Faraday Cage.'

'I read Classics,' Richter said. 'What exactly is a Faraday Cage?'

Baker looked at him with something approaching despair. 'In simple terms—'

'They're the best kind,' Richter murmured.

'In simple terms, it's an electronic shield. It stops any of the emanations from the computers being detected outside the building – in fact, outside this suite. We're going to sheath the entire building later this year, and then every office will be fitted with its own terminal.' He paused. 'Have you ever heard of TEMPEST?'

'No,' Richter replied.

'OK, it's a programme initiated by the Pentagon in the 1980s which covered electronic products used by government and defence agencies. It specifies things like radio frequency shielding, power-filtering on lines and so on. It's now been adopted by most other Western nations, and it's been fully implemented here.'

They walked through double doors into a very large room. The noise struck Richter first – a quiet, but quite distinct humming and chattering sound – and then Baker moved his arm in an expansive gesture. 'This,' he said, 'is my baby.'

Richter looked at the machine. Tall, dark blue cabinets, flashing red lights. It was huge, and he'd never seen anything like it before. 'What is it?' he asked.

Baker gave a very poor imitation of Clint Eastwood playing Dirty Harry. 'This is the most powerful super-computer in the world,' he said. 'This is a Cray–2.'

'OK,' Richter said. 'I'm impressed. What's a Cray–2?'

His ignorance was beginning to tell on Baker, and he shook his head sadly. 'In the 1950s,' he said, 'an American computer expert called Seymour Cray designed the world's first super-computer, which he called the Cray–1, and in 1976 he sold the first machine to a production plant in Chippewa Falls, Minnesota. The Cray–1 occupied only seventy square feet of floor space, but it weighed over five tons and contained two hundred thousand integrated circuits, nearly three and a half thousand printed circuit boards and sixty miles of wire. But what made the Cray–1 different from every other computer available then was its speed. It ran over one hundred times faster than the quickest IBM machine, and performed its calculations at the rate of two hundred and fifty mips.'

'Hold it,' Richter said. 'You're starting to lose me – again. What's a mip?'

'There's no singular form – it's a plural acronym that stands for a Million Instructions Per Second. To put that into everyday terms, that means the Cray–1 could transfer about three hundred and twenty million words – that's the text of about two and a half thousand average-size novels – every second. And that,' he added, 'was back in 1976.'

'I am impressed,' Richter said, and this time he actually he was.

'You should be. But this machine is the next generation. The Cray–2 operates at three thousand mips – that's twelve times faster than the Cray–1. You need government – American government – approval to order one, and it costs a bloody fortune to buy, but it's the best there is, and it's the only machine capable of doing some jobs.'

'What do you do with it?'

Baker looked somewhat sly. 'I'm not allowed to tell you the specifics,' he said, 'but I can say that we work in conjunction with GCHQ and SIS doing data processing.'

'OK,' Richter said. He felt they had drifted somewhat from the matter at hand. 'The Krutaya computer?'

'Oh, yes,' Baker said. 'Follow me.' He led the way through the main room and into a small office. It had a large desk, two upright chairs and a couple of armchairs. On the desk was another computer.

'Is this a terminal attached to the Cray?' Richter asked.

Baker looked slightly surprised. 'No,' he said. 'This is a pretty standard PC – personal computer. You can buy one of these in Dixons. We can't use the Cray for this job. We're limited by hardware considerations, and I'll explain that a bit later. We're also restricted in what outside links we are allowed to make with the Cray, for security reasons. Any hostile intelligence service would just love to tap into the

Cray's data banks, which is why we've got it hard-wired to only three other computers.'

Richter could see why some people thought Baker was a computer nerd. 'You mentioned outside links and hardware problems. Can you translate that into English for me?'

'Certainly,' Baker replied. 'What this computer is doing is looking for another computer in Russia. The outside links are the telephone lines it's using, and the hardware considerations are principally the speed of data transfer down those lines. The Cray is simply too fast and too powerful for this kind of work. The slowest part of the system is the telephone line. It's designed to carry analogue signals – the human voice – not data.

'The other problem is external noise,' he went on, 'the pops and crackles that you hear on most telephone lines. That can corrupt the data stream, which means that computers talk to each other using packets of data. Instead of sending an entire data file, the calling computer sends a packet of data and at the end of it a thing called a checksum. A checksum is a number that corresponds to the amount of data transmitted; the receiving computer adds up the units of data and calculates its own checksum. If that is the same as that sent by the first computer, it sends a message approving the transfer of the next data packet. If it isn't, then it asks for the previous packet of data to be sent again. That's the simplest method – there are a lot of much more sophisticated error-detecting protocols that can be used. All this, of course, is done by the computers – the operator is unaware that it's going on at all, but you can see how it slows data transfer down, especially on noisy lines.'

That more or less made sense to Richter. He looked at the computer screen. The background was blue, and there were three headings in red across the top – 'Code', 'Number' and 'Description'. White numbers were appearing in a vertical row below the 'Code' and 'Number' headings, about one every five to ten seconds, and immediately before the next number appeared, a line of text was generated under the 'Description' heading on the line above. 'What's it doing?' Richter asked.

Baker sighed. 'I've already explained that it's looking for another computer in Russia.'

'I know that. I meant how, exactly, is it doing that?'

'Ah, that's the clever bit.'

'I was afraid it would be,' Richter said, and sat down.

'It's running an auto-dialler program,' Baker replied. 'It's trying every possible telephone number within the Komi district of Russia.'

'That could take days,' Richter said.

'It's been running for several hours – since about an hour after you talked to General Modin, in fact,' Baker said. 'Actually it's not taking as long as I had calculated. The Komi district is pretty sparsely populated. A lot of it is swamp and the foothills of the Urals intrude to the east. About the only sizeable towns are Ukhta and Syktyvkar, and don't forget that telephones in Russia – especially rural Russia, which is most of it – are still pretty rare, so a high proportion of the possible numbers don't even exist.'

'What does it do when a number answers?'

'It listens,' Baker said. 'If it hears a voice, the computer breaks the connection and dials the next number in the sequence. If nobody answers after twenty seconds, or if it hears a fax tone – rarer still in Komi – it breaks the connection, but if it detects a modem, it logs the number for future action, and then breaks the connection.'

Light was slowly dawning. 'Isn't it a risk,' Richter asked, 'using a computer based here at FOE?'

Baker smiled happily. 'I was hoping you'd ask that, because it means you've been listening to what I've been saying. The answer is yes, it would be, if we were using this computer.'

'You've lost me again.'

'That's the really clever bit. What I've done is establish communications with a computer in our Embassy in Moscow – not in the Holy of Holies, of course. That computer in Moscow,' Baker went on, 'is actually making the calls. If anyone runs a back-trace down the line, Moscow is where the trail will stop.' A bell rang somewhere, and Baker excused himself to answer it. He returned pushing a small trolley covered with the files Richter had ordered from the Registry. He had requested all the files FOE held having any connection with the

Komi district, personnel files on known senior officers in the SVR and GRU, including Bykov and Modin, and on previous KGB and GRU operations. According to Baker, popular passwords in the Royal Navy include famous naval victories, like Trafalgar and Taranto, and Russian officers might well feel the same about past triumphs.

What appalled Richter was the size of the pile, but he sat down and started working his way through it.

Kutuzovskij prospekt, Moscow

The two cars parked directly outside the apartment building and seven men got out. They stood for a few moments in a group on the pavement, then entered the building together.

Genady Arkenko hadn't seen them arrive, but he heard them outside the apartment, just before they kicked down the door. His last act as a faithful friend and devoted lover of Dmitri Trushenko was to press the speed-dial code for Trushenko's mobile number and leave the phone off the hook and out of sight. That way, Arkenko hoped, Trushenko would hear what happened.

Hammersmith, London

Four minutes later, the computer emitted a single peremptory 'beep' and the numbers stopped appearing. Baker put down his mug of coffee and sat in front of the screen. 'Let's see what we've got.' He pressed a couple of keys and the screen display changed. The legend 'Autodial Record' appeared at the top, and under it the headings 'Number' and 'Identification if known'. There were fifteen numbers listed.

'Only fifteen?' Richter asked.

'It's about what I expected,' Baker said, and pointed at the right-hand column. 'Eight of these numbers have already been identified by the computer as belonging to the LPAR site at Pechora. As soon as a modem tone is detected, a sub-routine on the program accesses a database of known numbers and attempts a match. If it finds one, it displays the identification.'

'So there are seven unknown computers in the area?'

'Possibly,' said Baker. 'If you look at the numbers, we can probably eliminate one, because it's only two digits different from one of the known numbers at Pechora. I think we've only got six to try.' He pressed a key and the list appeared on a sheet of paper in the output tray of the laser printer sitting next to the computer.

'How will you know when you've got the right computer?' Richter asked.

'We'll know,' Baker said, 'because it won't want to let us in.'

Razdolnoye, Krym (Crimea)

Dmitri Trushenko answered the phone immediately. He had been watching the television, expecting news of the explosion at Gibraltar, and he had become increasingly agitated when he had heard nothing. He had logged on again to the weapon control system through his computer, but that had only confirmed that the firing signal had been sent by the mainframe and presumably, therefore, received by the weapon, not that detonation had actually occurred. 'Yes, Genady?' he said into the mouthpiece.

He heard no voice, just a splintering sound, then heavy footsteps, loud but indistinct voices, the sound of blows and then a single piercing wail of pain, abruptly silenced. He listened intently, trying to make sense of the noises. Finally, there was nothing but the sound of breathing, and then a click as the telephone handset was replaced on its cradle. Trushenko knew that the caller had to have been Genady, and that meant that his lover had been taken by the SVR. It also meant that the SVR had discovered his communications link and that, in turn, meant that *Podstava* was blown.

He sat for a few minutes, his eyes filling with tears at the thought of dear, gentle Genady. Then he made a decision. Genady Arkenko had been his lover for nearly forty years – longer than most marriages – and someone was going pay for what he was suffering. He would not fail him.

Trushenko walked across to the table, sat down and switched on his computer. He connected the telephone lead, loaded the communications software, auto-dialled the number through the modem and his mobile telephone and logged on to the distant mainframe.

Chapter Twenty-Six

Thursday
Hammersmith, London

Baker took manual control of the Moscow computer, and instructed the communications module to dial the first number. The screen cleared, and the terse message 'Dialing' appeared in the top left-hand corner, followed by the number. There was a brief pause, and Richter heard a faint warbling sound as the two computers communicated with each other, and then a symbolic representation of a computer appeared, and under it the message, in Cyrillic script:

WELCOME TO THE SYKTYVKAR BULLETIN BOARD
Type <?> for Help. If this is your first log on, use Username and Password
<GUEST>

Under that appeared 'Enter Username' with a flashing cursor. 'I take it that isn't it,' Richter said, as he translated the Russian text for Baker.

'No,' Baker replied. 'That definitely isn't it. That's just a bulletin board – a kind of electronic conference – run by a bunch of computer enthusiasts in Syktyvkar.' He looked down the list. 'I think we can skip the next number, because it's almost certainly a second line for the same bulletin board. Let's try the third.'

The fifth computer responded entirely differently to all the others. Once the number had dialled, there was no welcoming screen, no text at all, in fact, just a small flashing cursor in the top left of the screen. Baker looked at Richter. 'This is probably the one,' he said.

The Walnut Room, the Kremlin, Krasnaya ploshchad, Moscow

The junior SVR officer knocked respectfully on the door before opening it. He looked at the men seated round the table, approached Yuri Baratov, saluted and handed him a sheet of paper. The SVR chief scanned the paper, then spoke. 'Trushenko's in the Crimea,' he said, to the table at large. 'We've identified the cell his phone was using, and we've ordered the system to disable his phone card. Konstantin Abramov has instructed local units to pick him up.'

Hammersmith, London

'This is where I need your help,' Baker said. 'I don't speak Russian, and we'll need to use Russian to get in. Let's see if there's any help available.' He pressed the '?' key, followed by 'Enter'. A line of Cyrillic script flashed up. 'What's that?' he asked.

'It says "Bad command or filename",' Richter said.

'Typical,' Baker said, and pressed the 'F1' key. 'That's the normal "help" key,' he added. The same message appeared. 'It looks as if there's no help incorporated, on the very sound premise that they don't want anybody unauthorized gaining access to the system. It's probably waiting for direct entry of a username and password.'

'Try "*Podstava*",' Richter suggested. That didn't work either, and almost immediately afterwards the screen went blank and the message in English 'Connection terminated by gateway: reverse trace detected' appeared.

Baker looked at the screen thoughtfully. 'This is definitely the right machine,' he said. 'As soon as an invalid username was entered, the computer started a trace back along the telephone network to see who was calling it.'

'Is that going to be a problem?' Richter asked.

'Well, it certainly isn't going to help. I've programmed the Moscow computer – that's our gateway – to sever the connection each time it detects a trace, but it means we can only try one word per connection, which is going to add minutes to the time it takes us to get in. It also means that I can't use a password generator.' Richter nodded as if he knew what he was talking about, but Baker wasn't fooled. 'A password generator,' he said, 'is a routine that starts off with, say, AAAAAA and runs through all possible combinations of characters, including all the numerals and punctuation symbols, until it generates a username or password that the system will accept. The trouble is, you have to stay on-line to use it, and this set-up won't let us. So we have to get the username some other way. And the password that matches it.'

'A username is the real name of a person who is authorized to access the computer?'

Baker nodded. 'Normally, yes, although there's nothing to stop somebody who has a long name using an abbreviation to log on, as long as the system manager has approved it. If the user's real name was Oblavenkavich or something, he would probably be allowed to shorten it to Oblavo or even use a nickname.'

'And the password,' Richter asked. 'Is it always a name, or can you use anything?'

'Anything at all,' Baker replied, 'the more random and illogical the better. The most difficult password to crack is something like this –' he scribbled '%&reT34£' on a piece of paper '– but the trouble is that the user can never remember it unless he writes it down, which defeats the object of the exercise. So, as I said before, most people use names or birthdays or something like that. The other common passwords are Secret, Confidential, Keepout and Mine, all of which are moderately obvious, Fred and derf – fred backwards.'

'Why Fred?' Richter asked.

Baker grinned. 'Those letters are immediately adjacent to each other on the keyboard, and most computer users are lazy.'

Razdolnoye, Krym (Crimea)

Dmitri Trushenko stared at the screen of his laptop in irritation. The connection to the mainframe had failed, which meant that he had to re-dial and log on all over again. He pressed the keys angrily, and waited. The screen displayed the message 'Dialing' with the mainframe's telephone number beneath it. After two minutes, the screen message 'Connection timed out. Redial?' appeared.

Trushenko snatched up his mobile phone and unplugged the data cable. He input a number at random, pressed the 'Send' key and waited. Almost immediately he heard a beeping sound in the earpiece and the message 'Emergency calls only' was displayed on the phone's small screen. Instantly Trushenko knew what had happened. The SVR had identified his mobile telephone number, and disabled his phone's card. That also, he realized, meant that they knew more or less where he was.

He left the phone on the table – it was useless to him now, and would serve to mislead the SVR, as it would continue to show him as being in the Crimea as long as it remained switched on – quickly shoved the computer and his clothes into a suitcase, and walked outside.

Hammersmith, London

In the next half hour Baker tried every word Richter could think of connected with the Russian operation, including Gibraltar, the names of the French and German towns where Modin had told him neutron bombs were positioned, Modin, Bykov, Trushenko, Kremlin, Moscow, Lubyanka and Yazenevo spelt forwards and backwards, in upper case and lower case, KGB, GRU, SVR, GroupNord, and even the names of past Soviet heroes like Sorge, Abel, Philby and Blunt.

With a single exception, the screen blanked each time and the Moscow computer severed the connection. The exception was 'Modin', and when Baker entered that name, the system prompted for a password, but none of the suggestions Richter made were accepted.

'Let's take a break,' Richter said, 'and think about this.'

Baker made instant coffee in the corner of the office. 'Is it worth trying the Russian for secret and so on?' Richter asked, taking a chipped china mug.

Baker shook his head. 'I doubt it. This system will have an administrator who will have access to all passwords, and who should vet them. If he's doing his job correctly he wouldn't allow anything that simple to be used.' Baker shook his head. 'We need a name, or a word—'

Richter almost spilled his coffee. He had suddenly remembered something that hadn't really made sense before. 'Christ,' he said, 'I am slow.' He reached for the phone, dialled the Registry and told them to deliver the file on Graham Newman to the Computer Suite. 'I think I know what one password is,' Richter said.

Karkinitskiy Zaliv, Chernoye More (Black Sea)

The closest SVR area headquarters to the Crimea is at Odessa, but there are smaller SVR units at Sevastopol, Simferopol and Kerch. The message from SVR headquarters at Yazenevo had instructed that the two roads out of the Crimea, through Krasnoperekopsk and Novoalekseyevka, were to be closed to all motor vehicles, the two railway lines closed to all traffic, and ferry operations from the port of Krym to Kavkaz suspended. Stopping the ferry and closing the railway lines were easy – it took two phone calls – but the roads were different. SVR teams set out immediately from Simferopol to reinforce the roadblocks erected by the local police forces, but the traffic queues built up rapidly and there were angry confrontations.

Dmitri Trushenko was not a fool. He had chosen the Crimea deliberately because it is effectively an island, with very limited access and egress, and he had anticipated that if anything went wrong the SVR or one of the other authorities would block the roads. That was why he had bought the powerboat. Fifteen minutes after walking out of the *dacha*, Trushenko was two miles offshore and heading north-west at twenty-eight knots across the Karkinitskiy Zaliv towards Port-Khorly, where he had left a car. The trip would take him about forty-five minutes, and he anticipated that he could be back on-line to the mainframe, using an ordinary landline telephone, in a little over an hour.

10 Downing Street, London

The Prime Minister had used the hot-line and secure telephone circuits to talk to the President of the United States more often in the last three days than he had done throughout his entire term of office. The two men had enjoyed, almost from their well-publicized first meeting, a relationship that transcended the purely official functions of their respective offices and had turned into real friendship. And that friendship had helped the two of them face the similar, but in some ways very different, threats posed by Dmitri Trushenko's Operation *Podstava*.

It would be too much to say that Britain and America were working together to combat the Russian assault, because Trushenko had placed them in completely different positions – there were no pre-positioned weapons on British soil, but there were over two hundred in place in American cities – and the strategic assets of the two nations were wholly dissimilar. But both men had decided that the best way to combat the threat was to threaten the Russians just as hard, to take up a totally uncompromising, and non-negotiable, position.

'What targeting instructions have you given?' the President asked.

'A blanket assault,' the Prime Minister replied, 'aimed at Moscow, St Petersburg and Gor'kiy. No military targets at all, just the major civilian population centres.'

'And you've told the Russian ambassador? Sharov?'

'Yes. I'm certain he knew all about *Podstava* – you could see it in his face when I told him about the weapon we stopped in France. But what shocked him was that we'd also found and disarmed the one in Gibraltar. He knew there was going to be a demonstration, as that Russian bastard Trushenko put it, but he didn't know where. He's probably been talking to the Kremlin ever since, trying to find out what he's supposed to do now.'

'That was good work by your people,' the President said.

'Thank you. I hope that we may have some other good news for you later today,' he added. 'We have a team hard at work trying to break into the computer in Russia which we believe controls this entire operation.'

'You have?' the President's voice rose in hope and surprise. 'If you require any assistance, anything at all, just ask. We have some of the best computer scientists in the world working at the National Security Agency. I'm sure they could—'

The Prime Minister's soft chuckle interrupted him. 'Believe me, I've already offered your resources as well as our own, but the people involved have told me that outside assistance will not be required. I don't pretend to understand the technicalities of it, but apparently they can only use one line to access the Russian computer, so the two men who are working on it—'

'Two men?' the President interrupted. 'Only two men? Good God, I hope they know what they're doing.'

'I think they do,' the Prime Minister said smoothly. 'One of them is the man who stopped the road convoy in France and disarmed the weapon in Gibraltar.'

Hammersmith, London

When the courier arrived, Richter took the file and flicked through it until he reached the notes he had made following his meeting with Piers Taylor of SIS. As Richter read them, he realized that the answer had been staring him in the face all along, and that Graham Newman might have had an inkling that something was going on at Krutaya, even if he had no idea what it was. Richter thought he now knew why he had sent Andrew Payne to Sosnogorsk, and what the exchange of messages probably meant.

'The SIS Head of Station in Moscow sent his deputy – a man called Andrew Payne – out to Sosnogorsk in June,' Richter said. 'Officially, he was acting as a translator to a party of European businessmen, but the real reason he went was to contact a Russian called Nicolai Karelin and exchange messages. The messages,' he went on, 'consisted only of single words. He said *Schtchit* to Karelin, and the Russian replied with *Stukach* and *Chernozhopy*.'

Richter wrote the words on a piece of paper, together with the name of the Russian contact. 'Try *Schtchit* first,' Richter suggested.

Baker looked at the paper. 'What's that mean?' he asked.

'The actual meaning is "shield",' Richter said, 'but it has a more specific meaning to GRU personnel. It's a particular kind of double-exposure film that allows an operative to take two sets of pictures, one entirely innocent – the family playing on the beach, that sort of thing. The other set can be of anything he likes – classified documents, secret military installations or whatever. If the film is developed normally, all that the prints will show are the innocent pictures, but if the correct developing technique is used, the other images will appear.'

'All clever stuff and no rubbish,' Baker said, and watched the screen as the Moscow computer dialled Krutaya again. When the prompt appeared, he typed the word in, and they watched. Again, the screen went blank and the computer in the Moscow Embassy severed the connection.

'Shit,' Richter said. 'I really thought we had it. Try *Stukach*.' Baker typed in the word at the prompt, but again the screen blanked out as the connection was terminated. 'This is our last chance. Type *Chernozhopy*.'

'*Chernozhopy*,' Baker repeated, trying to get his tongue around it. 'What's it mean?'

'Literally,' Richter replied, 'it means "black-arses", but it's a GRU slang term meaning any foreigners.' Baker typed it, but the result was the same. 'Oh, shit.' Richter closed his eyes and leant back in the chair, then sat forward suddenly. 'A thought,' he said. 'Try the name of the Russian contact – Nicolai Karelin.'

Baker instructed the Moscow computer to dial the number again and tried 'Nicolai', without success.

'OK,' Richter said. 'Now try Karelin.' This time Baker typed in 'Karelin' at the prompt. The connection didn't break, and almost immediately another line of text appeared.

'Yes!' Baker said loudly. 'That's more like it. It looks like a password request.'

'That's what it says,' Richter agreed, nodding and leaning forwards. 'Try *Stukach*.' Immediately after Baker had typed the word, another line of text appeared. 'It says "incorrect password",' Richter said. 'Try *Chernozhopy*, then *Schtchit*. This really is our last chance.'

As Baker finished typing *Chernozhopy* and pressed the 'Enter' key, the screen cleared and a series of messages were displayed. Richter didn't understand what they meant, but they made sense to Baker. 'Thank God for that,' he said. 'We're in. It looks like it's UNIX-based – that's just a type of operating system, don't worry about it – and we are logged on.'

Richter pointed at the screen. 'There's the username Karelin,' he said. 'So Nicolai Karelin must be an authorized user of this system, and the name he passed to Payne was his password into the computer.'

'Excellent,' said Baker. 'Now we're cooking. Let's see what we can do. It all depends,' he went on, 'on Karelin's access level.'

'What's an access level?'

'It's a means of regulating the facilities which each user can access. In a business, for example, the higher management personnel will have access to all the data files, but the accounts staff only to accounts programs and associated data, and typists just to the word processor and the letter files. You can compartmentalize the computer's files in any way you like, but that would be a typical set-up. The most important user is the system supervisor or manager. He alone has access to everything – data and system files – at all times, and he can delete, copy or move files as he wishes, all as part of his job managing the network. What I'm hoping is that Karelin isn't just a low-grade user. I'm hoping he's the system administrator.'

'Is he likely to be?' Richter asked.

'Probably not,' said Baker. 'My gut feeling is that the administrator is probably based at Yazenevo. Anyway, we'll see in a couple of minutes.' While he'd been talking, Baker had been studying the screen. 'It looks like a fairly standard menu-based system,' he said. 'Can you just translate what these words mean for me?'

Richter looked at the screen. 'There are only two headings,' he said. 'The first means Satellite Maintenance, and the second Weapon Maintenance.'

Baker looked disappointed. 'I would have expected more than that,' he said. 'Still, let's have a look inside.' He selected Weapon Maintenance and Richter watched as a new screen of options was displayed. He ran down the list for Baker, translating each heading. Baker slumped low in the chair and shook his head. 'These are all low-grade functions – there's nothing here we can use to access the weapon control program. It looks as if Karelin is just a local operator, and he's locked out of all the other options.'

'Can you by-pass the security controls and access the weapon control functions?'

Baker considered this for a moment. 'Possibly,' he said, 'but it would take a hell of a long time – days, maybe. This system's been designed by someone who knew what they were doing, and I'd need to do a lot of playing around with it to get anywhere.'

'The clock's running,' Richter reminded him.

'I know,' Baker said, and looked across at him. 'I think we're up shit creek. Unless we can find another password – a password for the system administrator or some high-level user – I don't think we're going to crack this.'

Kherson, Prichernomorskaya Nizmennost' District, Ukraine

Captain Valentin Ivanovich Kabanov was a Ukrainian peasant by birth, and had spent all his working life in the SVR, most of it in and around Odessa. He had begun as a clerk, but his active brain and keen powers of observation had quickly elevated him, despite his lack of higher-level education, to field status.

When the alert message about Trushenko had arrived from Yazenevo, Kabanov had been directing a surveillance operation on the outskirts of Kherson, where the Dnieper drains into the Black Sea. The Odessa SVR operations room controller had called Kabanov on his mobile phone as a matter of course, but as the search for Trushenko was centred on the Crimea, there had been no obvious action for him and his team of five officers to undertake. At least, there had been no formal orders given, but Kabanov had not reached his present station in life waiting around for orders to be given.

He made two telephone calls to pull three of his team off the surveillance operation, then reached for a map of the Crimea and the Prichernomorskaya Nizmennost' District and studied it carefully. The alert message from Yazenevo had not been very specific, but as Kabanov looked at the map, the more sure he became that the roadblocks were in the wrong place. If he had been looking for a place to hide, the island that was the Crimea would have been a long way down on his list. Unless, of course, the rebel minister had another way out.

Fifteen minutes later, Kabanov was briefing the Odessa SVR duty officer on his mobile phone as his two-car convoy sped south-east through Tsyurupinsk on the main road from Kherson to Kalanchak and Port-Khorly.

Hammersmith, London

'I have a feeling,' Richter said, 'that I'm missing something here.'

'Apart from the system manager's password, you mean?' Baker said.

Something was bothering Richter. Something somebody had said, or hadn't said. Like a half-remembered dream, it was lurking at the very edge of his memory. He closed his eyes and leaned back in his chair, willing his mind to go blank, to become as receptive as possible.

Baker looked at him curiously. He had heard a lot about Richter – staff gossip was just as prevalent at FOE as in any other close-knit organization – and Richter's name had figured prominently in many of the stories he had heard or half-heard. Usually, the stories had involved violence of one sort or another; a mystic Richter was something altogether new.

Suddenly, Richter sat forward, his blue eyes snapping open. 'The phone,' he said. 'Give me the phone.'

Port-Khorly, Prichernomorskaya Nizmennost' District, Ukraine

Dmitri Trushenko nosed the powerboat slowly through the port entrance and eased it gently alongside the jetty. It was a big boat for one man to control when mooring, but Trushenko was an accomplished boat-handler and had no difficulty. The jetty was deserted, apart from one elderly man slumped against a bollard with a fishing rod across his lap. When Trushenko looked closely at him, he realized that his eyes were closed.

Trushenko had parked the car as close as he could to the jetty, but it was still ten minutes before he unlocked the door and slid behind the wheel. The engine fired at the first turn of the key; he slid the car into gear and headed towards the centre of Port-Khorly.

On the jetty, the elderly man put down the fishing rod, sat upright and looked round cautiously as soon as he heard the sound of Trushenko's receding footsteps. Then he climbed to his feet and walked towards the centre of the port, feeling in his pocket for some kopecks to make a local phone call. Like the KGB which preceded it, the SVR had eyes everywhere.

Hammersmith, London

'Good afternoon. American Embassy. How may I help you?'

'Roger Abrahams, please,' Richter said.

There was a brief pause, then the switchboard operator replied. 'I'm not sure we have anyone here of that name.' Standard procedure. None of the names of the CIA officers were a matter of public record, and the switchboard had standing orders to reject any caller who asked for a CIA officer by name.

'Lady,' Richter said slowly, 'this is an open line, which I know you're recording. I know Roger Abrahams personally. He's your Agency Chief of Station, and I need to speak to him immediately. If he's available, I would also like to speak to John Westwood, and you certainly don't want me to tell you who he is on this line.'

There was a short silence, and then a male voice spoke. 'Who is this?'

'Richter. Is that you, Roger?'

'Yup. What gives?'

Richter paused, choosing his words with some care. 'It's about that matter in France that John and I were involved in,' he said. 'We're trying to bring it to a final conclusion, and we need some help, right now. Our colleague from the east said something that we think might be important. He said,' Richter continued, 'that your Company and mine had to work very closely together, so I'm wondering if you've received something that we haven't.'

'Like what?' Abrahams asked.

'A word, a number, a name. Anything like that. We need it for access to the project we've been working on, if you see what I mean.'

'Stand by,' the American replied. 'I'll check.'

Port-Khorly, Prichernomorskaya Nizmennost' District, Ukraine

The other reason Trushenko had chosen Port-Khorly was because there were several small hotels and guesthouses there, catering to the crews of the ships which docked in the harbour. Trushenko parked the car in a side street and walked the final few hundred yards to his destination. As a government Minister, Trushenko had no need of travel passes or any other documentation, and he checked into the principal hotel without problems. He specified the largest room available, and insisted on a direct telephone line being provided through the hotel's switchboard.

Twenty minutes after he had walked away from his boat, he was ready to log on again.

Hammersmith, London

'You still there?'

'Yes,' said Richter.

'The only thing that we've received that might fit is a single word,' Abrahams said. 'It doesn't mean anything to us, but it might to you.'

'What is it?' Richter asked, picking up a pencil.

'The word is *Pripiska*,' Abrahams said, and spelt it.

'Thanks. Can you tell me where it came from?' Richter asked.

'From our source in the east. It came in a message, but without any explanation.'

'That's pretty much what I hoped you'd say. I'll get back to you, Roger,' Richter said, and put down the phone. Richter looked across at Baker. 'Here,' he said, sliding the paper across the desk. 'Try "Modin" again, then this.'

Prichernomorskaya Nizmennost' District, Ukraine

Valentin Kabanov knew Port-Khorly well. As a young man he had enjoyed sitting in the port, watching the ships arriving and departing and wondering to what exotic destinations they were bound. He also knew the local chief of police as a personal friend, and had telephoned him as soon as he had ended the call to Odessa. 'Any stranger – that means anyone not known personally to one of your officers or to a prominent local citizen – who has arrived in the town today by boat or car is to be apprehended,' Kabanov instructed.

'Why are you so sure he's here?'

'I'm not sure,' Kabanov replied. 'But I'm assuming this man is not so stupid as to allow himself to be bottled up in the Crimea. That means he had to have an escape route planned, and the only sensible escape method would be by boat. We know he was staying on the north-west side of the Crimea – somewhere in the vicinity of Razdolnoye or Krasnoperekopsk – so if he had a boat, Port-Khorly would be his most likely destination.'

'That makes sense,' the police chief responded, 'but finding him could take hours.'

'We don't have hours,' Kabanov said. The alert message had stressed the urgency of the situation. 'Use all available resources. Pull in all your off-duty officers, and call all your informers and agents. Call all the hotels and check all new registrations. Finding this man has the highest possible priority, and that instruction comes straight from Moscow.' The leading car made the right turn off the main road at Kalanchak as Kabanov terminated the call.

Hammersmith, London

Baker typed in 'Modin' at the prompt, and then '*Pripiska*', and immediately accessed the system. As with Karelin's log on, a welcome message was displayed at the top, but with a much larger options menu below it.

'That's different,' Richter said.

'Damn right it is,' Baker replied. He pointed at the screen. 'What's that say?'

Richter looked at the welcome message. 'It says "Welcome, General Modin",' he said. 'And the line below that translates as "Status – Principal User".'

Baker actually clapped his hands. 'Brilliant,' he said. 'This General Modin has high-level access – he's a principal user. We've really got them now.'

'I know I'll regret asking this,' Richter said, 'but what exactly is a principal user?'

Baker's fingers were flying over the keyboard as he accessed the menu system. 'It depends on what the administrator defined in his user categories, but it should mean he can do pretty much whatever he likes on the system. He can change settings and specifications, maybe even detonate the weapons. He can make almost any changes he wants without reference to anybody else. The only higher levels would be a super-user, the system designer and the administrator. I wonder,' he said, 'how the Americans got hold of his password?'

'I'll tell you later,' Richter said, and looked at the screen. Immediately he could see the differences in the displayed menu. There were five headings, not two, and he translated the new ones for Baker. 'That's Weapon Control,' he said, 'then there's Network Control and the last is System Utilities.'

Baker rubbed his hands. 'We'll start with the network, I think,' he said, and pressed a key. Richter always enjoyed watching an expert at work. His role was confined to that of translator, as Baker set about trying to disable the entire system. 'There are two stages,' he said, almost talking to himself. 'First we lock out the other users, then we sort out the bombs.' He turned to Richter. 'Could you feed me the right words when I ask for them? It doesn't matter much if we make mistakes now because we're actually in the system.'

Baker chose the Network Control menu item, looked down the list of choices and selected Current Log Ins, and watched as the screen changed. 'Two users on the system,' Baker said. 'We'll leave them until last. Now we'll try User Records.' That wasn't what he was looking for, but Username Table was. Baker printed a copy of all the usernames, plus the passwords for each one, then started to run down the list, changing each password as he went. He had barely started when a message appeared at the bottom of the screen.

Port-Khorly, Prichernomorskaya Nizmennost' District, Ukraine

Trushenko waited patiently, watching the screen, as the communications program logged on to the mainframe in Krutaya. Once he had connected, he instructed the computer to let him access the Weapon Control module.

Hammersmith, London

'What's that say?' Baker asked.

'"New logon",' Richter translated. 'The username is Trushenko. If that's the same Dmitri Trushenko who orchestrated this, he's trouble.'

'He's just logged on to the system,' Baker said. 'Maybe he's just another technician. Let's just see what his access level is.'

Baker scanned down the Username Table until he reached Trushenko. 'Oops,' Baker muttered. 'Trushenko is listed as a super-user.'

'Can you lock him out?'

'I don't know,' Baker said. 'I can change his password in the Username Table, which will stop him logging on again, but that won't affect what he can do now.'

Richter watched as Baker altered the password. 'What's he doing?' Richter asked.

Their principal-user access meant that they could literally look over user Trushenko's shoulders and see what actions he was performing. 'Oh, sweet Jesus,' Baker muttered. 'He's accessing the Weapon Control module.'

OVERKILL

The Walnut Room, the Kremlin, Krasnaya ploshchad, Moscow

'We missed him, Comrade President,' Yuri Baratov said. 'The local SVR officers found his mobile phone, still switched on, in a *dacha* at Razdolnoye on the north-west coast of Crimea.'

'What about the roadblocks?' the President asked.

Baratov shook his head. 'We think he left by boat. The police at Sevastopol have found records relating to the purchase of a high-speed powerboat in Trushenko's name. They're combing all the Black Sea ports for it now.' He paused. 'We'll find him, Comrade President,' he said, reassuringly.

The old Russian looked at him. 'Oh, I've no doubt you'll find him,' he replied. 'I just hope that when you do it won't be too late.'

Port-Khorly, Prichernomorskaya Nizmennost' District, Ukraine

Kabanov's phone buzzed as his car drove through the northern outskirts of Port-Khorly. 'Kabanov,' he said.

'We may have something,' the police chief said. 'A tall man was observed arriving here in a powerboat less than thirty minutes ago. We're checking the boat's registration—'

'Forget the boat,' Kabanov snapped. 'It's the man we're after. Where did he go?'

'At the moment, we don't know. Our informer thinks he drove away in a car, but can't be sure. He was too far away to see the suspect get into a car, but he is certain that a car was started and drove off a few minutes after the suspect reached the car-parking area.'

Kabanov absorbed the news in silence. 'What about the hotels?' he asked.

'We're checking them now. Nothing so far.'

'Let me know the instant you have anything,' Kabanov said. 'We've just arrived in the town, but we'll stay in the cars until I hear from you.'

*

Dmitri Trushenko paused, savouring the moment. Which one should he activate first? The first page of the Weapon Control module had three vertical columns. The left column listed ten American cities in alphabetical order, the second column showed the weapon yield, and the third the anticipated loss of life. There were twenty-three pages in all, listing two hundred and three weapons on American soil, plus fifteen in Europe.

Trushenko flipped through the pages until he came to the last one. Yes, he mused, that would be a satisfactory demonstration of the effectiveness of *Podstava*. He moved the cursor down the page until 'Washington D.C.' was highlighted. Then he pressed the 'Enter' key on his laptop and waited.

Hammersmith, London

Richter watched in horror as Dmitri Trushenko decided on the random annihilation of around a million people. 'Stop him, for God's sake,' he said.

'I don't know if I can,' Baker replied, and began scanning the options.

Port-Khorly, Prichernomorskaya Nizmennost' District, Ukraine

The screen on Trushenko's laptop changed and the boxed message 'Washington D.C. Weapon Enabled – Enter Authorization Code Three' appeared in the centre of it. Trushenko reached into his jacket pocket and extracted a slim diary. He opened it at the back page and placed the diary beside his computer.

Then he began to carefully enter on the keyboard the twelve random letters and numbers which constituted the first firing authorization code.

Hammersmith, London

Richter sat silent, because shouting wouldn't help. Baker was looking for any menu option that would enable him to disable the weapon or somehow override Trushenko's instructions.

'There's nothing,' Baker said, panic showing in his voice. 'There's no master override facility. I don't think we can stop this.'

Port-Khorly, Prichernomorskaya Nizmennost' District, Ukraine

At the first ring, Kabanov snatched up his mobile phone and pressed a button. 'Yes?'

'He's at the Hotel Metropole,' the police chief said. 'Room 25. It's on—'

'I know where it is,' Kabanov said. 'We're on our way.'

Hammersmith, London

'Wait,' Richter said. 'That code he's inputting.'

'Yes?'

'There must be a copy of it in the Krutaya computer. You know, to check that the right code is being input. Forget about looking for an override command – just change the system's authorization codes.'

'Brilliant,' Baker said, 'that's fucking brilliant,' and turned back to the keyboard.

Port-Khorly, Prichernomorskaya Nizmennost' District, Ukraine

The message on the laptop screen changed again. 'Authorization Code Three Accepted. For Final Verification, Enter Authorization Code Six'. Trushenko referred again to his diary and began carefully entering the letters and numbers.

Hammersmith, London

'What code has it asked for?' Baker demanded.

'Six,' Richter said.

Baker's fingers were moving rapidly over the keyboard. 'Got it,' he said.

Richter looked at the screen. The computer displayed the title 'Authorization Code List – Page One', and underneath it twenty horizontal lines of letters and numbers. Baker pressed the 'Print' button to save the original codes on paper, then swiftly moved the cursor down to Code Six. The last two digits were 'ДШ', so he altered them to 'ТД' and saved the change.

Port-Khorly, Prichernomorskaya Nizmennost' District, Ukraine

Trushenko sat back, puzzled. The laptop was displaying a message from the Krutaya mainframe – 'Authorization Code Six Not Accepted. Enter Authorization Code Ten'. He shook his head and referred again to his diary.

Hammersmith, London

'What code is that?' Baker asked.

The Cyrillic for 'ten' is 'ДЕСЯТЬ' – identical to 'ДЕВЯТЬ' – 'nine' – apart from one letter. Richter hadn't slept in something like thirty hours, and he was beginning to feel the strain. His eyes were tired and, because of his position slightly to one side of Baker, his view of the screen was somewhat distorted. All these factors combined into a single, dreadful mistake. Instead of the 'Ten' that the screen was displaying, Richter read the number as 'Nine'. 'Code Nine,' he said, and Baker obediently changed the last two digits on Code Nine.

'We can do this all day,' Baker said cheerfully, and leaned back in his chair.

OVERKILL

Port-Khorly, Prichernomorskaya Nizmennost' District, Ukraine

Trushenko had just entered the twelfth – and correct – digit of Code Ten when the hotel room door burst open. Three men stood there with drawn pistols. 'Minister Trushenko,' Captain Kabanov said, 'please step away from the computer.'

Dmitri Trushenko stood up to face them, and smiled. 'You are,' he said, 'too late. Much too late.' He turned away from the table, but then span back and hit the 'Enter' key.

Kabanov fired immediately. The first bullet hit Trushenko on his right arm, was deflected by the bone of his elbow, and shattered the screen of the laptop. The second shot entered Trushenko's left eye, killing him instantly As he fell, his arm caught the telephone cord and tore the plug out of the modem, breaking the connection a little under one hundredth of a second before the transmission of Code Ten was completed.

Chapter Twenty-Seven

'He's gone,' Baker said.

'Where?' Richter asked.

'No idea. The connection's been dropped. Right, with friend Trushenko out of the way, let's tidy this lot up.' Baker accessed the Username Table, selected 'Modin, General Nicolai', and changed the *'Pripiska'* password to '3tY&8$@Wq2#9', which he then carefully wrote down, checking it twice. 'They'll take weeks to crack that,' he said, 'if they ever do.' Baker checked Current Log Ins again, and found that the two other users had logged off the system. 'That's handy,' he said. 'It saves us having to wait until they've finished their day's work. They can't get back in because of the changes I've made. So, let's see what we can do.'

He selected the Network Control module and looked at the screen. 'Here we are,' he said. 'A schematic diagram of the whole network. The satellite uplink is at Pechora, and the network has only two permanent connections, to Yazenevo and a Moscow number.'

'Can you do anything about the permanent connection?'

'I already have done,' Baker said. 'The connections are only permanent in that the telephone lines link the Krutaya computer directly with those locations, rather than having to route through any exchanges. Anybody wanting to use the computer would still have to input a valid username and password and log in just as we did. As I've changed the passwords of all the listed users,' he added, 'they can't get into the system at all.'

478

Baker turned his attention to the Weapon Control module. He accessed the menu, and Richter translated the sub-menu choices for him. 'OK,' Baker said. 'What do you want?'

'Disarm them all, starting with Europe, except that one,' Richter pointed at the screen.

'The London weapon. OK, if that's what you want.' Baker concentrated on the screen while he navigated through the available options. He chose the Paris weapon, then looked at the options. 'Here we are. What do these mean?'

'This is Disable Sequence and that's Abort Sequence.'

Baker selected the Disable Sequence, pressed the 'Enter' key and looked at the screen. 'Another message. Can you translate it, please?'

Richter leaned over his shoulder. 'It says "Paris Device. Activation of the Disable Sequence will temporarily disarm this weapon. Are you sure you want to proceed?" That's not what we want,' Richter said. 'Try the Abort Sequence.'

Baker selected the other option, and they looked at the screen. 'OK,' Richter said. 'The message reads 'Paris Device. Activation of the Abort Sequence will permanently disarm this weapon. Are you sure you want to proceed?' I'd say yes, if I were you. In Cyrillic script that's "DA" – "ДА",' Richter added, 'so it's "D", not "Y".'

Baker nodded, pressed the 'D' key and then the 'Enter' key. The screen cleared, and another message appeared.

'Oh, shit,' Richter muttered.

'What?'

'It's saying "Operation failed. You require Administrator or System Designer access to modify the status of any weapon".'

The Walnut Room, the Kremlin, Krasnaya ploshchad, Moscow

'It's over, Comrade President,' Yuri Baratov said, smiling. 'Trushenko was found in Port-Khorly, near Odessa. We believe he was in the act of attempting to detonate a weapon. The SVR officer in charge opened fire, and the Minister did not survive the encounter.'

The Russian President smiled. 'Probably the best way, really. It saves any trial or embarrassment for us.' He nodded. 'Thank you, Yuri. Now I really do have something to tell the Americans.'

Hammersmith, London

'So now what?' Baker asked, sitting back in his chair.

'I don't know,' Richter replied. 'You're the computer expert, not me. First, and most important, can anyone else get into the system and detonate the weapons?'

Baker shook his head decisively. 'No way,' he said. 'I've changed all the passwords.'

'OK. So the only person in the system, or who can get into the system, is you?'

'I just said that.'

'I know,' Richter said. 'I just wanted to be sure because this is too important to cock up. OK, the system's secure so there's no immediate need to worry. If you can't get in and disable the weapons through the satellite, that can always be done on site – General Modin told me that the weapons can be deactivated locally. What we need is the precise location of each weapon, so we can advise the Americans and everyone else. Can you do that using Modin's access to the system?'

'Probably,' Baker replied, looking at the menu choices. 'Yes, here we are, I think.'

'"Weapon Locations (Europe)",' Richter read. 'Yes, print that, please.' A thought struck him, 'Can you also save the information on disk?'

Baker nodded, stuck a floppy disk into the drive and pressed a sequence of keys. The drive light illuminated and went out a few seconds later. Baker extracted the disk, wrote 'Weapons – Europe' on it and handed it to Richter.

The laser printer generated forty-five sheets, three for each weapon. Richter picked one up and scanned it. It was highly detailed and quite unambiguous, giving the precise location of the strategic-yield neutron bomb positioned at Toulouse, together with information about the power supply back-up routines, the location of the satellite dish and receiver system, and even the serial numbers of some of the pieces of equipment. If anyone needed documentary evidence of *Podstava*, those pages provided it.

Baker did the same for the American devices, first copying the information on to a floppy disk and then printing a hard copy. The process took longer because there were over six hundred sheets to print, and even at the six pages a minute that the printer was capable of, it took nearly two hours. Richter slumped, dozing, in his chair, a result of his lack of sleep and the somewhat soporific sound of the sheets of paper being fed through the laser.

At half past seven Baker leaned back wearily in his seat, then reached over and shook Richter awake. 'That's it,' he said. 'Can I break the connection now?'

'No,' Richter replied. He stood up, stretching his aching limbs and picked up the disk Baker had marked 'Weapons – America' and the plastic tray containing the printed sheets. 'I'm going up to see Simpson. Make another file copy of the weapon locations for our records so we can print the information whenever we need it. Keep trying to get into the module to disable the weapons. And when you get tired of trying to do that, there's one other thing I'd like you to do.'

Le Moulin au Pouchon, *St Médard, near Manciet, Midi-Pyrénées, France*

Hassan Abbas had been getting increasingly concerned. The last message he had received from Dmitri Trushenko had been a routine transmission, just a confirmation that the last two phases of the operation were proceeding on schedule, but there had been nothing since. He had anticipated a further message when the bomb convoy reached the English Channel, and certainly one when the London weapon had been safely delivered.

He had sent Trushenko an encrypted email by the usual route, just after six that afternoon and he had waited anxiously by the computer, his Internet connection active, for a reply. At nine, having heard nothing from wherever Trushenko had gone to ground, Abbas decided to check the status of the Krutaya computer through the dummy sex site in Arizona.

As usual, he accessed the page containing the hidden code, waited for the 404 error to be displayed and pressed the 'Refresh' button three times. His Internet connection was immediately transferred to the Krutaya mainframe, the screen cleared and the familiar winking cursor appeared in the top left-hand corner, waiting for his input. Abbas typed the single word 'manalagna' – the result of a private joke he had shared years earlier with Sadoun Khamil – and watched as his personal welcome message appeared on the monitor.

Hammersmith, London

Richter put the disk and plastic tray down on Simpson's desk and slumped wearily into a chair. Simpson looked at him questioningly.

'That's the complete list of the weapon locations,' Richter said. 'Those at the top are the European sites, the ones at the bottom are the bombs across the pond, and the floppy disk has file copies that the CIA can use.'

'Excellent,' Simpson said, and rang for a courier. 'I'll get them sent over to the Embassy right away so they can get their techies started on the disarming process.'

'You'll need these as well,' Richter said, handing over a couple of sheets of paper. 'They're copies of the instructions Professor Dewar gave me. If the Americans are going to dismantle the weapons manually they'll need to know the sequence of wires they have to cut to disable the anti-handling devices.'

Simpson picked up a couple of sheets from the plastic tray and glanced at the information printed on them. 'Remarkably comprehensive,' he murmured. 'I presume you've told Baker to keep a copy for our records?'

Richter nodded. 'It'll be in a file on the computer so we can print copies whenever we need them.'

There was a soft knock at the door and the courier entered. Simpson handed over the disk and the sheets relating to the American weapons and told him to take them straight to the American Embassy. The door had just closed behind him when the internal phone buzzed. Simpson picked it up, listened for a few seconds, then looked over at Richter. 'Right,' he said. 'I'll send him down.'

'What is it?' Richter asked as Simpson replaced the handset.

'That was Baker,' Simpson said, 'and we may not be out of the woods yet. He says a new user has just logged on to the Krutaya computer.'

'What? He told me that was impossible,' Richter said.

Simpson shrugged. 'No idea – it's not my field. We'd better get down there.'

Le Moulin au Pouchon, *St Médard, near Manciet, Midi-Pyrenees, France*

Hassan Abbas first checked to see if there were any other users on the system, but found only one – General Modin. That puzzled him, because he had been told by Trushenko that the general was one of the two senior Russian military officers who would be accompanying the last neutron bomb to London. The only way Modin could be connected to Krutaya would be through a computer at the London Russian Embassy, which meant that the bomb had to have been delivered already. Unless, Abbas rationalized, Modin had gone on ahead of the convoy for some reason. That could be it.

He checked the status of the London weapon and, as he expected, found that the system reported it as still being in transit. Then he accessed the network utilities module and checked the call origin. Modin's call to Krutaya had been placed from a London number, but routed through a Moscow exchange. That made sense. Obviously Modin had for some reason travelled ahead of the weapon and was now waiting in London for its arrival and positioning.

Abbas checked the overall system readiness, and then looked at the status of several of the individual weapons in both America and Europe, a routine he had followed many times before. All appeared to be in order, and he was about to exit from the system when something unexpected caught his eye.

Hammersmith, London

'How the hell did this happen, and who is he?' Richter demanded, walking into the Computer Suite two paces in front of Simpson.

Baker shrugged helplessly. 'He's a new user, but there's no record of him in the username table. That means he's got his own personal backdoor code.'

'In English, please, Baker,' Simpson snapped.

'A backdoor code is a shortcut most programmers use. They incorporate a specific code-word that's known only to them, and which will allow them back into the system at any time, without going through the normal log on procedure. I've effectively deleted all the authorized users by scrambling their passwords, but this guy –' he pointed at the screen '– just popped up out of nowhere, so that's the only possible way he could have got inside.'

'OK,' Richter growled, sitting down. 'Who is he and what can you do about him?'

'The first is easy. He's using identity "Dernowi", but that doesn't sound like a Russian name to me.'

Richter shook his head. 'It doesn't sound Russian because it isn't, as far as I know. Could it be a nickname?'

'Almost certainly, but that doesn't help. And the bad news is that because user Dernowi is using a backdoor code, I can't delete him, change the code or stop him getting into the system again. And the really bad news is he can definitely eliminate us if he wants to.'

'So what are you doing?'

'At the moment, absolutely nothing. I'm still logged on as Modin – which Dernowi has checked, by the way, so he knows we're here and also knows that we're calling from London – but I'm doing nothing else. I'm hoping he'll know Modin is an authorized user and he won't even think of altering his password or deleting his username.'

Richter sat silently for a moment, staring at the screen. 'The identity he's using,' he said, 'it doesn't sound like a contraction of a Russian word to me. Can you check it somehow?'

'I'm way ahead of you,' Baker said. 'I've been running a dictionary program for the last five minutes on my laptop.' He got up and walked across to the small desk in the corner. 'It's finished,' he announced, 'but I don't think it helps much. There's no exact match to "Dernowi", but the closest is in Yiddish, believe it or not, and it translates as "The Prophet".'

'Yiddish?' Richter said. 'That makes no sense. The Russians would never work with the Jews. This has to be someone's idea of a joke. OK, you said Dernowi had checked where Modin was calling from – can you do the same with him?'

Baker nodded. 'Probably. I'll visit some pages at random and include the network utilities section.' Two minutes later Baker passed Richter a post-it note on which he'd written an eleven digit number, starting with '33'. Richter looked at it then gave it to Simpson.

'France?' Simpson asked. 'He's calling from France? Southern France?'

'How do you know it's southern France?' Richter asked.

'The third digit,' Simpson replied. 'It identifies the region – I have a friend with a house in the Gers. You're sure of this, Baker?'

Baker shrugged. 'That's what the system's reporting. He's using a server in America – in Arizona, in fact – to bounce his call, but his actual origin is France.'

'This makes no sense,' Richter muttered, repeating himself. 'A new user, with backdoor access to a Russian weapon control system, with a Yiddish username and ringing from the South of France? What's he doing on the system?'

'No idea.'

'No, I meant what is he actually doing now?'

'Oh, OK. He's been checking the weapon readiness, but he hasn't moved off this page for a couple of minutes.'

'And what page is that?'

'The one for the Gibraltar demonstration weapon,' Baker replied. 'Which,' he added, 'shows that the device has already been detonated.'

Le Moulin au Pouchon, *St Médard, near Manciet, Midi-Pyrénées, France*

Abbas had been staring at the screen for what seemed like ten minutes, because what he was looking at simply didn't make sense. According to

the Krutaya computer, the Gibraltar weapon had already been detonated. But it obviously hadn't been, Abbas knew, because if it had there
was no way that he wouldn't have known about it. The detonation of a
nuclear weapon in a major population centre was something that simply
couldn't be kept secret.

Abbas opened a new window in his browser and typed
'www.cnn.com' into the address field. The CNN news site loaded almost
immediately, and he scanned the headlines. Nothing, or rather nothing
about Gibraltar. Despite what the Krutaya computer had reported, the
Gibraltar weapon had obviously not exploded.

That meant, Abbas realized, that there were only two possibilities –
either the weapon had misfired, which meant that the whole system,
weapons and firing mechanism, might be faulty, or somebody, somehow, had managed to disable the weapon at Gibraltar before the
detonation sequence had been completed. The successful test-firing of
the weapon on the tundra had proved the system worked, so on balance
the second possibility had to be the more likely. And that cast a whole
new light on the lack of communication from Dmitri Trushenko.

With almost frantic haste, Abbas opened the word processor and
began composing an email to Sadoun Khamil in Saudi Arabia.

47 Squadron Royal Air Force Special Forces Flight C–130 Hercules

The Hercules was virtually overhead Le Havre when the radio message
was received from Mazout Radar. The SAS troops had been delayed for
some time at the Rock because the aircraft had developed a minor fault
in one of its generators, and it was evening before the aircraft captain
had announced that they were ready to depart.

'Say again, Mazout.'

'Your operating authority has passed us a Class One mandatory
diversion message. You are instructed to re-route immediately to
Toulouse airport. Confirm you will comply, and advise when ready to
turn.'

The Hercules captain's voice was weary as he acknowledged the
message. 'Mazout, Charlie Whisky Three Seven. Ready to turn, and

requesting initial navigation assistance.' The crew were of course perfectly capable of plotting their own route to Toulouse, but it had been a long day and it looked as if it was a long way from being over.

'Three Seven, roger. Turn left heading one seven five, and climb to and maintain Flight Level one nine zero.'

'Roger, Mazout. Turning to one seven five and in the climb to level at one nine zero.'

As the aircraft's left wing dropped and the turn commenced, the co-pilot picked up the public address microphone. 'Gentlemen,' he said, 'we have no idea why, but we've been diverted to Toulouse, gateway to the Pyrenees. If we hear anything further, then I'll let you know. Otherwise, expect to be on the ground in about ninety minutes.'

Colin Dekker had been dozing in his seat, but his eyes opened immediately the Hercules began to turn. He glanced up as the co-pilot's announcement echoed round the cabin. 'It's Richter,' he muttered, to nobody in particular. 'Any money you like, Richter's behind this.'

Buraydah, Saudi Arabia

Sadoun Khamil read the email from Hassan Abbas for about the tenth time. He knew the contents by heart, and in fact had acted upon them within minutes of decrypting the message, but until he got a reply from Pakistan, there was nothing else he could do. And he wasn't expecting a reply soon. Arabs love to talk, and will endlessly debate even the most innocuous and mundane matters, and the request Khamil had made to the al-Qaeda leadership was neither innocuous nor mundane.

In his opinion, and in the opinion of his man on the spot, Hassan Abbas, the Russian operation had been discovered and its architect – Trushenko – either killed or captured. As far as he could see, the only option left to al-Qaeda was to immediately implement the final, and wholly secret, phase of the plan. That had been Khamil's recommendation, and that was what he was now waiting for the al-Qaeda leadership to approve.

The problem, Khamil knew, was probably not the actual implementation of the plan, but the time-scale. The idea had been to allow the

Russian operation – their *Podstava* – to run to its conclusion, with the ultimatum delivered to America and the West after the detonation of the weapon at Gibraltar. As far as the Russians were concerned, that would be the end of the matter. Faced with the weapons already positioned in the States, and the potent threat of the strategic-yield neutron bombs located throughout Western Europe, the Americans would have no option but to cooperate, to do whatever the Kremlin instructed.

That, Abbas had emphasized to Trushenko throughout the project, was what the Arabs wanted, was why they had been prepared to pay the millions of dollars that had been needed to fund *Podstava*. And Trushenko had believed him, had eagerly anticipated seeing an America cowed and humiliated by its impotence in the face of a brilliantly simple plot that at a stroke had negated all of America's military might, a country that would become the laughing-stock of the world, a super-power gone senile.

Then, and only then, would the Arabic component of the plan be implemented, the action that Sadoun and Abbas had privately labelled *El Sikkiyn* or 'the knife'. Then the Russians would learn why the Arabs had insisted, from the start, on having unrestricted access to the Krutaya computer, on having a backdoor code that couldn't be blocked or changed.

The leaders of all the Arab nations would be informed that a *fatwa* had been issued by al-Qaeda against America, Russia and the West – against, in fact, the entire non-Arab world – and that a *jihad* was about to start. Sufficient details of *Podstava* would be leaked to the West to ensure that everyone knew about the Russian plan. That would be fol-lowed by the simultaneous detonation of all the weapons positioned in American cities, a cataclysmic Armageddon that would incinerate tens of millions of Americans and leave the country crippled for years, pos-sibly for centuries.

The survivors would demand revenge, would force the American President, or whoever had survived in the administration, to respond in the only way possible to the obvious aggressor. A massive retaliatory thermonuclear attack on Russia would follow, as cer-tainly as night follows day. Then what was left of the Russian nuclear arsenal would inevitably be launched against America and then, probably, most of the British and French nuclear weapons would be fired at Russia.

And at a single stroke, the two superpowers would effectively eliminate each other, leaving the way clear for a unified Arab nation to arise behind the banner of al-Qaeda and impose a new world order upon the shattered remnants of humanity. That was the plan which had been conceived by Hassan Abbas so long ago, and which offered what was probably the last great hope for the Arab states.

All Khamil could do was hope that the leaders of al-Qaeda would see sense, would stop talking and act, before it was too late.

Royal Air Force Northolt, West London

The five Royal Air Force officers looked up as Paul Richter opened the door and walked into the aircrew briefing room. Richter hadn't slept or shaved for the better part of two days and was still wearing the jeans and shirt he'd pulled out of the cupboard in his office, augmented by his leather motorcycle jacket. 'Yes? Who are you and what do you want?' the squadron leader pilot snapped.

'I'm Richter – your passenger.'

The RAF officer muttered something that sounded suspiciously like 'Good God' under his breath but gestured to a seat at the back of the room before turning back to the other officers and the en-route planning charts spread out in front of them. Four minutes later the squadron leader stood up, glanced at his watch and announced, 'Briefing complete.' Then he turned to Richter. 'Ready, Mr Richter?'

Richter nodded, scrambled to his feet and followed the green-clad figure out of the room, across the tarmac outside and up the stairs into the cabin of the HS146. Richter was the only passenger so he chose the seat that offered the greatest legroom, sat down and strapped himself in. The co-pilot looked at him from the open door to the cockpit. 'Anything you want?' he asked.

'Yes,' Richter said, nodding. 'I want to go to sleep. Wake me up if an engine catches fire or a wing falls off, but otherwise don't call me until we're short finals. Oh, you may get two-way with a Special Forces Flight

Herky-bird out of Gibraltar that's heading for the same place we are. If so, pass on my best wishes and say I'll see them on the ground. I don't want to talk to them.' Two minutes later Richter was sound asleep.

American Embassy, Grosvenor Square, London

'So what the hell does all that mean?' John Westwood demanded.

Roger Abrahams had been called down to the Communications Suite fifteen minutes earlier, apparently to be briefed by the Secret Intelligence Service duty officer on a secure telephone link. In fact, he'd found himself talking with – or more accurately listening to – a man called Simpson, who'd declined to state his rank or department, but who had admitted that he was Paul Richter's immediate superior.

'It's bad news,' Abrahams replied. 'The British managed to hack their way into the Russian mainframe controlling the satellite and the weapons and changed all the passwords, and that should really have been the end of it. Unfortunately, just when they thought all they had left to do was locate each nuke and send in a bunch of techies to take it to pieces, somebody else logged on to the system, using what appears to be a Yiddish username and calling from France.'

'Oh, shit,' Westwood muttered.

'Exactly. According to this Simpson character, this new user – the name he's using is "Dernowi", which is close to the Yiddish for "The Prophet" – is using some kind of a backdoor code to gain access to the system, so there's no way of locking him out.'

'So what do we do now?'

'Simpson has already couriered us a disk copy of all the weapon locations in the States, and I've had the file sent by secure email to Langley. Apart from that, there's not a hell of a lot we can do. As soon as I got the message from Simpson I contacted Walter Hicks, and he's probably on his way to see the President right now. Obviously all our assets over there will stay at their current state of readiness, not that that will help if this Dernowi decides to nuke us all to hell.'

'So?'

'So the Brits have sent a team into France to locate Dernowi and take him out. It's the only way they can be certain of stopping an attack.'

Blagnac Airport, Toulouse, south-west France

The HS146 touched down smoothly just before eleven fifty, local time, and taxied off the runway to a parking area well away from the passenger terminal. With a sense of *déjà vu*, Richter looked across the hardstanding at the bulk of the C–130 Hercules with RAF markings standing a few yards away. Ross was waiting for him at the side door of a hangar. Richter greeted him briefly, then walked into the building. Colin Dekker was bent over a laptop computer which was hitched to a mobile telephone. 'Colin,' Richter said, 'we've got to stop meeting like this.'

Dekker looked up and grinned at him. 'Tell me about it. OK, your Mr Simpson has been busy while you've been poncing about over France in your executive jet. Where he got them from I've no idea, but there are three V6 Renault Espaces parked outside this hangar full of fuel and ready to go. They're our transport. Then he kicked Lacomte and Lacomte kicked France Telecom into action, so we now know the exact address this Dernowi guy is using. I got that a few minutes ago by email from London. We also,' Dekker added, 'know Dernowi's name, or at least the name he used when he applied for his landline telephone.'

'Which is?' Richter asked, as Dekker snapped the laptop closed and pulled out the data cable that linked it to the mobile phone.

'Abdullah Mahmoud.'

'An Arab. That makes a lot more sense. Anything known on him?'

Dekker shook his head. 'Nothing yet, but we've got traces running through all the allied databases. It's probably an alias, so I wouldn't hold your breath.'

'And where is he?' Richter asked.

'A charming little place called St Médard. Apparently, it's a hamlet near a village called Manciet, on the N124 beyond Auch, and it's about a hundred and ten clicks west of here on pretty average roads, according to the map, so we'd best get moving.'

Buraydah, Saudi Arabia

Sadoun Khamil had left his computer running, and the Internet connection open, but he'd left the room for a few minutes to instruct one of his men to prepare him some food and drink for what he anticipated would be a very long night. Three minutes after he'd walked out, his email client software emitted a soft double-tone that indicated receipt of an email, but it was another six minutes before he returned and checked the screen. Decrypting the message took a further four minutes, and then Khamil hunched forward and read the text with great care.

The response from Pakistan was all that he had dared hope. The al-Qaeda leaders had approved the immediate implementation of *El Sikkiyn*. The issue of the *fatwa* would follow, as would the leaked details of the Russian operation, but Khamil's instructions were clear and unambiguous – he was to instruct Abbas to complete the final phase immediately.

For a few moments, Khamil did nothing but re-read the message to ensure that he had made no mistake. He considered sending Abbas a message in clear, or even telephoning him, but decided that he would follow the agreed procedure. He composed two short paragraphs to Abbas, added the text he had received from Pakistan, and encrypted the entire message. He pasted the apparently corrupted text into an existing email marketing message, chose a suitable route and pressed the send button.

He left the computer running and the door to the room open, so that he would hear if any further email messages arrived for him. Then he walked into the main room where four of his men were sitting cross-legged on the floor watching an Arabic-language broadcast on the television. He instructed them to switch on the satellite receiver and watch the American CNN station. That, he knew from past experience, would probably be the first channel to break the news. If, that is, there was enough remaining of CNN to make any kind of a broadcast after *El Sikkiyn* began.

Chapter Twenty-Eight

Friday
Gascony

The roads were nothing like as bad as Colin Dekker had feared, and the three Renaults were able to hold their speed at well over one hundred and twenty kilometres an hour for most of the time. Richter claimed he was still half-asleep, which was not much of an exaggeration, so he navigated from the roadmap while Colin Dekker drove.

Like most of France after about seven in the evening, the villages that the convoy swept through appeared deserted, doors firmly closed, shutters secured, no lights showing. Léguevin, L'Isle-Jourdain, Gimont and Aubiet. Auch was different, simply because it was bigger, and they saw couples and small groups of people walking the streets. Then they were through the town and back on the empty country roads. St-Jean-Poutge, Vic-Fézensac and through Dému, and then an almost arrow-straight road to Manciet.

'According to this map,' Richter murmured, as Dekker pushed the speed up to just over one hundred and fifty kilometres an hour, 'this is an attractive country road with spectacular views to the south over the valley of the River Douze.'

'Fascinating,' Dekker replied. 'More to the point, how far have we got to go?'

'About six kilometres to Manciet, then another two up to St Médard. Eight clicks in total, which is just about five miles.'

Fifty-five minutes after driving out of Blagnac Airport, almost on the stroke of one, the three cars swept into the village of Manciet, headlights blazing, and immediately turned hard right onto the D931, north towards Eauze. St Médard lay two kilometres in front of them.

Le Moulin au Pouchon, *St Médard*, *near Manciet*, *Midi-Pyrénées*, *France*

Like Sadoun Khamil in Saudi Arabia, Hassan Abbas had left his computer switched on, waiting for the decision from al-Qaeda. Abbas received at least thirty emails every day, and eight times since he'd sent his message to Saudi Arabia he'd rushed back into the rear bedroom when he'd heard the warning announcing the receipt of an email. He'd checked, and then deleted, them all.

The ninth message was different, not least because its apparent origin was Germany, and Abbas scanned it swiftly, looking for the tell-tale 'corrupted' section of text. He found it about halfway down, highlighted and copied it, then ran the decryption routine to unscramble it. The plain text appeared on the screen and Abbas leaned forward to read it, simultaneously pressing the 'Print' button which would send a copy of the text to the Hewlett-Packard LaserJet. He read Sadoun Khamil's instructions, and the copy of the message from the al-Qaeda leadership, with increasing satisfaction. Then he read the whole email again, twice, just to be certain. 'Allah be praised,' he murmured, and stood up.

He removed the single sheet of paper from the printer and took it down the stairs and into the living room, where Jaafar Badri and Karim Ibrahim, two of his three bodyguards, were sitting watching a French game-show on the television. The fourth bodyguard – Saadi Fouad – was asleep upstairs.

'My friends,' Abbas said, his words ringing with the monumental significance of the announcement he was about to make, 'tonight we will strike a blow at the infidels from which they will never recover. Our leaders have instructed me to implement *El Sikkiyn* immediately. Within hours, America and Russia will be smoking ruins. Allah be praised.'

Abbas smiled in satisfaction as his companions echoed his prayer, then turned back to the stairs and the task he was going to perform.

St Médard, near Manciet, Midi-Pyrénées, France

Le Moulin au Pouchon took some finding, not least because, as appeared to be common practice in France, most of the streets didn't appear to have names and the houses lacked both names and numbers. Presumably the locals knew where they were going, and visitors just had to ask a local – easy enough at midday, but impossible after midnight.

The information from France Telecom had included a set of directions originally supplied by Abdullah Mahmoud, Abbas' alias, when he had applied for the landline to be installed. Though somewhat ambiguous, at least in the dark and silent village streets, the directions did eventually lead Richter and Dekker to a narrow, winding road that snaked away up the hillside. In the distance they could see a single light burning, but even through the night-vision glasses it was impossible to tell if it was from an uncurtained window or was simply an exterior light some farmer had forgotten to switch off.

The last thing they wanted to do was alert their quarry, so as soon as Ross was reasonably sure that they had identified the correct road, he ordered the three Espaces parked in a layby about a quarter of a mile from the village. Everybody climbed out and gathered round Ross and Dekker, who had the laptop open again and was re-checking the directions supplied by France Telecom. 'Any idea what the opposition strength is likely to be?' Ross asked.

Richter shook his head. 'At least one person, but we have to assume that there will be a team of people to support him. I'm guessing, but it could be anything from two or three to a round dozen. Obviously at least some of them, possibly all of them, will be armed.'

'Assault tactics,' Ross said, 'will have to be left until we see the location itself. All we got from France Telecom was the address of the house. We have no idea whether it's a new two-bedroom villa or a three-hundred-year-old six-bedroomed *maison de maître*. But it's fair to say that in this part of France old houses greatly outnumber the new properties, so the chances are that it will be an old stone property with solid doors and fairly small windows, none of which is good news from our point of view.'

'What about weapons?' Richter asked. 'I can see the Hocklers, but have you got anything heavier in case these comedians are living in some sort of fortified manor house?'

'We've got half a dozen G60 stun grenades left, plus one M79 launcher and three high-explosive grenades.'

Richter nodded. 'Excellent. That should make short work of any French front door.'

'The M79 is still in the car,' Dekker said.

'Get it, please,' Ross said, and a trooper trotted away obediently.

Richter glanced round at the faces of the SAS troopers. 'The weapon on the *Anton Kirov* was dangerous enough,' he said, 'but it was only one bomb, albeit a big one. This time we're playing for much bigger stakes – if this Arab decides to carry on where Trushenko left off, he could quite literally start a Third World War, effectively destroy America and return western civilization to the Stone Age. We don't mess with him. We have just one chance to do it right, and we have to stop him – permanently.'

Hammersmith, London

Baker still had the connection open to the Krutaya mainframe and had been working on the system ever since Richter had left the suite. He had been alternating his efforts between trying to locate Dernowi's backdoor code and getting into the weapon control module with Administrator status. Unfortunately, he had got precisely nowhere with both tasks.

Just after midnight, local time, he watched impotently as Derowi used his backdoor code to get into the system again.

St Médard, near Manciet, Midi-Pyrénées, France

Once they had all checked their weapons and equipment, Ross divided the men into two groups and led them silently up the twisting road towards the single light they'd seen from the edge of the village. All around them the countryside was dark and totally silent, as if nature herself was holding her breath.

When they were about two hundred yards from the light, they stopped, and Ross and Dekker used their night-vision glasses to inspect the target. What they saw was an L-shaped house with a single light burning above what was presumably the main door. They could see no lights in any of the rooms, no sign of life anywhere, and the shutters over all the windows were closed. Ross murmured orders through the radio, and the troopers began an even more stealthy approach, using the cover provided by the hedges and trees that lined both sides of the road.

Colin Dekker, who was leading the first group, suddenly stopped and stood erect beside one of the two stone gateposts that guarded the entrance to the property. 'This is the wrong house,' he said into his radio microphone.

'Are you sure?' Ross asked.

'Yup. Unless we've got the name wrong. According to this name plate –' he gestured at the stone pillar in front of him and the garden of the property beyond '– this house is called *"Les Deux Cèdres"*, and those two trees over there are probably the cedars in question.'

Le Moulin au Pouchon, *St Médard, near Manciet, Midi-Pyrénées, France*

Hassan Abbas was taking his time, relishing the moment. He accessed the weapon control module and chose the 'Total' option, which would allow all the weapons on American soil to be detonated simultaneously. Then he took out a small black leather-covered book from his pocket and, in response to the automated prompts from the Krutaya mainframe, began carefully inputting the two twelve-digit authorization codes that were required to activate each weapon in turn. Detonation would not take place until all two hundred and three nuclear weapons had been enabled.

St Médard, near Manciet, Midi-Pyrénées, France

Richer had left his mobile phone switched on, but with the ringer silent and the phone set to vibrate when a call was received. As Ross and Dekker regrouped their men and prepared to advance further up the lane, he felt the tremor in his pocket, pulled the phone out and pressed the button to answer the call. 'Richter.'

'You'd better be quick,' Baker said, his voice high and panicky. 'That bastard Dernowi's on the system again and he's just accessed the Weapon Control module.'

'Can't you change the authorization codes – you know, the same as you did with Trushenko?'

'No. He's got a higher access level then me. The moment I did anything like that he'd know I was an intruder. He'd simply delete Modin as a user, kick me off the system and then get on with detonating the weapons. It's better if I don't do anything. At least that way I can see what he's doing.'

'And what is he doing?'

'He's chosen simultaneous detonation. He's going to trigger all the American weapons at the same time.'

'Jesus Christ,' Richter said. 'OK – stay on the line.' He looked round and gestured urgently to Ross and Dekker. 'Dernowi's on the system again,' he said, 'and he's going to fire all the American weapons simultaneously. We have to act immediately. Are you sure this is the right road?'

Dekker nodded, his face visibly pale in the dim moonlight. 'If the France Telecom directions are right, yes.'

'Right,' Richter said. 'We can't do this with kid gloves, not now, so we have to risk alerting these fucking Arabs.' He pointed a few yards up the road at a telegraph pole and shone his torch at the cross-trees at the top of it. 'Those cables are probably the ones carrying Dernowi's transmissions. Shoot them off it.'

'Are you sure you want to do that?' Ross asked.

'Damn right I am,' Richter said. 'Do it now.'

Dekker gestured to a trooper who walked up, aimed his silenced Hockler at the top of the telegraph pole and squeezed the trigger. The weapon made a popping sound, alarmingly loud in the darkness, and wood splinters flew from the cross-trees. One cable fell, then a second, and the third and fourth together. Another trooper ran over, used his torch to locate the cables in the hedgerow, then severed each of them with his knife.

'You still there, Baker?' Richter snapped.

'Yes.'

'OK. We've just cut some telephone cables. Is Dernowi still on-line?'

There was a pause that seemed to last minutes as Baker looked at the computer screen in London. 'No,' he said finally. 'The connection's been dropped.'

Richter breathed again. 'Good. We're definitely in the right place,' he said. 'Baker, is Simpson still there?'

'Yes,' Baker replied shortly. 'I think everyone still in the building is here in the Computer Suite.'

'OK, just as a precaution, get Simpson to contact Lacomte and tell him to disable all the mobile phone cells in this area, as soon as possible.' Richter grabbed the map Dekker had been using. 'That's within, say, a fifty kilometre radius of Mont de Marsan, and for at least the next two hours. This bastard may have a mobile phone as well as a landline.'

'It'll take time,' Baker replied.

'I know, so best you get started. Disconnect now, but call me immediately there's any other sign of Dernowi.'

Le Moulin au Pouchon, *St Médard,* near Manciet, *Midi-Pyrénées, France*

Like Dmitri Trushenko had done in the Crimea, Hassan Abbas looked at the screen of the computer with considerable irritation. The double-computer icon in the Taskbar at the bottom right of the screen had abruptly vanished, taking his connection to the Krutaya mainframe with it. The sudden disconnection didn't surprise him because he had experienced similar problems in the past with France Telecom, and he knew perfectly well that line failures were by no means unusual in rural France.

He instructed the computer to re-dial his Wanadoo Internet access number, and watched as the Dial-Up Networking dialog box appeared in the centre of the screen. He pressed the 'Connect' button, and the system reported 'Status: Dialing'. Seconds later the status message read 'Disconnecting'. Abbas clicked on 'Details' and read the brief message 'There was no dialtone'. Something was wrong, he realized, with a sudden chill. Losing the connection to Krutaya was one thing, but losing the line completely was quite another. He grabbed the telephone beside the computer and pressed it to his ear. Silence. He depressed the receiver rest a couple of times, with no result.

Abbas was no fool. He got up, walked swiftly to the top of the stairs and shouted down. 'Arm yourselves. The house may be attacked imminently.' He walked into the main bedroom and paused beside the bed only long enough to shake Fouad awake, then moved swiftly over to the shuttered windows. He opened the window, then carefully eased one shutter open and peered out into the darkness, eyes and ears attuned for the slightest unusual sight or sound. Nothing, apart from the usual faint noises of the night.

Abbas pulled the shutter closed again and walked across the landing. Downstairs he could sense the tension, could hear his men murmuring quietly, and the metallic sounds as they checked and cocked their weapons.

'Lights out,' he called, 'and prepare.' Then he turned and walked back into the rear bedroom. He grabbed the leather Samsonite case containing the laptop computer and mobile phone, opened it and quickly checked that everything was there. Then he snapped the case closed, walked out of the bedroom, locked the door behind him and pocketed the key.

St Médard, near Manciet, Midi-Pyrénées, France

'That must be it,' Dekker muttered. 'Yes,' he added, swivelling his night glasses to the postbox standing by the roadside. The letters on the box were hand-painted, faded and weathered, and partially obscured by a bush, but he could just make out the last part of the name '*Pouchon*'.

They had followed the twisting road that climbed up out of the village to the north-east and were now the better part of a mile outside St Médard. In front of them, clearly visible in the faint moonlight, was a square white house sitting in a small garden just off the road on the outside of a right-hand bend. The walls were white-washed and looked as if they were solid stone and thick. The front door looked old and heavy, and Ross had been right about the windows – they were small and square and, predictably, tightly shuttered.

But there were some signs of life inside the property. Faint vertical and horizontal lines of light showed behind and through two of the shuttered windows on the ground floor on the left-hand side of the front door, but even as they looked the light was extinguished.

'Anyone here think they've just gone to bed?' Dekker asked.

'Not a chance,' Richter snapped. 'They've just lost the connection to the Russian mainframe and by now they'll also know that the landline has been cut. No doubt Dernowi or whoever's in charge has told the bodyguards to expect an attack. That, anyway, is the way I read it. They're certainly awake, and they'll be alert.'

'Right,' Ross said. 'Mr Beatty is probably right, but even if he's wrong we still have to assume that they know we're out here. Normally we'd wait and try to ascertain exactly how many of them there are inside, and where they're likely to be found. Tonight, we can't. I don't like going in blind, but in the circumstances I don't see we've got the slightest option. Colin – do you disagree with that?'

'No. We have absolutely no choice.'

'So, we use all the firepower we've got and try to finish it as quickly as we can.

Le Moulin au Pouchon, *St Médard, near Manciet, Midi-Pyrénées, France*

Abbas walked swiftly down the stairs into the tiny hall. A nightlight was burning in a power-point, and by its dim light he was able to check that his three bodyguards were ready. 'You are prepared?' he asked.

'Yes,' Karim Ibrahim replied. 'We have checked the explosives and set the tripwires. All is correct. We have put the extra ammunition in our bags.'

Abbas nodded his approval, and glanced at his watch. 'You are certain, *sayidi*?' Badri asked. 'You know we will be attacked?'

Abbas shook his head. 'No, and I hope I am wrong, but the telephone line is not working and that concerns me greatly, now that we are so close to success.' Abbas turned to Fouad. 'Saadi, set the floodlight time-switch for three minutes, then follow me. And switch off that nightlight – there is to be no light inside the house at all.'

Abbas turned and led the way into the kitchen. Fouad opened a wall cupboard and adjusted the floodlight time-switch as Abbas had instructed, then stepped across the hall and ripped the nightlight from its socket, before turning to follow the others out of the hall.

In the kitchen, Jaafar Badri hauled back the faded red carpet to reveal the flagstone floor below. Just off-centre in the floor was an old wooden trapdoor about three feet square, which Badri lifted. Then he reached down into the opening and clicked a switch. Dim electric lighting flickered into being, revealing a rusted steel ladder which descended into a rough-hewn vertical shaft, at the base of which Abbas could just make out the gleam of a trickle of water.

This was the unique feature of the property which had made Abbas select it. The house was called '*Le Moulin au Pouchon*', but unlike many other similarly named properties in France, the building had actually been a working mill until the end of the nineteenth century. The passageway into which Abbas was about to descend had then been the watercourse which had channelled water under the house to turn the long-vanished milling machinery.

Years ago, the stream which had supplied the water had either dried up or been diverted, but the stone-lined watercourse was still in good condition. More importantly, from Abbas' point of view, the watercourse led away from the house and up the hill to an old stone-built outhouse, some hundred metres distant, which had originally housed the sluices.

Abbas paused for a few moments before climbing down the ladder and looked at the three men with whom he had spent the last four months of his life. He shook hands with Badri and Ibrahim, but pulled Fouad into a close embrace before releasing him.

'*Inshallah* we will meet again, Saadi, my friend.'

'*Inshallah, sayidi* Abbas,' Fouad murmured respectfully.

'We should go,' Badri interjected. 'We may have very little time.'

Abbas nodded, but kept his eyes fixed on Fouad. 'Yes, you're right. Saadi – you know how much we are depending on you.'

Fouad nodded, but seemed to swell slightly at the implied praise. Abbas clapped him on the shoulder, then handed the Samsonite case to Badri and began to climb down the steel ladder. At the bottom he stood aside to let Badri and Ibrahim join him. Badri passed Abbas the

Samsonite, then moved away, up the old watercourse and towards the outhouse, torchlight dancing on the damp stone walls, his Kalashnikov in his right hand. Abbas followed and Ibrahim took up station behind Abbas.

Behind them, the lights went out and they heard the sound of the trapdoor in the kitchen closing. Fouad would remain in the house either until whoever had cut the wires actually attacked the property or until it became clear that it had been a false alarm.

St Médard, near Manciet, Midi-Pyrénées, France

Ross had divided his men into two teams, one to hit the front of the house and the second, led by Colin Dekker, to work around to the rear of the property to try to effect an entrance there. It was comparatively slow work for the second team, because of the absence of any plans of the property or knowledge of the terrain immediately surrounding the target, and twice the troopers had to move back and approach from a different angle when they encountered impenetrable vegetation. Finally Dekker announced that they were in position.

'Acknowledged,' Ross murmured. 'On my signal, we take out the front door, then get in and finish the job. As briefed, we'll take the upstairs rooms. Colin, get through the back door as soon as you hear the grenade, and clear downstairs. Everyone, be very careful of blue-on-blue – we don't want any more casualties. Wilson – don't forget to aim the grenade at the stone beside the front door, not the door itself, or it'll probably just go straight through it. Any questions, anybody not ready?'

There was silence on the net for a couple of seconds, then a blaze of light surrounded the old house as the eight exterior floodlights, installed as a precaution by Abbas almost as soon as they had moved into the property, kicked in.

'Jesus Christ,' someone muttered. 'That's fucked up my night vision good and proper.'

'Right.' Ross' voice was crisp and sharp. 'That's a clear enough indication, I think. They definitely know we're out here, so let's not keep them waiting any longer. Three, two, one. M79, go.'

Le Moulin au Pouchon, *St Médard*, *near Manciet*, *Midi-Pyrénées*, *France*

Saadi Fouad had rehearsed his actions many times before, and knew precisely what he had to do. Almost immediately they had begun their occupation of the house they'd spent some time moulding plastic explosive charges, studded with pounds of ball-bearings, nails and screws as a kind of rudimentary shrapnel, around the ground-floor doors and windows, to be triggered by simple tripwires. Those, they were confident, would eliminate the first wave of any assault, leaving them plenty of time and firepower to engage the remainder of the attacking force.

As soon as the floodlights switched on, Fouad ran swiftly up the staircase and crouched in front of the locked door of the small back bedroom, looking down the stairs and into the blackness of the hall over the barrel of his Kalashnikov assault rifle.

Abbas had briefed Fouad and the others very thoroughly. He didn't expect that the house would ever be assaulted, simply because of the security surrounding *Podstava* and *El Sikkiyn*, and he had always believed that if the French authorities ever tried to gain entrance to the house they would simply be dealing with a small group of gendarmes, effective enough at controlling traffic and handling normal French criminals, but hopelessly unprepared for the level of training, weaponry and dedication that his men possessed.

As the M79 fin-stabilized high-explosive grenade smashed into the stone wall immediately beside the door frame and virtually vaporized the front door of *Le Moulin au Pouchon* with a roar that shook the house to its foundations and showered him with debris, Fouad suddenly realized that in this matter Abbas had miscalculated, and very badly. Moments later he heard the flat crack as the plastic explosive around the doorframe detonated, the explosion precipitated by a section of the ruined door which had snagged on a tripwire, and flattened himself on the floor as the air filled with flying steel.

'Arwens, now,' Dekker called, and immediately two almost simultaneous explosions ripped through the night, tearing the rear door of *Le Moulin* off its hinges. As the door toppled outwards and crashed to the ground, the first troopers rushed inside the property, weapons at the ready, alert for the Arab terrorists they expected to find.

But the danger wasn't in front of them, it was behind. The home-made booby-trap placed by Abbas and his colleagues exploded less than a second after the first five men had dashed into the kitchen. Small but lethal steel missiles flew everywhere, bouncing off walls and ceiling, ripping into flesh, and all five men fell.

'Stop,' Dekker yelled, as his remaining troopers rushed forward. 'Second team – regroup outside. Cover the exits. Nobody goes in.' As his men scrambled into what cover they could find and sighted their weapons at the windows and the opening where the door had been, Dekker spoke again into his microphone. 'Ross, Dekker. The rear door was booby-trapped. I've five men down, injuries unknown. I'm going in alone.'

Seconds after the front door booby-trap detonated, Saadi Fouad heard another explosion at the back of the house, and realized that a second group of attackers must have smashed their way in through the rear door.

Two stun grenades bounced into the hall and Fouad barely had time to close his eyes and cover his ears before they detonated. Then dark shapes poured through the oblong hole where the front door had been, diving left and right into the shadows. Fouad scrambled to his knees and squeezed the trigger of his assault rifle. He poured a lethal stream of 7.62mm shells down the stairs at a rate of six hundred rounds a minute.

The problem he had was that he was by himself, and when the Kalashnikov fell silent as the thirtieth and last round was fired, he took over three seconds to unclip the empty magazine and snap on a full one. But by that time two of the dark shapes were half-way up the stairs, and less than one tenth of a second after that he was dead.

*

505

Dekker eased his way over the threshold of the kitchen door with exaggerated care, feeling with his feet and left hand for any tripwire or other actuating device. In his right hand he held his Hockler, and he was looking everywhere for any sign of the opposition. The faded carpet covering most of the kitchen floor was dark with blood, but he didn't look at that.

The door through to what Dekker guessed was the hallway was closed. He approached it cautiously, turned the handle and eased it open a crack, and peered out. By the dim light of the moon which was shining through the hole where the front door of the house had been, he realized he was looking straight down the muzzles of two Hocklers.

'Dekker,' he said with relief, and pushed the door wide. 'Where's the opposition?'

One of the troopers shrugged. 'There was one upstairs, but he's dead. Apart from him, the place seems deserted.'

'OK. I've got five men down in there,' Dekker said, gesturing back into the kitchen. 'Second team, this is Dekker. Target appears cleared. Enter with caution and render first aid. Establish a perimeter watch – there may be opposition players in the grounds.' He turned back to the troopers. 'Where's Beatty?'

'Upstairs, with the boss.'

St Médard, near Manciet, Midi-Pyrénées, France

Hassan Abbas and his two companions had barely reached the security of the derelict outhouse when the M79 grenade took out the front door of the old mill. The sounds of the plastic explosive and the stun grenades detonating were almost as loud, and then the staccato beat of the Kalashnikov carried clearly up the hill. Seconds later the weapon fell silent, and Abbas knew that they would not be seeing Saadi Fouad again, at least not alive.

Jaafar Badri moved a length of wood carefully to one side, making sure he made no noise, to clear a space for Abbas to sit on the floor. Then he and Ibrahim took up station in positions looking down the slope towards the mill, weapons at the ready.

Abbas opened up the Samsonite bag, pulled out the laptop computer and switched it on. It seemed to take an age to load the start-up programs, but he barely noticed because he had other things to do.

He opened the bag again and removed the mobile phone, which he switched on. Then he connected a data cable between it and the laptop and put the computer and phone on the bag, clear of the floor. He pulled the Glock out of his shoulder holster, removed the magazine and swiftly ejected each round on to the stone floor in front of him. Abbas reloaded the magazine, rammed it home into the pistol and worked the slide to chamber the first round, pulled out the magazine again and added a single round from his pocket to replace the one he'd just chambered.

The last thing he needed was a weapon jam, and past experience had taught him that a freshly loaded magazine was always more reliable than one in which the bullets had been sitting for days or weeks. He had two spare magazines attached to the webbing of his shoulder holster, and he swiftly unloaded and reloaded both of them as well. He left the pistol on the ground within easy reach of his right hand, then looked down at the laptop screen where the Windows ME desktop had just appeared.

Abbas smiled, placed his forefinger on the touchpad, slid the cursor across the screen to the Internet Explorer icon and double-clicked the left-hand mouse button. The program loaded almost instantly and the 'Connect to' dialog box appeared on the screen as the Dial-Up Networking utility accessed the mobile phone and began dialling Wanadoo. Abbas knew that within two or three minutes at the most he could begin the detonation sequence.

Le Moulin au Pouchon, *St Médard, near Manciet, Midi-Pyrénées, France*

'So where the fuck are they?' Dekker demanded.

'You're sure there would have been more than one terrorist?' Ross asked.

'Absolutely.' Richter was positive. 'There are four beds in this house, four prayer mats down in the living room, but only one dead Arab up here on the landing. An Arab's prayer mat is like his comfort blanket –

he never goes anywhere without it. Somewhere there are three more of these bastards, and we've got to find them.'

The rear bedroom door had yielded to a round from an Arwen but, apart from the glowing screen of the desktop computer, had revealed nothing of interest. No doubt Baker, when he got his hands on the machine, would have a lot more to say.

Richter's phone began vibrating again and he snatched it out of his pocket. 'Richter.'

'He's back,' Baker said shortly. 'He's calling from a mobile phone, and he's gone straight into the Weapon Control module.'

'You have to stop him,' Richter said urgently, 'because we can't find him. Change one digit on each of the firing codes. He might think he's mis-typed it when the system refuses to accept it, but even if he suspects that you're doing it, it will still take him time to get you off the system.'

'Right,' Baker replied, and rang off.

'He's on the system again,' Richter said. 'He's here somewhere, and we have to find him now.'

A trooper appeared at the foot of the stairs and called up. 'Boss, the kitchen, please, immediate.' Ross and Dekker ran down the stairs, Richter close behind. In the kitchen, five troopers lay flat on the floor, two obviously dead and three receiving treatment from their comrades. The faded carpet had been pulled back against the wall, and someone had opened the trapdoor.

'Their bolt hole,' Dekker breathed. 'Where does it go?'

'I've been down it, just to the bottom of the ladder,' the trooper said, 'and there's a passage that runs underneath the house, but they must have gone up the hill, because the downward passage has a metal grille fitted across it. It's real old, and real solid.'

Dekker looked at Ross. 'We don't go down it,' he said flatly. 'If they booby-trapped the doors, there's no way there isn't some sort of a nasty surprise waiting for us down there.'

'There's no point in going down there,' Richter said. 'They just used this to get out of the house. It has to lead to a building or just out into the fields somewhere.'

'Right,' Ross said. 'Back upstairs, and see if we can pick them up with the night-vision glasses.'

OVERKILL

St Médard, near Manciet, Midi-Pyrénées, France

Badri and Ibrahim had barely moved since they'd reached the derelict outhouse. They stood, silent as shadows behind the ruined walls, looking down the gentle incline towards the old mill, which now stood ominously silent in the faint moonlight. Behind them, crouched on the floor, Hassan Abbas was hunched over the laptop, still working on the detonation sequence. The first code he'd input had been rejected, which he had put down to a typing error, but when the second authorization code that he'd taken extreme care to get right was also rejected, he'd realized the system was being tampered with.

The only way that could happen was if the other user on the system wasn't actually General Modin, but someone who'd used his logon details to gain access, and who was altering the master list of authorization codes. And that, Abbas realized quickly, was something he could easily deal with. He exited from the Weapon Control module and checked the logged-on users. He found only one – Modin – which was itself unusual. Normally other users would have logged on, checked something or carried out some kind of maintenance task, and then logged off. But for the last several hours, only that single user had been on the system, and Abbas knew he had to be a *doppelgänger*.

That in turn meant that General Modin had been compromised and that some authority, presumably the same authority that had ordered its execution squad to attack the house, knew about *Podstava*. But what they didn't and couldn't know about was *El Sikkiyn*, although they were about to find out.

Hassan Abbas had a degree in computer science from Cornell University in the States, and was by any standards an expert. He had exactly the same authority on the Krutaya mainframe as the system designer, and could do anything he wished. He thought for a few seconds, then initiated a full system maintenance shut-down routine. This required the forced disconnection of all users apart from the initiator of the routine, and he watched in satisfaction as 'General Modin' suddenly vanished from the list of logged-on users. As a precaution, Abbas deleted Modin from the list of authorized users. Then he copied the list of modified firing authorization codes into the laptop's word processor program before turning his attention once again to the Weapons Control module.

Le Moulin au Pouchon, *St Médard, near Manciet, Midi-Pyrénées, France*

'There's definitely something there,' Dekker muttered, his eyes glued to the night-vision glasses in the darkened bedroom. 'About a hundred metres up the hill. It looks like a derelict building, but I can see at least one person in it, maybe two. I'm only seeing their faces.'

'That has to be them,' Richter said. 'Take them out.'

The bedroom had only one fairly narrow window with a view up the hill, and it was immediately obvious that two men wouldn't be able to shoot out of it at the same time. 'Take the first shot as soon as you can,' Ross instructed the sniper. 'With any luck the second target may show himself straight afterwards, taking a look down here.'

The trooper nodded, opened the window and rested his Accuracy International PM sniper rifle as comfortably as he could on the sill and stared up the hill through the Davin Optical Starlight scope.

Richter's mobile rang again, with the news that he had hoped not to hear. 'It's Baker. Sorry, but he ejected me from the system a couple of minutes ago, and I can't get back in – he seems to have deleted Modin as a user. It's all up to you now.'

'Thanks a bunch,' Richter said, and snapped the phone off. 'That was my computer man in London,' he told Ross. 'Dernowi has kicked him off the system, so we've got minutes at the most to sort this out.'

Even as he spoke, the sniper squeezed the rifle's trigger and immediately brought the weapon back on target. 'One down,' he said, never taking his eye from the sights.

St Médard, near Manciet, Midi-Pyrénées, France

Karim Ibrahim suddenly jerked backwards in a spray of blood and, in a slow motion that was almost graceful, span to the ground, his Kalashnikov clattering on to the stone floor beside him as the echo of the shot rang around the valley. Badri sprang across to his fallen comrade and looked down in disbelief. Ibrahim was dead, had been dead before he even hit the ground, a massive bullet wound in his face.

'A sniper,' Badri snapped, disgust in his voice, and rushed back across the outhouse to the ruined window. Keeping low and behind the wall, he pushed the muzzle of his Kalashnikov through the window and emptied the magazine down the hill towards the old house.

'Stop,' Abbas shouted, 'stop firing. Now they know where we are. You cannot hit them, and I need you alive to keep me alive. Reload, and stay down and out of sight.'

Almost reluctantly, Badri crouched low and fitted a new magazine to his Kalashnikov. 'Should we move on?' he asked.

Abbas shook his head. 'No. They would hunt us down like animals in the dark. To have killed Ibrahim like that, with a single shot, means they have image-intensifier sights and sniper rifles. They probably also have automatic weapons and grenades. We have two Kalashnikovs and three pistols. We have no choice but to make our last stand here.' Badri nodded, but said nothing. 'They cannot reach us directly from the house,' Abbas said. 'The undergrowth is too thick. Now they know where we are, they will try to work their way around and come upon us from behind.' Abbas gestured urgently to the dark hillside at the rear of the outhouse. 'Move over there and watch for them.'

Abbas had displayed an immediate tactical grasp of the situation, and of the intentions of Ross and Dekker. They'd both studied the terrain leading up to the outhouse through their night-vision glasses and had decided that it was effectively impassable without making their presence quite obvious, which would inevitably invite a stream of bullets from the surviving bodyguard. An approach from the rear was the only viable option.

Dekker and four troopers, followed by Richter, slid silently out of the front door of *Le Moulin au Pouchon* and ran up the road for about two hundred metres, then moved through the scrubby hedge and started up the hill.

*

Hassan Abbas leant back from the laptop computer, his fingers leaving the keyboard for the first time in what seemed hours, and for a few seconds he just sat there, deep in thought.

When *El Sikkiyn* had been conceived, the al-Qaeda leadership had insisted on the simultaneous detonation of all two hundred and three weapons placed on American soil. Abbas and Sadoun Khamil had both argued that it would be better only to detonate the majority of the weapons, leaving the others still in place and hidden, to be used as a lethal bargaining counter for the future.

But al-Qaeda believed that the only way that America could be induced to fire its entire nuclear arsenal at Russia, which was the prime objective of the plan, would be to ensure that America suffered an overwhelming nuclear attack, clearly originating from Russia. The American and Russian governments might be able to avoid a full-scale nuclear exchange if only a few weapons were exploded. They could, perhaps, negotiate some kind of reparation or settlement, particularly if the Russians could demonstrate that the attack had actually not been their doing. And that was not what al-Qaeda wanted. *El Sikkiyn* was designed to ensure the total destruction of both America and Russia, hence the single, massive strike.

The problem that Hassan Abbas was facing, as the executor of *El Sikkiyn*, was time. Ever since he had switched on the laptop, he had been trying to complete the detonation routine. But each weapon required the inputting of two twelve-digit codes – twenty-four digits – for each weapon. It was a safeguard the Russians had built into the system, and there had been no way Abbas could reasonably argue against it.

The other problem was that before any weapon could be detonated, the user had to select 'Individual', 'Group' or 'Total' to determine whether just one or a number of weapons were to be fired. Abbas had selected 'total', but he'd only enabled thirty-two of the two hundred and three weapons, and he knew that there was no possible way he could complete the authorization sequence for all of the devices before the unknown attackers would have worked their way around to the outhouse and killed him.

Abbas leaned forward again, decision made. If he couldn't carry out his orders, he would just have to do the best he could in the time he had left. At least, he thought, with a wry smile, nobody in al-Qaeda would be able to reproach him for it, because he knew with absolute certainty that he had only minutes left to live.

He flicked the touchpad and sent the cursor across the screen and cancelled the 'Total' detonation routine. With another swift movement he selected 'Individual' and chose the first target on the alphabetically sorted list – Abilene, Texas.

At the old mill, Ross looked at his watch for the eighth time since the group had left, then nodded to the sniper. The trooper squeezed the trigger of his rifle and sent the 7.62mm round screaming up the hill, to smash harmlessly into the solid stone wall of the outhouse. Then he reloaded and did it again, and again, and again.

Badri jumped to his feet as the first bullet smashed into the two-feet-thick stone wall beside him.

'That means they're coming,' Abbas called out, never taking his eyes off the screen of the computer. 'Ignore the sniper – he will just be trying to distract us from the men approaching. Prepare.'

With a grunt of satisfaction, Abbas pressed the last digit of the second authorization code for the Abilene weapon, flicked the cursor across the screen again, chose 'Albany, New York' and began inputting the first code requested by the system.

Abilene, Texas

The city of Abilene was founded in 1881 as the railhead for the Texas and Pacific Railway and as the new destination for the Texas cattle drives, taking over both the name and the business of the previous railhead – Abilene, Kansas. The city is situated in an area of low plains some one hundred and fifty miles west of Fort Worth, and straddles Taylor and Jones Counties. It is home to just under three hundred thousand people.

The two-metre satellite dish had been positioned on the roof of the small downtown office building, located a few blocks north of McMurry University, by a local company some six months earlier, and the co-axial feed cable had been run down into the smallest of the three rooms which comprised the office suite. There had been neither television set nor satellite receiver in the room when the installation had been completed, so the aerial fitters had aligned the dish with one of the commercial satellites, as they had been asked to do by the dark-skinned businessman who had leased the premises, and left, cash tucked in their pockets.

Three days, or rather nights, later, two men climbed on to the roof of the building with a signal strength meter and tools in their hands and re-aligned the dish to a more easterly satellite that didn't appear in any of the Clarke Belt charts.

Nobody noticed that the dish had been moved, and nor did any-body take much notice when the short, slim, dark-skinned businessman took delivery of a large and very heavy packing case two weeks later. And a month after that he left the office for the last time, heading for a new assignment on the west coast, in Los Angeles. The rent on the office had been paid a year in advance, much to the delight of the free-holder, and the utility bills were all settled direct from a company bank account, and what little mail arrived was automatically intercepted and forwarded to another address, so nobody had any need to go any-where near the office suite. Not that it would have made any difference if they had.

When Hassan Abbas input the final digit of the second authorization code for the Abilene weapon, the Krutaya mainframe began an auto-mated sequence of events. First it sent a 'system test' signal to the small computer attached to the selected weapon, which instructed it to carry out a check of all its circuits. Thirty seconds later the mainframe sent a 'prepare' signal, and thirty seconds after that the 'detonate' signal was sent via the satellite.

None of this, of course, was apparent to anybody in Abilene. Inside the large locked steel case in the back room of the deserted office suite, a small orange light illuminated. Thirty seconds later a red light came on, and after another half-minute a green light. The entire process up to that point had been completely silent, but within two seconds of the green light illuminating there was a barely audible click from within the steel chest. That single faint sound was the noise of the trigger assembly being actuated, and it was followed by an extraordinarily rapid sequence of events.

Within the case was a tempered-steel sphere which contained two sub-critical masses of uranium–235, surrounded by a shell of conventional chemical explosive. Outside this inner shell were further chemical explosives arranged as thirty-two critically shaped lenses. When these shaped charges detonated in a sequence that was accurate to the nearest millisecond, they focused shock waves which compressed and instantly ignited the inner chemical explosive shell, which in turn smashed together the two masses of uranium in the centre of the sphere, creating an immediate critical mass. Precisely one third of a second later the uranium tore itself to pieces as the fission reaction began.

The atomic weapon that was dropped on Hiroshima was only about 1.4 per cent efficient, but weapons technology has always been a growth industry and advances in the casing design and the shaping of the conventional explosive charges have greatly improved the efficiency of modern nuclear weapons. So although the Abilene weapon was only a fraction of the size of the Little Boy and Fat Man twenty-kiloton bombs that had devastated Hiroshima and Nagasaki respectively, it had almost exactly the same calculated yield. The yield of each weapon had been specified by Dmitri Trushenko to be sufficient to completely destroy the heart of the city in which it was positioned. Abilene, Texas, is a small city, and the weapon located there was one of the smallest of the *Podstava* devices and one of the few fission weapons that had been deployed.

Even so, its effects were immediate and devastating. The office building vaporized almost instantly, as did some four square miles of the centre of the city. Slightly over one hundred and seven thousand people died in less than one fifth of a second.

Half a second after the detonation, the temperature at the epicentre of the explosion reached several million degrees, and a massive fireball rose from the ground and expanded to cover most of the city of Abilene, starting innumerable ground fires that flared out of control, burning the living and incinerating the bodies of the newly dead.

Anything combustible burned. Garage fuel storage tanks, domestic gas supplies and automobile petrol tanks exploded, adding to the carnage. It was doubly unfortunate that a major part of Abilene's industrial area is given over to the production of natural gas and petroleum, and the explosion of these highly combustible fuels significantly increased the devastation caused by the fireball. A further thirty-one thousand people perished directly as a result of the fireball.

Another half a second later the shockwave from the weapon began to spread outwards at unbelievable speed in a circular pattern, demolishing the few remaining buildings and flinging vehicles and people high into the air. Its force would not be spent until it was well clear of the city limits, and even at the very edge of the city it was still strong enough to flatten houses. The shockwave killed another sixteen thousand people. Convection currents generated by the explosion sucked dust into the air, hauling it high above the shattered community and forming the terrifying and completely unmistakable shape of a mushroom cloud.

Almost everyone within three miles of ground zero who survived the detonation died as well, but more slowly, killed by the lethal but invisible fusillades of neutrons and gamma radiation generated by the explosion.

Even people several miles away from Abilene would die, even more slowly, over the succeeding weeks and months, killed by the fallout – the material vaporized in the fireball which would condense to form microscopically fine particles full of highly radioactive and long-lived contaminants like plutonium–239 and strontium–90. The final death toll from the Abilene weapon would top one hundred and eighty-five thousand, though nobody would ever be able to work out the exact number who perished, and the cost of the damage was quite literally incalculable.

Chapter Twenty-Nine

Friday
St Médard, near Manciet, Midi-Pyrénées, France

The trooper was within twenty yards of the outhouse before Jaafar Badri heard anything at all. This was partly due to the trooper's skill in silent movement, and partly because of the constant crackling of the unsilenced sniper rifle a hundred metres away and the smashing of its bullets against stone. All Badri heard was a faint slither, but it was enough. He crouched down almost to floor level, cautiously extended the muzzle of the Kalashnikov around the broken doorframe, and waited, eyes wide and staring into the darkness.

The trooper stopped moving, as he had been told to, lay flat on the ground and lobbed a small stone over to his right. Badri moved further out of the doorway, swinging his assault rifle to point at the sound he had just heard, and pulled the trigger. As the first round from the Kalashnikov crashed through the undergrowth, Colin Dekker, who had positioned himself to the left of the outhouse and with a clear view of the doorway, fired his silenced Hockler twice, hitting Badri in the chest and right shoulder.

The Arab crashed against the doorway, but with a supreme effort of will sat almost upright, pulling the muzzle of the Kalashnikov around towards Dekker. It didn't do him any good. Three Hocklers fired at him almost simultaneously, bullets ripping through his chest and torso, and he slumped to the ground, dead.

Abbas ignored the sounds behind him, and concentrated on inputting the second firing authorization code for the Albany device. He had only three digits to go when Richter shot him in the back.

517

North American Aerospace Defense Command, Cheyenne Mountain, Colorado

The normal silence of the NORAD control room was suddenly shattered by the sounds of warning bells and klaxons, and the giant vision screens flickered into life as lines of red text appeared. 'Nuclear detonation, nuclear detonation! Location is Continental United States, south-central region. Central Texas. Detonation confirmed by seismic sensors. Stand by for estimate of ground zero position.'

General Wayne Harmon ran from his office to the control room, sat down at his desk and snatched up his headset. There was a confused babble of voices, which he swiftly silenced. 'No way it was an ICBM. It had to have been sub-launched. Why didn't we get a launch detection?' he snapped.

'No idea. We saw nothing on radar from the DEW or anywhere else, and neither did the DSP birds.'

Missile launches are detected by one of three Defence Support Programme surveillance satellites in geosynchronous orbit twenty-two thousand three hundred miles above the surface of the Earth. One is positioned over Central America, the second over the middle of the Pacific Ocean and the last above the Indian Ocean, and they maintain a constant watch of the Asian landmass and the oceans. Each DSP bird is fitted with a massive infra-red telescope which can identify the heat flare of the missile's engines within one minute of launch. Only if there is heavy cloud above the launch site will the system not detect the missile until it clears the cloud tops. Launch and initial trajectory data are transmitted from the DSP satellite to the two Readout Stations located at Aurora, Colorado and Alice Springs, Australia, where the data is automatically compared with that from previous launches to determine whether or not the missile is on a 'threat fan' – that is to say, on a path ending in the United States or inside any allied nation.

'Bullshit. Play back the tape – there must have been something and we missed it,' Harmon said and reached for the JANET phone. 'JANET' is the Joint Chiefs of Staff Alerting Network, which links the National Military Command Center in the Pentagon and all other principal command headquarters.

'Ground zero location confirmed as Abilene, Texas. Initial estimates from the seismographs suggest a weapon size of around thirty kilotons.'

'Thirty kilotons? That's bullshit too,' Harmon snapped. 'The Russians haven't got any nuclear weapons that small – at least, none that they'd bother launching at us. This has just gotta be some kind of a screw-up.'

Camp David, Maryland

'There's been a what?' the President asked into the telephone, his face going pale. 'Where?'

'Satellite surveillance reports ground zero as Abilene, Texas, Mr President,' General Harmon replied, 'but the situation is still confused.'

'What do you mean "confused"?' the President snapped. 'Are you telling me you don't know if a nuclear weapon has been detonated or not?'

'No, Mr President. Detonation of a device definitely took place – the seismic data has already confirmed that – but the rest of the data doesn't make sense. First, we had no launch detection of any sort, so the weapon didn't arrive here on an ICBM or in a missile from a Russian boomer. We've checked the recorded data and all our systems, and there was definitely no launch. Second, the weapon is way too small. The seismic data puts it at around thirty kilotons, maybe even less, and all the Russian first-strike weapons are way up in the multi-megaton range. This thing was more like a tactical weapon.'

There was a pause as the President digested this information. 'Thank you, General,' he said. 'I'll be in touch.'

'Sir? What are your orders?'

'I said I'll be in touch. There are factors here that you will not be aware of, General, and I have to consider very carefully exactly what to do next.'

St Médard, near Manciet, Midi-Pyrénées, France

In the bedroom of *Le Moulin au Pouchon* the sniper suddenly stopped his rhythmic assault on the outhouse, but kept the rifle muzzle pointed straight up the hill as he stared through the Starlight scope.

'Are they there?' Ross asked.

'Yes. I can see four figures behind the outhouse, now all standing up.'

'Excellent,' Ross murmured, then spoke into his microphone. 'Dekker, Ross. SITREP?'

'It's over. One dead, we assume he was the bodyguard, and the other's wounded and out of action.'

'Right,' Ross said. 'I'll let London know.'

The bullet had taken Abbas just below the right shoulder and the force of its impact had tumbled him away from the laptop computer and against the wall. Richter gestured to Dekker to watch the Arab, and turned his attention to the laptop.

He was no computer expert, but it was obvious even to Richter what Abbas had been trying to do. He studied the screen for several seconds. At the top of the screen the heading 'Weapon: Albany, New York' was displayed. Below that appeared the message 'Authorization Code Six Accepted. For final Verification, Enter Authorization Code Two', and below that was an oblong horizontal box with space for twelve digits. Nine of the twelve spaces were already occupied by an asterisk symbol.

Richter touched the 'Esc' or 'Escape' key. As he had hoped, the screen display cleared and both the message and the oblong box vanished. The screen simply displayed the Albany weapon control page, but the system just sat there, waiting for his input.

'Thank God for that,' Richter muttered, and pulled out his mobile phone. He switched off silent ringing and punched in the direct line number for the computer suite. Baker answered almost immediately.

'Baker.'

'Richter. It's over. I'm looking at this Arab bastard's laptop, and we stopped him just before he detonated the weapon at Albany.'

Even over the mobile phone network, the sadness and horror in Baker's voice were unmistakable. 'Pity you didn't get to him a few minutes sooner,' he said. 'It's all a bit confused, but according to CNN a nuclear weapon has just exploded in Abilene, Texas.'

Richter said nothing, just sat back on his haunches, snapped the phone shut and put it back in his pocket. He looked across at Dekker, who was covering the Arab with his Hockler. Dekker had kicked Abbas' Glock well out of reach, and had hauled the wounded Arab up against the wall of the outhouse where he sat hunched and groaning, but conscious.

'We were too late,' Richter said. 'This bastard managed to detonate at least one weapon in the States. God knows how many people he's killed, or what the Americans will do now.'

Richter stood up, walked across the outhouse to where the Glock lay on the floor, bent down and picked it up. Showing no emotion, he walked back to where Abbas sat, placed the muzzle of the pistol against the Arab's left kneecap and pulled the trigger. The report of the shot echoed from the stone walls, and was followed immediately by a howl of pain from Abbas. 'That,' Richter said, 'is for Abilene.' He transferred the weapon to Abbas' right knee and fired again.

'Albany?' Dekker asked, looking at the information displayed on the laptop's screen.

'Albany,' Richter agreed. 'I know he didn't detonate it, but it certainly wasn't for want of trying.' As Richter squatted down in front of the groaning Arab, his mobile phone rang again. 'Richter.'

'It's Baker. It's only just dawned on me – you said that you had Dernowi's laptop?'

'Yes. It's right here beside me, connected to a mobile phone. When we took out the landlines I suppose he had no option but to use the mobile.'

'Yes, yes,' Baker said impatiently, 'but the point is that you have a link to the Krutaya mainframe using the laptop, and with Dernowi's access level you can disable all the weapons.'

'I can try,' Richter said doubtfully.

'It's not a problem. I can talk you through it right now.'

'OK,' Richter said, and sat down on the stone floor in front of the laptop.

'Right,' Baker said. 'first you access the—'

'Oh, shit,' Richter muttered, and looked in irritation at his phone. The battery strength was fine, but the signal strength read zero. He snatched up Abbas' mobile and looked at that. The battery was about two-thirds exhausted and, like Richter's Nokia, it was reading zero signal strength. Lacomte had taken his time getting the mobile phone cells switched off, but he had finally managed it.

There was nothing more Richter could do with the laptop, so he removed the data cable, switched off Abbas' mobile phone, and put the computer, phone and cable into the Samsonite case. Then he walked back to where Abbas was sitting groaning against the wall. He pushed the muzzle of the Glock under Abbas' chin and forced the Arab's head up.

'You're Dernowi, I presume. I've got a couple of questions for you. First, what's your backdoor code for the Russian computer?'

Abbas opened his eyes slowly and looked at Richter, then very deliberately he spat in his face. At first Richter didn't react at all, then he brought his left hand up, wiped the spittle from his cheek, then moved the Glock down and fired a bullet through Abbas' right thigh.

'Let's try that again, shall we?' he said, raising his voice over the Arab's screams. 'What's the backdoor code?' Abbas shook his head, still howling.

'You're going to die here,' Richter said, 'but it's up to you how. Tell us what we want and it will be a single bullet, then oblivion. Carry on like this and I'll just keep shooting bits off you until you pass out. Fun for me, but definitely not for you. So, what's your backdoor code?'

The Arab shook his head again. 'I will never tell you,' he murmured, his voice low and cultured, with a pronounced Home Counties English accent. Looking at him, Richter suddenly realized that he wouldn't, that he was looking at a committed martyr. 'OK, then why choose "Dernowi"? Why a Yiddish name for an Arab, and why "The Prophet"?'

Abbas almost smiled. 'It was an old joke,' he said. 'That was all.'

'And why all this? Why were you trying to detonate weapons the Russians had planted in America?'

Abbas was losing blood quickly from his multiple wounds, and Richter knew he had only minutes before the Arab lost consciousness for the last time. 'To start a war, of course,' Abbas said, his voice barely audible. 'The Russians were stupid. They knew nothing of our plan. They thought we just wanted to humiliate America, to threaten them with the bombs. We wanted America destroyed, but for Russia to be blamed and destroyed in her turn. At a stroke, we would eliminate the world's two superpowers, and allow the full blossoming of the Arab world. The Arab nations would arise as the new world leaders and we would finally fulfil our destiny. That is why we conceived this plan, and that is why we paid for everything, why we bought the Russians.'

Richter sat back, hardly believing what he had heard. 'So you and your camel-shit-eating masters were going to sacrifice the populations of America and Russia, and probably most of Western Europe, just so that a bunch of flea-ridden sand Arabs could rule the world?'

Abbas nodded. 'And we will make a much better job of it than you have,' he spat. 'It is our destiny. We will bring the word of Mohammed to the godless masses, if not now then later.' And then he added something which chilled Richter even more than Baker's news. 'I am not the only one who knows the backdoor code,' he said.

'Who else?' Richter demanded, but Abbas just smiled slightly and shook his head.

'I will not tell you,' he said. 'You will find out, and he will finish what I began. Your time is at an end.'

Richter nodded, decision made. 'And so is your time,' he said, and raised the Glock.

'You would not dare,' Abbas said. 'This is France, a civilized country. You cannot just execute me. I expect medical treatment. I want to talk to my Embassy in France.'

'Expect away,' Richter said, and shot Abbas twice in the stomach. The Arab's eyes widened with the sudden searing pain, and he began a keening, wailing sound as he toppled sideways, clutching his belly.

'One for Abilene, one for Albany,' Richter said, stood up and turned away.

'You want me to finish him?' Dekker asked.

'No,' Richter shook his head firmly, picked up the Samsonite computer case and walked out of the ruined building. 'Leave him there. Let him die slowly. It'll give him time to make his peace with Mohammed.'

Buraydah, Saudi Arabia

Sadoun Khamil looked at the television set with a broad smile on his face. The satellite receiver was tuned to CNN, and already the first still picture – shot from a safe distance, probably several miles away – of the characteristic mushroom-shaped cloud over what was left of Abilene was more or less a fixture on the screen. The correspondents were visibly appalled, and trying desperately to make any kind of sense of what they and the world were seeing.

American government buildings were already under siege from the news media, but there had been no announcements of any sort from any officials. Experts from various disciplines were being dragged into studios, or just stood in front of camera crews, and asked for their comments and conclusions, but the quite unmistakable fact was that nobody in America had any idea of what had happened or why. The best guess on the part of the CNN anchor was that it was just a terrible mistake – an American nuclear weapon had been accidentally detonated, with appalling loss of life and wholesale destruction.

Khamil smiled again as he heard this. 'There will be a few more such accidents,' he prophesied, and laughed out loud.

10 Downing Street, London

Sir Michael Geraghty sat down heavily in the leather chair opposite the mahogany desk in the Prime Minister's private office, and looked across at the grey-haired man who'd been roused from sleep by his staff minutes earlier when the news from Texas broke. His hair was tousled, and he was still in pyjamas, a mauve dressing gown wrapped tightly around him. Geraghty was uncomfortably aware that he didn't look much better himself, though he was fully dressed.

'This is appalling, simply appalling.'

'I can only agree with you, Prime Minister. You know that we in SIS did everything we could, and I have already congratulated Simpson on the performance of his people. The presence of this Arab –' he almost spat the word '– with a backdoor code into the Russian computer was completely unexpected, and something nobody could possibly have foreseen.'

'And what now?' the Prime Minister asked. 'After Abilene, what will the Americans do? The weapon was Russian in design, construction and placement. The fact that it was triggered by an Arab is probably, in this context, irrelevant. At the very least we can expect them to demand substantial reparation from Russia, and at worst they might decide on a surgical strike, to visit upon the Russian people the same sort of losses they have experienced.'

'That, Prime Minister, is why I'm here,' Geraghty said. 'Simpson has informed me that the SAS and his man successfully stopped the Arab terrorist from detonating any further weapons, although he was trying to do just that when they caught up with him. As far as we are aware, there is no further danger from any of the weapons that the Russians positioned on American soil. It would be a tragedy if America struck at Russia now, and precipitated any kind of a nuclear exchange. May I recommend, in the strongest possible terms, that you discuss the matter immediately with the American President and suggest that, for the moment, he does nothing precipitate.

'It may help if you advise him that we have evidence which definitely links al-Qaeda with the Abilene bombing. It was not, in the final analysis, the Russians who pulled the trigger, and any retaliation should probably not be directed towards them.'

Camp David, Maryland

'I hear what you say,' the President said, the secure telephone pressed close to his ear, 'and your views are not too dissimilar from my own. Of course, the hawks will want to strike back immediately, and I'll no doubt face a lot of criticism if I take no military action, but we have to think of the long-term consequences. And, as you rightly put it, the Russians didn't actually pull the trigger.'

St Médard, near Manciet, Midi-Pyrénées, France

Three of the troopers had been sent down the lane back to the village, and had returned with the three Renault Espaces.

They swiftly moved the bodies of the two dead SAS troopers into one of the vehicles, then Richter and Ross supervised the removal of almost everything portable in the house, from the computer in the back bedroom to the prayer mats in the lounge, taking anything and everything that could provide clues to the identity of the four dead Arabs. They stripped the bodies, collected their clothes, personal possessions, weapons and ammunition, and all the spent cartridge cases they could find. Everything went into the cavernous boots of the Espaces.

They photographed each of them, several times, full face and profile, even Ibrahim, who nobody, not even his own mother, would recognize. They worked quickly, aware that the noise they had created in assaulting the house would certainly have been heard by someone, and that quite possibly the gendarmes were already en route to the village. Confrontation with French law-enforcement officers would not be a problem, because one call by Richter to Lacomte should sort it out, but he and Ross had agreed that a swift and silent exit from the scene was by far the best option.

Twenty-eight minutes after Richter had shot Abbas in the stomach, the three vehicles began the descent down the hill into St Médard.

The Walnut Room, the Kremlin, Krasnaya ploshchad, Moscow

'This is appalling,' the Russian President said, unconsciously echoing the words the British Prime Minister had used just minutes earlier and almost two thousand miles away. 'You are absolutely certain of the facts?'

'Yes, Comrade President,' Yuri Baratov said, his familiar smile for once completely absent. 'A low-yield nuclear weapon was detonated in the American south-central region approximately one hour ago. Our initial estimate based on technical analysis and seismograph data suggests that ground zero was Abilene in Texas and this has been confirmed by the American news media. CNN, in particular.'

The President rubbed his chin thoughtfully. 'I am not familiar with American centres of population. What size city is Abilene?'

'The population of the city is around one hundred and twenty thousand,' Baratov said, 'and about a further one hundred and seventy thousand people live in the surrounding area.'

'And the weapon? What size device was used?'

'Again, Comrade President, we do not yet have accurate data, but we believe the weapon to be very low-yield, probably thirty kilotons or less.'

'So what sort of damage are we talking about? What casualties?'

Yuri Baratov spread his hands in a gesture of hopelessness. 'We can't begin to estimate it. The worst-case scenario would place the weapon in or near the centre of the city. That could produce a death toll of anything from one hundred thousand to two hundred thousand people. That's most of the population, but by American standards it's a small city. If the weapon was detonated some distance outside the city, perhaps half of those figures.'

'So many?' the President murmured, his voice shaking with emotion. 'But you said it was a low-yield weapon.'

'That is what we believe,' Baratov replied. 'But you must remember, Comrade President, that the weapon the Americans dropped on Hiroshima only had a yield of twenty kilotons, and that killed about one hundred thousand people.'

'And the question the Americans will want us to answer, no doubt, is why a Russian nuclear weapon was detonated in an American city. And I too want that question answered. There is no possibility that this was some kind of a terrorist attack, and nothing to do with that idiot Trushenko's *Podstava*, I suppose?'

Baratov shook his head. 'I have already talked with General Sokolov, and he has confirmed that Abilene was one of the cities targeted by

Trushenko, though he does not know either the calculated yield of the weapon or where it was located. But I do not believe in coincidence. This weapon was certainly one of the *Podstava* devices.'

'Which of course raises yet another question,' the President growled. 'Modin and Bykov have just been placed under armed guard at the Embassy in London. Sokolov is here in Moscow in a cell in the Lubyanka and Trushenko is dead, killed in the Ukraine, so who fired the weapon?'

Again Baratov spread his hands wide. 'I have no idea,' he said.

'Well, one thing is quite certain,' the President said, getting to his feet. 'I will have to go and talk to the Americans. Immediately.'

Vic-Fézensac, Midi-Pyrénées, France

'There's a phone box – stop the car,' Richter called, and Dekker obediently hauled the Espace into the side of the road. Richter had been checking his mobile phone for the last eight minutes, ever since the idea had come to him, but the signal strength had stayed obstinately at zero. The box in Vic-Fézensac was the first public telephone he'd seen on the road since they'd left St Médard. He jumped out of the Espace, ran back to the phone box and lifted the receiver, feeding Euros into the slot as he did so. The phone rang only twice before Baker answered.

'It's Richter. The Arab who was calling himself "The Prophet". It's just occurred to me that perhaps his backdoor code could be the same, but in a different language. His screen name or whatever you call it was Yiddish, not Farsi or Pashto, which we would have expected of an Arab. Maybe he ransacked the languages of the world, using obscure words in dialects spoken by only a handful of people. He seemed to think the name "The Prophet" was some kind of a joke, so it's possible he thought it was so funny he used it twice, if you see what I mean.'

'Yes, maybe,' Baker said doubtfully. 'I've already tried accessing the system using "Dernowi", but that didn't work. I'll run the word "prophet" through the dictionary program and see what it comes up with. I'll call you.'

'Right,' Richter said. 'You'd better make that your first priority – the Arab said that somebody else knew the backdoor code to the Krutaya mainframe, and I don't think he was joking about that. Oh, and ask somebody there to get Lacomte to re-activate the mobile phone cells down here as soon as he can.'

'Right. Is that it?'

'No. Is Simpson there? I need to brief him on what we got out of the Arab. Some of what he said will certainly interest him, and I'm sure the Americans will be fascinated.'

Buraydah, Saudi Arabia

Sadoun Khamil was still sitting in front of the television set, but his smile had vanished and he was puzzled. The screen now showed long-distance television pictures of the ruins of Abilene, taken from a news chopper that was keeping some miles back from the devastation, presumably because of the danger from the fallout. That wasn't what was puzzling him. By now, he had expected there to be news of other detonations, from all across the United States, but it was beginning to look as if the Abilene weapon was an isolated incident.

He would, he decided, wait only a further hour, and then he would have to contact al-Qaeda. In the meantime, he strode across to his computer to compose an urgent email, sent direct and this time in clear, to Hassan Abbas.

The Walnut Room, the Kremlin, Krasnaya ploshchad, Moscow

'An Arab?' Yuri Baratov could not keep the incredulity out of his voice. 'Why would some fucking raghead have access to a Russian weapons computer?'

'According to the American President, because the fucking ragheads, as you describe them, actually paid for it to be built. If the Americans are to be believed,' the Russian President continued, 'the Arabs – and by that the President actually means the al-Qaeda group – conceived the *Podstava* operation, behind which their own plan was hidden, and they also paid for the construction and placement of all the weapons, here in

Europe as well as in America. That bastard Trushenko was the recipient of the funds, and no doubt he had a nice little nest-egg salted away somewhere. Your people can no doubt find out exactly where he chose and recover the funds for us.'

Baratov nodded, then shook his head. 'I still don't believe it,' he said.

'Well, the Americans do, and so do the British, who actually stopped the al-Qaeda operation. The Arabs' intention, according to the President, was to detonate over two hundred nuclear weapons in America at the same moment. This, they believed, would be certain to initiate a massive retaliatory attack on us, and to which we would respond with whatever weapons we had left. In a little over twenty-four hours both Russia and America would have been effectively destroyed. The only good thing, if you can call it that, is that Trushenko and the others involved apparently had no idea what the Arabs actually had planned.'

Baratov was noticeably pale in the face, and his voice shook slightly as he replied. 'But why? Why would the Arabs do that?'

'Again according to the Americans, because that would provide the Arab world with the opportunity to arise as the new world leaders, to bring the word of Mohammed to the godless East, and the far-too Christian West.'

'And now?' Baratov asked. 'What will the Americans do about the bomb that detonated in Texas?'

'Nothing,' The Russian President said, with a smile of relief. 'At least, no military action, though we will certainly have to make financial and other reparations – it was, after all, a Russian weapon. That, I have assured the President, we will be more than happy to do.'

Hammersmith, London

Fifty-three minutes after he'd received the call from Richter, and thirty-eight minutes after the dictionary program had delivered the results of its worldwide language search, Baker leaned back from the screen of his computer. 'Well, I'll be buggered,' he muttered.

He had just tried yet again to log on to the Krutaya mainframe, and the word he had tried this time from the printout in front of him produced results. The screen display showed two lines of text, but only one of them was comprehensible to Baker. The first line read, in English, 'Welcome, Prophet. I await your commands.'

The reason Baker couldn't read the second line was because it was written in Dari, the Afghan dialect of Farsi, which is spoken by about one third of the population of Afghanistan, and is used as a kind of lingua franca between speakers of different languages in that country. Baker was well versed in all the major computer languages, but was barely literate in English and he had no knowledge whatsoever of any other spoken language. In fact, the second line was only a repeat of the first, with the addition of a single word – '*Inshallah*'.

Baker grabbed the phone and dialled Richter's mobile, which rang instantly. Obviously Lacomte had got the cells working again.

'Richter.'

'It's Baker. I'm in.'

'Thank God for that. What was the backdoor code?'

'You were right. I ran the dictionary program, and this was about the thirtieth word I tried. It's "manalagna".'

'What?'

Baker spelt it phonetically. 'Just like all the others it means "The Prophet", and the language is Ilongo, from the Philippines.'

'OK,' Richter said. 'Start disabling the weapons, and be quick about it, just in case this other Arab bastard tries to get in to finish off what Dernowi started. But don't,' he added, 'disable the London weapon – we've still got plans for that.'

Buraydah, Saudi Arabia

The hour was up, and still there had been neither word from Hassan Abbas nor any further weapon detonations in America. Khamil had even tried to telephone Abbas using both the landline number and his mobile phone; the former had resulted in a 'number unobtainable' message, while the mobile was apparently switched off.

Four years of planning, Khamil realized, and the operation had gone wrong in a spectacular fashion at the eleventh hour. But there was one thing he could do to retrieve it. He was not a computer expert, but he was competent, and Abbas had shown him the Weapon Control program on the Russian mainframe computer. He could read enough Cyrillic script to decipher the various options, he had a copy of the firing authorization codes and, most importantly, he knew the backdoor code. If Abbas had been killed or captured, he could do it instead. *El Sikkiyn* would be implemented a little late, but it would be implemented.

Khamil crossed to his laptop computer and touched the space bar to remove the screen saver. He pulled a small notebook from his pocket, opened Internet Explorer and typed in the name of the Arizona sex site. When the site had loaded, Khamil moved swiftly to the link that generated the 404 error, and clicked the 'Refresh' button several times.

The screen went blank apart from the flashing cursor. Khamil referred again to his book, then carefully typed in 'manalagna' and watched the screen. The welcome message in English and Dari that he was expecting did not appear, and he stared, puzzled, at a message in Cyrillic lettering for some moments. Then he opened a drawer on his desk, extracted a small Russian-English dictionary and laboriously began to translate the message.

Four minutes later, he sat back, his face ashen. Now there could be no doubt, no doubt at all, that his gamble had failed. The message read simply: 'Duplicate log-on attempt. This user is already registered on the system. Please check your username and password and try again.'

Hammersmith, London

At eleven thirty that morning Richter climbed wearily up the stairs, walked into Simpson's office and sat down. He'd flown back from Toulouse in the HS-146 and there had been a car at Northolt to meet him. Simpson looked at him and closed the file he had been reading.

'Is it done?' he asked.

'Yes, it's done,' Richter replied. 'Baker got in using Dernowi's back-door code and disarmed all the American bombs, and all the strategic neutron bombs apart from the London weapon.'

'Is that a permanent disarming procedure?' Simpson asked.

Richter nodded. 'I think so. According to Professor Dewar, the weapon includes a circuit to physically burn out the actuating coils in the trigger unit, and he presumed that the circuit was included as part of the abort routine. If he's right, then the only way to arm the weapon again is to fit an entire new trigger assembly. That,' Richter added, 'is the case with the neutron bomb that he examined in France. We obviously haven't had a chance to examine any of the weapons placed in America, so I don't know if the abort sequence works the same way on those.'

'That's something the Americans can sort out,' Simpson said. 'They've had the details of the weapon locations since last night. And the London device?'

'That was the last thing I asked Baker to do,' Richter said. 'We've locked out all the other users from the Russian computer, and as things stand the only people that can access it are us. No doubt they will try and get back into the system any time now.'

'As a matter of fact, Baker said that user Dernowi tried to get back on-line while he was actually disabling the weapons. And as Dernowi was dead at the time,' Richter added, 'either that's definite proof of life after death or there was somebody else – probably another bloody Arab – who knew the backdoor code. Anyway, he couldn't get in using the "manalagna" code because Baker was already logged on as Dernowi.'

'I wonder who he was,' Simpson mused.

'It doesn't matter now,' Richter said. 'The weapons are just lumps of metal and the Arab plan is defunct. Right, I don't pretend to understand the technicalities of it, but I asked Baker to write what he called a sub-routine and include it in the Russian system. What it means is that, with effect from the end of next week, the computer will accept any of the previous log ins and passwords, but the new code he's written will divert all users away from the existing system and into Baker's little routine.

'His program will tell them that all the weapons but one have been disabled, and that control of the firing program, and of the satellite, have passed into Western hands. The kicker is the last section, which tells them that the London weapon is in full working order, armed and ready, and is now residing in Her Britannic Majesty's Embassy at Sofiyskaya naberezhnaya 14, Moscow, which is, as we all know, just across the Moskva River from the Kremlin. The access delay Baker built-in will allow plenty of time for the weapon to be physically placed in the Embassy.'

Simpson smiled – a rare and not particularly attractive sight. 'A real cuckoo's egg,' he said, 'right in the heart of Moscow, and one we can hatch any time we like. Nice to know that the Diplomatic Bag system works as well for us as for them.'

'Will it be armed?' Richter asked.

'Of course not,' Simpson replied. 'We can't have some simple-minded Embassy hack fiddling about with it. Dewar assures me that it can be armed in about ten minutes, if you know what you're doing, so it's still a viable threat.' He paused. 'So that's it. The Prime Minister and "C" are waiting to hear from me, so I'd best get moving. We've got a couple of nuclear submarines stuffed full of missiles more or less lurking at the mouth of the Moskva River, and I think the Navy would like to get them back, or at least get them back into deep water. I take it,' he added, looking at Richter's red-rimmed eyes, 'that you don't want to come with me?'

Richter shook his head. 'No thanks. What about Abilene? What's the latest?'

'The PM and the American President have agreed there's going to be no military retaliation. In fact, it looks as if the official response will be to write it off as a tragic accident – an American nuke was accidentally detonated.'

Richter grunted in disbelief. 'Will the American people wear that? With, what, around a quarter of a million dead?'

'The spin doctors will sort it out, and I don't actually think it will be that difficult to do. Don't forget, there was no launch vehicle involved, so they can argue that it couldn't have been an act of aggression by any other nation, and the bomb itself was really small, by Russian standards, and they can prove it. And there's even a convenient American Air Force base – Dyess – which is within about four miles of ground zero, down to the south-west of Abilene. They'll probably say the epicentre of the explosion was there, and blame it on some maintenance glitch or a freak weapon control malfunction.'

'Very convenient. Does Dyess store nukes?'

'I'd be very surprised if it didn't; about half of America's B-1B bomber force is based there.'

'And the Russians?'

'Oh, they'll pay, there's no doubt about that. The Americans will seek punitive damages for every life lost and every building flattened, and they'll get exactly what they ask for. Russia will be in debt for years.'

'And what about the selection of little incidents on our side of the pond? The SAS killing Russian seamen in Gibraltar, nuclear bombs in Russian trucks on French autoroutes and dead Arabs scattered all over southern France. Am I going to read about them in the paper tomorrow?'

Simpson shook his head. 'If I've got anything to do with it,' he said, 'none of these little episodes will ever make any paper. They'll be far more use to us as bargaining counters with the Russians in the future, not to mention the clout it'll give us with the CIA and the rest of the American intelligence community. Don't forget, we – or you, in fact – saved America.'

'Yeah, right. But you'll have to tell the press something. You can't keep incidents like these under wraps – here or over in the States.'

Simpson waved a hand airily. 'Abilene is going to dominate the news for weeks, maybe months, just like New York did after the nine eleven attacks. Nobody's going to take any notice of some minor and unrelated incidents in Europe. If anybody asks, we'll just say, oh, that the Russian ship was carrying arms for the IRA, the Russian truck was stopped as part of a routine security exercise, and the Arabs were terrorists who were killed by a rival faction. Something like that. No further details available due to the security classifications of the incidents and the ongoing investigations.'

'The usual crap, in fact?'

'Yes, the usual crap, but that and the Official Secrets Act, and if necessary a handful of D-Notices, will ensure it's all kept nice and quiet.'

Simpson paused and looked over at Richter. 'Look,' he said, 'why don't you push off and take some leave? You must have some crumpet lurking around somewhere.'

'Two things,' Richter said. 'I wish you wouldn't call any woman under the age of forty "some crumpet", and there's still one loose end that needs to be tied.'

Richter told him what he wanted to do. When Simpson started to argue, Richter told him why.

'I'm sorry,' he said. 'I didn't know.'

Richter shrugged his shoulders. 'No reason why you should. It wasn't on file anywhere, and until this business it really wasn't relevant. But you do see why I have to do it?'

'Yes. Let Tactics and Equipment know what you want and if they give you any flak refer them to me. Just don't tell me all the details.'

Buraydah, Saudi Arabia

When Sadoun Khamil finally plucked up the courage to contact the al-Qaeda leaders to tell them that their plan, which had taken four years to prepare and cost literally millions of dollars, had come to almost nothing, he had been prepared for furious anger.

To his surprise, the reaction from Tariq Rahmani was much less violent than he had expected. He guessed that the al-Qaeda leaders had realized that detonating the Abilene bomb was a considerable achievement in its own right, overshadowing even the destruction of the World Trade Center buildings in New York, and with a huge loss of life.

He expressed his sorrow at Hassan Abbas' failure, but assured Rahmani that there would be other targets, other opportunities and, above all, other successes. If he had been less nervous, he might have wondered at one remark made by the man on the other end of the scrambled telephone link.

Just after seven that evening, local time, as Khamil was preparing to go to one of the nearby restaurants for a light meal, he was grabbed from behind by three men, wrestled to the ground and bludgeoned into unconsciousness.

When he came to, he was lying naked on his back somewhere out in the dunes and tied spread-eagled to a rough wooden frame. An hour or so later, a small procession appeared. It was led by Tariq Rahmani, Khamil's conduit to the very highest echelons of al-Qaeda, and a man he had only seen twice before in his life. Rahmani walked across until he was a few feet from Khamil, looked down at him, shook his head and then stepped back.

From behind him, another figure appeared, moving slowly and with deliberate purpose, and as Khamil heard the click of a knife being opened and saw Rashid's swarthy features, he suddenly remembered the remark he had heard, but not registered, on the telephone.

Tariq Rahmani had said, 'It is not Hassan Abbas that we blame for this failure.'

Chapter Thirty

Monday
London

On Friday night Richter slept like a log, and dozed off and on all Saturday. On Sunday he felt more like a going concern, but didn't leave his flat, even to buy a paper. He watched the news programmes on the television and ate out of his freezer.

At seven fifty on Monday morning he climbed out of the minicab at Heathrow Terminal One and walked in, carrying an overnight case and a slim black briefcase bearing a gold crest. Around his neck was a blue tie bearing a small silver greyhound motif, the symbol of the Corps of Queen's Messengers.

The Queen's Messengers are diplomatic couriers who spend their lives ferrying documents from embassy to embassy and back to Britain. Their travels are conducted under the auspices of the Treaty of Vienna and, as diplomatic personnel, their luggage is exempt from search at borders. Every week a Queen's Messenger, sometimes with an assistant, flies from London to Moscow to deliver and collect the diplomatic mail. All that is necessary is for the British Embassy in Moscow to inform the Russian authorities forty-eight hours in advance who is flying in or out, and the Queen's Messenger invariably travels on a diplomatic passport.

The Moscow British Embassy had been informed the previous Friday that a Queen's Messenger named Beatty would be arriving on Monday with urgent documents, and notice had been duly given to the Russians.

At the Enquiry Desk Richter asked if there were any messages for him, and received a manila envelope in return, together with a sympathetic look at his still battered face.

'Car accident,' he murmured, and headed for the gents' toilet. Sitting fairly uncomfortably, Richter opened the envelope and scanned the contents. There was a first-class return ticket on the direct Heathrow–Moscow British Airways flight in the name of Beatty to match the diplomatic passport that he still held. In a sealed envelope was a letter addressed to the British Ambassador, the contents of which Richter knew, because he had told Simpson what to write. He also found another permit issued by the Metropolitan Police, this time endorsed by someone in the higher echelons of British Airways, authorizing the carriage of the Smith and Wesson, and another personal search exemption certificate, which would avoid the pistol shorting out the metal detector in the departure lounge.

Richter flushed the toilet, disposing of the manila envelope, then checked his suitcase in at the BA counter, and bought a paperback at the book shop – it was going to be a long flight, and he didn't want to spend all the time thinking about the job he had to do in Moscow.

They called the flight five minutes early and the aircraft took off on time. Richter watched the streets of London dwindle in size until the Boeing 767 went through a cloudbank and he could no longer see the ground.

Moscow

As for all arrivals in Moscow by Queen's Messengers, there was an escort from the Embassy waiting for Richter at Sheremetievo. He looked a little surprised at Richter's haggard appearance, but was obviously far too well trained to comment. Richter followed him through passport control with a minimum of fuss, and they avoided Customs altogether on the strength of the Beatty diplomatic passport. A black Rover was waiting, and they drove swiftly through the streets of Moscow, heading for the Embassy. Richter said little to the driver or the escort. He was still feeling the after-effects of both his encounter with Yuri and the Kalashnikov round in his chest, not to mention the succession of sleepless nights that seemed to have accompanied them, and he really didn't want to make conversation.

Richter ate a light lunch at the Embassy, then went down to meet the Ambassador. When he found out this couldn't happen, because the Ambassador had left the Embassy on Friday morning to spend a four-day weekend in Germany, Richter had no option but to renew his acquaintance with Secretary Horne.

That afternoon, Horne was late and Richter sat twiddling his thumbs in his office until almost two. When Horne walked in, he didn't seem at all pleased to see his visitor. 'Who let you in? What do you want?'

'We met a short while ago, after Mr Newman's death, remember?' Richter said.

Horne looked at him with suspicion. 'My secretary advised me to expect a Mr Beatty this afternoon, not you.'

Richter tossed the Beatty passport onto his desk. 'That's me as well. As you may have guessed, I'm not an insurance company representative.' Richter passed Horne the envelope with the Ambassador's name on it. 'Would you please read that. I need help from some of your staff, and I need it today.'

Horne turned the envelope over suspiciously in his hand. 'Now look here, Mr Willis or Beatty or whatever your name is, you can't just push your way in here and start ordering me around. I'll have you know—'

Richter stood up, leaned across the desk, fixed Horne with an unblinking stare and spoke very quietly. 'Secretary Horne,' he said, 'I'm through asking; I'm telling. Any obstruction from you, and I can have you shipped out of this Embassy in less than twenty-four hours, with no job, no pension and no "sir" at the front of your name.'

All of which was a grotesque exaggeration, of course, but it seemed to do the trick, because Horne sat down without another word and tore open the flap of the envelope. Richter resumed his seat while Horne glanced at the single sheet of paper it contained, then read it.

When he'd finished, he folded the page and looked up at Richter. 'I've never heard of this Richard Simpson or his organization,' Horne said, 'but I do recognize the counter-signature on this letter. I do not,' he added, 'wish to know what you are doing here in Moscow. Payne will provide you with whatever assistance you need.' Richter nodded and Horne reached out his hand to the telephone. 'Get me Payne, please. It's urgent.' He put the receiver back in its rest and looked in a hostile manner across his desk at Richter.

Andrew Payne, still the acting SIS Head of Station, arrived three minutes later. Horne introduced 'Mr Beatty', told Payne to give him whatever assistance he required, and then dismissed them both with a certain amount of relief. Payne was a tall, sandy-haired individual in his late thirties, who appeared puzzled at Richter's presence in Moscow, and still more perplexed when he had explained what he wanted.

'It's not that I can't tell you exactly what I'm doing,' Richter said, 'it's more that I don't think you'd really want to know.'

'As you wish,' Payne said, somewhat stiffly. 'So all you actually want SIS to do is provide you with a car for the day – not an official car, just an ordinary saloon – plus maps of Moscow and so on. Then you'll be meeting this man Gremiakin late this evening, and flying back to Britain tomorrow.'

'That's about the size of it,' Richter said.

'Are you expecting a little trouble at this meeting with the Russian?'

'No,' Richter replied. 'I'm expecting a lot of trouble.'

'I see. Do you require a weapon of any sort? We have a small armoury here, of course.'

'Thank you, no.' Richter opened his jacket to show him the butt of the Smith and Wesson. Payne nodded absently, and five minutes later Richter was inspecting his transport for the day in the Embassy car park. It proved to be a VAZ, like that in which Mr Newman's unfortunate *doppelgänger* had met his end. Richter hoped it wasn't an omen. He checked the boot first, to confirm that what he expected to find was actually there, then he unlocked the car and climbed in. Richter spent a few minutes getting used to the controls before starting it and driving out into the light mid-afternoon traffic of Moscow. He didn't really know where he was going, but he knew that he would recognize what he wanted when he saw it.

Moscow is encircled by two ring roads, both centred more or less on the Kremlin. The first describes a circle about three miles in diameter and encloses the heart of the city; the second is ten miles out, and follows the Gorod Moskva district boundary. Richter would be meeting Leonid Gremiakin at his apartment in the Shaydrovo district, about eight miles to the south of the city centre and just to the east of the main road which runs on south to Tula and Orel and, if you follow it far enough, eventually to Sevastopol in the Crimea on the northern shore of the Black Sea. Shaydrovo seemed a good place to start, so Richter turned the VAZ on to Ljusinovskaja at Serpuhovskaja ploshchad and headed south.

He drove past the western loop of the Moskva River, where it flows past Yuzhnyy Port and Nagatino before turning north for the centre of Moscow, and on through the thinning suburbs, through Belyayevo and on to Krasnyy Mayak. Then Richter turned left and circled round to approach Shaydrovo from the south. The maps Payne had provided were no more than adequate, and did not, of course, identify individual apartment buildings, but he had plenty of time in hand, and within two hours he had found exactly where Gremiakin lived.

Richter headed west out of Shaydrovo, turned north and drove almost as far as Belyayevo on the main road, then turned left towards Vorontsavo. About a mile along the road he turned left again, past the outskirts of Kon'kovo and on towards Tëplyystan. By the time Richter reached the turning for Uzkoye, he had identified three sites that were suitable, so he carried on south to Yazenevo, past the access road that leads to SVR headquarters, and then drove east to the main road and turned north, back towards the Embassy.

Richter only needed one more item, and he found that on a derelict building site as he approached the inner ring road. Richter stopped the car, picked it up and put it in the boot, and drove the VAZ back into the Embassy car park.

At seven Richter went down to the dining room for an early meal. When he'd finished eating it was seven thirty, and by a quarter to eight he was sitting in the driving seat of the VAZ and heading south again. He reached Shaydrovo a little after eight, drove to Gremiakin's apartment building and parked around the corner. Richter climbed the stairs to the second floor and knocked on the door. After a minute or so it opened, and a stooping, grey-haired man with twinkling blue eyes peered out, looking at him quizzically.

'Comrade Gremiakin?' Richter asked, and the Russian nodded. Richter proffered an SVR identity card which was absolutely genuine. He knew it was genuine because it had formerly been the property of

Colonel Vladimir Orlov, deceased, but it now bore Richter's picture and a different name. 'I'm Lieutenant Nicolai Teplov,' Richter said. 'General Modin has requested I deliver you this letter and then take you to him. An urgent matter has arisen and he requires your services.'

Gremiakin smiled, took the letter which Modin had written beside the autoroute in northern France and opened it. He scanned its contents, looked carefully at the signature, and then handed it back to Richter. 'I'll just get my jacket,' he said. Two minutes later he locked the apartment door behind him and followed Richter down the stairs. 'I've not seen you before,' Gremiakin said, as they descended the final flight.

'No, Comrade. I've only worked for the general for a few weeks.'

'You have an unusual accent, Lieutenant,' the Russian continued. 'Where are you from?'

'Georgia,' Richter said.

Gremiakin was silent for a few moments, but then as they emerged on to the pavement and walked towards the corner around which Richter had parked the car he spoke again. 'Probably not Georgia,' he said, and the way he said it made Richter stop and look at him. Gremiakin had removed his right hand from the pocket of his jacket, and Richter could see that he was holding a small automatic pistol. 'More probably one of the counties of northern England, Mr Willis. Or should that be Mr Beatty?' Gremiakin said.

Something, somewhere, had gone badly wrong. In the quiet of the evening Richter could faintly hear the sound of a car engine at high revolutions, still a long way off, but rapidly getting closer. Obviously Gremiakin hadn't just been finding his jacket in his flat – he'd also been making a telephone call, and the cavalry was on its way. Richter had probably less than a minute to sort things out.

Gremiakin was smiling with pleasurable anticipation. 'I was talking to General Modin this afternoon – most of the afternoon, in fact,' he said with a chuckle, 'and he told me all about you.'

'I see,' Richter said, and turned as if to walk away. Then he pivoted on his left heel and span round, dropping and kicking out, hard, with his right foot. His kick caught the side of Gremiakin's right knee, and he fell like a pole-axed ox. As he tumbled, Richter crouched forward and punched him with the side of his hand, below and behind the left ear, and the Russian was unconscious before he reached the ground. The VAZ was only about fifty yards away. Richter put his arms round Gremiakin's chest, dragged him to it and manoeuvred him into the passenger seat. The noise of the approaching car was much louder, and Richter expected it to arrive at any moment.

What Gremiakin wouldn't have been able to tell them was what Richter was driving, because he had parked the VAZ out of sight of the flat, and Richter was keen that they shouldn't find out. Gremiakin was still out cold. Richter started the engine of the VAZ, put Gremiakin's pistol – a 9mm Makarov PM, modelled on the German Walther PP – in his pocket and walked back to the corner to wait for the cavalry.

Richter took the Smith and Wesson out of the shoulder holster and checked the cylinder. He knew it was fully loaded, but it never hurts to check twice. Then he just waited.

The car – a VAZ, similar to the one Richter was driving – came round the corner in front of him on no more than three wheels, headlights blazing, and lurched to a stop in front of the apartment building. Four men got out and ran for the entrance doors. Richer had no quarrel with any of them, so he waited until they were inside and, he guessed, at least halfway up the stairs, before he did anything.

Then Richter took careful aim with the Smith and fired once at the car. The pistol kicked high, and the left front tyre blew with a satisfying bang. Richter lowered the weapon again and put two rounds through the engine compartment. If a .357 Magnum bullet hits the side of an engine block, it's quite capable of going right through it. Richter couldn't guarantee that he'd destroyed the motor, but he was quite sure the car wouldn't be able to follow him.

Richter holstered the Smith, ran back to his car and drove away as quickly as he could, watching the rear-view mirror very carefully. The first of them came round the corner of the building when the VAZ was about eighty metres down the road, and just as Richter made a turn to the right. At that range Richter was certain he would not have been able to read the car number plate. He would no doubt have identified the vehicle as a VAZ, but that was hardly a problem – every second car on the streets of Moscow was a VAZ.

Gremiakin was beginning to stir, so Richter waited until the road straightened up, then took out the Smith, reversed it, and hit him smartly on the head with the butt. Gremiakin lapsed into unconsciousness again, and Richter concentrated on getting to where he wanted to go.

It was a little after eight forty when Richter drove up a narrow track off a side road to the south-east of Kon'kovo. He parked the car in a small clearing well off the road and facing back the way he had come, stopped the engine, got out and just listened. In the twilight Richter heard bird song, occasional rustlings of small animals in the undergrowth, and the wind in the treetops, but no voices, no indication of any human presence. Satisfied, he opened the boot and dragged out the tarpaulin he had liberated from the building site that afternoon, and spread it out on the ground behind the car and next to a small tree. Then he took out the toolkit and the jack handle and put them beside it.

Richter dragged Gremiakin out of the car and laid him out on the tarpaulin. He was beginning to come round, which suited Richter fine. He opened up the toolkit and took out a roll of thick black sticky tape, a length of which he stuck across Gremiakin's mouth as a makeshift gag. Richter didn't want him to talk, only to listen. Richter used a couple of plastic cable ties to lash the Russian's wrists together behind the tree, leaving him in a sitting position. He removed Gremiakin's shoes and socks, found a stout tree branch about three feet long and used more cable ties to secure his ankles to it, one at each end.

Ten minutes later Gremiakin was fully awake and staring at Richter. Richter stared straight back. 'You shouldn't have come with me,' Richter said. 'You knew who I was, and you must have guessed what I wanted. You should have stayed in your flat.'

Gremiakin blinked, his blue eyes watery. 'You said you talked with General Modin. I presume that meant you talked with him in your professional capacity?' The Russian's nod was just perceptible. 'He was under suspicion because of what happened to the London weapon, I suppose? Recalled by the Kremlin, or possibly Bykov put the finger on him?'

The Russian shook his head. 'That's a surprise,' Richter said. 'And because you were involved, I presume that the general is now no longer with us?' Again the slight nod. 'Another tick in your records?' Richter said, and Gremiakin looked puzzled. Richter waved a hand. 'Never mind,' he continued. 'I didn't come about the general.'

Richter opened the toolbox again and took out a claw hammer. Then he walked behind the tree and smashed it as hard as he could, twice, into the back of Gremiakin's right hand. The skin ruptured, and bones splintered, showing white against the up-welling blood.

Richter walked back to the end of the tarpaulin and sat down. He took a tissue from his pocket, cleaned the debris off the end of the hammer and put it on the tarpaulin beside him. Only then did he look at Gremiakin. The Russian's face was pale and bloodless, and tears were running down his cheeks.

'It stings, doesn't it?' Richter said. 'Perhaps before you die you'll appreciate a little of what your subjects have suffered at your hands over the years. I'm only sorry,' he added, 'that I don't have the sophisticated instruments that are available to you in the Lubyanka.' Richter smiled mirthlessly at Gremiakin, and dragged the toolbox towards him. 'So we'll just have to make do with what we've got in here, won't we?' he said.

Richter took a pair of heavy wire-cutters, walked behind the tree again, severed two of the fingers from Gremiakin's left hand and tossed them on to the tarpaulin in front of him. The Russian was groaning and barely conscious, so Richter cleaned up the cutters and waited a few minutes for him to recover.

'This is really just a taster,' Richter said. 'You'll die within the hour, very painfully, but you'll still have had an easier ride than most of the people you've questioned.' Richter picked up the hammer again and Gremiakin flinched. 'Your feet next, I think,' Richter said, then put the hammer down. 'You probably want to know why,' Richter continued. 'You want to know why you're here, and why I'm doing all these terrible things to you – terrible things that you would normally expect to be doing to somebody else. You probably think I'm a sadist, but I'm not. But I do believe in retribution, and if anyone I've ever met deserves retribution, it's you.

'You,' Richter continued, 'are a sadist, without question. You probably see yourself as a technician, just a man doing an important job for the KGB and then for the SVR that nobody else wanted to do.

But you're wrong, because you enjoy your work, and that's the difference. It probably gave you a particular thrill to see General Modin lying naked in front of you this afternoon, strapped to the table and hoping to die quickly. He was a decent man who didn't like you, and never made any secret of it, and I'm sure that added extra spice to your work.'

Richter took the hammer then and hit the side of Gremiakin's left foot as hard as he could. Blood flowed and bones broke. Even through the tape gag Richter could hear the Russian's howl of anguish. 'That,' Richter said, 'is a small return of service for General Modin.' He cleaned the head of the hammer again. 'But as I said, I'm not here because of the general.' Richter put the hammer down and looked at Gremiakin.

'I'm here,' Richter continued, 'because of an Englishman. A man called Newman, Graham Newman, who received your attentions earlier this year. He was, as the SVR quite obviously knew, the British Secret Intelligence Service Head of Station here in Moscow. General Modin was quite forthcoming when I asked him. Newman was snatched by the SVR, not because of anything he knew, but because of something he might have found out about.'

The Russian stared at him. 'You questioned him. According to General Modin, it took you several hours, and I cannot even begin to imagine the agony Newman went through before he finally died. You can, of course, because you were entirely responsible for it.' Gremiakin shook his head. 'Normally, of course, we professionals accept that kind of thing as being all part of the game, one of the risks a man runs if he gets involved in the clandestine world.

'But Newman was different,' Richter continued, 'at least to me.' Gremiakin was still staring at him. 'Graham Newman,' Richter said, 'was my cousin.' The Russian recoiled as if Richter had hit him. 'So you see,' Richter said, 'this is nothing to do with professional ethics or morals or anything else. This is just a simple family matter.'

He reached into the toolbox again, took out a six-inch screwdriver and walked towards Gremiakin.

*

Richter left the site at a little before ten. What was left of Gremiakin was lying in the undergrowth, wrapped in the tarpaulin, and it might be days or weeks before anybody found the body. Richter had thoroughly cleaned all the tools, and was confident that there was nothing in the vehicle that could link the VAZ either to the site or to the body. He wouldn't have been so certain in the West, but Russian forensic science is fairly rudimentary.

He returned to the Embassy without incident, parked the car and went to bed.

Tuesday
Moscow

Richter saw Payne the following morning, told him that his business in Moscow was completed, and asked for a car and escort to Sheremetievo airport that afternoon to catch the British Airways afternoon flight back to Heathrow.

'Why an escort?' Payne asked.

'Because I have reason to believe that I have been compromised and my possession of a diplomatic passport may not be sufficient to guarantee my safe passage out of the country.'

This burst of officialese was actually understating the case. Gremiakin had known exactly who Richter was, and his telephone call to his minders had presumably included a statement of Richter's identity. Even a cursory check of the departure flight schedules would reveal that a 'Mr Beatty' was booked on the London flight.

Reverting to Richter's real name and genuine passport, which he had sewn into the lining of the bottom of his overnight case, wouldn't help. Russian bureaucracy is slow but thorough – they have, after all, had a lot of practice. Before a Mr Richter could fly out of Russia, a Mr Richter would have to fly in to Russia; the two sections of the visa have to match.

Richter's best hope was that Gremiakin had not had time to disseminate the information properly, and that he would be able to slip out before the hunt was really under way. The escort from the Embassy might help if this turned out to be as forlorn a hope as Richter expected.

Payne elected to come in person, together with the Second Secretary, and they climbed out of the car at Sheremetievo Terminal Two at fifteen thirty, allowing the usual two hours before the flight's departure time. Richter hadn't noticed any unusual police or militia presence outside the airport, and the terminal appeared much as normal. He was beginning to think it was actually going to work when he saw a face he knew approaching him.

'Mr Beatty. Leaving us so soon?' Viktor Grigorevich Bykov was dressed in the uniform of a full general, a change from the civilian suit he had been wearing when Richter had last seen him beside the autoroute in France. In the background Richter could see two junior officers in uniform, both carrying sidearms and clearly awaiting instructions from Bykov.

'General Bykov,' Richter said, and forced a smile. 'Congratulations on your promotion. Yes, I'm hoping to leave.'

'I'm sure you are,' the Russian chuckled, 'and I'm here just to see you off. But first,' he said, 'come over here. We have some matters to discuss.'

Richter motioned to Payne and the Second Secretary to stay close, and followed Bykov to a seating area. 'So,' Bykov said, 'why did you come here? Despite your smart new tie –' Bykov gestured towards the silver greyhound motif '– you have not, I am sure, been reduced to taking a job as a Queen's Messenger.' Richter shook his head. 'Perhaps, then, you came to see our famous art treasures?'

Richter shook his head again. 'I'm not a tourist, General.'

Bykov's smile vanished. 'I know that, Mr Beatty. I know why you came, or I think I do.' He paused, leaned forward and looked steadily at the Englishman. 'I should have you killed for interfering with our operation. It took over four years of work to set it up, to get all the weapons constructed and positioned, and you came along and ruined it in just a few days.'

Richter shook his head. 'I won't say I'm sorry, General, because I'm not.'

'I didn't expect that you would be,' Bykov said.

'And I didn't think,' Richter said, 'that it was entirely your operation. We were surprised when a bunch of Arabs appeared out of the woodwork with their own world domination plan. Which,' he added, 'might well have worked if the American weapons had been exploded as they had intended.'

Bykov grimaced. 'You weren't anything like as surprised as us,' he said. 'They were obviously Minister Trushenko's personal little secret, but neither he nor anybody else here suspected their hidden agenda. In fact, for stopping them, we owe you and the Americans a debt of gratitude. And we are genuinely sorry about Abilene. You must believe it was never our intention to actually pull the trigger – the weapons in America were just a threat, pawns, as it were, to be played in our long-running game of international chess.'

After a moment, Bykov spoke again. 'Comrade Gremiakin has not reported for work today.' He looked at Richter expectantly, and the Englishman could feel the net closing around him.

'Perhaps,' Richter said, 'this Gremiakin is unwell.'

Bykov looked at him appraisingly. 'His apartment is empty, and nobody has seen him since last night. He called his security guards to report an armed intruder, and they thought he might have been driven away in a VAZ saloon.' He stared at Richter. 'Where were you yesterday evening, Mr Beatty? Doing paperwork at the Embassy, perhaps? Something like that?'

'Yes,' Richter said. 'Something like that.'

'You can produce witnesses, no doubt?'

'If necessary,' he replied, 'I probably could.'

Bykov nodded. 'I'm sure you could,' he said agreeably. Then his tone hardened. 'Do you know what Gremiakin did yesterday afternoon, Mr Beatty?' Before Richter could answer, Bykov shook his head. 'No, of course you don't. Let me tell you. He was instructed to terminate General Modin. The general and I were ordered by the Kremlin to fly back from London almost as soon as we had disclosed that the weapon had been seized in France. Because of General Modin's part in the project he knew that he would inevitably be blamed for its failure, and he could probably guess what would happen to him.'

Holy Russia – *Rodina* – exerts a compelling pull on her children, a pull which is impossible for a non-Russian to comprehend. Time and again in the history of the country, citizens have returned voluntarily, knowing without a shadow of a doubt that they were facing certain – and often extremely painful – death.

'Gremiakin did terminate the general,' Bykov continued. 'It took him nearly three hours, and when he'd finished they had to send a squad into the cellar to hose down the walls and the ceiling. You cannot imagine what he did to Modin, and nor would you want to.' Bykov leaned forward. 'Gremiakin could be unwell, Mr Beatty,' he said softly, 'but I hope he's not. I hope the bastard's dead in a ditch somewhere.'

Richter sat silent, not knowing what to say.

'Between ourselves, Mr Beatty, you have actually done me a favour. Operation *Podstava* has failed, that we know. Like General Modin, I had my doubts, but unlike him I did not voice them. Perhaps,' he added thoughtfully, 'that is why I am alive and enjoying my promotion, while he is dead.

'Following the death of General Modin under interrogation yesterday,' Bykov continued, 'I was immediately promoted. The failed plan was deemed to be the fault of Minister Trushenko and General Modin; the Minister for a totally unauthorized operation and for negotiating with, and accepting funds from, the Arabs, and General Modin for failing to realize that the operation was not approved by the Kremlin. But no blame was attached to General Sokolov or to me.' He smiled. 'That is the favour you have done me, Mr Beatty.'

'And Gremiakin?' Richter asked.

Bykov's face clouded and his voice dropped. 'Gremiakin,' he said, 'was nothing more than an animal, a hideous example of the worst excesses of the Stalin era. The trouble was, he was also very senior, and had powerful friends. There was no way to curb him, to stop what he called his "work". For the removal of Gremiakin,' Bykov concluded, 'for I am sure you were responsible, I also thank you.'

Richter nodded, but said nothing. Bykov looked at his watch, and stood up. 'Come, Mr Beatty, or you will miss your flight.'

'I thought,' Richter said, getting to his feet, and still unsure of the situation, 'that making me miss my flight was why you were here.'

Bykov shook his head and smiled. 'No, no, Mr Beatty. I really did only come to see you off. Oh, and to warn you that it might be better if you stayed away from Russia for a while. As I said, Gremiakin had some powerful friends.'

Viktor Bykov stood silent for a few seconds, looking at Richter, then held out his hand. And after a moment Richter reached out and shook it.